In The Care
Of Evil

In The Care
Of Evil

A FOSTER CHILD'S BRUTAL
TALE OF SEX, VIOLENCE,
GREED, AND BETRAYAL

Dewey Reynolds

4609-REYN

To order additional copies of this book, contact:
Xlibris Corporation
1-888-7-XLIBRIS
www.Xlibris.com
Orders@Xlibris.com

Contents

In Loving Memory Of:

Aurora Lee Bryson (My Eternal Sweetheart)
Aunt Jackie Wylie (You're Greatly Missed!)
Uncle Booker T. Porter (A Great Uncle)
Gerald Lee Posey (Miss Ya Always, Gerald)
Michael McFadden (My Brother, Always)
LaTonya Ammons (My Little Sister, Always)
LaKenya Ammons (You're With The Angels)
Mrs. Dorothy White (The Knowledge Was Invaluable)
Mr. David "Hugo" Hughes (Your Wisdom Was Priceless)
Bobby DeBarge (Thanks For The Great Music)
Mr. Holly Denson (We Had Great Talks)
Lois Matthews (We All Miss You)

May You Rest In The Bosom Of The Almighty

When my father and my mother forsake me, then the Lord
will take care of me.

Psalm 27:10

IN THE CARE Of Evil is a compelling account of the brutal experiences that a group of foster children and handicapped men encounter in a foster home located on Chicago's south side. After surviving the drug dealing, bootlegging, and prostitution, which took place in their parent's home, Vernon, Valerie, and Vincent are placed in the care of Bessie Mae and J.D. Willingham, along with numerous other foster children by the state of Illinois.

Vincent is one of the many foster children who is brutally beaten at the hands of J.D. Willingham with the use of a long brown extension cord. This same extension cord leaves some very painful whelps all over his body, which have a tendency to leak blood like a sore. Because of a virtually uncontrollable bedwetting problem, he dreads getting beatings on a daily basis. His older and wiser brother, Vernon, leaves this foster home because of the abuse and neglect. He joins the Air Force immediately following his graduation from high school.

The home is scrupulously unsanitary, surrounded with extreme filth as many piles of laundry soiled with raw urine and defecation, many mice and rats, as well as thousands of cockroaches and fly maggots, all nesting throughout different areas of the home. Some of these foster children encounter health-related problems from these unsanitary conditions. Despite their longing to inform child care authorities, these foster children procrastinate, fearful that their punishment will become more severe.

The evil foster father, J.D. Willingham, proves to be extremely abusive. First, he brutally rapes Valerie, one of his helpless foster daughters, and then he pushes his limits and continues the cycle of abuse of by impregnating another one of his foster daughters, which took place several years after the rape incident. Though social service authorities are apprehensive about bringing more foster children to the Willingham home, two more foster boys, Gilbert Curry and Jose Underwood, are brought to live there. Gilbert is the one foster child who displays a militant side, constantly trying to convince Jose and Vincent that they should run away or contact the proper authorities about all the abuse surrounding the home.

Bessie Mae suspects that her husband is guilty of both rape and child molestation, but because of her unconditionally blinding love for him, she tries to ignore his sinnister deeds. But until the one foster daughter comes forward and reveals that she has given birth to the baby son that J.D. fathered, Bessie Mae finally comes to her senses and confronts him for taking advantage of the two foster girls. J.D. experiences a nearly life ending encounter when Bessie Mae slips into an anger frenzy and plants a .38 calibre handgun to his head. J.D. denies any allegations brought against him and continues to abuse anyone in his path.

Bessie Mae suffers a fatal stroke from all the years of deception that was perpetrated by her husband, J.D. The appropriate child care services are contacted and the Willingham's notorious foster parenting home is finally put out of business. Vernon, Valerie, and Vincent, all come back to pay their respects to Bessie Mae. For Vincent, the one foster child who remained at the home, he no longer have to tolerate the abuse. The tumultuous lives of these foster children and handicapped men have been skillfully captured with this novel, In The Care Of Evil.

Acknowledgements

F IRST AND FOREMOST, I give all honor and praise to the one force who controls everything living and breathing in the universe, God Almighty. A great love for my family, which includes my beautiful neices Sarah, Gloria, and Marquita, my handsome and intelligent nephew Isaac, my other nephews Antoine and Xavier, my wise and wonderful sister-in-law Sharon. I mustn't forget about my big brother William, b.k.a. *"Mack"*, for his guidance and support throughout the years, all the pep talks when things didn't work out the way I wanted them to, and for showing his concern when no one else seemed to care. Love ya unconditionally big brother.

To my little brother, b.k.a. *"Jimmy"*, who first taught me how to wrap a tie around my neck. I'm still laughing about that to this day. We'll have to do better at keeping in touch with one another. As long as planes still soar across the sky, buses still zoom down the highway, or trains still jet down the tracks, nothing can keep us apart. Love ya also unconditionally little brother.

Every ounce of love goes out to my sister Fran, whom I love more than life itself. We want you to know that we're always there for you, no matter what happens. God is always watching over you big sister. For all of my siblings, I want you to be careful, be watchful, stay prayerful, stay strong in the midst of the storm, and always stay in touch with me.

To my extended family, William "Wild Bill" Lacey, his son "Little Bill", Big Bubba, Gretchen, Angela, Donnell,

DeWayne, Squeaky, Leaky, Shelia, Tyrone and Marcus. Also, to my cousin Angela Wylie and her son and grandson, Big and Little Nathan Wylie, Annetta Washington, Uncle Bill Wylie, cousins Ethal Mae, Lonnie, and Vanessa.

The acknowledgements wouldn't be complete without thanking two very strong women that I've had the pleasure of meeting in my crazy lifetime, Karen Jackson and Sandra Juancito. Thank you Karen for your powerful words of encouragement and the drive to bust through concrete walls. (Think we'll get a number one hit from this one, Karen?) Thank you Sandra for being the mouthpiece and attentive ear during turbulent times. You are true sweethearts, Karen and Sandra.

To my big brother on the East Coast, Hank Hamlette, the same big brother that I don't recall asking for, but we're stuck with one another now. I'm still trying to get back to New York City, right there in "Money Making Manhattan", just to see you Hank. Oh yes, the Yankees won another dreamer. (Where's my championship shirt?) Smile, Hank.

To my buddy since the days of the IRS, Nicole Wiley, a young lady who I admire greatly for having a vision and fighting diligently to keep that vision alive. Keep on fighting, Nicole, it's never over! To Mitchell Wright, another priceless mouthpiece and attentive ear who kept the encouragement coming non-stop. Good luck with your business and any future endeavor, Mitchell.

I simply can't forget about the man with the silky smooth and mega-platinum voice, Mr. Howard Hewett, for so many years of encouraging and spiritually uplifting music. It's through your powerful music, Howard, that I feel as though there's nothing that I can't do. Your God-Ordained voice remains in a class all by itself.

Love, hugs, kisses, and great admiration for my sophomore English teacher, Mrs. Emma Stewart, for the great English skills, and who also told me that she really enjoyed

reading my story, and encouraged me to push further with the project. For every student who passed through Central High School and who passed through your class, we will always admire you.

To all of the people in my hometown of Kansas City, Missouri, the same ones who prayed very hard for me, wished me well no matter what path in life that I chose, as long as that path was legal, ethical, and moral, and an endless love for those who walked through the fire with me. Peace to everyone in Kansas City, both sides of the river, Missouri and Kansas.

To all of the foster children, past, present, and America hopes not future, the caseworkers and social workers who work tirelessly in trying to make the system work for all those involved, you've truly inspired me to write this story and I hope that all of your dreams come true.

Before I sign off, I just wanted to tell all of the men and women in America and across the planet, that if you're man and woman enough to lie down and make children, then be man and woman enough to stand up and take care of your children, because we all know that no one on this Earth asked to come here. To make a long story short, when it comes to your children, take care of your responsibilities. If there's anyone else that I've forgotten, please forgive me. Just stand up, shout very loud, wave your hands high in the air, so that I'll know that you've been accounted for.

(1931-1999)

I dedicate all of the years of hard work involved in this book, every tear that I cried, every drop of blood that I shed, and every sweat that I broke, to the the memory of my late mother, my dearest always, Mrs. Alla Mae Reynolds.

The Entire Reynolds Family

First Row from left to right: Janice, Elmer, Coleman, Lydia, Leona Mae, Samuel, Peggy Ann, Ervin, Margeurite, and Stella Marie.

Second Row from left to right: Doris, Margeurite, Lloyd and son John, Pop Reynolds, Mom Reynolds, Stella Juanita, Marion and son Stephen, McCoyd and son Butch, and Thelma and daughter Monica.

Third Row: Evelyn, Armand, Shirley, Chloe, Leota, Barbara, Kenneth, Al, Dewey, Nathan, S.E. Marie, and Toka.

Book I

Procrastinators are creative in making excuses, even if they can't do anything else. The question they always get from people around them is, "What are you waiting for?"

—Stedman Graham

Chapter 1

DECISIONS

THEY CAME FROM different areas of Chicago, Cicero, Hyde Park, Chicago Heights, and the west and south sides. They made many requests. Many knocked at the door of 3233 Fitzgerald on the infamous North side. An Italian-American outlaw named Vito Carvelli operated illegal vice activities, such as purchasing and selling various narcotics and bootleg whiskey, as well as soliciting prostitution.

"Hey, Vito, my wife and I are separated and I really need a good fuck from one of your girls," said a faithful customer, who stood in the front room of this corrupt residence.

"Give me a dime bag of coke with a pint of that Jack Daniels whiskey," another one of the loyal neighborhood drug addicts and alcoholics demanded of Vito, while he reached into his pocket for a roll of fresh bills.

"Think I can do a threesome with two of your girls, Vito?" a more well-to-do customer asked, shortly after the second customer walked out with his drugs and alcohol. Of course, he referred to the selection of beautiful prostitutes who worked for Vito. It wasn't uncommon for the men to have a kinky rendezvous with three and four of Vito's whores at the same time. As long as the price was right, they could get whatever they wanted.

He wasn't operating this house by himself. His wife, Marion, an attractive, well-built colored woman, made sure law and order was maintained among the prostitutes. All of the whores behaved themselves accordingly. Their house

was blue and white, made from sturdy wood and plaster. It was four stories high with six bedrooms. Not only was it used for unlawful vice activity, but also a residence for the Carvelli couple and their three children. Besides the three large bedrooms on the third floor, which had king sized beds, portable black and white televisions, dark oak dressers, and were used for sexual delights, there were two large rooms on the second floor that Vito and Marion, as well as a guest from time to time, occupied.

On the first floor, all the way in the back, was where the children stayed. In case of an emergency, Vito thought that it would be wise to have them near the back door. They could be rushed to safety if danger arose.

It was just another day of business at the house of corruption. Whenever a customer wanted to have sex with one of the several prostitutes, Marion brought them up to the third floor. They were colored, white, hispanic, and even one oriental girl worked there. They would always report directly to Vito whenever they came to the house. She collected their money, took them upstairs, and introduced them to one of the gorgeous ladies of the evening. After the rules of the house were explained, she'd tell them to enjoy themselves. Many of the customers and whores referred to her as *Madam Marion.*

Meanwhile, while Marion took care of her responsibilities, Vito was busy in the basement unboxing bottles of Jack Daniel's, Johnny Walker Red, Canadian Mist, and different brands of vodka. Because of public demand, he never ran low on any scotch, bourbon, or whiskey. He used a small scale to weigh the small quantities of marijuana, heroin, and cocaine. Small plastic bags were used to stuff the narcotics inside and then sold to the customers at ten, twenty, and on up to fifty dollars. Vito adopted the same philosophy as the world's most famous gangster, *Scarface* Al Capone: *"I make my money by supplying a public demand. If I break the law, my customers are as*

guilty as I am. I call myself a business man. "Vito's supplies were provided by small-time organized crime figures throughout Chicago. Their supplies were provided by big-time organized crime figures.

   The children, Valerie and Vernon Ramirez, and Vincent Carvelli, weren't aware that their parents operated a bawdy house. Valerie and Vernon were from Marion's first marriage to a criminally insane Cuban named Raoul Ramirez, who fled to Miami immediately following his release from a state penitentiary in Illinois. When it was reported that Raoul never became a U.S. citizen, not even after he supposedly married Marion, the Immigration and Naturalization Service issued a deportation order for him to return to his native Havana, Cuba. Marion always emphasized that she would never become involved with colored men. *"Colored men don't know how to treat their women,"* she'd often say to her colored friends and associates. *"They're abusive, irresponsible, and inconsiderate."* Despite the myth that white America supposedly gave birth to, women from other racial backgrounds believed that all men were potentially abusive, irresponsible, and inconsiderate. But nothing would change Marion's mind over the years. Men who led dangerous lifestyles, who were of an opposite race, certainly attracted her to them.

   Vincent was one of Vito's many biological children. It was rumored that he fathered more than forty children from women all over the United States, all during his illustrious criminal career. Fathering illegitimate children by women from different racial backgrounds became his trademark. Unlike Valerie and Vernon, who had a dark olive complexion and somewhat coarse jet black hair, Vincent had a very bright complexion and large brown curly locks. The Negro and Caucasian features displayed themselves across his face. While the six month old Vincent lay asleep in his crib, Valerie and Vernon played happily together. They rolled a large green plastic ball across the floor to one another. The traffic

of customers continued, as the echoes of knocks on the door
sent either Vito or Marion to answer. There were times when
customers would be in the front room making unlawful trans-
actions with Vito or Marion. Valerie and Vernon would be
right there to witness everything. They were never fully aware
of what went on.

The Carvelli family lived in this house for more than two
years. They made lots of illegal money. The time had come
when policemen cruised up and down Fitzgerald. They'd
slow down and look up at the Carvelli residence. They browsed
at Vito's sharp Cadillac. There were a total of seven prostitutes who came to the house dressed in tight-fitted dresses.
They wore thick layers of makeup and different colored wigs.
Marion suggested that Vito have them dress differently or
come through the back door.

"Through the back," Vito thought. "The kids don't need
to see our girls. Even though they're just children, they're a
little aware of what might be going on. I know that Valerie
and Vernon have peeked out of their room a couple of times
and seen some things that they shouldnt've seen."

Bam! Bam! Bam! Someone knocked very hard on the
door. They knocked like they were in desperate need of
something. Vito answered, one of his many pistols concealed
under his pants, and it was a customer wanting to know how
long he would be able to spend with one of the women. Vito
took his right arm and moved Marion to the very back of him,
something the Italians believed in doing. He carefully explained things to the anxious customer, a man with gray and
receding hair, along with a body odor strong enough to
drive away a colony of flies.

"Twenty dollars will get you two hours with one of our
girls," Vito said, smiling generously to the potential customer.
"All of our girls are aimed to please. The more you spend,
the more you get. If you want more than just a good fuck,
you'll have to pay more. But right now, give my wife Marion

twenty dollars and she'll take you upstairs so you can meet one of the girls."

The smelly customer reached into his pocket. Two crisp twenty dollar bills unfolded from the palm of his grimy left hand. "I've worked hard all week for this money. I wanna spend it the best way I can." The horny man had to explain that to Vito.

"Oh, you'll get more than your money's worth," Vito assured him. "Trust me on this one, pal."

Marion escorted him up to the third floor. The first two rooms were being occupied. The tricks were in there enjoying all the steamy sex that they could. The sounds of hardcore fucking traveled into the hallway. She knocked on the door to the third room. It was three soft knocks. The door opened and a vuluptuous hispanic woman, with curves that could match that of a well-crafted hourglass, stepped into the hallway. She had long and jet black hair, with a small mole below her right eye that complimented her creamy complexion, which was as smooth as porcelain. She sensually wore black and red evening wear.

"Sir," said *Madam Marion*. "This is one of our girls named Chili Pepper. She's one of the beautiful women that my husband was telling you about."

The man's breathing was heavy, like he was about to have a serious heart attack. One look at Chili Pepper, and any man's heart was set on fire. A sudden rise from the top of his dirty pants was a sign that he was ready to dive deep into some pussy.

"Sweet Jesus!" said the overly excited, under-sexed customer. "She's . . . she's . . ."

"Beautiful," Marion added, hoping that this trick would spend more than the forty bucks.

"Yeah, yeah, that's what I was trying to say."

"Enjoy."

Chili Pepper took him into the room and closed the

door. Marion went downstairs to check on the kids. She approached the room and noticed that Valerie and Vernon were stirring up lots of noise.

"Cut out all that noise before you all wake up Vincent!" Marion told her son and daughter in a real motherly fashion. "It took me a long time to get him to sleep, and I don't wanna be listening to him screaming and crying right now."

The customers continuously came to the front door. Many had asked Vito for their favorite brand of bourbon, vodka, or whiskey. Some asked for their ten, twenty, and fifty dollar bags of cured marijuana or pure cocaine and heroin. Vito sold only the best. His suppliers made sure that he had the best. The redbud marijuana soaked in the Earth from the West Indies, heroin processed in Italy and parts of Asia, pure uncut cocaine that was ground from the coca plant in the fertile soils of South America. They wanted it; Vito had it. There were never any complaints from his sinful customers.

"Dam, Vito!" a customer cheered in an elated voice. "Man, you've got the real shit" He walked out the door with a large, fifty dollar bag of marijuana.

Another customer came right behind him. "Goddam, Vito! You've got some of the strongest whiskey in Chicago. Hell, I don't think I could go to the backwoods of Tennessee or Mississippi and find no whiskey like yours. The last drink I had almost knocked fire from my ass!"

After one of the tricks and hookers left, the first room on the third floor wasn't being occupied. Marion decided to go into the room with a broom, a large trashbag, and a dustpan. She wanted to clean the room up so she would have something to keep her occupied until another trick came to the door. She walked into the room and witnessed a total disaster. There were used condoms across the bed and on the dresser. Small drops of fresh semen were all over the sheets and on the shiny wooden floor. Several bottles of whiskey and scotch were scattered over the room. Wet rings from the

liquor covered parts of the sheets. Large balls of hair and an open pornographic magazine were at the head of the bed. What a total disaster!

Marion's job served as sort of the *clean up lady*. She cleaned up behind the customers and their women proteges. She didn't mind, but the room that she stood in was absolutely wrecked. The last two customers got more than twenty dollars worth of sex. It would be more work than anticipated. She didn't want to touch any of the filth, such as the worn condoms and balls of hair. She swept everything up with the broom and scooped it into the dustpan. Marion dumped the trash into the trashbag and dragged it out of the room.

While bringing the bag downstairs, Marion noticed Vito in the front room talking with one of his lifetime friends named Tony Castellano. Tony hissed out warnings to Vito about the police. They were beginning to drive up and down Fitzgerald within the last few days. Tony possessed good looks that made him the envy of other men, an Italian man with a set of charming eyes and thick dark eyebrows that sent a woman into a dreamworld. He explained to Vito that things had gotten heated up. There were jealous rivals who wanted him dead or doing some serious time in jail. He told him to be especially cautious of those individuals who weren't regular customers, those who looked somewhat suspicious.

"Shit!" sighed a somewhat concerned Vito. "So, you think I should be looking out for unfamiliar faces who wanna buy a little dope or liquor here and there, or those horny bastards coming here for a piece of ass?"

"Hell, yeah!" Tony cautioned. "I just have a gut feeling that some undercover punk on the Chicago Police Department, who's gonna be on somebody's payroll, is going to have you shut down. Could be some cocksucker working for those lowlife punks Bennie Caputo and Fat Tony."

"Luckily, it wouldn't be Ness and his boys," Vito giggled,

thinking back to the days of Al Capone and his Chicago crime syndicate.

"Now you're going way back."

"Bennie Caputo. Fat Tony," Vito said, shaking his head and laughing as though their names were an insult to be mentioned in his house. "I've always been at peace with Bennie and Fat Tony. Why would they wanna have me set up?"

"Listen to me, Vito," Tony paused. "Them cocksuckers are jealous of you. You're inside this house making all this big money with Marion, and they don't like it. Especially, since Marion is a colored woman. Rats are everywhere, watching your every move."

Tony and Vito knew that Bennie Caputo was the strong arm of the prostitution business. It certainly didn't take the madams and pimps of Chicago long to realize that when Bennie's boys came by for their protection money, it was advisable to pay them. Those who weren't so wise, were intimidated, beaten, and even killed. Vito never paid protection fees to anyone. He separated himself from the small-time mobster hoods who were spread out across Chicago. *Fat Tony* Torio played a major role in the illegal liquor distribution trade. He and Bennie had strong alliances with Midwest crimes families that included Kansas City, Cleveland, and Milwaukee.

"Let's see now," Vito said calmly to Tony. "My neighbors and my customers are the only ones who know that my old lady and our kids live here. The neighbors watch the customers come to and go from this house and never gave me a sign that they knew what was going on. You know, Tony, you've really gotten all of my attention. I'm gonna start being more careful."

"Especially of Bennie and Tony," Tony added, staring right at Vito with those bedroom eyes. "Remember this, Bennie and Tony's got operations that are legal and illegal.

They've got something to fall back on if the law decides to move in on them. Those two cocksuckers are out to control everything around them. The whores, the booze, the dope, and probably some of these gambling joints. Everything, Vito! So please, be real careful."

"Will do," Vito assured Tony, who also operated some of the small-time rackets on Chicago's west side.

Tony patted Vito across the back and then gave him the old traditional Italian kiss on the right cheek. Their discussion ended and Marion stood in the kitchen against the stove. She worried about the vital information that she overheard. After Vito escorted Tony out the front door, Marion came into the front room and told her fearless husband that they needed to have a serious talk.

Baby Vincent cried loudly. She rushed into the back room where Valerie and Vernon were lying across their bunkbeds sound asleep. The baby was in the process of waking them up. She picked him up out of his crib and took him into the kitchen. She grabbed a bottle out of the refrigerator and placed it in a pan of water on the stove. While the bottle heated up, she went back into the front room to have the much needed talk with Vito. Complete silence filled the room. Marion straightforwardly told him how much she feared for the safety of their children.

"What are you worried about?" Vito asked his worry sick wife. "We've been living here for more than two years and nothing has happened yet. I've got everything under control, everything on the inside and outside of this house."

"We don't know what could happen tomorrow," Marion whined. "We don't know what could happen the next hour. We know that that old Jewish woman next door is always peeking out of her window and coming out on her porch to watch the customers come up to the house. She stays up at all times of night to see what's going on. She might be the one who's got the police watching this house."

"Now look, Marion," Vito purred, speaking soft and low to console his wife. "Nothing is going to happen to anyone in this house. Mrs. Goldstein is old and senile and don't have nothing better to do since her husband died. For chrissake, she's not a threat to us."

"You're saying that because you're only concerned about making more money. Our children are more important than all the money in the world."

The short discussion ended and the overly satisfied customer walked downstairs fastening his pants. Chili Pepper walked beside him, palming his droopy ass with her left hand. They came to the bottom of the stairs. He had an exciting report for Vito.

"Sweet Jesus!" the dirty old man growled, sounding like he released the worries of the world from his body. "I had a helluva good time. This senorita can fuck better than any hooker that I've been with in any of the whore houses around Chi-town." It appeared that he would be another one of Vito's loyal customers.

"That's what we're here for," Vito smiled prosperously, especially knowing that this new customer also liked to drink. He purchased two pints of whiskey. Chili Pepper walked him to the front door and grabbed his dick, a sort of reminder for him to return soon. There weren't going to be any more acts of prostitution. Marion told Chili Pepper to get her belongings and head for home. Other whores were also on duty. A young colored girl named *Honey Mamma*, a white girl named *Booby Trap*, who achieved the nickname from having a set of perfect boobs that could trap most men into giving her anything she wanted, and the short and petite oriental girl named *Fee Fee*. They all walked behind Chili Pepper towards the front door.

Marion was aware that they would be available for the remainder of the week. "Bye bye, Madam Marion," all four women said to Marion as they walked out the door, going to

their respective residences throughout Chicago. After they left, Marion took Vincent back into the room and laid him inside his crib. A gentle turn on his side with the bottle planted between his bright red lips put him to sleep. She patted him on his rosy red cheeks. Someone knocked real hard on the door. Immediately, Marion became alarmed. The sudden fright caused her to run to the basement and alert Vito.

"Vito!" Marion shouted down the basement stairs. "Someone's acting like they're wanting to knock the door down."

"Wait a second, Marion," Vito said, throwing a half-pint of Johnny Walker Red down on top of one of the boxes.

Without hesitation, he grabbed his pearl handled .38 revolver and .22 pistol from a secret compartment behind the boxes of liquor. The .22 was placed down the middle of his pants and the .38 was held firmly in his left hand. Vito had plenty of hardware to protect him and his family. He ran past Marion and straight towards the front door. Gradually, he pulled the short curtains back. Tony stood on the porch anxiously wanting to talk. Vito cautiously opened the door and they walked into the kitchen. Tony tried slowing his heavy breathing before explaining his reason for making a commanding second appearance.

"You're gonna have to listen to me, Vito," he whistled, lowering his head as he placed both hands across his chest. "I mean listen very, very carefully. Bennie and Fat Tony got dope-thugs and pimp-thugs working for them. They're gonna get their boys to try and move in on your turf." Tony wanted to warn Vito with every ounce of information that he obtained. They were like close brothers. True bloodbrothers. Tony's father, Enzo Castellano, was Vito's godfather.

"What makes you think that Bennie and Fat Tony are gonna finish me off in this sweet, notorious fashion?" Vito asked Tony, as an uncertain grin came upon his handsome,

man-child face. "I don't understand it, Tony. I thought that
we were all on the same side here."

"Bennie and Tony are the lowest of backstabbing
sonofabitches in all of Chicago," Tony advised his up and
coming racketeer friend. "When you're in this business,
hardly anyone's on the same side. When one guy makes more
money than the other, and starts controlling everything
around him, those jealous bastards come out of the
woodwork." Tony certainly was on the streets more than Vito.
He knew that men like Bennie and Fat Tony and other
racketeers were out to control turf.

"I don't care about those rogue-punks who want me
rubbed out!" Vito exploded, allowing his hot temper to soar,
raising his already high blood pressure. With a wavering finger, he pointed towards the front door. "If they come to this
house, right here, fucking with Marion and the kids, I'm
gonna pump some hot lead in their asses! That goes for
Bennie Caputo, Fat Tony, Nick Morelli, Rudy Broncato, and
even their dope peddlers and pimp-thugs. Goes for them
all, Tony."

"Vito, calm down," Tony said, then throwing his arm
around the friend that he grew up with in the brutal
Brownsville section of Brooklyn, New York. "For God's sake,
don't let your hot head get you and your family killed. These
guys are very serious. They're a bunch of ruthless punks.
They wouldn't care about killing you and Marion and three
little innocent kids. Do yourself a favor and get out of here
fast. Do it for yourself, Marion, and above all, do it for the sake
of the kids."

Marion stood behind the kitchen door. She looked worried out of her senses. Her children's safety was in jeopardy.
Unfortunately, Vito had a bad case of stubbornness. Before
leaving, Tony told Vito about a possible drive-by shooting of
their home. The rumors that circulated out on the streets

always got back to Tony. Since he was Vito's friend, his best interest was always with the Carvelli family.

"If you can, move as soon as possible. Rudy Broncato and Nick Morelli done spread the word that you've been interrupting their business. They're supposedly gonna send some of their henchman down Fitzgerald and shower your house."

"Thanks, Tony," said Vito, moving closer to give Tony a kiss on the right cheek.

Tony left their home and Vito returned to the basement to finish preparing more liquor and drugs. Marion went into the room to check on the kids. She watched her three sleeping children. They seem to rest very peacefully. She traveled to the basement where Vito unboxed more liquor and weighed more bags of dope. He stood above the small scale that he purchased from one of the merchants down in Little Italy.

"Tony wouldnt've come around here a second time if things weren't as bad as he said," Marion reminded Vito, expressing herself in a voice that pleaded for attention.

"Tony may know a lot of things about what's going on out there on the streets, but he don't know everything," Vito reiterated to his worried wife. "He doesn't know how, when, or where anybody's gonna move in on me."

"Like you would know?" Marion asked sarcastically.

"I might."

"I think that it's time to follow Tony's advice. He's into the rackets just like us."

"I've heard enough advice from enough people for one day," spoke the big ego of Vito, which caused him to have a blatant disregard to what she was trying to say.

"Tony was sent here by God to warn us," Marion rippled. "We'd better take heed to that warning. Me, you, the kids, and anything else that's breathing in this house."

"Are you getting sanctified on me, Marion?" Vito asked, thinking of how Marion would speak so strongly of God when she lived an awfully sinful life.

"I wouldn't call it sanctified, but using God-given common sense."

"Why would you mention God at a time like this?"

"He works in mysterious ways and sends whoever he wants to be his messenger."

"So, Tony's the messenger?"

"Could be."

"Tony came by here because he's my friend. He's like the brother that I never had."

"Don't you even believe in God, Vito?" Marion questioned, like Vito was a true non-believer of religion.

"Yes, I believe in God," Vito answered roughly. "My old man and dear mother were Roman Catholic and we went to church every Sunday."

"Is that a fact?" Marion asked. "Well, my family were Southern Baptists, and I still say God used Tony as a messenger. Goddammit, Vito, were gonna end up all shot to death in this house."

"Damn you, woman!" Vito roared loudly, then throwing a pint of bourbon back into the box. "Your family was nothing but a bunch of poor dumb niggers from the white man's south! Let's get off this religious bullshit and get back to trying to make some more money. Can we do that, please?"

"What did you say?" Marion blasted back, her eyes bucked with sheer astonishment, slinging her left arm around her waist. "What was your family? A bunch of poor dumb dagos from the white man's Italy? Huh?" Neither Marion nor Vito thought that they would live to see the day that they would engage in a heated argument that would eventually become malicious with racism.

"Marion, I'm sorry," Vito apologized, sorry that he ever insulted her family in such a manner. "Honey, I'm sorry. I swear to you, I didn't mean to say those things."

"Yeah, I'll bet you're sorry."

"We'll worry about those things later. Let me finish what I started."

Vito had several boxes of liquor stacked against the wall. He had two large bags filled with marijuana and large cellophane bags of heroin and cocaine. He also had lots of work, trying to decide how the liquor and drugs would be evenly distributed among his many customers. Marion didn't want to continue arguing. She left the basement and went straight to the front room. She took a peak out the front door window. Much to her surprise, there were two blue and white police cars parked down the street. Those unoccupied squad cars were from Chicago's North area district. Marion suddenly became paranoid. She rushed back to the basement to tell Vito. Together, they came upstairs and observed from opposite sides of the curtain. They assumed that the police were probably taking care of a call from somewhere else on the block. Vito returned to the basement to finish his work.

*   *   *

During the early morning hours, an earlier model Chevy cruised down Fitzgerald with the windows rolled down halfway. A sudden burst of gunfire from this car began spraying up the Carvelli residence. Everyone inside the house were awakened and greatly alarmed at the shredding of plaster and wood and the shattering of glass. After the shooting stopped, Vito and Marion rushed downstairs to make sure the children were okay. Vincent cried loudly as Marion cuddled him in her arms. Valerie and Vernon were shook up from all the pandemonium.

"Are you two okay?" Marion asked, staring down at the broken glass near the bed.

"I'm alright, mamma," Valerie answered, stepping up to Marion and embracing her leg.

"Are you okay, Vernon?"

"Yes, mamma."

After calming the baby Vincent down, and consoling

Valerie and Vernon, Marion left their room with Vito. Frightened out of her wits, she turned to Vito and said, "Honey,
we've got to get out of here."

"You're right, Marion," Vito agreed, total submissiveness
in his voice. "Tony told us that it would happen and now it
came to pass."

"Thank God nobody was hurt."

"We're packing up and getting the hell out of here in
the morning."

Vito and Marion didn't care about the damage that the
massacre did to their home. They planned on leaving before
an even worse massacre would occur. This was probably a
small message of warning from Bennie Caputo and Fat Tony
and some other rival mobster hoods.

Chapter 2

SUSPICION

VALERIE AND VERNON sat at the table eating breakfast. Marion sat on the sofa feeding Vincent. Suddenly, Vito stormed through the front door with a fresh copy of *The Chicago Tribune* curled under his right armpit. He was breathing like he was an olympic sprinter. During the early morning hours, Vito suspected henchman associated with Bennie Caputo and Fat Tony drove by and shot up the whole Carvelli residence. Luckily, no one was hurt. Valerie and Vernon rested their spoons in their bowls of cereal. They stared aimlessly at a very restless Vito.

"He really knew what he was talking about," Vito recalled, not able to stop talking about the warning Tony had given him.

"What are you talking about?" Marion asked Vito, squeezing baby Vincent under her right arm.

"The word's out on the streets that Nick Morelli and Bennie Caputo had this house shot up."

"What are we gonna do? Where are we gonna go?"

"Take this newspaper and try and find someone who'll keep the kids until we find another spot," Vito instructed Marion, unfolding the paper and placing it on her lap.

Marion sat Vincent at the end of the sofa. She opened the paper to the child care section and paced the floor with her head covered. She took a ballpoint pen and glanced up and down the child care columns. One column after another, Marion attentively searched for someone who would care for the children. Was there someone in a safer location

who didn't mind keeping Valerie, Vernon, and Vincent until Vito and Marion found another home?

There were man daycare houses and babysitters throughout the metropolitan Chicago area. These houses and sitters basically cared for children on a five day, work week basis. It was the usual 9:00 a.m. through 5:00 p.m., Monday through Friday schedule. Meals and recreational activities were provided. Marion realized that it wouldn't be easy finding someone who would keep the kids while Vito made plans of relocation. Neither Marion nor Vito had relatives or friends who would watch their children. She continued her search until she came across an ad that had an appeal to it. Halfway down the third column of the lengthy child care section, Marion read an ad that could be the answer to her prayers. The ad read as follows:

Child care, flexible hours. Number of children and length of stay negotiable. Meals and recreation provided. Contact Bessie Mae Willingham at 742-8286.

Marion couldn't find a better offer anywhere else in the paper. The length of stay being negotiable is what she found most eyecatching. She moved the telephone over to her lap and dialed those crucial digits. The phone rang at the Willingham residence. It rang several times before a tenor-voice woman answered. There was someone in the background screaming loudly, like they were being beat viciously. The loud screaming carried over from another room. Marion explained to the strange woman that she had three children who needed someone to care for them until they found another home.

"I don't have a problem with that," Bessie Mae

Willingham told Marion. "If you leave clean clothes for the kids, that'll be fine."

"I must tell you that I have a six month old baby," Marion added, speaking slightly hesitant. "My other two children are four and six years old."

"Bring them over and we'll be glad to keep them until you find a place."

"Well, who all lives in your home?" Marion asked.

"There's a few people, as you'll see when you get over here," Bessie Mae said woefully.

"Where do you live?"

"Do you know where Milwaukee Parkway is?" asked Bessie Mae.

"The Milwaukee Parkway that's not too far from Rush Boulevard and Lowell Avenue?" Marion recalled quite well, mapping the streets out in her mind.

"Exactly," Bessie Mae said. "Where are you coming from?"

"We're coming from around Thirty-Second and Fitzgerald." Marion was sort of reluctant to reveal their address.

"If you drive south on the expressway, you can't miss Milwaukee. We're in a dark green house at the corner of Thirty-Ninth and Milwaukee."

"We'll be over shortly."

"Okay."

Marion walked up to the second floor to let Vito know that she had found someone to watch their children. Hopefully, it would be a more comfortable and safer place. After having a long discussion, Vito decided that it wasn't such a bad idea to take the children over to the Willingham's child care residence, at least until they figured out their next move.

Marion left the room to start gathering their belongings. She packed clean clothing, fresh diapers, toys, milk, and several infant toiletries. Maybe it would be enough until they returned. Their bags were filled. The children were bathed and everyone was ready to take off. Vito was across the street

warming up his sparkling red, 1964 Cadillac Sedan de Ville. Marion walked behind Valerie, who swung her long braid back and forth. Vernon carried his brother in his left arm, along with a baby bag in the other. Vito was proud to have his family riding in his spanking brand new automobile. His car definitely stood out. It had white leather seats, an immaculate red paint job, an eight track player, and fancy tires with rims, which had the Cadillac emblem sculptured in the middle. While Vito started the car up, he listened to the mesmerizing tunes of Sam Cooke. Once everyone climbed inside, he began driving south on the expressway. Sam Cooke sure had the silky smooth voice that could soothe the soul.

Since the tune, "*You Send Me*", was one of Vito's favorites, he sang along with the tape, grasping Marion's left leg. It wasn't unusual for an Italian like Vito to listen to soul singers like The Temptations, The Platters, Nat King Cole, and James Brown. Frank Sinatra and Tony Bennett were also some of his favorites. He had to remind himself that he had several previous convictions for traffic violations from all over the Chicago area.

These convictions mainly involved drunk and careless driving. He drove with caution. Vincent playfully tossed and turned in his mother's lap, while Valerie and Vernon leaned against the back of the front seats. Vito turned up the volume on the song that became a monstrous hit for Sam Cooke.

"Where are we going, mamma?" Valerie asked Marion, slightly talking over the music.

"We're going to take you and your brothers over someone's house," Marion explained. "You're going to stay there until we find another home." It wasn't easy explaining things to her curious daughter. Marion turned to give Vito a glare of uncertainty. Vito grew up in a home where a child was taught to stay in a child's place. He believed that they shouldn't ask too many questions. But Valerie still had a right to know.

"How long we're gonna stay there, mamma?" Vernon asked, leaning over the middle, resting between both front seats.

"I don't know," Marion answered, not able to give her son any assurance. "I really don't know, Vernon."

After driving out the expressway, Vito drove to a stop sign at the corner of Milwaukee Parkway. Marion looked slightly to the left and there was a large green house. The lower half was constructed entirely of solid brick. A large brick chimney overshadowed the roof. This house appeared to be the largest one on the block. It was spooky looking and could scare the life out of anyone. There was a dark green Cadillac Fleetwood and a black Chevy truck parked beside one another in the front yard.

Vito took a hard look at all the houses and automobiles. He assumed that the people who resided in the neighborhood were all coloreds. It wasn't uncommon for some of the coloreds in Chicago to drive those fancy Cadillacs. There were other houses up and down Milwaukee that were constructed like the one on the corner. The left and right sides of the block had houses with flat yards and small trees standing in front of each house. When the traffic was clear, Vito made a sharp left onto Milkwaukee Parkway.

He parked in front of the very house that Bessie Mae Willingham had described over the phone. He came around on the passenger's side to help carry some of the bags. Marion instructed Valerie and Vernon to grab one side of a large bag that was stuffed with Vincent's toiletries. She held Vincent in her left arm and carried a small bag in the other. As they approached the house, people at surrounding houses came to their front doors. They stepped out on their porches and peeked between the cracks of the concrete columns. They were observing the interracial couple who made their way up to the Willingham residence. Next door, a colored couple and their small children watched the Carvelli family like

they were people from another planet. The entire neighborhood was predominantly colored. Vito, Marion, and their
children were basically frowned upon as though they were
not welcome.

"What in the hell are they staring at?" Marion charged in
an explosive voice. "These nosy people act like they've never
seen a colored woman with an Italian man. I'd wish they
would go back into their houses and mind their own dam
business!"

"You have to understand one thing," Vito said to his wife
of nearly four years. "We love each other and that's all that
counts."

Vito knew that you could never please everybody. Inside
his mind, love had no color, especially since he had sampled
women of practically every nationality. But how was it that he
ended up falling madly in love with a colored woman?

Generally, his philosophy was: *"You can please some of the
people sometimes, but you can't please all of the people all the time."*

At times, he wished that he could've taken Marion and
the kids back to New York, but he realized that there was too
much money to be made in Chicago.

"Did you lose something?" Marion said, smarting off to
the entire family next door. They stared at the Carvelli family
in the most disapproving manner.

"Marion! Marion!" Vito said to his angry wife. "Let them
look all they want, honey. As long as they don't put a hand on
any of us."

Vito and Marion knew that they were against incredible
odds when they first decided to marry in the early spring of
1960. Not only did the coloreds around them disapprove,
but other racial groups, such as the Italians, Jewish, Polish,
Dutch, and Irish, all disapproved of anyone marrying out of
their ethnic background.

Vito was once told by a well-known Italian vice lord named

Ross Vignelli, who once supplied him with some of his liquor and dope:

"You're in serious trouble, Vito."
"Why?" Vito asked Ross.
"You're taking it upon yourself to marry a colored woman?" Ross said in a tone that made it seem that Vito was not only disgracing himself, but all Italian people.
"So, what's wrong with that?" Vito questioned, not even concerned what others had to say.
"Everything's wrong," Ross warned. "You can't even live like normal people. They'll look at both of you and wonder what is a nigger and a dago doing married to one another.
"I don't care, because I love Marion."
"Okay, it's your life, Vito."

They came up on the porch to this creepy residence. Vito tapped lightly on the screen door with his rock hard knuckles. A medium complexioned colored woman limped to the front door. She was about forty-five years old and large-boned. Her left leg was slightly deformed. It was shorter than normal as a result of an improperly set broken hip at age two. It didn't cause her pain or restrict her movements. Tiny black moles covered her lower left and right cheeks. Like her neighbors, she was surprised to see the interracial couple. She strongly concealed her facial expression.

"May I help you?" the southern accented woman asked.

"Are you Bessie Mae Willingham?" Marion wanted to know.

"Yes, I am," she answered with apprehension, like the Carvelli family were at the wrong house.

"I'm Marion Carvelli and this is my husband Vito Carvelli."

I spoke with you on the phone about bringing my children over."

"Oh yeah, come on in," Bessie Mae replied, smiling deceitfully into the faces of Marion and Vito.

"We're pleased to meet you," Vito said as walked into the front room with the children.

Bessie Mae told them to take a seat. She excused herself to go back into the kitchen of the very spacious home. While she walked away, Vito and Marion watched her left leg. It was badly deformed, causing her to walk unevenly, limping up and down in vertical motions.

Bessie Mae limped to the doorway of the kitchen and leaned her right arm against the door. Her mother, Ida Lou Pierson, who was better known around the house as *Granny Dear*, was a heavyset woman of a much darker complexion. She was restricted to a wheelchair as a result of severe arthritis throughout her body. Granny Dear leaned back in her wheelchair, wondering why her daughter stood in the doorway speechless.

Bessie Mae's husband, Jesse Dewayne Willingham, was known by many friends and relatives as *J.D.* He was very dark complexioned, rather heavyset, almost to the point of being obese, and bald over his entire shiny head. In short, J.D. Willingham was labeled as being *big, black, and ugly*. Like Granny Dear, J.D. wondered why his wife stood perfectly still with her lips locked. She had some very shocking news for their attentive ears.

"J.D. and Granny Dear, guess what?" Bessie Mae said in a pumped up voice.

"What?" J.D. answered before Granny Dear could say anything.

"You all remember that woman who called about bringing her kids over here to stay awhile?"

"Yep," said J.D., waiting for her to continue.

"They're in the front room and guess what?"

"What?" said Granny Dear, gripping the sides of her wheelchair and leaning forward. "C'mon and tell us." Her voice also had a strong southern accent.

"She's a colored woman and he's a white man," Bessie Mae mentioned unfavorably. "He looks like one of them dam dagos that we buy fruit from down in Little Italy." As soon as they came to the front door, Bessie Mae could recognize Vito's Italian features.

"Colored gal? White mane?" J.D. responded with a twist of his mouth. He knew that interracial couples were a *no no* in his hometown.

"Isn't that what I said?"

"I'm fum Mississippa, and anybodies know dat a colored gal and white mane ain't spose ta be'gether." J.D. spoke in an illiterate dialect.

"Huh!" Bessie Mae chuckled. "I don't even see why they're together." Bessie Mae tried keeping her voice at a low tone to keep the Carvelli couple from hearing their discussion.

"Dey got chilluns?" J.D. asked.

"They've got three. Two boys and a girl."

"What dey chilluns look like?"

"Since the mamma's colored and the daddy's white, the baby boy looks like one of those half-breeds, like a trick baby. The older boy and girl look like they got a different daddy." Bessie Mae gave her best observation of the children.

"Twick baby, huh," J.D. chuckled. "I thank most half-beed chilluns are twick babies anyway."

Being that Bessie Mae and Granny Dear were both natives of Memphis, Tennessee, and J.D. was a native of Clarksdale, Mississippi, their attitudes towards interracial dating and marriages and bi-racial children were definitely dissenting. J.D. walked behind Bessie Mae, pushing Granny Dear's wheelchair towards the front room. They stepped into the front room and Bessie Mae introduced Marion and Vito to

her husband and mother. They shook hands and made one another's acquaintances. J.D. opened the floor to questions.

"So, whadda you do fo a libbing?" J.D. asked Vito straightforwardly, not even caring if he sounded nosy.

"Could you repeat yourself?" Vito asked, leaning forward and moving his head sideways, because J.D.'s improper English had thrown him way off guard.

"Whadda you do fo a libbing?" J.D. repeated, not able to express himself any clearer.

"I'm sorry, but I still can't understand the question," Vito said, as he sort of gave J.D. a friendly frown, still not understanding the badly broken English in his southern speech. There was every indication that J.D. had very little education. "You're asking me what I do for a what?"

"I said, whadda . . . ya . . . do . . . fo . . . a . . . libbing?" This time, J.D. drug his words very slowly, badly mispronouncing the word *living*.

"Oh, you're asking me what do I do for a living?" Vito understood J.D. a lot clearer this time.

"Yep."

"Well, I run my own business."

"What kind'a bizness is dat?"

"I sell goods out of my house."

"What kind of goods is dat?" J.D. felt the need to grill Vito to no apparent satisfaction. He wanted to question him like he had to know everything about him.

"Cigarettes, clothing, and food. You name it, I've probably got it." Vito had to lie in every way possible, wanting J.D.'s stupid ass to stop asking so many questions.

Bessie Mae didn't want her husband to sound like inspector Dick Tracy. She threw up a hand signal for him to end the chain of questions. Suddenly, there were two men walking down the stairs facing the room they occupied. They came to the bottom of the stairs and Bessie Mae called them into the front room. She wanted to introduce them to the

Carvelli family. The man in the very front had a very strong and compact body. He had a reddish, Indian like complexion, and a very low shadow haircut.

"Vito and Marion, this is George Braun," Bessie Mae said, introducing one of her male occupants. "He's a mentally retarded man that I've been keeping for awhile. He's real helpful around the house. Everybody around here calls him Braun. I don't know what I'd do without him."

"Good to meet you, Braun," said Vito, reaching forward to shake Braun's hard chapped hand. Braun did much housework for Bessie Mae and his worn hands were proof.

"Yeah! Yeah!" Braun spoke back in a hyper voice, then smiling at Vito and Marion with a set of badly rotten teeth. Old food particles and tobacco kernels were also smeared across them. "I'm pleased to meet you, too."

Vito and Marion made immediate eye contact. They frowned distastefully at one another. How did that guy's teeth get that bad? They could only wonder what happened to them. The man behind Braun trotted slowly across the blue carpet with a set of glossy eyes. He stared deep into space. His build was very thin, and his complexion was oily but clear. In the same style and length as Braun, this man's haircut was low and trimmed. After several minutes, his eyeballs and eyelids were motionless.

"Vito and Marion, this is another mentally retarded man that I've been keeping for a few years," Bessie Mae explained, holding the second man by the middle of his left arm. "His name is Raymond Bolton, Jr., but everybody around here calls him Junior."

"How are you doing, Junior?" Vito and Marion asked, respectively, as they both reached to shake his hand.

"How are you doing? How are you doing?" Junior repeated twice, nodding his head and looking forward without a single blink of his eyes.

"Quit repeating what they just said," Bessie Mae ordered,

speaking as though she had total control over him. "Just tell them that you're doing fine."

"Tell them you're doing fine. Tell them you're doing fine."

"You'll have to excuse Junior," Bessie Mae explained once again. "Like I first told you, Junior is mentally retarded and repeats everything."

"That's understandable," said Vito, then turning to look over at Marion.

It was rumored that Junior lost his mind after he witnessed both parents shot to death by a man whom Junior's father, Raymond Bolton, Sr., owed thousands of dollars to. The validity of this rumor remained in question. After being confined to several mental institutions and homes for the mentally retarded, Junior ended up in the Willingham residence. At this point, Vito and Marion suspected that these two men had something in common. Bessie Mae excused them. As they were leaving the room, J.D. observed something that deeply angered him.

"Put yo goddam shirt tail in yo britches, Joanyer!" J.D. shouted at Junior. He gained the immediate attention of everyone present. His strong bass voice frightened the children. Vito tuned in tightly to the threat that J.D. lashed out at Junior. And pronouncing Junior's name in the most screwed up manner left him curious. Joanyer? It was like adding *yer* to the name *Joan*. Dumb bastard!

"Shirt tail in britches. Shirt tail in britches," Junior replied submissively, then walking away whining. He swung his right arm to the back and shoved his shirt down into his pants. J.D. would nearly breathe fire like a dragon whenever he saw someone with their shirt hanging over the back of their pants.

Vito and Marion wondered why J.D. shouted such cruelty at the frail and mentally retarded man who seemed to be meek in nature. While Braun and Junior were stepping onto

the porch, a little girl walked into the front room patting her chest. Bessie Mae grabbed her by the arm and introduced her to the Carvelli family.

"Everyone, this is a foster girl of mine's named Carmen Taylor," Bessie Mae told Vito and Marion. "I've been keeping her since she was a baby."

"Foster girl?" Marion asked Bessie Mae, surprised that she kept two kinds of people in their home. "Do you keep foster children too?"

"Sure do," she replied, a calibre of greed coming out in her voice. "I'm licensed by the state of Illinois to care for foster children and the handicapped."

"So, this is a home for both foster children and handicapped people?"

"It's been that way for a long time," Bessie Mae said. "As a matter of fact, my husband and I would like to have more foster children come and stay with us."

"Why's that?" Marion inquired, not for sure if Bessie Mae viewed foster children as property.

"You know, the parents these days don't care for their children the way they should. So many of them end up in group homes and orphanages and foster homes."

"Do you have any children of your own?"

"No."

"You never wanted any of your own?"

"One of my tubes was scarred when I was young. It ruined my chances of having any children."

"Is this girl Carmen the only foster child that you have in your home?" Marion asked, thoroughly checking things out at the Willingham home.

"Right now she is," Bessie Mae said. "But like I said, I'd like to have more children come and stay with us." Bessie Mae had spelled it out. She could not admit that more foster children meant more money. This issue concerned Marion deeply.

Carmen found the baby Vincent irresistable. She wanted to hold him in her little arms. Marion lifted him up from her lap and handed him over to her. The dark complexioned girl with high cheek bones bounced him around in her arms. Carmen was given to Bessie Mae and J.D. by the family services when she was three days old. Her parents could no longer keep her. The Willinghams didn't have legal custody papers on Carmen, because her father had considered marrying again. The woman he wanted to marry would have been a good mother to her.

Carmen lifted Vincent up and down towards the ceiling. Valerie and Vernon smiled up at their baby brother. While she circled the room with the baby, Bessie Mae and J.D. volunteered to show Vito and Marion their enormous home. The children would have time to become better acquainted. Bessie Mae started this tour by limping back into the kitchen, where there was a long red curtain that covered a doorway. Beyond this doorway was Granny Dear's room.

The room had a comfortable queen-sized bed, an eight drawer dresser, a portable black and white television, and a small dusty coffee table. Since they were in the kitchen, Bessie Mae pointed to the cabinets that housed the dishes and cooking ingredients. An oval shaped table with four iron cast chairs sat in the middle of the floor. A tall refrigerator and a four burner stove sat against the adjacent walls near Granny Dear's room. She limped into the dining room and pointed to an area that had a long, solid oak table which could seat six people. The table had matching oak chairs with padded seating. There was a black lacquer china cabinet in the corner behind the kitchen door. It had expensive chinaware inside, like plates, cups, and saucers. A shelf to the right of the table had plates with U.S. presidents and historical landmarks painted in the middle.

Bessie Mae took them into the den and showed them her expensive antique furniture and collectibles which

decorated that whole area. From the number of new pieces of furniture, and new decorative items appearing in the Willingham home, Bessie Mae and J.D. were living to the limits of their incomes. Marion and Vito thought it must be a severe financial strain on them.

"Wow!" said Vito. "All this stuff must've cost a fortune. Where did you buy all these nice things?"

"I have a friend who's into the antique business," Bessie Mae said with pride. "She gives me a discount on everything."

"Man!" Vito snorkled. "This stuff looks like it could decorate the homes of rich people."

Bessie Mae limped past a bathroom and to a doorway that went down a hallway towards the front room. Vito and Marion were only a few steps behind her. J.D. was only a few steps behind them. She opened a door that led down a narrow set of stairs. The stairs were old, made of a thin wood that was beginning to rot. Since there were two set of stairs, everyone took a sharp left down the other half.

Vito and Marion moved closer to the bottom of this area. Quickly, their heads jerked back. J.D. was a couple of stairs behind, watching their swift head movement and sour facial expressions. There were many piles of dirty laundry that covered the floor. An electric washing machine and dryer stood against the wall to the left. Some of this laundry wasn't a pretty sight to behold or to smell.

"Gosh!" Vito thought to himself, slowly nodding his head, biting his lower lip, and then squeezing every muscle in his face. "Look at all those underwear and pants with shit and piss smeared everywhere!"

There was a place for filth in the Willingham household. Directly past the laundry room, there was a large room that had three unoccupied beds, dressers, and a closet over

in the far left corner. Bessie Mae took them down a short hallway and into a small room. There was a young man who sat in a chair with his head down. He rocked back and forth in the sturdy wooden chair, looking real sad, as though something was troubling him. He made swaying motions, like he wanted to fall asleep.

"Shone!" J.D. yelled, who happened to be standing behind Bessie Mae. He clutched tightly onto the large black strap around his waist. "Sat yo muttapucking ass up in dat chair wight!"

Vito and Marion turned to lock eye contact once again. They frowned into one another's face. They wondered why J.D. went around cursing at the occupants in their home. Vito noticed that J.D. couldn't even use profanity the correct way, which left him awfully curious.

"How much education did this dumb nigger have?" Vito silently speculated, a street-oriented, but semi-educated man who knew very well that you didn't say 'sat yo', but rather you say, 'sat your'. Where did he get the word 'muttapucking'? Isn't it supposed to be 'motherfucking'? Did this big black country sonofabitch even make it past the first grade?"

Bessie Mae had the strange man to stand and be introduced. "Vito and Marion, this is another handicapped man that I've been keeping for a while. His name is Sean Randle and he's a fairly bright young man. He can be stubborn at times, but my husband usually straightens him out."

"We're pleased to meet you, Sean," said Vito and Marion in a perfect unison. They both reached forward to shake his hand.

Sean wasn't quite mentally retarded. His left hand was totally useless from paralysis. It had a deformity that gave it a

shape like the top of a crowbar. Sean was known to have spells and was given medication. A strong slant in his walk caused him to drag his feet. He shooks hands with Vito and Marion and everyone left the basement. Vito wondered how the people at the Willingham residence were being treated. J.D. had outlandishly cursed at another handicapped occupant. Who was next on his hitlist of insults?

Bessie Mae took the tour up to the second floor. This floor had four rooms, three of which were occupied by the Willingham couple, Carmen, and Braun and Junior. The last room at the end of the hall was unoccupied. Bessie Mae and J.D.'s room was furnished with a lavish king-sized bed, a long solid oak dresser, a large RCA television, matching oak coffee tables, and two portable radios. There was a large linen closet next to their room. A full restroom was across from the linen closet.

Bessie Mae made sure that Vito and Marion wouldn't see the other commodities in their room. She wanted to end this tour of their very large home by leading Vito and Marion back to the front room. Carmen was sucking all over Vincent's rosy red cheeks. She kissed him in the dead center of his bright red lips.

"Carmen!" Bessie Mae shouted at her foster daughter. "Quit kissing all over the baby like that. He ain't no dollbaby for you to be kissing all over!" Carmen sure thought that she had a dollbaby in her arms.

Before leaving, Vito and Marion gave their children many hugs and kisses. Marion wanted them to behave themselves while they were gone.

"When are you coming back, mamma?" Valerie asked in a whining tone.

"Mamma'll be back when we find another home," Marion explained to her adorable daughter. "Now, you be good and do what Mr. and Mrs. Willingham tell you."

"I wanna go with you, mamma," Valerie insisted, then shedding a light tear.

"You can't go right now. Give me a kiss and be a good girl."

Valerie and Vernon walked up to Marion and planted a kiss on her left and right cheeks. Marion moved to where Carmen stood and gave Vincent a kiss. The Willinghams walked out on the porch with the Carvelli couple. The children waved goodbye. Carmen raised Vincent's arm and shook it in a waving motion. Bessie Mae assured Vito and Marion that the children would be in good hands until they returned. She told them to call if any changes occurred. Though Vito and Marion were extremely apprehensive about leaving their children with the Willinghams, they also realized that they would probably be much safer in a house that wasn't being shot up by rival gangsters. J.D. stood near the front door. He gave Vito a grimacing look that was much too noticeable. Vito knew a knavish man when he saw one. J.D. Willingham fit that description. The Carvellis said goodbye to the Willinghams. They got into their car and drove northbound down Milwaukee Parkway.

Chapter 3

FOR THE RECORD

SEVERAL WEEKS PASSED and the Carvelli couple didn't return for their children. They didn't leave a phone number or address. Bessie Mae kept wondering where they were and how she could get into contact with them. She cared for Valerie and Vernon and the baby Vincent as though she were their legal guardian. She wasn't too happy, mainly because she provided three well-balanced meals a day, extra old clothing, and milk and diapers for Vincent.

When the Willinghams were told a few days, they weren't expecting to keep the children longer than a week, two weeks at the most. They discussed it with Vito and Marion. While expressing no interest in the children and no true desire to have them in the home, J.D. considered the children and handicapped men Bessie Mae's responsibility. He remained aloof from much of the home interaction.

Bessie Mae felt that she couldn't wait any longer, especially after getting the notion that the children had been abandoned. She made an attempt to contact The Department of Children and Family Services in the south region of Cook County.

Valerie and Vernon played happily with Carmen on the front room floor. They waited for "*Leave It To Beaver*" to come on. Eddie Haskel made everyone laugh with all his funny jokes. Vincent lay sound asleep on a blanket in the den. Bessie Mae limped to the back of the kitchen door in search of a phone book. She found the white pages for the greater Chicago area buried under some old newspapers.

She went into the den and flipped through the city and
state government pages. Her finger trailed up and down the
pages for the state government agencies. It would have been
easier for her to go upstairs and find the number for Carmen's
caseworker in her personal phone directory. Bessie Mae
limped everywhere she traveled. Going up and down the
stairs was murder on her already strained legs. The children
made loud chuckling sounds. They kicked their feet against
the sofa and slammed their fists down on the floor. Eddie
Haskel was on "*Leave It To Beaver*" making insulting wise cracks
at Wally and The Beaver. It tickled Valerie, Vernon, and
Carmen's funny bones.

"Cut out all that dam noise!" Bessie Mae yelled into the
front room. She informed the children that she had to make
an important phone call. She dialed the number for social
services. The phone rang at the main switchboard inside the
downtown office of The Department of Children and Family
Services. Bessie Mae waited a few seconds and one of the
supervisors in the twenty-four hour child abuse and neglect
division took the call.

"This is Helen Bartlett," the woman said, a tiresome spark
in her voice. "How may I help you?"

"Yes, my name's Bessie Mae Willingham," Bessie Mae
mentioned. "I have three children who've been living in my
home for the past several weeks. Their parents haven't come
back for them."

"What are the children's names?" Helen asked.

"The oldest boy's name is Vernon Ramirez," Bessie Mae
paused. "The girl's name is Valerie Ramirez. The baby boy's
name is Vincent Carvelli."

"What are their parent's names."

"Vito Carvelli and Marion Carvelli," Bessie Mae said re-
sentfully, sort of giving Helen the idea that she wished that it
was unlawful for such a marital union. "She's a colored woman

and he's an Italian man." Helen really didn't have to know that information.

"I assume that Valerie and Vernon have a different father than Vincent?"

"Yes, they do."

Helen knew that this was a possible case of abandonment. As a thirteen year veteran of the family services, she had dealt with many similar cases. She informed Bessie Mae that she would have to follow through with a couple of procedures. First and foremost, she would have to contact The City of Chicago Police Department Internal Affairs Division. They would have to be informed that the Carvelli couple abandoned their children. Police must determine Vito and Marion's whereabouts.

Bessie Mae hung up and went into the kitchen. Granny Dear had dumped leftover food into a ten gallon white bucket. The large bucket was used to dump food slop from breakfast, lunch, and dinner. J.D.'s beagle hounds were fed this collection of different food groups. They were in the backyard barking very loudly. Bessie Mae told Granny Dear that she was waiting for an important call, which would tell her where Vito and Marion were. She sat at the kitchen table taking hard puffs from her Pall Mall Red cigarette. Unexpectedly, Vernon came to the doorway to inquire about his parents.

"When is my mamma and daddy coming back?" Vernon asked, a sorrowful tone to match the sorrowful facial expression.

"They should be back soon," Bessie Mae told the curious juvenile, finding it hard to give a genuine answer. It was ironic that Vernon would ask that question. Bessie Mae was overly anxious to find out herself.

It was late in the afternoon and Vincent was in the den crying. He was awake and everyone knew it. Bessie Mae

mashed out her cigarette and limped into the den. Carmen
and Valerie were in the front room watching him cry his lungs
flat. Bessie Mae picked him up and stuck her right hand
between his diaper. He was soaking wet. The phone rang
and it was proably the call that she'd been waiting on. Since
Carmen had knowledge of how to change a baby's diaper,
she was told to change him. Bessie Mae limped back into the
kitchen. She answered the phone and it was Helen Bartlett.

"I hope that you have a patient ear, Mrs. Willingham,"
Helen told Bessie Mae. "I made a call over to the police
department and found out some information on Vito and
Marion Carvelli." Helen flipped through a stack of papers
which had notes that she had taken. "Let me start with some
information on Vito Carvelli that I obtained from an
investigator named Anthony Zahorsky from the 8th District
Headquarters of The Chicago Police Department."

* * *

*Vito Carvelli is an ex-convict born in New York City on 4-25-20 to
Salvatore and Maria Carvelli. Since he is of Italian descent, records
indicate that he has been involved with small-time Chicago organized
crime racketeers, men such as Antonio Torio, Rudolpho Broncato,
Benedito Caputo, Anthony Castellano, Ross Vignelli, and Nicodemo
Morelli. These men are believed to be his source of illegal vice activities,
which he operated in a house for vice at 3233 Fitzgerald. Vito's
criminal files shows 52 criminal convictions prior to 10-24-64. These
arrests include suspicion of highway robbery; burglary; larceny; drunk
and careless driving violations; investigation of prostitutional
activities, which includes being a procurer and renting out rooms for
illegal and immoral purposes; disturbing the peace; assault and battery;
possession of illegal firearms; gas rationing violations during World
War II; cashing bogus checks; possession of narcotics with the intent to
distribute; selling liquor without a permit; suspicion of murder;
loansharking; gambling; and failure to appear before the courts. Vito*

was recently arrested for selling liquor without a permit and being in the company of prostitutes who were well-known throughout the Chicago area. In the past, Vito has been confined to state, county, and federal correctional institutions. No known occupation has ever been shown for him, and he has always made his living illegally. His criminal record is so extensive until it would be impossible to read over all the documentation.

* * *

Bessie Mae was practically blown through the ceiling after listening to Vito's long and illustrious criminal career. "Goodness gracious!" Bessie Mae crooned, slowly wiping sweat from under her neck. "He must've spent the majority of his life in and out of jail or the penitentiary. When my husband asked him what he did for a living, he told him that he was a businessman who sold products out of his home. Now I see what kind of products he sold out of his home."

Bessie Mae pulled the phone away from her ear to stop Carmen from rubbing on Vincent's tiny genitals.

"Stop that, girl!" Bessie Mae shouted. "You were supposed to be changing his diaper, not playing with his wee wee."

"I wasn't playing with his wee wee, Mrs. Willingham," Carmen lied, now putting the finishing touches on the new diaper.

"I'm sitting right here and watching you."

"I'm sorry, Mrs. Willingham."

"Finish what you're doing and put the baby down."

Bessie Mae placed the phone back up to her ear. After she paused a few moments, Helen moved on to explain Marion's criminal career.

*   *   *

A check of the record bureau from the 8th District Headquarters, has revealed some information regarding a Marion Denise Carvelli. She is also an ex-convict born here in Chicago, Illinois on 8-30-33 to Earl and Willa Mae Baker. According to the records on this subject, now on file in the Chicago Police Department records bureau, Marion has been arrested, charged, and found guilty on charges of prostitution since she was sixteen years of age. Numerous reports read in her file by Investigator Zahorsky, where she was found in the company with white men on or near the 3200 and 3300 blocks of Fitzgerald. She would be stopped by police on suspicion of prostitution. White men driving by in their cars admitted that they had just been propositioned by a definite price for an act of prostitution or had just been given a price for performing an act of prostitution on the body of other prostitutes. Marion's arrests are too numerous to dictate, and, as they all pertain to the investigation of vice activities. Her file cards have been thermofaxed by Investigator Zahorsky and forwarded on to a caseworker for further information. Judging from the information that I received, Marion has been in and out of jail for prostitution, soliciting rooms for illegal and immoral purposes, being an inmate of a bawdy house, and selling liquor without a permit. Marion was recently arrested along with her husband, Vito, for the solicitation of prostitution, selling liquor without a permit, and renting rooms for illegal and immoral purposes. Vito and Marion are being held in the Cook County Jail until they can meet their bond.

*   *   *

Bessie Mae was absolutely speechless. Did the police and investigators find any of the narcotics that Vito had stashed in his basement? Did Vito find a place to hide the drugs before they raided the house? The organized crime unit and the prostitution and obscene matter unit were only able to charge them with selling liquor without a permit and

compulsory prostitution. Bessie Mae didn't know which direction to turn after she listened to the perennial records of three helpless children's parents. She was definitely concerned about spending more money to provide the children's necessities.

The uncertainty about the ability to provide adequate financial support to Valerie, Vernon, and Vincent, over an infinite period of time without some state-supported assistance, sent Bessie Mae's blood pressure soaring. She was already popping four blood pressure pills a day. In a very loud voice, she cried, *"I need money for these kids and I need it right now!"* It sure seemed like Vito and Marion's criminal records could stretch a real long way.

Bessie Mae didn't know what to do until they got out of jail. Helen Bartlett enlightened her that Vito and Marion would be summoned to appear at The Cook County Juvenile Detention Center immediately following their release from jail. Bessie Mae confirmed that she and J.D. would try to satisfactorily meet the children's needs until the court decided where the children would live.

Chapter 4

LONG LIVES A LIE

J.D. WALKED through the front door at 5:00 p.m. wearing a dark blue uniform covered with small patches of tar. He carried a large silver lunchbucket and had an evil look on his shiny black face. As a roofer, he stepped in melted tar all day long. The tar fumes gave him a head rush and usually sent him home with a major headache. His greatest fear was facing a white man who sat behind a desk gliding a pen across a piece of paper, someone who called all the shots and determined the direction of his fate. J.D. resented the fact that he only had a first grade education, and putting roofs on houses and businesses for minimal wages was all he could do. Illusions of any white man's face always sent him into anger frenzies, filling his sinnister mind with the most hateful thoughts.

I ain't neva gone git head cause of da white mane.
White folks done kep colored folks back long nuff.
White mane done cheat us, beat us, and fucked our colored gals.
Dat's why we got all dese half-beed chilluns runnin round here.
Got too many chilluns lookin like dey halves white.
Colored folks gittin pimped by da white mane everyday.
We been dey hoes long nuff.
We still livin in slavery.
Dey still using whips and chains on us and we ain't got nuff sense ta see it.
Colored folks ain't got nuff sense ta stand up fo deyself.
One day I'm gone git back at'em.
Watch what I tell ya.

My day gone come.
I'm gone git back at every white mane dat eva done ma wong.
It's gone happen soon nuff.

Bessie Mae stood in the hallway near the basement. She rushed J.D. back into the kitchen to give him the news of the day. He took a seat at the end of the kitchen table and fired up one of his Pall Mall Gold cigarettes.

"Guess what, J.D.?" Bessie Mae said to her exhausted husband, pulling a Pall Mall Red from the pack for a smoke break.

"What's on yo mind?" J.D. answered, sending long drags of smoke from both of his wide dark nostrils.

"Remember that Italian-White man named Vito and that colored woman named Marion Carvelli?"

"Talkin bout da ones who ain't came back fo dey chilluns?" J.D. commented unfavorably. "What bout'em?"

"They're in jail."

"In jail!" J.D. replied surprisingly, nearly coughing from the sudden news. "What dey in jail fo?"

"Ready for this?" Bessie Mae paused. "They had a house on Thirty-Second and Fitzgerald that they were using to sell liquor, dope, and running whores in and out of."

"How ya find all dis out?"

"Wasn't hard it all, J.D.," Bessie Mae made clear, limping over to the other side of the table to mash out her cigarettte. "I just called down to the family services and they told me everything that I needed to know."

"Dey told ya everythang?" J.D. asked, even longer drags blowing from his nose.

"Everything."

"I knew sumthang was crooked bout both of dem."

"I knew something was crooked about both of them, too," Bessie Mae added. "He had the nerves to talk about selling

products out of his house. He couldn't come straight out and tell us that he was nothing but a bootlegger, dope dealer, and pimp."

"Shit!" J.D. squealed. "We should'a known dat dat Italian mane and dat colored woman was nuttin but trouble." J.D. always felt that interracial couples meant nothing but trouble. He wasn't even allowed to look at white women while growing up in his native home of Clarksdale, Mississippi during his younger years, fearing that his life would end by a possible lynching by a group of extreme racists white men. Before speaking another word to Bessie Mae, a quick flashback entered his mind, a bad memory of threats directed at him by racist Mississippi white men.

*   *   *

"Keep your eyes to yourself, nigger boy!" J.D. often heard from the southern white men while growing up in the late nineteen twenties Clarksdale, Mississippi.

"Yes suh," J.D. replied frightfully, nearly closing his eyes and moving at an accelerated pace. "I keeps my eyes to myself, suh."

"Don't let your eyes send ya to your grave, you worthless nigger!"

"Yes suh, yes suh," J.D. said, walking so fast until dirt was being kicked up along his trail. "I keep my eyes to myself, suh."

"You better, boy!"

*   *   *

The colored boys down in Mississippi constantly heard threatening remarks from the klansmen who protected their white women, watching every move they made. The Willinghams remained on standby until Helen Bartlett contacted them about the court hearing.

Chapter 5

COURTS AND DOCUMENTS

FOUR MONTHS PASSED and the Willinghams never heard from Vito or Marion. Bessie Mae and J.D. weren't aware that they were released from Cook County Jail. They were summoned to appear at a hearing that had been scheduled for the following week. Vito was sent a certified letter from the circuit court for the County of Cook, state of Illinois at Chicago. The letter was written as follows:

Circuit Court for the county of
Cook, state of Illinois at Chicago

In the interest of
Vincent Carvelli (Plaintiff)

S.J. Pucci (Petitioner)
No. 37260 "B"

Vito Carvelli (Defendant)

Order of Publication of Notice
The state of Illinois to defendant Vito Carvelli:
You are hereby notified that an action has been

commenced against you in the circuit court for the
County of Cook, state of Illinois, at Chicago, the object
and general nature of which is a termination of all
your parental rights in and to Vincent Carvelli, a
child under 17 years of age. You are further notified of
your right to have counsel, and if you request counsel
and you are unable to employ counsel, counsel shall
be employed by the court for you as provided by section
411.368, C.N. IL., 1957. The names of all parties to
said suit are stated above in the caption hereof and the
name and address of the attorney for the plaintiff is
legal and society. You are further notified that, unless
you file an answer or other pleading or shall otherwise
appear and defend against the aforesaid petition within
45 days after the 19th day of November, 1964,
judgement by default will be rendered against you at a
hearing in the Cook County Juvenile Court. It is ordered
that a copy hereof be published according to law in the
daily record, a newspaper of general circulation
published in the County of Cook, state of Illinois.
Witness my hand and the seal of the Circuit Court on
this 19th day of November, 1964.
Carlo Terranova (Circuit Clerk)
Mary Jacobson (Deputy Clerk)

*   *   *

Within these four months, Helen Bartlett made a summary of contacts. These contacts included home visits, interviews with the Willinghams and the three children, telephone conversations with Bessie Mae, relentless efforts to try and contact relatives of the children, relatives who could possibly take them into their custody; (which seemed to be a hopeless search). Warrants were issued for the whereabouts of

Vito and Marion. Marion was also sent a certified letter from the circuit court which read as follows:

In the circuit court of Illinois, seventeenth judicial circuit juvenile and domestic relations, division "A"

In the interest of:

Vernon Ramirez: birthdate: 3-11-58

Valerie Ramirez: birthdate: 7-26-60

Vincent Carvelli: birthdate: 4-04-64

Order

Now on this 19th day of November, 1964, it appearing to the court that diligent efforts have been made to locate Marion Denise Carvelli, mother of the above-named children, and the court being satisfied that after thorough investigation that it is impractical to serve summons personally, or by registered mail, the address of the mother being unknown, and it is appearing to the court that termination of the rights of the mother to each child have heretofore been filed in the above-numbered and titled causes; and that service of process may be had by publication in the manner prescribed in section 427.249 T.P. IL., 1957, and the issues in said three causes being the same and involving the same parents. It is therefore ordered by the court that the above entitled causes be, and the same are hereby, consolidated so that the notice of publication to the mother may be incorporated in a single notice of publication published as provided by law.

*   *   *

It was the day of court and the Willinghams prepared themselves to drive down to The Cook County Circuit Court. Bessie
Mae profiled a two-piece, green and yellow plaid outfit. A
bright yellow blouse complimented the suit. J.D. sported a
pair of gray polyester slacks with a black rayon shirt. Before
they left the house, Bessie Mae limped into the kitchen to
tell Granny Dear to make sure everyone was fed breakfast.
They got into the car and J.D. drove north on Milwaukee
Parkway.

He turned left onto a street named Jefferson Avenue, a
street which stretched several miles east and west. J.D. cruised
up to a busy street named Rush Boulevard, which ran north
and south. Rush Boulevard was well known for its many liquor
stores, cleaners, bakeries, service stations, grocery stores,
restaurants, and run down hotels. The line of corrupt vice
activities, such as prostitution, drug trafficking, car theft,
robbery, burglary, and even murder, made this street a well-
known haven for criminals. The native Chicagoans of this
area were contentious, territorial, and possessive. For those
who didn't know, the slogan of Rush Boulevard was: *Don't ever
be a beginning hustler in this red light district.*

A set of lights at Rush Boulevard turned green and J.D.
proceeded up to another busy street named Lowell Avenue.
Lowell was known for its bevy of hookers. Many called it the
'sex district'. Ask J.D., because he left home several times to
purchase some sex from one of the hookers when he felt that
his sex life was suffering. At times, Bessie Mae just couldn't
satisfy him. This strip was controlled by a small-time mobster
known as Nicodemo "Nick The Kick" Morelli. Nick earned
his nickname because he didn't mind using some of his
henchmen to break their feet off in someone's ass.

J.D. turned off the expressway and drove down Michigan
Avenue. They arrived at the heart of downtown Chicago. The

sidewalks were crowded with men, women, and children from all types of backgrounds. They strutted quickly in different directions. There were city, county, state, and federal buildings lined up and down the many streets. The Willinghams arrived at the Cook County Circuit Court. J.D. parked across the street in a lot filled with Buicks, Oldsmobiles, and Cadillacs. Once inside the circuit court building, Bessie Mae searched the glass enclosed board for the juvenile section.

She guided her finger down the glass until she discovered that they needed to go to the third floor. She told J.D. that they would take the elevator to where the hearing would be held. Before the elevator arrived on the third floor, Bessie Mae grabbed J.D.'s hand. She clutched it tightly. There was something that she had been wanting to say since they rode in the car.

"You know, J.D.," Bessie Mae thought. "If they give us custody of Valerie, Vernon, and Vincent, that'll mean that we'll have three more checks coming in." Bessie Mae smiled joyfully into J.D.'s rough dark face. The vision of dollar signs raced through her corrupt and money-hungry mind.

"Yep."

"Do you know what we could do with three more checks?" she asked. "We could put them with the other checks and buy some things that we've always wanted."

"What kind'a thangs?" J.D. asked, big dollar signs also racing through his mind.

"Like take a trip or buy a new car." There was no denying that Bessie Mae only wanted to keep foster children and handicapped men to increase their monthly revenue, which would enhance their material comforts.

"I thank ya wight," J.D. agreed, then sliding his left hand up to Bessie Mae's large breasts, massaging them in vertical motions. "Three mo checks would hep us git dose thangs faster."

"Maybe the state will give us some more foster children."

"You thank so?"

"Sure do."

They continued to discuss ways to handle their finances. Valerie, Vernon, and Vincent were only going to be *foster child property*. The elevator stopped on the third floor. They walked down the hallway looking for courtroom F.

"Here da coatroom, Bessa Mae," J.D. directed Bessie Mae, pointing to the large "F" above the courtroom double doors. Bessie Mae limped behind J.D. and they walked inside the courtroom. Helen Bartlett stood near the judge's bench. She was decked out in a two-piece blue polyester suit. The suit had a corporate, professional type of look to it. The stylish outfit complimented her neatly permed hair and smooth melon tone skin.

To Helen's left, near a long wooden table, stood a man named David Feinstein. David served as the prosecuting attorney for the upcoming abandonment case. The table was covered with lots of paperwork. Documents of the subpoenas and certified letters served to Vito and Marion were stacked neatly near the middle. David scanned the courtroom to see who was already in attendance. An expensive watch and rings graced his wrist and fingers. A wealthy Jewish background allowed him to have ritzy taste.

To the right of Helen was the court reporter. She sat at her stenotype, awaiting another long or short court session. She stood up and walked over to the long table. The lustful eyes of J.D. penetrated the dim lighting of the courtroom. Her shapely figure caused his heart to pound faster than the average man who observed beautiful women. Staying reserved was his best defense mechanism against Bessie Mae catching his eyes wandering. She truly had a vuluptuous figure. Helen came on the other side of the wooden railings to greet the Willinghams. She informed them about the current whereabout status of Vito and Marion.

"I'm not for sure if you were aware that Vito and Marion Carvelli were summoned to appear at this hearing?" Helen asked, thumping a pen at the tips of her knuckles.

"No, we weren't," said Bessie Mae. "Of course, we haven't heard from them since they dropped the kids off at our house. Do they really want their kids?"

"We'll see."

Helen looked at her watch. The hearing was due to start in a few minutes. She walked over to Barbara and they browsed through some of the documentation. These papers would be read before the presiding judge. It was 9:00 a.m. and the judge stepped up to the bench.

"All rise for the honorable Albert Frantiano, judge of division number five!" the baliff shouted before the nearly empty courtroom.

Judge Frantiano took a seat. He told everyone present that they could be seated. Helen and David were informed by Frantiano that he read over the complaint concerning the abandonment of Valerie, Vernon, and Vincent. David told the judge that Vito and Marion have presently made no appearance and were summoned several times prior to the court hearing. Helen was told to take the floor and read over the documentation that she put together at The Department of Children and Family Services. Bessie Mae and J.D. sat quietly. They were pressed to one another's side. Their fingers and legs were crossed like a traffic-jammed intersection. Helen prepared for her speech. She cleared her voice and clamped the documents in her right hand. She stood in the middle of the floor and read before the courtroom:

*   *   *

"On this date in accordance with the section of 221.690, revised statutes of Illinois, the Illinois division of welfare was notified of a hearing that is presently held in the interest of Valerie and Vernon

Ramirez and Vincent Carvelli. This petition alleged that the Children's parents have failed to provide them with the support and other care necessary for their well-being. The complaintants, Mr. and Mrs. Jesse Dewayne Willingham, stated that the children have been left in their custody for over a four month period. The juvenile court has obtained a complete social history on this family that isn't in attendance at the time of this court hearing. Vito Carvelli is the natural father of Vincent Carvelli and the stepfather of Valerie and Vernon Ramirez. We have no information of Mr. Carvelli's early childhood, but we are aware that he has an extensive criminal record, in which some of these convictions have occurred in other states. He is a Caucasian male, of Italian ancestry, who stands five feet seven inches and weighs approximately one-hundred and fifty-five pounds. The mother of all three siblings, Marion Denise Carvelli, is a colored woman who weighs approximately one-hundred and fifteen pounds, who stands about five feet three inches. Both were arrested for operating a house of vice activity, located at 3233 Fitzgerald, in which they were selling liquor without a permit and soliciting prostitution."

Helen took a moment to take a sip of water and clear her dry throat. While she fine-tuned her voice, Judge Frantiano gradually moved his eyes closer to the paragraph which clearly stated the nationalities of Vito and Marion. An Italian man and a colored woman? An interracial couple living in Chicago in the nineteen sixties? He lifted his head and stared around the courtroom with a noticeable frown on his face. Did he look upon it as a tragedy? The biggest mistake of a lifetime? As an eighteen year veteran with the Cook County Circuit Courts, he had never presided over an abandonment case that involved an interracial couple. Judge Frantiano was also an Italian-American, a man who knew that if Italian men wanted to be with colored women, they would do it behind closed doors, in the darkest room of the darkest house. Italians reasoned that there was far too much shame brought

upon their race. She assumed her position and picked up
where she left off.

*   *   *

*"The siblings: Valerie and Vernon Ramirez and Vincent Carvelli, are
three very attractive children. Vincent is a vivacious little boy of Negro
and Caucasian parentage, with loose curly hair and a very bright
complexion, that one would expect from a child known to have a
Caucasian father. The Negroid features appear especially in his mouth,
nose, and hair. Valerie and Vernon are of a slightly darker complexion, with black and brown eyes. All three are in good health and their
physical growth has been within normal range for their ages. Presently, residing at the licensed agency foster home of Bessie Mae and
Jesse Dewayne Willingham are ten year old Carmen Taylor, sixty-two
year old Ida Lou Pierson, who is the elderly mother of Bessie Mae
Willingham, forty-six year old George Braun, thirty-eight year old
Raymond Bolton, Jr., both of whom are mentally retarded, and twenty-
eight year old Sean Randle, also a handicapped individual."*

*   *   *

Helen completed reading over the information. David was
told to come forward. The watch and rings sparkled from the
bright lighting as he stepped to the middle of the floor. He
glanced over at Bessie Mae and J.D. Smiles with hopes of
gaining custody of the children brought optimism to the
Willinghams. He opened a manila folder and spread some
documents over the table. The silent courtroom listened to
the following information from David:

*   *   *

*"Now on this day, this cause coming for a hearing in the interest of
Valerie and Vernon Ramirez and Vincent Carvelli, who are under the*

age of seventeen years, and those in need of the care of and services of foster home placement, and that the court has jurisdiction over the said children, under the provisions of section 914.319 L.M. IL as amended. The mother of the said children, Marion Denise Carvelli, has been duly summoned, and she appears not. The father of Vincent Carvelli and the stepfather of Valerie and Vernon Ramirez, having also been duly summoned, has not made an appearance. With evidence having been heard, the court has been duly advised and finds that the natural mother and father of the said children both have criminal records. A petition of abandonment has been filed, stating that the parents willfully, substantially, continuously, and repeatedly neglected the children and refused to provide them with the necessary care and protection. The court further finds that it is in the best interest of the said children, that the parental rights of Vito and Marion Carvelli be terminated. It is further ordered that the temporary custody of the three children , Valerie and Vernon Ramirez and Vincent Carvelli, be continued in the Illinois Division of Welfare for permanent foster home placement with Bessie Mae and Jesse Dewayne Willingham. Your honor, I have no further documentation to read over at this time."

*　　*　　*

David read over the documents and Judge Frantiano told everyone to approach the bench. He told Bessie Mae and J.D. that the children would be turned over into their custody. Provided that they meet all the required standards of the Illinois state codes for the well-being of the children, the Willinghams would remain their foster parents. Helen and Barbara were all smiles. The children now have foster home placement. Judge Frantiano adjourned the court session.

He told Bessie Mae and J.D. that some documents would have to be signed in order to make everything official. Helen, Barbara, and the Willinghams signed the required documents and everyone left the courtroom cheerful. Naturally,

the Willingham couple was excited. Excited for all the wrong reasons. They stepped inside the unoccupied elevator and gave one another the tightest hug.

"We've got three more checks coming in, J.D.!" Bessie Mae cheered, throwing her arm around J.D.'s massive waist. She planted a big kiss on his dark chapped lips.

"Yep!" J.D. sighed. "Three mo checks we could use."

"We're gonna get more things that we want."

"My tuck need new tires."

"We'll get'em, J.D."

Bessie Mae and J.D. were happier than children on Christmas day.

Chapter 6

CONFRONTATIONS

EVERYTHING WAS SMOOTH sailing at the Willingham's residence of foster and handicapped care. Carmen just had her thirteenth birthday. Vernon turned twelve, Valerie was seven, and Vincent was a ripe three years old. Bessie Mae had been trying to toilet train Vincent with extreme difficulty. When he wanted to use the restroom, he wouldn't tell her until it was too late. An impatient Bessie Mae would ask her foster son on a continuous basis, *"Do you have to boo boo? Do you have to pee pee?"*

She would be furious when he would get off the small white potty and then release his body waste. She claimed that he knew better, but wouldn't cooperate. The four foster children in the Willingham home seemed to get along very well, and so far, had not shown that they had any behavior problems. Since Bessie Mae also cared for the handicapped men, who had a tendency to roam around the house with no supervision, the children became alarmed at the disfigured hand of Sean and the mental retardation of Braun and Junior.

J.D. was responsible for keeping Braun and Junior shaved and their hair cut. It took them a while, but Valerie and Vernon became adjusted to their new home. They had to stop asking questions such as, "Where is my mamma and daddy?" "When is my mamma and daddy coming back?" "When are we going back home?"

They found Carmen to be the perfect playmate. Carmen found Vincent to be the perfect little foster brother, the ideal little boy. She would always bounce him up and down, clamp

her fingers onto his large curly locks, and spin him around in circles. While the children played in the front room, Bessie Mae was in the kitchen with Granny Dear preparing dinner. She stood over the stove cutting up pieces of salt pork into a large pot of boiling water. Granny Dear leaned over into her wheelchair, as she sorted through a large pile of pinto beans. While the salt pork floated around the edges of the pot, Bessie Mae gathered all the ingredients for some cornbread. She placed a couple of eggs and some milk on the table and greased a large square pan with Crisco cooking oil. The clock above the stove said 1:45 p.m.

It was the first of the month and Bessie Mae was excited. Every check from the state of Illinois for the people that she kept was on its way, not to mention a special check that she received for taking care of her elderly mother. Bessie Mae was thrilled about meeting the mailman out on the porch. She quickly limped that direction and waited patiently for the man in the light blue uniform.

Everyone along Milwaukee Parkway knew when it was the first part of the month. They looked out their doors and saw their neighbor, Bessie Mae Willingham, sitting on the porch, all stretched out in her favorite fold-up chair. Anywhere between 1:00 p.m. and 1:45 p.m., at the first of the month, the neighbors watched her wait. The timing was perfect. The short and stocky-built mailman walked up to the Willingham residence.

"Hello there, Mrs. Willingham," said the always happy postman. He reached into his bulky mailbag for a handful of mail.

"Hello, Mr. Tucker," Bessie Mae said, her legs gyrating nervously. "How's it going today?"

"Doing just fine, Mrs. Willingham," postman Tucker said, holding the bundle of mail firmly in his right hand. "Let's see what I have for you today."

"Hope it's not a bunch of bills."

"We've got one, two, three, four, five, six, seven, and eight," Tucker counted consecutively, then handing Bessie Mae five more letters from other places.

"Thank you, Mr. Tucker!" Bessie Mae cheered, her eyes lighting up like a bright Christmas tree. "Thank you very, very, much, Mr. Tucker! Have a nice day, now!"

"You do the same, Mrs. Willingham," postman Tucker responded, then walking south up Milwaukee Parkway.

Bessie Mae limped back into the kitchen. She fired up a Pall Mall Red and started opening the checks with a small steak knife. A sparkle beamed in her eyes as she watched the stack of checks before her.

She studied the dollar amount of every check and tried calculating the total inside her head. The phone rang and she limped over by the stove to answer. The digits had her hypnotized and practically left her speechless. Finally, she answered by saying, "Hello, what can I do for you?"

"Yes, can I speak with Bessie Mae Willingham?" a familiar voice said.

"This is Bessie Mae Willingham," she replied, the man's tone immediately catching on.

"How are you doing, Bessie Mae?"

"I'm fine," she answered speculatively. "May I ask with whom am I speaking?"

"This is Vito Carvelli," Vito said. "I really need to talk with you."

"Vito who?"

"Vito Carvelli," he reiterated. "I'm the guy who left my three kids with you and your husband."

"Yes, yes, I remember you now," Bessie Mae recalled too well. "May I ask, why are you calling here?"

"I'm calling because my wife and I want the kids to come

back home," Vito explained, making her believe that he was really sincere.

"Home?" Bessie Mae huffed. "I just know that you didn't say home?"

"Yeah, that's right," Vito clarified, his voice raising a couple of octaves. "I'll say it again, my wife and I want our kids to come home."

"Your children are at home. They're at our home," Bessie Mae strongly emphasized. "They're gonna be at this home until they get old enough to move out on their own. Do you understand?"

"No, I don't understand."

"Anyway, you and your wife probably don't have a home for them to come to."

"Say what!" Vito rebounded furiously, shouting loudly into Bessie Mae's already sensitive ear. "Are you trying to tell me that your crippled, knaving ass has gotten custody of our children? You and your black, country, non-talking husband?"

"Hold on!" Bessie Mae strongly intervened. "Hold on one goddam minute! First of all, I know everything about you and your wife. I know all about the crap that you all are involved with. All the liquor and dope and whores that was part of that house that you all had over on Thirty-Second and Fitzgerald. You were doing all that filth around your three children. Second of all, the courts had summoned you and your wife several times. They had court hearings to see who would get custody of the children. Did you and your wife show up? Hell no you didn't! Did you answer any of the certified letters that the prosecutors and caseworkers sent you? Hell no you didn't! Apparently, this would tell anybody with common sense that you didn't want the children anyway. Anybody would know that you don't have no respect for your children or for yourselves. Please, Vito, don't ever call here talking crazy to me anymore."

"Where in the hell did you get your information?" Even

Vito was surprised that Bessie Mae gained knowledge of his dangerously criminal lifestyle.

"Don't worry about where," Bessie Mae assured him. "You were dealing with those other dagos who are into that mafia shit like you."

"What the hell do you know about my business?" Vito felt that Bessie Mae was surely raising a few eyebrows.

"I know about you dealing with Bennie Caputo. I know he's got that whore hotel up on Rush Boulevard, letting all those whores make money for their pimps in front of his hotel. He's nothing but a dago-pimp, just like you."

"Who are you calling a dago-pimp!" Vito blasted, growling into the phone like an angry lion.

"I'm not a stupid woman. I know a lot more about what's going on around Chicago than you think I know."

"Who fed you all those lies?"

"Never mind who," Bessie Mae insisted. "Anyone who would leave their children the way you and your wife did, should not be able to see them, more less get them back. You don't respect yourself, the people around you, and you definitely don't respect your children. Is that the way that you dagos are raised? Polluting the streets with all that liquor and dope and whores?"

"You crazy, crippled bitch!" Vito snarled, insulting Bessie Mae in the harshest manner. "Don't ever talk about me like that again. Do you understand, you crippled nigger-bitch!" If given his choice, Vito would jump straight through the phone and choke the life out of Bessie Mae.

"Go straight to hell!" Bessie Mae shouted. "You dope-dealing dago-pimp!"

"Fuck you!"

"No, fuck you!" Bessie Mae reciprocated, then slamming the phone down in Vito's ear. The furious conversation finally ended. Bessie Mae limped away from the wall. She was huffing and puffing rather strongly. Her blood pressure had

soared after arguing with Vito. Slight tears of anger streamed from the inner corner of her eyes. She fired up a cigarette and quickly swallowed four blood pressure pills. Vito's harsh words were unwillingly planted in her mind. She mixed the cornbread up and spread it evenly across the greasy pan.

"What's wong, Bessa Mae?" Granny Dear asked, noticing the tears drying on her face.

"That dago bastard!" Bessie Mae charged. "Had the nerves calling here trying to confront me about getting custody of the kids."

"What he gone do fo dose chilluns?" Granny Dear commented, using the exact type of illiteracy in her dialect.

"He can't do nothing for those children."

Bessie Mae had to leave the kitchen to cool off. Granny Dear was left with the duty of baking the cornbread and watching the pot of beans. She nursed a hatred for some of the Italian people, especially when she witnessed their influence of the underworld in ghetto economic life in Chicago. She became deeply angered when she sat and watched the nickel and dime rackets of organized crime rake in millions of welfare client dollars every year, the same Italian underworld czars who peddled drugs to the coloreds as their antidote to relieve despair. Even as a foster parent and caretaker of the handicapped, a woman who spent most of her time performing house chores, Bessie Mae knew that the immoral gangsters had control in the neighborhood that she resided in. Vito didn't do much to polish the tarnished image of some of the Italians.

*   *   *

Carmen and Valerie were on the sidewalk playing jumprope with two other neighborhood girls. Vernon was playing catch with a football with a little boy from across the street. The hot sun had drained all of their energy. The scorching fury

caused them to come up on the porch. Bessie Mae sat on the porch puffing on a cigarette. Marilyn Walker was one of the neighborhood girls who lived two doors down. She came up on the porch with Carmen and Valerie. Her oval-shaped head kept swaying side to side.

"Are you and Valerie real sisters?" Marilyn asked Carmen, staring directly into her face.

"I don't know," Carmen answered uncertainly, only knowing that she and Valerie were foster sisters.

"Why are you dark-skinned and she's light-skinned?" she questioned, making a comparison in their skin contrasts.

"Why does she have long hair and you have short hair?"

"I don't know," Carmen repeated, then looking at Valerie and making her own comparison.

Bessie Mae couldn't listen to any more questions from the girl two houses down. "Honey, Carmen and Valerie are foster sisters. They don't have the same parents."

Marilyn's mother called from down the street. She quickly ran off the porch to see what her mother wanted. Bessie Mae told her foster daughters and foster son to go into the house and wash up for dinner.

Chapter 7

NO WHITES ALLOWED

Besides purchasing items from department and wholesale stores, Bessie Mae bought items for their large home from door-to-door salesmen. She would buy brooms from a blind man named Bobby Franklin. Bobby was short, bow-legged, and medium complexioned. He wore nice two-piece suits, with a matching brim and dark sunglasses. He sold brooms throughout the greater Chicago area. An armful of brooms and his black cane guided him up and down the street. Today was the day for him to visit the Willingham residence. He tapped lightly on the screen door. Bessie Mae limped to the front door and allowed him to come inside.

"Hey there, brother Franklin," Bessie said, brushing up against his cluster of brooms. "How's the broom business?"

"Oh, just fine," Bobby told Bessie Mae, tapping his cane down on the floor and slowly walking ahead. "I'm just trying to sell the rest of these brooms before I call it a day." He held his head to the ceiling and pushed his dark-shaded glasses closer to his moist face.

Bessie Mae took him into the kitchen. Granny Dear grabbed him by the arm and told him to take a load off his feet. She pulled a chair out from the table. The hot sun had him drenched from being under his dark suit. They offered him cool refreshments, like water, lemonade, or a frosty bowl of vanilla ice cream. Bobby agreed to a large glass of ice water. Granny Dear rolled over to the refrigerator and sink for some ice cubes and water. Bessie Mae remembered that her car was always dirty. She inquired about a couple of whiskbrooms.

"Got any whiskbrooms left, brother Franklin?"

"I think I got some under my large brooms," Franklin told Bessie Mae. After running his left hand along the.cluster of brooms, he landed on the smaller set of brooms and he pulled them from under the larger ones.

Everytime Bobby came to the house, Bessie Mae would buy at least two large brooms and two whiskbrooms. Today, she decided to buy three large brooms and four whiskbrooms. This way, she could save herself time and money. Bobby was a reasonable man. Scrupulously honest. The previous brooms were always worn from rigorous housework. Sweeping the bathrooms, kitchen, sidewalks, porch, and parts of the rug inside the front room and the den, took its toll on the broom straws. Bobby guzzled down the water and folded the money in his pocket. Granny Dear offered him something to eat, but he refused. It was part of her southern hospitality. He felt that the development of stomach cramps would plague him if he mixed food with a belly filled with water. Granny Dear said goodbye and Bessie Mae led him to the front door.

"You take care now, brother Franklin," she told him, watching him step onto the porch.

"Okay, sister Bessie Mae."

"Stay cool out there."

"I will."

Bobby walked south on Milwaukee while his cane tapped on the hot sidewalk. Everyone around that neighborhood had great respect for him. Known as *the blind man who sells all those brooms,* he was determined to make an honest living for himself despite his blindness.

*   *   *

It was late in the afternoon. Bessie Mae allowed the beans to simmer until they became tender. Granny Dear pulled the cornbread out of the hot oven and slid the pan on top of the

stove. The doorbell rang and Carmen and Valerie rushed to answer it. On the other side of screendoor, which was covered with fingerprints and hot breath, was a tall and cleancut white man. Brown wavy hair rippled across the top of his head. He wore a sharp blue leisure suit, carrying a very large black case that dangled down by his side.

"Are the people in charge at home?" he asked both Carmen and Valerie, who were standing there looking up at the tall man.

"Yes," Carmen answered hesitantly, slightly afraid because she rarely saw white people who came to the Willingham residence. Only the caseworkers who came to visit with the foster kids were white.

Bessie Mae limped towards the front room. She noticed that Carmen and Valerie were watching the strange man from the opposite side of the door.

"Get away from that door!" she shouted politely. They stepped back and she opened the door for the man to come inside. She directed him into the den. They cordially introduced themselves.

"My name's Douglas McIntosh," he said in a gargled voice. "I'm with The Chicago Division of World Class Sewing Machines."

"My name's Bessie Mae Willingham," Bessie Mae said. "My husband and I run a home for foster children and handicapped men."

"That's interesting."

"Something interesting happens everyday."

Douglas was an aggressive salesman. He tried selling sewing machines at lower than retail department store prices. The black case was opened and he showed Bessie Mae a large beige sewing machine. He wanted to give her a demonstration of his product. An electrical outlet was needed within a twelve foot radius. Bessie Mae searched the den for one that wasn't in use.

Granny Dear rolled her wheelchair to the kitchen doorway. She peeked into the den and wanted to know what Bessie Mae and Douglas were in the den doing. What a nosy elderly woman she turned out to be. Like Valerie and Carmen, Granny Dear was surprised to see Douglas visiting. White people coming to the Willingham home was an extreme rarity. Granny Dear knew that, so she locked her wheelchair in place at the edge of the door. She leaned forward to watch his every move.

Bessie Mae found an outlet over by the bookcases. She unplugged a lamp and slid the cord into the outlet. Within seconds, power flowed to the machine. Douglas began showing her all the extra features that the machine had. Unlike other sewing machines found in department stores, stores like "Sears and Roebuck" and "J.C. Penney", he wanted to show her all the benefits that his machine had to offer.

He reached into the spacious case and took out a piece of blue polyester material. Fancy stitch designs were sewn onto the material. Sewing happened to be one of Bessie Mae's favorite past times. She took pride in sewing together rips and tears in J.D.'s clothing. This machine would possibly make a good investment for her. She became excited after watching all the magnificent features that Douglas' product offered. Douglas continued to discuss the time and money Bessie Mae would save.

J.D. galloped through the front door wearing his tarred up blue uniform. His lunchbucket swung back and forth. He walked through the front room and glanced into the den. He gave Douglas a very evil stare. It was rather uncomfortable. J.D. wondered why a white man was in the den talking to his wife. A white man with authority over him, the ones who proudly carried a gun and a badge, and the ones who were educated and possessed a great wealth of knowledge, remained his worst nightmare. He simply hated white people! The more he stared into Douglas' face, the anger only inten-

sified. Since his past wouldn't dismiss itself, he experienced a sudden flashback of his youth while growing up in the racist city of Clarksdale, Mississippi.

* * *

J.D. rummaged through an old store for a jar of molasses and some cornmeal for his parents. One of the store clerks, an extreme racist who was probably part of the local Klan, who threw sheets over his body after closing of the store, watched the young J.D. trot up and down the aisles. The clerk ran from behind the counter to confront J.D. He was parading around the store and not showing any interest in buying anything.

"What ya looking for, boy?"

"My mammy and pappy sent ma ta da sto ta buy some molasses and meal, suh."

"You in here trying to steal something, boy?"

"No suh," J.D. answered with terror. "I ain't doing no such thang, suh."

"You got any money, boy?"

"Yes suh," J.D. said, unfolding his hand and showing the clerk his money.

"Do you know what I'll do to you, boy, If I catch you stealing?"

"No suh."

"You don't?"

"No suh."

"I'll break off each and every one of those greasy crusty fingers of yours. Do you understand what I'm saying to you, boy?"

"Yes suh."

* * *

J.D. took a seat at the dining room table and tuned in tightly to the conversation that Bessie Mae and Douglas were having. Bessie Mae seemed thoroughly impressed with everything

Douglas had shown her. She wanted to know the cost of the machine. He reached into the case and pulled out a small sheet of paper. The blue and white piece of paper resembled a business invoice. He pointed to some dollar figures.

"Well, now," Douglas paused. "The total cost will be one-hundred and fourteen dollars and sixty-two cents."

"Sounds like a good deal," Bessie Mae smiled, admiring the structure of the sewing machine.

"Mrs. Willingham, this is the best bargain that you'll get on a machine as good as this one."

"What type of warranty comes with it?"

"One year, which includes parts and labor."

"That's a deal."

The den and dining room were close to one another. J.D. clearly heard the total cost of the sewing machine. Immediately, he jumped up from his chair and rushed into the den. Bessie Mae had been married to J.D. for several years. She knew when he was about to explode. It was almost like an atomic bomb. His eyes became watery. His lips puckered inwards. His large chest poked outwards.

"You mean ta tell ma dat dat machine coss dat much?" J.D. said abruptly. "Let ma show ya out of my house." J.D. had erupted on Douglas like a volcano. He mispronounced words so badly until Douglas barely understood him. He only knew that J.D. was upset. That was obvious.

"But sir, this machine is really a bargain," Douglas tried explaining, frightened from the strong bass in J.D.'s voice.

"Out da door!" J.D. shouted, pointing directly at the front door, his arm trembling and eyes shedding tears of fury.

"But . . ."

"But nuttin."

"But sir, I . . ."

"I ain't gone let no white mane cheat ma wife."

"Sir, I'm not trying to cheat your wife."

"I reckon ya are tying ta cheat'er."

"I'm an honest businessman."

"Git outta ma house."

"But, sir . . ."

"Now!"

"If you insist, sir."

"Yep, I reckon I do."

J.D. gave Douglas the look of, *"Here's my one and only chance to show all white people how I really feel about them."*

Douglas had been humiliated. Insulted in the most vulgar manner. He quickly packed his machine into the case. Bessie Mae limped to the front door with him. Had Douglas had known that J.D. was uneducated, illiterate, and just plain bullheaded, maybe he would've overlooked him. It was just another classic example of J.D. abusing his authority in the household. Had he known that he was a native of Clarksdale, Mississippi, a man who openly expressed his hatred for whites, maybe he would've never come to the Willingham residence.

Bessie Mae and Douglas stepped onto the porch. She felt that it was part of her duty to apologize for the insulting nature of her husband.

"I'm very sorry for the way that my husband acted," Bessie Mae pardoned, holding on to the morals that she had.

"That's quite alright," Douglas replied, his face expressing sheer sadness." In this line of business, I've dealt with those types of people before."

"And what kind is that?" Bessie Mae asked, hoping that Douglas wouldn't say rude and obnoxious things about all Negro men.

"The outspoken kind with no manners."

"Do me a favor, please?" Bessie Mae said, sweetly talking to the ambitious salesman.

"What's that?"

"Don't go around hating all colored men because of my husband's bad attitude."

"Trust me, I won't," Douglas assured Bessie Mae. "I don't lable all colored men the same, Mrs. Willingham."

"Well, that's certainly good to know."

"I'm a very rational man, mam."

Douglas got into his dark red Oldsmobile Cutlass and rushed north down Milwaukee. The beans were simmering and tender enough to be served. Bessie Mae took the plates out of the cabinet and placed them on the table. J.D. remained at the dining room table. He mumbled words of fury about the price of the sewing machine. Why couldn't he just let it go? Who cared that he had a malicious hatred towards all white people? The fact reamained that everytime that he showed up at his roofing job; there was going to be a white man staring him right in the face.

"Can't bleeves dat white mane gone come round here trying to cheat somebody," J.D. commented in a low voice, reaching into his shirt pocket so he can fire up a Pall Mall Gold.

"J.D.!" Bessie Mae hooted strongly. "You didn't have to talk to that man that way."

"I talk ta anybody anyways I wanna."

"He was a nice man," she said, pushing a Pall Mall Red out of the packet so she could join J.D. in a smoke break.

"I ain't neva known no nice white folks."

"That's where you're wrong."

"All of 'em crooks."

"That's not true."

"Ya always takin sides wit da white folks."

"I'm not taking sides with nobody. He was only trying to sell a sewing machine."

"Ya turnin out ta be one of dose uncle tom negro folks."

"That's a dam lie and you know it."

"Dat white mane was tying ta steal yo money, Bessa Mae."

"You need to stop having so much hatred for white people."

"I shuddin allow white folks round dis house."

"That's not nice, J.D."

"I don't lack it when dose white folks come here fo dese falsta chilluns."

"Now you know that the caseworkers have to visit this home."

"We runnin thangs in dis here house."

Anyone who came into contact with J.D. could tell that his educational level was low. According to some of the racist and facist whites, he was recognized as a *poor dumb nigger from the south*. Would he have recognized a bargain if it slapped him in the face? Before calling everyone to dinner, Bessie Mae limped into the dining room to give J.D. the news of the day.

"Guess who called today?" Bessie Mae chuckled, then blowing a long stream of smoke towards J.D.

"Who?" asked J.D., then returning a long stream of smoke back in Bessie Mae's direction.

"Vito."

"Veedo who?"

"Vito Carvelli."

"Dat Italian-White mane?"

"Yeah."

"Dey daddy called, huh? What he want?"

"Called here talking about he wanted the kids to come back home."

"Well, I say," J.D. said, nodding his head. "He gotta whole lotta nerves callin here."

"I told that dago-pimp that the kids were at home. I told him that they were at our home."

"Dat's wight."

Bessie Mae begin calling everybody to dinner and another day at the Willingham residence would soon come to an end.

Chapter 8

FOOD FOR ALL

OPERATING A FOSTER home meant having the necessary skills to feed the many occupants. Bessie Mae was a country girl. She basically made all of her meals from scratch. Cooking food on a daily basis for all of the foster children and handicapped men was an all day chore. There was a certain skill that she possessed. This skill cut down on hours in the kitchen. There would be times when Bessie Mae and J.D. would go down to Little Italy. They would buy large crates of fruit and vegetables around the long lines of stands. J.D. would load the food commodities into the car while Bessie Mae bargained with the many Italian and Irish merchants.

They were all lined up in small tent areas. She would buy crates of apples, peaches, pears, green beans, corn, and squash. The crates of fruits and vegetables were placed on the kitchen floor. Bessie Mae created *culinary magic* in the kitchen. She had five boxes of Ball Jars stacked on the kitchen table, close to where Granny Dear's wheelchair was sitting. Vincent stood in the doorway of the kitchen. He wondered what his foster mother was going to do with the box of jars.

Bessie Mae limped over to the drawers near the sink. She pulled out two large butcher knives. The large trash barrel was brought closer so she and Granny Dear could have access to it. The crates of apples and peaches were to be used first in this cooking project. Granny Dear moved forward in her wheelchair to slide the crate closer. Bessie Mae peeled the apples while her elderly mother went to work on the peaches.

Vincent was the only child around the house. Carmen and Valerie were outside playing hopscotch. Vernon was down the street playing with other kids along Milwaukee Parkway. Vincent decided to stand in the doorway and watch his foster mother and foster grandmother perform their tasks. He couldn't find other kids his age to play with.

They peeled and peeled until every piece of fruit was completely skinned. Apple and pear peels were everywhere, from the floor to the table, and even in Granny Dear and Bessie Mae's laps. Bessie Mae limped over to the cabinets below the sink to bring out two large pots. These pots resembled the ones used in military mess halls to feed a multitude of soldiers. She filled them with warm water. The peaches and pears were placed in the sink under cool running water. Friction from Bessie Mae's hands was used to remove the dirt particles. She limped over to the stove with the cleaned fruit, and it was dumped into the boiling water. The tops were placed over the pots.

Bessie Mae wanted to take a cigarette break. The doctor had warned her about smoking. Not only was smoking hazardous to her health, but her diet also became a threat, eating foods high in fat and sodium. The blood pressure pills didn't seem to work efficiently, because her blood pressure soared to the top whenever stress hit. She fried everything in lard.

Granny Dear roamed around inside the refrigerator. She tried to find a bowl of collard greens that she placed in there several days ago. Vincent watched her lean forward into the spacious refrigerator. Maybe he wanted a peanut butter sandwich with jelly. Granny Dear found the bowl of greens. She rolled over to the slopbucket. It was already filled to the top. From the day before, and from the present day breakfast and lunch, food floated around inside. Neckbones, oatmeal, biscuits, cornbread, beans, bacon, scrambled eggs, milk, rice,

and now the greens that Granny Dear dumped inside. This combination of food were to be fed to the dogs.

"Braun!" Bessie Mae shouted from inside the kitchen. "Come and feed those dogs right now."

Braun rushed into the kitchen from upstairs. As always, he was beating the middle of his hand with one of his thick wires.

"Put that dam wire up, Braun!" Bessie Mae yelled. "Don't be outside trying to find no cigarette butts."

"Okay, okay, I won't be outside trying to find no butts."

"You better not."

"I won't, I won't. I'm not gonna be out there trying to find not butts."

"We'll see."

Braun grabbed the heavy bucket with all the dense food inside and carried it with his powerful left arm. He turned the corner heading towards the hallway to the front room.

Steam blew from under the tops of the large pots. Bessie Mae limped over to the stove to check on the simmering apples and pears. The one-time white colored fruit was ready for some fruit pectin and spices like cinnamon and nutmeg. They cooked for another hour and a half. Bessie Mae limped back to the stove. The apples and pears were dark brown and drooped at the edges. The aroma filled the entire house. Vincent watered at the mouth and his stomach signaled that hunger approached.

Braun returned to the kitchen with the spotless slopbucket. The bucket was placed in the corner and he turned around to leave the kitchen. Bessie Mae glanced down at his bulging left pants pocket. She quickly became suspicious. Like a radar, both of her eyes moved in closer to that one pocket.

"Come here, Braun," Bessie Mae said, crushing out her cigarette and reaching for Braun's left pocket.

"Yeah, yeah, you want me to come to you?" Braun asked

nervously, staring up at the ceiling as though he was the only one in the kitchen."

"I said come here."

"You want me to come to you?"

"Yeah, come here," Bessie Mae said calmly, stretching her arm further to get closer to his bulging pocket.

"Yeah, yeah, you want me to come to you?" Braun repeated frantically, trying to avoid stepping closer to Bessie Mae.

"Shut up and bring your ass to me!" Bessie Mae shouted, scooting closer to Braun.

"Okay, okay, I'm coming to you."

Braun stepped up to Bessie Mae and she quickly shoved her hand down his left pants pocket. She pulled out a handful of old cigarette butts. It was enough to start falling out of her palm. The writings of Pall Mall Gold, Pall Mall Red, Lucky Strike, Camel, and Marlboro, were written above the filters on these butts. Bessie Mae knew that pedestrians walking past their home also thumped cigarette butts into the yard. Anything besides Pall Mall Gold and Pall Mall Red came from somewhere else.

"I'll be dam!" Bessie Mae thundered, highly disappointed because her efforts were worthless in trying to keep a mentally retarded man like Braun from eating the old tobacco out of cigarette butts. "Look at this, Granny Dear. Braun thought he could sneak past me with these butts. Didn't you, Braun!"

"No, no, I didn't think I could sneak nothing past you," Braun replied, showing signs of embarrassment.

"Yes, you did."

"No, I didn't."

"You're lying, Braun!" Bessie Mae said, holding her hand open with the different brands of cigarette butts. "Don't you ever get tired of eating these nasty butts? You're going to die from having all that tobacco crap in your stomach. That's why all of your teeth are rotted inside your mouth. Every single

one of them. You can't even spit without something black or brown coming out of your mouth. Now, you take your nasty retarded ass over to the trash barrel with these filthy butts and dump them."

Bessie Mae was furious, but she was also concerned about Braun's health. Braun didn't have to be caught with any of the butts in his pockets. She sometimes noticed the fresh tobacco kernels smeared across his front teeth.

"Okay, okay, I'll dump the butts in the trash," Braun responded timidly, grabbing the butts out of Bessie Mae's hand and then dumping them into the barrel.

"Don't let me catch you with this junk in your pockets no more!"

Finally, Bessie Mae calmed down. She turned the fire off the pots and placed the jars in the sink for a quick rinsing. A steel tray was placed at the back of the stove. Six jars were lined up on top of the tray. They were to be filled with the warm fruit. With a large dipper spoon, Bessie Mae dipped into the pots and leveled the jars with the fruit only. She poured the juices over the fruit and allowed the jars to cool off. After the jars were filled, she took them over to Granny Dear, who screwed on the tops. Granny Dear lined the jars up near the middle of the table. Bessie Mae made several trips to and from the stove. She filled over twenty jars. To make sure Braun wasn't outside searching for more cigarette butts, she limped over to a window facing the backyard. She called him back into the kitchen to help her take some of the jars to the basement. There were empty cabinets over by Vincent's bed where the jars were stored.

It was up the stairs. It was down the stairs. They carried every jar of fruit from the kitchen to the basement. Sean came to the kitchen to see if it was dinnertime. In a harsh manner, Bessie Mae told him that dinner was more than an hour away.

"Get out of this kitchen!" Bessie Mae shouted. "You know good and well that I'll call you when it's time to eat."

Bessie Mae loved telling most people in the home that dinner wouldn't be ready until she said it was ready. Sean rubbed his nose with his paralyzed hand. He walked out of the kitchen pushing his partially handicapped body back to the basement. Was it like Sean didn't exist in the Willingham home? They hardly ever showed him any concern. After a long day in the kitchen, this ended another day of food preparation for Bessie Mae and Granny Dear.

Chapter 9

STEAMY SEXUAL SECRETS

VERNON AND VINCENT sat in front of the television watching *Batman and Robin*. It was late in the evening and their eyes were glued to the set. Valerie was in the corner playing with her doll. Bessie Mae and J.D. were at the grocery store. Granny Dear was in her room watching television. She sat calmly in her wheelchair. Braun was upstairs in their room beating the middle of his hand with a broken off piece of hanger and talking to himself. Junior sat across from him staring straight ahead, his glossy eyes not blinking one bit. Sean was in the basement, sitting in the dark, feeling for himself and others around him. You couldn't blame him much, especially when he was being treated like an outcast.

Carmen paced the floor, from the kitchen to the living room, and back into the kitchen. Vincent had a blast watching *Batman and Robin* take on villans like The Joker and The Riddler.

"Get'em Batman! Get'em Robin!" Vincent cheered, swinging his fist at the television everytime Batman or Robin hit The Joker or The Riddler. He watched the action words light up the television screen. He recovered from a tragic day, because earlier that morning he received a terrible beating from J.D. for wetting the bed. Though he had fun watching his favorite program, he was cautious about pressing up against the red whelps across his back.

Carmen walked into the front room to tell Vincent to settle down. She didn't realize that he might've thought that he was Batman or Robin and his sense of reality was gone.

Vernon looked over at him. He cut a slight grin, then glanced over in the corner where Valerie was combing her doll's hair. Carmen stood over them with her eyes planted on top of Vincent's head. She went back into the kitchen and leaned against the sink, her arms crossed in suspense and index finger pressed on her lips.

Granny Dear had ears that could hear a feather drop. She rolled her wheelchair to the curtain to see who was hanging around the kitchen. The *guardian of the kitchen* stuck her head from around the edges of the curtain. Carmen was leaned against the sink. She stared into her own dreamworld, no expression on her face whatsoever. Granny Dear rolled back into her room when she saw no one trying to go into the refrigerator or in the cabinets.

*   *   *

Carmen returned into the living room and stopped at the stairs going to the second floor. She had broken out into a heavy sweat. Her fingers twirled around the inside of her sweaty palms. Vernon felt someone in his presence. The electricity sent charges around the room. He looked to his immediate left and Carmen stood between he and Vincent. He noticed that something was unusual about her behavior.

"Are you alright, Carmen?" Vernon asked, Carmen standing there looking nervous, sweating heavy, and eyes spelling nothing but mischief.

"Of course I'm alright," she answered smoothly, wiping sweat off her moist face.

"Are you sure?"

"Of course, I'm sure. What makes you think that something's wrong?"

"You're sweating a lot and your eyes look . . ."

"Look what?" Carmen replied quickly. "Don't worry about me, Vernon. I'm doing just fine."

Vernon agreed with Carmen since she convinced him that nothing was wrong. He looked up at the clock and it was late. He walked down to the basement to prepare himself for school. Carmen took a seat on the sofa. She continuously perspired. Her lucious lips were licked in perpendicular motions. The upper portion of her legs were rubbing together. Add all of this together, and you came up with a *horny teenage girl in heat.*

Valerie looked in the direction of Carmen and froze the moment in time. Like Vernon, she noticed something strange about Carmen's behavior. It stemmed from her giving Vincent those lustful looks. The electricity sent greater charges around the room.

"What's wrong, Carmen?" Valerie inquired, studying the deprived eyes of Carmen.

"Why does it have to be something wrong?"

"I don't know."

"Mind your business and finish combing your doll's hair."

"Okay."

It was time to move around again. Carmen traveled back into the kitchen. Everything in there remained quiet. Granny Dear was in her room falling asleep at the edge of her wheelchair. She snored loud, like others in the house who were in a deep sleep. Carmen made soft and short steps. She crept back towards the front room. She stopped near the basement stairs to watch Vincent. *Batman and Robin* had gone off the air and it was time for cartoons. Vincent sat on the floor rotating his head in circular motions. His eyes opened and closed. He struggled to stay awake, nearly falling sideways to the floor. Carmen stepped to the middle of the front room floor."Bedtime, Valerie." She looked up at the clock and it said 9:30 p.m.

"Can I stay up longer?" Valerie asked Carmen.

"It's past your bedtime, so you've got to hit the sack."

"Why can't I stay up tonight?" Valerie questioned, pouting by throwing her doll down on the floor.

"You have to go to school tomorrow."

Since Valerie knew that she had to go to bed, she moved over to Vincent, who was on the verge of being totally asleep, and shook him across the shoulders. "Vincent, get up and go to the basement."

Carmen jumped in as though Valerie had offended her. "Don't worry about Vincent. I'll make sure he gets to bed. You just carry yourself upstairs and get in bed."

She pointed to the top of the stairs. Valerie was frightened by the sudden uproar in Carmen's voice. She rushed upstairs and everyone had cleared the front room. Vincent remained on the floor. Still, he fought to stay awake. Several minutes had passed and Carmen decided to shake him a few times.

"Come upstairs," Carmen instructed Vincent, tightly wrapping her hand around the back of his shirt.

"Why do I have to go upstairs?" Vincent asked. "I thought I was supposed to go to the basement."

"Not tonight."

"That's where me and Vernon go when it's bedtime."

Carmen didn't need a reminder of where he slept. Tonight, there would be a change of plans. "Come on upstairs." She jerked him by the arm and pointed to the top of the stairs.

"Why?"

"Bring your high yellow ass upstairs, boy!" Carmen got her point across by squeezing him tighter.

Vincent stood up and they walked up to the second floor. Carmen told him to stand near the linen closet. She cautiously closed the door to Valerie's room, who was stretched out in her bed, with her head planted in the pillow. Braun and Junior were in the room next door snoring like two grizzly bears during hibernation season.

Carmen saw that everyone was sleeping rather heavily. A perfect time to make her move. She grabbed Vincent by the

waist and they journeyed into the bathroom. The lock was turned quietly to minimize the clicking noise of the metal slot. She guided him over by the toilet. The lid was placed down and Vincent took a seat on top. Carmen moved him against the head of the bathtub. She gently lifted his shirt up and pulled his pants and underwear down. He may have fallen alseep earlier, but was presently in for the *rudest awakening*.

"What we're about to do," Carmen said, pointing her wavering finger to middle of his eyes. "You better not tell anybody. Do you understand me?"

"Yes," Vincent answered frightfully.

"I'm serious, boy!" she snarled, sounding as though she was making a death threat.

She told Vincent to lift up his feet while she removed his socks and shoes. The question that entered Vincent's mind was, *"Why is she undressing me?"*

He was almost certain that Carmen wasn't about to give him a bath, especially during that time of night. Once she fully undressed him, he glanced around the uniquely decorated bathroom. It was painted sky blue with an assortment of scented soaps and monogrammed terry towels. Bessie Mae and J.D. were always given first priority to this bathroom.

Carmen began undressing herself. It was the very beginning of the nineteen seventies and many Negro teens around America were wearing large afros, bellbottom pants, thick-heeled platform shoes, polyester shirts with large butterfly collars, and bead necklaces. Many emulated their style from the dancers on the popular musical television show *Soul Train*. Carmen simply wore straight permed hair, straight leg jeans or polyester pants, and button up or pullover shirts. She simply dressed *Chi-town style*.

Six and a half year old Vincent was absolutely astonished. He sat there watching his older foster sister undress herself.

More than twenty minutes had passed and Carmen and Vincent were still engaged in *teenage girl to little boy* sexual intercourse. She had both arms locked around his tiny neck. Her wide legs were wrapped around his lower body. The moisture from her dark lips smeared onto his thin red lips. Slapping and smacking noises traveled into the steamy air. His small penis slipped from in between her well-defined legs. Carmen knew that Vincent was too small and her pussy was too large. She lifted his head and looked him directly in his fearful eyes. In a voice that had a serious tone, she said, "I love high-yellow boys like you. I love this pretty curly hair that you have. I love these little juicy red lips that you have. I love everything about you, Vincent!"

This may have been her lifelong fantasy. Since she couldn't find a teenage boy who was light complexioned with a fine grade of hair to have sex with her, she found the next best thing. Her foster brother, who also happened to be light complexioned with a fine grade of hair, who also happened to be much younger. She wanted to spice up their unusual intercourse by kissing, rubbing, sucking, pressing, and grinding. By now, the bathroom was steamed up with sheer passion. Someone unexpectedly knocked on the bathroom door.

"Shhhhh!" Carmen whispered to Vincent. "Who is it?"

"It's Valerie," Valerie answered, drowsiness ringing in her voice.

"What do you want?" Carmen asked, her voice timid, sitting on the stool frozen like a glacier.

"I have to use the bathroom."

"Go downstairs."

"I can't go downstairs."

"Why can't you go downstairs?"

"Granny Dear don't like nobody using that bathroom downstairs."

"Shit, girl!" Carmen shouted in rage. "You better go

downstairs and use that bathroom! Plus, I won't be finished for awhile."

"Granny Dear'll be mad at me for using that bathroom on the first floor," Valerie whined, pressing tightly against the door.

"Tell her I said that you can use it."

Valerie began sniffing around the edges of the bathroom door. The odor from inside had came out into the hallway.

"What's that nasty smell?" Valerie asked, fanning the foul odor away.

"What smell?" Carmen said, afraid that she might have been busted.

"Smells like somebody's butt."

"Get away from the door, Valerie."

"Did somebody boo boo out in the hallway?"

"Don't make tell you no more."

Valerie walked away stomping her feet and hitting her hand against the wall. She was in the process of using the bathroom on herself. When she came to the bottom of the stairs, Vernon stood there wanting to know where Vincent was. She didn't know of his whereabouts. He hadn't been seen since they left the front room. Valerie looked in the bathroom near the dining room. Vernon went into the kitchen and pulled back the curtain to Granny Dear's room. He made a sudden inquiry about Vincent.

"I ain't seen Vinsun since suppatime," said Granny Dear, preparing herself to climb out of her wheelchair and into the bed.

"You haven't seen him hanging around the kitchen?"

"Naw."

"What about the dining room?"

"Naw, I ain't," Granny Dear said, nearly falling out of her wheelchair. "Yall keep hunting fo him, yall'll find'em somewhere round dis house."

"Okay, we will."

They roamed the house calling his name. Vernon traveled up to the second floor. He stuck his head inside Braun and Junior's room. They remained asleep. Braun vibrated the walls and the floor with his aggressive snoring. He went next door and looked inside Valerie's room. Vincent wasn't inside there. No one could go inside Bessie Mae and J.D.'s room. Their door was padlocked whenever they left the house. Bessie Mae complained that her belongings kept disappearing. She blamed the thief on a cousin from Memphis, Tennessee named Clara Martin. She put Clara in a juvenile home for girls after a large sum of money and jewelry came up missing.

"That thieving bitch done stole from me again!" Bessie Mae would shout in fury everytime her valuables did a disappearing act. *"I'm gonna have her locked up so she won't steal from nobody else!*

"Vincent!" Vernon called, his voice ringing out in search of his little brother. "Where are you, boy!"

Carmen had Vincent's mouth cuffed tightly with both hands. Silently, they waited in the muggy bathroom. They listened closely to Vernon's tardy footsteps. Vernon proceeded down the dark hallway. He noticed the bright light that was shining from under the bathroom door. He knocked several times. Naturally, he wanted to know who was in there.

"Vincent!" Vernon called. "Are you in there?" He pressed his ear against the door for any signs of his little brother. "If you're in there, come on out so we can stop looking all around this house for you." Still, no one answered. Carmen held a tighter grip over Vincent's mouth. She was afraid that she might've been caught in the act. Vernon knocked several more times. He jerked on the doorknob and twisted and turned it until he saw that it was useless.

"Vincent!" he called, fury in his tone. "I'm not gonna ask you no more to come out of that bathroom. If you're in there, then come out now." He pressed his ear up to the door a second time. Both of his hard fists pounded on the shallow wood of the door. Just as Valerie had noticed, Vernon detected the foul odor coming from the other side. He jumped back and rubbed his nose.

"Who's there?" Carmen asked dreadfully. Finally, she let Vernon know that someone was in there. Vincent stood suspended between her legs. Both of her hands cuffed his nose and mouth. She wasn't aware that she was nearly suffocating him. Anything to keep him from squealing a word.

"It's Vernon." He would've never suspected in his wildest dreams that his little brother and older foster sister were inside the bathroom in the absolute nude. Their bodies were drenched with sweat. They had just finished a crazy form of sexual intercourse.

"What's the matter?" Carmen said. "You sound like something just happened."

"Valerie and I were trying to find Vincent," Vernon mentioned. "Have you seen him anywhere around this house?"

"Have you checked on the first floor?"

"He's nowhere down there," Vernon said, partially covering his mouth and nose, as the foul odor began to set in.

"What about the basement?"

"I just came from down there."

"Have you asked Granny Dear?"

"She said she haven't seen him since dinnertime."

"Check outside."

"At this time of night?"

"Check anyway, Vernon."

"After that real bad whipping that he got from Mr. Willingham, I don't think he would be outside this time of night."

"Go out there and check anyway," Carmen said mild-manneredly, anxiously awaiting Vernon to leave the second floor.

The longer Vernon stood at the bathroom door, the stronger the odor became. It became unbearable to his sense of smell. "What's that smell, Carmen?"

"What smell?"

"Smells like booty or coochie or something."

"It's probably coming from Braun and Junior's room."

"No, no, it's coming from right at this door."

"It's probably coming from Mr. and Mrs. Willingham's room."

"I know my nose isn't playing tricks on me."

"I don't smell it, Vernon."

"Is somebody in there fucking, Carmen?"

"Say what!" Carmen jolted. "Watch your mouth, Vernon."

"Well, have they?"

"Don't ask no silly questions like that."

"Sorry."

Vernon returned to the first floor. Carmen quickly got dressed. Deep sunken fingerprints were around the edges of Vincent's mouth. She informed Vincent to hurry up and get dressed. She pointed to his pants and underwear and shoes and socks. Vincent picked up his clothes that were scattered across the bathroom floor and dressed himself. Valerie called for her little brother down on the first floor.

"Vincent! Vincent!" Valerie yelled out. "Where are you at? Quit playing and tell us where you're at."

Carmen stood at the edge of the bathroom door. She peeked between the cracks near the hinges. Cautiously, she pressed the lock between her thumb and index finger. She grabbed Vincent closer and said, "Don't ever tell anybody what we just did. Do you hear me?"

"Yes," Vincent answered humbly, sweat rolling down his innocent face.

"I'm not playing with you," Carmen reinforced. "Don't never tell anybody what we just did in this bathroom. Because if you tell anybody, I'm going to hurt you. Do you hear me, boy?"

"Yes," Vincent replied, fright entering his mind.

"Do you?"

"Yes."

The bathroom door opened about halfway. The coast couldn't have been clearer. Carmen slowly stepped out of the bathroom. She stared down the dark hallway, watching for someone who might've came up the stairs. Vincent walked behind her while she quietly crept to the top of the stairs. She glanced over the bannisters to see who was down on the first floor.

"Remember, don't say nothing to nobody," Carmen said, drilling it inside his mind like it was a matter of life or death. "I'll hurt you if you do. Do you understand?"

"Yes."

"Don't say nothing to Braun, Junior, Valerie, Vernon, Granny Dear, Sean, or Mr. and Mrs. Willingham."

"Okay."

"Run all the way to the basement and jump in the bed."

The opportunity couldn't have been greater. Vincent ran down the stairs that went to the first floor. No one was on the first floor. He dashed down the basement stairs and jumped into his bed, throwing the covers over his head. Surprisingly, he wasn't seen by Valerie or Vernon. They continued their search in other areas of the house. Vernon decided to search in the basement again. He stepped past the laundry room and couldn't believe his eyes. He came to the middle of the room and threw both arms around his waist.

"Where were you at, boy!" Vernon scorned, angrier than ever. "We've been all around this house and outdoors looking for you."

"I was down . . . uh . . ."

"Down where?" Vernon asked, expecting a logical reason for his absence.

"I was down here." Right then, immediate flashbacks raced through his mind.

"You're lying!"

"No, I'm not."

"Why do you wanna lie to me?"

"I'm not lying."

"I came through this basement looking for you a lot of times."

"I was down here."

"Why are you sweating like that?"

"It's hot in here."

"You stink, Vinnie."

"I don't stink."

"You smell like somebody's ass."

"No, I don't."

"Shut up and go to sleep."

Vincent couldn't uphold his integrity. He turned away in silence and went to sleep. Valerie came to the top of the basement stairs to see if Vincent had been found. When she knew that he had been found, she went upstairs and got into her bed.

The front door opened and Bessie Mae and J.D. barged through carrying two grocery sacks a piece. It was perfect timing. Carmen executed a master plan that would sneak Vincent in and out of the bathroom before they were caught. Very clever move on her behalf! Vincent lay stretched across his bed thinking about the horrible sexual encounter that he had just experienced. Thoughts flashed through his mind. Sex with a fully developed teenage girl. There was the possibility that he would be scarred for life. Would he take this secret to the grave with him? Was it sexual pleasure as well as sexual abuse on Carmen's behalf?

Once Bessie Mae and J.D. had put all the groceries away,

they made sure that everyone was asleep. While traveling up to the second floor, they noticed the same foul odor coming from the bathroom. They stopped at the top of the stairs and looked around. Bessie Mae turned to J.D. and asked, "Where is that smell coming from?"

"Probably fum da bathwoom."

"Somebody forgot to wash their ass?"

"It sho do stank."

"Let me find some air freshener."

"Thank Brawns forgot ta wipe Joanyer?"

"Who knows?"

"Spay evry'where ya can, Bessa Mae."

"I plan to, J.D."

Carmen and Vincent did more than leave evidence behind. Bessie Mae unlocked their door and rushed back out into the hallway spraying some strawberry air freshener. She went into the bathroom and nearly sprayed the whole can. She was determined to get rid of the nasty odor. J.D. checked to make sure the doors were locked and all the lights were out.

Chapter 10

SOAKING WET NIGHTMARES

CASEWORKER REPRESENTATIVES FROM The Children and Family Services for Cook County continued to make contacts by home visits and phone calls. An issue was raised about Bessie Mae often keeping unrelated children at the Willingham residence. Children were everywhere. Most didn't belong in the home. Whether or not Bessie Mae had a city license for daycare or to exchange services with other people, remained in question. Whenever a caseworker questioned her about keeping other children, she always maintained that it was for that day. After several home visits with Valerie, Vernon, and Vincent, one of the caseworkers made observations of the three children:

Children's adjustment to the licensed agency foster home of Bessie Mae and Jesse Dewayne Willingham.

Vernon Ramirez

Vernon is now fourteen years of age. He has lived with Bessie Mae and Jesse Dewayne Willingham, his foster parents, since the age of six. Vernon is a bright boy. He will be a freshman at George Washington Senior High in the fall. He mows lawns and does other odd jobs during the summer to make additional money to use during the school year. Since Vernon is the oldest of the three, he felt emotional pain more severely towards his mother's lack of interest and his step-father's

insensitivity. Vernon had definite negative feelings toward his mother and stepfather.

Valerie Ramirez

Valerie is an attractive girl of eleven years of age. Valerie has lived with Mr. and Mrs. Willingham since the age of four. She does not do as well scholastically as Vernon. She was promoted to the sixth grade; however, her teacher stated that Valerie did not do her work well in class and that she had a somewhat arrogant attitude.

Vincent Carvelli

Vincent is the half-sibling of Valerie and Vernon. Marion Carvelli is the natural mother and Vito Carvelli is the natural father. Vincent has lived with Mr. and Mrs. Willingham since infancy, thus looks to them as his natural parents. He is very close to Valerie and Vernon and holds opinions similar to theirs. Although Vincent did not live with his natural mother long enough to remember feelings of rejection by her, he has heard comments from Valerie and Vincent that they have no desire to build a relationship with his natural mother or father. Vincent is a good student in school. He will be in the second grade this fall. He enjoys reading a great deal.

*   *   *

Though a caseworker had made several observations of these three siblings, there were some personal problems that they had experienced. They never knew that Carmen had used Vincent as a *bathroom sex object*. The risk became too high for her to keep sneaking him in the bathroom. She found a steady boyfriend and he seemed to satisfy her intense sex drive.

*   *   *

A certain remark came from Vincent at the same time every night or early in the morning: *"Oh god, I've done it again!"* He would make this statement often, always reminiscing on the edge of his bed. A large wet ring covered most of the sheets and mattress underneath. Vincent lied on top of this wet ring. Consequently, he knew that the beatings would continue. When Bessie Mae or J.D. came to the basement to check his bed, they would pull the covers back. They would tell him to roll out of the bed to see if a large wet ring covered the sheets. A wet bed meant another beating. A dry bed meant that he was waking up in time and going to the restroom.

Vincent sat at the edge of his wet bed. His light blue pajamas were soaked. The dark yellow urine spot began drying. Looking up at the ceiling only gave Vincent thoughts of getting another beating with J.D.'s long extension cord. This long brown cord was painful, especially when it was stroked across his wet pajamas. It caused a stinging sensation everytime it made contact with his body.

Frightening memories came crashing back through his mind about J.D. looking down on his soaked bed and asking all kinds of questions:

"Why can't chu git yo ass up and go to da bathwoom?"
"I don't know," Vincent answered, not able to give the angry J.D. straight eye contact.
"Dunno?" J.D. replied.
"No sir," Vincent cried, trembling from fear of another vicious beating.
"Why ya keep pissing in da bed?"
"I don't know," he whined, hoping J.D. would show mercy.
"You gone know when I beat yo ass!" J.D. said, wasting no time beating Vincent with his extension cord.

Vincent felt that his bedwetting problem was virtually uncontrollable. He leaned his head against the steel post at the foot of his bed. Brainstorming might have been a way to resolve this dreaded problem. In a whispering voice, he asked himself the questions:

"Is Vernon Willing to keep waking me up in the middle of the night?"

"I wonder if I can get Mr. or Mrs. Willingham to feel sorry for me and I'll stop getting beatings?"

"Would they stop beating me if I told them that I can't help myself?"

These thoughts of sympathy diminished. Vincent felt that there was no solution. Vernon was across the room sleeping peacefully. The spreads covered his entire body. There was complete silence and darkness in Sean's room. Vincent sat in the dark, at the very end of his bed. He felt hopeless! Truly helpless! The agonizing burden of having bedwetting problems reflected directly on him. His head hung low in despair. A bright light shone through the window above the area where Vernon slept. It beamed directly down on the dark yellow spot. Darkness and silence embraced the entire basement. A seven year old foster boy sat in mass confusion.

"Wait!" Vincent whispered. "Wait a minute here! There's a linen closet with fresh sheets on the second floor."

This closet was located down the hall from Bessie Mae and J.D.'s room. Sheets, pillowcases, towels, washcloths, and old draperies filled every shelf to capacity. Vincent took a moment to think. Was the risk worth it? Would a trip up to the linen closet on the second floor save him from another morning of getting beat?

He arose from the soaked bed. Sean snored loudly under his thick spreads. Vernon gracefully slept the hours away. Vincent walked over to the basement stairs. The squeaking noises from the stairs traveled back into the room. He didn't want to awake Vernon. Taking each stair slow and easy was wise. The pattern was to take one stair and stop. Take another stair and stop again. The goal was to keep stepping until he reached the top of the stairs.

The basement door met him face first. Vincent turned the knob on the door with great ease. He made sure the noise from the rusty bolts didn't travel into Granny Dear's room. Granny Dear could hear a mouse creeping in the midst of a massive explosion. Not bad for sixty-something elderly woman.

Vincent made it to the first floor. The hallway that led towards the dining room was pitch black. The air was void. The wooden antique clock in the front room said 3:25 a.m. The heartpounding challenge, along with the great risk of getting caught, was being able to travel up to the second floor. The clean bed linen had to be taken with caution. Vincent's little heart pounded against his chest like a jackhammer pounding on concrete. He had broken out into a mild sweat. His left leg was placed on the first stair. The crucial part of this task was to avoid the squeaking noises that carried up to the second floor. The same stair was pressed with little impact. There wasn't enough acoustic to distract anyone's sleep.

Vincent began his risky journey up to the second floor. He took three soft steps and stopped. The thick carpet on the stairs absorbed any sounds from heavy impact. Unlike the decaying basement stairs, he knew the chances of getting upstairs without being heard were good. The pattern was to take a step and then stop. Take three more steps and stop again. After several more steps, he reached the landing that separated the two flight of stairs.

The door to the Willingham room opened. Vincent quietly raced for a narrow corner to his left. The corner was formed by three connecting walls. The massive shadow of a man wearing droopy boxing shorts faltered into the hallway. A pair of heavy feet slowly dragged across the carpet. J.D. stopped and glanced down the set of stairs. Something looked rather suspicious to him. He walked halfway down the stairs and stopped.

Vincent's small frame was curled in a stooped position. Was fate on Vincent's side? Had the corner not been there for him to run and hide, he would have had to run down the entire flight of stairs going towards the first floor. Getting caught by J.D. would not have been a pretty sight. There was barely enough space in that corner for him to hide. J.D. had poor eyesight, especially in dark surroundings, but something still aroused his curiosity.

"Who down dere?" J.D. asked, looking around to see if he could spot anything. No one answered and he went back to the top of the stairs. Vincent remained motionless in the corner. Keeping his composure under that type of pressure was hard. A pounding heart and butterflies racing through his stomach caused him to shiver. Heavy perspiration saturated his face and armpits. Anyone who had to stare at someone as *big, black, and ugly* as J.D., especially in the dark, would become frightened senselessly.

Part of Vincent's leg was showing from the corner. Since J.D. wasn't looking that direction, it wasn't noticeable. Silence encompassed the first and second floors and J.D.'s pair of solid feet were heard pouncing across the floor. Vincent sat, waited, and listened for any kids of footsteps. J.D. entered the bathroom and the top of the stool could be heard dropping onto the rim.

Brmmmmmp! Brmmmmmp! Bmmmmmp! Those were the sounds that J.D. made after strong gaseous noises shot straight out of his large black ass and echoing from around the rim of

the stool. These were the farts that he had held in since dinnertime. Those pinto beans had gone to work on his system. They continued to sound off loudly, one right after another. Vincent shook his head wildly in that corner everytime he heard the gas shooting off and water splashing. No one could stand to step into the bathroom after J.D. had a strong bowel movement. They'd walk in the opposite direction.

Squealing noises traveled through the cracks of the floor. J.D. stepped into their room and closed the door. The odor from the bathroom had come out into the hallway.

"Dam, he stinks!" Vincent whispered. "Mr. Willingham's dooky always smells real bad!"

The Willingham's door was completely shut. Vincent looked into Braun and Junior's room. They snored loud enough to awake the living and dead. He hesitantly crept over to the linen closet. The door was opened gently. There were exactly eight shelves in the linen closet. They were occupied with bathroom and bedroom linen. Vincent looked up at the top shelf and moved down to the bottom. Trying to find the right sheets and pillowcase that would fit his bed proved time consuming. Among the king, queen, and twin bed sizes, it was difficult deciding which one of the folded ones belonged on his bed.

Vincent pulled pillowcases and other sheets from under the other linen and cuffed them under his arm. Vincent knew that he had to hurry. The door to the Willingham room turned softly. A crack in the door sent a flash of light out into the hallway. Vincent was firecely alert! He heard the beginning of footsteps coming into the hallway. There wasn't

time to run to the first floor or hide in the corner near the landing.

The door leading to the third floor was the perfect hiding place. Bessie Mae limped out of their room and down to the bathroom. Vincent knew it was her. The off-balance, rhythmic footsteps, that pressed twice as hard into the thick carpet, gave her away every time. Behind that door, he was quieter than a soldier behind enemy lines. Through his slim nostrils, he was breathing rather heavy. He held the bed linen up to his mouth to silence the noises.

Bessie Mae flushed the stool and returned to their room. After she closed the door, Vincent began his journey back to the basement. The bed linen that would save him from further severe punishment was folded under his right arm. The trip up to the second floor was taken with precaution. The trip back to the basement was taken with lesser precaution. He simply walked down the stairs like he normally would. Once he arrived on the first floor, he crept to the doorway of the basement. He paused momentarily to glance down the dark hallway going towards the dining room.

When he gently turned the knob to the basement door, his mission was nearly complete. The door opened and he tiptoed down the stairs. The laundry room was mobbed with piles of filthy clothes. Vincent stepped over the tall piles and walked over to his soaked bed. The sheets began drying. It was only a short period of time. The sky blue fitted sheet and top sheets were pulled back. The heavily soaked mattress displayed a large yellow spot from the head of the bed and slightly past the middle.

The consumption from all of Vincent's bodily fluids saturated the already badly damaged mattress. He was an active child, drinking five to seven glasses of water everyday. The wet spot covered most of the area where his body lied. He placed his hand in the middle of the mattress. It was still heavily saturated with his urine. Placing the fresh sheets on

the bed wasn't a good idea. Vincent was well aware of this. The saturated mattress would cause the urine to penetrate the sheets. He was smart enough to know that he didn't want to defeat his purpose. Finding anything that would protect the sheets was an alternative. There had to be something to separate the soiled mattress from the clean sheets. Vincent looked into Sean's dark room. Sean simply snored the hours away.

Vernon tossed and turned under the bed spreads. He walked softly up the basement stairs. Bessie Mae kept newspapers in the dining room near her antique china cabinet. The clever mind of Vincent told him that newspapers would serve as a sponge once he placed it across his bed. The urine wouldn't make contact with the sheets.

"I can keep the piss from getting on the sheets," Vincent whispered, looking down at the wet bed.

His wet body was suspended in motion on the dark stairways. Thoughts were fresh inside his mind. The basement door was pushed open gently. He crept slowly into the dining room. The kitchen was slightly to the left, which meant extreme caution had to be taken. Anyone knew better than to awake Granny Dear. He walked around the dining room for several minutes. The china cabinet was on the other side of the kitchen door. A stack of old *Chicago Tribune* and *Chicago Sun-Times* newspapers were spread across the floor.

Vincent wasn't sure how much would be needed to cover the soaked mattress. He reached down and grabbed a handful. Quickly, but rather softly, he rushed past the kitchen. Granny Dear made a loud groaning noise. She was trying to clear her throat. Vincent stopped in the dark narrow hallway. She logically couldn't catch him, being that she wouldn't

have enough time to jump into her wheelchair and roll herself into the dining room.

Vincent returned to his room. He was back to the old drawing board. The newspapers were spread across the mattress in neat sections. Vincent's bed had different sections of *The Chicago Tribune* and *The Chicago Sun-Times* going from the head and on down to the foot. The fitted sheet was placed over the neatly spreaded papers. The pillowcase was removed and a fresh one replaced it. Most people like Bessie Mae and J.D. wanted their pillowcases and sheets to match. It didn't matter to Vincent, especially since his only concern was both foster parents checking a clean dry bed the next morning. The fluffiness of the pillow caused difficulty while trying to slide it on. It stubbornly wouldn't slide on. Vincent pushed and pushed until it finally slid under the pillowcase.

"Shew!" Vincent whispered, a breath of relief coming out like steam. "I'm finally done with changing these sheets and pillowcase."

His mission wasn't fully accomplished. He asked the unpardonable question:

"What am I going to do with these pissy sheets?"

A question such as that suddenly popped up inside his mind. It made him believe that his efforts were useless.

"Maybe I can ball up these sheets and pillowcase and stick them in with the piles of other dirty laundry?"

Vincent questioned himself while holding the sheets and pillowcase under his right armpit. He knew it wouldn't be wise to bury the soiled linen under the rest of the laundry. Bessie Mae observed every piece of laundry before stuffing it into the washing machine. She was fully aware that Vincent was the only one in the entire household who had a bedwetting problem.

"Maybe I can stick the sheets and pillowcase between the mattress and boxspring? Mr. or Mrs. Willingham would never find them under there."

Vincent thought about it twice. Maybe even three or four times. He bent forward to lift the mattress to stare down at the already ripped up boxspring. It wouldn't be wise to bury the soiled bed linen between the mattress and boxspring. Sooner or later, Bessie Mae or J.D. would pick up the foul scents like a foxhound picked up blood scents. Urine spoiled and the odor would definitely seep from in between that tight area.

"Maybe I can throw the sheets in the washing machine after Mrs. Willingham left the basement to go and smoke a cigarette?"

Vincent thought of a lot of different suggestions. While deep in thought, he didn't move a muscle. Would it be wise to take the risk of getting caught? Bessie Mae rarely left the basement while doing laundry. There was the conscious mind. There was the subconscious mind. His conscious mind made suggestions. His subconscious mind objected. He thought further into the confusing mind. He quietly

rationalized about the options left open. Throwing the sheets and pillowcases into the trash would make things a lot simpler.

There was a large trash barrel in Sean's room. The barrel was filled with trash from house cleaning duties. Vincent shoved the balled up sheets and pillowcase inside. A moaning noise came from over at Sean's bed. His head lifted as he turned over to another side. Vincent ran out of his room. The rambling from the trash inside the barrel might've awakened Sean. When the snoring resumed, he knew that Sean had gone back to sleep. Vincent was totally exhausted after two well-executed trips were made upstairs.

The extreme wetness of the mattress even penetrated the newspaper. The slight wetness of the newspaper barely penetrated the clean sheets. The dark color of the sheets helped camouflage the yellowish color of the urine. Would the bed have dried by the time Bessie Mae or J.D. came to the basement to make their check? This creeping, grueling, sheet-changing, mind-boggling, heartpounding, and remarkably risky task was not over. Wearing soiled underwear and pajamas would reveal that he wet the bed.

Back to the drawing board. Bessie Mae or J.D. would notice the discoloration on his light blue pajamas. They would smell the bad odor. Vincent went to the third drawer of his dresser. He searched for clean sleepwear. There was a pair of green *winnie the pooh* pajamas and *fruit of the looms* underwear. He slipped into the clean ones.

Kids often teased Vincent at school. The odor of raw urine would travel into the atmosphere of the classroom. He resented splashing soap and water on his body before leaving for school. Didn't Bessie or J.D. smell him before he left the house? Vincent had painful memories of those kids at school teasing him:

"Pissy Vinnie! Pissy Vinnie!" a group of rowdy children shouted right in Vincent's face.

"Leave me alone!" Vincent cried loudly, trying to run away from those who teased him.

"Peabody Vinnie! Peabody Vinnie!"

"That's not my name!"

"You smell just like piss, Vinnie!"

"Your mamma smells like piss!"

"Pissy boy! Pissy boy!"

"I don't smell like piss!"

"Yes you do, you pissy peabody!"

"Go home and leave me alone!"

*   *   *

Where could he hide the wet pajamas and underwear? The sounds of birds chirping, dogs barking, and loud car engines came from out on Milwaukee Parkway. A big burst of sunlight beamed through the window above Vernon's bed. It was every indication that morning had arrived. Vincent didn't want to throw away the soiled pajamas and underwear. They were balled up and stuffed between the mattress and boxspring. He could care less if Bessie Mae or J.D. smelled the urine near his bed. Maybe they would. Maybe they wouldn't. Maybe he could throw them in the washing machine if Bessie Mae took a break from doing laundry.

The hours traveled around the clock. Vincent spent most of the night traveling around the house. The main objective was trying to save himself from another vicious beating. He finally lied in a clean bed. He didn't have to worry about his foster parents throwing the covers back and staring down at a soaked bed. Several minutes passed and the beaming sun brightened the whole room. The basement door opened and squeaking noises echoed past the laundry room.

Vincent lied in a supine position. The mystery person stepped into the laundry room. They trampled through the piles of dirty clothes and into the middle of the floor. They

gradually stepped towards Vincent's bed. Heavy breathing circulated into the air. Vincent opened his eyes and J.D. stood there with both hands rested around his large waist. The long brown extension cord was clutched in his large fist. He leaned forward and reached for the top of the covers. Dark blood vessels in his watery eyes signaled that he was angry. His evil red eyes traveled from the head and down to the foot of the bed. Vincent lied perfectly still. Any sudden movement would reveal that the newspapers were spread underneath.

"Well," J.D. hummed, leaning forward to take a second look. "You finally went wittout pissin in da bed. Who woke ya up dis time?"

"Nobody," Vincent lied, cautiously moving his head towards J.D. "I woke myself up." The rest of his body remained motionless.

"You betta git yo ass up every night and go to da bathwoom," J.D. warned. "You hear ma, boy?"

"Yes sir," Vincent said, meekness in his voice.

"I will keep beatin yo ass wit dis stanching code."

Vernon woke up and looked across the room. He whispered to himself, "This black motherfucker is always coming to the basement to check and see if Vincent done pissed in the bed again. He's always looking for an excuse to beat on somebody."

J.D. took a few more seconds to inspect Vincent's bed. He returned upstairs and they prepared themselves for school.

Chapter 11

DENIAL

INFORMATION ABOUT VITO and Marion continued to flow into the Children and Family Services division. Over a course of time, Helen Bartlett and David Feinstein sent letters to them. They knew of their address and sent a brief letter that read:

> Dear Mr. and Mrs. Carvelli:
> We would like to talk to both of you in the interest of Valerie and Vernon Ramirez and Vincent Carvelli. Please telephone me at 745-2580 any weekday, between the hours of 8:00 a.m. and 5:00 p.m., so that we may set up an appointment time. Your prompt response is greatly appreciated.
>
> > Very truly yours,
> > Helen Bartlett

Helen learned about the harsh words between Bessie Mae and Vito. Contacts with Vito and Marion weren't arranged without the knowledge of a child welfare aide. Helen explained that should Vito and Marion make a change in their lives and wanted to visit the children, they would have to contact her office and set up a visit. If they wanted the children returned, they would have to show the courts that they

would be able to take care of their children by meeting all of their needs.

Bessie Mae was convinced that Vito only wanted the children back in order to increase his so-called phony social secuirty benefits. Was this another scam that Vito was trying to run on someone? Would he bring his children in the middle of this scam? Some people were heartless and would follow through on something as sinnister as using children to get social security checks.

*   *   *

It was a very sunny Wednesday afternoon on the playground of Abraham Lincoln Elementary. Vincent and his classmates played kickball on a circle drawn with white paint. The circle was at the north end of the playground. He came up to the plate to kick the ball. Other classmates waited impatiently for their turn. Those who waited in the outfield, shouted harsh and insulting remarks at Vincent.

"Come on and kick the ball, white boy!" yelled a group of outfielders.

"I'm not a white boy!" Vincent yelled back, grabbing the ball that was rolled to him. The ball was thrown back to the sweet little girl who rolled it to him.

"We're gonna kick your white ass after school."

"Quit calling me white."

"You're a white boy and you know it."

"No, I'm not."

"Yes, you are."

Vincent hated when his classmates called him names like, *"white boy"*, *"white honky"*, and *"white snow"*. Being bi-racial and having a bright complexion, with a fine grade of curly hair, made him stand out from all his other classmates. According to the laws of American society, if a person had any black blood in them, they were still considered to be

black. James Brown let it be known that being black was beautiful and anyone who was black should be proud. The classmates of Vincent continued making their insulting remarks.

"Your mamma's a white honky! Your daddy's a white honky!" they shouted furiously. "That makes you a white honky just like them, Vinnie!" These classmates were going on the assumption that both of Vincent's parents were white. Kids were cruel and it was moments like these that made Vincent realize it.

The ball was rolled to Vincent a second time. He cocked his right leg back and kicked it high up in the air. He used every ounce of engery to make the ball land far into the out-field. The ball flew right towards another circle and ended up at the south end of the playground. One of the outfield-ers ran towards the other circle and the red blubbery ball landed in his cradled arms.

Seconds later, the bell rang for recess to end. Everyone walked towards the front of the school. There was no teacher supervision and the students made lots of noise. They trampled through the front acting very undisciplined. Those who were on the same team as Vincent weren't too happy with him making the last out. They formed a small group and began shouting outlandish remarks about him being bi-racial.

"White boy, white boy, you don't shine! You call me a nigger, I'll beat your behind!" barked a group of unruly classmates who had closed Vincent in.

"Leave me alone!" Vincent sneered, protecting himself from his classmates.

"Vinnie is a white boy! Vinnie is a white boy!" paraded yet another circle of his classmates.

"Leave me alone and go inside the school!"

"Shut up, white honky!"

"I'm not a white honky!"

"Shut up, white boy!"

"I'm not a white boy!"

"We don't like white boys like you."

"Stop it!" Vincent shouted. "Stop calling me that!"

For Vincent, attending Abraham Lincoln Elementary was like being an only white kid attending an all black school in the heart of an urban Chicago ghetto. His feelings were shattered after all the insults were lashed out at him. Many black scholars who were experts on the subject of racial injustice and the color stratification of blacks, admitted to the fact that dark complexioned blacks may have had an inferiority complex towards brighter complexioned blacks with the fine grades of hair, resenting the fact that they have been called names like *tarbabies, spooks, nappy headed buckwheats, jiggs, porch monkies, and blackies,* which was something that dated all the way back to slavery. And Vincent was experiencing some of this same resentment from his much darker complexioned classmates. Had he called any of them those names, would they retaliate with voilence?

*   *   *

Everyone walked into the classroom. They were restless and were still whispering insults about Vincent. The poor guy just wasn't accepted by them. Their teacher was Mrs. Alberta Hoffman. She was a short woman with a fair complexion and tinted hair. She clapped her hands three times and told the class to settle down.

"Recess is over, students," Mrs. Hoffman said. "Do any of you want to go to the principal's office?"

"No, Mrs. Hoffman," responded the entire classroom.

"Then sit up straight and pay attention to class."

"Yes, Mrs. Hoffman."

Vincent sat at his desk with his face partially covered. Alberta wasn't aware that her students had gotten rowdy on

the playground and inside the school building. She instructed everyone to take out their English textbooks. Despite all the uproar, the insults continued. Two of Vincent's classmates, Jerry Grayson and Clinton Marks, sat in the row to his left. They were heartless. Jerry had very nappy hair, a wide pugged nose, a very dark complexion, but teeth were whiter than winter snow, which complimented his shiny dark complexion. He kept an afro comb and loose change jingling in his back pocket, wanting everyone at Abraham Lincoln to know that his mother always gave him spending money.

Clinton was heavyset and had a stomach that overlapped past his waistline. His oily face had a shine from him having too much hair grease in his head. Jerry whispered over to his attractive classmate named Anita Davidson. Anita dressed adorable, wearing her dark hair in a ponytail, with red ribbons to match her red velvet dress. She had the cutest babydoll face, with a glowing coppertone complexion to compliment it.

"There's a lot of names that you can call Vinnie," Jerry whispered over to Anita, checking to make sure Mrs. Hoffman wasn't looking.

"What kind of names?" Anita asked, moving her desk closer.

"Peckerwood, redneck, honky, half-breed, cracker, and white boy." Jerry said those derogatory names with no problem. Like many other black youths, he lived in a home with angry black parents who detested racist whites who had oppressed them for many years. They even detested the biracial blacks who could pass for white and flaunted their high-society status.

"Who told you all those names?" Anita inquired, moving closer to Jerry's desk.

"My daddy and uncle told me."

"Wow!"

Vincent didn't pick up on their conversation. He glanced

their direction and made eye contact with Jerry. Several outlandish remarks were made about his bright complexion. His mixed-parentage status seemed to annoy those at their school. Jerry's insults were lethal. They kept pouring in. Alberta Hoffman took a break from writing on the blackboard. She turned around and caught Jerry whispering in Anita's ear. She came over to their desks and wanted an explanation. They had to explain why they weren't listening to the lecture.

"Jerry was telling me some jokes," Anita explained. "I'm sorry for not paying attention, Mrs. Hoffman."

Mrs. Hoffman turned her attention to Jerry. "Would you like to tell the classroom some of these jokes?"

"I don't have no more jokes," Jerry said, hoping that he wouldn't be sent to the principal's office. "I'm sorry, too, Mrs. Hoffman, for not paying attention."

"You know that I don't tolerate disruptive behavior?"

"Yes, Mrs. Hoffman," Jerry answered.

"Wait until school lets out," Mrs. Hoffman told her students. "Do you understand me, Jerry?"

"Yes, Mrs. Hoffman."

Alberta Hoffman returned to the chalkboard to finish writing sentences from the English textbook. The bell rang shortly afterwards and school was finally out. Everyone grabbed their textbooks and school supplies. They rushed towards the front door that faced Milwaukee Parkway.

Vincent walked behind everyone else. He was frightened to step out of the school building. There were several of his classmates who stood near the fence and steps in front of the building. Vincent stepped onto the playground and a congregation of boys and girls were stomping their feet, clapping their hands, swinging their arms high in the air, and rocking their heads from side to side. The atmosphere became flooded with more harsh remarks about his mixed-race heritage.

"Vinnie is white boy! Vinnie is a white boy!" yelled a group of about ten boys and six girls.

"I'm not a white boy!" Vincent shouted back, tears rushing out of his weary eyes.

"Vinnie is a white honky! Vinnie is a white honky!" barked even more children who joined in with the others.

"I'm not a white honky!" Vincent cried, a voice that rung along Milwaukee Parkway.

Vincent was closed in by a multitude of kids. They pressed up close to one another and kept him from trying to run away. He wondered where these group of black elementary children were taught to say all those racial slurs. Were they viciously picking on Vincent because he was a product of the white race? Like Jerry Grayson, they lived in households where their parents would say detestable things about the white race.

They clapped and stomped and shouted to a rhythm that resembled a jamboree celebration. Vincent desperately tried penetrating his way through the crowd of *unruly* elementary kids.

"Let me out!" Vincent roared, shoving his arms at those who wouldn't move.

"You're not going anywhere, you half-breed honky!"

"Go home and leave me alone!"

"Don't run, you white half-breed!"

"Stop it! Stop it!"

The chaos became more intense. They continued to coldheartedly disrespect him. One of the fourth grade teachers, whose room was located near the front, walked onto the playground. She made the students leave the playground. By now, tears were rushing down Vincent's face. The little feelings that he had were crushed. He ran out on Milwaukee Parkway to escape the group of *young savages.*

Those cruel classmates weren't anywhere in sight after he ran for more than a block. His tears had dried up. Cars drove up and down Milwaukee playing loud music. They blasted the smash hit, *"What's Going On"*, and the airwaves were flooded with the mega-hit by Marvin Gaye. Practically

every word of Marvin's politically conscious song made sense to Vincent. He definitely could relate. His mother, Marion Carvelli, was somewhere in Chicago crying. She was sorry for leaving him in a foster home. His father, Vito Carvelli, though he was an utterly ruthless man, was somewhere within the city limits feeling sorry for leaving his children in a foster home.

Vincent walked out Milwaukee until he reached closer to home. The light at the corner turned red. Someone was trailing him and the feeling was inevitable. The light turned green and he crossed the street. He instantly became curious. He looked back and Jerry Grayson and Clinton Marks were walking less than a block behind. They lived in the opposite direction, several blocks west of Abraham Lincoln. The journey continued out Milwaukee. Vincent looked back again and Jerry and Clinton had smiles of mischeviousness on their faces.

Vincent put more speed in his pace. Regardless of how fast he walked, they were able to keep up. They were hot on Vincent's trail. He came to the very corner where his residence was. The most humiliating sight ever was on the side of the house. Braun, Junior, Sean, and a new handicapped man named Morris Wesley, who was paralyzed from the waist down and confined to a wheelchair, all sat near the side door going into the basement.

Morris was medium complexioned with short and graying hair. Thick bags under his eyes and wrinkles on his skin showed signs of aging. He made his debut at the Willingham residence the day before. One of the Chicago handicapped foundations agreed to let Bessie Mae keep him on a trial basis. Junior stared straight across the street without moving an eyebrow or an eyelid. His near vegetative state was revealed to those who walked up the street. They assumed that he was probably mentally retarded.

Braun waved his long arm and spoke to every single person who walked up the street. His black, tobacco-smeared teeth smiled at them. They watched him beat the middle of

his right hand with one of his broken off hangers. Bessie Mae sure had a lot of hangers missing around the house.

Sean leaned back in his chair with his legs crossed. His paralyzed hand slid across his lap while he used his other hand to wipe his face. Like Braun, Morris spoke to everyone walking up the street. In his dark green wheelchair, he moved his handicapped-stricken body to a position that was more comforting. Braun's long arm kept going up everytime he saw someone.

"Hey, how ya doing there?" Braun said to a teenage girl and her teenage boyfriend.

"We're doing fine, sir," spoke the young man. He paid close attention to Braun beating the middle of his hand with the wire. The black teeth in Braun's mouth brought a frown on his face. The teenage couple faded away and a group of high schoolers were coming up the street.

"Hey, hey, how ya doing there?" Braun asked, slapping his hand at an accelerated pace.

"We're doing okay," some the youngsters answered, wearing their big afros, bellbottom pants, and platform shoes. They all frowned when they saw his disgusting black teeth.

Vincent stood frozen at the corner. He stared at the handicapped men who lived at the same residence as him. It came as a shock to see them sitting out there. Braun and Sean usually attended an institution for the handicapped. Junior and Morris usually sat somewhere in the house. Vincent watched them closely. They watched the people coming up the street. Jerry and Clinton were watching Vincent. They also stood near the corner. They waited for his next move. Vincent always wanted to be home at a certain time. Television programs such as *"The Flying Nun"*, *"Green Acres"*, *"Gilligan's Island"*, and *"Bewitched"*, aired during the early and late afternoon hours.

"Do you live in that house on the corner?" Jerry asked Vincent, talking from a short distance.

"Nope!" Vincent denied, watching one of the houses from across the street, scoping it out like he lived in one of them.

"Yes, you do," Jerry argued, then turning to lock eye contact with his buddy Clinton.

"No, I don't."

"You're lying!" Clinton spoke, quickly pulling his sagging pants up around his obese frame. "You live in that house with those funny looking men. Don't you, Vinnie?"

Did Jerry and Clinton know that two of those funny looking men were mentally retarded and the other two were simply handicapped?

"No!" Vincent objected loudly, turning red all over the face.

"Yes, you do," Jerry insisted.

"No, I don't!"

Jerry pointed to the side of the house. Braun beat the middle of his hand harder. His jaws and teeth went to work on a piece of chewing gum that was weeks old. He kept old balls of chewing gum hidden in his dresser drawers, right under a pile of folded clothes. Clinton knew that something had to be unusual about a man who slapped the middle of his hand with a broken off piece of hanger.

"If you don't live in that house, then where do you live?" Clinton asked.

"I live down the street," Vincent answered repulsively.

"Down the street where?"

"Down by . . ."

"Down by where?"

"On the next corner of Milwaukee."

"In which house?"

"That big yellow house," Vincent replied nervously.

"You're lying!" Jerry said furiously. "You live in that foster home with those retarded men. Don't you, Vinnie?"

"No!" Vincent yelled.

"Show us the house that you live in," said Clinton.

How in the name of God did they find out that Vincent was in a foster home? Being in a foster home was a secret that he wanted to keep from his classmates. It was embarrassing living in a foster home. Shame was brought to those children who became *wards of the state.*

Most kids who lived with their biological parents believed in an old cliche which said:

"If someone lived in a foster home or an orphanage, then that meant that their mother and father didn't want them or they gave them away and then ran off."

Vincent was totally confused. Jerry and Clinton caught him off guard. These two cruel classmates insisted that he show them the house that he lived in. He crossed the street and they followed him.

"Look at that man with the funny looking hand," Jerry said, pointing at Sean and laughing up a storm. "Hey, look at that man who's looking without blinking his eyes."

Courtesy was one area that both of these boys failed in. They had a blast insulting the four handicapped men who lived at the Willingham residence. Vincent didn't know what to do. He didn't know where to walk to. He obviously was too ashamed for Jerry and Clinton to know that he lived in the foster home on the corner. Bessie Mae limped onto the porch and he proceeded down the street. She came out to check on the group who were on the side of the house.

Vincent continued down Milwaukee until he came to the corner. He made a left at the corner and crossed the street. There was a gray and white house halfway up the block. It appeared to be vacant. Vincent went up on the porch, sitting his books and school supplies on an old lawn chair. He pretended as though he lived there, like he might've been locked out or

wanted for someone to come home. Jerry and Clinton weren't about to give up. They stood directly in front of the house.

"I thought you said that you lived in that big yellow house," Jerry said, trying to verify if Vincent was telling the truth or not. He pointed at the very large house that had several cars parked in the driveway

"I . . . do . . . live . . ." Vincent stuttered, maybe caught in the biggest lie ever. Someone in the big yellow house were playing the tune by the Jackson Five, "*I'll Be There.*"

"Where?" Jerry asked, chopping him off in mid-speech.

"In that yellow house."

"Quit lying, punk!" Jerry snarled. "You live in that foster home up on Milwaukee."

"No, I don't!" Vincent exploded. "Why don't you all go home and leave me alone?"

"Where's your real mamma and daddy?" Jerry incremented, leaving Vincent speechless for a few seconds. Would Vincent admit that his mother and father, Marion and Vito Carvelli, abandoned him at six months old? Luckily, Jerry and Clinton weren't aware of that.

"They're at home."

"Why do you keep lying?"

"I do live with my real mamma and daddy."

"No, you don't."

"Yes, I do."

"I said that you didn't, punk!" Jerry shouted.

"I said that I do, punk!" Vincent shouted back.

The shouting match caused an elderly woman, someone who appeared to be in her late sixties, to step onto the porch. She wore a bushy gray wig to cover her naturally thinning gray hair.

"Why are you sitting on my porch?" the elderly woman asked Vincent.

"I don't know, mam," Vincent replied, alarmed that she made a sudden appearance.

"Don't know," she said. "You've got to have a reason for sitting on my porch."

"I was tired and wanted to have somewhere to sit down."

"Well, I'm sorry," she apologized. "I usually don't allow strangers to sit on my porch. You'll have to find somebody else's porch to sit on."

"Yes mam."

"Sorry, son."

"That's alright."

Vincent was aware that he had to be home at a certain time. He started walking towards Milwaukee. Jerry and Clinton possessed a persistence that was unbelievable. They wouldn't stop trailing Vincent if they were paid dearly to do so. He journeyed up Milwaukee with staggering footsteps. Someone kicked a rusty soda can and Vincent quickly turned around to give his full attention.

"Hey, white boy," Jerry called. "You lied to us. You told us that you didn't live in that foster home with those retarded dudes."

"I didn't lie," Vincent declared, wanting to build up enough courage to walk towards his real home.

"Yes you did, you white honky."

"Your mamma's a white honky."

"What did you say?"

"Your mamma's a white honky," Vincent repeated, balling up his fist, ready for battle with Jerry.

"Don't let me catch you coming to school tomorrow."

"I'll be there."

"I'm gonna catch you on the playground and beat your white ass."

The front door to the Willingham residence opened. Bessie Mae stepped onto the porch and looked out towards the street. She called for Vincent to come inside the house.

Chapter 12

PUBLIC EMBARRASSMENT

CASEWORKERS FROM THE Department of Children and Family Services finally made contact with Vito and Marion. They made several trips to their home and made the following observations:

Mr. Carvelli said that he wanted the children back. I told him that we needed to talk more about this issue, should he come back into the office. He said that I could talk with his wife, as he was reluctant to leave his so-called place of work. He said that he was working under another name, as the name of 'Carvelli' has been misused, because that given name couldn't be used when trying to get a job. He said that they have no phone. Mr. Carvelli came into the office for an interview. He began the interview by saying that he had been working with the Goodwill Industries for several months. He said that he was a collection box maintenance man who earned $3.00 per hour. He went on to say that he is working there under the assumed name of Vito Carson. I saw his Illinois Chauffeur's License and social security card with his name on it. Mr. Carvelli said that he and his wife bought a new home three months ago. He said that they also purchased an old apartment building which was sold at a public auction. He's been letting things settle down for the last few years. Mr. Carvelli said that he thought the children would be happy with their mother, except possibly Vincent, who never knew his mother or father. He believed that he could turn the basement of the new home into two bedrooms or simply add on to the house.

There was a separate caseworker who visited with and interviewed Marion Carvelli. Vito wasn't present when she made the following observations:

*   *   *

The Carvellis live on a street on Chicago's south side that is only a block long. The homes are old and in need of repair. It is in a Negro neighborhood. The Carvellis live in a three story house. To reach the front door one has to go up a few steps. Mrs. Carvelli came to the door after several knocks. She was still in her housecoat, as she had been doing some cleaning. Mrs. Carvelli welcomed me in, after I explained to her who I was. I told Mrs. Carvelli that I wasn't for sure what name she went by. She said that people knew them by their real names. Because of bad things connected with the Carvelli name, Mr. Carvelli changed his name several times. Mrs. Carvelli asked how long would it be before they could get their children back. I told her I couldn't say, depending on their continued interest in the children and how the children were getting along at the Willinghams, in reaction to the visits. I explained to her that she and her husband would be like strangers to Vincent. She said that she realized this. Mrs. Carvelli asked if she should buy any school clothes for the children. I told her that it would be impossible to have the children returned before school started. She seemed relieved that she wouldn't have this financial responsibility. I talked with Mrs. Carvelli about having future visits with the children arranged through our office. She agreed to this and said she would not try to see them again unless it was arranged properly. Mrs. Carvelli is a medium complexioned Negro woman. She has a smooth complexion. Her house had a neat and clean appearance, but it was crowded and the rooms were small. Even though Mr. and Mrs. Carvelli are still wanting the children back, Mrs. Carvelli impressed me as not being eager for them to be returned. She seemed somewhat relieved when she learned that she wouldn't have to buy their school clothes, nor did she seem anxious to have them returned during the school year. Were Vito and Marion trying to live legitimate lifestyles?

The courts were apprehensive about returning Valerie, Vernon, and Vincent to them.

*   *   *

Smoke bombs and black snakes caused clouds of different colored smoke to travel into the air. Firecrackers exploded inside the tiny holes in the front yard of the Willingham residence. Bottlerockets lit up the bright sky and fell into the neighbor's yards up and down Milwaukee. Valerie, Vernon, and Vincent were in front of the house using their favorite fireworks. Other neighbors along the block joined them.

Braun, Junior, Sean, and Morris were on the porch watching them stir up lots of noise. It was the "Fourth of July" and everyone celebrated in their own way. Vernon and Vincent were near the side of the house. They stuck firecrackers down into large soda and beer bottles. After the firecrackers were lit, they would run for safety. Seconds later, pieces of glass were blown everywhere. These were dangerous measures that Bessie Mae didn't approve of.

"Quit putting those firecrackers in those bottles!" Bessie Mae yelled out to her two foster sons from the side of the porch.

"Yes mam."

"That glass will pop in somebody's face and put their eyes out." Bessie Mae knew that their stunts were dangerous. Valerie was lighting snakes on the sidewalk facing Milwaukee. She lit smoke bombs and ran in circles. The smoke from these harmless fireworks caused her to have blurred vision. She waved the smoke out of her face and coughed out the fumes.

"Stand away from all that smoke before it goes down your lungs and make you sick!" Bessie Mae shouted out at Valerie.

While they created all this glorious chaos, Granny Dear

was in the kitchen preparing their "Fourth of July" picnic dinner. The dinner included chicken, beef, and pork ribs, baked beans, sausage links, potato salad, hamburger patties, coleslaw, potato chips, and a twenty gallon cooler filled with lemonade. Granny Dear had all the food inside the pans and bowls.

They were wrapped with aluminum foil and ready for takeoff. Bessie Mae called everyone from the yard to come inside, so they could start loading the food in the back of J.D.'s truck. Everyone arrived in the kitchen and Vincent reached for the pan of sausage links and hamburgers. Vernon grabbed the pan of ribs and Valerie took the bowls of potato salad and baked beans.

They came to the truck and J.D. was there taking the food. He placed it against the board that kept it from turning over. Since the truck was parked on the side of the house, Braun was summoned to help bring Morris down the side stairs. Vernon remembered that the pan of chicken was on the kitchen table. He went back to the kitchen before the truck was fully loaded. Bessie Mae told Valerie and Vernon to get inside the car. The others started walking towards the side of the house.

Braun and J.D. lifted Morris' wheelchair down the side stairs. They strained every muscle they had. Carrying that solid steel wheelchair and Morris' compact, handicapped body, took a lot of muscle work.

"Brawns!" J.D. shouted, badly mispronouncing Braun's name. "Liff dis chair high enough in da air." J.D. felt that Braun didn't lift the wheelchair high enough to elevate above the stairs.

"Okay, okay, I'll lift the wheelchair up high, J.D.," Braun replied, straining extra muscles to lift the back of Morris' wheelchair.

"Liff dis chair up higher, Brawns!" J.D. shouted a second time.

"Alright, alright, I'll lift it up higher, J.D."

"Shut da fuck up, Brawns!"

"Okay, okay, I'll shut up, J.D."

"Shut yo goddam mouth, Brawns!"

"Okay, okay, I'll shut my mouth, J.D."

"Dun let ma tell ya no mo ta shut da fuck up!"

"Yeah, yeah, I'll shut up, J.D."

One of the characteristic traits that Braun possessed, which was clever and unique, was having the last word with anyone. J.D. thought that he was being stubborn on his behalf. No one could ever get the last word in when it came to Braun. Periodically, Bessie Mae had to remind J.D. that Braun was mentally retarded and that he didn't know any better. She once got angry and told J.D., *"Don't you know, you dumb bastard, that you don't argue with a man who's got the mind of a five year old child?"*

After they made it to the truck, Morris was lifted inside the back of the camper. Braun, Junior, and Sean were told to sit on the flatboards that J.D. used as seats. The food and handicapped men were arranged properly. Valerie, Vernon, and Vincent were seated in the front and back of Bessie Mae's black and white Cadillac Sedan de Ville. It was time for take-off. Before J.D. could start up his truck, Granny Dear had rolled her wheelchair over to the window in the kitchen that faced the side of the house. She reminded him that the cooler of lemonade was being left behind. Some type of fluid was needed to wash down all the food they were going to eat.

J.D. didn't want to delay time. He went into the kitchen and threw the cooler in the back of the truck. Everything was placed in order. Bessie and J.D. cruised out Milwaukee Parkway and continued southbound. They were destined for Lincoln Park. They had to travel a few short miles out Milwaukee until they came to Lincoln Avenue.

Bessie Mae leaned back with one hand on the steering wheel. The other hand rested on the armrest. She

nonchalantly watched the many rows of large houses that resembled the one that she operated. She watched the row of small trees that graced the small strip of grass. About four car lengths behind, J.D. had his radio turned to station WBBM. Some of his favorite blues music, which included the likes of B.B. King, Muddy Waters, Bobby Blue Bland, and Albert King, filled the front of his truck with *a good old down home blues of a good time.*

True southerners like J.D. could relate to the message in blues music, especially since he felt that white people gave him the blues all the time. Milwaukee Parkway ended and Bessie Mae drove past a set of traffic lights that crossed over into Lincoln Avenue. The trip continued as they drove to another set of lights. Across the street there were signs that gave directions to the many picnic shelters in Lincoln Park.

There was a large swimming pool, a zoo, a shelter for animals, and a wide fishing lagoon. Bessie Mae made a sharp left and drove slowly to try and follow the signs that led to a large shelter. Her foster children and the handicapped men needed room to roam around.

J.D. was right behind her. A huge area that covered many acres was to his right. They drove further into the park, passing shelters that were occupied by large groups of people. Many of them played outdoor games like frisbee, baseball, tennis, and football. Lincoln Park accomodated many people for different cultural activities. The main drag of Lincoln Park included shops, restaurants, and theatres.

While the children played throughout the park, their parents had grills fired up. Loud music blasted through speakers and many tables were filled with packs of soda, beer, and hard liquor. The sounds of "Earth, Wind, and Fire", "The Commodores", and "Parliament-Funkadelic", jaunted through the air. They were some of the hottest soul groups of

the seventies. It was a day of independence and everyone felt real good.

Vincent became excited when he saw the children having barrels of fun. They played basketball on some of the basketball courts and baseball on some of the baseball diamonds. Bessie Mae and J.D. drove by many occupied shelters, all surrounded by large grassy areas and cooking grills.

There was an empty shelter house that sat far off into the grass. Bessie Mae didn't hesitate to drive her long Cadillac up in the grass. J.D. pulled up behind her and everyone started getting out. The back of the camper was opened and Braun assisted J.D. with lifting Morris out. Junior and Sean stepped out of the camper and onto the grass. J.D. handed Valerie, Vernon, and Vincent the pantries of food. They carried it to the picnic table near the shelter. People at surrounding shelters watched them walk through the grass. They noticed something different about Braun, Sean, and Junior.

Braun pushed Morris' wheelchair through the grass. Vernon didn't pay much attention to the people who stared his direction. Valerie and Vincent felt eyes looking at them from every direction.

"Why are they looking at us like that?" Vincent asked Valerie.

"I think I might know," said Valerie, then turning her head to avoid the lethal stares from others.

"Why?"

"They're looking at Sean's crippled hand. They're wondering why Junior's eyes aren't blinking."

"People are gonna be laughing at us, Valerie."

"Now they're looking at Braun push Morris over to the shelter," Valerie noticed, tilting her head in shame.

Valerie and Vincent knew that being in the company of men who were either crippled or mentally retarded brought

on unexpected humiliation. Some of the men, women, and children at surrounding areas covered their mouths and hid their faces. They tried disguising the outburst of laughter. Didn't anyone teach them that you didn't laugh at people who were born with a certain birth defect? People who were mentally retarded or crippled? Didn't they know that they could've been born the same way?

Bessie Mae limped through the grass. She carried the large bowl of potato salad over to the picnic table. There were those same people at other picnic areas who watched her limp up and down on her deformed leg. She became the immediate center of attention. After many years of being teased, with children calling her 'hop-a-long', she learned to ignore the unwelcome stares and insults.

Everyone came to the shelter area and the food was spread out over the table. While Bessie Mae unwrapped the food, J.D. went to his truck to turn up some loud blues music. His music couldn't nearly drown out the other music because of the powerful speakers. Valerie and Vincent stood on the left side of the large grill. People continued to stare their direction, like they didn't belong at Lincoln Park. They brought on a sense of uneasiness.

Vincent's eyes wandered towards the sky. Not long ago, he was followed home by two classmates, who discovered that he lived in a foster home with handicapped men. These same men were present at a "Fourth of July" picnic that Bessie Mae and J.D. arranged. At times, shame seemed endless. Vincent wondered how much shame was ahead. He snapped out of the brief flashback to glance around the park.

Bessie Mae looked over at Valerie and Vincent and sensed that something wasn't right. When she turned her head, they went over to the truck and climbed inside the camper. The camper was dark and hollow. Their heads hung low. They grew tired of others spectating them.

No one attended a picnic on "The Fourth of July" to be

looked upon as an outcast. Minutes later, Bessie Mae looked around. She noticed that Valerie and Vincent had disappeared.

"Where's Valerie and Vincent?" Bessie Mae asked Vernon.

"They walked over by the truck," Vernon told Bessie Mae, pointing to the back of the camper.

"Where at over by the truck?"

"Somewhere towards the back."

Bessie Mae limped over to the back of the camper. Valerie and Vincent were given a rude awakening shortly afterwards.

"Get out the truck!" Bessie Mae yelled furiously at Valerie and Vincent, pointing directly to the outside. "Get you all's yellow asses out of this truck right now! Get over there with everybody else!"

With Bessie Mae being the true southerner from the old school, she identified many bright and fair complexioned black people as *'yellow'*, *'high yellow'*, or *'red'*.

"What the hell's wrong with you?" Bessie Mae asked Valerie.

"I'm not feeling good, Mrs. Willingham," Valerie whined, holding her stomach in a pretentious position.

"What's the matter with you, girl?" By now, Bessie Mae had gained the attention of many surrounding shelters.

"My stomach's hurting."

"How is it that your stomach starts hurting all of a sudden?"

"I don't know."

"Well, what's wrong?"

"I think it's something that I ate for breakfast."

"You never get sick after breakfast."

"I think the rice made me sick."

"There's nothing wrong with your stomach. Get out of the truck right now."

Valerie and Vincent jumped out of the camper and strolled through the grass. Valerie pouted and it was in a rather noticeable manner. She mumbled words under her

breath. Bessie Mae noticed her every move. Her belligerent ways had gone too far. Uncooperative foster children was something that Bessie Mae didn't tolerate. She was blowing steam by now. Dirt was kicked from under the thick grass, because she quickly approached a wide tree on the other side of the shelter. The tree had long and thick branches. Seconds later, she limped towards Valerie and Vincent.

"Alright, goddammit!" Bessie Mae roared, shoving the long flexible switches in their faces. "I'm not gone put up with no more bullshit from no high yellow heifer and no high yellow and half-breed fuckers like you all! Do you want me to call your caseworkers to come and get your asses?"

"I don't know," Vincent answered sorrowfully, tears rolling down his red face.

"What do you mean you don't know?" Bessie Mae asked. "I can call your caseworker and have her haul your yellow ass away from my foster home!"

"I don't wanna go to another foster home, Mrs. Willingham," Vincent weased, crying as though Bessie Mae had the power of the state of Illinois in her hands. Actually, part of his fate was in her hands.

"You all better straighten your asses up!" Bessie Mae warned. "I try and take you somewhere and this is how you act. You all act like a couple of dam clowns!"

"I don't wanna go to another foster home, Mrs. Willingham," Vincent repeated remorsefully, frightfully emphasizing his point.

"Ain't no other foster home is gonna want you. They're gonna end up putting your ass in a boys home."

"I don't wanna go to a boys home." Vincent had become attached to Bessie Mae and J.D.'s foster home after all those years.

"Then you better straighten your ass up!"

Valerie, Vincent, and including Bessie Mae, had become the trio of unwelcome attention. The spotlight on them was

brighter than any star of Broadway. Bessie Mae threatened to put any foster child in a boys home or a girls home whenever she felt they were being disruptive. That's how she always played her game, a serious mind game that made helpless foster children feel as though they would end up on the streets if they were taken away from her home.

Bessie Mae instructed Valerie and Vincent to grab a plate and join everyone else. They fixed a plate and sat at the end of the benches. They ate very slowly. It was much slower than they had eaten at home. Bessie Mae watched them closely. Nothing irritated her more than watching someone pick over their food. She charged Valerie and Vincent with the thick switches. They were given three quick strokes across the back and shoulders.

Valerie accidentally dropped some potato salad onto her lap. Vincent jumped up crying. The body parts that were struck caused him to feel a burning sensation. He rubbed those parts to ease the pain. Valerie massaged her right shoulder and lower right arm. Bessie Mae really meant business! More embarrassment was brought to her two foster siblings. One of Bessie Mae and J.D.'s favorite slogans was: *A good old-fashioned ass whipping would change anybody's mind and make them straighten up and act right.*

"Me and Granny Dear didn't cook all this food for you all to mess over!" Bessie Mae made clear to Valerie and Vincent. She pointed down at the two plates that had food splattered everywhere. Maybe she could change Valerie and Vincent's mind about acting right.

"I was eating, Mrs. Willingham," Valerie said, tears rolling down her face.

"No, you weren't, girl!"

"I was just eating slow."

"Quit your lying, girl!"

Now they had really become the center of attention to those at the nearby shelters. People had discontinued what

they were doing. They stopped their sporting activities. They quit eating to watch Bessie Mae discipline her two foster children. Quick rushes of tears rolled down their flushed faces. They tried eating faster to please Bessie Mae. Vernon journeyed away from the picnic area. There were many attractive young ladies around the park. They wore their hot pants, towering afros and pressed hair, halter tops, which showcased their firm breast prints, and tight bellbottom jeans.

Vernon grew up to be a handsome teenager himself. He sported a large curly afro and began growing a thin mustache. The open-face gold in his mouth and handsome face attracted young women from everywhere. One of the girls from the other shelters was a contender for his girlfriend. He was at the age where he wanted to date the opposite sex. J.D. turned up the music inside his truck. Blues music was his religion. There were older generation people at the park who also enjoyed his brand of music. Bessie Mae sat at the picnic bench with the switches clutched in her right hand. While they ate their food, Valerie and Vincent were being watched closely. Valerie was dragging her fork slowly through the baked beans. Bessie Mae watched the fork move from one end of the paper plate to the other. Not eating your food in a timely fashion irritated her even greater. Vincent had a sausage link at the end of his mouth. The sausage had been planted between his lips for several minutes. Bessie Mae became furious! She galloped towards the end of the table with the switches stretched forward.

"I've had enough of this shit!" Bessie Mae erupted loudly, drawing her right arm backwards, ready to strike Valerie or Vincent at any second. "I'm sick and tired of a high yellow bitch and a high yellow, half-breed bastard like you all acting up! You come out to this park trying to show your high yellow asses to everybody!" Of course, with Bessie Mae, it was always 'high yellow this' or 'high yellow that'. According to her and many

other deep-rooted southerners, bright complexioned blacks were all considered 'yellow' and 'red'.

"We weren't doing nothing wrong, Mrs. Willingham!" Valerie cried, feeling like Bessie Mae only picked on her and Vincent.

"I will beat you all the way home!" Bessie Mae threatened, fury burning in her eyes.

"But I wasn't doing anything."

"I will beat you from yellow to black, girl!"

People around the park were using their fireworks. They played a game of throwing firecrackers at one another. Bottlerockets were shot into the air. Sparkles were waved into circles. No one at the Willingham residence was allowed to bring any fireworks. Valerie and Vincent watched the other youngsters have a blast. Morris scooted around in his wheelchair. He laughed everytime he saw a bottlerocket race across the sky or a firecracker burst into shreds of smoke and paper. Sean and Braun watched the people from other picnic areas look over at them.

Braun's black teeth were visible from far away. He didn't have his broken off hanger to relieve tension. Sean's paralyzed hand put a frown on the faces of those nearby. They stared profusely. Why couldn't they understand that he was born that way? It was no one's fault when they were born a certain way.

Crickets chirped and the sun began to disappear. Bessie Mae told everyone to walk towards the car and truck. Vernon came towards the car with phone numbers written on several pieces of small paper. A lot of girls were going to await his phone call. Valerie and Vincent walked towards the car as quickly as possible. They covered their heads with an empty bowl and meat pan. It was extremely embarrassing being at that picnic.

A final observation of the four handicapped men were taken by the group of people at other picnic areas. Sean's

paralyzed hand, Braun's black teeth, Junior's eyes and eyelids that never blinked, and Morris' paralyzed body curled
up in the wheelchair, made others believe that they belonged
with *The Ringling Brothers and Barnum Bailey Circus*. No they
weren't some kind of freaks who belonged in a circus, but
men who were dealt a bad hand in life.

   Bessie Mae brought the rest of the empty cookware to
the camper. Braun and J.D. lifted Morris inside. No one really had a good time at this picnic. Everyone was being
watched the whole time that they were at the park. Bessie
Mae stayed mad at Valerie and Vincent. They stayed embarrassed every second that they were there. Vernon found plenty
of girls his age to mingle with. J.D. ate most of the picnic away.
There was enough blues music played to keep him company. Everyone made it home and Milwaukee Parkway was lit
up with fireworks. Every firework imaginable sounded off
from the beginning to the end of the block. Bessie Mae
rushed back into the kitchen to tell Granny Dear the news
about the picnic.
   "Let me tell you, Granny Dear," Bessie Mae paused, reaching into her pack for a Pall Mall Red. "We got out to the park
and Valerie and Vincent showed their yellow asses. They
acted like they didn't wanna eat the food that we cooked."
   "And why's dat?" Granny Dear asked, holding on to the
refrigerator door in search of more leftovers.
   "I think they were too ashamed to be around Braun, Junior, Sean, and Morris," Bessie Mae speculated, but was absolutely correct at the same time. Valerie and Vincent were
never aware that she knew this. Instincts led her to believe it
at first.
   "What dey shame of?"
   "Worried about what other people think."
   "Utter peoples?"

"Those negative-minded negroes!"

Bessie Mae wasn't remorseful when it came to saying racially offensive things about her own black people.

"Folks sho do act funny."

"They kept staring at us, like they wanted us to leave the goddam park."

"Well, I say."

"We had every right to be there as them."

Negative-minded negroes was another term that Bessie Mae used whenever she described black people who had negative attitudes, those blacks who thought negatively when other blacks tried thinking positively. A hot bath and a good rubdown would be enough to suit Bessie Mae just fine after a grueling and hot "Fourth of July".

Chapter 13

THIEF OF VIRGINS

A SUMMARIZATION OF caseworker services were documented on Vincent's behalf. Caseworker Marcia Dewberry made the following summarizations:

1. GOALS AND OBJECTIVES

The goal on this case has been the movement of the individuals own home from institutional or community based care. The objectives have been to insure the well-being of the individual, providing a health-ful child development.

2. DESCRIPTION OF CHILD
A. APPEARANCE AND PERSONALITY

Vincent Carvelli is an attractive 10 year old boy. Vincent is a bit brighter than his half-brother and sister, who are in the same foster home. He does appear to be a bi-racial child. Vincent is usually rather quiet when caseworker Dewberry is around and usually does not speak unless asked a direct question or told to do so. He is usually very pleasant and polite.

B. HEALTH

During this dictation period, Vincent was in good health. He did have a physical in the earlier part of this year.

C. SCHOOLING

Vincent just finished the fourth grade at Abraham Lincoln Elementary school. Vincent was doing above-average work there. His foster mother, Bessie Mae Willingham, had him to go to summer school.

3. ADJUSTMENT TO FOSTER CARE
A. FEELINGS TOWARDS FOSTER FAMILY

Vincent is fairly close to his foster parents. He does not know anyone else as his parents. He has been in this foster home since he was six months old. Mr. and Mrs. Willingham never expressed a desire to adopt Vincent or his half-brother Vernon Ramirez. Because there still seems to be some problems in the foster home as far as the people who live there and also the relationship between the Willinghams and Vincent's sister, Valerie, nothing has been done about a possible adoption.

B. FEELINGS TOWARDS NATURAL PARENTS,

Vincent has no emotional ties to his natural parents. Vito and Marion Carvelli, whatsoever. He is very close to his natural half-brother and sister, who are in the same foster home. Parental rights were terminated between Vincent and his natural parents.

C. RELATIONSHIP WITH CASEWORKER

Caseworker Dewberry and Vincent have a very friendly relationship.

4. PROTECTIVE SERVICE OFFERING

During this dictation period, there was an Administrative Review. A hearing was held by Mr. Arnold Brewer at the Cook County Juvenile Center. Mr. Brewer recommended that this present order remained in effect. He also recommended that continued work be done on an

adoption. The next Administrative Review will be planned accordingly.

5. *The main problem in this case is the situation between Vincent's half-sister, Valerie, and the Willinghams. Valerie seems to display a lot of insubordination. Because of her behavior, the Willinghams have no desire to adopt her in the future. Another problem in this case is that there seems to be a big question about the number of people living in the licensed agency foster home of Bessie Mae and Jesse Dewayne Willingham. They continued to keep a number of mentally retarded men who roam around at their own will, throughout every level of the house. Mrs. Willingham also cares for some elderly boarders, plus her own elderly mother. There seems to be some question about the number of people in the house who all demand the Willinghams care and affection. Because of these uncertain incidents in their foster home, any future adoption would not be taken to court.*

6. **PLAN**

   The plan on this case is to continue Vincent in foster care until the right adoptive home can be found for him.

Bessie Mae earned extra money by allowing elderly boarders to live in their home. Legally or otherwise, she took in elderly men and women without future notice. The Department of Children and Family Services should have been notified everytime a new individual boarded at their home.

The phone rang several times and no one was around to answer. Seconds later, Bessie Mae limped up the basement stairs. Sweat drops had spread over her face. The laundry was piled up, and she worked continuously to clean clothes. She limped to the kitchen to answer the phone.

"Hello," Bessie Mae answered in an exhausted tone.

"Hey, Bessie Mae!"

"Booker T.? Is that you, Booker T.?"

"Yeah, it's me," Booker T. said, his voice groaning, making him sound very depressed.

"What's wrong?"

"I'm sick, Bessie Mae."

"What else is wrong?"

"I'm broke!" Booker T. moaned. "I need you to come down here to Memphis and help me out."

Bessie Mae now realized that Granny Dear's younger brother had fallen into a serious crisis. He started crumbling, both physically and financially. She knew that he only called when he wanted something. They knew that Memphis and Chicago were many miles apart.

"What happened to your girlfriend, Booker?"

"Oh lawd!" Booker sighed. "She left me a long time ago. She went back down to Mississippi to live with her folks."

"You tried asking Cousin Bobbie Jo for help?"

"Bobbie Jo's broke too."

Bessie Mae realized that her uncle's condition sounded serious. It wasn't quite life-threatening, but she told him to stay put anyway. The first flight out of Chicago to Memphis had to be arranged. Bessie Mae limped to the curtain of Granny Dear's room to inform her that her younger brother was sick and without any money.

"Booker T. gone be alwight?" Granny Dear asked.

"Hoping so."

"Wonder what he done came down with?"

"He wouldn't say."

Bessie Mae would do anything for her uncle Booker T. After all, he helped raise her after her father had died while she was growing up in Memphis as a little girl.

J.D. sat in the front room watching television. Valerie traveled to and from the porch. She took wet towels from the second floor bathroom to be dried out in the sun. During

each trip, J.D. had his eyes glued to her developing and shapely body parts. Valerie had grown to be an attractive fourteen year old girl. Her long dark hair, soft facial features, and curvy figure, had drawn the attention of boys everywhere.

Everytime she went out on the porch or back up to the second floor, J.D. took his eyes off the television program to inspect her well-proportioned buttocks and firm breasts. In the most unusual way, he kept staring at her. He continued to lust for her, but when Bessie Mae came into the front room to give him the news about her health-stricken uncle, he pretended as though his eyes were glued to the television.

"What's wong wit'em?" J.D. asked, clearing his head from sexually explicit thoughts about Valerie.

"He's real sick and he's without any money," Bessie Mae said. "He don't know what he's come down with."

"You gone go down ta Memfuss to see bout'em?" J.D. said frantically, reaching into his pack of Pall Mall Golds for a fresh cigarette.

"I really need to," Bessie Mae said compassionately, sticking her hand down into her bra for her pack of Pall Mall Reds. "He was there for me when I needed him. He's the best uncle that anybody could have."

Bessie Mae and J.D. timed their smoke breaks perfectly. He would fire up first, and she would fire up seconds after him.

"Dat'll be a nice twip fo ya, Bessa Mae."

Time was crucial! Bessie Mae immediately limped up to their room to start packing. She pulled out her blue Samsonite suitcase and began stuffing all of her toiletries, socks, underwear, and other miscellaneous items inside. The unplanned trip wouldn't be complete until she made reservations. She left the room to go back into the kitchen to make a call to one of the airlines.

Bessie Mae explained to one of the ticket agents for TWA that her uncle was extremely ill, that she had to travel to

Memphis, Tennessee as soon as possible. The agent checked for the next available flight.

"Let's see, now," said the polite and proper speaking ticket agent, tapping lightly on her monitor. "Let me check my list of schedules for the next available flight to Memphis, Tennessee out of O'Hare International Airport."

Bessie Mae limped around the kitchen searching for a pen and some paper. She needed to write down the schedule information. Granny Dear rolled out of her room with a pencil and a small piece of paper. Bessie Mae limped frantically around in circles with the phone pressed to the side of her face. Granny Dear handed her the pencil and paper.

"The next available flight departing Chicago's O'Hare International Airport will be on Wednesday at 6:00 p.m., arriving in Memphis, Tennessee at 8:35 p.m., with a thirty-minute layover in St. Louis, Missouri."

"What gate do I have to come to?" Bessie Mae inquired, because it was her first time ever flying down to Memphis. She usually drove when she wanted to take the trip.

"Come to terminal four and you'll be departing from gate eleven," the helpful agent told Bessie Mae.

"Thank you."

"You're welcome, Mrs. Willingham. Have a safe trip to Memphis."

"Thank you."

Time mattered greatly to Bessie Mae. It was Saturday evening, and she grew more worried about Booker T. She went upstairs and rambled through her drawers for some money. Safeguarding her money in the house was the least of her worries. With that large padlock on her door, a .38 calibre handgun, and with her thieving cousin Clara gone, someone had to kick the door down to get in there to get what they wanted. The top drawer of her dresser was filled with several five, ten, and twenty dollar bills. The drawer below was filled with one dollar bills and piles of loose change. Whenever

Bessie Mae needed small change, she went to her large coca cola bottle that was filled with hundreds of pennies, nickels, and dimes.

*   *   *

Wednesday arrived and it was exactly 5:00 p.m. Booker T's condition had gotten worse. One of Bessie Mae's philosophies was: *You can never tell if people care about you until you're on your sick bed or when you don't have a penny to your name.*

One of the greatest philosophies that she learned in her native home of Memphis, Tennessee was: *When you're broke or real sick, you don't have no friends and you're stuck on a dead-end street.*

On the front porch, Valerie was conversing with the next door neighbor, Mrs. Eleanor Purvis. Eleanor was short, fair complexioned, wore thick glasses, and kept hair nets on her head to keep her graying wavy hair in place. She was only seen when going to work or planting flowers in her flowerbed around Springtime. Valerie was out of school and wanted to wait to start on her homework.

Inside the front room, J.D. constantly turned his head towards the porch to watch Valerie in her form-fitting shorts. He slowly turned back to watch television. Normally, when *"Sanford and Son"* was on the television screen, he never turned away to watch anything else. Fred Sanford and Lamont Sanford were enough to keep him laughing the whole half-hour.

J.D. perversely developed a slight erection. His young and attractive fourteen year old foster daughter was a girl who was to be desired sexually. J.D. tried disguising his erection by crossing both legs and placing both hands towards the middle of his lap. A rock hard dick was something that he barely achieved, especially since Bessie Mae didn't excite him and they didn't have sex too often.

The blubbery body of J.D. moved back and forth on the

sofa. He fidgeted until Bessie Mae called from upstairs. As he walked towards the stairs leading to the second floor, Valerie stepped into the front room. He took a quick glance at her lucious body parts. His eyes respectively traveled from her breasts, to her hips and thighs, and on down to her perfectly round buttocks.

Their eyes met momentarily. It frightened the living daylights out of Valerie. J.D.'s evil glossy eyes were enough to frighten anyone. Could J.D. be trying to seduce his foster daughter? Valerie stood there frozen like an icecube.

"What's wrong, Mr. Willingham?" she asked.

"Ain't nuttin wong."

"You scared me."

"You ain't got no weason ta be fraid of me."

He went to the second floor and Bessie Mae explained that he would have to drive her out to the airport. She gave him the price of the ticket and the time of departure. The clock said 5:00 p.m., letting them know that the time was drawing near. The trip to O'Hare airport would take close to an hour. That was certainly pushing it.

Bessie Mae slammed the suitcase shut, reached for her purse, locked their door, and limped behind J.D. Granny Dear rolled her wheelchair into the kitchen to receive instructions from Bessie Mae. She was truly pressed for time.

"Make sure everybody is fed," Bessie Mae told Granny Dear. She already knew that Granny Dear could cook all the meals by herself. "Make sure Valerie and Vincent stay around this house, and make sure Braun or Vernon feed the dogs."

"I ain't gone forget," Granny Dear promised. "You make sho you call ta let us know dat you made it dere okay. Let ma know how Booker T's doing."

"I will," Bessie Mae said. "Make sure the house is tended to."

"Gone now, Bessa Mae. You gone miss yo pane."

"You're right, I don't wanna miss this plane."

Bessie Mae planted a bursting kiss on Granny Dear's left cheek and limped out of the kitchen. She and J.D. knew they had to start their journey out to the airport, so they started walking towards the car. They stepped out on the porch, where Valerie was sharing a laugh with Eleanor.

"Where are you going, Bessie Mae?" Eleanor asked, noticing the large Samsonite suitcase in her hand. "Looks like you're in a rush."

"I'm going to Memphis, Tennessee," Bessie Mae told Eleanor, walking cautiously down the porch stairs to avoid a fall.

"Memphis, huh?"

"I'm going to see about my sick uncle."

"What's wrong with him?"

"He came down with some type of sickness."

"What kind of sickness?"

"He couldn't tell me exactly what it was."

"How long will you be there?" Eleanor asked, not wanting to sound as though she was prying into the personal life of Bessie Mae.

"A few days."

"Hope your uncle gets well."

"Thanks."

"Have a safe trip."

"Thank you."

Bessie Mae knew that The Department of Children and Family Services would question her about any lengthy time away from her foster care home.

While her head was turned towards the car, J.D. looked back to lustfully observe Valerie. J.D. still found her to be a treat to watch. Her thighs were spread out across the fold-out chair. Her fully developed breasts, which showed a slight nipple print from her form-fitting blue halter top, and wide hips, that were pressed against the bar that supported the

armrest, all of which kept a sparkle in J.D.'s eyes. He grabbed the suitcase and threw it in the backseat.

Bessie Mae climbed in on the passenger's side while J.D. started up the car. Before he backed out onto Milwaukee Parkway, he took another quick glance at Valerie. The magnetism that he had for her was too intense. It was early Fall and they didn't have to wait for the car to warm up. He started their trip out to the airport. They traveled north down Milwaukee Parkway until the red lights at the corner of Rush Boulevard changed.

It was Wednesday afternoon and the weather was fairly decent. Most people around Chicago found it to be another busy day. Playday was everyday for those individuals who were into the *hardcore street scene.* There were many people hanging out all along Rush Boulevard.

"What they hit for?" asked one of the young teenagers, who strutted up the street with no shirt, with braids running through his head, rattling dice in his right hand, hoping that he would find a crap session on one of the street corners.

"Come on so I can break your ass," replied another teenager, looking just as hardcore as the others who ran in their circle.

Directly across the street, there were packs of dragqueens, known to others as transvestites, and prostitutes who tried flagging cars down. They viciously competed against one another to see who would interest the tricks who were driving past, pushing and shoving as some of the cars slowed down. J.D. stared at them and nodded his head.

"Look at dem sissy boys and nasty gals," J.D. said, pointing to one of the dragqueens and prostitutes, respectively.

"I see them," Bessie Mae said. "There's a whole lot of them out here. Every since I can remember, it's always been a lot of whores and those sissy boys hanging around Rush."

"Dem sissy boys look betta dan dose women," J.D. disclosed,

his eyes planted on one of the drags who had a rough face and street-worn body.

"That's why those men have to be careful."

"Dat's wight."

"Sometimes, I wonder how those men can tell when they're really men or women."

"I can tell."

"How?"

"Dem fake titties."

"You can't just go by their breasts, J.D."

"Dem fake booties, too."

"I've seen men whose asses stuck out like women."

"Dem big muscle thangs in dey throat, too."

"The adam's apple?"

"Yep."

In so many words, J.D. was telling Bessie Mae that if you carefully analyzed the artificial breasts, an unusual shape of their buttocks, and the large muscle in some of their throats, then you would be able to separate the wannabe women from the real women. Bessie Mae looked over at the opposite corner and saw a massive crowd of young teenagers engaged in a crap session, slamming dice and dollar bills on the concrete.

"Look at all those niggahs on this corner gambling, J.D.," Bessie Mae exclaimed. Her heart cried out when she witnessed so many young, gifted, and black men wasting their lives away on a dangerous street corner.

"What niggahs?" J.D. asked, waiting impatiently for that long traffic light to change. They had to continue their journey out to the airport.

"The ones over there shooting dice."

"Where bouts, Bessa Mae?"

"Right there, J.D.," Bessie Mae pointed, directing J.D.'s attention to the right.

"Now, I see."

"Negroes are always talking about the white man is keeping them down," Bessie Mae told J.D. without remorse, never afraid to call the shots the way she saw them. "They try and blame the white man for everything that happens to colored folks. Blame him for this! Blame him for that! It's not the white man who's keeping us down."

"You don't thank so?" J.D. asked, never hesitant to say something negative about the white race.

"It's niggahs keeping other niggahs down!"

"Where da police at?"

"Who knows."

"I thank it is da white mane's fault dat dese boys're out here shooting craps."

"Whatever, J.D."

The light finally turned green. They proceeded across Rush Boulevard and were immediately stopped by another red light at the corner of Lowell Avenue. There were even more prostitutes soliciting their bodies on this street. More teenagers and grown men gathered around the corner shooting craps, throwing their bills on the ground everytime they placed bets.

Several pimps drove past in their Cadillacs and Lincoln Continentals. They kept a watchful eye on what they considered to be their *walking goldmines*. Black exploitation movies, such as *"Superfly* and *"The Mack"*, which had come and gone from box offices across America, epitomized the urban pimp scene. Going northbound, about halfway up Lowell Avenue, there was an adult theatre that had the letter 'X' in a bright red neon color, sitting right above an old red brick building. Adult theatres had become popular at the beginning of the nineteen seventies, because pornography and adult entertainment were steadily on the rise.

J.D. stared real hard at the theatre that had posters of X-rated movies placed out front. The light turned green, but he continued to stare over at the theatre. There were two

other cars behind them. The other motorists pounded hard
to sound their horns. J.D. couldn't seem to take his eyes off
the theatre. He was a porno fanatic and it showed.

"J.D.!" Bessie Mae yelled directly into his ear, shaking his
leg and pointing at the green light. "Come on and make this
light so we can get out to the airport on time. Plus, we've got
people behind us."

"Don't wush me, woman!" J.D. shouted back. "We gone
git to da airpoat."

"It'll help if you put your foot on the gas."

"Alwight, alwight, I'm going."

J.D. quickly drove across Lowell Avenue and took another quick glance at the theatre. Bessie Mae stared him
straight in the face. She tried figuring out what might have
captured his attention so strongly. He drove to the expressway, which would take them right to O'Hare International
Airport.

Bessie Mae kept expressing how much she hoped that
Booker T. would make a speedy recovery. Since there were so
many sights to see in her native home of Memphis, she told
J.D. that she would try to see as many as possible. He hadn't
heard a word she said. After leaving the house, his mind
became corrupted. Where had his illiterate mind traveled
to? Did the display of the X-rated movies fill his already perverted mind with senseless bullshit? Bessie Mae wanted an
explanation for all the silence.

"Why are you so quiet, J.D.?" Bessie Mae asked, studying
the blatant expression on his face.

"I ain't got much ta say wight now, Bessa Mae," J.D. said
calmly, leaning closer to the driver's door and holding the
top of the steering wheel.

"What's bothering you?"

"Nuttin."

"Come on and tell me."

"Ain't nuttin wong, Bessa Mae."

"Got something on your chest?"

"Naw."

"Okay, if you say so."

J.D. looked down at his watch. It said exactly 5:45 p.m. and Bessie Mae's flight was due to leave at 6:00 p.m. He applied much pressure to the accelerator. They traveled to a sign that said the airport would be the next exit to the right. After spinning around a sharp curve, Bessie Mae pointed to the concourse for TWA, in which her flight would be departing soon. J.D. parked and she quickly limped to the ticket counter. She gave the agent her name, address, and a rather thick stack of bills. The agent counted the money and handed her the ticket. J.D. walked towards the ticket counter swinging her suitcase. His eyes circled parts of the enormous airport.

Bessie Mae might have thought that he was brain dead. Not hardly! The adult theatre on Lowell Avenue had his every thought suspended. With the ticket held firmly in her right hand, Bessie Mae was anxious for the departure out of Chicago. She hadn't had a trip since she and J.D. went to Las Vegas. Her sick uncle was the perfect opportunity to get away for a few days. She turned around, only to notice that J.D. continued to act strange. His unusual behavior was sudden and she noticed every minute of it.

"Why are you acting so different today, J.D.?" Bessie Mae inquired, trying desperately to pick her way through his wasted mind. "You've been acting real strange since you started driving me out to the airport."

"I ain't acking funny."

"Yes, you are."

"How am I acking funny?"

"You're real quiet and staring off into space."

"I'm just thanking bout something I gotta do when I git home," J.D. answered falsely, barely snapping out of his perverted dreamworld, smiling deviously at Bessie Mae.

"What do you have to do when you get home?"

"Oh, it ain't nuttin."

"Come on and tell the truth, now."

"I'm tellin da truth."

"I don't want to have to find out later."

"Yo pane gone be leavin fum da airpoat soon."

"You're right, I've got a plane to catch."

Bessie Mae wasn't aware that his mind was filled with corruption. She didn't know that his thoughts were polluted with all manifestations of ungodliness. The official announcement was made over the loud intercom.

"All passengers boarding for St. Louis, Little Rock, Oklahoma City, Memphis, Birmingham, Jackson, Atlanta, and Memphis, should board at gate eleven at this time."

Bessie Mae stood a few feet away from the terminal, then limped to the gate and gave J.D. a quick kiss. Before handing her ticket to the flight attendant, they gave one another a final kiss and hug. She limped her way towards the inside of the plane. Bessie Mae was off to Memphis, Tennessee.

J.D. sat in front of the airport doing some heavy thinking. He thought about where to go now that Bessie Mae was going to be in Memphis for a few days. It was time to get out and play! Most men could think of a thousand places to go when their wives left town. J.D.'s mind traveled over to the wicked streets of Lowell Avenue.

*   *   *

The pimps, prostitutes, drug dealers, drug addicts, crap shooters, dragqueens, rapists, murderers, burglars, drunks, and other hardcore street personnel, had J.D. trying to decide if he should go out and play in the immoral street playground. The street scene was nothing new to him. Two of J.D.'s eldest sons were pimps out in California. Some of the

most vicious criminals were a part of his family. The letter 'X' flashed around inside his mind. It was *X, X, X,* and more *X's.*

Since J.D. had a wallet filled with money, he got back on the expressway, on his way to Lowell Avenue. When he arrived there, he pulled up in front of the same adult theatre that weighed so heavily on his mind. A very cunning looking hooker paraded towards the Cadillac. She was a short woman with a well-rounded and vuluptuous figure. She had a smooth, honey-melon complexion that was buried under layers of makeup. Her curve-hugging mini-skirt was dark burgundy and it complimented the long burgundy wig that hung down to her curvaceous buttocks. She would try an irresistable proposition to J.D.

"Hey there, big fellow," the hooker said kindly to J.D. "Do you wanna have a real good time tonight?" She was sweet talking J.D., using a sort of *false and whorish* tone, but knew it could prove effective if executed right.

"I dunno yet," J.D. replied, checking out her shapely body. "I'm gone go intide dis pace and watch a dutty movie. When I come out, I'll let'cha know something."

"Dirty movie, huh?"

"Yep."

"We can make our dirty movie together."

"How much?"

"Twenty, baby."

"I dunno."

"You'll be good and horny after watching a movie," the experienced hooker said, always there to meet the sex-craved men who walked in and out of the theatre with their dicks harder than U.S. penitentiary steel. She smiled at J.D. with her one-time glamourous face.

"I'm horny wight now!"

"Then let's go up the street and make it go away."

"Let me go intide first."

"Okay, I'll be right here waiting for you."

"Alwight."

J.D. walked up to the booth near the front entrance. A crispy five dollar bill was folded neatly in his right hand. The clerk noticed his wide body standing in the front of the glass.

"Will you be going inside one of the private booths or inside the theatre?" asked the clerk, a honey blonde who had a large dragon tattoo on her left shoulder.

"What's da diffence?" J.D. asked, clamping the five dollar bill down onto the counter.

"The difference?"

"Yep."

"The private booths are sectioned off for your private viewing pleasures," she explained clearly. "There's a monitor that shows four adult films, with an approximate running time of thirty-minutes each. The theatre is open to the public."

The theatre sounded good to J.D., so he walked that direction. As soon as he opened the double doors to the theatre, he looked around at several men who tossed and turned in their seats. They were restless and horny men. Some of them were masturbating and dropping their semen on the floor. How disgusting these lowlifes were! The only light inside the spacious theatre came from the big screen. What caught J.D.'s attention were the couples who were sitting towards the front. It couldn't have been a better opportunity for them to boost their sexual morale. They were kissing and grinding and nearly in the process of having sex right there in the theatre.

J.D. took a seat on the right side, the second row from the back. After several minutes of viewing the movie, he rushed out of theatre and straight towards his car. The same hooker tried propositioning him again. She happened to be the same hooker who worked for Vito Carvelli several years ago, right upstairs in his house of hookers, dope, and liquors.

'Honey Mamma', who earned the nickname from having a glowing, honey-brown complexion, couldn't give up the

hooker business. She opted to the streets after Vito and Marion had been shut down by the police for their vice activities. She didn't even have a pimp. This proved extremely dangerous on the mean streets of Chicago. There were plenty of jealous pimps out there. Her face and body could still turn heads. She earned enough to support herself, even supporting her mild drug and alcohol addiction.

Honey Mamma massaged J.D.'s large chest. His left pocket bulged from his wallet being loaded with money. Her soft hands slid down his left pants leg, scratching the surface of his wallet with her long and sharp fingernails. J.D. smiled at her graciously. She wanted him to feel more manly. Sex from a hooker was never free. J.D. knew that, but wasn't ready to spend any money for a good time.

"I gotta go," J.D. told Honey Mamma, working up a serious erection from her enticements.

"Come on, big fella," Honey Mamma said. "Don't you wanna buy yourself some of this good and hot, wet, juicy, pussy?" She tempted him over and over, pinching the side of his obese waist.

"I gotta wife," he admitted honestly, but knowing he would buy some pussy in a quick second.

"Where's your wife right now?" Honey Mamma asked, purposely trying to poke out her large breasts for J.D. to see.

"I juss dropped her off at da airpoat."

"Where's she going?"

"She had ta go down ta Memfuss."

"What, a vacation?"

"She had ta see bout her sick uncle."

"Memphis, Tennessee, huh?"

"Yep."

"So, what do you do for a living?"

"I'm a woofer," J.D. said, speaking very illiterately. He fired up a Pall Mall Gold and planted his eyes on Honey Mamma's jiggly breasts.

"You're a who?"

"A woofer," J.D. repeated. "I put woofs on buildings and folks houses."

"Oh, you're a roofer," Honey Mamma smiled, understanding J.D. slightly clearer. She was thinking he could be a potential trick who was loaded with lots of money.

"Yep, dat's what I do fo a libbing."

"What does your wife do for a living?" Honey Mamma asked, getting awfully personal with J.D. The more she knew about him, the more she could entice him into possibly spending some money.

"She runs a falsta home fo kids and keep tarted folks."

"She runs what kind of home?"

"A home fo falsta chilluns and tarted folks."

"Did you say a home for foster children and retarded people?"

"Yep."

"My son's in a foster home," she confessed sadly, her face fading to no expression at all.

"You gotta a little boy?"

"Yeah, I do."

"How old's he?"

"Eleven."

"Why's he in a falsta home?" J.D. asked, already knowing how many children ended up in foster care. There were many different reasons, but Honey Mamma had her own personal reasons.

"Can't you see why?" she answered wittingly, her facial expression growing even sadder. "I got hooked on dope and liquor and started back whoring. They took him away from me and wouldn't tell me what foster home he was in."

"Dat's too bad," J.D. said sympathetically, then blowing smoke over the top of her head.

"How many foster children do you and your wife keep?"

"Thwee."

"Three, huh?"

"Yep."

"Did you say that you also keep retarded people?"

"Yep."

"How many of them do you keep?"

"Five."

"You've got a house full, don't you?"

"Sho do."

"I sure wish I could get my boy back."

"Why can't chu?"

"I need to get off dope and liquor and get my shit together."

"What falsta home yo boy's in?"

"The state won't tell me."

"Where bouts his daddy?"

"In jail?"

"Fo what?"

"Killing somebody."

"Muddah?"

"Yeah, they've got him locked up for murder."

"How long he gone be in dere?"

"He got life."

"Goddam!" J.D. said, nodding his head in disapproval. "Who he kill?"

"Shot and killed a white man."

"Colored folks know dey shuddin kill white folks," J.D. frowned. "Dey lock ya up fo da west of yo life."

"He had to find out the hard way."

Honey Mamma was tired of all the talk about her son and the home where J.D. resided. She wanted to make some money quickly.

"Come on and buy yourself some of this good pussy!" Honey Mamma said, rubbing the print on the front of her short skirt. "It's got your name written all over it."

"Naw, dat's alwight."

"I've got some rubbers in my purse."

"Naw, I'm alwight fo now."

"Then, what's wrong?"

"Ain't nuttin wong?"

"Okay, suit yourself."

Would J.D. have ever guessed that Honey Mamma once worked for Vito Carvelli, the same man who was the father and step-father of his three present foster children? He looked down at his watch and it said 12:30 a.m. It was well past midnight and he knew that it was time to head home.

The car pulled up in the front yard. The lights and ignition went off. Darkness surrounded the inside and outside of the house. J.D. came inside the house and the rooms were even darker. He strolled through the front room and glanced into the den. The silence was intense! Squealing noises made by J.D.'s obese frame seeped through the cracks of the floor, which eventually traveled into the dining room. Granny Dear was asleep in her room, launching away loud snores. Amazingly, she wasn't awakened by the squealing noises.

J.D. stood at the bottom of the stairs leading to the second floor. He stared past the set of bannisters and the hallway going to the dining room. He slowly walked up to the second floor and peeped into Braun and Junior's room. They were under the covers, snoring loud and moving every which direction. Who, at the Willingham residence, didn't snore?

Taking a couple of more steps to the left, he peeped into Valerie's room. Strangely, Valerie slept on top of the covers at the foot of her bed. In a bright yellow nightgown, she lied in a curled position, showing part of her pink pastel panties. J.D. stood at the corner of the doorway, caught in a deep trance. His wet tongue rolled around his dark and chapped lips. Excessive movement and breathing pushed

his broad chest and large stomach outwards. Dark red veins and water filled his lustful eyes. Scalp oils from the top of his bald head rose to the surface, causing his head to shine from the beaming moonlight, which came through the windows in Valerie's room.

J.D. became excited as he watched his fourteen year old foster daughter lie asleep. Sexually explicit thoughts caused him to develop an erection. Valerie moved restlessly on top of the bed covers. She made the type of groaning noises heard when someone was in a deep sleep.

J.D. stood in the doorway with his left arm stretched across the top. He quietly crept into his room and raised the mattress to the king-size bed. A stack of pornographic magazines were spread out evenly across the top of the boxspring. This was the sexually explicit literature that he purchased from an adult bookstore near Lowell Avenue.

As he flipped through the pages, he had flashbacks of the movie that he had just seen in the adult theatre on Lowell Avenue. Honey Mamma's voluptuous figure quickly entered his mind. The X-rated movie wasn't nearly enough! He flipped through every magazine, page after filthy page. The women inside spreading their legs, holding their breasts, palming their buttocks, got J.D. heated up like a coal fire. He was ready to have some serious sexual intercourse! The corner of the mattress was lifted high. The magazines were spread out evenly, placed far apart, where Bessie Mae wouldn't feel any bumps in the mattress.

If Bessie Mae only knew that she was sleeping on top of a bunch of porno magazines every night. It never occurred to her why J.D. was the only one who changed their sheets. He would do anything to prevent her from finding out.

The alarm clock on the coffee table said 1:00 a.m. It was early Thursday morning and throughout the house everything remained silent. J.D. calmly crept back to the doorway of Valerie's room. Valerie turned facing the doorway. Her

nightgown eased further up her legs, showing more of her pink panties. J.D. began having wild sexual fantasies about Valerie: "*I want dat redbone, gal!*" *J.D. whispered with sheer desire, using the term 'redbone' when he referred to Valerie being a delectable, bright complexioned black girl. He wanted her so desperately.* "*I know I can fuck'er and ain't nobody gone stop ma.*"

Through the midst of the thick darkness, he peeped into Braun and Junior's room. Their snoring sort of distracted J.D. Next, he opened the door to the third floor and glanced up the dark stairways. No one had slept up there since Carmen moved out. After leaving the second floor, J.D. went into the kitchen. Granny Dear was in her room sleeping like a log floating down a peaceful stream. He left the kitchen to head for the basement. He gradually turned the knob and pulled the rusty-hinged door to the tip of the wall. His heavy feet pressed one stair at a time.

The laundry room had more piles of filthy clothes. J.D. stepped to the middle of Vincent and Vernon's room. Vincent lied flat on his back, sleeping on top of a dry bed. J.D. was quite surprised when he glanced over at his bed. Vernon wasn't present. One of his many girlfriends allowed him to spend the night when she found out that her parents were leaving town for a few days.

J.D. walked into Sean's room and stood at the foot of his bed. Almost everyone in the house had the *snoring syndrome*. Sean sucked in air through his nose and mouth at the same time. Morris was in the very last room, also vibrating the floor and walls with his snoring.

J.D. left the basement and went back to the second floor. The door to Braun and Junior's room was closed. The door to Valerie's room was wide open. He stood at the far left corner, breathing like his life was coming to an end. Like Bessie Mae, he smoked too much and ate too much fried and fattening foods. They both knew that it wasn't good for their hearts.

Walking up and down all those stairs sent his heart pumping full speed. He tried resuming normal breathing.

After checking every room on the floor, J.D. was conspiring an unlawful and sinful act. His breathing got heavier. The print of his rock hard dick became more noticeable. The blood vessels in his evil eyes became redder, while more water was secreted over the vessels. Beads of sweat trickled down his dark face.

J.D. stepped into Valerie's room and stopped at the middle of the floor. As he moved further towards her bed, his eyes scanned her panties. A small wet ring appeared at the middle of his pants. Without any warning, J.D. slammed his obese body on top of Valerie. Her mouth was clamped by both of his strong and callous hands. Immediately, she was awakened and greatly alarmed.

"You betta not squeam!" J.D. threatened, applying much pressure down on Valerie's shapely, petite frame.

Valerie tried screaming from under J.D.'s large hands. In a cluttered voice, she pleaded for him to lift his heavy body off her.

"Please, please, don't hurt me!"

"Shut up, gal!"

"You're hurting me, Mr. Willingham!" Valerie pleaded, kicking her legs from under J.D.'s bulky legs. She tried to alleviate some of the pressure from his dense weight and tight grip.

"Don't try ta squeam, gal!"

"I'm not going to scream!"

"Don't make no noises!" J.D. responded unmercifully, staring right into the fearful eyes of Valerie with his set of demonic eyes.

"I won't make no noises."

"Ya tell anybody, I'm gone kill ya!"

"I won't tell nobody."

"Ya unnastands me, gal?"

and rushed out of the room, pulling up his underwear and pants. After he rushed down to the first floor, he ran outside and jumped into his truck, speeding off down Milwaukee.

*   *   *

Valerie sat at the middle of her bed crying. The sheets were grossly stained with her blood and the semen of J.D. She trembled excessively. Rolls of tears trickled down her face. After being raped by her foster father, she was absolutely startled. It's a shame that Braun and Junior couldn't come to Valerie's rescue. They neither heard nor seen anything. Could two mentally retarded men have prevented a rape?

Valerie momentarily went into a mild state of shock. Mass confusion clutched her whole body. She walked tardily down the stairs leading to the first floor. She stepped into the kitchen and pulled back the curtain to Granny Dear's room. Granny Dear raised up and pushed the light switch on with her long brown cane.

"Why ya waking me up dis time of moaning?" Granny Dear asked, noticing the startled look on Valerie's face.

"Mr. Willingham did it to me," Valerie gurgled, tears flowing constantly down her face.

"What ya mean he did it to ya?" Granny Dear needed a much better explanation.

"He jumped on top of me and did it to me."

"What chu talking bout, Vallaray?"

"When I was sleep, Mr. Willingham jumped on top of me and stuck his thang in me?"

"Stuck his thang in ya?"

"Yeah!"

"Ya tying ta say dat J.D. waped ya?"

"Mr. Willingham raped me!"

"I don't bleeves ya, Vallaray."

"Why not?"

"Why would J.D. wanna do sumthang lack dat?"

"I don't know!" Valerie cried intensely, her head hung low in despair. She sucked in her tears as she had horrifying flashbacks of what had just happened to her.

Granny Dear had lived in the same household as J.D., almost since the time that he and Bessie Mae first got married. She couldn't believe that he was perverted! Cold-hearted! A motherfucker who was capable of raping a fourteen year old girl.

"I thank ya lying, gal."

"I'm not lying!"

Granny Dear stood in J.D.'s honor. The lowlife bastard had no honor! Something had to be done to find closure to this ordeal.

Chapter 14

EVIDENCE

At 2:15 A.M. Carmen walked through the front door jingling her car keys. The only time she ever visited the Willingham residence was to borrow money or collect some of Bessie Mae's antique furniture for her apartment. She walked back into Granny Dear's room, where Valerie sat on the edge of her bed, still frightened out of her senses.

Carmen stood behind Granny Dear's wheelchair. She watched Valerie tremble, with endless tears rolling down her face. If this matter was to be resolved, Valerie was to explain everything that happened. Carmen came and sat beside her, throwing her arm around her waist. Valerie shut her eyes tightly and threw her head down. More tears fell onto her nightgown like raindrops.

"He . . . ," Valerie stammered, shaking like someone caught in sub-zero weather.

"He did what?" Carmen asked, holding her tighter, making her feel important during this time of crisis. "Take your time and tell us what happened."

"Mr. Willingham jumped on top of me and covered my mouth."

"What happened after that?"

"He pulled up my gown and pulled down my panties."

"Okay, what happened after that?"

"He stuck his thang in me and started doing it to me."

"What happened after he started doing it to you?"

"It started bleeding down by my private," Valerie said,

the rush of tears shooting out of her eyes like bullets shooting out of a gun.

"What, blood started coming out of your coochie?"

"Yeah, it did."

"Keep telling me more, Valerie," Carmen said, as though her story was intriguing. Was she asking all of these questions because she was sympathetic, or was she just interested in listening to a bunch of details?

"He shot that nasty stuff out of his thang."

"Cum?"

"Yes."

"What happened next?"

"He ran out of my room pulling up his drawers and pants."

"Where were Braun and Junior when all of this was going on?"

"I don't know!" Valerie weeped strongly. "I think they were sleep."

"Where do you think he went after he ran out of your room?"

"I don't know!"

Carmen went up to the second floor and looked into Braun and Junior's room. They were sound alseep, snoring loud under the covers. She hesitantly stepped into Valerie's room. She moved slowly towards the bed. When she bent forward to view the sheets, Carmen quickly jumped back. The large blood stain and pool of thick semen had formed a large circle in the middle of the sheets. The grotesque sight caused Carmen to rush out of the room.

A pornographic magazine was lying at the doorway to the Willingham room. J.D. forgot to put it away only minutes before the rape occurred. Carmen didn't waste a second telling Granny Dear what she had seen.

"Granny Dear! Granny Dear!" Carmen yelled loudly, untangling herself out of the thick red curtain.

"You gone wake da whole house up," Granny Dear said. "What done happen?"

"Valerie really was raped by Mr. Willingham," Carmen informed the elderly mother of Bessie Mae.

"Waped? How?"

"Look at this nasty book that I found on the floor."

"So?"

"It belongs to Mr. Willingham."

"How ya know it belongs ta J.D.?"

"Who else in this house would be looking at nasty books?"

"Ain't no tellin."

"It was close to Valerie's room."

"So?"

"So?" Valerie said, holding the porno book up so Granny Dear can clearly see it. "He was looking through it before he raped Valerie."

"Ya can't go round cusing folks."

"Nobody's falsely accusing Mr. Willingham. The facts are upstairs in the room."

"What chu talkin bout?"

"There's blood on the sheets."

"Blood?"

"There's cum on the sheets, too!" Carmen said disbelievingly, her eyes widened with graceful amazement.

"What chu say, Coremen?"

"Ooops! I didn't mean to say that, Granny Dear," Carmen said, covering her mouth with a look of disgust across her perspiring face, but also well aware that Granny Dear knew what the word *"cum"* meant.

"I don't bleeves J.D. could do no such thang."

"Well, believe it," Carmen said. "He's a lowdown dirty black dog!"

"Watch yo mouth, gal."

"I'm sorry, but he's what he is."

"What chu gone do now?"

"I'm taking Valerie to the hospital so the doctors can look at her."

"Ain't no hospital gone see yall dis time of moaning."

"Hospitals are open at anytime of morning, Granny Dear."

"No, dey ain't."

"Yes, they are!" Carmen argued, strongly concerned, as though the rape had happened to her.

"No, dere ain't."

"How would you know?"

"I know, alwight."

"I can't argue with you," Carmen said. "Valerie has been raped, and I know there is a hospital somewhere in Chicago that'll look at her."

Carmen told Valerie to get dressed. Her nightgown and panties were left in the room for evidence. As they drove towards the hospital, Carmen urgently needed to ask Valerie something.

"Why did Mr. Willingham do this to you?"

"I don't know," Valerie answered uncertainly, finding it difficult to take her mind off the grueling experience.

"Lowdown black dog!"

As they cruised to the hospital, they listened to the Jackson Five tune, *"Never Can Say Goodbye"*.

*   *   *

Carmen drove up to Cook County Hospital and parked close to the emergency entrance. They walked inside and Valerie was taken to the emergency entrance. Nothing but bright lights and busy hospital personnel were seen. Carmen told the nurse at the desk that she would like to speak with one of the head nurses or physicians. A head nurse named Marsha Shinholster came walking past the emergency doors. She took them into a more private section of the hospital.

Marsha had light brown hair that had a coiffure style like international singer Phyllis McGuire of the famed McGuire sisters. Her face was sweet, as innocent as a child, and very

much smooth. She was a thirteen year veteran with the Cook
County Hospital system. After listening to Valerie's story about
the tragic rape, Marsha interpreted the story clearly. Carmen
explained to Marsha in her own words, in very clear details.

"My foster sister was raped by her foster father," Carmen
said to the experienced nurse, speaking with a serious face.
"She was lying in her bed and he jumped on top of her and
forced her to have sex with him."

"Were there other people in the house when she was
raped?" Marsha inquired, listening close to Carmen's version
of the incident.

"Oh yeah!" Carmen assured the nurse. "There were lots
of other people in the house. But, I believe that he planned
the whole thing."

"How?"

"He waited for everybody in the house to go to sleep."

"To make his move?"

"More than just a move."

"So he could take complete advantage of Valerie?"
Marsha concluded, a woman who had dealt with enough rape
cases to know the pattern that a rapist followed.

"Mr. Willingham knew that she was helpless."

"Sounds real familiar."

"How?"

"I've seen similar cases here at Cook County Hospital."

"Similar cases?"

"Babies being molested by their mothers and fathers,"
Marsha explained. "Little children being sodomized by their
sick'o fathers or other relatives. Unfortunately, other similar
cases come in here all the time."

"What other kind of cases?"

"Teenage girls being raped by her foster father."

"What do you think'll happen?" Carmen asked, hoping
J.D. would be brought to justice for his serious crime.

"Personally, I think foster homes, along with the foster

parents, should be investigated more closely," Marsha retorted, wishing she had the power to change some things in the foster care system.

"Why?"

"A lot of the abuse and neglect in these homes go unreported," Marsha added. "Those children grow up to live dysfunctional lives."

Marsha took Valerie into one of the rooms down the hall for examination. Meanwhile, Carmen sat in the lobby filling out some paperwork. The results of the examination showed there was damage done to Valerie. There were expert lab technicians who examined the blood, pubic hairs, and semen under the powerful zoom microscope.

Test after test, the technicians tried putting together information that would prove helpful in the sexual assault on Valerie. There were also forensic experts from the sexual unit of The Chicago Police Department.

Some of the nurses in the small room tried consoling a crying and confused Valerie. The results of any lab findings would take time. Carmen was called into the room with Valerie. Marsha and one of the physicians had examined the area where the forced entry occurred. There was severe redness and swelling around Valerie's vaginal area.

Over at The Chicago Police Department, the fifth area district, Detective James Bucci of the sex crimes unit was notified about the rape. Copies of lab results were going to be sent to him. He wasted no time getting the investigation underway.

Valerie had fallen alseep. Carmen embraced her foster sister warmly. She turned to look up at the bright lights in the ceiling. Thoughts of the times that she had taken Vincent into the bathroom to satisfy her own sexual delights raced through her mind. Why would her mind wander several years back during this present-moment crisis? The six year old

Vincent. The unusual sexual intercourse that took place in
that steamy bathroom.

>   *"Oh yeah, feels so good to me!" Carmen said pleasurably, entering*
> *another orgasmic stage. "Does it feel good to you, Vincent?"*
>   *"Yes," Vincent said, his face expressionless.*
>   *"Do you like it, Vincent?"*
>   *"Yes."*
>   *"Do you love it, Vincent?"*
>   *"Yes."*
>   *"Say you like it, baby!"*
>   *"I like it."*

*   *   *

Carmen never considered having sex with Vincent any form
of sexual assault. She presently felt a sense of guilt. Did the
horrific rape that happened to Valerie conjure up those
heartpounding memories? Was she as just as guilty as J.D.?

"Carmen," Marsha called quietly from outside the door.
"I'm on the phone with detective James Bucci over at the
fifth area district and he's requesting some information from
you." Carmen left the room to speak with detective Bucci.
Marsha handed her the phone from inside the nurse's station.

"Hello, detective Bucci," Carmen said exuberantly.

"Yes, is this Carmen?" Bucci replied, anxiously awaiting
some information.

"Yes."

"Could you give me the name and a full description of
the man who raped Valerie Ramirez?"

"His name is Jesse Dewayne Willingham," Carmen said.
"Most people who know him call him J.D. He's very dark
complexioned, stands about five feet eight. He's got a shiny

bald head and he's very heavyset with short gray sideburns and a mustache."

"An accurate description, indeed."

"Thank you."

"I'll get back with you."

*   *   *

Not long after their conversation, detective James Bucci ran a thorough background search on J.D. Willingham. Carmen waited anxiously at the hospital with Valerie. Several hours later, Bucci called the hospital and gave Carmen a criminal history background on J.D. He had been a known felon for quite some time. Carmen listened closely as detective Bucci read her the following information:

"The mentioned subject, Jesse Dewayne Willingham, was sentenced to ten months in a Clarksdale, Mississippi correctional institute for assault and battery. He later served a two year sentence for possession of large quantities of marijuana. Less than a year following this conviction, he was sentenced to nine years in a Mississippi prison farm for strong arm robbery and parole violation. Following his release from prison for this conviction, he was arrested for soliciting prostitution and possession of narcotics, with the intent to distribute. He was also sentenced to a brief six month sentence for the mistreatment of a child. Jesse Dewayne Willingham has been arrested numerous times for crimes such as car theft, burglary, vagrancy, solicitation of prostitution, tampering, possession of narcotics with the intent to distribute, and vandalism. He has an extensive criminal career and has been a known felon since the age of sixteen."

Carmen couldn't believe what her ears had just heard. She never knew that J.D. had committed all those crimes. Several questions arose in her mind. Were those crimes committed before he moved to Chicago and married Bessie Mae? Was Bessie Mae hiding J.D.'s dark past from everyone? Maybe Bessie Mae knew about his past and felt that it wasn't important and that he would probably become a changed man?

"Jesus Christ!" Carmen said, breathing deeply. "I never knew that Mrs. Willingham was married to a man like him."

In so many words, Carmen was trying to tell detective Bucci that Bessie Mae was married to a *lowlife-penitentiary-street-thug*. Yes, he was a thug who had done serious time in more than one penitentiary.

"Do you possibly know of J.D. Willingham's whereabouts?" Bucci asked.

"Whereabouts?"

"Yes, like some of his favorite hangout spots."

"I sure don't," Carmen answered, wishing J.D. would be caught and locked up forever.

"You don't have a lead as to where he might have fled after the rape occurred?"

"It's hard to say," Carmen recollected. "He knows a whole lot of people around Chicago."

"Do you know the names or addresses of some of these people?" Bucci pressed strongly. He didn't consider that Chicago was a massive city.

"I don't think that he would go over to any of those people's houses at that time of morning."

"Can you think of any of his favorite hangouts around Chicago?"

"I'm sorry, detective Bucci," Carmen apologized. "But I can't think of any place in particular that he would have gone."

She gave the detective the notion that she was tired and frustrated.

"That's okay," Bucci said. "I think we have enough information."

The case couldn't go any further until the assailant, the notorious J.D. Willingham, was arrested. A warrant was issued for his arrest. Carmen hung up the phone and Valerie jumped up screaming. She screamed very loud.

"Help me!"

"It's okay," Carmen said, consoling her foster sister as much as possible. "We're here for you, Valerie."

"Help me somebody, please!"

"Nobody's going to hurt you."

While still in a mild state of shock, she glanced around the room, holding her chest, trying to hold back a rush of tears in her water-filled eyes. She licked her tears from the rim of her mouth. Her head bowed in shame. The horrifying rape became traumatic.

*   *   *

Carmen drove Valerie over to Tamara Davidson's house. Tamara was a respected church member who lived on Chicago's south side. They cruised up in front of Tamara's two bedroom home and parked in the short narrow driveway. Carmen knocked on the door three times and waited. After waiting a couple of minutes, no one answered. She knocked three more times and waited diligently for someone to answer.

"Wait a minute!" shouted the voice of a woman, making it seem as though she was racing towards the front door. "I'm coming, just give me a second. Who's there?"

"It's Carmen and Valerie, Sister Tamara," Carmen answered calmly.

"Carmen and Valerie from St. Mark's?" Tamara asked. "Sister Bessie Mae's foster girls?"

"Yes mam, it's us."

"Wait a second."

"Okay."

Tamara slowly turned the deadbolt locks and lifted the chain off the door. In order to see who she was letting through the front door, she peeked between the cracks. Everything looked okay, so she allowed Carmen and Valerie entry. She locked the door and turned around to observe the *sexually assaulted* Valerie. Tamara had a bad feeling that something had happened. She leaned back in her black leather recliner, patting lightly on the large pink rollers in her head.

"What can I do for you young ladies?" Tamara asked.

"Something really bad happened last night," Carmen said, partially explaining the story.

"What happened?"

"Something very bad happened over at the house last night, Sister Tamara."

"The foster home over on Milwaukee Parkway?"

"Yes, that home."

"Well, tell me what happened, sista girl," Tamara said, who could tell that something had happened to Valerie, but just couldn't tell exactly what it was.

"I mean to tell you," Carmen paused exhaustingly. "Something really, really, really, bad happened in that house over there." She stalled for time, nearly crying from just thinking about the graphic bed on the second floor that she looked upon.

"Will you tell me what happened!" Tamara yelled Christianly, wanting Carmen to just spit out the rest of her words.

"It's like this, Sister Tamara," Carmen snorkled. "Last night, Valerie was . . . she . . . was . . ."

"She was what?"

"She was raped," Carmen finally admitted, fighting back a few drop of tears.

"By whom?"

"Mr. Willingham."

"Oh my god!" Tamara shivered, covering her mouth with both hands and moving over towards Valerie. "Sister Bessie Mae's husband?"

"Yes."

"Sweet Jesus!"

"We just came from Cook County Hospital."

"What did the doctors or nurses say?"

"They checked her out."

"And?"

"She . . . ," Carmen cried, pouring out all of her emotions for Valerie.

"Take your time, sista girl."

"She was all messed up."

"Messed up? How?"

"It was all red and swollen by down her private." Carmen couldn't but help discharge a rush of tears.

"Where's Sister Bessie Mae?"

"She's down in Memphis, Tennessee."

"Memphis?" Tamara inquired. "What's she doing in Memphis?"

"She had to see about her uncle."

"What uncle?"

"Her uncle Booker T."

"What's wrong with him?"

"He's real sick."

"Who was around when this man raped Valerie?"

"A lot of people."

"Didn't nobody hear anything?"

"Everybody was alseep when it happened."

"Nobody heard nothing or seen nothing?"

"Not really."

"What about Sister Bessie Mae's mother?"

"Granny Dear?"

"The old woman who sleeps past that curtain."

"She's in a wheelchair and sleeps on the first floor. She couldn't have done anything, even if she heard something."

"Why in God's name would that man wanna hurt this poor little helpless girl?"

"I asked myself the same question."

"I'll probably be looking in the newspaper and be reading about a foster father raping his foster daughter."

"This is not the first time you've heard about something like this happening?" Carmen questioned Tamara. She was a church youth counselor who had a heart made of pure love.

"It happens all the time," Tamara explained. "Some of these foster homes don't care two cents about the foster children that they keep. As long as they're getting that money from the state every month, they don't care."

Tamara may have been speaking of Bessie Mae and J.D. She only knew her from attending church. Many people close to them knew that Bessie Mae waited faithfully for her checks at the first of every month.

"That's weird," Carmen said, snapping her finger loudly.

"What's weird?"

"A nurse named Marsha at the hospital was saying the same things that you're saying about foster homes."

"It's true," Tamara added. "Some of them feel like the children that they're keeping aren't their biological children anyway, and they end up treating them like they're some kind of property that they're leasing, like a contract that'll expire with the state."

"You're right, Sister Tamara."

"You know, I never liked Sister Bessie Mae's husband."

"Mr. Willingham?"

"When I first laid eyes on him, I knew that he was evil."

"Why?"

"The eyes are the windows to the soul."

"They say that the eyes don't lie."

＊   ＊   ＊

It was 10:45 a.m. and the forensic medical experts from the sex crimes unit were walking out of the Willingham residence. They carried the badly stained sheet from Valerie's bed, Valerie's yellow nightgown, a cervical scraper, samples of pubic hairs from J.D.'s scrotum, and dried up semen. Carmen and detective Bucci were standing in the front room discussing J.D.'s character. James Bucci had true matinee idol looks. He was a handsome Italian man. The Rudolph Valentino type! A smooth olive complexion, deep dark eyes, jet black wavy hair, and a tall and well-built frame, would make one think:

"Why is this guy a police detective? Why isn't he a model or out in Hollywood making millions of dollars as a movie star?"

"What kind of guy is this J.D. Willingham?" detective Bucci asked.

"Let's see now," Carmen shrugged. "He curses a lot."

"A lot?"

"I mean, almost every word that comes out of his mouth is a curse word."

"Is he physically abusive?"

"Very abusive!" Carmen mentioned strongly. "He's been abusive towards all of the foster children who've come and gone from this home every since I can remember."

"Including, you?" detective Bucci questioned, taking notes on a small white notepad.

"Never!" Carmen answered offensively. "I was left in their foster home when I was a baby, but Mr. Willingham never beat me for anything."

"He never raised his hand to you?"

"No!"

"Are there any children in the home that he presently abuses?"

"Valerie's little brother, Vincent."

"For what type of things?"

"When he wets the bed, Mr. Willingham beats him with an extension cord."

"Wow!" Bucci quivered. "That's a painful punishment."

"I mean, he beats him real hard," Carmen explained. "Leaves these red marks all over him."

"Okay, Carmen," Bucci said. "You've told me about the physical abuse. Does this J.D. Willingham verbally or mentally abuses anyone?"

"Remember when I told you he curses a lot?"

"Yes, I remember."

"There's a mentally retarded man named Braun who stays on the second floor, and Mr. Willingham curses at him for not understanding something and for eating cigarette butts. This man, Braun, has a nervous condition, where he beats the middle of his hand with a thick hanger wire, and Mr. Willingham curses at him for that."

"Cigarette butts? Hanger wire?" Bucci said, straining every facial muscle, then taking a deep swallow. Braun sure seemed to be an interesting character to the detective. "If this guy is mentally retarded, then why would J.D. Willingham say harsh things to him?"

"My question, exactly," Carmen concurred. "Braun can't help himself, but Mr. Willingham just doesn't care."

"Very interesting," said detective Bucci, pausing momentarily to internalize all the information that Carmen had just given him. "Didn't you mention that this guy named Braun and another mentally retarded guy stayed in the same room right next to the one where Valerie stayed?"

"Yes, I did," Carmen said. "The other man's name is Junior."

"Do you think Braun could answer a few questions?"

"Possibly."

Carmen stood at the bottom of the stairs and summoned for Braun to come down. He rushed down beating the middle of his right hand with one of his hangers and chewing wildly on a piece of chewing gum that was several weeks old. Bucci extended his hand forward to greet Braun. "How are you doing, Braun?"

"Hey, hey, how ya doing there?" Braun replied, showing all of his black teeth with the moist gum caught between the front ones.

"I'm fine, Braun. Did you notice anything unusual upstairs in the early morning hours?"

"No, no, I didn't notice nothing unusual."

"Do you know who J.D. Willingham is?"

"Yeah, yeah, I know who J.D. is."

"Do you know who Valerie Ramirez is?"

"Yeah, yeah, I know who Valerie is?"

"Did you see J.D. go into Valerie's room last night?"

"No, no, I didn't see nobody go into her room last night."

"Did you hear anyone walking around up there last night?"

"No, no, I didn't hear nobody walking around upstairs last night."

"Thank you, Braun," Bucci said, extending his hand forward to shake Braun's rough and chapped hand. It wasn't easy keeping his composure while viewing Braun's badly rotten teeth.

"Yeah, yeah, you're welcome, sir."

Bucci realized that he was questioning someone who was mentally retarded. He turned his attention back to Valerie. "Why hasn't anyone reported any of the abuse?"

"I've always wanted to," Carmen divulged, hit with another strong memory of the times that she'd take Vincent in the bathroom for sex. Her past had come back to haunt her

constantly. Bucci noticed Carmen's sudden change of demeanor.

"Something wrong, Carmen?"

"Oh no, everything's alright."

"You were saying that you've always wanted to report the abuse."

"Oh yeah!" Carmen recollected. "I've always been scared that if I told one of the caseworkers what Mr. and Mrs. Willingham were doing, they would beat me on the outskirts of Chicago."

"You and a lot of other foster kids."

"You're right."

"I must tell you," Bucci paused, flipping over a full page of notes. "After being involved with investigative police work, foster homes aren't the safest places to be, especially when you've got foster parents who don't show special interest for the children."

"What makes you say that, detective Bucci?" Carmen asked, admiring every striking feature on his alluring handsome face.

"Some of those children are intentionally abused and neglected. Is it the love of children or the love of money that motivates these foster parents?"

"Good question."

"Makes a person wonder."

"You're the third person that I heard say something like that."

"It's true."

"Three things that tie in together," Carmen said. "The abuse, the neglect, and the love for money."

"Sounds about right to me."

"There was a nurse at the hospital and a church youth counselor who were telling me almost the exact same thing."

"It's a real sad thing." Detective Bucci spoke with passion in his voice.

"I'm curious."

"About what?"

"Have you ever dealt with a case like that of Valerie's?" Carmen asked.

"Worse!" Bucci nodded. "About five years ago, we investigated a case that involved a nine year old foster girl who was brutally beaten and raped by her foster father. This animal had been burning the little girl with cigarettes and irons."

"What did they do to this cruel man?"

"He got some jail time."

"How much time?"

"Three years."

"That's all?"

"The bastard should've been given life!"

"Or the death penalty."

"It's people like him and J.D. Willingham who make the world an unsafe place to live in."

Bucci and Carmen continued their discussion as the phone began suddenly ringing like crazy.

4609-REYN

Chapter 15

SISTER TELLS BROTHER

VERNON WALKED THROUGH the front door with several dark bruises around his neck. They were those noticeable passion marks. He came home after a long night of *teenager to teenager intimacy*. He took advantage of quality time with one of his many girlfriends.

"Who put all those marks on your neck?" Carmen asked, moving towards Vernon with aggression, thinking someone could play connect the dots with his neck.

"I'll tell you about it later," Vernon said, noticing detective Bucci's presence in the front room. There stood a tall Italian man wearing a sharp gray suit, with a .38 calibre, which was held in a brown leather holster to his right side. Anyone other than a black person remained to be a rarity at the Willingham residence.

Vernon knew that this man was Italian. For the most part, their features usually gave them away.

"What happened?" Vernon asked Carmen.

"Hold on, Vernon," Carmen replied. "I'll let you know a little later."

Carmen had polite manners and thought it would only be sensible to introduce strangers to one another. "Detective Bucci, this is my foster brother. His name is Vernon Ramirez and he's been living at the Willingham residence for quite some time."

"Hello, detective Bucci," Vernon spoke with great respect, extending his right arm to exchange handshakes. "How are you doing today?"

"How are you doing, young man?" Bucci responded, firmly grasping Vernon's whole hand and extending a very warm smile.

"I'm doing okay."

"You must be Valerie's brother?"

"How did you know that?"

"Well . . ."

"I'll feel more at ease when somebody tell me what's going on." Vernon was anxious to know what had happened. The detective and squad cars out front told part of the story.

"I'll let Carmen explain it to you," Bucci said.

"That's fine."

If the case was ever to be solved, detective Bucci had lots of work to do. After the forensic lab contacted him, or if J.D. was apprehended, he told Carmen that he would contact her. As soon as the detective left the home, Vernon took a seat on the sofa. He was restless from a long night of wild sex. He stared up at the ceiling, lightly pounding his feet onto the carpet. Carmen came over to the sofa and pressed her body next to him. Her long fingers ran through the tight curls in his large afro.

"Why was that detective Bucci here?" Vernon asked, touching the dark circles on his neck with his fingertips.

"Which one of your girlfriends put those passion marks on your neck?" Carmen asked, smiling cleverly to avoid Vernon's inquiry. She too, pressed her fingertips on different areas of Vernon's neck.

"I'll tell you about these marks later. Tell me why that detective was here."

"Tell me about those dark passion marks first."

"Alright, alright," Vernon whisked, finally giving in. "This girl named Daphne Sinclair went wild with her tongue."

"She used your neck as a lollipop."

"Yeah, you could say that."

"Sounds freaky to me."

"Real freaky," Vernon said with a big grin.

"Who's Daphne Sinclair?"

"My girlfriend."

"Where did you meet this girl?"

"Come on, Carmen!" Vernon snapped."Forget about my neck, the freaky stuff, and Daphne Sinclair. For God's sake, forget about all that crap. Will you go ahead and tell me what happened?"

"How can I explain it?" said Carmen, moving further down the sofa. She sucked in a strong breath and then exhaled from her puffy jaws. "I'm going to explain it to you the best way I know how."

"You what?"

"I . . ."

"Go ahead and tell me."

"Last night, Mr. Willingham . . ."

"He what?" Vernon asked, hoping Carmen would let the words shoot out of her mouth.

"Mr. Willingham raped Valerie."

"He did what!" Vernon screamed, jumping up from the sofa and sinking his teeth into his lower lip. He turned red all over his face.

"Calm down, Vernon."

"How in the fuck did that happen!"

"He raped Valerie when everybody in the house was sleep." Carmen made sure that she kept her distance from Vernon, just in case he went wild and started throwing things. She never underestimated his temper.

"Where's my sister right now?"

"Valerie's over at Sister Tamara's house."

"Where's the lowdown black sonofabitch that raped her?"

"Mr. Willingham's out in the streets somewhere," Valerie explained. "Maybe he's riding around or over somebody's house."

"It get it, Carmen," Vernon incriminated. "The fat black

motherfucker couldn't face up to what he did!" For some strange reason, Vernon could envision the actual rape incident. Anger had painted the perfect picture for him.

"Take it easy, Vernon."

"Is detective Bucci gonna go out and try to find the black greasy motherfucker?"

"Yes," Carmen said. "The police are probably all over this part of Chicago looking for him."

"Forget about the police," Vernon added. "You know what I wish I could do?"

"What?"

"I wish I could take him in the woods, tie both of his hands behind his back, hang him upside down by his feet, pull his pants and underwear down, and then take a giant butcher knife and cut his dick and balls off. Maybe even slice his motherfucking throat afterwards!"

"Vernon, that's cruel."

"I don't care, Carmen."

"You don't need to be getting yourself into any trouble."

Vernon never would have imagined in his wildest nightmares that his sister would have been brutally raped by their foster father. Carmen wanted him to calm down and tone down on some of the profanity. It made her flesh crawl from just listening to him make brutal threats towards J.D. His homicidal fantasies were similar to those that had been carried out by ruthless Chicago mobsters, men like Rudy Broncato and Nick Morelli and Fat Tony Torio. His vision of doing destructive things had him pacing the floor with both fists balled up. Carmen knew that anger had taken over his mind.

Vincent was awakened from all the uproar. He came into the laundry room and tried listening to all of the confusion. Little did he know that his sister, Valerie, had been raped by J.D. Willingham. Carmen and Vernon had developed a big appetite.

"I'm hungry, Carmen," Vernon said.

"What do you have a taste for?" Carmen asked.

"McDonald's."

"Jack In The Box sounds better."

"Okay."

They left and would return later and would wait for detective Bucci to call. While listening to the remainder of the
conversation, Vincent kept hearing the word *rape*. He wanted
to know the definition of the word. Inside one of the book-
shelves in the den, he took out a large Thorndike Barnhart
dictionary. Dust and spiderwebs had accrued over the years.
After dusting off the front cover, Vincent flipped through
the yellow and crinkly pages. He turned to the section where
the word *rape* was found.

In small bold print, Vincent stared right at the definition of
the word: *Forcible sexual intercourse by way of seizing and violation.*
He tried making sense of the word that had his juvenile
mind wandering aimlessly. The question that arose in his
mind was, *"Did Mr. Willingham force Valerie to have sexual intercourse with him?"* There was plenty of time for him to find out
what happened.

*   *   *

Two days following the rape, there were policemen who were
assigned to search around parts of Chicago for the notorious
J.D. Willingham. Several officers were paired off. The search
was massive. The search was long. But in the end, J.D. had
been apprehended. Police spotted him coming out of an
old rundown hotel with a hooker on the west side.

J.D. waited restlessly in a small jail cell on the third floor
of the Cook County Jail. He paced the floor nervously, smoking

one Pall Mall Gold cigarette after another. He felt no remorse for the crime that he had committed, only concerned
about being freed.

Over at the fifth district headquarters, detective Bucci
waited for the crime lab division to bring the lab results to his
office. After the papers were brought to his office, he received a call from the interrogation room over at the jail. He
left the district headquarters for a worthwhile trip to the jail.

Inside the small and dim room, there stood another man
from the sex crimes unit. Also from the fifth area district, was
detective Jeremy Rosenthal, a thirteen year veteran with The
Chicago Police Department. He stood in a commanding pose
to the left of J.D. Detective Rosenthal was the total opposite
of Bucci. He wore cheap clothes, cheap cologne, scraggly
hair stubble piercing through his puppy dog face, and a
bushy hairstyle suited him just fine. Despite his semi-wealthy
Jewish background, Rosenthal was scrupulously conservative.
Bucci opened up the interrogation process by firing away
with the questioning.

"Mr. Willingham," Bucci said. "Where were you between
the hours of 11:00 p.m. and 1:00 a.m. on Wednesday night?"

"Lemme see, now," J.D. replied nervously. "I went to da
lickka sto bout dat time."

"You went to what type of store?" asked Bucci, barely able
to understand the extreme illiteracy of J.D.'s words.

"A lickka sto."

"Did you say liquor store, Mr. Willingham?"

"Yep, dat's what I'm tying ta say."

"What's the name of this liquor store?"

"I dunno."

"Come on, you remember."

"I can't memba."

"Why can't you remember?"

"I dunno."

"Where's the liquor store located?"

"On Wush."

"Rush Boulevard?"

"Yep."

"There's a lot of liquor stores on Rush."

"I know."

"Was it Bertolli's?"

"Can't memba."

"Vanzetti's?"

"Yep, I thank dat's it."

"Do you think someone who works in the liquor store can recognize you?"

"Yep."

Bucci and Rosenthal were giving J.D. some repugnant stares. They sensed that his educational level was the lowest of low. His dialect was a total wreck! J.D. slipped into a brief trance and his weary mind traveled back to his younger years of living in Clarksdale, Mississippi. Police constantly harrassed the Negro boys who walked along the dirt trail during the late night hours.

*   *   *

"Where you going, nigger boy?" one of the racist cops asked a young J.D., who walked along a dirt trail kicking rocks with his bare feet.

"Suh, I'm going to ma house."

"What you doing out this late at night?"

"Suh, I been working in da fields with da utter negro folks."

"Do you know what happens to nigger boys who walk down dark streets at night?"

"No, suh," J.D. answered frightfully.

"You don't know, nigger boy?"

"No suh."

"If you don't want yo mammy and yo pappy to find you hanging from no tree, then you betta get your ass to yo house."

"Yes suh! Yes suh!" J.D. replied obediently, putting much stride in his steps.

"Hurry up, you coon."
"Yes suh, I'm gone be gettin home wight now!"
"Run, run, you black jigg."
"Yes suh, yes suh, I runs on home!"
The cops in the cluttering squad car began cocking their rifles to sort of frighten J.D. even moreso.

*   *   *

Detective Rosenthal stepped into the interrogation process. He circled the room with a cup of piping hot coffee. "Where did you go after leaving the liquor store?"

"I went back to ma house," J.D. said.

"What did you do when you got back to your house?"

"I drank ma beers out in my twuck."

"How long did you sit in your truck?"

"Bout, ten minutes," J.D. answered smoothly, making sure he could get his story straight.

Bucci stepped back into the interrogation. "Where did you go after leaving your truck?"

"I went ta bed afta dat."

"You went to bed?"

"Yep."

"Approximately, what time was that?"

"Bout, quota ta twelve."

"About a quarter to twelve, huh?"

"Yep."

Bucci raised his voice slightly and moved further into the black greasy face of J.D. He wanted to grill the lowlife to no apparent satisfaction. "I'm going to present some evidence before you, Mr. Willingham. According to hospital and lab records, Valerie Ramirez, a fourteen year old female, was the victim of a brutal rape. There were pubic hairs and semen left around her genitals after the rape occurred. There was blood and semen left on the bed sheets and the nightgown

of Valerie Ramirez. The crime lab took sample pubic hairs from you, Mr. Willingham, and the DNA samples matched exactly with the ones that the hospital removed from the genital area of Valerie."

When Bucci finished, J.D. threw him a gnarling stare and said, "What chu tying ta say?"

"All the evidence is not in your favor, Mr. Willingham."

"I ain't waped nobody."

"You're lying and we're going to prove that you did."

"I ain't got no weason ta lie."

"I think you waited for the opportune time to take advantage of a fourteen year old girl."

"Dat ain't true."

"How can you live with yourself?"

"Lack I always been doing."

"You're a liar, a rapist, a child molestor, and you're guilty of a crime, Mr. Willingham," Bucci said straightforwardly, using his gorgeous bedroom eyes to stare right into the watery and veiny eyes of J.D. "It's people like you who destroys the moral fiber of our country. It's people like you who ruin the lives of children with promising futures. It's people like you who give all men a bad name, and I won't quit until I know that justice has been served."

With Bucci saying that, it was enough to shut J.D. up. Anyway, who was J.D. trying to fool? James Armand Bucci was a criminal justice graduate from the University of Notre Dame. Jeremy Rosenthal was a criminal justice law graduate from UCLA. Both men knew all of the Illinois rape laws, from criminal sexual assault, aggravated criminal sexual assault, criminal sexual abuse, aggravated criminal sexual abuse, and right down to spousal rape.

The interrogation process came to a close. J.D. was absolutely stunned! Detectives Bucci and Rosenthal left him speechless. Since he had committed an act of sexual misconduct against Valerie, who was under the age of seventeen,

they wanted to charge him with aggravated criminal sexual abuse, a class 2 felon under Illinois code 5/12-16.

Later that day, Bucci contacted Carmen to inform her that in order to proceed, Valerie or a legal guardian would have to press charges. Detective Bucci was informed that Bessie Mae would be returning from Memphis, Tennessee soon.

Chapter 16

MOTHER MUST KNOW

MONDAY MORNING ARRIVED and Vincent awoke in another bed soaked with his own urine. The thick layers of newspaper and thin plastic that Bessie Mae used to cover her dry cleaned clothes, were enough to stop the urine from reaching the sheets. The wall next to his bed was covered with large black waterbugs. Mice ran from one end of the room to the next. J.D. hadn't exterminated in months. The bed changing chore became agonizing, because he had to prepare his bed every night. Luckily, Bessie Mae kept large volumes of newspaper around. Anything to prevent another beating was worth it.

Had he pissed in the bed anyway, Vincent had nothing to worry about. J.D. was behind bars and Bessie Mae hadn't returned from Memphis. Vincent raised out of his bed and rolled the newspaper and plastic into a tight ball. The soiled paper and plastic were thrown into the same barrel in Sean's room.

Granny Dear was in the kitchen cooking a large pot of oatmeal, along with a wide pan of biscuits in the oven and bacon and eggs frying in a large black skillet. Since she was short of help, breakfast was going to be late. The aroma from the kitchen traveled to the basement. Vincent loved the taste of buttery biscuits. The smell of a hearty breakfast caused his tastebuds to activate and saliva to form around the edge of his mouth.

After Granny Dear prepared everyone's plate, the phone rang. She quickly rolled her wheelchair to the other side of

the stove. She stood on her arthritis-stricken legs to answer. Bessie Mae had unexpectedly called from Memphis.

"How're things going around the house?" Bessie Mae asked Granny Dear.

"Dey okay," Granny Dear said, her voice low-spirited, gradually falling down into her wheelchair.

"What's wrong, Granny Dear?" Bessie Mae said, detecting the bitterness in her voice.

"Sumthang bad happened da utta night."

"The other night?"

"Yep."

"What happened?"

"I thank ya betta wait till ya come home, Bessa Mae."

"Why?"

"You betta wait."

"Is it that bad that you can't tell me over the phone?"

"Sho ain't good."

"Why did something have to happen when I left town?"

"How's Booker T.?"

"He's doing fine."

"What was wong wit'em?"

"He came down with a mild case of the pneumonia."

"So, he gone be alwight?"

"He'll be just fine," Bessie Mae said. "He's taking some medication and getting better everyday."

"When ya comin home?"

"My plane leaves later this morning."

"Okay."

"Tell J.D. that I'll be at the airport around four o'clock."

"J.D. can't pick ya up, Bessa Mae," Granny Dear confessed honestly.

"Why?"

"You gone have ta find out when ya git home."

"Oh lord!" Bessie Mae grunted. "Sounds like something terrible happened."

"You gone find out."

"Who's gonna pick me up from the airport?"

"Carmen can pick ya up."

"Tell her what time I'll be there."

"Alwight."

Bessie Mae hung up worried. She couldn't wait to get on the next plane for Chicago. Moments after talking to Bessie Mae, the phone rang again. Granny Dear wasn't too happy about answering it. As she rolled over to the phone, she was grinding together her well-fitted dentures. This was every indication that she was angry.

"Hello."

"Will you accept a collect call from J.D. Willingham?" a fast and sassy talking operator asked Granny Dear.

"Naw."

Granny simply told the operator that she wouldn't accept the charges. She dropped the phone on the receiver and fell back into her wheelchair. J.D. was calling collect from Cook County Jail. The only person he needed to speak to was Bessie Mae. The phone rang several minutes later and Granny Dear refused to answer again. She suspected that it was J.D. She allowed it to ring until it stopped.

Once Bessie Mae was picked up from one of the TWA terminals out at O'Hare International Airport, Vernon stored her suitcase in the trunk. Carmen drove down the busy expressway looking straight ahead. Her attentive eyes concentrated on the cars driving in her lane. Vernon sat quietly in the back seat, checking out the view of the downtown skyscrapers.

Carmen's strange behavior caused Bessie Mae to shift her head to the left, observing the blank expression on her face. Through the rearview mirror, she glanced at the absent expression on the face of Vernon. She continuously gyrated her head to the left, up to the mirror, and over to the right side. The silence in the car had to come to a cease.

"Why are you all so quiet?" Bessie Mae asked, wanting Carmen or Vernon to finally open their mouths.

"I don't have much to say," Carmen spoke. "How were things in Memphis?"

"Fine."

"How's Uncle Booker T.?"

"Booker's doing fine."

"How's everybody else down there doing?"

"They're fine."

Carmen was playing a serious game of trying to elude questions about J.D.

"Did you go down Elvis Presley Boulevard and see Elvis Presley's Graceland Mansion?"

"We rode down Elvis Presley Boulevard a few times."

"I know exactly what you saw out front."

"What?"

"A bunch of white people waiting outside Graceland to see him."

"There's always a real long line of white people," Bessie Mae said. "Most of them be wasting their time standing out there."

"Why's that, Mrs. Willingham?"

"Elvis is almost never there."

"Where does he be?"

"Out in California making movies or somewhere overseas."

"Mrs. Willingham!" Carmen jolted, suddenly pounding on the steering wheel. "Remember the story that you told us about the black woman and Elvis Presley?"

"What story?" Bessie Mae asked, not knowing what Carmen was speaking of. She was a true native of Memphis who knew several stories about Elvis.

"The story about the black woman who was standing in the car lot."

"And?"

"Elvis supposedly walked up and asked her if she liked the car."

"Yeah, I remember that story."

"Did it really happen?"

"Elvis bought her that car, too."

"Said he paid cold cash for it."

"He sure did."

"Why come things like that never happen to me?" Carmen asked.

"Who knows."

"I get excited talking about that story."

Despite that story, which was on a positive realm, Bessie Mae knew that Elvis had supposedly said that the only thing that colored people could do for him was shine his shoes and buy his records. Needless to say, long before Elvis Presley became an internationally famous superstar, the colored boys would take him around to the blues and jazz clubs in Memphis, right there on Beale Street, and give him the chance to study the vocal styles of the colored entertainers. But ask some of the colored people from the old school, the ones who didn't care about Elvis one way or another, they would tell anyone that in their opinion, Elvis was nothing but a poor white boy from the backwoods of Mississippi.

*   *   *

Carmen continued to elude any conversation leading to J.D. "Did you go down Beale Street?"

"Yeah, yeah, we drove all over Memphis and parts of Mississippi," Bessie Mae answered irritably. "I'm back in Chicago now and I wanna know why J.D. didn't come and pick me up."

Carmen and Vernon were afraid to give Bessie Mae the disheartening news. How could they explain to her the horrible crime that her husband had committed? Their tongues

were locked between their gums and teeth like a vice grip. Bessie Mae became impatient! Was she talking to them or to the car?

They arrived at the house and Carmen parked behind Bessie Mae's Cadillac Sedan de Ville. She handed the keys to Vernon and he went into the truck to take out the suitcase. Bessie Mae limped towards the house carrying her suitcase. Carmen and Vernon stood around the car for a quick pep talk before giving Bessie Mae the bad news.

"How are we gonna tell Mrs. Willingham?" Carmen asked Vernon, not knowing where to start.

"I don't know," Vernon said, his shoulders humping in curiosity."But I do know what I would like to do to Mr. Willingham."

"What?"

"I wanna kill the fat black motherfucker for raping my sister!" Vernon snapped. "I wanna give him cement shoes and dump his greasy black ass in the river." Vernon's blood continued to boil after the rape incident.

"You can tell Mrs. Willingham when we get in the house."

"I don't wanna tell her."

"Why not?"

"I'll get mad and start cursing."

"Then don't curse."

"I'll hear her mouth about me disrespecting her."

"You're a man, and a man should tell her."

"You're a woman, and it's better for a woman to tell her."

"Valerie's your sister."

"So?"

"Mrs. Willingham'll listen since she is your sister."

"Why don't you tell her woman-to-woman?"

"Somebody's got to tell her."

"You're right."

Bessie Mae took a seat at the dinnertable in the dining room. A worried look came upon her face. She picked dirt

from in between her fingernails. She fired up a Pall Mall
Red and blew smoke every which direction. Carmen and
Vernon took a seat on opposite sides of the table. They moved
their chairs closer to where Bessie Mae sat. Finally, Carmen
came forward with the truth.

"Something really bad happened upstairs," Carmen
huffed. "And it happened not long after you left for
Memphis."

"Granny Dear already told me that something
happened," Bessie Mae disclosed. "Will somebody go ahead
and tell me what happened?"

"It's not easy telling you this, Mrs. Willingham."

"What?"

"Mr. Willingham, he . . ."

"He what?"

"He went upstairs and . . ."

"He did what?" Bessie Mae asked, releasing a long thick
cluster of smoke into the air.

"He raped Valerie."

Bessie Mae screamed from the top of her voice. The
outcry was heard throughout the entire house. "J.D. did what!"

"He snuck upstairs and raped Valerie."

"When did this happen?"

"The same night that you left for Memphis."

"Are you sure, Carmen?"

"I'm one-hundred percent positive, Mrs. Willingham."

At that moment, Bessie Mae's blood pressure soared
higher than ever. She coughed out spurts of smoke. "Where's
J.D.?"

"He's in Cook County Jail."

"Where's Valerie?"

"She's over Sister Tamara's."

"How long J.D. been in jail?"

"A few days, now."

Bessie Mae began feeling a strong sense of cold and

numbness through her body. She could hear her own heart
beating as silence gripped the dining room. "Can they prove
that J.D. raped Valerie?"

"There's all kind of evidence against Mr. Willingham,"
Carmen said. "You can talk with a nurse named Marsha
Shinholster at Cook County Hospital."

"What does she know?"

"Her and some doctors looked Valerie over after she was
raped."

"And?"

"She was messed up down there."

"Down where?"

"Her private."

"How in the name of God could J.D. do something like
that?"

"A detective named James Bucci with the sex crimes unit
at the Chicago Police Department has proof, too."

"What does he know?"

"He can tell you all about the investigation and the lab
tests."

"What tests?"

"The blood, the cum, the hairs, and other things they
found on the sheets and Valerie's nightgown."

"What did you say?"

"What do you mean, Mrs. Willingham?"

"When you said cum?"

"Oh, I'm sorry."

"Don't say that nasty word around me no more."

"I'm sorry."

"Don't you have any respect for your elders?"

"Yes, I do."

Carmen had an easy time saying something like *cum*.
She heard the word after first entering high school and it was
hard to use words that were synonymous. The long discussion
surrounding the tragic dilemma ended.

*   *   *

Hours later, Carmen brought Valerie back to the house to sit and talk with Bessie Mae. She sat at the table and explained everything, detail by hardcore detail. Detective Bucci spoke with Bessie Mae about the possible charges being filed against J.D. He filled her in on all the details about the rape and DNA tests from the blood, semen, and pubic hairs.

Bessie Mae was thoroughly convinced that J.D. was guilty of raping Valerie. In less than three hours, she had smoked two packs of cigarettes. She popped four blood pressure pills with two tall glasses of water. Thinking about her husband being a rapist ripped her heart into pieces. The phone rang and Bessie Mae jumped up to answer. It was J.D. calling and he was ready to explain. Was she ready to listen to a lot of lies and deceit? Everyone sat around the table. They anxiously awaited to hear what Bessie Mae had to say to J.D. She held the phone tightly with another cigarette planted between her fingers.

"Will you accept a collect call from J.D. Willingham?" the operator asked cordially.

"Yes, I will," Bessie Mae replied, cockiness ringing in her voice.

"How ya doing, Bessa Mae?" J.D. asked, his voice cranking with sympathy.

"Bad!" Bessie Mae shouted into the phone. "Real, real, bad!"

"What's wong?"

"What do you have to say for yourself?"

"What chu means?"

"You know goddam well what I mean!"

"Naw, I don't."

"What possessed you to do such a lowdown thing?"

"Lowdown thang lack what?"

"Why, J.D.?"

"I ain't did nuttin, Bessa Mae."

"Don't play dumb with me, man!"

"I ain't paying dumb, Bessa Mae?"

"Fucking me wasn't good enough?"

"What chu talking bouts?"

"You had to fuck our own foster daughter?"

"Dat's a lie."

"You left your cum on the sheets."

"I ain't leff no comb on no seets, Bessa Mae."

"Man, I know what that sticky shit is!"

"It ain't none of mine's."

"You forced your dick up in Valerie!" Bessie Mae grumbled ferociously, allowing raw anger to speak for her.

"Don't bleeve nuttin dat gal sayin."

"You made her bleed real bad."

"Ain't nobody made dat gal bleed."

"You're the most lowdown, the most trifling, the most knaving bastard in the world."

Bessie Mae finished the first cigarette of her third pack. Hostility took over and began speaking for her. "You waited for me to leave to Chicago, didn't you?"

"Naw, I didden."

"Why did you pull some shit like that?"

"Shit, lack what?"

"Raping Valerie, niggah!"

"Ain't nobody did nuttin to dat gal," J.D. said, trying to convince Bessie Mae in every way possible.

"You're lying, niggah!"

"I ain't lying."

"The nurse at the hospital and the police detective don't have no reason to lie!" Bessie Mae confirmed strongly. "You fucked her and you can't try and squeal your way out of this!"

"It's my word ginst hers."

"You don't have no word, J.D."

"Lissen to ma, Bessa Mae."

"You could've bought you some pussy."

"Dat gal lying on ma, Bessa Mae."

"Lowell Avenue's got plenty of whores," Bessie Mae said. "You could've went up there and bought all the pussy you wanted. You took it upon yourself to rape a fourteen year old girl."

"Dat little yella bitch is lying on ma!" J.D. yelled into the phone, his anger surfacing strongly.

J.D. told Bessie Mae one lie after another. Valerie interrupted the argument. She wanted her chance to prove that J.D. was a professional liar. Bessie Mae handed the phone over to Valerie.

"You did rape me!" Valerie shouted aggressively, tears forming at the edge of her eyes. "You jumped on top of me and stuck your thang in me."

"Why ya lying to Bessa Mae?"

"The cum is still on the sheets," Valerie retorted, using the word *cum* because it seemed like the only sensible word to use. By now, it was being misused.

"What comb ya talkin bout, gal?"

"The sticky messy stuff that you left behind after you raped me."

"Ain't nuttin on no seets."

"You're the liar, Mr. Willingham!"

"Naw, ya da one lyin."

"You ran out of the room after you raped me."

"Quit lying, gal."

"Mrs. Willingham already talked with the nurse."

"So."

"And she talked to the police detective, too."

"So."

"You're a filthy liar, Mr. Willingham."

"And you a lying ass, yella bitch!"

"I hate you!"

"Dat's yo problem."

"I will always hate you!"

Bessie Mae quickly reached for the phone. Valerie bent over the table and shoved the phone in her hand. She was almost finished with her second cigarette from the third pack.

"You can sit your black ass in jail."

"Lissen to ma, Bessa Mae."

"No, you listen!"

"What?"

"Sit your ass in jail and think about what you did."

"I ain't did nuttin."

"Whatever!" Bessie said, then slamming the phone down in his ear. She sat at the table with her feelings totally shattered. More blood pressure pills and Pall Mall Reds couldn't calm her nerves. This was the type of devastation that she thought she would never encounter.

* * *

Bessie Mae spent several weeks talking to Valerie. The fact that J.D. had raped Valerie still didn't set in. After playing fierce games of psychology, Bessie Mae convinced Valerie to change her story and drop all the charges. They went to the bishop at the church they attended, talked through counseling sessions, and she eventually changed her story. Bessie Mae stood by her man, for better and for worse.

Carmen and Vernon, along with others, like Marsha Shinholster and James Bucci, weren't too happy with the decision that she made. The need to keep extra help in the house to run things smoothly wasn't acceptable. Bessie Mae didn't want to run a busy foster home by herself and she definitely refused to be without a man. But worst of all, she refused to accept the fact that her husband was a rapist and a child molestor.

Valerie and her caseworker walked out the front door of the Willingham residence carrying her belongings. Vernon

and Vincent stood near the sidewalk as they sadly watched their sister leave the same foster home that all three had come into at the same time. They walked to the car and both gave their sister a hug.

"What foster home are they taking you to?" Vernon asked, shedding a light tear for his sister.

"I don't know," Valerie answered sadly, holding onto his hand tightly.

"Call us sometimes."

"I will."

"Maybe it's better you're leaving this jacked up foster home," Vernon said. "Who wants to live in a home with foster people like Mr. and Mrs. Willingham?"

"You're right, Vernon."

"I know I'm right."

"I love you, brother."

"I love you, too, sister."

Valerie smiled over at Vincent and extended her loving arms. "Come here, Vincent."

"Okay."

"I'm going to miss you, Vincent."

"I'm going to miss you, too, Valerie."

"I'll call you and Vernon, okay."

"Okay."

"Bye bye."

"Bye."

Valerie and her caseworker placed her belongings in the backseat and got into the front. They began waving goodbye to Vernon and Vincent. Her caseworker drove off down Milwaukee Parkway. Vernon and Vincent turned to look up on the porch and there sat J.D. with a mischevious smirk on his shiny black face. In the end, he became the victorious one. A villan who had squealed his way out of a tight jam. But Vernon felt that someday he would get even.

"I hate that fat black motherfucker!"

"Why did he do that to Valerie?" Vincent asked, also noticing how J.D. sat up on the porch with a devious expression on his face.

"He's no good, Vincent."

"I hate him, too."

"Someday, somebody, somewhere, somehow, will punish that sonofabitch for all the dirt that he's ever done."

"I really hope that they do, Vern."

"What goes around, will definitely come back around."

Vernon sucked it in and went about his business. Vincent didn't understand fully, but as he would mature over the years, he would get a better understanding.

Chapter 17

NEW RECRUITS

CASEWORKER REPRESENTATIVES from The Department of Children and Family Services made the following documentation during this period of dictation at the Willingham residence:

Status of work with own parents toward making permanent plans for Vincent Carvelli and Vernon Ramirez:
Parental rights were terminated.

Feelings of children about their parents:
Vincent and Vernon were never close to their natural parents. Vincent has lived with Mr. and Mrs. Willingham since the age of six months. Vernon has lived with them since the age of six.

Conclusions and Recommendations:
Mr. and Mrs. Willingham are proud to have Vernon and Vincent in their foster home. The Willinghams didn't make any plans to adopt Vincent and Vernon. A few weeks after the termination hearing, Valerie accused Mr. Willingham of rape. After Mr. Willingham was arrested, she admitted that the accusation was a lie. At that time, it was discovered that Mr. and Mrs. Willingham had some marital problems. They denied that the problems existed and have refused to accept counseling. For this reason, we have not proceeded with the counseling. For this reason, we have not proceeded with the adoption. Because Vincent and Vernon have been in the home most of their lives, we are hesitant to move them. They are doing well in the home and want to

stay there. Therefore, we recommend that Vincent and Vernon remain in foster care.

*   *   *

Vincent sat in a warm classroom at Abraham Lincoln Elementary anxiously awaiting for the bell to ring. Like always, his classmates were making insulting remarks towards him. They never grew tried of making harsh remarks about his mixed-race identity. The bell rang for school to end and Vincent rushed down the long set of stairs. As soon as he stepped onto the playground, there was the usual group of rowdy classmates, led by Jerry Grayson and Clinton Marks, waiting to shout cruelty into his face.

"White boy! White boy! You don't shine!" yelled the group of hyper kids. "If you call me a nigger, I'll beat your behind!"

"Go home and leave me alone!" Vincent snarled, trying to weave his way through the dense crowd.

"Where're you going, you white honky?"

"None of your business."

"You're not going nowhere, you half-breed honky."

"Get out of my way!"

"Shut up, white boy."

"Leave me alone!"

"Be quiet, white honky."

"Stop it!"

Vincent finally penetrated his way through his classmates. It was his daily walk home with books and supplies hanging down by his side. He walked into the house and Bessie Mae was sitting on the sofa talking with a white woman, who had long and stringy brown hair and a deep cleft in her chin. She had a milky white complexion and a short, narrow face. On opposite sides of Bessie Mae and this woman were two young boys. Suitcases and trashbags were sitting on the floor at opposite ends of the front room. The boy to the left of Bessie

Mae was short, medium complexioned, and slender built. He had an unusually keen nose, stretching far out from his face, and a thick lower lip that was pinkish in color. His hair stood tall and dirt particles were caught between the kinky strands.

The boy to the right of Bessie Mae was tall for his age, also medium complexioned, with a low and well-trimmed haircut. A slight case of cross-eyedness made it seem that he looked a different direction than what others perceived. Vincent stood by the door gasping for air. Bessie Mae opened the floor for introductions.

"Vincent," Bessie Mae said. "This is Sandra Maloney from The Department of Children and Family Services."

"Hello, Mrs. Maloney," Vincent said politely, stepping closer to shake her hand. Caseworkers only visited the Willingham residence when they were either bringing children there or taking them away.

"How are you, Vincent?" Sandra asked, holding his hand firmly with her soft hand.

"I'm okay."

"How long have you been in Mrs. Willingham's foster home?"

"Since I was a baby."

"A baby, huh?"

"Yes, mam."

"Then I take it you like it?"

Vincent couldn't answer that question right away. He stared over at Bessie Mae and she had the look in her eyes as though he'd better say: *"I love this home more than any other place in the world. There's no other place I'd rather be."*

"Yes, mam."

"That's good," Sandra said. "Then you're happy being here?"

"Yes, mam."

"I'm glad to hear that, Vincent."

Bessie Mae wanted Vincent to become familiar with the two boys sitting on the sofa.

"Vincent," she smiled. "These are your new foster brothers. Their names are Gilbert Curry and Jose Underwood. They'll be sleeping in the basement with you and Vernon."

"Hello, Gilbert. Hello, Jose," Vincent replied, reaching forward to shake their hands individually.

"Hello, Vincent," Gilbert said, scratching some of the filth out of his head. "I'm glad to be your new foster brother."

"I'm glad to be your new foster brother, too."

Jose looked at Vincent and said, "Hello, Vincent. I'm glad to be your new foster brother, too."

"Me, too."

Bessie Mae wanted Vincent to help his new foster brothers carry their belongings to the basement. She and Sandra wanted to discuss some matters about foster care. Vincent grabbed one of the trashbags and a small suitcase. Gilbert and Jose followed him down the basement stairs with the rest of their belongings. Before coming to the other half of the stairs, Vincent overheard Bessie Mae tell Sandra Maloney, "When my husband gets home, he's going to put some beds together for Gilbert and Jose."

"That'll be great," Sandra responded.

"They'll have nice beds to sleep on."

"Oh God!" Vincent thought to himself. "I hope they don't use those boxsprings and mattresses in the backyard. Nobody wants to lay their heads down on no shit or no piss."

At one time, there were four beds in the room where Vincent and Vernon slept. Bessie Mae sold them because she never would have thought that two more foster children would be coming to their home.

Gilbert and Jose came to the bottom of the stairs dragging their belongings. The piles of clothes surrounding the
laundry room had amassed. The floor, the washing machine,
and the dryer, were covered with filthy laundry. The socks
and underwear had molded and a strong ammonia odor
circled through the air.

"Where did all these clothes come from?" Gilbert asked.

"Mrs. Willingham," Vincent grunted, cutting a slight grin.
"She has to wash clothes for a lot of people around this house."

"A lot of people live here?"

"Yes."

"What's that black stuff on those blue shirts and blue
pants?"

"That's tar."

"Who wears those clothes?"

"Mr. Willingham."

"Who's he?"

"He'll be home soon."

Since they didn't have any beds, Gilbert and Jose sat
their things on the floor. The long day of being moved had
them tired. They took a seat on Vincent and Vernon's beds.
At first, the room was filled with silence. Gilbert kicked his
feet against the steel rail on the side of the bed frame. Jose
moved further up on the bed and whistled up at the ceiling.
Vincent observed the shyness of his two new foster brothers.
The opportunity to make one another's acquaintances arose.

"Why did you have to be put into a foster home?" Gilbert
asked bluntly, then taking in a deep breath. Vincent was expecting him to inquire about something like that.

"It's kind of a long story," Vincent sighed. "My mother
and father were doing some bad things."

"Like what?"

"Selling dope and liquor and having whores in this
house."

"How old were you when this happened?"

"A baby."

"Tell me more."

"Me, my sister, and my brother were brought to this foster home."

"What happened after that?"

"They never came back to get us."

"They just left you here?" Gilbert asked in amazement. "They never called or nothing? Never came by to see if you were still here?"

"Yes."

"Where's your mother and father now?"

"Somewhere."

"You don't know where?"

"No."

"You haven't seen your mother and father since you were a baby?"

"No."

"Why?"

"Mrs. Willingham said they didn't want to see us."

"Dam!" Gilbert said, a quick nodding of the head. "That's messed up."

The room became dead quiet again. While they waited for someone else to speak, Vincent mumbled words to himself. A host of questions entertained his mind.

"Why did you have to come to this foster home?" Vincent asked Gilbert.

"This is not the first foster home I've been to," Gilbert verified.

"How many foster homes have you been to?"

"Five."

"Five?" Vincent squeaked. "Why did they put you in five foster homes?"

"Because of my mother and father."

"What were they doing?"

"Fighting all the time."

"Why?"

"My daddy came home drunk all the time and beat up my mother."

"Did he beat her up real bad?"

"Yes."

"How bad?"

"He would give her black eyes and busted lips."

"That's terrible, Gilbert!"

"One time he knocked out three of her front teeth."

Vincent didn't want it to seem that he was prying deeply into the troubled past of Gilbert, but he was curious as to why a child would transfer around from foster home to foster home.

"Do you wanna go back and live with your mother and father?"

"No!" Gilbert answered in a charged voice.

"Why not?"

"My father used to beat on me after he beat on my mother."

"Why couldn't you stay in one foster home?"

"I didn't like any of them."

"Why not?"

"I didn't like the foster parents and the foster kids."

"Why not?"

"The foster parents were mean and the other foster kids were bad."

Gilbert wanted Vincent and Jose to know that he had had a hard time adjusting to any foster home. He lived in foster homes where other foster children started fires, soiled their clothing, wet the bed constantly, and engaged in unnatural sex with one another. By now, he had lived with ten foster parents and many other foster children. Since Vincent and Gilbert had already explained their past, they were curious about Jose's story.

"Why did you have to go into a foster home?" Gilbert questioned Jose.

"My mother got real sick," Jose explained.

"Boy!"

"My father ran off and left us," Jose said, strong resentment in his voice.

"What wrong with your mother?"

"She's got a bad heart."

"She had a heart attack?"

"I think so."

"She's in the hospital, now?"

"I don't know."

"Will you go back home when she gets better?"

"I don't know."

"Where's your father?"

"Fuck him!" Jose whisked. "I don't know where he is and don't care."

"Is this your first foster home?"

"No."

"How many have you been to?"

"This is the third one."

Gilbert turned back to Vincent and asked, "Didn't you say that you had a brother and sister?"

"Yes."

"Where are they?"

"My brother is over his girlfriend's house."

"What about your sister?"

"She's in another foster home."

"Why?"

"Promise you won't say anything?"

"I promise."

"She was raped."

"By who?"

"Mr. Willingham."

"Mrs. Willingham's husband?"

"Yes."

"The foster lady upstairs?"

"Yes."

"You're scaring me, Vincent," Gilbert said. "Is he real mean?"

"You'll see."

"He doesn't fuck little boys in the ass, does he?"

"No."

Vincent took Jose and Gilbert into the next room to meet Sean. The first thing they noticed was his paralyzed hand. "Gilbert and Jose, this is Sean."

"Hello," Sean said, showing signs of sadness.

"How are you?" Gilbert and Jose replied respectively, glancing at the bent shape of his left hand.

"I'm okay."

Sadly, Bessie Mae made Sean sit in his room with no one to talk to. He sometimes sat in the dark with his head hung low. He never had any companionship and was treated as a total outcast in the household. The basement door opened and Bessie Mae yelled for Gilbert and Jose to come upstairs. As they trampled through the piles of dirty laundry, Gilbert noticed a gross sight that caused him to bite down hard on his thick lower lip.

"Yuck!"

"What's wrong?" Vincent asked.

"Look at all those shit stains in those drawers."

"I see that everyday."

"Somebody forgot to wipe their ass?"

"There's mentally retarded people who live here," Vincent explained.

"And you see that everyday?"

"Several times a day."

"I don't wanna get none of that stuff on my shoes."

"Watch your step."

"Looks like it's done turned hard inside those drawers."

"That's nasty!"

Gilbert and Jose had to be made aware that special laundry

had to be done for occupants like Sean and Junior. Because of his hand being handicapped, Sean had trouble wiping himself. If Braun didn't come into the bathroom after Junior got off the toilet, then he would forget to wipe himself. Vincent didn't feel proud about his new foster brothers witnessing such unpleasant sights in that filthy laundry room. They returned to the front room where Bessie Mae and Sandra were standing at the front door. With time running short and deadlines having to be met, Sandra informed Gilbert and Jose that she would make regular visits.

"I hope you guys like your new foster home," Sandra said, smiling jubilantly at Gilbert and Jose.

"Thank you, Mrs. Maloney," Gilbert replied falsely, disguising a frown.

"Well, I have to run guys."

"Bye, Mrs. Maloney," said Gilbert and Jose.

Gilbert thought to himself, *"Yeah, I hope I like this new foster home, too."*

Sandra left and Bessie Mae took Gilbert and Jose into the kitchen to meet Granny Dear. They stood on opposite sides of the doorway. They watched Granny Dear stand over the stove on her arthritis-stricken legs. With a long handle spoon, she stirred a large pot of turnip greens. Gilbert stepped up to her wheelchair to be introduced.

"What's yo name, young mane?"

"What did you ask?"

"What's yo name?"

"My name is Gilbert Curry," Gilbert said cordially.

"Yo name Gillbutt, huh?"

"Yes, mam."

Granny Dear wasn't conscious that she had badly mispronounced Gilbert's name. It may have been close enough for him.

"My name's Ida Lou Pierson. Folks round here call ma Granny Dear."

"Pleased to meet you, Granny Dear."

"You sho is a fine young mane."

"Thank you."

Granny Dear turned her wheelchair around to direct her attention towards Jose.

"What's yo name, young mane?"

"My name is Jose Underwood."

"I beg yo pardon."

"It's Jose Underwood."

"Awe, so yo name's Holezay?"

"Yes, mam."

"You sho a fine lookin boy."

"Thank you."

Like Gilbert, Granny Dear had badly mispronounced Jose's name. She only had a first grade education and spent most of her working years laboring for white people around the Memphis, Tennessee and Tupelo, Mississippi areas.

The glass and tin metal around the frame of the front door rattled. J.D. stormed through the door with a toothpick in his mouth. More tar covered his dingy blue uniform. Judging by the way he swung his lunchbucket, and dragged his heavy feet across the carpet, it was a long and hard day at work. His relations with white co-workers had gotten worse. He marched right into the kitchen, which was where Gilbert and Jose were standing near the kitchen table. Bessie Mae embraced them under both arms. She kindly introduced them to J.D.

"J.D.," Bessie Mae smiled. "These are our new foster boys who came to live with us today." Dollar signs were swimming around inside her head, as she smiled into the innocent faces of Gilbert and Jose.

"New falsta boys, huh?" J.D. said, reaching into his shirt pocket for a cigarette. "What's yo name, young mane?"

"I'm Gilbert Curry, sir," Gilbert replied in a frightened voice.

"Gillbutt, huh?"

"Yes, sir."

"We gone be glad ta have ya here."

"Thank you, sir."

J.D. turned to Jose with his black face shining more than ever before.

"What's yo name, fella?"

"My name is Jose Underwood, sir," Jose said, also frightened from J.D.'s evil-looking appearance.

"Yo name's Holezay, huh?"

"Yes, sir."

"Glad ta have ya here, Holezay."

"Thank you."

Granny Dear and J.D. seem to speak with the exact same dialect. Their deep southern roots lingered on to them like molasses to a ripe oak tree. J.D. looked Gilbert and Jose over thoroughly. They looked him over thoroughly. They felt bad vibes about their new foster father. The *big, black, and ugly* appearance of J.D. threw warning signs up. Before she left the kitchen, Bessie Mae had to remind J.D. to put beds together for their new foster sons.

Gilbert and Jose followed Bessie Mae to the stairs leading to the second floor. She called Braun and Junior to come to the first floor. Junior trotted slowly down the stairs. His eyes stared deep into space. When he came to the bottom of the stairs, Bessie Mae embraced him around the waist. She began to introduce him.

"Gilbert and Jose, this is Junior," Bessie Mae said. "He's a mentally retarded man that I've been keeping for awhile."

"Hello, Junior," Gilbert and Jose replied in unison. They stared straight into Junior's face, noticing that his glossy eyeballs and eyelids weren't bulging. They reached forward to shake his hand and Junior never moved a muscle near his eyes.

"Say hello to Gilbert and Jose," Bessie Mae instructed Junior.

"Hello to Gilbert and Jose. Hello to Gilbert and Jose," Junior repeated, his head swinging up and down.

"Tell them that you're pleased to them," Bessie Mae advised, talking to Junior like he was someone programmable.

"Tell them you're pleased to meet them. Tell them you're pleased to meet them."

"No, no, Junior, don't repeat what I said."

"Don't repeat what I said. Don't repeat what I said."

Bessie Mae excused Junior and Braun came walking down the stairs beating the middle of his right hand with a thick and silverish wire from one of the old hangers. Bessie Mae became irritated everytime she heard the sounds of that thick hanger pounding onto the thick skin of his right palm.

"Braun!" Bessie Mae shouted. "Quit slapping your hand with that goddam wire!"

"Okay, okay, I'll stop slapping my hand with the wire."

"I've somebody I want you to meet."

"Alright, alright, you've got somebody for me to meet."

Braun shoved the wire down into his pocket and stood motionless at the bottom of the stairs. Gilbert and Jose glanced at his mouth as he began to smile. They cut a slight frown after seeing his dark and rotten teeth, and the brown saliva that had dried around the rim of his mouth. Feelings of speculation encompassed them.

"Braun," Bessie Mae said, pausing briefly. "This is Gilbert Curry and Jose Underwood. They're new foster boys who'll be staying with us for awhile."

"Hey, hey, how'ya doing there?" Braun said in a friendly manner.

"Fine," Gilbert and Jose said.

They were hesitant at first, but they stepped forward to shake his hand. It was the same right hand that had a long dark streak in the very center of his palm. Layers of skin had been ripped away from him beating his hand on a daily basis. He opened his mouth with a big smile and Gilbert and Jose

noticed the tobacco kernels and old food particles between his black teeth, which were almost ready to fall right out of the gums. Gilbert and Jose walked away frowning.

Bessie Mae reminded Braun that J.D. would need help putting the two beds together. Vincent was called into the kitchen to feed the dogs. When he entered the kitchen, J.D. was sitting at the table crushing out one of his cigarettes. His angry black face had that evil look of: *You better rush out of this kitchen with that slopbucket and hurry back.* The slopbucket was quite heavy and required Vincent to use both arms. Inside the dense bucket, there was molded cornbread, spoiled milk, a big lump of oatmeal, rock hard biscuits, crusted macaroni and cheese, a mound of pinto peans, frozen neckbones, and some rotten tomatoes.

Granny Dear decided to dump some of the leftover food out after being in the refrigerator for several weeks. Bessie Mae would have to force her to bring some of that old food out of the refrigerator. As he walked through the front door, Gilbert and Jose noticed the bucket that had a collection of distastefully looking food inside. Dinner wasn't going to be ready for awhile, so Bessie Mae had Gilbert and Jose to return to the basement.

In the meantime, Vincent was out at the dogpen. The mass of food was dumped into the large pan for the Beagle Hounds. The four hungry beagles wasted no time shoving their heads down into the pan, sinking their strong teeth right into the oatmeal and molded cornbread. They growled and barked at one another. It was their own way of telling one another to stay at your end of the pan.

To this day, Vincent never knew how the beagles survived off leftover table scraps. No one ever fed them regular dog food. To avoid stepping in some of the moist defecation, Vincent circled the pen and jumped over a wooden board near the gate. Once the gate was locked, he went to the waterhose and sprayed the inside of the bucket. Anyone who

fed the dogs was required to spray out the remaining food particles that stuck to the sides and bottom of the bucket. Vincent returned to the kitchen, where Granny Dear was pulling a large pan of cornbread out of the oven. J.D. sat at the table sinking his teeth into a large bowl of turnip greens and sprinkling salt over them at the same time. Granny Dear placed a hot piece of buttered cornbread on a saucer and sat it right next to his bowl of greens. Vincent sat the slopbucket against the wall at the end of the sink.

"Dat bucket clane?" J.D. asked Vincent.

"Yes, the bucket's clean," Vincent answered submissively.

"Lemme see," J.D. requested, swinging his chair around to glance inside the bucket. "Why da hell you so wet?"

"Spraying out the bucket."

"Spaying out da bucket?"

"Yes, sir."

"Quit lying."

"The water from the hose made me wet."

"Ya shuddin git dat wet fum spaying out dat bucket," J.D. said. "Gone and git yo ass out of dis kitchen."

"Yes, sir."

Vincent returned to the basement. Gilbert and Jose were sitting on Vincent and Vernon's beds. They were trying to become more familiar with one another and their new foster home. The different physical appearances and personalities at the Willingham residence had them curious, somewhat timid.

"Can I ask you something, Vincent?" Gilbert said.

"Yes."

"What's wrong with Mrs. Willingham's leg?"

"What do you mean?"

"Why does she limp around like that?"

"I really don't know."

"You don't?"

"No," Vincent said. "I think she had a real bad accident when she was a little girl."

Jose now took command of the floor by asking some questions.

"What about that man named Junior?" Jose asked.

"What do you want to know?"

"Why does he stare for a real long time?"

"Junior is mentally retarded."

"He never blinks his eyes."

"No, he doesn't."

"Why does he repeat everything that someone says?"

"Again, because he's mentally retarded."

"Not all retarded people repeat everything."

"Junior can't help himself."

"Guess you're right."

"I've been living around him all of my life."

"That's really weird."

Gilbert took the floor back because he had more questions to ask Vincent.

"What's wrong with that man Braun?" Gilbert asked.

"What do you mean?"

"What's wrong with his teeth?"

"Braun eats cigarette butts."

"Cigarette butts?"

"Yes."

"You're lying."

"No, I'm not," Vincent said. "He eats out the tobacco part of cigarettes."

"That's some nasty shit!" Gilbert snarled, frowning strongly from the thought of it.

"Real nasty."

"It looks like he ate a lot of black jellybeans," Gilbert joked.

"Or drunk a gallon of black motor oil," Vincent added.

"Maybe even smeared tar all over his teeth."

They found ways to joke about Braun's badly rotten teeth.
But in reality, it wasn't no joke, because that type of poor
dental hygiene led to diseases of the gum and other parts of
the mouth.

"Does he ever brush his teeth?"

"I don't think so."

"Why does he beat the middle of his hand?" Gilbert asked,
then staring at both of his palms.

"Like Junior, Braun is mentally retarded."

"Where did he get that wire from?"

"He's got a drawer full of those wires."

"I know it probably hurts everytime he pounds that wire
up against his hand."

"He's used to it by now."

"Where does he find them?"

"In the trash, after Mrs. Willingham throws hangers away."

"He rips them apart and makes them into wires?"

"Yes."

Jose began to ask questions now that the room became
momentarily silent.

"Why does this foster home have handicapped people?"

"I don't know," Vincent answered.

"When I was in the last foster home, they never had handicapped people."

"Really?"

"Our foster mother wanted to bring retarded people
there and the family services people wouldn't let her."

The noise from the squeaky hinges on the basement
door revealed that someone was coming down the stairs. The
sounds of two sets of footsteps carried into the basement. J.D.
and Braun were walking through the laundry room. They
were on their way to the backyard. Vincent warned Gilbert
and Jose to never sit on the bed. J.D. would never hesitate
cursing them or beating on them.

J.D. and Braun brought two boxsprings, mattresses, and

bed frames into the basement. They were ready to assemble two beds for Gilbert and Jose. Gilbert displayed a slight frown on his face. The yellow and brown discolorations on the boxsprings and mattresses indicated that urine and defecation had dried on the surface and wasn't removed. The bed parts were absolutely unsanitary! After J.D. hammered the steel frames into place, Braun lifted the boxspring and mattresses on top. J.D. informed Gilbert and Jose to get bed linen from Bessie Mae. When J.D. and Braun returned upstairs, Gilbert and Jose stepped over to the beds they would have to sleep on. Gilbert wasn't too enthused about his upcoming sleeping arrangements.

"Do we have to sleep on those beds?" Gilbert croaked to Vincent, glancing strongly at the rings of dark yellow urine and small patches of brown human defecation.

"Yes," Vincent told Gilbert, straightforwardly.

"Why?"

"Everybody in this house sleep on beds like these."

"But they're nasty."

"I know."

"Everybody does?"

"Sure do."

"Does Mr. and Mrs. Willingham have to sleep on beds like these?"

"Maybe not them."

"I bet their beds don't have shit and piss stains on them."

"You're probably right."

Gilbert used one of his shoes to try and brush off a patch of dried defecation waste. He openly expressed his views about his unsanitary surroundings. He circled the room with his weary eyes and discovered yet another filthy sight.

"Where did all those roaches come from?"

"They're all over this house," Vincent explained.

"Do they crawl into your bed at night?"

"Sometimes," Vincent admitted.

"There must be a thousand of them on that wall."

"Probably so."

"Do they ever spray?"

"Spray?"

"You know, exterminate."

"Sometimes."

"Well, they need to do it again, soon."

"You're right."

Jose had his eyes planted on the mattress to the bed where he was to sleep.

"What about those spit stains?"

"What spit stains?" Vincent asked.

"Right there," Jose pointed.

"I see it now."

"It's got yellow snot stains, too."

Jose noticed the thick saliva and dried yellow mucous at the head of the mattress.

"We never had beds like these at my other foster home."

"Really?" Vincent said.

"They were cleaner."

"I'll bet they were."

Gilbert and Jose resented the fact that the Willinghams gave them filthy beds to sleep on. Where in Heaven's name did Bessie Mae and J.D. find those boxsprings and mattresses? Did they go to the worst rummage sale or garage sales to find them? Bums out on the street slept on better boxsprings and mattresses. For Gilbert and Jose, it had been a day filled with surprises, a day of being initiated into a new foster home. In an almost loud and passionate voice, Vincent was telling them, *"Gilbert Curry and Jose Underwood, welcome to a foster home that is full of irregularities!"*

Chapter 18

IN-HOUSE DESTRUCTION

VINCENT WAS HAPPY to have Gilbert and Jose as new foster brothers. Every since he went to the drive-in to see *"The Exorcist"*, he slept with the lights on for several weeks, wishing he had someone besides himself to keep him occupied in that dark and creepy basement. Thoughts of green vomit being shot out of a demon-possessed girl's mouth, crept into his sleep almost every night.

Since Vernon rarely stayed at home, Gilbert and Jose's company was much appreciated. Several months passed and they were still trying to adjust to their relatively new foster home. Living around handicapped men and new foster parents wasn't an easy adjustment.

The rain pounded hard against the windows above the beds of Gilbert and Jose. Their bellies were filled with the fried chicken and spaghetti that Bessie Mae and Granny Dear cooked especially for J.D. Jose lied across his bed comfortably. Gilbert circled the floor, passing gas and popping his knuckles. Vincent sat quietly in the middle of his bed with his legs crossed.

"I'm bored," said Vincent. "I'm bored, I'm full, and I want something fun to do."

"I'm bored, too," Gilbert agreed.

"You need to stop farting."

"Why?"

"You're stinking up the whole room."

"I can't help it."

"Yes, you can."

"No, I can't."

"You've got it smelling like spoiled spaghetti in here."

"Sorry," Gilbert apologized.

"I'll bet you are," Vincent said, covering his nose to avoid the foul smell.

The room became quiet and the only sound heard was farts coming from the end of the room where Gilbert was. The rain pounded even harder, with high winds whistling between the window seals. Gilbert snapped his finger and ran to the middle of the room.

"That's it!"

"What's it?" Vincent asked.

"I just thought of something."

"What?"

"Something that we used to do at one of my other foster homes."

"What's that?"

"Ready for this?"

"Yes."

"We used to have what was called 'throwing fights'," Gilbert explained to Vincent and Jose. He was excited like a bolt of lightning had just hit him.

"Throwing fights?"

"Yeah."

"What are throwing fights?"

"It's a game where everybody throw things at one another."

"What kind of things?" Jose asked.

"Socks, shoes, cups, rocks, books, newspapers, pennies, nickels, or anything that you could find."

"Where would you be when this throwing fight was going on?"

"We'd hide behind our beds."

"But you're not in that other foster home," Vincent reminded Gilbert.

"I know."

"It's scary to think about doing something like that."

"I just wanna have some fun."

"What if Mr. Willingham caught us?"

"He won't."

"That fat, black niggah might bring his bald-headed ass down here and beat the skin off us." Vincent knew more about J.D.'s beatings than anyone in the Willingham residence. His disciplinary actions weren't nice at all.

"Somebody should go upstairs and check to see if Mr. and Mrs. Willingham are up there," Gilbert suggested.

"Good idea."

Gilbert and Jose waited patiently while Vincent went upstairs to look around. He walked into the dining room. There was no one left at the dinnertable. Inside the kitchen, Granny Dear was storing more leftovers in the refrigerator. Once she placed all the bowls inside, she rolled back into her room to watch television. Vincent went halfway up the stairs leading to the second floor. The Willingham's door was closed and padlocked. A good sign for Gilbert, Jose, and Vincent. This simply told Vincent that Bessie Mae and J.D. weren't present in the home.

Braun was in his room beating his hand and talking to himself. Junior stared at the wall straight ahead. He listened to Braun tell him stories about Joe Louis, "The Brown Bomber", and his life of growing up in St. Louis, Missouri. Braun may have been mentally retarded, but he still recalled some of his childhood memories.

Vincent returned to the basement to inform Gilbert and Jose that Bessie Mae and J.D. were gone.

"What if Vernon came down here?" Jose asked.

"He's not going to say nothing," Vincent assured Jose.

"Are you sure?" Gilbert asked.

"Yes, I'm sure."

"Vernon's not a snitch?"

"No way," Vincent said. "He hates Mr. Willingham."

They started collecting objects for their upcoming *throwing fight*. Gilbert believed that plastic cups from the kitchen would serve as the perfect ammunition. Vincent warned him about the supersonic ears that Granny Dear had. He tiptoed into the kitchen and pulled out six plastic cups from the cabinets. Vincent and Jose searched the room for anything that could be used for ammunition. The various size schoolbooks, dirty socks from the laundry room, chips of plaster from the wall, large wingtip shoes from a closet near Vincent's bed, empty soda cans from the trashbarrel in Sean's room, pennies scattered all over the floor, sections of old newspapers, and an old rusty antenna, were collected from inside their room.

Gilbert returned from the kitchen with the plastic cups. Vincent and Jose had already gathered their ammunition. While Gilbert collected the rest of his ammunition, they pulled their beds away from the wall. Respectively, Vincent and Jose's beds were positioned at the east and west ends of the room.

Behind Vincent's bed, there were four black wingtip shoes, two chunks of large plaster, his English and math textbooks, eight pennies, three crusty tube socks, and ten pieces of balled up newspaper. Behind Jose's bed, there were two brown wingtip shoes, three mashed up soda cans, five blue dress socks, six dingy tube socks, ten pennies, and a large red dictionary that was falling apart from the cover.

Gilbert managed to collect five pieces of small plaster, three dress socks, his social studies and math textbooks, seven pennies, eleven balled up pieces of paper, one black wingtip shoe, and the rusty antenna. He had his bed positioned at the far north end of the room.

Actually, neither one of them knew what the other person had. Gilbert, Jose, and Vincent hid behind their beds. They were apprehensive about making any sudden moves. Gilbert raised his head slightly above his bed with the only

shoe cocked in his left hand. Jose gradually moved his upper body above his bed. The large dictionary was cuffed under his right arm. They hastily exchanged fire and ducked to the floor. No one made contact.

Gilbert and Jose were preparing for another round and Vincent was behind his bed trying to gain enough courage to raise up and strike one of them. He held on tightly to one of the shoes. Gilbert grabbed the social studies textbook. Surprisingly, Gilbert and Vincent rose at the same time. Their arms were drawn back far. Their hands trembled with the textbook and the shoe.

Vincent hesitated to throw. Gilbert hesitated to throw. Silently, they called one another's bluff. Who would make the first move? They fired at one another and no contact was made. In the wall facing Vincent's bed, a small hole was made from the impact of the textbook. The thin plaster was easily penetrated. As a result of the accident, Vincent had chunks of plaster to use as ammunition, not to mention the textbook that Gilbert had thrown.

Gilbert took all of the pennies and balled them up in his hand. Vincent already had two chunks of plaster in his hand. Jose also held all the pennies he had in a tight fist. All three came up at the same time, throwing their ammunition as quickly as possible. Pennies and plaster were flying all through the air! The pennies thrown by Gilbert struck Vincent on the right cheek and in the middle of his forehead. Vincent struck Jose in the chest with a chunk of plaster. None of the ammunition thrown touched Gilbert. The name of the game was: *Throw your objects and duck as quickly as possible.*

Vincent sat on the floor massaging his cheek and forehead. The stinging sensation set in strongly. Jose pampered the middle of his chest with both hands. Gilbert had built up much confidence. He had scored and wasn't hit in the process. He decided to try and use two plastic cups, holding one

in each hand. Jose reached for two flat soda cans, pressing them firmly between his thumbs and forefingers. Vincent felt that a wingtip shoe would be appropriate ammunition.

From under their beds, they studied one another's leg movements. Like three enemies fighting in the same war, they jumped up at the same time. Their arms were cocked with shoes, cups, and cans. The challenge was on.

"Go ahead," Gilbert said, daring Vincent and staring fiercely with the plastic cups.

"You go ahead," Vincent objected, ready to fire the shoe his direction.

"No, you go ahead."

"Throw yours, first."

"No, throw yours."

"I'll throw mine's when you throw your's."

"I'm not stupid."

"Yes, you are."

"We'll see about that."

At the same time, Gilbert, Jose, and Vincent fired both shoes, cups, and cans at one another. Since Gilbert and Jose aimed in the direction of Vincent, he was hit with the cups and soda cans across the arms and chest. Jose was struck with one of the shoes on the right shoulder blade. As for Gilbert, he didn't even receive a graze anywhere on his body. 'MR. UNTOUCHABLE' he had become. He must've known the game very well.

The sounds of the squeaky hinges on the basement door traveled down into the basement. The door opened and all three waited to see who might have been coming towards their room. They could only pray that it wasn't J.D. Gilbert threw up a hand signal for Vincent and Jose to cease from throwing any more objects. They didn't hear any footsteps or see any shadows reflecting off the laundry room wall.

"What yall down dere doing?" Granny Dear asked, her wheelchair parked at the top of the basement stairs.

"Nothing," Gilbert answered timidly, his arm suspended in the air, indicating for Vincent and Jose to remain silent.

"Yall down dere making a whole lotta racket."

"We're not doing anything wrong, Granny Dear."

"Yall betta be quiet down dere."

"Yes, mam."

"I'm gone send J.D. down dere afta yall," Granny Dear warned them.

"We're sorry for making a lot of noise."

"Yall know J.D. will come down dere and beat da skin off yall's hides."

"Yes, mam."

Granny Dear rolled her wheelchair back into the kitchen. She was no fool. Her room was not too far above their room. She could hear the objects pounding on the walls. Despite her objections, they resumed their throwing escapades.

Vincent wanted to use some lighter ammunition, so she reached for the socks. Jose reached for one of the shoes thrown his direction. Gilbert switched ammunition by reaching for the long antenna. This antenna had been broken off one of Bessie Mae's old Cadillacs and left in the closet with a lot of other junk. They rose up and down, trying to study one another's moves. Jose stood up with the shoe cocked in his right hand. Gilbert stood up with the antenna cocked in his left hand. There was no bluffing this time around. They quickly discharged their ammunition. Gilbert threw the antenna like a javelin competitor in the olympics. Jose threw the shoe like a quarterback making a touchdown pass to his receiver.

The exchange of fire was ugly! First, the sharp end of the antenna stuck directly into the middle of Jose's forehead, deeply piercing the skin and causing blood to rush down his forehead. The shoe made a large hole in the wall behind Gilbert's bed. Gilbert and Vincent came to Jose's rescue.

"Take your hand off your forehead," Gilbert told Jose, grabbing him around the wrist.

"I can't, it's bleeding!" Jose cried, bending his head forward as a stream of blood trickled between his fingers.

"Let's see where the antenna stuck you."

"No!"

"Let me see."

"I told you, it's bleeding!" Jose shouted, rocking his head back and forth, blood now dripping onto the floor.

"Let me see how bad it is."

"No!"

"Come on, Jose."

Gilbert desperately wanted to see how much damage the antenna had done.

"Get away from me!" Jose snapped. "It's your fucking fault!"

Jose removed both hands to show Gilbert and Vincent the minor laceration that was slightly below his hairline. They escorted him into the bathroom that was on the other side of Sean's room. They placed a cold washcloth on the cut and held it strongly up to his head. There was a bottle of alcohol in the medicine chest above the sink. Gilbert saturated part of the washcloth with some of the alcohol and placed it back on his forehead. A big circle of blood appeared on the washcloth. Sean rose out of his seat and asked, "He alright?"

"Yeah, I think he's going to be alright," Gilbert said.

"What happened?"

"We were having a throwing fight and an accident happened."

"What's a throwing fight?" Sean asked.

"It's something that we used to do at one of my other foster homes."

"That's where all that noise was coming from?"

"Yeah."

Gilbert instructed Jose to continue holding the washcloth in place, applying as much pressure as possible. He wasn't a paramedic, but he knew that in order to stop the

bleeding, the cut had to be pressed upon. Their room was a total disaster! Surrounding the entire floor were every object that they had thrown or had collected.

"We're in trouble," Gilbert said.

"Why?" Vincent asked.

"Look at this mess."

"If Mr. Willingham came down here and saw all this shit on the floor, he'd beat the color off our black asses." Vincent and his two foster brothers had something to really worry about.

"The floor?" Gilbert wailed. "What if he see those holes that we put in the walls?"

"We've got to find something to cover them up."

"With what?"

"Something."

"But, what?"

"We've got to hurry up!"

"We need to think of something."

Gilbert, Jose, and Vincent were in a state of panic. Time was quickly ticking away and they had to think of something. They searched the room for anything to cover up the holes. With the washcloth pressed to his forehead, Jose paced the floor, picking up most objects that were thrown at him and around him. There was an old stack of newspapers that Vincent had used to cover the top of his sheets. They were used as part of his *bedwetting preventive method.* Gilbert felt that newspaper was too thin and J.D. would raise issues about it.

"What about pages from your social studies book?" Vincent suggested to Gilbert.

"Are you crazy!" Gilbert said.

"What about pages from my English book?"

"No way!"

"What about pages from that dictionary?"

"Forget about it, Vincent."

Gilbert disapproved of every idea that Vincent presented.

Pages from their school textbooks would cause Bessie Mae or J.D. to rip them off. Gilbert decided to ramble inside the same closet that they found the shoes in. Inside a large box in the very back, there were old dusty stacks of *Ebony* and *Jet* magazines.

An early nineteen sixties issue of *Ebony*, which had a glamour shot of the astonishingly beautiful actress Dorothy Dandridge on the cover, was surprisingly at the top of the stack. Gilbert wasted no time pulling the magazines out. While he flipped through the inside pages, Jose and Vincent formed a close-knit circle around him. There was a treat for their eyes on that front cover.

"Boy!" Vincent said, greatly admiring the awesome beauty of Dorothy Dandridge. "She looks real, real good."

"Who is she?" Gilbert asked.

"She's the lady who plays in movies," Vincent told Gilbert, studying her alluring good looks.

"What movies?"

"I can't remember the names."

"She's beautiful!"

"She can sing good, too."

"I wish she was my girlfriend."

"Mine's, too."

Dorothy Dandridge was definitely one beautiful black woman! Gilbert, Jose, and Vincent just couldn't take their eyes off the gorgeous actress with flawless, cocoa brown skin, pearly white teeth that were perfectly straight, silky black hair that was styled to perfection, and a figure that would make a man's heart drop to the bottom of his feet.

"We could use these pictures to cover up the holes," Gilbert suggested.

"Good idea!" Vincent agreed strongly.

"Let's start putting them on the walls."

"We better hurry."

Vincent and Gilbert tore off the front cover and the pages

inside. They used some of J.D.'s electrical tape that had been stored in the closet.

*   *   *

Bessie Mae and J.D were coming through the front door with sacks from "Sears and Roebucks". The heavy thunderstorms had them shaking water from their matching raincoats. As they traveled into the kitchen, trails of water were left on the carpet. Granny Dear was sitting at the edge of her wheelchair. A concerned look was marked across her aged face. Bessie Mae and J.D. stepped over to the kitchen table and placed the wet sacks aside, then dropping their drenched raincoats on the back of the chairs. They took a seat and fired up a Pall Mall Gold and a Pall Mall Red. Within minutes, the entire kitchen was congested with smoke. Bessie Mae noticed the strange attitude that Granny Dear conveyed. "Everything okay, Granny Dear?"

"Naw."

"What's wrong?"

"I thank dey down in da basement tearing thangs up."

"Tearing things up?"

"Yep."

"How?"

"I thank dey throwin thangs ginst da walls."

"You could hear it from up here?"

"Dey was making a whole lotta racket down dere."

Bessie Mae and J.D. suspected that Gilbert, Jose, and Vincent were downstairs doing something wrong. For J.D., a trip down to the basement sounded like a good idea. The basement door opened, the wood-rotted stairs squeaked, and the sounds of heavy breathing and strong footsteps, all carried into the lower portion of the basement. Gilbert, Jose, and Vincent dashed towards their beds. They straightened every wrinkle and bump on the covers of their beds. Gilbert

and Vincent opened their social studies and English text-books and sat at the edge of their beds. Jose sat on his bed with the washcloth pressed to his forehead.

J.D. made his entry and glanced around the room. The room was perfectly straight. The floor was spotless and the walls had the striking pictures of Dorothy Dandridge taped neatly over the holes. J.D. walked over to the side of the room where Vincent slept with his long brown extension cord clutched in his left hand. He bent forward to glance at the cover of the *Ebony* magazine.

The breathtaking beauty of Dorothy Dandridge had him wishing he could stand in the same room with a woman of her calibre. But what would she want with someone as poor and as black as J.D.? Dream on J.D. Willingham, dream on. J.D. strutted from one side of the room to the other. Gilbert, Jose, and Vincent remained in awe as he inspected their room. Their young hearts pumped with sheer nervousness as he kept his eyes planted on the pictures on the wall.

"Ganny Dear tells ma and Bessa Mae dat yall down here making a whole lotta racket," J.D. said, confronting all three of them.

"We weren't making any noises," Gilbert spoke courageously, closing his social studies book and raising up off his bed.

"Ganny Dear say yall down here throwin thangs ginst da walls."

"We weren't throwing things."

"You callin Ganny Dear a liar?"

"No, sir."

"Den what yall down here doing?"

"We weren't doing anything."

"Don't lie to ma, boy!"

"I'm not lying."

"Don't make ma use my stanching code."

"Yes, sir."

Gilbert, Jose, and Vincent knew that J.D. wouldn't hesitate bringing his extension cord to the basement and start
whipping lots of ass. J.D. never questioned why Jose had the
cloth pressed to his forehead. Vincent knew to be afraid.
Actually, all three of them were afraid. When J.D. left the
basement, they released a wind of relief.

Book II

Do not go where the path may lead, go where there is no path and leave a trail

—Les Brown

Chapter 19

OPPOSITION

THE BRIGHT SUN beamed through a window in the kitchen and down onto the table, where Granny Dear sat in her wheelchair dicing up a large white onion. A large pot of pig feet and pig ears was on the back of the stove boiling. An even larger pot of stew was simmering on the front of the stove. Steam from both pots jetted from under the tops and into the kitchen atmosphere, causing an almost unbearable humidity.

Bessie Mae sat next to Granny Dear dicing up a large bell pepper. She removed the top from the pot of pig feet and pig ears and dumped the onions and peppers inside. They floated around the top, sending an aroma into the air that smelled like freshly cooked pig stock. Bessie Mae knew that dinner wasn't far away, so she limped over to the cabinets and brought out the bowls and plates. Granny Dear searched the refrigerator for more leftovers. She found a large bowl of week-old great northern beans.

"Bessie Mae, we should woam dese beans up fo dinna," Granny Dear suggested, rolling her wheelchair from around the refrigerator door and showing Bessie Mae the bowl of beans.

"No," Bessie Mae disagreed, staring at the white mold that formed around the edge of the bowl. "Somebody could get sick if they ate some of those beans, Granny Dear."

"Dey look fine ta me."

"Those beans done spoiled," Bessie Mae said. "I don't have time to be running nobody to the hospital."

"What chu want ma ta do wit'em?"

"Get rid of them."

"You sho?"

"Definitely."

Bessie Mae placed the bowls and plates in the center of the table. Granny Dear rolled over to the slopbucket and dumped the beans inside. She wasn't too enthused. Being told to throw away leftovers from weeks ago was like telling Granny Dear to throw away a fortune in priceless treasures. Bessie Mae stirred the beef stew with her long handle spoon.

Gilbert, Jose, and Vincent rode their bicycles down the steep hill on the side of the house. Along with other neighborhood kids, they made loud horn noises, pretending as though their bicycles were eighteen wheeler trucks speeding down the highway. On the back of their bicycles, they had clothespins and playing cards attached to the side of the frame. The playing cards were clamped between the clothespin and they brushed against the spokes inside the wheels.

This was the era of experimenting with bicycles. Some kids had turned their bikes into choppers, placing car steering wheels up where the handlebars were, mounting mirrors with fur around the rim on the side of the handlebars, and some even had decorations around the spokes.

The beagle hounds were barking continuously inside their pen. The irritating noises traveled into the kitchen, causing Bessie Mae to limp over to the window facing the side of the house. While the children raced down the hill, Bessie Mae noticed the clothespins and playing cards on the back of their bicycles. She held a freshly lit Pall Mall Red close to the window screen.

"Hey, hey!" Bessie Mae bellowed. "Stop all that dam noise!"

The other children, who didn't belong in her foster home, looked up at the window and had an expression of: *You ain't none of my mamma and you can't tell me what to do.*

"Vincent was making all the noise, Mrs. Willingham," Gilbert snitched, pointing directly into the face of Vincent.

"No, I wasn't, Mrs. Willingham," Vincent spoke in his own defense, glancing up at the smoke-filled window, trying to see the face of Bessie Mae.

"Yes, you were."

"No, I wasn't."

"You know good and well you were."

"You know good and well I wasn't."

The other children stood in silence as they watched Gilbert and Vincent debate over who made the loudest noises. They got off their bikes and pushed down the kickstands. Bessie Mae sort of pressed her face against the screen.

"Shut up, before I make you all put those bikes up," Bessie Mae ordered. "Where did you all get those clothespin from?"

"We found them in the backyard," Gilbert answered truthfully.

"In the backyard?"

"Yes, mam."

"Where?"

"On the clothesline."

"Don't you know that I use those clothespins to hang clothes out to dry?"

"No, mam."

"Where did you get those cards from?"

"We found them in the dining room."

"Where, in the dining room?"

"On the China cabinet."

"Dammit!" Bessie Mae thumped. "Those are the cards that me and J.D. use to play card games with."

"I'm sorry, Mrs. Willingham."

"I should get J.D. to beat you all into a coma."

"We didn't know, Mrs. Willingham."

"Take my clothespins and cards off those bikes."

"Yes, mam."

"Right now!"

"Yes, mam."

Gilbert, Jose, and Vincent went around collecting all the clothespins and playing cards that they gave to other children to put on the back of their bicycles. Bessie Mae checked to see that the clothespins were still in good condition. She ordered Gilbert to clamp them back on the clothesline in the backyard. Since the playing cards were ruined from the friction against the metal spokes, she had Jose to throw them in the trash.

Matters calmed down and the children decided to have races going down the street. More than twelve bicycles were lined up at the top of the hill. Vincent gave the official announcement. They slammed their feet down onto the pedal of their three, five, and ten speeds. Gilbert, Jose, Vincent, and other kids from up the street and around the corner, were racing right beside one another. They laughed and shouted and tried bumping one another. Their legs pumped pure energy to try and win the race.

Bessie Mae stood in the same window in the kitchen. From the top of the hill to the bottom, she watched Gilbert, Jose, and Vincent use the bottom of their sneakers as brakes. The brake shoes on their bicycles were worn from constant friction against the front and back tires. The soles of their sneakers were already in bad condition. When they returned up the hill, Bessie Mae rudely got their attention.

"Hey!" she called abruptly. "When you wear out those sneakers, I'm not going to buy you all anymore."

"We weren't doing anything," Gilbert said, keeping both feet planted firmly on the concrete.

"You're lying, boy!" Bessie said strongly. "I'm sitting in this window watching you all stick your feet on those tires to stop the bicycle with. I don't care if you walk around barefoot."

"We already need a new pair of sneakers," Gilbert reminded Bessie Mae. "My toe is sticking through these old ones."

"Who's going to buy them?"

"I don't know."

Bessie Mae left the window to check on the pots. Gilbert, Jose, and Vincent were leaning against their bicycles as leverage to turn their sneakers upwards. There was much damage that had been done to the soles. Long tire tracks, starting from the toes to the very back, were engraved deep into the rubber of the sole.

Knowing that dinner was approaching, Bessie Mae limped back to the window to tell Gilbert, Jose, and Vincent to put their bicycles away and get washed up. They ran up on the porch, where Braun was beating the middle of his right hand with one of his long silver wires.

"Hey, hey, how'ya doing there, Vincent?" Braun said.

"I'm okay, Braun," Vincent answered in a childish fashion, still somewhat afraid of Braun after all those years of living with him.

"Hey, hey, what'cha doing there, Vincent?"

"I'm not doing anything, Braun," Vincent spoke cordially, watching the rhythm of Braun beating his hand.

"Okay, okay, you're doing nothing."

Braun may have been mentally retarded, but Vincent still considered him to be his elder.

Junior sat in one of the fold-up chairs staring directly at the houses across the street. As soon as they walked into the house, the intense aroma hit Gilbert. He sniffed his way towards the kitchen. The aroma smelled too familiar. Steam rushed across the stove and out the kitchen doorway.

"Whew!" Gilbert said, inhaling the scent from the kitchen. "That smells just like something that we used to eat at one of my other foster homes."

"There you go again," Vincent said.

"What?" Gilbert asked.

"You're always talking about your other foster homes."

"So what."

"What does it smell like?"

"It smells like pig feet and pig ears."

"Pig feet? Pig ears?" Vincent repeated, stepping around Gilbert to take a stronger sniff.

"Yeah!" Gilbert snorkled. "It's definitely pig feet and pig ears. My foster mothers at the last two foster homes used to cook them all the time."

"I don't know what it is, but we'll find out at dinnertime."

Gilbert grabbed the keys to the toolshed. Along with his own bicycle, he volunteered to put Jose and Vincent's bicycles inside. Inside the compacted toolshed, he pushed aside J.D.'s tools and the lawnmower to find room for all three bicycles. In the far right corner, the scratching of a shovel surface and low squealing noises indicated that something was trying to crawl it's way out of the toolshed. Suddenly, Gilbert became frightened. He rolled his bicycle halfway out of the shed.

From behind a group of shovels and the wide lawnmower, two large rats jumped out. Gilbert quickly dropped his bicycle, jumped over the other two bicycles, and raced for the middle of the backyard. His heart pounded with pure fear! He stood hysterically in the grass holding the middle of his chest.

"Whoa!" Gilbert said to himself, shivering and stepping further away from the toolshed. "That's the biggest dam rat that I've ever seen in my life. That sucker had teeth and a tail like a beaver."

Once he gained enough courage to throw the bicycles inside, he rushed into the house to tell Jose and Vincent. Vincent listened to the description that Gilbert gave of the large rats. He gave him some advice for future occurrences.

"Hee! Hee!" Vincent chuckled, but turning to a more serious demeanor. "Those rats that you saw in the toolshed?"

"Yeah," Gilbert said.

"They're not the only ones."

"You're lying!" Gilbert shook. "Are you saying that those weren't the only big rats running around out there?"

"There's a whole lot of them," Vincent validated. "They're in the backyard, on the sides of the house, and in front of the house."

"What about inside the house?" Gilbert asked frightfully.

"Yes, there are."

"You're lying!"

"No, I'm not."

"I'm scared."

"Granny Dear and Mrs. Willingham set up those big rat traps."

"How do they get into the house?"

"They dig tunnels."

"That's scary."

"Some are big and some are little. Some are brown and some are black."

"Boy!" Gilbert quivered. "I don't wanna go to sleep at night."

"You have to be careful."

"Why?"

"They'll bite you."

"Rats got rabies."

"And carry diseases, too."

With a long fork, Bessie Mae stood over the stove poking at the pig feet and pig ears. The sharp teeth of the fork easily pierced through the leathery skin, telling her that the ears and feet were tender enough for eating. She removed the top from the stew and a cloud of steam rushed into her face. Dinner was done and Bessie Mae was ready to service everyone.

"Braun! Junior!" Bessie Mae called from the edge of the stairs that led to the second floor. "You all come down here

and eat." She limped the opposite direction of the front room and opened the basement door.

"Gilbert! Jose! Vincent! Sean!" Bessie Mae yelled strongly, her voice traveling down the hollow stairs. "You all come on up here and eat."

Bessie Mae had a voice that traveled far. Simultaneously, everyone arrived at the kitchen doorway. Because they knew that they would be the first ones to eat, Braun and Junior stood at the front of the door. Vincent and Sean stood behind them, while Gilbert and Jose were in the very back. Braun stepped further into the kitchen while Granny Dear prepared his bowl.

"Git back, Brones!" Granny Dear hissed towards Braun, pausing from preparing a bowl of stew to tell him to step out of the kitchen. "You sho acking like you starving."

Granny Dear never hesitated to let someone know if they irritated her. If you were anxious about eating, then that was too bad.

"Okay, okay, I'll get back," Braun said, brushing against Junior to step on the other side of the door.

One by one, Granny Dear fed the three foster boys and the handicapped men, standing on her arthritis-stricken legs to prepare bowls of stew and plates of pig feet and pig ears. Everyone but Sean went to the table carrying the bowl in one hand and the plate in the other. Spills were made on the carpet. Who cared? Bessie Mae had the carpet cleaned every four months.

Everyone was assembled at the dinner table. Gilbert, Jose, and Vincent weren't too happy with this particular dinner. They liked the beef in the stew, but could do without the vegetables. They hated the large chunks of carrots, onions, and celery. Bessie Mae's motto was: *Eat and eat whatever I cook and keep eating until you can't eat no more.*

On the right side of the table, Sean allowed his paralyzed hand to rest in his lap. His strong teeth sunk into the skin of

a pig feet. Known as a man with a ferocious appetite, Braun left nothing but bristles on the feet and ears. He slurped quickly through his bowl of stew. Those badly decayed teeth went to work during meals.

After spending several minutes picking through their bowls of stew, Gilbert, Vincent, and Jose had placed the carrots, onions, and celery on the side of their plates. Their pig feet and pig ears became soggy and cold. Gilbert took his fork and poked through the thick leathery skin.

While Junior stared down at his bowl, he circled his spoon around the stew, never raising the spoon up to his mouth. The mild steam coated his eyes, which caused them to appear glossier. Granny Dear leaned forward in her wheelchair. From the end of the kitchen table, which was near the refrigerator, she closely watched Gilbert, Jose, and Vincent. In order to get a better view of the dining room, she rolled her wheelchair further away from the table.

"Git yall's feet off dem chair rinds," Granny Dear said directly to Gilbert, Jose, and Vincent.

"Our feet aren't on the chair rinds," Gilbert said, talking in a smartalecky tone.

"Boy, I'm sittin wight here looking at'cha."

"You just want something to fuss about."

"What chu say, boy?"

"Nothing."

"You smartin off at me?"

"No, mam."

"I'll git J.D. ta beat da skin off yo hide."

Gilbert, Jose, and Vincent immediately removed their feet from the wooden bars between the lower section of the chair. Resting your feet on that bar always irritated Granny Dear or Bessie Mae. Everyone at the dinnertable was eating at a moderate rate but Junior.

The front door opened softly, but was slammed hard enough to send vibrations into the den and dining room.

Someone burping and farting repeatedly carried into the dining room. The sound of a lunchbucket swinging could also be heard. Gilbert, Jose, and Vincent immediately sat up straight in their chairs. Their spoons were put into fast motion.

J.D. stepped into the dining room and stopped. Fearful expressions crept upon the faces of everyone at the table. When J.D. looked over at Junior, his eyes became red and watery, his black chapped lips puckered up like dried prunes, and whole upper-body began breathing out sheer cruelty.

"Eat yo muttapucking food, Joanyer!" J.D. growled ferociously, then stepping closer to the dinnertable. He had many threatening tactics to use on anyone.

"Eat the food! Eat the food!" Junior repeated sadly, nodding his head and shoving his spoon down into the bowl of stew. He brought up big chunks of beef and vegetables.

"You can eat fasta dan dat, Joanyer!"

"Eat faster than that, Junior! Eat faster than that, Junior!"

"Blow yo goddam food, Joanyer!" J.D. snarled furiously, unbuckling his belt and jerking it from around his waist.

"Blow your food, Junior! Blow your food, Junior!"

"I'll beat yo muttapucking ass if ya don't eat fasta, Joanyer!"

"Eat faster, Junior! Eat faster, Junior!"

Junior did have a problem with blowing hot food before putting it into his mouth. But the man simply couldn't help himself. Even a mentally retarded person like Junior had feelings. J.D. didn't care if he had insulted him or not. Once again, someone had fallen victim to the insensitivity of J.D. He left the dining room and was greeted with royalty inside the kitchen. Gilbert, Jose, and Vincent were all looking around at one another. They moved their chairs closer to one another.

"What does muttapucking mean?" Gilbert asked, whispering over to Vincent and cautiously watching the kitchen door.

"It's that 'MF' word that people say," Vincent answered softly.

"What '*MF*' word?"

"Motherfucking," Vincent said, his voice as low as possible. He also watched the kitchen door with caution.

"Oh!" Gilbert said. "You're saying that Mr. Willingham was trying to say '*motherfucking*'?"

"Yeah."

"But instead he said something stupid like, '*muttapucking*?"

"Exactly."

"Can't he even curse the correct way?"

"No."

"I knew he was a dumb, black fool."

"And ugly, too," Vincent added.

Sean continued sucking the meat off the pig feet and pig ears. He made good use of the hand that was available. Inside the kitchen, Bessie Mae was preparing J.D.'s dinner. A large bottle of Louisiana hotsauce, a salt and pepper shaker, and fresh chopped onions, were all placed on the side of his bowl and plate. J.D. sprinkled nearly one-third of the hotsauce into his plate. The pig feet and pig ears looked like they were bleeding. It wasn't uncommon for him to shake lots of salt and pepper on his meals. The Willinghams knew that these were true blood pressure elevators.

"How was your day, J.D.?" Bessie Mae asked, sliding her pack of cigarettes across the table.

"Alwight, I guess," J.D. answered low-spirited, sucking on those feet and ears like a vacuum cleaner sucking up dirt. Hotsauce dripped down his chin. His bottom lip looked like it was bleeding.

"What's wrong, J.D.?" Bessie Mae questioned, firing up one of her Pall Mall Reds.

"It's dose white folks."

"What did they do?"

"Dey working my black ass lack a slave."

"Why do you feel like that?"

"Dey do."

"There's a reason you feel like that."

"Dose white boys get da easy work."

"They do?"

"Dey make all da black folks do da hard thangs."

"Like what?"

"We walk in mo tar dan dem white boys."

"Oh, really?"

"I git tired of steppin in all dat goddam tar!"

"I know what you're saying, baby."

"My goddam feet be burning."

"Do you ever tell your supervisor about it?"

"My who?"

"Your boss."

"I sho be wanting ta tell dose white folks bout deyself."

"That's how most jobs are," Bessie Mae said. "They work the colored folks like dogs and give the white people the easy jobs. The white folks always get paid more money and the first ones to get promotions."

"Dey sho do," J.D. agreed, gulping down a spoonful of stew.

"Just don't make no sense."

"Colored folks ain't got nuff sense ta set dem white folks straight."

"Hah! Hah!" Bessie Mae giggled. "We're running this home here and ain't no white person gonna come here and tell us what to do. I wish one of those white persons at The Department of Children and Family Services would come here and tell us what to do." Bessie Mae felt that she had *bragging rights.* She felt threatened by no one. Maybe it would have been good if some decent white person from the family services did come to their home to see how they operated things. As he sucked strongly on a pig ear, J.D. encountered another bitter memory about his turbulent past in Clarksdale,

Mississippi. The extremely racist whites were always saying or doing something to destroy his self-esteem:

"Ain't you got enough sense to follow simple instructions, boy!" a racist cottonfield owner asked a young J.D.

"Yes suh, yes suh, I do as I told, sir," J.D. said, lifting a large bale of cotton and then throwing it up on a large wagon.

"It's dumb niggers like you who give all of your people a bad name."

"I git to it, suh. I'm gone git to it, suh."

"Didn't yo mammy send you to school, boy?"

"No, suh, my mammy sent ma ta work in da fields when I was a youngen."

"Well, well, I knew that's all a dumb nigger like you would be good for."

"Yes suh, I'm a good nigger."

*   *   *

J.D. would always resent the fact that he never received an education and would have to obey the commands of the white man. Sometimes Bessie Mae felt that if he stopped his complaining about how vicious the nature of the white man was, and took some classes on how to read and write, maybe even learn math, he could get further than he already was. What if every black in America blamed the white man for every single one of their problems? There probably wouldn't be any progressive blacks in America.

Granny Dear sat at the opposite end of the kitchen table staring into the dining room. She was on another one of her watchful missions. Her wheelchair moved away from the table.

"Git yall's feet off dem chair rinds," she reminded Gilbert, Jose, and Vincent a second time, grabbing the spokes on the wheels to guide herself towards the kitchen door. She

became frustrated after seeing their feet resting on those wooden bars. According to Granny Dear, chairs were easily worn down when shoes rested on those bars. They quickly removed their feet and placed them in front of the table. Surprisingly, Bessie Mae or J.D. never responded to the complaint made by Granny Dear. Everyone sat at the table trying to finish their meals. Junior was barely eating. Granny Dear noticed from inside the kitchen. She, too, made sure that the humble, mentally retarded man ate his food at a moderate rate.

"Eat yo food, Joanyer!" Granny Dear shouted.

J.D. stopped eating, because he couldn't imagine that Junior wasn't eating.

"Eat the food! Eat the food!" Junior repeated quickly.

"Put dat spoon in yo mouth, Joanyer!"

"Put spoon in mouth! Put spoon in mouth!"

"You eating too slow, Joanyer!"

"Eating too slow! Eating too slow!" Junior said, nodding his head and scooping up large helpings of the stew. Did Junior have to eat at a certain pace? Why did they rush him through his meals?

Braun's bowl and plate were almost empty. Judging by the way he was putting the finishing touches on the stew, he appeared to want more. From all the hard manual labor that he performed around the house, his appetite stayed strong. There were times when Bessie Mae allowed him to have seconds and thirds, depending on how much food was left.

Vincent wanted to get rid of his pig feet and pig ears. Since the plate and bowl near Braun was empty, he contemplated on dumping his food onto the empty stoneware. A plan such as this one had to be executed precisely. Vincent felt it was a time of desperation. To make sure Granny Dear wasn't watching, he stood up and leaned towards the kitchen door. Her attention was directed towards her bowl of stew. With much discrection, he picked his plate up off the table

and dumped the pig feet and pig ears onto Braun's plate. Braun surely didn't mind. This wasn't the first time someone dumped food onto his plate. Gilbert and Jose glanced at Vincent. Their faces wore an envious expression. They also wanted to get rid of their pig feet and pig ears. Vincent was sympathetic to their needs. Provided that he sat next to Braun, he agreed to help by having them slide their plates down the table. It would be risky! Gilbert and Jose sat towards the end of the table, which was facing the kitchen. Both plates were slid down to Vincent and dumped onto Braun's plate.

Granny Dear saw nothing. Two empty plates missing from in front of Gilbert and Jose worried Vincent. Wouldn't it seem odd to anyone passing through the dining room? Since Granny Dear wasn't watching, he slid the plates back to Gilbert and Jose. Broth from both plates spilled on the snow white tablecloth. What if Bessie Mae saw the brown stains on the tablecloth? She had a license to be a *bitch!* Bessie Mae *bitched* about this! Bessie Mae *bitched* about that!

Gilbert and Jose felt that Vincent deserved a medal of honor for such bravery. Braun's plate was filled to capacity. Pig feet and pig ears were stacked on top of one another. It appeared that he almost had a whole pig to tackle. Sean finished his meal and took his plate and bowl inside the kitchen.

Brmmmmp! Brmmmmp! Loud gaseous noises came from the chair where Jose was sitting. Gilbert and Jose immediately stopped eating. Their angry faces glanced in the direction where Jose was sitting. In an upright position, Jose had his ass turned up. He had just released a couple of strong farts. He waved his left hand down by his rear end, wanting others at the table to smell his gas. Gilbert and Vincent became highly upset. The foul odor from Jose passing gas surrounded the table. They covered their noses and moved their chairs away from the table. Jose sat in his chair laughing. Someone needed to teach him some etiquette.

"Boy, you stink!" Gilbert reciprocated. "If you had to fart, you should've left the table." He began scooting his chair further away from Jose.

"You can't talk about me," Jose charged. "You fart all the time."

"I don't be farting at the dinnertable."

"What's wrong with that?"

"It's nasty."

"You can't smell my farts."

"Yes, I can."

"I don't smell nothing."

"Everybody's farts stink."

"Not mine's."

"You fanned your's so everybody could smell it."

"I couldn't hold it."

"Yes, you could."

"You're lying, punk!"

"No I'm not, punk!"

"Your mamma's a punk!"

"Your daddy's a punk!"

Once their voices rose to higher levels, the altercation between Gilbert and Jose proceeded into the kitchen. Bessie Mae limped out of the kitchen and straight into the dining room. Gilbert and Jose were exchanging bad words and spitting in one another's faces.

"What the hell are you all in here doing?" Bessie Mae asked.

"Jose farted at the table," Gilbert responded. "He fanned it so everybody at the table could smell it."

"No, I didn't."

"Yes, you did."

Bessie Mae jumped in and shouted, "Shut up, the both of you!" She moved closer to the dinnertable. For a few seconds, she was dead silent. She stood over Jose with both hands

rested around her waist. "Did you sit at the table and pass gas?"

"No, mam," Jose said, a big lie scribbled all over his face.

Gilbert jumped back in and said, "He's lying, Mrs. Willingham. Vincent heard him fart and saw him fanning it over the table."

Bessie Mae limped around to the chair where Vincent was sitting. She stood over Vincent with her left hand wrapped around the back of the chair.

"Is Gilbert telling the truth, Vincent?" Bessie Mae questioned Vincent.

"Yes, mam," Vincent answered truthfully.

"Are you sure?"

"Yes, mam."

"Don't lie, now."

"I'm not lying."

Bessie Mae limped back over to the chair where Jose was sitting. She pointed right into Jose's face and shouted, "Get your ill-mannered ass away from this table!"

"Yes, mam," Jose replied sadly.

"You nasty bastard!"

"I'm sorry."

"Sorry's never good enough for somebody who breaks wind and laughs about it."

"I couldn't hold it."

"As a matter of fact, I want everybody to get up from the table when you're finished eating."

Everyone walked into the kitchen carrying their bowls and plates. Junior was left at the table eating by himself, still trying to bite into the skin of the pig feet. Unlike the black and rotten teeth inside the disgusting mouth of Braun, Junior didn't have a single tooth in his mouth. A set of pinkish gums were the only tools used for eating.

While they stood around the slopbucket, Bessie Mae reminded Gilbert to feed the dogs. When J.D.'s plate became

empty, he departed from the kitchen. Junior remained at the table. He gnawed down on the same pig feet. A senselessly angry J.D. stopped at the seat next to Junior. His eyes became red. His lips puckered up. His heavy breathing became intense.

"Eat yo goddam food, Joanyer!" J.D. scorned, then unbuckling his wide black belt.

"Eat your food, Junior! Eat your food, Junior!" Junior whined, biting down harder into the pig feet.

J.D. stepped closer to Junior with the belt looped in his right hand. "You can eat fasta dan dat!"

"Eat faster than that! Eat faster than that!"

"Quit peating everythang I say."

"Quit repeating everything you say! Quit repeating everything you say!"

"Shut yo goddam mouth, Joanyer!"

"Shut the mouth! Shut the mouth!"

A few more bites and Junior was finished. J.D. pointed towards the kitchen while holding his belt tightly. "Now take yo pate in da kitchen."

"Take the plate in the kitchen! Take the plate in the kitchen!" Junior repeated as usual, staring at his plate and bowl without blinking.

J.D. watched Junior from behind. "And put yo goddam shirt tail in yo britches!"

"Put shirt tail in britches! Put shirt tail in britches!"

Where did it end? When did it end? For J.D. Willingham, everything had to be *goddam this* or *goddam that*. Didn't he know that taking God's name in vain was a sin? Why did eating slow and a person's shirt hanging over the back of their pants irritate J.D. to no apparent satisfaction?

The table was cleared and had to be wiped down. Granny Dear rolled into the dining room with a wet dishcloth and a small pan. She circled the table, wiping away the crumbs and scrubbing the cloth to lighten up some of the spills.

"Dey sho made a mess in here, Bessa Mae."

"They always make a mess in there."

"Not lack dis."

"Don't worry about it, Granny Dear."

"You gone need a new tablecloth."

"Probably so."

Granny Dear rolled back into the kitchen to dump the crumbs into the slopbucket. Like always, the slopbucket was nearly full.

"Somebody gone have ta feed dose dogs," Granny Dear told Bessie Mae.

"The bucket's full again?" Bessie Mae asked.

"Yep."

"Everybody's finished eating?"

"I thank so."

"Junior's finished eating?"

"Yep."

"I'll make sure somebody gets in here to feed the dogs."

Bessie Mae opened the basement door and shouted down the stairs. "Gilbert, come up here and feed the dogs!"

Gilbert came rushing up the basement stairs. The slopbucket was filled with chicken bones, grits, eggs, biscuits, macaroni and cheese, spoiled buttermilk, molded rice pudding, frozen okra, and the bristles from the pig feet and pig ears. Gilbert lifted the slopbucket off the floor and it was rather heavy. The beagle hounds were in for quite a treat.

A monopoly game that hadn't been used since Carmen moved out sat in a corner over by the china cabinet. It had collected much dust. Starting a game after he fed the dogs had crossed Gilbert's mind. Having those *throwing fights* had gotten old and much too risky.

Gilbert was out at the dogpen surrounded by a group of hungry hounds. He abruptly shook the food out of the bucket. Thoughts of those large rats that he saw earlier in the toolshed had crossed his mind. He wanted to get in and out of the dog

pen as quickly as possible. The rats had drilled tunnels around the dog pen and toolshed. They welcomed themselves to the food that the beagles left in the pan.

Gilbert wasn't aware of it, but there were many rats sticking their heads out of the tunnels. Surely, there were more bellies that craved the variety of slop from inside the Willingham residence. Gilbert rapidly left the pen and went to the waterhose on the side of the house. While spraying the bucket out, he noticed that the beagles were barking wildly. They occasionally fought over the food. But this time, they fought to keep the pack of rats from eating their meal. Four beagle hounds versus a band of large hungry rats.

This confrontation occurred almost on a daily basis. Bessie Mae had always talked about calling The City of Chicago, The Rodent Control Division, from the street sanitation department, wanting them to bring out bait to kill those disgusting rats. The fear of the beagles eating some of the poison put her plans off for a later date.

Gilbert came through the front room swinging the slopbucket. Vernon was sitting on the sofa with his arm wrapped around a very attractive young lady. With her long set of dark eyelashes, oval-shaped head, slim and curvy frame, and long dark hair, she reminded someone of a make-up or fashion model right out of *Ebony* or *Jet* magazines. Vernon sure had taste when it came to women.

They sat at the opposite end from where J.D. was. J.D. boiled over inside, because he knew that a handsome teen like Vernon was a true ladies man. Having a strikingly handsome foster son who could get practically any girl that he wanted, created a serious problem for him. Girls from everywhere flocked to Vernon. They were from his high school, the neighborhood, and some were from the church he attended.

Every since the dilemma surrounding the rape of Valerie, Vernon and J.D. didn't have much to say to one another.

Vernon even threatened to kill J.D. if he ever got out of line with him. They were like total strangers living under the same roof.

A very shook up Gilbert ran into Bessie Mae on his way into the kitchen. Water drops were all over his clothes. The bucket was cleaner than normal.

"Guess what I saw out at the dog pen?" Gilbert told Bessie Mae.

"What?" Bessie Mae asked.

"A whole bunch of rats."

"Really?"

"They were trying to eat the dog's food."

"Did they come out of those holes?"

"Yes, mam."

"Those rats were out there before we moved here."

"I've never seen rats that big before," Gilbert confessed. "When I was at those other foster homes, I never saw any rats." His flesh began to crawl from just thinking about the eery rodents.

"There's rat bigger than them," Bessie Mae said. "People are always talking about the rats here in Chicago. When I was in New York visiting one of my uncles, I saw a rat jump out of a dumpster that looked like a puppy."

"A puppy?" Gilbert fretted. "Do they get that big?"

"Yes, they get that big."

"I'm scared to feed the dogs now."

"Be careful!" Bessie Mae warned. "They'll bite you and give you rabies. Rats are some nasty son-of-a-guns."

Gilbert remembered the Monopoly game in the dining room. He anxiously wanted to get a game started. He went to the basement to encourage Jose and Vincent to join him in a game. They agreed and all three returned to the dining room.

"I sort of forgot how to play Monopoly," Jose told Gilbert.

"It's not hard to learn again," Gilbert assured his foster brother.

"I don't know, Gilbert," Jose hesitated.

"Come on, I can teach you again."

"Okay."

Gilbert grabbed the game and placed the board in the middle of the dining room table. Vincent took a seat in the chair that Braun normally occupied. Jose sat to his left and Gilbert sat to his right. Gilbert was placed in charge of handling the money. Vincent was in charge of the chance and community chest cards and Jose in charge of the real estate cards. Gilbert numerically counted the money and placed it neatly inside the slots. Now that the community chest and chance cards were placed on the board, they were ready to begin a game.

According to the rules, all three had to throw the dice to find out which order they would roll throughout the game. Gilbert threw the dice down on the board and came up with the lucky number of seven. Tapping the board lightly a couple of times, Jose rolled a ten. Rattling the dice in his right hand like a well-known gambler in a Las Vegas or Atlantic City casino, Vincent slammed the dice down on the board and came up with eight.

Because Jose was the first person to officially start the game, he grabbed the dice and threw them towards the center of the board. The small metal shoe was tapped on the board until he reached community chest. A twinkle came to his eyes when the card instructed him to pass GO and collect two-hundred dollars.

"That's just beginner's luck," Gilbert said, a sense of jealousy detected in his voice.

"So what," Jose boasted. "I've got two-hundred dollars added to my money."

"I bet you that I'll make more money than that."

"We'll see."

"Yeah, we'll see."

Vincent was getting the dice warmed up for his roll.

After hitting eleven, his small horse galloped down the board, landing on property that he wanted to purchase. The cost was reasonable, so he handed the money over to Gilbert.

"You can't buy any property until you pass GO," Gilbert explained, making his own rules since he was in charge of handling the money.

"You must be crazy," Vincent charged. "You don't have to pass GO to start buying property."

"No, you're the one who's crazy," Gilbert rebounded. "The rule book says that you have to pass GO at least one time before you start buying property."

"Forget the rule book," Vincent said. "I'm gonna buy some property and you can't stop me." He watched Carmen, Vernon, and others play Monopoly for years and took notes on how they played.

"Why don't you listen to me? Jose's the only one who can buy property."

"Why?" Vincent asked.

"Because he's already done passed GO."

"I don't care, I'm still gonna buy some property."

"You see!" Gilbert snuffed. "It's always punks like you messing up the game."

"Who are you calling a punk?"

"I'm calling you a punk," Gilbert acknowledged, sliding the money tray further away from the board.

"Your daddy's a punk!"

"Your mamma's a hoe!"

"You funny-nosed sissy."

"You pissy-peabody fag."

"That's why your mamma and daddy put you in all those foster homes," Vincent bantered, locking strong eye contact with Gilbert. He was greatly insulted by Gilbert's comment about his bed-wetting problem.

"How can you talk about me?" Gilbert snarled. "That's

why your mamma and daddy left you in this foster home, here, and never came back to get your half-white ass!"

"That's why you can't even comb your nappy hair."

"That's why you keep pissing in the bed."

Insult after insult, Gilbert and Vincent continued exchanging harsh words, mentioning things about each other's past and present. As a result of the arguing, Bessie Mae limped into the dining room. She stood at the opposite end of the dining room with a Pall Mall Red planted between her dark lips.

"What the hell are you all in here doing?" Bessie Mae asked, blowing a quick drag of smoke over the table.

"Gilbert called me a punk, Mrs. Willingham," Vincent said, then pointing to Gilbert, waving the cloud of smoke out of his face.

"No, I didn't, Mrs. Willingham," Gilbert falsified, turning to stare ferociously into the eyes of Vincent.

"Yes, you did!"

"No, I didn't."

"You're lying, Gilbert."

"You're the one who's lying, Vincent."

Bessie Mae couldn't stand to hear anymore shouting across the table. She limped further up towards Gilbert and Vincent. "Shut up! Both of you all!" she rudely interrupted them. "Don't let me send J.D. in here. Do you understand?"

"Yes, mam," answered Gilbert, Jose, and Vincent in a humble unison.

"He'll get his extension cord and beat the skin off your asses."

"Yes, mam."

Bessie Mae left the dining room and they resumed their game of Monopoly. Before Gilbert took his turn, Vincent agreed to not purchase any property before he passed GO. Gilbert rolled a five and handed the dice over to Jose. Jose rolled an even twelve, which took him on the other side of

the board. Gilbert, Jose, and Vincent viewed Monopoly as a game where the players wanted to become prosperous through owning property; therefore they all took the game very serious. Trying to accumulate as much property as possible required several trips around the board.

Vincent had hotels on Boardwalk and Park Place. Gilbert and Jose were especially afraid to land on his property. When it came time for Jose to roll, he juggled the dice, blew into his fist, and threw them down on the board. Much to his surprise, he landed on property that was one space over from Boardwalk. Jose rolled and came up with an even ten. With the money that had been accrued, he bought more property.

The dice were handed over to Vincent, who rolled a six, thus moving down to Atlantic Avenue. Atlantic Avenue was a good investment, so he purchased the property with his somewhat massive fortune.

It was Gilbert's turn again. He was almost too nervous to pick up the dice. Boardwalk and Park Place were close by. Gilbert clattered the dice, blew his hot breath into his fist, and then tossed the dice up in the air. He dreadfully landed right on Boardwalk. He knew that he had to pay dearly.

"Shoot!" Gilbert complained. "I just had to land on that fucking Boardwalk!" He was disgusted after trying to avoid landing on that property.

"Pay up buddy," Vincent insisted, holding his red palm out in front of Gilbert.

"Do I have to pay you all of it?"

"Yes siree. All of it, buddy."

"Let me pay you some of it now."

"No way."

"I'll pay you the rest of it later."

Gilbert tried his hardest compromising, but the disappointed look on his face didn't make Vincent change his mind.

"I want all of my money."

"But . . ."

"Right now!"

Vincent sounded like a loanshark expert showing up on payday.

"When we played Monopoly at the other foster homes, we used to let each other pay some of it now and pay the rest later."

"Your other foster home this! Your other foster home that!" Vincent reiterated. "You're always talking about what you used to do at your other foster homes. Well, you're not in your other foster homes. Will you pay me all of my money?"

"Come on, Vincent," Gilbert pleaded. "Let me pay you half of it now."

"Give me all of my money."

"You're gonna leave me broke."

"Too bad," said Vincent. "Give me my money right now."

"Since you wanna get smart, I'm not giving you no money."

"Yes, you are, punk!" Vincent said.

"No, I'm not, punk!" Gilbert said.

"Then we're going to kick your ass out of the game."

"No, you're not."

"Yes, we are."

Gilbert and Vincent weren't aware that their voices carried into the front room. Bessie Mae wanted them to put the Monopoly game away. But first, she had to make a trip back into the dining room.

"Alright!" Bessie Mae angrily halted. "Who talked about kicking somebody's ass out of this Monopoly game?"

"Vincent!" shouted Gilbert and Jose, pointing their wavering fingers right at Vincent.

"Vincent," Bessie Mae said. "Did you talk about kicking somebody's ass out of this game?"

"Yes, mam," Vincent answered honestly, holding his head down in shame from the opposite direction.

"Get in the bathroom."

"The bathroom?"

"Yeah, the bathroom, you yellow bastard!"

"Why?"

"You'll find out when you get in there."

Bessie Mae escorted Vincent into the bathroom that Granny Dear normally used. She instructed him to go over by the sink and turn on the faucet.

"Now pick that soap up and foam your hands up real good."

"For what?" Vincent questioned Bessie Mae.

"Foam your hands up!" Bessie Mae shouted. "Don't ask no more questions, you yellow bastard!"

Vincent worked up a thick lather until the soap covered every area of both hands.

"Stick both of your hands in your mouth."

"I don't want to, Mrs. Willingham," Vincent cried, tears forming in his eyes.

"Stick your hands in your mouth, boy!"

"It's not enough room."

"Yes, it is."

"No, it isn't."

Bessie Mae limped out of the bathroom to go back into the front room. She rushed back with the black leather strap that J.D. used to threaten Junior with.

"Stick your hands in your mouth."

"Okay."

"Further."

"Okay."

Vincent had both hands shoved halfway through his mouth. Bessie Mae was moments away from striking him with the belt. He stroked his teeth, gums, and tongue with the lather. Soap dripped down his chin and onto his shirt. Water began spilling all over the floor.

"Scrub all around your filthy mouth," Bessie Mae ordered.

"My mouth's burning!" Vincent cried, trying to spit out some of the suds. Tears rushed down his red face.

"I don't care."

"This soap's burning!"

"Me and J.D. are the only niggahs in this house who can curse."

"Can I spit this stuff out, Mrs. Willingham?"

"Not yet."

"Please."

"Shut up and keep scrubbing."

"Alright."

Bessie Mae felt that Vincent had had enough. She told him to bend down and rinse his mouth out. His teeth, gums, and tongue were squeaky clean. Residue from the soap had his mouth dry. He was barely able to swallow. Bessie Mae had Vincent to return to the table with Gilbert and Jose.

J.D. cut through the den and entered the dining room. Through the hallway leading to the dining room, Bessie Mae limped that direction. She stood behind J.D. The matriarch and patriarch of the Willingham foster care residence stood at the doorway that separated the den and the dining room. Expressions of *non pity* framed their faces. Besides the television playing in the front room, complete silence embraced the entire first floor. When J.D. became angry, everyone around him knew it. The red and watery eyes! The puckered lips! The intense breathing! He held tightly onto his long brown extension cord.

"I'm gone tell yall dis one time," J.D. said, swinging the extension cord down by his leg. "If yall muttapuckers don't stop makin all dat goddam noise, I'm gone come back in here wit dis stanching code and beat all yall muttapucking asses!"

"We're sorry, Mr. Willingham," Gilbert, Jose, and Vincent apologized gracefully, their eyes greatly filled with the glow of fear. All three visualized J.D. coming into the dining room with that extension cord, ready to whip some ass all over the place.

"Me and Bessa Mae tying ta watch tv."

"Yes, sir."

"I'm gone kick yall's asses if I hear sum mo noise."

"Yes, sir."

J.D. may have been a man with only a first grade education, someone who spoke badly broken English and used wreckless profanity to the maximum, especially when he was angrier than ever, but could effectively convince the foster children that he would beat them senselessly. Gilbert, Jose, and Vincent sat frozen in their chairs. Bessie Mae and J.D. left the dining room and the Monopoly game was over.

Chapter 20

HAND-ME-DOWNS

Worrying escalated for Bessie Mae when The Department of Children and Family Services were sending her letters concerning the relicensing of her foster home. She began taking other medication besides her daily blood pressure pills. Bessie Mae received the following letter from a social worker supervisor named Annette Spizziri:

Mrs. Bessie Mae Willingham
3838 Milwaukee Parkway
Chicago, Illinois 60609

Dear Mrs. Willingham:

You recall that a request was made for vital information necessary for the agency to relicense your home. To date, we have not received your medical information and we have Vincent Carvelli, Vernon Ramirez, Gilbert Curry, and Jose Underwood, who are in your custody, residing in your home. According to Illinois state regulations, we cannot continue payments for children in an unlicensed home. We realized that Vincent and Vernon have been in your home so long, that both you and them consider it their home. Gilbert and Jose are considered transient foster children. For this reason, we would like to discuss plans and alternatives in permanent planning for their futures. We will be

expecting to hear from you very soon, Mrs. Willingham. However, we will find it necessary to discontinue foster care payments on behalf of Vincent, Vernon, Gilbert, and Jose. We do thank you for your cooperation. Please call either myself at 773-5890 or my immediate supervisor at 773-5847.

*   *   *

Another schoolyear approached for Gilbert, Jose, and Vincent. They were badly in need of new school clothes, mainly because their present ones were worn from the many extracurricular activities that they were involved with. Baseball, football, kickball, and racing around the block were some of the activities that they played with other neighborhood boys.

When one spoke of clothing, Gilbert, Jose, and Vincent constantly opened and closed their drawers, searching for clean clothing that they hoped were in good condition. After doing chores around the house, they would bring pants and shirts out of their drawers that were ripped at the seams, several buttons missing, holes under the armpits, and tube and dress socks that were badly discolored with holes at the toes.

Jose and Vincent stood out on Milwaukee Parkway. They pointed and shouted at fancy automobiles driving up and down the street. They played a silly game of, *claim that car before the next person does.*

"Oooh! Oooh!" Vincent shouted. "That's my car right there!" An expensive blue Mercedes-Benz was traveling south out Milwaukee.

"There go my car!" Jose exclaimed. "I'm gonna drive a car like that one day." He jumped up and down as the shiny red Cadillac Fleetwood sped north up the street.

"It's my car."

"It's mine."

"I saw it before you."

"No you didn't. I saw it before you saw it."

"You know good and well I saw it before you."

Bessie Mae stood in the doorway observing all the shouting and jumping and pointing. She didn't know that fantasy could be taken to that level. Jose and Vincent weren't aware that they were drawing unwelcome attention from other neighbors who couldn't stand all the pandemonium.

"Quit yelling at them dam cars!" Bessie Mae shouted from the front door. "Come on up here so I can take you all somewhere."

"Where are we going?" Vincent asked.

"Does it matter?"

"No, mam."

"Then get on up here."

"Yes, mam."

Jose and Vincent quickly ended their *fancy automobile claiming* excursion and left the sidewalk. Bessie Mae limped towards the car carrying her long brown purse. She started the car up after Gilbert, Jose, and Vincent got inside. They had no idea where they were going.

Bessie Mae drove several miles until they arrived on the far west side of Chicago. On a street in a semi-impoverished neighborhood, she made a right turn and drove up into a driveway on the east side of the street. A dark blue house, trimmed in white around the windows and doors, graced with a light blue awning on the side of the house, was one of the largest houses on the entire block. Written on the front of this awning in large white letters was: *Loretta's Thrifty House of Bargains.*

Bessie Mae parked in front of the awning and turned the car off. She limped up to the door with Gilbert, Jose, and Vincent behind her. Gilbert and Jose were curious as to why they were coming to this strange house. When he was much

younger, Vincent recalled coming to this exact house. Bessie Mae knocked several times before a rather short woman with a bright complexion opened the large wooden door. She was wearing a pair of thick bi-focals that covered most of her face.

"Hey, Bessie Mae!" she said with a burst of energy, throwing her short arm around Bessie Mae's waist. "Girl, it's so good to see you again."

"Loretta!" Bessie Mae cheered. "Girl, you sure are looking good. I'm so glad to see you, too."

"Girl, what can I do for you?" Loretta asked.

"It's close to schooltime."

"Sure is."

"I came by to pick out some school clothes for my three foster boys."

"Are you looking for anything in particular?"

"Well, now," Bessie Mae paused. "I'm looking for some pants, shirts, shoes, socks, maybe even some hats."

"We've got all that."

"Good."

"Ready to start looking?"

"I'm ready."

The owner of the house, Loretta Walker, held the door open for Gilbert, Jose, and Vincent to walk through. The bottom of this house was like a neighborhood thrift store, which mainly attracted families from disadvantaged backgrounds. Gilbert, Jose, and Vincent walked to the middle of the floor. They observed the old and worn clothing that hung on a set of racks and were folded neatly in boxes. A set of books were stacked on a shelf on the other side of the room. Small appliances, miscellaneous furniture items, toys, and generic jewelry, were placed further off into the room.

"These are your foster boys?" Loretta asked, inspecting Gilbert, Jose, and Vincent like they were some kind of misfits.

"Yeah," Bessie Mae nodded. "That's all three of them."

DEWEY REYNOLDS

"I think I remember the little light-skinned one," said Loretta, referring directly to Vincent.

"Yeah, that's Vincent," Bessie Mae snorted. "I've been keeping him since he was a baby."

"Doesn't he have a brother that you keep in your foster home?"

"Vernon?"

"Yes, that's his name."

"He still lives with me."

"Doesn't he have a sister, too?"

"Valerie?"

"Yes, that's her name."

"She's in another foster home," Bessie Mae answered bitterly.

"Why?"

"It's a long story."

"I see."

"I'll tell you about it some other time."

Bessie Mae tried putting the past behind her. She knew that J.D. raped Valerie and she was still in denial.

Gilbert, Jose, and Vincent browsed around the thrifty house while Loretta traveled upstairs to bring down more boxes of old clothes. She returned with a box of smelly and wrinkled clothes.

"Hey, Bessie Mae," Loretta said. "Do you think any of your foster boys can fit any of these clothes?"

"They should."

"What size are they?"

"Good question."

"Do you know?"

"They're different sizes."

Loretta hung pants, shirts, socks, and underwear across her arm. These particular clothing were faded in color, rips and tears under the arms and along the inseams, and with plenty of buttons missing. She handed Bessie Mae three pairs

of polyester, double-knit pants. Many threads were coming out at the inseams. From the top to the bottom, the pastel design shirts were missing almost every button. From where the moths had eaten, the socks had holes at the back and near the toes.

Gilbert, Jose, and Vincent frowned with every muscle in their faces. Ripples formed in their foreheads like an angry elderly person. They quickly straightened their faces when Bessie Mae rose up to hand them a pair of the faded polyester pants. Since there was only one bathroom in her house, Loretta took Vincent towards the back to use it.

Vincent tried the pants on and they were tight, to the point of nearly cutting off the circulation in his legs. The zipper only came halfway up. When he walked out of the bathroom and towards Bessie Mae, she approved of the leg-hugging pants. Gilbert was handed a pair of brown pants that were also polyester and double-knit, which appeared to have been bleached too many times. Jose was given a pair of navy blue pants that had more wrinkles than a cotton shirt coming out of a hot dryer. They went into the bathroom together to try on the pants.

Like the ones that Vincent showed Bessie Mae, they weren't too happy about stepping out in the open. Wearing skin-tight pants, which had threads hanging around the lower leg was the ultimate embarrassment. Unlike other boys who attended Abraham Lincoln Elementary, Gilbert and Jose weren't allowed to wear the latest contemporary fashions. They always glanced through department store catalogs that Bessie Mae had sitting around the house. They wished they could wear clothing from stores like *Sears and Roebuck, JC Penney,* and *Montgomery Ward.*

"No way," Gilbert said, barely able to move his legs in the pants.

"What's wrong?" Vincent asked.

"I'm not going to wear these funny looking pants."

"What will you wear?"

"I'm going to stuff these motherfuckers in my drawers."

"You'll get into trouble."

"I'm going to pretend that I can't find them."

"I'm going to do the same thing," Jose assented, pinching the middle of his pants to see if he could have walking room.

"I hate these pants!" Gilbert grunted. "They make me look like a clown or something."

"We can't even fit these pants," Jose said.

Bessie Mae bent down to sort through more of the *hand me downs*. Vincent stood above her with a discontented look that framed his reddish face. Bessie Mae abruptly rose up and caught that sour look on his face. The pair of pants that she was going to have Vincent try on was thrown back into the box. She literally exploded after that.

"What the hell's wrong with you, boy!" she screamed, kicking the box aside to turn and face Vincent.

"Nothing, " Vincent answered bitterly.

"Something's wrong with you, boy!" she yelled louder. "Don't lie to me, Vincent."

"There's nothing wrong."

"Don't make me slap the shit out of you!"

"I don't wanna wear these ugly pants to school."

Bessie Mae got Vincent to confess. He turned his head sideways to avoid eye contact with his furious foster mother.

"Why?" Bessie Mae asked angrily. "You think you're too good to wear something out of Loretta's place?"

"No, mam."

"Then, tell me why."

"The other kids."

"What other kids?"

"The other kids at school are gonna laugh at me."

"Why are they going to laugh at you?"

"They'll have better clothes than me."

Vincent knew that he was raising Bessie Mae's blood pressure. One thing that she didn't tolerate was an ungrateful foster child.

"Guess what, Vincent?"

"What?"

"You know why they'll have better clothes than you?"

"No, mam."

"Look at me, boy, when I'm talking to you!"

"Yes, mam."

"Other kids at your school aren't in a foster home," Bessie said harshly. "The state isn't supporting them like they're supporting you. Do you understand, boy?"

"Yes, mam."

"Their mammas and daddies probably have good jobs. Do you understand what I'm saying?"

"Yes, mam."

"Them other kids got parents who can afford to buy them nice clothes. Do you know what I'm trying to say to you, boy?"

"Yes, mam."

"Don't you know that the state doesn't give me enough money to buy you all no nice clothes?"

"Yes, mam," Vincent whined, standing there with his head hung low.

"You listen closely to me, boy," Bessie Mae squeaked. "Do you think that your real mamma and real daddy is going to give me any money to buy you some new clothes with?"

"No, mam."

"Guess what, Vincent?"

"What?"

"You're going to get these clothes whether you want them or not. Do you understand me, boy?"

"I don't know," Vincent answered uncertainly, mumbling as his face went from a sad expression to a very much mad one.

"I said, do you understand?"

"I don't know."

"Speak up, boy."

"Yes, mam."

"You kids today make me sick," Bessie Mae said. "I'm not about to come out of my pocket to buy you all those fancy, name brand clothes that those children just wear to show off. Do you hear me, Vincent?"

"Yes, mam."

"Get that frown off your face before I slap it off!"

"Yes, mam."

"You better straighten up," she charged. "I'll get J.D. to annihilate your high-yellow, half-breed ass with his extension cord when we get home."

The long and brutal lecture that Bessie Mae dished out at Vincent was finally over. Her adrenalin got to flowing and she couldn't stop telling him about a pair of pants that should've been thrown away a long time ago. She handed the pants to Vincent and told him to try them on. On the way towards the back, he passed Gilbert and Jose. Similiar to the same problems as Vincent, Gilbert and Jose had a hard time trying to walk in the pants that they considered to be leg-hugging and vein-squeezing.

They arrived in the front and Bessie Mae wanted them to walk in front of her. In order to give her a good view, they had to walk side by side and around in circles. Bessie Mae was an expert at reading facial expressions. She detected negative attitudes like a metal detector sensing gold or silver. She sensed that Gilbert and Jose weren't too happy about her being in the process of purchasing the worn clothing from Loretta's. Gilbert had that look on his face of: *"I don't wanna wear these weird looking pants when school starts"*.

"What's wrong with you, boy?" Bessie Mae interrogated Gilbert, slamming a couple of shirts back into the box.

"There's nothing wrong with me," Gilbert answered, swiftly removing the sour expression from his face.

"Then why are you acting like that yellow bastard, Vincent?"

"I'm not acting like Vincent."

"Are you trying to call me a liar?" Bessie Mae asked. "I saw that ugly look on your face."

"What ugly look?"

"Don't even try it."

"Try what?"

"You're trying to make me look like a dam fool."

"No, I'm not."

"You're trying to say that you weren't twisting your face all up?"

"No, mam."

"Like I told Vincent," Bessie Mae said. "I'll get J.D. to beat some sense into your black ass with his extension cord. Do you understand, boy?"

"Yes, mam."

"Take these shirts and try them on."

"Yes, mam."

"You kids these days get on my goddam nerves!"

Loretta came downstairs to see how everything was going. Because of all the animosity towards her foster sons, Bessie Mae shook her head continuously. Loretta cracked a smile after she listened to the self-proclaimed rhetoric of Bessie Mae. She silently expressed her condolences for Gilbert and Jose. They stood in the middle of the floor looking like two rejects from a lost society. They desperately wanted to get out of those tight pants.

Bessie Mae handed them two shirts each and sent them towards the back. Vincent stepped out of the bathroom in another pair of tight and faded polyester pants with the double-knit stitches on the side of the leg. Before walking towards the front, he immediately disguised the noticeable frown on his face. He remained disappointed despite his

opposition to wearing the pants. Bessie Mae would never know it.

While he walked around, Bessie Mae observed the pants closely. She agreed that they would fit him perfectly. They would be set aside with the other clothes. Gilbert and Jose walked out showing Bessie Mae the shirts, which had large holes under the armpits, every other button was missing, dark ink spots had covered most of the front, and threads hung around the sleeve. Bessie Mae approved every piece of clothing that was presented before her. Gilbert and Jose returned to the back. Vincent stood over the face bowl in the bathroom with the pants dangling down by his side.

"What's wrong with you?" Gilbert asked Vincent, stepping closer to the face bowl.

"I don't wanna wear these funny looking pants," Vincent objected strongly, ready to throw the pants in the trash.

"I've got an idea."

"What idea?"

"Let's throw these dingy pants away when we get home."

"Don't forget about tight," Vincent added.

"Yeah, and tight, too."

"What about these shirts with holes under the arms and buttons missing?" Jose asked.

"These clothes are worse than the ones we already have at home," Gilbert scrutinized, disgusted from just being present at Loretta's.

"I would rather keep wearing the ones at home," Jose said.

"They're gonna laugh at us when school starts," Vincent said.

"When school starts?" Gilbert said.

"I'm gonna throw this shit away."

"What about when you run out of clothes?" Vincent asked Gilbert.

"I'll just have to run out," Gilbert amended. "There's no

way that I can be seen wearing something like this." He held the shirt up for Jose and Vincent to observe.

"You're going to keep wearing the same clothes?"

"I guess so."

"These clothes are older than dirt," Jose said.

"I wonder how many people wore them before us?"

"At least ten."

"Maybe more," Vincent added.

"We're going to have to wear these clothes."

"Says who?" Gilbert asked, his militant attitude surfacing.

"You forgot about Mr. Willingham and his extension cord," Vincent reminded Gilbert, the thought of that painful cord making his flesh crawl.

"You're right."

"That black, bald-headed niggah's gonna make us wear them anyway."

Before they continued their discussion, Bessie Mae called from up front. As they began exiting the bathroom, Gilbert said, "I've got something to tell you all when we get home."

"What?" Vincent asked.

"I'll tell you."

The clothes were handed to Bessie Mae and she waited for Loretta to ring up the total price. Loretta didn't own a cash register. She figured everything up on a small sheet of paper. The total came to fifteen dollars and twenty-seven cents. Bessie Mae reached into her purse and handed Loretta a crispy twenty dollar bill. After she received the change, business was finished at *Loretta's Thrifty House of Bargains*.

*   *   *

Once they returned home, Gilbert, Jose, and Vincent rushed to the basement. Gilbert revealed some information that was truly enlightening.

"What did you have to tell us?" Vincent asked Gilbert.

"About what?"

Gilbert had forgotten what he had to tell his foster brothers, as he was stretched across his bed with his pillow buried under his chin.

"You wanted to tell me and Jose something when we were at that thrift house."

Gilbert's memory was refreshed. "Now I remember. It's something about when I was at those other foster homes."

"Oh god!" Vincent squalled. "There you go talking about your other foster homes. Your other foster homes this! Your other foster homes that! You're acting like you wish you were back in those other foster homes."

"You know what?" Gilbert asked. "After being in this crazy foster home, I sort of wish I could've stayed in the last one."

"I bet you do."

"But, listen to this."

"What?"

"Mrs. Willingham is supposed to be buying us new clothes."

"How do you know that?" Jose asked.

"How?" Gilbert frowned. "When I was at those other foster homes, the state-welfare people used to give the foster parents clothings stamps or clothing vouchers to buy us brand new clothes for school."

"You're very smart, Gilbert," Vincent said.

"Thank you."

"Maybe this foster home is different," Jose said.

"Different!" Gilbert objected, grabbing a pair of the old and faded pants from Loretta's Thrift House and holding it up for Jose and Vincent to view. "All the foster parents in every foster home are supposed to buy the kids new clothes."

"You're right," Jose agreed. "Not taking us to no house to buy clothes that should be thrown away."

"Let me ask you this?" Vincent said. "Do you think our

caseworkers gave Mrs. Willingham some of those stamps or vouchers to buy us new clothes for school?"

"What do you think?" Gilbert replied sarcastically.

"I don't know," Vincent nodded. "That's why I'm asking you."

Jose lifted up one of the shirts from Loretta's, holding it right before Gilbert.

"Use your brain, dummy."

"There you go calling me a dummy," Vincent confronted Gilbert.

"I'm sorry for calling you a dummy," Gilbert apologized."But, just think about all that nice shit that Mr. and Mrs. Willingham have."

"Shit like what?" Jose asked.

"Like what?"

"Yeah."

"Are you blind or what?" Gilbert foiled. "Shit like that brand new Cadillac, those cold-blooded fur coats, dresses, suits, and jewelry that Mr. and Mrs. Willingham be wearing to church and out to dinner, and that real nice antique furniture. That shit costs lots of money."

"I get it now," Jose replied attentively. "They buy all those things with the stamps and vouchers."

"Not just the stamps or vouchers. But, think about all the checks that they get for keeping everybody in this house."

"Does Mrs. Willingham get money for keeping Granny Dear?" Vincent asked, who has always been curious if Bessie Mae received a check for having Granny Dear in the home.

"Like I said, everybody."

"Granny Dear's her mother," Vincent turned to tell Gilbert and Jose.

"It doesn't matter," Gilbert said. "I'll bet you she still gets money for keeping her here."

"I think Gilbert's right," Jose pondered. "One time, I saw the mailman give Mrs. Willingham a thick stack of brown

envelopes. I think they were a bunch of checks from the state-welfare people."

"I know I'm right. Mrs. Willingham waits outside around the first of the month for those checks to come."

Several clothing vouchers were given to Bessie Mae from The Department of Children and Family Services, Division of Welfare, Cook County Office. These vouchers came from *Sears, Roebuck, and Company* and *JC Penney*.

Inside the bottom drawer of Bessie Mae's bedside table, there were a stack of copies of these vouchers. From the credit layaway clerk at *Sears, Roebuck, and Company*, each letter read:

Dear sir:

This will introduce Mrs. Bessie Mae Willingham, who has been authorized to make a one-time purchase of clothing for the following: Vincent Carvelli, Gilbert Curry, and Jose Underwood. The total purchases are not to exceed the amount given. On each sales slip, please ask Mrs. Willingham to write the name of the child for whom the purchase is made, and to sign the sales slip. She will be shopping at your store on August 23. These purchases are to be charged to account number 669-257-146-0, which is the number assigned to the Child Welfare Services, Cook County Office of the Illinois Division of Welfare. We have called the District Controller's Office and talked with Mrs. Darci Galloway, telling her of these intended purchases.

Approved by: Catherine O'Bannion
Social Service Supervisor I

*   *   *

There were several reasons why Bessie Mae hid the copies of these vouchers. Somehow, she cashed them over and used the money for her own personal spending ventures. It was amazing how a boy Gilbert's age knew about the adulterated schemes that Bessie Mae executed. When neglect hit him in the face, Gilbert knew it. Trying to get Jose and Vincent to realize that they were living in a poorly operated foster home wasn't hard.

Wouldn't someone know how the foster care system was supposed to be run? Living in other foster homes beforehand made Gilbert an expert. Bessie Mae was a materialistic woman. She was unreasonably greedy. Her assets included expensive perfumes, genuine diamond rings and pearl necklaces, lavish fox, rabbit, and coon furs, costly hairdos and manicures from her personal beautician, fine chinaware and antique furniture, not to mention the countless trips back and forth to Memphis, Tennessee and Las Vegas, Nevada.

Gilbert believed that all of this was done at the expense of neglecting the foster children and handicapped men. Overpowering thoughts of negligence had Gilbert, Jose, and Vincent sitting across their beds in deep meditation. Without any body motion or facial expression, they wondered about their future at the Willingham's foster care home.

Chapter 21

FREE AMONG THE JUNGLE

THE AUTUMN BREEZE blew through the open windows inside the classrooms at Abraham Lincoln Elementary. Gilbert, Jose, and Vincent listened to their individual instructors give lectures on different subject matters.

Inside the sixth grade class where Jose sat, he listened to his instructor, Mrs. Carrie Westbrook, give instructions on how to add rows of double mathematical figures. She stood at the blackboard writing the numbers with a long piece of white chalk in her right hand. Her wide-built body covered almost everything she wrote on the board or she pointed to.

Whenever her back was turned, her roistering students pressed their lips together. They made low noises that resembled someone passing gas. Carrie turned around to look at the class and they quickly removed their hands from their lips. Once she added up the right side of the figures, she turned around to show her students how to carry the remainder to the other side. When she turned around to face the board, they pressed their lips together and made the imitation farting noises.

"Booty lips! Booty lips!" her students chanted in a whispering voice, vibrating their lips and sending mists of saliva into the air.

Carrie turned around quickly and asked, "Why are you students saying *'booty lips'*?"

No one could give her a straight answer, so she continued with her lecture. Carrie Westbrook had very thick lips that

were curled outwards. A set of lips like hers really did resemble the shape of someone's ass. She would have never guessed that her students were mocking her while her back was turned. Without any humor in the classroom, her students would have been bored out of their senses. They continued to poke their lips out and imitate their instructor.

On the same floor at Abraham Lincoln Elementary, three doors down the hall from Jose, Gilbert listened to his instructor, Mrs. Marlena Kravitz, give a lecture on sex education. These sixth graders were getting an early lesson about sex and it's consequential possibilities. Gilbert and his classmates sat patiently, while Marlena stood in front of her desk holding a pamphlet that gave information about all facets of sex.

The thirty-page white booklet raised awareness about veneral diseases, such as gonorrhea and syphillis, heterosexual, homosexual, and bi-sexual activities, teenage and unplanned pregnancies, and birth control and condoms. Marlena flipped through the pages before her students. They were shown illustrations of condoms, the gonococcus and spirochete bacterias, and various birth control pills.

On the tenth page, about halfway down the second paragraph, the literature talked about homosexuality. It intellectually explained how men and women were known to have sexual intercourse with someone of the same sex. Marlena skipped over words or phrases that she found somewhat explicit. Although they were sixth graders, she wanted to leave room for their imaginations. They were premature and didn't have to know everything about the *birds and bees* or the *do's and dont's* of sex.

The further she read, the more her students glanced around at one another, allowing their curiosity to wander aimlessly. At their desks, they tossed and turned. They slid over to ask one another questions, which really didn't allow Marlena to exercise her knowledge on the subject. She continued reading until the pamphlet ended. Pausing

momentarily, she caught her breath and landed her eyes over at the desk of Gilbert. He was whispering in the ear of Yolonda Gates. She was the tallest girl in their class. She stood five feet seven as a sixth grader. Other classmates referred to her as *Miss Walking Stick.*

"Mr. Curry!" Marlena lightly shouted. "Do you have something that you'd like to share with the class?" She stepped away from her desk to stand at the center of the class.

"No, Mrs. Kravitz," Gilbert replied in a meek voice.

"Did you have something important to tell Yolonda?"

"Yes, Mrs. Kravitz."

"Would you like to share it with the class?"

"Yeah, but . . ."

"But, what?"

"It's kind of nasty."

"I'll decide if it's nasty."

"It's about that homosexuality thing."

"What about it?"

"I was asking Yolonda something about dogs."

"What about dogs?"

"I was asking her if dogs could be homosexuals."

Gilbert sat up as straight as possible in his seat. The entire classroom broke out into a thunderous laughter. They became somewhat rowdy until Mrs. Kravitz made them settle down. Gilbert gripped the sides of his desk and tucked his big bottom lip inward, simply because he was nervous about asking his instructor such a question.

"Whew!" Marlena blushed. "Well now, I've never seen or heard of an act of homosexuality occurring among the animal species. What made you ask Yolonda a question as strange as that one?"

"I saw this one male dog pumping this other male dog in the booty," Gilbert said before the entire class. "I saw it happening when I was outside playing with some of my neighbors."

Again, the entire classroom broke out into great laughter, bamming their fists down on their desks, scratching their shoes across the hard wooden floor, and falling out of their seats. The answer that Gilbert gave tickled their every funnybone.

"Settle down, students."

"Yes, Mrs. Kravitz," the classroom responded humbly.

"I'm sure you're not the only one who's ever seen something of that nature," Marlena told Gilbert. She found no amusement behind something as vulgar as that. Gilbert witnessed one male dog fucking another male dog in the ass and wanted to share it with the class. Who cared? Marlena Kravitz sure didn't.

Three doors up the hall, back in Carrie Westbrook's class, the noise broke the concentration of the students who tried adding the double figures from the blackboard. Jose stopped to listen to the uproar that came from Gilbert's classroom.

On the floor below Gilbert and Jose, in a classroom near the middle of the hall, Vincent sat at his desk with his chest leaned against the lid. His instructor, Mrs. Pauline Nizzi, gave a lecture about great Italian figures during the Renaissance era. Columbus, Leonardo Da Vinci, Michaelangelo, and Amerigo Vespucci, were discussed during this lecture. Colorful pages inside their hardbound world history books, showed the great art masterpieces of Da Vinci and Michaelangelo. Pictures of the fresco paintings in *The Sistine Chapel, The Last Supper, The Statue of David, The Mona Lisa,* and *The Pieta,* were shown on consecutive pages near the end of the textbook. As they turned the pages with Pauline, Vincent and his fellow classmates were fascinated with the glossy pictures.

"Why is that man naked?" Vincent asked Pauline, pointing right at the page which had *The Statue of David.*

"What man?" Pauline asked, flipping back and forth between the pages.

"The man with the curly hair."

"Oh!" Pauline recalled. "You're speaking of The Statue of David."

"Yes, yes, that's what I'm talking about."

"Michaelangelo was also a sculptor and that's how he chiseled out the marble."

Gilbert, Jose, and Vincent received their separate lectures. The final minutes of school approached and the mild breeze continued to blow into their classrooms. Autumn leaves floated around the playground and up towards the windows. The bell sounded on every floor at Abraham Lincoln. School ended and students from all four floors rushed towards the double doors facing Milwaukee Parkway.

Carrying his math and English textbooks under his arm, Vincent walked down the stairs leading to the front entrance. Four classmates, two from previous classes and two who were presently in Pauline Nizzi's class, walked behind and on the sides of Vincent. They barely allowed him enough room to walk. They repeatedly giggled and whispered into one another's ears. As soon as Vincent stepped onto the playground, two of his old classmates, Jerry Grayson and Clinton Marks, jumped in front of him, ready to lash out harsh remarks.

"You white honky!" Jerry gruffed, showing his insulting side before everyone who was present on the playground.

"I'm not a white honky!" Vincent yelled, shoving his way around the rowdy students.

"I said you were one."

"No, I'm not."

"Yes, you are."

Vincent thought the days of being insulted by Jerry were over. They were far from being over. But he could see that history was only repeating itself.

"Leave me alone!" Vincent screamed, turning red all over his face.

"Where are you going, white boy?" Jerry asked, pushing Vincent strongly in the middle of his chest.

"I'm going home," Vincent replied sorrowfully, wanting every bit of pity he could get.

"What home, half-breed honky?"

"My home."

"You're going to that foster home."

"So what!"

"You're going to that home with those retarded men."

"Get out of my face, Jerry!"

"Shut up, you white punk."

"Stop calling me that!" Vincent yelled furiously, trying to penetrate around the disruptive kids.

"Be quiet, you white orphaned-punk."

"Stop saying that, before . . ."

"Before what?"

"I'm going to . . ."

"You're not going to do anything."

Jerry, Clinton, and a host of others formed a tighter circle around Vincent. If he dared to brush his way out of their circle, a fight was sure to start.

"White boy! White boy! You don't shine! If you call me a nigger, I'll beat your behind!" shouted those who were right up in Vincent's face.

"White honky! White honky! You can't ride my donkey! You can't ride my donkey, because it don't like nobody white and funky!" shouted those on the outside of the circle.

The series of insolent remarks continued. They stood around on the playground making up harsh remarks and

rhymes about the very much noticeable Caucasian background of Vincent. With many students surrounding him, Vincent was closed in like a *prisoner of misery.*

"Leave me alone!" Vincent cried, slinging tears from under his eyes, then becoming redder in the face.

"Shut up, you half-breed, white honky!" Clinton remarked, pressing his finger into the thin chest of Vincent.

"Why don't you all go home and leave me alone!"

"Hell no!" Clinton snarled. "You half-breed sissy."

"Stop it!"

"Shut up!"

Gilbert and Jose stepped onto the playground. Momentarily, they watched Jerry, Clinton, and the others humiliate Vincent. Enough was enough! Gilbert walked into the midst of the barbaric bunch. He slammed his books onto the playground and shoved some of the crowd away from Vincent.

"Hey, fat boy!" Gilbert roared. "If you call him one more name, I'm gonna knock some of that fat off your ass!" Gilbert pointed right into the center of his face.

"I was only playing with him," Clinton shrugged, gradually stepping away from Vincent.

"It don't look like you were playing to me."

"But, I was."

"Not calling him *white this* and *white that.*"

"We always play with Vincent like that."

"Sure looks like Vincent don't like those names you all be calling him."

Jerry moved around Clinton to make his presence known. "Why are you taking up for this white honky?"

"He ain't no white honky," Gilbert bluffed, never hesitant to stand in the defense of Vincent.

"I said he was."

"I said he wasn't."

"Why are you biting all up in his ass?" Jerry asked Gilbert, bucking up to him like he wanted to go a few rounds.

"Because I'm about to kick off into your ass."

"You're going to let a white honky get your ass kicked?"

"Go ahead and call Vincent another white honky," Gilbert said, both fists balled up and ready to battle with Jerry.

"What?"

"You heard me."

"Who is he to you?"

"He's my foster brother?"

"Foster brother?"

"Yeah, niggah!"

"You're in the same foster home with him?"

"That's right, niggah!"

"Where those retarded men live?"

"You heard right, niggah!"

"You're an orphaned just like Vincent?"

"What did you call me?"

"I said . . ."

"Say it again, punk!" Gilbert challenged Jerry, drawing his arm back, ready to strike at any second. "Call me another orphan."

"Hey man, I don't want to fight you."

"I know that you don't," Gilbert objected. "I'll knock all the black off your shiny tarbaby ass!"

"I see that you can't even take a joke."

"Anyway, you're jealous of Vincent."

"Jealous?"

"That's right."

"What are you talking about?"

"You're jealous because you don't have good hair like him."

"I don't have no reason to be jealous."

"Get out of my face before I knock all the black off your ass."

Jerry, Clinton, and the other rowdy ones didn't want to

test the fighting abilities of Gilbert. Everyone went their separate directions. Vincent stood there relieved. Did Gilbert finally put an end to their *name-calling* charades? He helped Gilbert pick up his books and they started their journey home.

While they walked up Milwaukee, kicking leaves along their paths, Vincent stressed how much he admired Gilbert's courage. The after school journey continued until they came to the house. Bessie Mae waited anxiously for them to cross the street. Braun came up the stairs beating the middle of his hand and talking to himself. Students from the junior and senior high schools strutted up the street, watching Braun pound the middle of his hand with the wire.

"Hey, hey, how'ya doing there?" Braun spoke to the group of teenagers, showing all of his black teeth as they walked past the house.

"Fine," the teenagers replied, alarmed at the grimy black substances smeared across his teeth.

A woman and her three children walked up the hill carrying some sacks from the grocery store.

"Hey, hey, how'ya doing there?" Braun spoke to the woman.

"Doing just fine," she replied, concealing a frown after watching his teeth. "How are you doing today?"

"I'm doing okay, today. Yeah, yeah, I'm doing okay, today."

Once the woman and her children got to the corner, one of her three children asked, "Mamma, what's wrong with that man's teeth?"

"He probably chews tobacco, honey," the woman said.

"His teeth looks like one of those monsters in a scary movie."

"Don't talk about his teeth, honey."

"Okay."

Gilbert, Jose, and Vincent walked through the front door and glanced over at the sofa. There were three stacks of *The*

Baldwin Express papers sitting there. This was a black newspaper that came out every Friday. It was named after the late great black philanthropist and political activist named Lawrence Baldwin. Features in this important paper was sports, entertainment, business, medicine, and politics. Born and raised in the inner-city of Chicago, Lawrence Baldwin made significant contributions within the black community.

This issue featured a cover story on the well-known black activist, Reverened Jesse Jackson, and his Operation Push campaign. The article covered a unique blend of revivalist assemblies and political strategists, which featured nationally prominent leaders as guest speakers at Reverened Jesse Jackson's headquarters on Drexel Boulevard. Gilbert went over to the sofa and flipped through one of the stacks. The large black and white photo of Jesse Jackson showed clearly across the front of every page. Gilbert assumed that Bessie Mae had the three separate stacks waiting for them. They went to the basement and changed out of their outdated and tight-fitting school clothing, and into their outdated and tight-fitting play clothing. When they returned upstairs, Bessie Mae was standing over the papers. She was ready to explain the new work assignment to her *eager to work foster sons.*

"These are The Baldwin Express," Bessie Mae told Gilbert, Jose, and Vincent, grabbing one from the stack and holding it up in mid-air. "Don't ever sell these papers for less than a quarter. When you get out on the street, you all need to split up. You will sell them faster that way. If you try and work the same places, you will end up rushing the same customers."

"What if they need change?" Gilbert asked.

"If they need some change," Bessie Mae paused. "Then ask them what they need change for?"

"What if they don't have change? What if we don't have change?"

"Well, then you can't sell a paper."

"Shucks."

"That happens, you know."

"What if people ask us for money?"

"Don't ever give anybody money," Bessie Mae stressed. "I don't care who they are or what kind of shit they're talking. Don't ever give them one red cent."

"What else should we do?"

"Oh, and always remember this."

"What?"

"Always tell the customer 'thank you' after they've bought one of your papers."

"Okay."

Vincent was hesitant about selling The Baldwin Express. He had to speak up about the location for selling the papers. "Where will we go to sell The Baldwin Express?"

"On Rush Boulevard," Bessie Mae said.

"Rush!" Gilbert whisked, afraid to even hear that street name."

"That's where you can make the money."

"Yeek!"

Bessie Mae knew that Rush Boulevard was infested with pimps, prostitutes, drunks, druggies, murderers, armed robbers, car thieves, dragqueens, and any other type of hustlers.

"Watch out for those street punks," Bessie Mae warned her three foster sons."

"What street punks?"

"The ones who'll try and rob you."

"I didn't know about them."

"They'll try and pull you in one of those alleys and beat you up and take your money."

"Really?" Gilbert asked.

"Yes."

Bessie Mae knew that Rush Boulevard came to life on Fridays. She explained all the details for selling The Baldwin

Express. It was now up to Gilbert, Jose, and Vincent to go out and distribute the paper in the black community.

Carmen walked through the front door wondering why the stacks of papers were on the sofa. She seductively undressed Vincent with her lustful eyes. Her desire for him since he was that six year old boy that she'd take in the bathroom to have sex with hadn't changed after several years. She had had several boyfriends since those bathroom rendezvous' with Vincent, but that meant nothing. She still had a silent passion for him. Everytime he saw her face, the memories would always resurface. To this day, he blamed her for introducing him to sex before it was his time. Long after Carmen left the Willingham residence to move in with her boyfriend, Vincent still had nightmares about their bathroom sexcapades.

Gilbert, Jose, and Vincent pulled their stack of papers off the sofa and walked down Milwaukee Parkway. Carmen stepped onto the porch. She stared at Vincent as he walked down the street. She succulently licked her lucious lips. She massaged her throat in a vigorous manner. The feelings were definitely still there.

Vincent was familiar with the areas that were close to Rush Boulevard. He had lived on Milwaukee Parkway long enough to know the other streets that surrounded these busy streets. Gilbert and Jose were informed to follow him until they reached Rush. When the nineteen seventies hit, it became one of the undisputed kings of all the hustle areas around Chicago.

* * *

Things were awfully busy on this late Friday afternoon. The heavy traffic and multitude of hustlers allowed Gilbert, Jose, and Vincent to witness how others earned their illegitimate living. From several blocks away, they saw every hustler

imaginable. They scanned the blocks cautiously, trying to see where they could start selling the papers.

Near the corner where Gilbert, Jose, and Vincent stood, there were several rogues crowded around shooting dice. They made their bids, throwing every bill they had down on the concrete, calling one another *niggah this* and *niggah that*. The papers became heavy. The walk to Rush Boulevard was long, and they wanted to take a load off their shoulders.

Halfway up Rush, going towards the north end, there was a small bank. Several liquor stores and a few restaurants were further down the street. A building constructed from a dark brown stone, housed The First National Bank of Chicago. This was the only bank along the extremely busy boulevard. Inside the bank, there were four tellers, three loan officers, two security guards, and one customer representative.

On the next three corners, Bertolli's Liquors and Sundries, Nicoletti's Handy Stop, and Vanzetti's One-Stop Liquors, were busy with customers trafficking in and out, stocking up on their favorite beers and liquors for the weekend. Could this turn into a moneymaking haven for Gilbert, Jose, and Vincent? Were they three eager young men who wanted to start some beginner's luck?

People walked up to the bank carrying their bank books, purses, and payroll checks. As they strolled towards the front entrance, they picked through their towering afros with their afro forks and afro rakes, some even spraying afro sheen in their hair with the smaller carry-around cans.

Vincent stood near the front entrance of the bank, almost afraid to ask his first customer to purchase the paper. Gilbert and Jose stood near the drive-thru, also afraid to ask anyone who came their direction. Jose glanced across the street at Bertolli's Liquors. Several men and women walked out of the store. Eventually, Jose and Gilbert would end up rushing the same customer. Bessie Mae's advice was to

separate from the same location. Jose took heed to her advice by traveling across the street.

Instantly, he gained business from the customers going in and out of the liquor store. Quarters came from every direction. He was selling the papers quicker than he thought. Customers stood in line, reaching down into their purses and coin holders. What a wise choice Jose made. They took a hard look at the front cover picture of Jesse Jackson.

From across the street, Gilbert and Vincent watched Jose sell lots of papers. Several customers walked towards the bank. They carried their ink pens on top of their bank books and payroll checks, preparing to deposit or withdraw money or cash their checks. Once they got closer, Gilbert flipped up one of the papers to their faces, hoping they would get a full view of Jesse's photo.

"Would you like to buy one of The Baldwin Express, sir?" Gilbert asked the first person, speaking in a very cordial voice.

"I'll buy two of them when I cash my check," said a tall and fair-complexioned man, deep, well-trimmed sideburns on the side of his face.

"Okay, sir," Gilbert cheered. "I'll be standing right here when you come out." He was simply flabbergasted after making his first sale.

Approaching the bank were two elderly women. Vincent stepped in front of them with a paper held high.

"Mam," Vincent paused. "Would one of you all like to buy The Baldwin Express?"

"Let's see, sonny," said the first elderly woman. "How much is this Baldwin Express paper?" She stared hard with her narrow-framed glasses that covered most of her wrinkling face.

"It's a quarter, mam."

"You're a well-mannered young man."

"Thank you."

The elderly woman turned to her friend and said, "Look

here, Betty Jo. They've got a picture of Jesse Jackson on the front page."

"Jesse Jackson," Betty Jo replied. "Ain't Jesse gone be speaking somewhere around Chicago?"

"I reckon so," she said. "Them white folks been talking about it on the television."

"Where he gone speaking at?"

"Chile, I heard 'em say, but I can't remember to save my life."

"Gone and buy one of them papers so we can find out."

"I reckon so."

Both elderly women gracefully slapped a quarter in the pinkish palm of Vincent's right hand. They walked away reading the article about Jesse Jackson. Before they entered the bank, Vincent had something important to tell them.

"Thank you, mam," Vincent said, smiling from ear to ear.

"You're welcome, sonny," both women said.

Vincent sold two papers and it was forty-eight to go. As far as Gilbert was concerned, he waited anxiously for the man who promised to purchase two of his papers. Things weren't taken out of stride, because more customers drove up into the bank parking lot. Countless cars drove up and down Rush Boulevard. They made left and right turns into the bank and liquor stores and restaurants down the street.

Because it was Friday around the great windy city of Chicago, for most people it was *payday, playday, partyday, shopping day,* and a day for *paying bills, paying dues,* and *paying attention.*

With two quarters jingling inside his left hand, the same man who promised to buy two papers from Gilbert, stepped out of the bank. They exchanged the papers and the quarters and Gilbert was one happy youngster.

"Thank you, sir," Gilbert said, showing an expression of sincerety.

"You're welcome, son."

"I'll be here next Friday, too."

"Okay, I'll remember to be looking for you."

"Thanks again."

Customers were coming. Customers were going. In front of Bertolli's Liquors, Jose continued selling his papers. He held them up high, making sure the customers wouldn't miss the photo of Jesse. It proved to be an attention-getter, therefore boosting sales. Many black people around Chicago wanted to see and hear Jesse Jackson speak. Of course, The Baldwin Express gave all the information needed, including the date, location, and time of his prominent speech.

Back over at the bank, a dark blue, 1969 convertible, Oldsmobile Cutlass Supreme, drove into the parking lot. The mint conditioned automobile was occupied by three gorgeous black girls. As they cruised across the parking lot, they had all of the undivided attention of Gilbert and Vincent. Their lips created strange movements. Tantalizing thoughts entered their minds.

It wasn't too often that they were allowed to leave the Willingham residence unsupervised, so they closely watched the strikingly beautiful girls. All three girls had long and dark silky hair that hung down their backs. Though it was late in the Fall, they wore different colored hotpants, which clung to their curvaceous hips and tight buttocks.

The vultures riding down Rush had come out of nowhere. The chaotic noises of horns sounding, tires peeling rubber, and cars fishtailing, were every sign that these three young ladies had drawn much attention. For them, it was certainly unwelcome attention. Many guys stuck their heads out of their car windows. Obscene and disrespectful comments were made at the attractive high schoolers. When they approached the bank, Gilbert and Vincent were too afraid to ask them to purchase a paper, taken in by their dangerously beautiful faces. But in return, these three young

beauties weren't too afraid to inquire about The Baldwin
Express.

"How much does The Baldwin Express cost?" one of the
three girls asked in the sweetest voice, wearing a pair of black
hotpants, like she was on a mission to tease a man.

"It costs . . . uh . . . ," Vincent said incoherently, his heart
pumping fast.

"How much?" she asked again.

"It costs a quarter."

"Do you have change for a dollar?"

"Not right now."

"Let me cash my check first."

"Okay."

"I'll buy one then."

"Alright."

Vincent shivered as he watched her walk away. The other
two girls would buy one when they returned outside. As they
were walking into the bank, a car full of male joyriders pulled
up in front of the bank, sitting right in front of a no-parking
sign. The man in the front, sitting on the passenger's side,
smiled at the attractive girls and was showing nothing but a
lot of missing teeth. Every other tooth was missing from his
top and bottom rows.

He held up a tall can of Budweiser and outlandishly
said, "Hey girls, I just love all three of you all's tooty, fruity,
juicy, booties, that's always on their duties."

"Take a hike," said the young lady in the blue hotpants.

"Don't be so mean, baby," said the nearly toothless man,
reaching his arm out of the car like he wanted to grab her ass.

"We don't have time for drunks like you."

"Can I go with you all?" the man begged, intoxication
ringing through his voice.

"Hell no!"

"Please."

"Get lost."

"Why, baby?"

"I'll tell you what you could do?"

"What's that?"

"Put some teeth in your mouth."

"Now see, you're wrong."

"No, I'm not."

Gilbert and Vincent were standing there nearly laughing their heads off their shoulders. Maybe the drunk man was asking for it. One of the security guards who patrolled the bank stepped out on the sidewalk and the car of joyriders sped off. They knew that they were parked in a no-parking zone. Gilbert and Vincent just couldn't stop laughing.

"Did you see that dude's teeth?" Gilbert asked, patting his chest from so much laughter.

"Yes, I saw it."

"His teeth almost looked like Braun's teeth."

"Sure did."

"Except, Braun's teeth may be black, but he still got all of them."

"You're right."

"That dude's mouth was like, a tooth here, and skip, skip, skip. A tooth there, and skip, skip, skip."

"That's funny, Gilbert!" Vincent chuckled wildly, his papers sliding from under his arm.

"If you went inside his mouth, you could play hopscotch."

"Hee! Hee!"

Several minutes passed and the three attractive girls came out of the bank to buy The Baldwin Express from Gilbert and Vincent.

"Wow!" said Gilbert, rubbing his fingers around her palm as he reached for the quarter. "You all look good. I mean, you all look real, real good." After living at the Willingham residence for awhile, he rarely got the opportunity to see any attractive girls.

"Why, thank you," rendered the young beauty in the burgundy hotpants, purposely trying to blow Gilbert's mind.

"What's your name?" Gilbert asked, flirting at the same time.

"I'm Violet," she said. "What's your name?"

"My name's Gilbert."

"Gilbert what?"

"Gilbert Curry."

Violet turned away from Rush Boulevard to keep her attractive rear end from being seen.

"That's a nice name."

"Who are those other two girls that you're with?"

"They're my cousins."

"What's their names?"

"Monique and Renee."

"Your cousins are pretty."

"Thank you."

"And so are you."

"You're so nice."

Violet turned away to look the opposite direction. She wanted to make an inquiry.

"Who's the light-skinned boy with the pretty curly hair?"

"He's my foster brother."

"You're who?"

"Foster brother."

"What's his name?"

"Vincent."

"He's cute."

"He already knows that."

"Where's this foster home at?"

"It's on Milwaukee Parkway."

"Is your foster brother mixed?"

"Yes, he is."

"With what?"

"His mother is black and his father is Italian."

"Black and Italian, huh?" Violet said. "Mixed kids always come out cute."

"Do you live with your real mother and father?" Gilbert asked.

"Yeah," Violet smiled. "Why did you have to be put into a foster home?"

"Shew!" Gilbert snooted. "My father kept beating up on my mother and then he would beat on me real bad. They would take me away everytime my father would beat on me and my mother. I've been to a lot of different foster homes."

"I'm sorry."

"That's okay."

"Do you like the foster home that you're in now?"

"Fuck no!" Gilbert blasted, locking serious eye contact with Violet.

"Why not?"

"Our foster parent's are real mean to us."

"Mean? How?"

"They curse at us all the time," Gilbert explained. "They're always talking about beating us with an extension cord. We have to sleep on beds that have dried up shit and piss and snot stains on the mattress and boxspring."

"Yuck!" Violet frowned. "That's nasty!"

"Sure is."

"That's too bad."

"We have to lay our faces on that junk every night."

"Have you ever thought about running away?"

"All the time?"

"Are there a lot of other people in this foster home?"

"Let's see," Gilbert thought. "There's Vincent over there, Vincent's big brother, Vernon, our other foster brother, Jose, who's across the street, both of my foster parents, Mr. and Mrs. Willingham, an old woman named Granny Dear, and some handicapped men."

"Handicapped?" Violet asked. "What's wrong with them?"

"Two of them are mentally retarded."

"Really?"

"There's another man who's got a paralyzed hand."

"If you don't like that home, can't you call those people?"

"What people?"

"You know, the ones who take foster kids to different foster homes."

"Caseworkers?"

"I guess."

The story that Gilbert was telling Violet about the Willingham residence seemed quite interesting to her. He could go on for hours telling her about all the horrible details. She didn't want to cut him short, but she had other engagements. Vincent sold two papers to Monique and Renee. Before walking towards the parking lot, they surrounded a very shy Vincent. They twirled their fingers around his large curly locks. Quite naturally, he blushed and his heart pounded like a barritone drum. His cheeks turned rosy red. The experience was mind-blowing because it was a rarity for three good-looking teenage girls to show him that much attention. As they drove out of the parking lot, they waved, smiled, and even winked back at Gilbert and Vincent.

"You lucky ass fool!" Gilbert acclaimed. "I wish that I had that good hair like yours."

"I'm not lucky," Vincent said, never making an ordeal out of the fine texture of his hair.

"Yes you are, and you know it."

"How am I lucky?"

"Girls love light-skinned dudes with good hair," Gilbert defined.

"I never thought it was my hair or my skin color."

"You fool!" Gilbert charged. "What else could it be?"

"Quit calling me all those fools," Vincent confronted Gilbert.

"Ooops!" Gilbert remembered. "I didn't mean to call you a fool. Those three girls looked good and they had some big booties, too."

"Yes, they did have some real big booties."

"Check this out," Gilbert said. "When I was living at one of those other foster homes, there was this light-skinned dude with real good hair who lived up the street. I started hanging around him because he got all the girls."

"Why do you keep talking about your other foster homes?"

"I don't know, I just do."

"I don't like being light-skinned with good hair," Vincent resented, always wishing that he could change his racial identity.

"Why not?"

"Because of those people at Abraham Lincoln."

"What they do?"

"Calling me all those *white boys* and *white honkies* and *half-breed honkies.*"

"So what."

"I hate it when they call me those names."

"They're just jealous."

"Are they?" Vincent asked.

"Especially that black, tarbaby motherfucker whose ass I was gonna kick."

"Jerry Grayson."

"Whatever his name was."

"He's always calling me those names."

"That black motherfucker is jealous!"

"Of what?"

"He wished he had that good, curly hair like yours."

One of the guards came to the double glass doors of the bank and stuck a key in the lock. Gilbert came up to the doors and pressed his face up to the glass.

"What time is it?" Gilbert asked the guard.

"It's 4:50," the guard told Gilbert, tilting his watch to the glass so he could see the time for himself.

"Are you closed?"

"Yes."

"When will you be open again?"

"Tomorrow morning," the guard said. "The doors'll open about 9:00 a.m."

"Thank you."

"You're welcome, young man."

The parking lot was nearly empty. Cadillacs and Lincoln Continentals drove up and down Rush Boulevard. Inside these fancy automobiles, which had donut whitewalls on the tires, lightly tinted windows, gold and silver angels gracing the front of the hoods, loud eight track tape players, were men at the steering wheels who wore big straw brims, fancy three-piece suits, with pure silk shirts that were unbuttoned halfway down their broad chests, showcasing their jewelry, dark sunglasses, and permed hairdos.

On the passenger's side, and in the back, there were women wearing different colored wigs, make-up covering their aging faces, large looped earrings, form-fitting dresses or hot pants, drooped halter tops, which revealed prints of their large and small breasts.

Gilbert suggested that they travel further down Rush Boulevard. They had hopes to sell the rest of The Baldwin Express before nightfall. Vincent looked across the street, trying to locate Jose. He wasn't over there, so they journeyed into a restaurant further down Rush Boulevard.

Written in large red letters, on the front window of a neighborhood dining spot, was *Mickey's Restaurant and Lounge.* Gilbert walked inside with his papers hanging down by his right side. Vincent followed him and they discovered a buffet that faced the opposite direction of the dining area. The walls were proudly displayed with framed portraits of Dr. Martin Luther King, Jr., Malcolm X, Andrew Young, Medgar Evers, Marcus Garvey, Jesse Jackson, and other black leaders. The owner, Mickey Cartwright, threw up a hand signal to Gilbert. He walked past the buffet, thinking about all that food.

"How much is The Baldwin Express?" Mickey asked Gilbert, digging into his deep left pocket for loose change.

"They're a quarter," Gilbert said.

"Let me get four of them," he requested, sorting through a handful of pennies, nickels, and dimes.

"Thank you, sir," Gilbert said graciously, dropping the four quarters down his pocket.

When Gilbert walked past the buffet again, his tastebuds were ready to go to work. Fried chicken, green beans, macaroni and cheese, beef brisket, corn-on-the-cob, spaghetti, hot buttered dinner rolls, beef stew, pork steak, and an assortment of deserts like pies, cakes, cobblers, cookies, and ice cream, were some of the tasty food that sat in the long and deep trays. The cashier called Vincent over to her register. She wore a net over her head to protect the food.

"How much are you selling The Baldwin Express for?"

"A quarter," Vincent said in a business tone of voice.

"Let me get two of them," the cashier requested, feeling around both pockets for some change. In exchange for the two papers, she handed Vincent two shiny quarters.

Instantly, people around the dining area were reaching into their purses, coin holders, shirt pockets, all holding up quarters. Gilbert and Vincent traveled over to their individual tables. From one table to the next, they sold more papers with pride. Most people around the neighborhood knew that *Mickey's* was an excellent place. The food was great, the atmosphere was pleasant, and dining time was unlimited. There was a lounge on the other side for alcoholic beverages and a jukebox for musical listening pleasures.

Two couples sitting at the back of the restaurant called Vincent over to their table. Both men reached over the table with quarters clamped between their fingers. Vincent handed them their papers, and as always, he thanked them. From the front of the restaurant, a man called for Vincent. He glanced

that direction, but Gilbert had already rushed towards the same table. Gilbert made the sale, leaving Vincent fairly angry.

"You punk!" Vincent confronted Gilbert. "You know good and well that that man wanted to buy one of my papers." He wanted to snatch the quarter right out of Gilbert's hand.

"I was closer."

"So."

"So, I went ahead and sold him one of my papers."

"But you know that he called me over to his table."

"It doesn't matter."

"Yes, it does."

"No, it doesn't."

"As long as he got a paper, that's all that counts."

"You're jealous!" Vincent responded angrily.

"Of what?"

"You know I can sell more papers than you."

"You can't stand no competition."

"That's a lie."

Since most people had left *Mickey's*, Gilbert and Vincent stepped out on the sidewalk. Both had several choices as to where they would go to finish selling their papers. Vincent looked up the street, where the bank was closed. Gilbert looked the opposite direction, right where Bertolli's Liquors was still busy with many customers.

Gilbert and Vincent strolled over to Bertolli's. Panhandlers, drunks, and druggies were everywhere, desperately trying to support their drinking and drug habits. Stepping onto the sidewalk was the store owner, a rather slim-built and gray-haired man named Paul Bertolli. Occasionally, Paul checked out front to make sure that law and order was kept among the vagrants who loitered in front of his store. With a sawed-off shotgun and several handguns behind the counter, he never worried about a random robbery or those who wanted to create a ruckus.

Change jingled inside the loose pockets of Gilbert and

Vincent. They watched the panhandlers and dopeheads beg the customers for money. One of the men wearing the filthiest clothes, and whose breath smelled like a shutdown distillery, trotted towards Gilbert. Gilbert studied his body movement closely, making sure that he didn't have a gun or a knife. A long bottle covered with a paper sack hung to his right side.

"Can you help a brother out with some change?" the alcoholic asked Gilbert, his intoxicating voice slumbering with words.

"I can't give you any of my money," Gilbert explained, moving a few steps away from the strange man, avoiding his annoying body odor.

"Can you help a brother out with just a little change?"

"This isn't my money."

"Whose money is it?"

"My foster mother."

"Help me out, brother man."

"I can't."

"She won't know if you spare me a little change," said the drunk hustler, trying his hardest to extort money from Gilbert. He nearly fell to the ground from being senselessly intoxicated.

"Yes, she will."

"No, she won't."

"Sorry."

"All I need is a little change."

"Can't help you, sir."

"I need to buy me something to eat."

"I'm not stupid."

"What're you talking about?"

"You want to fill your belly with more liquor."

"I'm not gonna do no such thing."

"Yes, you are."

"You sure are smart."

"Thank you."

"How old are you?"

"Twelve, going on thirteen."

"Help me out, youngblood."

"If I gave you some of this money, my foster mother would get my foster father to beat me with an extension cord."

Gilbert kept trying to stress his point. He hoped that the bum would just disappear.

"Did you say extension cord?"

"Sure did."

"Them dam extension cords hurt!" the drunk said, his state of intoxcation nearly diminishing. "They hurt like a sonofabitch! My daddy beat me with an extension cord a long time ago. They leave them marks on you that hurt real bad. Hell, it hurts from just thinking about that beating that I got."

"I don't wanna get no beating when I get home."

"Keep your money, little brother," the drunk advised. "I wouldn't want my worst enemy getting beat with no extension cord."

Long after he begged and bargained, Gilbert still wasn't about to give away his hard-earned money. Because more drunks hung around Bertolli's, staggering up to people and begging for money, Vincent suggested that they travel down Rush Boulevard. Nicoletti's Handy Stop and Vanzetti's One-Stop were crowded with more panhandlers and druggies and drunks.

Less than two blocks down from Vanzetti's, on the opposite side of the street, a large hotel sat in the very middle of the block. In bright green and yellow neon colors, a sign above the hotel read, *Bennie's Town and Country Hotel*. Parked directly in front of this hotel were long rows of exotic and expensive automobiles. Sitting comfortably behind the wheel of these Mercedes-Benzes, BMWs, Rolls Royces, and Jaguars, were well-dressed white men, ready to spend some big money.

Groups of women from all racial backgrounds stood in

front of *Bennie's Town and Country Hotel*. They aggressively approached the cars, some of them being black, white, and hispanic. From the passenger's side, they stuck their heads through the windows, seeking a date with one of the big-spending tricks. These women reminded Gilbert and Vincent of the same ones who had rode up and down Rush Boulevard in those fancy Cadillacs and Lincoln Continentals.

"Let's ask one of those men across the street to buy a Baldwin Express," Vincent suggested, ready to cross the street and start selling the rest of his papers.

"Those white dudes?" Gilbert asked.

"Yes."

"No way!" Gilbert dejected. "White people don't buy The Baldwin Express."

"They might."

"Are you talking about the ones in those bad cars?"

"Yes."

"They won't buy one."

"Let's ask some of those women over there."

"In those funny looking clothes?"

"Yes."

"They're not gonna buy one, neither."

"Why not?" Vincent asked. "They should, some of those women are black."

"And guess what?"

"What?"

"They're prostitutes," Gilbert explained. "They're out here trying to make money like us."

"What are prostitutes?"

"Oh no!"

"What's wrong?"

"You don't know what prostitutes are?" Gilbert asked, bursting out in total laughter.

"No," Vincent said. "What are they?"

"They're women who sell their pussy for money."

"For money?"

"Yes."

"Why do they sell their pussy for money?"

"I can see that Mr. and Mrs. Willingham done locked you up in that house for too long."

"Go ahead, tell me, Gilbert."

"I don't know."

"I thought if a dude wanted to fuck a girl, he could do it for free."

"Not in this world."

"I didn't even know that."

"Now you know."

"Those white men are over there showing them lots of money."

The flashing of money brought a sparkle to the eyes of Gilbert. They crossed the street and stood in the midst of the gangs of prostitutes. A short man with a beak nose and dark, slicked back hair, stepped out of the hotel like he was the king of the universe. Standing barely five feet tall, he wore a fancy blue silk shirt with a pair of heavily starched khaki pants. This man was well respected and greatly feared within his turf! He was the hotel's owner, Benedito *'Big-time Bennie'* Caputo. Among some of his street associates, he was also known as, *'The king of the pimps'*.

Bennie operated this transient hotel for men who wanted to rent room for illegal and immoral purposes. When law enforcement wasn't patrolling the area heavily, or cracking down on prostitution, he allowed the pimps and prostitutes to solitcit to the tricks, and the distribution of narcotics was done at the back of the hotel. Of course, in return, everyone had to pay Bennie protection fees, keeping the law at bay so the money could be distributed evenly and fairly.

Bennie saw Vincent and Gilbert walking around asking everyone to purchase The Baldwin Express.

"Hey guys, come here," Bennie signaled to Gilbert and

Vincent, waving his right hand in the air. "I don't mind you guys selling your papers in front of my hotel, but don't stand around the front door."

"Can we try and sell our papers to those men," Gilbert asked.

"What men?"

"The white men sitting in those cars."

"Sure," Bennie agreed."But please, don't bumrush any of those guys. I don't need you scaring any of these people away."

"How do you want us to sell our papers?"

"Just hold the papers up and ask them if they'd like to buy one," Bennie instructed the two youngsters. "That's all you have to do, son."

"Would you like to buy a Baldwin Express?"

"Sure, why not?"

Bennie searched his left pocket for some change. Since he wanted to purchase two papers, he came up with four dimes and two nickels, handing Gilbert two of the dimes and one of the nickels, and then handing Vincent the rest. Gilbert and Vincent remembered the advice that Bessie Mae gave them when a customer bought a paper.

"Thank you, sir," Gilbert said.

"You're welcome, son."

Little did Bennie Caputo know that Vincent was the son of one of his old rivals, the same man that he and Fat Tony and others had double-crossed. Vincent resembled Vito slightly, but not enough for Bennie to know the difference. Years after the dispute over turf, the bad blood was never cleaned up between Bennie and Vito. Vito always knew that Bennie and Fat Tony had he and Marion delivered over into the hands of the law on a framed case. He swore immediate revenge, but whether or not he would ever get even with Bennie and Fat Tony, was still pending.

The mass of prostitutes swarmed the many cars that

parked in front of *Bennie's Hotel*. These women were truly a
sight to see. From the back of their hotpants, their buttock
cheeks hung out. Their high heel shoes made them appear
much taller. Long wigs hung down their backs and thick
layers of makeup were packed on their abused faces. During
this time of evening, particularly on Fridays, Rush Boulevard
looked like a circus of freaks. As the cars pulled up, street-
oriented jargon clouded the air.

"Hey, baby," one of the regular tricks said. "How much
for a good time?"

"How much you're spending?" replied a hooker with a
killer body.

"Whatever you need, baby."

"Then, I'll do whatever you want."

"Anything?"

"That's right."

"Can you turn some good tricks, baby?"

"Sure can, honey."

"What will you do?"

"I'll do some things that you never had done before."

"Like what?" asked the sex craved white man, ready to
throw out a roll of money at the tall and curvaceous hooker.

"I'll suck your dick and make you cum like a guinea
pig."

"You can make me cum real hard?"

"Real, real hard, baby!"

"What else?"

"I'll blow up through your asshole and make your toes
curl back to your heels."

"Tell me more, baby, tell me more!"

"I'll juggle your balls around in my mouth like ice cubes."

"Can you make me feel good?"

"I'll make you scream for mercy, sugah."

"Can you give me the best time of my life?"

"I'll have you coming back for more of this good stuff."

"Let's go, sugah," the horny man told the hooker. He threw his arm around her waist and opened the door to the hotel.

At the front desk, inside the old hotel, Bennie's nephew, Johnny Caputo, was sitting down watching television. The bell on top of the desk rang, and he arose from his chair. It wasn't uncommon for him to see a flashy white man with lots of cash, and a black hooker who worked the streets of Rush Boulevard, to eagerly stand in his presence, ready to rent a room.

"How long do you wanna rent a room?" Johnny asked the flamboyant man, someone who was wearing an expensive suit.

"Couple of hours," he said, then flipping out a wallet that was holding a thick stack of high bills.

"Twenty-five dollars," Johnny said, writing up a ticket and then reaching for a key on the wall.

The man handed Johnny two fresh twenty dollar bills and told him to keep the change. Johnny handed him the key to the room and said, "Enjoy."

"Thank you."

Outside the hotel, Gilbert and Vincent waited patiently to try and sell the rest of their papers. Vincent made serious eye contact with Gilbert. Listening to the conversation between the hooker and the trick had startled his mind.

"What's a trick?" Vincent asked.

"I don't know," Gilbert said.

"Were they talking about doing some type of magic trick?"

"How am I supposed to know?"

"What did they mean?"

"That lady was a prostitute."

"Was she?"

"She definitely wasn't no magician."

"I think she talked about sucking that white dude's dick."

"I know you know what that means?"

"Yes, I do."

"Like I said, Mr. and Mrs. Willingham done had you locked up in that house for too long."

"But I'm learning some things now."

"Yes, you're finally learning about life."

Gilbert may have been correct. Shutting Vincent out from the many things that went on out in society may have been the wrong thing to do. He wasn't used to this early street education that was being thrown his direction. But the time had surely come for him to experience some things outside of the Willingham residence.

With one or several women around their arms, the big spending tricks continued walking in and out of the hotel. Since sexual gratification had taken place, or was about to take place, everyone wore big smiles on their faces. The hookers outnumbered the tricks, leaving several women standing in front of and on the side of the hotel, anxiously awaiting more cars to pull up.

A shiny black Cadillac Fleetwood with red leather interior and donut whitewalls parked directly in front of the hotel. Stepping out of this fancy automobile was a tall man with diamond rings on every finger and gold chains around his skinny neck. Covering his lean body, from head to toe, was a white fedora, a white double-breasted suit, a black shirt with a matching black hankerchief, a white silk tie, all coming from top designers, and a pair of white Stacey Adams. A pair of black shades that were trimmed in white disguised his sleepy eyes. Bennie stepped out of the hotel to check on the flow of hookers and tricks. The sharply dressed man walked towards the front entrance.

"How's it going, Jawbone?" Bennie said to the known street pimp, a man known for having a bevy of beautiful whores working for him, recruiting for women near high schools and nightclubs.

"I can't complain," Jawbone said, extending his long arm

to greet Bennie. "How's it going with you, Big-time Bennie?" He towered over the short Italian man.

"Everything's cool, man."

"How're the girls doing tonight?"

Jawbone always inquired about his women as soon as he arrived in front of Bennie's Hotel.

"Doing fine."

"Fuzz been riding through?"

"Don't worry about the fuzz," Bennie told Jawbone. "I've got most of'em paid off. They're right inside my hip pocket."

Bennie always bragged about the legal protection that he had with the police department. As a smart businessman, he kept a hefty payroll for the cops who rode past his hotel and looked the other way.

"I'm gonna try and send you some more customers."

"Sounds good."

Bennie Caputo didn't mind crossing ethnic lines. As long as he could make lots of money and exercise power, it was no problem whatsoever for the many of pimps to solicit their whores in front of his hotel. They both profited greatly this way. While Bennie and Jawbone stood around discussing their business, another fancy Cadillac Sedan de Ville drove up. A tall and dark complexioned man, wearing a charcoal gray, double breasted suit, with a matching gray fedora, stepped out and was styling and profiling. Like Jawbone, he wore diamonds on every finger and thin gold chains around his neck. Bennie and Jawbone were like his business associates. They greeted him as though he was royalty.

"What'cha know good, T-Slick?" Bennie asked the debonair pimp, admiring the taste that he and Jawbone had when it came to fashion.

"I don't know no good," T-Slick said. "How're you feeling, Big-time Bennie?"

"Feeling good, my friend."

"The girls doing okay tonight?"

"They doing just fine."

"Fuzz been bothering anybody tonight?"

"Like I told Jawbone, I've got them boys taken care of."

"Sometimes you make me wish that I was Italian."

"And get blamed for all the crime in America?"

While Bennie, Jawbone, and T-Slick continued discussing their street business, Gilbert and Vincent paced back and forth, hoping they could sell the rest of their papers. Jawbone and T-Slick knew they were holding The Baldwin Express.

"Say, young brother," Jawbone said to Gilbert, looking his direction.

"Yes, sir," Gilbert answered.

"How much is The Baldwin Express?"

"A quarter."

"Whose picture is that on the front?"

"Jesse Jackson."

"Oh yeah," Jawbone said. "Isn't Jesse supposed to be speaking somewhere here in Chicago?"

"Yes, sir."

"Jesse's the man."

"Do you wanna buy a paper?"

"Yeah, let me get two of them."

T-Slick didn't want to leave Vincent out, so he bought two from him. They walked away pointing to the large photo of Jesse Jackson. The front door to the hotel opened and several more hookers walked out with their tricks. In order to remain viewed as honest citizens, some of the tricks, who were clergymen, doctors, lawyers, accountants, engineers, and business owners, rushed to their cars and sped off down Rush Boulevard.

*   *   *

In a secretive room in the very back of the hotel, Bennie and some of his organized crime associates were having an important meeting. Thick cigar smoke filled the room that was occupied by ten of the major players in the liquor, gambling, narcotics, and prostitution business. On one side of the long and oval shaped table, there were five men who controlled most of the liquor and narcotics around the profitable streets of Rush Boulevard and Lowell Avenue.

There was Salvatore "Razor Tongue" Brunelli, Paul "Fast Dealing" Coletti, Francisco "Big Bank Frank" Petrelli, Nicholas "Nick The Kick" Morelli, and Joseph "Joey Batters" Capezio.

Assembled on the opposite side of the table were five other mobsters who controlled the gambling and prostitution business, also around Rush and Lowell. There was Rudolpho "Rudy Butterball" Broncato, Anthony "Fat Tony" Torio, James "Jimmy B" Bruccola, Bobby "Greasy Fingers" Marcello, and of course, the king of the pimps himself, Benedito "Big-time Bennie" Caputo.

One of the reasons for the meeting was because Francisco Petrelli wanted to expand into the narcotics business. Prostitution and liquor were already bringing in major dollars, but Petrelli knew that narcotics like heroin had potential for making huge profits.

"Listen to me fellas," Petrelli spoke generously to his mobster colleagues. "I don't want to turn into no money-hungry sonofabitch. I need about thirty-thousand to make a heroin buy." He took a deep drag from his Cuban cigar and glanced around the room.

"Hey, Frankie," Brunelli said, someone who could use his sharp tongue to cut in on any profitable deal. "What kind of return would you make on that kind of buy?"

"We're guaranteed at least a hundred and sixty-thousand out on the streets."

"Let's hope that our greed don't get our dicks chopped off," Brunelli joked, lowering his head into the shadows of the gloomy room. "What would be our cut off this buy?"

"Let's see how my brain's working," Petrelli said. "If you, Nicky, Joey, Paulie, and myself, put up the thirty-thousand, we could split it at twenty-percent each."

"What a deal!" Brunelli conceded. "If we put up six-thousand a piece, we'll make over a twenty-three thousand dollar profit."

"Absolutely," Petrelli said, a slight swaying of his head.

"What about protection from the police?" Brunelli asked.

"Bennie's got that all taken care of as far as this part of Rush is concerned."

"What about Lowell Avenue?"

"Nicky's got everything under control over on Lowell."

"Any new customers on the scene?"

"We're getting new customers all the time."

"Like who?"

"Dam near all of them are the niggers."

"Sounds about right."

"They'll do just about anything to stay high."

"All the time."

"They always bring more customers to us."

"That's good."

"The hookers and queenies and junkies who hang out on Rush are like walking goldmines."

"We definitely need to keep the hookers supplied."

"They turn their tricks on to the junk and get them hooked."

"That's major bucks there."

"Absolutely."

Evidently, these men preyed on the plight of Chicago's blacks. Most of the black people were poor and disenfranchised. They knew who their loyal customers would be. At times, narcotics use was their only outlet. While the *bad boys of*

crime continued their meeting, Gilbert and Vincent waited patiently in front of the hotel. Walking from the south end of Rush Boulevard, were two more hookers. One was black and the other was hispanic. Most of the tricks were already occupied inside the hotel, which made these two women late arrivals. Now Gilbert and Vincent were able to see why Bessie Mae called *Bennie's Town and Country Hotel* a "whore hotel". It's the only reason why the hotel existed in the first place, catering strictly to the pimps and whores and tricks who came to wallow in sin.

Ironically, the hispanic woman was the veteran hooker named "Chili Pepper". Vincent wasn't aware that once upon a time Chili Pepper worked for his father. After many years of selling her body on the hardcore streets of Chicago, the wear and tear showed across her face and all over her body. How many dicks could one woman have shoved up in her in one lifetime? Eleven and a half years later, Chili Pepper didn't know that she stood in the midst of the son of Vito and Marion Carvelli. She gestured seductive signs as she walked toward Gilbert and Vincent.

"How much have you made?" Chili Pepper asked Gilbert.

"Money?" Gilbert said.

"From selling The Baldwin Express."

"We haven't counted our money yet."

"Pull it out."

"What?"

"Let's see how much you've made."

"I can't."

"Why not, baby?"

"I'll get in trouble."

"No, you won't."

"My foster mother don't want me showing my money to nobody."

"Why?"

"Because I'll get a beating with an extension cord."

"Do you wanna have a good time?" Chili Pepper asked, watching the bulging left pocket of Gilbert.

"What do you mean?"

Chili Pepper was very desperate for money and it showed. For the price that she was asking to show a man a good time, she was practically giving her pussy away.

"Do you wanna buy some pussy?"

"No!" Gilbert dejected.

"Have you ever had any?"

"Yes."

"Not like mine's."

From the shadows of nowhere, Bennie Caputo kicked open the left side of the double glass doors to his hotel. His nephew Johnny was right behind him.

"What the fuck are you doing! What the fuck are you doing!" Bennie blasted two times at Chili Pepper, his wavering finger pointed at the middle of her face, grinding his teeth together like he was going to bite her head off.

"I wasn't doing nothing, Bennie," Chili Pepper jumped, afraid that Bennie would hurt her severely. She wasn't aware that Bennie stood at the door listening to her trying to solicit sex to Gilbert.

"You're out here trying to sell a piece of ass to a kid! For chrissake, he's nothing but a young boy."

"I'm sorry, Bennie," Chili Pepper apologized. "It'll never happen again."

She stood on the side of the hotel frightened out of her mind.

"I know it'll never happen again," Bennie assured her. "If I catch you in front of my hotel again, I'm personally gonna kick your ass up and down Rush."

"I'm so sorry."

"Then I'll have the cops haul your ass off to jail for trying

to solicit to minors. Do you understand where I'm coming from, bitch!"

"Yes, yes, I understand, Bennie."

"Do you?"

"Yes, Bennie, I do."

"Now, get the fuck away from in front of my hotel," Bennie said. "You perverted lowlife spick-cunt!"

There was a sensitive side to Bennie Caputo. Why would an older hooker try and sell sex to a minor like Gilbert? Chili Pepper and her street associate ran up Rush as quickly as possible. Things cooled off and Bennie and his criminal associates walked out through the back of the hotel. Petrelli, Brunelli, and the others agreed that they would make the heroin purchase and distribute to the blacks along Rush and Lowell streets and possibly other urban ghettos throughout Chicago.

Crickets began making those annoying revving sounds. The traffic on Rush Boulevard got heavier. Darkness filled the sky, telling Gilbert and Vincent that it was time to head towards Milwaukee Parkway. Inside their sweaty palms, they held the remainder of their papers. After standing around for several hours, they were really tired. They returned home and Vernon was sitting on the porch with one of his many girlfriends.

She was very attractive indeed. Her face was beautiful and innocent. She had a body that was truly curvaceous. It never came as a surprise how Vernon ended up with the gorgeous girls, simply because he was a very handsome teen. Whispering jokes in one another's ears, and touching the private body parts, had Gilbert and Vincent wishing they had the midas touch that Vernon possessed. They went into the kitchen and took a load off their feet. Bessie Mae had them to empty their pockets so she could count the money.

Chapter 22

IT'S A COLD WORLD!

Heavy snow fell throughout Chicago and the accumulation piled up around the sidewalks, streets, and yards of the residences up and down Milwaukee Parkway. Along with Granny Dear's help, Bessie Mae was in the kitchen preparing lima beans with neckbones. While Bessie Mae stood over the stove stirring the beans, Granny Dear mixed up the cornbread inside a large plastic bowl. The beans had formed a thick, yellowish gravy and the neckbones were well done. The aroma traveled to the basement, seeping through the nostrils of Gilbert, Jose, and Vincent. They were in Sean's room observing his handicapped hand.

"How did your hand get like that?" Gilbert asked Sean, bending forward to study the bent shape of his left hand.

"I was born like this," Sean explained low-spirited, wishing he could change his handicapped status.

"Do you like being in this home?"

"No, I don't."

"Why?" Gilbert asked.

"Mr. Willingham, he curses at me all the time."

"Do you wish you were at another home?"

"Yes, I do," Sean answered like there had to be a better home than the Willingham residence.

"So, do I."

At the edge of Sean's bed, Gilbert, Jose, and Vincent watched the snow get deeper. Gilbert believed that money could be made from shoveling the snow out of the neighbor's yards and driveways. Bessie Mae would probably allow them

to use the shovels out in the toolshed. If they could shovel yards or driveways and make money, she would probably be all for it. Gilbert felt that it wouldn't hurt to ask. He raced up to the kitchen, where Bessie Mae paced back and forth from the stove and sink. She and Granny Dear were putting the finishing touches on the dinner.

"Can we use the shovels in the toolshed?" Gilbert asked Bessie Mae, hoping she wouldn't shout at him.

"For what?" Bessie Mae asked.

"To shovel people's yards and driveways."

"How far are you all going to go?"

"Just up and down Milwaukee Parkway."

"I'm sure J.D. won't mind," Bessie Mae thought. "How much are you all going to charge these yards?"

"At least ten dollars for their sidewalks."

"What about their driveways?"

"Ten dollars."

"What if they want both shoveled?"

"Twenty dollars."

Bessie Mae tested the business skills of Gilbert. He was a bright youngster who knew how to add dollar figures, especially when it came to earning himself some money.

"Go ahead and use the shovels," Bessie Mae permitted. "I want you all to make lots of money."

"Yes, mam."

"And come back home right after you're finished."

"Yes, mam."

Gilbert ran back to the basement excited. He informed Jose and Vincent that Bessie Mae had approved. For the almost blizzard-like weather, they got suited down. They covered their bodies with two shirts, two pairs of pants, and the thickest socks that they could find. Once they were fully dressed, they walked like someone with stiff and aching joints.

Since Bessie Mae never bought them any gloves, they went into the laundry room looking for socks. Any type of

socks to keep their hands warm from the blistering frostbite were sought. Gilbert, Jose, and Vincent were finding real crusty socks, ones that were deeply embedded with dirt. To bring some of the dirt and stiffness out, they beat the socks against the wall, sending clouds of dirt and dust into the air. Afterwards, their hands slid right up to the toe section.

"Dam!" Gilbert sniffed disapprovingly. "These socks stink real bad. Our hands are gonna be smelling like somebody's funky feet."

"Like, who?" Vincent asked Gilbert, also holding socks close to his nose for a quick whiff.

"Probably Mr. Willingham," Gilbert joked. "He's got big, black, and musty feet."

They observed the width and length of the socks.

"Ha! Ha!" Jose laughed. "Somebody should take a gun and shoot Mr. Willingham's stinky feet."

"Kill that funky smell, huh?" Gilbert said.

"Or cut them off," Vincent said.

They threw on their winter parkas and headed towards the toolshed. Giving directions as to where they would start, Gilbert led Jose and Vincent up the south end of Milwaukee Parkway. Some of the houses had flat yards, while others had hills. To make things easier, Gilbert suggested that they start with the flat ones. At the third house from the corner, Vincent knocked on the door. A middle-age couple, approximately in their early forties, answered the door.

"Yes, what can we do for you young man?" the man of the house asked Vincent, slightly cracking the door to keep the cold draft from coming into his house.

"Would you like your yard shoveled, sir?" Vincent asked.

"How much would you charge to do my sidewalk and driveway?"

"Twenty dollars."

"Okay," the man agreed. "You've got yourself a deal, young man. If you do a good job, I might throw in some extra bucks."

"Yes sir!" Vincent cheered. "There won't be one drop of snow left around your sidewalk or driveway."

"Alright, young man."

Minutes after Vincent began shoveling, Gilbert and Jose were a half-block up the street shoveling an elderly woman's sidewalk. The yards were finished, and they trampled through the snow, traveling further south up Milwaukee. They continued to make bids on other people's sidewalks and driveways. The deep snow was like *white gold*. It became handsomely profitable for Gilbert, Jose, and Vincent.

They weren't exactly aware of how much money they had made, but they planned to have it counted before going back home. For three youngsters who had bent and strained their backs and withstood the strong winter winds, Gilbert wanted to call it a day. The thick clusters of flakes started up again. The sky was overshadowed with dark clouds.

Gilbert, Jose, and Vincent reached into their pockets and pulled out the money that they had made. Before counting the crinkly bills, they removed the socks. Gilbert and Jose counted twenty-five dollars each, and ironically, it was all in five dollar bills.

"I'm going to keep twenty and give five to Mrs. Willingham," Gilbert explained to Jose and Vincent, separating the bills by placing four five dollar bills in one hand and one five in the other.

"Are you crazy?" Vincent objected, the cold frost from his breath blowing directly into the hardened face of Gilbert.

"No, I'm not crazy," Gilbert said. "I'm keeping some of this money."

"You're going to hide some of it from Mrs. Willingham?"

"Sure am."

"Why?"

"I've worked hard for this fucking money."

"You're right, Gilbert."

"She's not going to take all of it."

DEWEY REYNOLDS

"I hope that you don't get caught."

"Doing what?"

"Trying to hide that money from her."

"You've been living in that foster home for too long."

"You keep reminding me."

"I won't get caught if you or Jose keep your mouth shut."

"Neither will we."

"Exactly."

"You're a smart dude, Gilbert."

"I froze my black ass off to make this money."

"Guess what?"

"What?"

"We wouldn't have to say nothing to Mrs. Willingham about the money."

"Why's that?"

"She'll figure out that we made more than five dollars."

"How?"

"We've been out here a long time."

"So what."

"She sniffs out money like a rat sniffs out food."

"Fuck Mrs. Willingham!" Gilbert exploded, the cold winter draft forming dark red patches across his brown complexion. "That crippled bitch ain't getting all of my money, no matter how good she is at sniffing out money. She's already taking all of our money that we make from selling The Baldwin Express. We can't even keep a single dime of our money, and I'm tired of the shit."

"What is she doing with our money?" Jose asked, ready to follow the advice given by Gilbert.

"Spending it on herself."

"You think so?"

"Or that fat, black, bald-headed Mr. Willingham!"

"Mr. Willingham?"

"Yes, his black greasy ass!"

"What are you going to do?" Jose asked Gilbert.

"You can give her all of your money," Gilbert said. "She's only getting five dollars, and that's all it is to it."

Vincent was in total agreement with Gilbert. "Where are you gonna hide the rest of your money?"

"I've got a secret hiding place."

"I know she goes through our drawers when she stick our clothes in there."

"That's why I've got this hiding place."

"What if Mrs. Willingham finds out about this secret hiding place?"

"She won't find out," Gilbert assured Vincent, cleverly learning new tactics the longer that he stayed at the Willingham residence.

"Why do you think she won't find out?"

"Nobody's ever around when I stick my money in this hiding place."

"Where's this secret hiding place?" Jose inquired.

"It's on the other side of my bed."

"Where?"

"Under a flipped up piece of tile."

"That's cool!" Jose rejoiced. "How much you've got up under there?"

"I don't know," Gilbert said."But I've got a lot of tips that I made when I was selling The Baldwin Express."

"You've made tips?"

"All the time."

"You might get caught, Gilbert," Vincent predicted, struck with sudden fear.

"How?"

"Remember what Vernon told us about Mrs. Willingham?"

"What did he tell us?"

"Mrs. Willingham can smell money like a bloodhound smells blood."

"Yes, I remember."

"Remember what else he told us?"

"What?"

"That she would never let us keep any of our money."

"I remember that, too," Gilbert recalled. "No matter how many times we go out and sell The Baldwin Express, rake leaves, cut grass, shovel snow, or run errands for those old people, that crippled bitch is going to take every dime that we make. We've got a greedy foster mother and that's why I'm keeping some of my money."

"I'm with you, Gilbert," Vincent said.

"I'm with you, too," Jose said.

Before they went into the house, Gilbert, Jose, and Vincent stood on the porch stuffing the money into separate pairs of pants. They walked back into the warm kitchen and gave Bessie Mae five dollars each. They knew that it was five dollars that they would never see again. Bessie Mae unfolded the bills and stuffed them into her coin purse. Unsurprisingly, she stared at the money and began wondering about the length of time they spent out there.

"Is this all the money that you all made?" Bessie Mae questioned her three foster sons.

"Yes, mam," Gilbert said, praying that she wouldn't start checking their pockets.

"I thought you were charging at least ten for sidewalks or driveways."

"The people on Milwaukee were only paying five dollars."

"Cheap ass people!" Bessie Mae said, buying the lie that Gilbert had just told.

A black Chevy truck came down the hill on the side of the house. J.D. was turning into the driveway. He parked and came around to the camper with a twelve gauge rifle in his left hand, allowing his beagle hounds to jump out of the camper and return to their pen. With a strong grip of his right hand, he held three dead rabbits by their hind legs.

His yellow hunting jumpsuit was bloody and had small twigs attached all over.

Occasionally, J.D. and other skilled hunters would travel to the wooded areas on the outskirts of Chicago to hunt for rabbits and deer, using as many beagle hounds as possible. The rabbits were placed on the side of the porch and J.D. came into the house searching for Braun.

"Brawns!" J.D. called in an angry voice from the bottom of the stairs, whisking rabbit hairs from between his fingers.

"Yeah, yeah, you looking for me, J.D.?" Braun answered intensely, coming down the stairs beating the middle of his right hand with one of his wires, and sucking food and tobacco kernels from between his badly rotten teeth.

"Put dat goddam wire up!" J.D. shouted, pointing up the stairs towards the second floor. "I'm gone need ya to hep ma skan dose wabbits."

"Okay, okay, I'll help you skin the rabbits, J.D.," Braun replied humbly, placing the wire in his pocket and rushing towards his room. Amazingly, someone mentally retarded like Braun could understand the illiteracy in the totally wreckless dialect of J.D.

J.D. jerked open the basement door, slamming the knob against the wall. He sent a loud echo down into the basement. Gilbert, Jose, and Vincent ran to the head of their beds. They pretentiously straightened wrinkles from the covers, opened their school textbooks, or picked up objects from the floor. Like always, they had to act innocent whenever an evil bastard like J.D. came through the basement. J.D. stepped to the middle of their room and pointed towards the backyard.

"Git up off yall's asses," J.D. told Gilbert, Jose, and Vincent.

"Yes, sir," all three answered.

"I want yall ta git dose shuvels fum da shed."

"What do you want us to do, Mr. Willingham?" Gilbert asked.

"I want yall ta shuvel round dis house."

"Where do you want us to start?"

"Start toads da backyard."

"Towards the backyard, Mr. Willingham?" Vincent asked.

"Ain't dat what I said?"

"Yes, sir."

"And don't be out dere paying round."

"We won't be playing around, Mr. Willingham," Jose said, rushing towards the closet with Gilbert and Vincent to grab his parka.

They walked through the front room and out to the toolshed. J.D. traveled into the next room, where Sean was crushing up a ballpoint inkpen. The pen had broken into different sections across his lap, with a big ink spot having spread across his left pants leg. Sean was angry and his anger had to be taken out different ways. It became severely depressing living at the Willingham residence.

"Why ya baking dat pen up?" J.D. asked Sean, the red and watery eyes, puckered black lips that stayed chapped, and heavy breathing, all coming to the surface.

"It was mine's," Sean replied defensively, rubbing the black ink across his lap.

"I don't care," J.D. said. "Why ya gittin smart wit ma?"

"You're getting smart with me."

"How Bessa Mae spose ta git dat ank out of dose pants?"

"I don't know how Mrs. Willingham is supposed to get the ink out."

"You done messed up a good pair of britches."

"I don't care."

"Don't git smart wit ma no mo, boy!" J.D. said, the redness in his eyes more concentrated. He couldn't believe that Sean would bravely stand up against him, because J.D. was feared by everyone at the Willingham residence.

"You got smart with me, first. Remember?"

"Where ya git dat pen, anyways?"

"None of your business."

"You juss wait, boy," J.D. brisked. "Afta I skan dose wabbits, I'm gone come back down here wit ma stanching code and make ya tell ma why ya spill all dat ank over yo britches."

J.D. returned outdoors to where his truck was parked. Since they forgot to cover their hands with socks, Gilbert, Jose, and Vincent held the shovels between their legs. Their hands were cold and they sought refuge by blowing their warm breath onto their crossed fingers. Braun waited by the camper for J.D. to give him instructions. He was ordered to hold the rabbits by their hind legs. While J.D. pulled the coat from the first rabbit, starting from the forelegs and on down to the head, the rabbit slipped from the hands of Braun.

"Hold da wabbit up wight, Brawns!" J.D. said angrily, using the same technique to skin every rabbit that he's ever killed.

"Okay, okay, I'll hold the rabbit up right, J.D.," Braun said, bringing the rabbit back into the tight grip of both hands.

"And shut da hellup!" J.D. snarled, jerking harder on the coat of the rabbit.

"Alright, alright, I'll shut up, J.D."

"Shut da fuck up, Brawns!"

"Yeah, yeah, I'll shut up, J.D."

"Shut yo muttapucking mouth, Brawns!"

"Okay, okay, I'll shut up, J.D."

"Don't let ma tell ya no mo!"

"Alright, alright, I'll be quiet, J.D."

"Don't make ma slap ya in yo goddam mouth!"

J.D. wanted to have the last word. Braun wanted to have the last word. Didn't J.D. ever stop and consider that Braun was mentally retarded? Maybe J.D. possessed a mind that wasn't any more developed than that of Braun. Finally, Braun allowed J.D. to have the last word. When all three rabbits were skinned, J.D. took his large hunting knife and slit them down the middle of their stomachs. Small pools of blood

dripped from the rabbits, soaking right through the snow. The organs fell out of their bodies and onto the ground.

Gilbert, Jose, and Vincent shoveled their way up the hill. They had a long and cold work assignment ahead of them. J.D. wanted the front, back, and side of the house shoveled. Large snowflakes began to fall. It only meant extra work for them. Vincent was the shortest of the three and the snow had elevated to his knees. Scoop after scoop, they threw the snow to the side of the sidewalk. They periodically stopped to rub their mildly frostbitten hands. J.D. turned to look their direction and they quickly shoveled again.

The rabbits were skinned and gutted. For an outstanding job, J.D. rewarded his beagle hounds by gathering the organs and throwing them over the fence. The hungry hounds wasted no time sinking their teeth into the hearts, livers, stomachs, and intestines. Blood drooled down the side of their mouths as they swallowed some of the organs whole. After watching his dogs dine on the rabbit organs, J.D. went to check on his three foster sons.

From the edge of the camper, he stood and observed them. Suddenly, they stopped to warm their hands. Vincent slid his hands under both armpits, using as much friction as possible to create some warmth. From his dehydrated mouth, he gushed out warm air onto his frostbitten hands.

No relief was accomplished, because his mouth was coated with cool air. As a result of the thick mucous running from his nose, his upper lip had stiffened. Gilbert tried sucking in the dripping mucous from under his nose and around his lips. Jose had both hands between his legs. He rubbed them at the knees, also trying to create some warmth. Nightfall was approaching, and J.D. wanted the sidwalks shoveled in a reasonable amount of time.

"Yall betta keep on shuvlin," J.D. strongly ordered Gilbert, Jose, and Vincent, pointing at them individually.

"My hands are real cold, Mr. Willingham!" cried the

pitiful voice of Vincent, shedding light tears from his blurry eyes.

"I don't care," J.D. said unmercifully. "Keep on shuvlin, boy."

J.D. looked over at Gilbert and noticed that his shovel wasn't moving. "What's wong wit ya, Gailbert?"

"My hands are real cold, too, Mr. Willingham!" Gilbert weeped, trying to shake off some of the cold from his numb hands.

"Ain't nuttin wong wit yo hands, boy!" J.D. snarled, kicking snow up towards Gilbert's face.

J.D. moved over by Jose and also noticed that his shovel wasn't moving. "Why ain't ya shuvlin lack I told ya, boy?"

"My fingers are frozen, Mr. Willingham," Jose reproached, rubbing his fingers together, while blowing his breath into the palm of his blistering cold hands.

"Ain't nuttin wong wit yo fangers."

"They feel like they're about to start bleeding."

"I don't care," J.D. said. "I want yall ta keep shuvlin dis goddam snow!"

The hands of Gilbert, Jose, and Vincent had become severely numb. Vincent's hands became especially red. Their faces were flushed from the strong winter winds. The soles of their feet were like stones, because the cold air penetrated their thin sole sneakers. The shoes they wore were very cheap ones that were bought at "Loretta's Thrifty House of Bargains".

Every chance they got, they tried warming their bitterly cold hands. Without caution, J.D. turned around and caught them resting their shovels on the ground. He demanded that they keep shoveling. They begged J.D. to allow them to go inside and get warm. No sympathy whatsoever came from J.D. Standing on the side of his truck, he waited to see if they would resume their harsh task.

The cold winter draft blew into his already red eyes. They appeared as two flaming red marbles. His chapped and

cracked lips were like sun-dried prunes. Beneath all that body fat, J.D.'s blood boiled with sheer rage. He wanted to prove to his three foster sons, which he considered uncoop- erative, that he truly meant business. He kicked his way through the deep snow and started up the stairs going to the porch. Obscene words were mumbled silently. When J.D. was no longer in sight, Gilbert ran over to Jose and Vincent.

"Mr. Willingham's going to get his extension cord," Gil- bert told Jose and Vincent, his face having turned seriously red.

"How do you know?" Jose asked.

"I heard him cursing when he was walking up the stairs."

"So."

"You know what that means."

"What?"

"Whenever that fat black motherfucker gets mad," Gil- bert reiterated strongly. "He runs and get that extension cord." Gilbert was only trying to warn Jose and Vincent that they might be in danger.

"Is he going to come out here and beat us?" Jose asked.

"He might."

"In the snow?"

"We never know."

"Then let's start shoveling."

"My hands feel like stones," Gilbert said.

"Mine's feel like frozen iron," Vincent said.

"I've got an idea."

"What?"

Gilbert, Jose, and Vincent ran inside the basement and rushed straight towards the laundry room. They threw dirty clothes everywhere, searching for anything to protect their hands from the merciless cold. To assure complete warmth for his hands, Vincent slid on two pairs of dress socks and two pairs of tube socks. Gilbert and Jose slid on two pairs of thick

tube socks. Time was crucial! They rushed back outdoors to resume their task.

Through the heavy snow, J.D. came walking with a long brown extension cord clutched in his right hand. To see if they had made any progress, he stood over one of the brick platforms. They were paranoid! Gilbert peeked from the corner of his eyes, hoping that J.D. wouldn't notice the socks covering his hands. J.D. paced up and down the sidewalk like a *master drill instructor.*

The extension cord swung down by his right leg. Snow was maliciously kicked out of his path. For anyone who didn't want to bend their backs and shovel, J.D. was delightfully ready to sting their backs with a lash of his extension cord. Gilbert, Jose, and Vincent bent, scooped, and threw snow off to the side. They finally reached the top of the hill, ready to start shoveling the sidewalk in front of the house.

Inside the kitchen, Bessie Mae had turned off the fire to the lima beans. She limped over to the window facing the side of the house. She smeared the fog away from the window to watch J.D. stand guard over their three foster sons. She lifted the window up and wasn't too pleased with the way that Gilbert was shoveling.

"Get that pile of snow, Gilbert," Bessie Mae said, poking her finger on the screen.

"What pile, Mrs. Willingham?" Gilbert asked, looking up at the window and trying to move his shovel at the same time.

"Watch the tone of your voice, boy!" Bessie Mae hollered down at Gilbert. "J.D. is standing right there."

"I wasn't getting smart."

"Can't you see that pile on the side of your leg?"

"No, mam."

"You dumb bastard!" Bessie Mae barked. "On your left side, dummy."

"Okay, I see it now."

Gilbert and Jose shoveled further down the sidewalk. J.D. circled the area where Vincent shoveled.

"Git dat pile of snow wight dere," J.D. told Vincent, pointing with the same hand that held the extension cord.

"What pile, Mr. Willingham?" Vincent asked, swaying his head from left to right.

"Wight dere, ya dummy."

"Right where, Mr. Willingham?"

"Don't pay dumb wit ma, boy."

"I'm not playing dumb, Mr. Willingham."

"You blind, boy?"

"No, sir."

"Why can't you see dat snow wight dere?"

"I'm trying, Mr. Willingham."

"Don't make ma hit ya wit dis stanching code," J.D. threatened, jerking his extension cord back, holding the tightest grip ever.

"Yes, sir, I'll get it, Mr. Willingham!" Vincent dismayed, rapidly scooping every drop of snow near his radius. "I'll get it right now, sir!"

J.D. kicked a pile of snow with his right foot that caused flakes to land in the already blurry eyes of Vincent. "I don't wanna see not one dop of snow out here."

"Yes, sir, there won't one drop left out here."

Gilbert, Jose, and Vincent tried ending this brawny winter task. At times, they believed that J.D. didn't have an ounce of sanity. He must have been possessed by demons to do some of the things that he would do. In their opinions, to stand in blistering cold weather with an extension cord gripped in his hand, making sure that his three foster sons shoveled snow at a satisfactory pace, had to be totally insane. After he left, they slowed down their pace. The kitchen window facing the side of the house came up again. The scratching of old wood reflected out to the sidewalk.

"Get back to work!" Bessie Mae shouted down to Gilbert,

Jose, and Vincent, blowing thick cigarette smoke through the screen.

"We're working, Mrs. Willingham," Gilbert responded, pausing to look up at the window.

"I'm not blind, boy!" Bessie Mae validated. "I'm looking right through this window at all three of you."

"I'm tired and my feet are cold, Mrs. Willingham," Vincent said, resting his shovel between his legs to look up at the window.

"I don't care, keep shoveling the snow until it's all gone."

"My arms are tired."

"From what?"

"Lifting the snow with this heavy shovel," Vincent said, holding his exhausted arms down by his side.

"Do you want me to send J.D. back out there?"

"No, mam."

"I'll get him to beat you out there in the cold."

"I don't want him to come back out here."

"Then get back to shoveling that snow."

Bessie Mae's mentioning the extension cord was enough for Gilbert, Jose, and Vincent to put more stride in shoveling the snow. The job was completed and they returned to the basement. J.D. was in the next room arguing with Sean. Still, they quarreled about the breaking up of the ink pen. Lots of ink had spread across the leg of the pants. Sean stubbornly refused to tell J.D. why he broke the pen up. J.D. felt that Sean may have wasted some of their money by ruining a good pair of pants.

"What's yo muttapucking problem, Shone?" J.D. asked Sean in the harshest voice, standing at the foot of Sean's bed with the extension cord in his right hand.

"I don't have a problem," Sean said, staring up at the fire red in the eyes of J.D. "What's your problem, Mr. Willingham?"

"Why ya bake dat pen up?"

"It was mine's."

"Why ya spill dat ank everywhere?"

"I wasn't trying to spill the ink."

"You done messed up a good pair of britches."

"So."

"Dat's it!" J.D. gruffed. "Git yo clothes off."

"Get my what off?" Sean asked in a surprised voice, fright rushing straight to his heart.

"I said, git yo clothes off!"

*   *   *

J.D. was about to practice an old family tradition that was harsh, a brutal tradition that occurred during his upbringing in Clarksdale, Mississippi. He was about to brutally beat Sean in the total nude with the extension cord. Many wondered why J.D. was so abusive, and where the abuse may have stemmed from, severely punishing anyone at his whim.

As Sean bent down to untie his shoes, J.D.'s evil mind traveled back to his early years of growing up in Clarksdale, Mississippi. He remembered the vicious beatings that his father would give him. Clarksdale was largely a cotton growing section of Mississippi that had a vast whiteness of cottonfields, using Negroes to pick most of the crop.

J.D.'s mother, Callie Mae Willingham, a very, very dark complexioned woman, with a wide nose that spread across most of her shiny black face, who dressed in some of the gleaming white cotton that she picked, returned home from one of the stores with corn meal, salt pork, sugar, coffee, and black molasses. During this time of day, J.D. hadn't been around to help his mother carry any of the cooking ingredients home from the store.

J.D.'s father, Henry Joe Willingham, also very, very dark complexioned, a man who dressed in white cotton shirts with vests and matching pants, returned from the cottonfields on a horse. Like his son, he had a severely limited vocabulary and an innocence of grammatical niceties. Long bales of cotton hung over the horse's back.

Along the streets that were abruptly cottonfields, Henry emerged into the shaded open country of bright willow trees. He came up to their large, worn down frame house, with wide front galleries.

"Where bouts J.D., Callie Mae?" Henry asked his wife, brushing dirt from his clothes.

"J.D. spose ta be out in da fields, Henry," Callie answered, pouring the slow black molasses into one of the large jars.

"I'm gone beat da skan off his hide," Henry said. "He spose ta be heppin ma take dis cotton to da white folks over yonder."

"Dat niggah dun wanna mind nobody," Callie Mae told Henry, like J.D. had become very disobedient. "J.D. wuss spose ta hep ma brang dis supper on home."

Callie Mae and Henry must have conjured up J.D. He walked into the house sweating profusely. Henry was furious at his teenage son.

"Where bouts you been, J.D.?" Henry asked, the energetic J.D. standing there breathing heavy.

"I been out in da fields, pappa."

"Dun lie ta ma, niggah!"

"I ain't lying to ya, pappa," J.D. said, wiping sweat from his shiny black face. "Mista man had us Negros folks pickin cotton late today."

"You spose ta tell dose white folks you got thangs ta tend to," said Henry. "Ya know you wuss spose ta hep yo mammy wit some stuff fore suppatime."

"But pappa . . ."

"But nuttin niggah!" he yelled. "Git out doze."

"I ain't did nuttin, pappa."

"I'm gone beat da skan off yo hide, boy!"

Henry made J.D. strip down to absolutely nothing and tied him to the trunk of a tree in their wide open backyard. With some of the thick branches from the willow trees, Henry started beating his son. He and Callie Mae didn't tolerate J.D. coming home late to perform his duties.

"Don't beat ma, pappa!" J.D. screamed, trying to squirm his way out of the tight rope that Henry had used to wrap large bales of cotton.

"You gone mind ma, boy?" Henry asked J.D., taking long and hard strokes with the thick willow branches.

"Yes suh, pappa!" J.D. screamed, feeling the severe sting of the branches across his nude body.

"You gone mind yo mammy, boy?"

"Yes suh, pappa! Yes suh . . . !"

"You gone mind me and Callie Mae, aint'cha boy?"

"Yes suh! Yes suh!" J.D. shouted loudly, his cries strong enough to be heard by others in the cottonfields nearby.

Henry stopped the beating and untied J.D. He ran around the backyard screaming with puffy whelps all across his body. These were some of the same harsh practices that slavemasters used to discipline their slaves into submission. Negroes passed this same brutal discipline down from generation to generation, not consciously aware that it was a continuous cycle of abuse. Callie Mae came through the back door and pointed straight at J.D. "Git yo naked behind in da house, J.D."

"Yes, mam!" J.D. replied, still screaming from the painful beating.

"Dat'll teach ya a good lesson."

Slowly, Sean got undressed. He unbuttoned his shirt with his useful hand while resting his paralyzed hand on his lap. He stood up to unbutton and unzip his pants. Gilbert and Jose gathered around the bed of Vincent. They looked into the next room as Sean undressed himself. Quizzical gestures framed their youthful faces.

"Is Mr. Willingham gonna beat Sean?" Gilbert asked.

"I think he is," Vincent said, whispering close to his ear.

"With all of his clothes off?"

"Yes."

"Would he beat somebody handicapped like Sean?"

"Yes, he would."

"Not with all of his clothes?"

"Mr. Willingham's mean."

Sean was down to his underwear. J.D. walked into the bathroom to throw his cigarette into the toilet. He came back into Sean's room, tightly holding the extension cord in his right hand. When he saw that Sean had stalled for time, J.D. shouted for him to take the rest of his clothes off. Sean stood up and pulled down his underwear. J.D. grabbed him by his functional hand and wildly swung the extension cord across his nude body.

Vincent sat in a chair next to his dresser, pretending as though he was reading from his English textbook. He slightly raised his head to glance into the next room. J.D. was brutally beating Sean! Long and hard strokes were taken across his body. Sean was penned to the ground with the powerful left leg of J.D. He was crying and slobbering and begging for the mercy of J.D. He trembled like he was caught nude in the cold weather that was right outside of his room. From the top of his lungs, he screamed like he had never done. Thick mounds of saliva ran down his mouth.

"Please, stop!" Sean begged, twisting and turning his nude body across the floor.

"Why ya bake dat pen up?" J.D. interrogated Sean.

"I don't know!" Sean screamed.

"You ain't gone bake up no mo pens, aint'cha?"

"No, sir!"

"You ain't gone spill no mo ank, aint'cha?"

"No, sir!"

"You ain't gone mess up no mo britches, aint'cha?"

"No, sir!"

Sean continued screaming loudly while taking the severe beating, painstakingly feeling the lashes from the extension cord. J.D. visualized his father, Henry Willingham, beating him in the nude while tied to one of the willow trees. Every lash that J.D. gave Sean, he pictured his father, Henry, giving him a lash. Everytime Sean screamed, he could hear himself screaming from his beatings of the past.

"Ya ain't gone git smart wit ma no mo, aint'cha?"

"No, sir!" Sean yelled, his entire body turning bloody red.

"Ya know what's gone happen next time?"

"Yes, sir!"

"Ya know, dont'cha?"

"Yes, sir!"

"Dont'cha?"

"Yes, sir!"

J.D. held the tightest grip around Sean's right arm, stroking the extension cord up and down his chest, back, buttocks, and legs.

In the opposite room, tears of sympathy rolled down the face of Vincent. He sobbed over the beating that a helpless, handicapped man was receiving. In his twelve years at the Willingham residence, he had never witnessed something as unjustifiable as that. Gilbert and Jose crept back over to the side of the room where Vincent was. From the wall that was adjacent to the hallway leading into Sean's room, they watched J.D. inflict severe punishment upon Sean. Spread over the floor, and jerking his body from side to side, Sean continued to beg J.D. for mercy. J.D. continued beating him long and hard.

Gilbert, Jose, and Vincent shook everytime they witnessed J.D. strike Sean with the extension cord. Their eyes opened and closed, and frowns of pity came upon their faces, with every contact made to his body. The impact from the extension cord made Sean feel like his body was being burned with a hot iron. The burning and stinging was almost unbearable! Tears began to swell the sympathetic eyes of Vincent.

"Why are you crying?" Gilbert asked Vincent.

"He doesn't have to beat Sean like that," Vincent answered, a slow tear rippling down his face.

"Nobody should be beat like that."

"I can hardly sit here and watch."

"Mr. Willingham is nearly beating him to death," Jose said, shivering as he witnessed the brutal beating.

Vernon came down the basement stairs and stopped at the end of the laundry room.

"Who's that screaming like that?" Vernon asked, tuning in closely to the loud screams.

"It's Sean," Gilbert said, moving away from the wall and closer towards Vernon.

"What happened?"

"Mr. Willingham's beating him for breaking up an ink pen."

"An ink pen?"

"And spilling ink all over his pants."

"I need to hurry up and get the fuck out of this foster home."

"I wanna be right behind you," Gilbert added.

"It's hard to believe that someone would beat a handicapped person like Sean."

"And, he's beating him with all of his clothes off."

"You're lying!"

"No, I'm not."

Vernon had a female companion waiting upstairs. He grabbed some change from his dresser and left the basement. Stroke after painful stroke, J.D. thrashed Sean until he became too tired to inflict any further punishment. Sean continued screaming after the beating was over. J.D. had worked up a serious sweat. His shirt was soaking wet. He rewarded himself by reaching into his shirt pocket and pulling out a Pall Mall Gold. A severe beating well-executed!

Gilbert, Jose, and Vincent felt the presence of J.D. about to enter their room. They laid their tablets and school textbooks across their beds, pretending as though they had schoolwork to do. J.D. walked into their room with beads of sweat all over his greasy black face. He stopped in the middle of the floor, raising up the extension cord, like he wanted to brutally beat someone

else. Individually, Gilbert, Jose, and Vincent were given the evil look of, *If I catch any of you all doing something wrong, you're going to get the same punishment that Sean got.*

J.D. left their room and went upstairs. To make sure he had left, Jose walked over by the laundry room, looking up the stairs, listening for anymore footsteps. Everything looked okay, so they ran back into Sean's room to witness the ugly aftermath.

There were swollen red welts across Sean's back, chest, legs, and buttocks. His entire body was marred with those ugly red welts. They resembled blisters that were clotted with dark red blood. On some of the badly swollen areas, blood began to leak out and run down his arms and legs. Sean may have needed serious medical attention, but neither Bessie Mae nor J.D. cared.

"That fat, black motherfucker!" Vincent commented strongly, kicking the steel frame of Sean's bed, then stepping closer to Sean to observe the nasty marks.

"Somebody should shoot that fat, black bastard!" Gilbert furiously added. "He didn't have to beat Sean like that. That just doesn't make no sense at all."

"I hope that black ugly punk goes straight to hell for this!" Jose said, using the tip of his fingers to lightly touch the welts on Sean's arm.

"We should call The Children and Family Services people on Mr. Willingham," Gilbert said.

"Do you think they'll put Mr. Willingham in jail for beating Sean like this?" Jose asked.

"They should."

"He'll get away with it," Vincent interjected.

"Why do you think he will?" Gilbert asked.

"He got away with raping my sister."

"I remember you telling us that when we first got to this foster home."

"It's true."

"If he did get put in jail, I wonder how long they'll keep him there?"

"Hopefully, forever."

"Lock him up and throw the key away."

"Why does Mrs. Willingham let him do mean stuff like this to Sean?"

"Everybody knows why," Gilbert said.

"Why?" Vincent asked.

"Money."

"You're right, Gilbert."

"That crippled bitch only cares about two things."

"What's that?"

"Money, and more money!"

"I'm scared," Vincent admitted, shrieking everytime he looked upon the welts on the arms of Sean.

"Scared of what?" Gilbert asked.

"Being in this insane foster home."

"Mr. Willingham gets away with too much shit."

"He could've killed Sean when he was beating him with the extension cord."

"Is there anything that we can do about it?"

"Hell yeah!" Vincent boldly replied.

"Like what?"

"Calling our caseworkers."

"Good idea."

"Tell them that we want to get out of this fucking foster home."

"What if your caseworker tells you no?"

"We can always run away."

"And get a very vicious beating?"

"Not if they don't find us."

"They've probably ran out of foster homes for me," Gilbert thought.

"You're right."

Gilbert and Vincent moved closer to Sean and payed close attention to the blood that continued to leak. They wished they were physicians who could attend to the helpless, handicapped man.

"This blood won't stop!" Gilbert shrugged. "We've got to find something to stop the bleeding."

"What about in the bathroom?" Vincent inquired.

"I've got an idea."

"What?"

"Let's do the same thing to Sean that we did to Jose."

"What's that?"

"Remember when Jose got hit with the antenna?"

"In his forehead?"

"Right."

"When we were having the throwing fight?"

"Right."

Now was not the time for Gilbert to be mentioning the tragic incident when Jose was struck with the car antenna in the center of his forehead. He turned to stare at Gilbert as though he wanted immediate revenge. Gilbert and Vincent went into the bathroom and searched through the medicine cabinet above the sink. They were fortunate enough to find a bottle of green alcohol that was nearly empty. They grabbed one of the washcloths from the racks and soaked it with cold water. The alcohol was dropped onto the washcloth and they returned to Sean's room to pamper his wounds. Close attention was paid to the areas where blood trickled out. Sean began to smile again, knowing that someone at the Willingham residence cared. It wasn't easy recuperating from his harsh beating, but Gilbert, Jose, and Vincent were there to give him all the moral support they could.

Chapter 23

TORTURE

MONTH AFTER MONTH, changes constantly occurred at the Willingham residence. First, Sean was removed from the home and taken to a home strictly for the handicapped. Occasionally, the beatings kept coming, because J.D. needed someone to take all of his frustrations out on. Gilbert, Jose, and Vincent were exceptionally glad to see him leave, depart from a house of injustice.

On the sidewalk in front of the house, Vincent shouted for a kickball that Gilbert had kicked up in the air. The ball landed in the middle of a neighbor's yard. Vincent threw the ball to one of the neighborhood girls, Marlo Dickerson, a rather cute girl who wore a long ponytail.

Jose came up to kick and Marlo slowly rolled the ball to him. He had drawn his right leg backwards, kicking the ball with all of his power, sending it several feet over the head of Vincent. Like a young runaway freight train, Jose ran around those bases. Vincent grabbed the ball and threw it to Marlo in time to hold him at third base.

A walnut tree in the grassy strip was used as third base. Before she rolled the ball to Gilbert, Marlo turned to look up at the porch. Vernon stepped out on the porch wearing a black and white tuxedo with a shiny pair of black platform shoes. Looking real surprised, Jose stooped down against the tree. Gilbert and Vincent stared up on the porch. Vernon considered himself to be the sharpest dressed man in Chicago. Neighbors up and down Milwaukee came out on their porches to get a glance at a very handsome Vernon.

Mr. Vernon Ramirez was on his way to his senior prom. He stood on the porch combing through his towering afro. Bessie Mae limped out of the house with her polaroid camera. She wanted him to pose for a quick snapshot. The perfect picture was Vernon posing with both arms crossed and his head tilted to the side.

The camera's flash gave off a brilliant glow, which caused their kickball game to be delayed. Braun walked from the backyard with his pockets bulging. Like the others, a surprised look framed his face. Vernon was never seen in a well-fitted tuxedo before. As Braun walked towards the front door, Bessie Mae noticed the bulge in his pockets.

"Come here, Braun," Bessie Mae told Braun, throwing up her hand as a signal.

"Yeah, yeah, you want me to come to you?" Braun said, going into a nervous stage.

"Empty your pockets, Braun," Bessie Mae said, pinching the side of his pants to bring him closer.

"Okay, okay, you want me to empty my pockets?"

"That's what I said."

"Yeah, yeah, there's nothing in my pockets."

"I'll decide that."

"No, no, I don't have nothing in my pockets."

"Come closer to me, Braun."

"Yeah, yeah, you want me to come closer?"

"Shut up and let me see what's in your pockets!"

Bessie Mae pulled Braun closer. She shoved both hands down both of his pants pockets. She jerked out a handful of cigarette butts that she and J.D. had thumped on the side of the house.

"What the hell are you doing?" Bessie Mae asked.

"What, what, I'm not doing nothing."

"What are you doing with all these butts in your pockets?"

"Nothing, nothing, I'm not doing nothing with any butts."

Braun timidly stepped away from Bessie Mae. She felt steam coming out of her head.

"You were going to eat these butts? Weren't you, Braun?"

"No, no, I wasn't going to eat any butts," Braun said, shooting spurts of black saliva onto Bessie Mae's arm.

"You're lying!"

"No, no, I'm not lying to you," Braun replied, foamy dark saliva dropping on Bessie Mae's pants.

"Quit spitting that black shit on me!"

"Alright, alright, I'll stop spitting the black stuff on you."

"You're around here hunting for butts. Aren't you, Braun?"

"No, no, I wasn't going to do no such thing."

"Open your mouth."

"Yeah, yeah, you want me to open my mouth?"

"Shut up and open your dam mouth!"

Braun gradually opened his mouth and Bessie Mae jumped back. Moist tobacco kernels were smeared all along his upper and lower rows of rotten teeth. His mouth appeared as though he had shoved a large mound of tobacco into it.

"Do you remember what I told you?" Bessie Mae asked.

"No, no, I don't remember what you told me."

"You're going to eat these butts until you die."

"No, no, I don't want to eat no butts until I die."

"They're going to have to pump your stomach."

"Yeah, yeah, they'll have to pump my stomach."

Vernon patiently sat on the porch for his date and ride to the prom. Marlo's eyes were glued to the strikingly handsome face of Vernon. Most youngsters like her were at the perfect age to have crushes.

Once they resumed their kickball game, Gilbert was ready to kick. A blue and white, 1976 Cadillac Sedan de Ville drove up in front of the house. A beautiful young lady came from the driver's side of this classy automobile. She had a glowing caramel complexion and long silky black hair. Her figure was well-proportioned and it complimented the long black dress that she wore. The black platform shoes that she wore

matched the dress perfectly. She came off the street and walked towards the Willingham residence. Gilbert, Jose, and Vincent were stunned at her breathtaking beauty.

"God!" Gilbert huffed. "She is very pretty."

"She's got a big booty, too," Jose added, directing all of his attention to her attractive rear end.

"And some big titties, too."

"I wonder where my brother met her?" Vincent asked.

"I don't know," Gilbert said.

"I wish she had a sister who looked just like her."

"Me too."

"Vernon gets all the girls."

"He sure does."

It never surprised them how a handsome guy like Vernon ended up with the gorgeous girls who had heavenly bodies. Vernon was their idol, a definite mentor when it came to choosing women. She came up on the porch and Vernon introduced her to Bessie Mae.

"Daphne," Vernon said. "This is my foster mother, Mrs. Bessie Mae Willingham."

"How are you, Daphne?" Bessie Mae said politely.

"I'm fine, Mrs. Willingham," Daphne replied cordially.

"Boy!" Bessie Mae smiled. "You sure are a very pretty young lady."

"Thank you."

"What's your last name?" Bessie Mae asked.

"It's Sinclair.

"Are you related to the Sinclairs on the west side?"

"Yes, I am."

"There's a lot of them."

"You're talking about Ronnie, Roland, Ricky, Rudolph, Raymond, Reggie, Rochelle, and Rachel," Daphne mentioned consecutively, just to name a few from the large family, still not running out of an ounce of breath.

"Girl, yeah!" Bessie Mae chuckled. "I used to keep Ronnie, Roland, and Ricky in my foster home."

"I do remember them saying that they stayed in a foster home on Milwaukee Parkway."

"You are dressed so nice."

"Thank you," Daphne blushed.

"I want you all to have a good time."

"We definitely plan to."

"You all will be the cutest couple there."

"Thank you very much."

"Nice meeting you, Daphne."

"Nice meeting you, too, Mrs. Willingham."

Time had ticked away while they conversed with Bessie Mae. The prom was due to start in less than a half-hour. Vernon and Daphne said goodbye to Bessie Mae. Marlo went into a daze as she watched the attractive couple walk to the car. Looking back over his shoulders, Vernon blew her a kiss and winked. For Marlo, those gestures were mind-blowing, sending her heart to pounding.

Further down the street, Gilbert, Jose, and Vincent were admiring how debonair Vernon really was. The beautiful face of Daphne and shapely body couldn't be ignored. They watched her plump ass until she faded away on the driver's side. Everyone waved at them as they drove down Milwaukee Parkway. Jose remained on third base and Gilbert was about to kick the ball. Marlo looked back to make sure Vincent had resumed his position. When Gilbert rushed forward to kick the ball, a deep voice shouted out to the sidewalk.

"Yall git up on dis poach," J.D. told Gilbert, Jose, and Vincent, holding a Pall Mall Gold in his left hand, pointing to the front of the porch.

"Can we play one more game, Mr. Willingham?" Gilbert asked, pressing the ball under his right foot.

"Hell naw!" said J.D. "Git up on dis poach wight now."

"Can Marlo come up on the porch with us?"

"I said, hell naw!"

"Please, Mr. Willingham."

"Don't make ma go and git ma stanching code."

"Yes, sir."

Gilbert grabbed the ball and they said goodbye to Marlo. J.D. and Bessie Mae were leaving. Before they got into the car, they informed their foster sons to stay up on the porch.

"Where are they going?" Gilbert asked.

"Probably to the store," Jose guessed.

"That's where we should go," Gilbert suggested.

"For what?"

"To get some candy."

"Are you stupid?" Jose said. "Mr. Willingham kept telling us to stay on this porch. Do you want us to get a beating or what?"

"We won't get a beating."

"Yes, we will."

"We don't know how long they'll be gone."

"True."

"They might be gone for a real long time."

"Or they might not."

"Don't worry, Jose."

"Is there a store that we can run to?"

"Yes."

"Can we make it back before Mr. and Mrs. Willingham?"

"Vanzetti's."

"On Rush?"

"Yes."

"Vanzetti's is at least a mile."

"It's not that far."

"I don't know, Gilbert."

"If we run there, we can get back before Mr. and Mrs. Willingham."

"Run?" Jose shrilled. "I don't wanna run way up there."

"Come on."

"I don't know."

"We'll be back in time."

"Are you sure?"

"Yes."

"Okay."

Jose and Vincent were willing to follow their courageous foster brother to *"Vanzetti's One-Stop Liquors"*. Actually, they pictured Gilbert's plan working, especially since he knew of a shortcut. Accepting tips from the customers while selling The Baldwin Express, allowed them to have pockets full of change. On the way to Vanzetti's, they hopped and skipped and sang. They were supposed to run, but nonchalantly, they observed the *hardcore* scenery on Rush Boulevard. Since it wasn't too often that Bessie Mae and J.D. allowed them to leave the home, they released all their inhibitions.

They arrived at Vanzetti's and had to step around all the drunks and druggies and vagrants. Inside the liquor store, behind a long counter, there stood a short and bulky man with a dark olive complexion. A bushy mustache covered the lower portion of his bridged nose.

Gilbert, Jose, and Vincent had spread out to search for the candy section. Gilbert walked down the aisle that had the potato chips, dip, and canned goods. Jose had traveled into the aisle that had all the candy that they would ever need. He signaled for Gilbert and Vincent to come over to where he stood. They paced up and down the aisle, staring at the assortment of candy bars, lemonheads, Boston baked beans, now and laters, and sweet and sour tarts. Footsteps onto the white tile floor, and over into the aisle where they walked up and down, were heard very clearly.

"What're you boys gonna get?" asked the store owner, Sam Vanzetti, standing at the end of the aisle watching them closely.

"We haven't decided yet," Gilbert answered intellectually, staring down at the boxes of candy bars.

"First of all, do you boys have any money?" Sam questioned, who felt that since he operated this liquor store for

several years, he could study those people who did and didn't
have any money. Too many drunks and druggies came into
his store without a dime to their name, only to be thrown
back out on Rush Boulevard.

Instantly, Vincent turned red in the face. Sam might've
asked him the wrong question.

"None of your business!" Vincent replied sarcastically,
reaching down for a pack of cherry now and laters.

"You little punk!" Sam erupted. "How about if I made it
my business to throw your ass out of my store?"

"You can't put me out of here."

"Like hell I can't."

"You don't own this store."

"You wanna bet?" Sam interjected strongly. "This is my
store, and I can put anybody out that I wanna. Do you
understand me, you little punk!"

"I'm not a punk," Vincent said, not consciously aware
that he was arguing with a grown man, maybe even disrespecting his elder. What would Bessie Mae and J.D. think of
something like that?

"I just asked you a simple question."

Gilbert had to step forward to try and end the altercation. "Yes sir, we have some money."

"That's all your friend had to say."

"He's my foster brother."

"Whatever."

Vincent became offended, because he didn't know
whether or not Sam wanted a group of black boys standing
around loitering in his store. Samuel Joseph Vanzetti, who
was referred to as "Sammy V" by friends and associates, didn't
have a prejudice bone in his body. To Italians like him, money
was only one color. Mean green!

Sam returned to the front counter. He was blowing steam
off behind the belligerency of Vincent. Against the shelves,
where all the liquor sat, he thumped his fingers. The candy

items of Gilbert and Jose were rung up first. When Sam came around to ringing up Vincent's items, he snatched the money right out of his small palms. They stepped out of the store and Vincent quickly tore open the pack of cherry now and laters. The drunks couldn't resist begging for change.

"Say brother, can you spare a little change?" a grimy looking drunk asked Gilbert.

"I just bought a lot of candy, sir," Gilbert said. "I don't have no more change."

"Can you spare just a little something?"

"Sorry, I can't."

"Come on, youngblood."

"Can't help you, sir."

They walked down Rush eating their candy. Gilbert had become worried about Vincent. The nasty scene in Vanzetti's could have gotten worse.

"You shouldnt've gotten smart with that man," Gilbert advised Vincent.

"What man?"

"The man in Vanzetti's."

"Why not?" Vincent asked.

"He was Italian."

"So," Vincent said. "I don't care if he was Italian."

"You should care, Vincent."

"Why?"

"Those Italian men are crazy."

"Crazy? How?"

"There was something bad that happened in front of a liquor store."

"What liquor store?"

"When I was living at one of those other foster homes."

"There you go again," Vincent disapproved. "You're always talking about what happened at your other foster homes. Everytime we talk about something, you're always telling us some kind of story that happened at your other foster home."

"Won't you listen to me?"

"Okay, I'll listen."

"This is how the story goes," Gilbert said. "There was this Italian man who owned this liquor store close to where my last foster home was. He beat this black dude across the head with a baseball bat."

"For real?" Vincent frowned, moving away from Gilbert with an ugly frown on his face.

"Yes, for real."

"That's crazy."

"We stood around and watched that Italian man bust the black dude's skull open with that long bat."

"Didn't nobody help the black dude?"

"It was too late."

"Why?" Vincent asked.

"The black dude's brains were lying on the sidewalk."

"That's nasty!"

"It looked like brown cottage cheese."

"Yuck!"

"Blood was all over the sidewalk."

"What did this dude do?"

"He tried to steal something and run out of the store."

"How could you have stood around and watched that?"

"I left before the police and ambulance got there."

"Are Italians like white people?"

"I don't think so."

"My father's Italian."

"That's right, Vincent."

"Do you think the man in Vanzetti's would've beat me with a bat?"

"I don't think so."

As they walked out Rush, Gilbert's jaws worked up much friction. Brown juices from the snicker bar ran down the side of his mouth. Jose slammed a few Boston baked beans down his mouth. Vincent unwrapped a couple of the cherry now

and laters and stuck one on each side of his mouth. Happily, they chewed and smacked and swallowed their delicious candy. Their mouths worked like engines in a car, dripping juices around their lips and chins, forming sticky coats everywhere. The late Spring breeze blew into their young faces. They approached Milwaukee Parkway and Gilbert wanted Jose and Vincent to stop. He insisted that they hear a rhyme that was bouncing around in his mind.

"This is a rhyme that me and the other foster kids used to say at my other foster home."

"What rhyme?" Jose asked.

"Promise you won't laugh?"

"I promise."

"Are you ready to hear it?"

"Yes, go ahead and tell us."

"Okay," Gilbert said. "This is how it goes." He took a deep swallow.

"I went downtown to see James Brown. He gave me a nickel and I bought me a pickle. The pickle was sour so I bought me a flower. The flower was dead, so I turned around and said: 'Oh my! I wanna piece of pie! The pie's too sweet, so I wanna piece of meat. The meat's too tough, so I wanna ride the bus. The bus is too full, so I wanna ride the bull. The bull's too fat, so I want my money back."

"Where did you learn to say that?" Vincent asked, overly impressed with the flow of the rhymes.

"My foster brother at my last foster home taught it to me."

"I wish I could make up something like that."

"It's not hard to remember."

"No, it's not."

They continued their journey out Rush until they came to Milwaukee Parkway. From halfway up the block, Gilbert

spotted Bessie Mae's Cadillac. The car that he was hoping wouldn't be there. It was parked in the grass near the front. Their hearts nearly dropped to the bottom of their feet! Jose and Vincent became angry with Gilbert. Weren't they supposed to run to the store and run right back? Choosing to walk slow and not paying any attention to time may have proven costly.

"There's Mrs. Willingham's car," said Jose, perspiring from nervousness.

"I know," Gilbert said. "I didn't think they would be back already."

"It's all your fault," Jose blamed Gilbert, shoving him aside so he could walk in front of everybody.

"Who's fault?"

"Your's."

"Don't blame me."

"I knew I shouldnt've walked to the store with you."

The trio of foster brothers could only think the worst. A vicious beating! They crept to the side of the house, where Braun was on the hunt for more cigarette butts to eat. Reluctantly, they walked to the side of the porch and stopped. Gilbert gradually stepped up on the porch, with Jose and Vincent right behind. They were frightened to walk in the house.

Inside the front room, Bessie Mae and J.D. were watching the popular television series, *"The Six Million Dollar Man"*. The volume on the television was turned up loud. J.D. enjoyed watching Steve Austin jump over high fences, go through concrete walls, run faster than any olympic sprinter, throw men high into the air, and use his bionic eye to see far away distances.

"Look, Bessa Mae," J.D. said, pointing at the television screen. "Million dolla mane beating dose folks up."

Steve Austin was taking on a legion of ruthless criminals.

"Isn't that something, J.D.," said Bessie Mae. "They give

that man all kinds of bionic parts and he be doing some unbelievable crap."

"Ya wight, Bessa Mae," J.D. agreed. "I memba dat time when da millen dolla mane ran cross dat field."

"I remember, too."

"You memba?"

"He looked like a rocket running across that wheat field."

Bessie Mae and J.D.'s attention were directed at *"The Six Million Dollar Man"*. Gilbert, Jose, and Vincent loitered around near the porch. Gilbert moved his head towards the screen door. He tried to see if Bessie Mae had left the room. Jose stepped around Gilbert to get a better view of the front room. From two separate directions, clouds of smoke filled the air. Bessie Mae and J.D. puffed on their Pall Mall Gold and Pall Mall Red cigarettes. Gilbert, Jose, and Vincent knew that they couldn't loiter around on the porch forever.

"Let's go inside the house," Jose suggested, showing every sign of fright.

"No," Gilbert said. "You go inside the house."

"We've got to go in there sooner or later."

"I know, but I'm too scared to go in front of Mr. and Mrs. Willingham."

"You shouldn't be scared," Jose said. "You're the one who talked us into walking to the store."

"You didn't have to walk to the store."

Hesitantly, Gilbert, Jose, and Vincent walked up to the screen door. They came inside the house and were quickly stopped in the middle of the front room.

"Stop right there!" Bessie Mae demanded, crushing out her cigarette and blowing the irritating smoke right in their faces. "Where have you all been?"

"Down the street," Gilbert spoke up, standing there more nervous than a minister caught screwing in a whorehouse.

"Down the street?"

"Yes, mam."

"Where?"

"At Marlo's house."

"You lying bastard!" Bessie Mae opposed. "I called down there and Marlo's mother told me that she hadn't seen you all."

"We were down at Marlo's," Gilbert fabricated, his fingers trembling from great fright. "Marlo's mother didn't see us down there."

"You're lying, boy! I had that woman to look all around her house."

"Really, Mrs. Willingham, we were down at Marlo's house."

"Do I look like one of your fools?"

"I . . ."

"Huh?"

"No, mam."

"You all aren't going to lie your way out of this, boy."

Gilbert, Jose, and Vincent were told to go into the dining room. While they stood around shaking, their dreadful eyes traveled from the ceiling, to the walls, and on down to the floor. J.D. took a brief trip up to the second floor. He returned to the dining room with his long brown extension cord. Respectively, J.D. pointed to Jose, Vincent, and Gilbert, using the same arm that held the extension cord.

"Git yall's clothes off," J.D. told Gilbert, Jose, and Vincent, wanting them to strip down in the total nude.

"All of our clothes, Mr. Willingham?" Gilbert asked, absolutely stunned from the sudden news.

"All yo clothes, boy."

"All of them?"

"Ain't dat what I say?"

"What did we do wrong?" Gilbert asked, listening to the sound of his own heart pumping.

"Shut da fuck up and git yo clothes off!"

"But we . . ."

"Shut up, boy, and do lack I tell ya!"

Looking over one another's shoulders, Gilbert, Jose, and Vincent knew that they were going to get a rendition of J.D.'s *birthday suit beating.*

Like shock waves traveling through their central nervous system, they trembled repeatedly. They unbuttoned their shirts, pulled down their pants, and slid off their shoes and socks. Standing side by side, they were left in their underwear, dreadfully awaiting for J.D. to call one of them forward.

J.D. had his back turned to the windows on the other side of the dining room. He swung his extension cord down by his right side, just like a rodeo cowboy swinging a lasso. With all three of them extremely frightened, Gilbert, Jose, and Vincent wondered who would be the first to pull their underwear down. Silently, they waited near the wall facing the kitchen. They hoped and prayed that J.D. would never turn around. J.D. suddenly turned around and saw his fearful foster sons shaking in their underwear.

"I said, git all yo goddam clothes off!" J.D. warned Gilbert, Jose, and Vincent, clutching the extension cord even tighter.

"Do we have to take all of our clothes off, Mr. Willingham?" Gilbert whined, wishing this was just a bad dream.

"What ya thank, boy?"

"I don't know, sir."

"Den, git all yo clothes off."

Gilbert, Jose, and Vincent slid their underwear off and threw them into their individual pile of clothes. Gilbert took a few steps towards J.D. and jumped back. Vincent stepped in front of Gilbert and ran on the other side of Jose. Jose reached his arm out to J.D. and jerked back. They moved forward and backwards, then forward again, until Gilbert courageously allowed J.D. to grab him around his right arm.

Raising his right arm back as far as it would go, J.D. gave Gilbert a hard lash across his back, leaving the first unattractive whelp. Though Gilbert was trying to jerk loose, J.D. had

him penned between his strong legs. Several lashes across his chest, back, buttocks, and legs, caused a rush of tears to come out of Gilbert's eyes like raindrops.

Gilbert screamed mercifully! The stinging from the extension cord was severe. More and more ugly marks were added to his body. Gilbert tried breaking away from J.D.'s tight grip, but there was far too much power in J.D.'s *Mississippi Bred Body*. Every second of his punishment was like a repititious pattern. J.D. took a stroke across Gilbert's nude body and drew back even harder. He took much stronger strokes and didn't care where the extension cord landed on Gilbert's wiggling body. Bessie Mae was in the front room smiling, happy that she got her husband to do her dirty work once more.

*   *   *

Instantly, J.D. remembered back to his teenage years in Clarksdale, Mississippi, when his father, Henry Willingham, was beating him in the total nude, while he was tied to the trunk of a large tree in their backyard. For each lash that Henry used to give J.D., he gave Gilbert an equal or harder lash. J.D. recalled very well when his father would ask those questions while beating him senselessly.

"J.D., why can't chu do lack yo mammy tell ya?" Henry asked the young J.D., beating him hard with the thick willow branches.

"I do what yall tell ma, pappa!" J.D. cried loudly, trying to jerk loose from the tight grip of the rope tied around the tree.

"Wassamatta, J.D.?" Henry said. "Can't chu tell dose white folks dat Negro folks got thangs ta do, too?"

"Yes suh, pappa! Yes suh, pappa!" J.D. screamed extremely loud. "I tells dose white folks dat ma mammy and ma pappy need ma round da house fo suppatime!"

"You gone mind me and yo mammy, aint'cha, boy?"

"Yes suh!"

"Aint'cha, boy!"

"Yes suh! Yes suh!"

"Me and yo mammy da only ones round here runnin thangs. You unnastands, boy!"

"Yes suh, pappa!"

As hard as J.D. tried forgetting, the memories of his father's horrible beatings always came crashing through his mind. It was unfortunate that he carried on the same animalistic traits of Henry Willingham. The fact remained that he was severely abused as a child and his only outlet was to abuse others.

*   *   *

J.D. held Gilbert tightly with his powerful arm. He swung the extension cord wildly and used harder strokes.

"Why ya leave fum in funt of dis house?" J.D. asked Gilbert, stroking even harder and dropping sweat from his active body, only to mix with the tears that Gilbert dropped on the floor.

"I don't know, sir!" Gilbert screamed, sounding off from the top of his lungs, twisting and turning and jerking everytime he felt the impact of the extension cord.

"What ya say, boy?"

"I didn't mean to leave from in front of the house!"

"What ya mean ya didden mean to?"

"I don't know, sir!"

"Didden Bessa Mae tell yall ta stay in funt of dis house?"

"Yes, sir!" Gilbert yelled higher, his eyes nearly out of tears.

"What ya say, boy!"

"Yes, sir!"

"I can't hear ya."

"Yes, sir!"

"Ya ain't gone leave fum in funt of dis house no mo?"

"No, sir!"

"Not less Bessa Mae tell ya?"

"No, sir!"

"What?"

"No, sir!"

"Ya gone mind, aint'cha?"

"Yes, sir!"

"Aint'cha?"

"Yes, sir!"

"Ya ain't gone be hardheaded no mo?"

"No, sir!"

"Aint'cha?"

"No, sir!"

J.D. knowingly swung the extension cord right towards the mid-section of Gilbert, striking him right on the head of his penis. Sweat rushed down his face like he had worked all day in a boiler room. For J.D., beating on someone was like an extracurricular activity. Gilbert's screaming had Jose and Vincent over by the wall scared to death. They hadn't received their punishment, but they were crying like they had.

J.D. literally tried to beat the very life out of Gilbert's body. Thick saliva dripped from his mouth. While they were on standby for their torment, Jose and Vincent could nearly feel the infliction put on Gilbert. Intimidation came upon their faces and fear crossed through their minds.

J.D. continuously stroked harder and Gilbert screamed louder. The tears and saliva had formed small wet rings on the carpet. J.D. finally turned Gilbert's hand loose, pointing towards the basement. Once he grabbed his clothes, he rushed down the basement stairs crying his lungs flat. J.D. was sweating and gasping for breath.

He recuperated and pointed right at Vincent. He knew he had to face his foster father, who was possessed with sheer anger. He stepped towards J.D. trembling. He stopped in the middle of the floor and then moved back. He took a few steps forward and moved back again. J.D. slammed his fist down on the dining room table. He insisted that Vincent

came all the way. The red, watery eyes, puckered lips, and much heavier breathing, indicated that J.D. was angrier than ever.

"Git over here, Vinsun!" J.D. said, intense anger causing his bull nostrils to spread and sweat to roll down the middle of his shiny bald head.

"I'm scared, Mr. Willingham!" Vincent shook, frightened like he was about to be sentenced to death.

"Don't let ma come afta yo ass."

"I don't want no beating, Mr. Willingham."

"Git over here, boy!"

"I don't want to."

"I ain't paying wit'cha, boy!"

Vincent repeatedly stepped backwards and forward. He slid across the carpet and J.D. quickly grabbed him by his right arm. He began swinging the extension cord up and down Vincent's nude body. Red marks began to form across his chest. Since Vincent had a small frame, J.D. was able to pen him down on the carpet. The hard soles of J.D.'s shoes were pressed into the middle of his chest. The tight grip was held onto his right arm. Like Gilbert, Vincent tried breaking the hold, screaming loud enough to be heard on the outside of the Willingham residence.

*   *   *

Again, the unstable and wandering mind of J.D. traveled back to his disturbing beginnings in Clarksdale, Mississippi. For those who were very bright complexioned as Vincent, J.D. had a strong resentment. During the slavery years, the bright complexioned slaves with fine grades of hair were given preferential treatment over the very dark complexioned slaves, being assigned light house duties while the others were assigned hard duties out in the field. Even after slavery ended, J.D. and other negroes in the deep south, felt that the blacks who could pass for white were still given preferential treatment. Everytime J.D.

looked at Vincent, he felt nothing but bitterness. He saw nothing but the white race in his foster son, which he had nursed a hatred for all of his life. Some of the extreme racist white men in Clarksdale often made slandering comments about J.D.'s very dark skin and nappy hair. He walked along a dirt road carrying some items for his mother, Callie Mae.

"Where ya going, you shiny dark coon?" asked a racist white man driving an old rusty truck along the dirt road.

"I gets home to ma mammy and pappy, suh."

"Boy, you so dark, I barely could see ya."

"I stands off da road next time, suh."

"I nearly ran your nigger ass over, boy."

"I leaves da road to ya, suh."

"Get on home, you nappy headed coon."

"Yes suh, I gets on home to ma mammy and pappy."

"Hurry up, you shiny black, nappy headed coon!"

"Yes, suh! Yes, suh!"

*   *   *

Vincent grabbed the extension cord and held a tight grip.

"Let go dis stanching code!" J.D. shouted at Vincent, trying to jerk the extension cord away from the tight grip of Vincent.

"It hurts, Mr. Willingham!" Vincent cried, tears running off the side of his flushed face, and right down onto the carpet.

"Let go, boy!"

"The extension cord hurts, Mr. Willingham!"

"I'm gone stomp a mudhole in yo ass!"

J.D. threatened to stomp Vincent through the floor if he didn't release the extension cord.

"Don't whip me no more, Mr. Willingham!"

Vincent refused to let go of the extension cord. J.D. jerked on the cord until it was snatched right out of his hand.

After picking up where he left off, J.D. continued torturing the nude body of Vincent, taking harder strokes across his chest and back. Vincent jerked away from the tight grip of J.D. and rolled out from under his powerful foot. While running around in circles, he stampeded around the dining room, screaming and crying to ease the burning sensation. Afraid to receive any further punishment, Vincent stood on the opposite side of the table.

J.D. rushed his direction and he ran into the kitchen. At opposite ends of the kitchen table, they studied one another's moves. Granny Dear rolled her wheelchair out of her room to see what was going on. She was stunned to see a nude Vincent standing at the end of the table that was closest to the refrigerator.

"Git yo naked behind out of dis kitchen!" Granny Dear snapped at Vincent, waving her hands as a signal for him to take his beating.

"Help me, Granny Dear!" Vincent cried. "Help me, please!"

"Gone," Granny Dear said. "Git yo naked behind way fum me."

J.D. had Vincent cornered near the refrigerator. Vincent ran out of the kitchen and J.D. thrashed him a couple of more times. He told him to head for the basement. He grabbed his clothes and ran down the basement stairs screaming. Two foster sons were already badly beaten, and it was one more to go.

Cuffing his mid-section with both hands, Gilbert was sitting across his bed in his pajamas. He and Vincent sat quietly, listening to Jose scream and cry and pound the floor, almost in the same manner as they did. After several minutes of stroking the extension cord across the nude body of Jose, J.D. sent him to the basement. Once he got downstairs, all three sat around discussing the harsh beating that they just received.

They tried pampering the individual swollen marks, which were all across their backs, chests, arms, legs, and buttocks, almost the exact marks that were inflicted upon Sean. Blood began leaking out of the arm of Vincent and chest of Gilbert. They would have never expected J.D. to beat them with all of their clothes off. Anyone who resided in the Willingham residence knew that they could expect the worst. Gilbert pushed his pajamas and underwear outwards to observe some of the marks left on his more private body parts.

"I can't believe it," said Gilbert, bending closer to get a better view of the small ugly marks.

"Believe what?" Vincent asked.

"That black motherfucker hit me on my dick!"

There were small, blistering marks on the head and shaft of Gilbert's penis. How disgusting it was!

"On your dick!" Vincent grudged.

"Yes."

"Did he do it on purpose?"

"I know he did."

"You should call Mrs. Maloney."

"Really?"

"Tell her what Mr. Willingham just did."

"What's Mrs. Maloney's number?"

"I don't know."

"We can find it in the phone book."

"It's in there."

"What if we call her and tell her what happened?"

"I don't know."

"She'll call back and tell Mr. and Mrs. Willingham that we talked to her."

"So!" Gilbert boasted. "I'm sick of this motherfucking foster home!"

"Do you think Mrs. Maloney will put you in another foster home?"

"Maybe," Gilbert said. "I really don't know."

"Gosh, Gilbert!" Jose thought. "They probably don't have anymore foster homes for you to go to."

"They probably don't."

"What will you do?"

"I wish Mrs. Maloney will take me somewhere else."

Vincent arose from his bed and stood towards the middle of the floor. "I think he tried to hit me on my dick, too."

"What did you do?"

"I grabbed the extension cord."

"What did Mr. Willingham do?"

"Snatched it out of my hand."

The basement door opened and Jose jumped up to cut off the lights. They jumped in their beds and threw the covers over their heads. Walking like they were trying not to fall, someone stepped slowly into the laundry room. Judging by the rhythm of the footsteps, Gilbert, Jose, and Vincent could usually tell if Bessie Mae or J.D. were coming down there. Underneath their covers, they lied motionless.

The light inside the laundry room came on and the silhouette of someone with a blasting afro reflected off the wall inside the other room. Vernon stepped to the middle of the room and glanced over at their beds. They pretended as though they were asleep. They weren't aware that everything was okay and they could come from behind their covers. Sluggishly, Gilbert slid his covers back and took a quick glance. He rose up to tell Jose and Vincent that everything was in the clear.

"Whew!" Gilbert exhaled strongly. "I thought you was Mr. Willingham coming down here to beat us again."

"Beat you all for what?" Vernon asked, loosening his tuxedo tie and taking off his jacket.

"For walking up to Vanzetti's."

"On Rush?"

"Yes."

"The liquor store up on Rush, right?"

"Right."

"It's close to Bennie's Hotel."

"We walked up there to get some candy."

"I see that Mr. Willingham's still beating on people for no real reason."

"Has Mr. Willingham ever beat you for anything?" Gilbert asked.

"Never!" Vernon stressed strongly. "Not in a million years."

"Never?"

"Not since I've been living in this foster home."

"Are you serious, Vernon?"

"I wouldn't lie to you."

"Why hasn't he?"

"I let him know a long time ago how I felt about beatings."

"What's that?"

"If he ever hit me, I was going to kill him."

"You're serious?"

"Mr. Willingham knows to stay out of my face."

"What if he comes up in your face?"

"I'll kill him with the same belts and switches and extension cords that he throws up in my face."

"What if he tried it anyway?"

"They'll find him in the river with cement shoes."

"That's what those mafia dudes do to people."

"Exactly."

"When are you gonna leave this foster home?"

"Right after I finish school."

"Wow!"

"Maybe sooner than that."

"When will you be finishing school?"

"A few months."

"Who was that pretty girl that you took to the prom?" Gilbert asked, still admiring her unforgettable beauty.

"Her name's Daphne Sinclair."

"Where did you meet her?"

IN THE CARE OF EVIL 393

"She's in some of my classes at school."

"Were there a lot of other dudes wanting to go to the prom with her?"

"Oh yeah!"

"Daphne looks good, Vernon."

"One of the finest girls at school."

"She's got some big titties," Gilbert said, blushing as he turned his head away.

"And one of the nicest asses, too," Vernon added.

"Does she know that you're in a foster home?"

"Of course she does."

"You weren't embarrassed to tell her?"

"Embarrassed? For what?"

"I don't want people at school knowing that I'm in a foster home."

"Why not?"

"They talk about you real bad."

"So."

"It happened all the time when I was at those foster homes."

"Why would they talk about you?" Vernon asked.

"Because, Vernon."

"Because of what, Gilbert?"

"They lived with their real mothers and fathers."

"So."

"They laugh at us."

"Laugh? Why?"

"Because our mothers and fathers gave us away."

"Let me tell you this much," Vernon said, the most serious face. "When somebody is truly your friend, they're not going to laugh at you or put you down for being put into a foster home. You couldn't help it that your mother and father had to give you away. It's just like me and Vincent's mother and father had to give us away. Those same people who are

talking about you and laughing at you, the same thing could've happened to them."

"What did you and Daphne do after the prom?"

"That's private."

"Come on, tell me."

"We checked into a hotel."

"Hope it wasn't Bennie's Hotel."

"No way!" Vernon dejected. "I would never take a nice girl like her to no hotel with a bunch of pimps and whores and drunks."

"Did you two have sex?"

"You're all into my business."

"Did you?"

"What do people do on prom night?"

"Have sex?"

"You've got it."

"Did she have some good pussy?"

"Dam, Gilbert!" Vernon nodded. "Do you have to know all of my business?"

"Did she?"

"The best."

"Are you going to have sex with her again?"

"What do you think?"

"Yes."

"What do you know about sex, anyway?" Vernon asked.

"I know a whole lot," Gilbert assured Vernon.

"Have you ever had some pussy?"

"Well . . . I . . . almost . . ."

"Almost what?"

"This girl wanted to give me some."

"Quit lying, boy."

"I'm not lying."

Gilbert, Jose, and Vincent came over to Vernon's bed to show him their swollen marks from the horrible beating. He

shook his head and frowned, feeling great sympathy for all three of them.

"Mr. Willingham must've beat you all real bad," Vernon commented sympathetically, lightly touching the welts across the arms of Gilbert.

"He was trying to kill us," Gilbert said, still massaging the area down by his penis.

"With that extension cord?"

"What else?"

"It looks like blood is trying to come out of those blisters."

"We tried putting alcohol on them."

"I remember the time he beat Sean with that same extension cord."

"He beat us just as hard," Gilbert disapproved strongly. "He hit me right across my dick with that fucking extension cord."

"One day, we should all come back to this foster home and beat his ass with our own extension cords."

"That sounds like a good idea."

"I can picture all of us whacking away at his fat ass."

"Me too," Gilbert smiled, palming the head of his penis gently, trying to soothe some of the stinging.

Vernon turned his attention to Vincent. "How bad did he beat you, Vinnie?"

"Just as bad as he beat Gilbert and Jose," Vincent mentioned unfavorably, showing Vernon the ugly looking red welts across his arms and chest.

"Dam!" Vernon snorkled, gently gliding his fingers across the welts. "Mr. Willingham is trying to be a murderer."

"When is somebody gonna call the family services people?" Gilbert asked.

"Good question, Gilbert."

"We've got to get out of this home before he tries and kill one of us."

"I thought they would stop bringing foster children here," Vernon said, glancing around the room with vengeful eyes, his pain almost as lethal as Gilbert, Jose, and Vincent.

"Why'd you say that?"

"After Mr. Willingham raped my sister, I was thinking they would close this foster home down."

"Yeah, I remember Vincent telling us that when we first got here."

Vernon and the others hoped someday that they would make headway to get out of the Willingham's foster home.

Chapter 24

GREED

VERNON WAS AT Roselli's Market standing on the other side of the checkout counter sacking customer's groceries. A short, well-built, fair complexioned young lady stood at the end of the line. She waited patiently for her groceries to be rung up. While she waited, Vernon gave her strong eye contact. There was that expression as though he was truly interested. Vernon sacked her groceries and she went to the end of the counter to pick them up.

"What's your name?" Vernon asked flirtatiously, gently placing her groceries in one of the carts.

"My name's Tyletha," she answered seductively.

"Tyletha what?"

"Tyletha Adams. What's your name?"

"Vernon Ramirez," Vernon said, never taking his eyes off the attractive teenage girl.

"Are you Mexican?"

"My father's cuban and my mother's black."

"What a combination!" Tyletha acclaimed. "God knew what he was doing when he made you." She admired the smooth and handsome face of Vernon.

"Tyletha is a pretty name."

"Thank you."

"Do you have a phone number?" Vernon asked, wanting to hurry and help the other customers who were coming through the checkout line.

"I sure do," Tyletha said happily, reaching down into her purse for a pen and some paper.

While she wrote her phone number down, a cashier named Marsha Bohannon was at the cash register shaking her head. She knew that Tyletha was one of the many girls whose phone number Vernon had collected. Tyletha handed him the small piece of paper and pushed her groceries out of the store.

"Vernon!" a barritoned voice called from the back of the store.

"Yeah," Vernon answered, stopping the sacking of groceries to figure out who had called him.

"I need you back here, son."

"I'm coming."

Marsha agreed to call another sacker up front until he returned up there. Vernon weaved his way through the checkout line and traveled back into the freezer section. The owner of the store, Virgil Roselli, a tall and well-compacted Italian man, with a set of dark and bushy eyebrows, was sitting on a set of milk crates.

"Did you need to see me, Mr. Roselli?"

"I need you to stock some of this pork."

"Where?"

"At the far end of the meat section."

Virgil was flipping through a stack of magazines.

"Mr. Roselli!" Vernon rumbled. "Your wife Vickie's up front." He tried warning his boss while he flipped through a stack of *"Playboy"* and *"Penthouse"* magazines.

"I don't care."

"What if she comes back here in the freezer?"

"Then she comes back here," Virgil said, directing all of his attention at the beautiful centerfolds.

"You don't care?"

"Vickie's my wife, not my boss," Virgil made clear to Vernon. "I'm her boss and she does whatever I say. Do you understand, son?"

"Yes sir, boss."

"The woman shouldn't be the boss."

"Yeah, I used to hear the old people say that."

"Well, they're right."

Virgil left the freezer and Vernon took a small sharp knife to cut open the box of pork sausages. This brand of sausage always sold well at Roselli's Market. He grabbed the two-wheeler against the wall and pushed the boxes out to the meat section. Today, Vernon was performing his duties with extra pride. It was Saturday and payday and he wanted to go to the drive-in. Tyletha remained on his mind. Maybe he would ask her to the drive-in.

One by one, he emptied the boxes of sausage and placed them neatly in the meat section. In the very back of the store, the boxes were thrown in a dumpster. Two large German Shepards were chained to a fence several feet away from the dumpster. They barked loudly, mainly because they weren't too familiar with Vernon.

He returned inside the store and went up and down the aisles. Canned goods like pork and beans, greenbeans, corn, and spinach, had run low on the shelves. They were some of the hottest canned good commodities purchased at Roselli's Market. Vernon rolled the two-wheeler to the storage section and brought back the necessary items. As he filled the shelves, two very attractive girls walked down the same aisle. Vernon appeared attracted to them. They appeared attracted to him. They pushed their cart up to the two-wheeler and stopped.

"What time will you be free tonight?" Vernon asked one of the attractive girls standing to the left of the cart.

"I'm not sure," she smiled.

"You didn't answer my question."

"Probably, later on. Why'd you ask?"

"I wanted to go to the drive-in with someone."

"To see which movie?"

"Now, which movie is everybody in Chicago and America going to see?"

"I don't now, tell me."

"That new disco movie."

"What disco movie?"

"Saturday Night Fever."

"Yeah!" she bellowed. "I want to see that movie so bad."

"I've heard that it was real good."

"Found anybody to go to the drive-in with?"

"Nobody, right now."

"The drive-in will probably be packed."

"Yeah, it will."

"A lot of people want to see that movie."

"Yeah, they do."

"What's your name?"

"My name's Vernon. What's your name?"

"My name's Cheryl."

"Where do you live, Cheryl?" Vernon was hinting around for someone to attend the drive-in with.

"Cabrini-Green."

"Whoa!"

"What's wrong?"

"Nothing's wrong."

"Are you sure?"

"I've heard a lot of bad things about Cabrini-Green."

"Bad things? Like what?"

"All kinds of things," Vernon confessed. "I've heard that somebody gets killed over there everyday. A friend of mine's told me that he went to visit somebody over there, and when he came outside, his car was sitting flat on the concrete. They say that there's snipers on the roofs, shooting at people who look like cops and snitches."

"It's got some bad points."

"I agree."

"Thugs do move fast."

"I'd say so."

"Do you want my phone number?" Cheryl asked Vernon,

trying to evade the conversation about the notorious Cabrini-Green.

"Sure, give it to me."

Cheryl handed Vernon her phone number, and she left the aisle. Since there weren't any customers coming through the checkout line, Marsha left the register. She walked down the aisle where Vernon was stocking the rest of the canned goods.

"How many girlfriends do you have?" Marsha asked Vernon.

"Too many, I guess," Vernon answered blatantly, keeping his head turned towards the shelves to avoid looking into her eyes.

"You're dam right, too many!" Marsha accused Vernon. "Since I've been working here at Roselli's, I've seen you get over a hundred different girl's numbers."

"I can't help it, Marsha," Vernon said. "I like being with more than just one girl."

"You can help it, alright," she grinned. "Find yourself one good girl and tell those others girls that you're taken."

"There're so many girls who like me. There're so many girls who I like. I can't tell them no when they want to talk to me."

"You're still young and have lots of time to find *Ms. Right*," Marsha explained to the young Vernon.

"Exactly."

"Are you screwing all those girls?" Marsha outlandishly asked Vernon.

"Why'd you ask me that?"

"Answer the question, Vernon."

"What kind of question is that?"

"I'm waiting on an answer."

"Some of them."

"Do you use a rubber?"

"Sometimes."

"Why not all the time?"

"I don't know."

"Aren't you scared of getting the drips?"

"The drips?"

"Syphilis, gonorreha, or the claps?"

"Of course I'm scared."

"Have you ever heard of Al Capone?"

"Everybody's heard of him," Vernon mentioned. "He was that big-time gangster right here in Chicago."

"Do you know how he died?"

"He got shot?"

"No."

"How?"

"He died of syphilis."

"Really?"

"Syphilis ate him up real bad."

"Yeek!" Vernon shrugged.

"Ate his brain up and made him lose his mind."

"That's too bad."

"Had those nasty red sores all over his body, too."

"How did he get syphilis?"

"Screwing all those women up in those whorehouses."

"Really?"

"He was a well-known pimp right here in Chicago."

"I don't wanna end up like that."

"Be careful."

"I'm not a pimp who's screwing a bunch of whores."

"You can still catch it."

"Really?"

"A lot of other famous people had syphilis and gonorreah."

"Are you serious?"

"Very serious."

"How do you know all of this?"

"I read a lot."

"Maybe I need to start doing a lot of reading."

"Read and use a rubber when you're messing around with a lot of girls."

"You're right."

Marsha returned to the cash register so Vernon could finish stocking the shelves. The clock on the wall above the freezer said 7:30 p.m. Vernon had a few more minutes to empty the boxes and wait for his next assignment. Virgil came down the aisle to remind him that the floor had to be swept and mopped. When the canned goods were arranged neatly on the shelves, Vernon glided the push broom up and down every aisle, behind the checkout counter, and near the front entrance. Hot water was ran in a bucket in the back of the store. A half-bottle of ammonia was added to the water. Vernon dipped the mop down into the bucket and pushed it up and down the white tile floor.

Virgil was in the back of the store signing payroll checks. Marsha was in the ladies room powdering her face. Once the floor was mopped, Vernon took off his dirty apron and stood near Virgil's office. He anxiously awaited to get paid. Virgil came out and handed him his paycheck.

He rushed out to his 1966, sky blue Plymouth Fury III. He sped up the street blasting his radio. A song entitled, *"Disco Inferno"*, a monstrous hit by a soul group called "The Trammps", was playing over the airways. It was the age of disco and popular disco groups and individual singers like "The Bee Gees", "KC and The Sunshine Band", "Gloria Gaynor", and "Donna Summer", were burning up the music charts.

Vernon was elated to know that his evening would be filled with excitement. He sang along to the words of *"Disco Inferno"*. After making a right turn onto Milwaukee Parkway, Vernon lowered the music. Policemen were always hiding somewhere to catch drunk drivers and teenage joyriders. Because Vernon was so popular at school and in the

neighborhood, winning class president two years in a row, people all along Milwaukee Parkway waved at him, calling out his name loudly. He made it home and went into the house for a bucket of soap and water.

His car was soaped up and sprayed down thoroughly. Using one of the whisk brooms from the trunk, Vernon swept out the front and back of his car, which included the floors, seats, and dashboard. A touch of chrome cleaner was applied to the bumpers and tire rims. When Vernon went out on a date, his Plymouth had to be sparkling. The inside would always be smelling like strawberry and cherry incense.

Bessie Mae stood in the doorway facing the side of the house. She watched Vernon put the finishing touches on his car. A large pot of chicken and noodles was boiling on top of the stove. The fire was turned down low to minimize the cooking time. Bessie Mae's health condition had gotten worse. She was taking five different medications for her high blood pressure. She worried herself about things that were senseless. Money was always her biggest worry. She never got enough of it! Her doctor warned her that she had developed essential hypertension. A lack of exercise, her enormous intake of salt and fat, smoking all those packs of Pall Mall Reds, being a black woman, and even her age, were all factors working against her.

Granny Dear's rheumatoid arthritis had been bothering her lately. While she slept, her joints and muscles had stiffened. Symptoms, such as fever, fatigue, and loss of appetite, had come about. Injections of immunosuppressants were used by her doctor to reduce the symptoms. It was difficult, but Granny Dear coped with her arthritis. Bessie Mae stood over the stove stirring the chicken and noodles. The heat in the kitchen had her perspiring heavily.

"I wonder if Vernon got paid at Roselli's Market today?" Bessie Mae asked Granny Dear, using the top of her shirt to wipe away some of the sweat.

"You ought ta ask'em when he come intide."

"I believe he gets paid on Saturdays."

"Ain't t'day Saturday, Bessa Mac?"

"Yes, it's Saturday."

"Call up dere and find out."

"Yes, I'll do that."

"Dat's da only way ya gone find out."

Bessie Mae limped over to the phone and called up to Roselli's Market. If she was lucky, she might have caught someone before the store was closed. The phone rang back in Virgil Roselli's office. No one anwered. It rang several more times before someone picked up.

"Roselli's," a deep-voiced man answered, sounding like he had been awaken from a deep sleep.

"Can I speak with the owner?" Bessie Mae asked.

"This is Virgil Roselli. How can I help you?"

"I'm Vernon Ramirez's foster mother."

"What can I do for you?"

"I want to know if Vernon was paid today."

"I can't give out that information."

"Why not?"

"It's a policy that I have here at the store."

"I have to know if Vernon was paid or not."

"I'm sorry, miss."

"It's urgent that I know."

"Why don't you ask him when he gets home?"

"Why don't you go to hell!" Bessie Mae shouted into the phone, then slamming abruptly into Virgil's ear.

She limped away from the wall and took a seat. Her blood pressure had elevated to a much higher level. "Them goddam dago-wops are all the same!"

Vernon walked into the basement with wet spots all over his clothes. Gilbert, Jose, and Vincent were in their room fixing a flat on the back tire of Vincent's bike. Vernon had an

DEWEY REYNOLDS

expression on his handsome face that conveyed a message of happiness.

"Why are you so happy?" Gilbert asked.

"I got paid today," Vernon said.

"I'd be happy, too."

"I'm supposed to be going to the drive-in tonight."

"What movie are you going to see?"

"Saturday Night Fever."

"Everybody wants to go and see that movie."

"Sure does."

"The dude from 'Welcome Back Kotter' is playing in it."

"Vinnie Barbarino?"

"That's him!"

"I'm excited."

"Who are you going to the drive-in with?"

"A girl that I met at Roselli's today."

"You're not taking Daphne?"

"I don't think so."

"Why not?"

"She's out of town."

"Does this girl live by us?"

"She lives in Cabrini-Green."

"Cabrini-Green!" Gilbert shivered, dropping the wrench on the floor and wiping oil on his shirt. "Aren't you scared to go over in Cabrini-Green?"

"Hell yeah, I'm scared!"

"I heard the police are scared to go over there."

"I heard the same thing."

"Is this girl cute?"

"Fine!" Vernon cheered.

"Man, Vernon, you better be careful over in Cabrini-Green."

"Believe me, I will."

"If you have to, you better take a razor or a gun."

"Maybe."

Bessie Mae stood at the top of the basement stairs listening to their conversation. Boasting about the fruitful fortunes of Vernon had deeply angered her. She limped down the basement stairs and trampled through the laundry room. Gilbert, Jose, and Vincent were told to take the bike out of the basement. This left Bessie Mae and Vernon in the room by themselves.

"Did you get paid at Roselli's today?" Bessie Mae asked Vernon, her tone of voice having a bit of greed in it.

"Yes, I did," Vernon replied in a low voice, holding his curled paycheck in his right pocket.

"Did you cash it yet?"

"No, I didn't."

"Why not?"

"I just didn't."

"I want you to cash it."

"I will, sooner or later."

"I want you to give me all of it."

"Excuse me?"

"You heard me."

"Why do you want my whole paycheck?"

"I'm feeding you."

"So."

"I'm giving you a roof over your head."

"Feeding me?"

"That's right."

"A roof over my head?"

"You're not deaf."

"You're getting paid to do all of that."

"Not enough."

"The Department of Children and Family Services is sending you a lot of checks every month."

"Says who?"

"Says those caseworkers who work there."

"Those white folks aren't paying me enough."

"Why aren't they paying you enough?"

"I've got all these bills to pay around here."

"Then take that up with somebody else."

"I just bought a new furniture set upstairs."

"So."

"I have to feed you all and pay these bills."

"That's not my problem, Mrs. Willingham."

"I hardly have anything left for me and J.D."

"You and J.D, huh?"

"That's right."

"Is it all about you and J.D.?"

"You've got it."

"What about the foster children and handicapped people?"

"What about them?"

"You never cared about anybody but yourself."

"That's not true."

"It's all about the money, isn't it?"

"That's a lie!"

"It's all about waiting on those checks, isn't it?"

"You're talking what you don't know."

"It's all about waiting on the first of the month, isn't it?"

"Watch your mouth, boy!"

"You know that I'm telling the truth, Mrs. Willingham."

"I don't have time to argue with you."

"Then go back upstairs."

Vernon had confronted Bessie Mae in the most shocking manner. He knew that she played *money games*, a woman who was consumed with greed.

"Give me that paycheck, Vernon."

"I'll just leave this foster home."

"Go ahead, leave."

"I will."

"You don't have nowhere to go."

"You wanna bet?" Vernon bluffed.

"I wanna bet that paycheck that you've got."

As soon as Bessie Mae limped up the stairs, Vernon jerked out all four drawers to his dresser and dumped everything on top of his bed. Using two large laundry bags that he bought, he stuffed all of his clothes inside. The basement door was kicked open and he popped the trunk to his car. He slammed both laundry bags inside. During the second trip, he went into the closet near Vincent's bed and grabbed his coats and a box of music albums and cassettes.

Gilbert and Vincent helped him take the two-hundred pound concrete weight set out to the car. During the third and final trip, he cleared off the top of his dresser, placing his colognes, soap, deodorant, toothpaste, and other personal toiletries inside a small box on the floor. Jose had gathered his shoes from under the bed. The trunk and back seat of his car were filled to capacity. Angrily, he mashed down the trunk and kicked both of the back doors closed. He erupted in a loud voice and shouted, "This is one fucked up foster home ran by some fucked up foster people!"

"It must've not been that fucked up!" Bessie Mae retaliated, poking her finger onto the screen, blowing a long drag of cigarette smoke out the window.

"I only stayed because I didn't know any better."

"You've stayed here this long, niggah."

"That's alright," Vernon said. "I'm getting the hell away from here."

"Where you gonna go, niggah?"

"Don't worry about it."

"Who's gonna let you come and stay in their home?"

"None of your business."

"You'll be on the streets."

"I've got somewhere else to go."

"Where, niggah?"

"Somewhere much better than this house."

"I'll see you out there on them streets."

"That's what you think."

"You'll be nothing but a drunk or a dopehead."

"We'll see about that."

"You'll be all messed up."

"Keep believing that, okay."

"You'll end up like your high yellow sister."

"What did you say about my sister?"

"You heard me, niggah."

"Let me tell you something," Vernon said, pointing right up to the window. "Don't ever say nothing bad about Valerie. I'll pull your crippled ass right out of that window."

"Can't stand the truth, huh?"

"Valerie wouldn't be out there if it wasn't for Mr. Willingham."

"Go ahead and blame J.D."

"He'll burn in hell forever for what he did to Valerie."

"Shut your mouth, boy!"

"If you were on your job, she never would've been raped."

"Close your mouth, boy!"

"I should send some of the caseworkers out here."

"What're they gonna do?"

"Close this foster home down."

"Those white folks can't tell me how to run this home."

"They've got more power than you."

"Me and J.D. are the queen and king that run this castle."

"You think so?"

"I know so."

"You all are more like two demons running a hellhole."

"I should burn your tongue with this cigarette for saying that," Bessie Mae challenged, holding her Pall Mall Red close to the screen.

"I'll see you later, Mrs. Willingham," Vernon said. "You're not qualified to run no foster home."

Vernon's final words left Bessie Mae speechless. She couldn't stand to listen to anymore remarks. She left the

window to finish stirring the chicken and noodles. Gilbert, Jose, and Vincent gathered around Vernon on the side of the car. Before speaking one word, he looked up at the window.

"Remember this," Vernon spoke quietly. "Whenever you all go out and rake yards, cut grass, shovel snow, deliver groceries to people's houses, or sell those Baldwin Express papers, keep every penny of your money."

"I always keep my money," Gilbert added. "I've hidden a lot of my money in my secret compartment near my bed.

"Do you ever get to spend any of it?" Vernon asked.

"Sometimes."

"That's good."

"I don't wanna spend too much of it."

"Why not?"

"Mrs. Willingham might start getting suspicious."

"You're right."

"She'll get nosy and start asking a lot of questions."

"Where are you gonna go?" Gilbert asked Vernon, very sad to see him leave, someone who'd been like his mentor.

"A couple of friends."

"Friends?"

"They've been wanting me to come and stay with them."

"How long will you stay with them?"

"Until I graduate from school."

"Where will you go from there?"

"I don't know, we'll see."

Vernon got inside his car and jerked the ignition to start the car. Before driving off, he told Gilbert, Jose, and Vincent to remember his advice. Bessie Mae came back to the window.

"Come and feed the dogs."

"Is the slopbucket full?" Vincent asked.

"It don't matter."

"Okay."

"Come and feed them anyway."

Vincent came into the kitchen and walked over to the

slopbucket. Molded cornbread, neckbones, oatmeal, pork sausage, biscuits, sweet potato pie, chicken bones, and rice covered in gravy, some of the food from weeks ago, filled the bucket to capacity. Vincent lifted the bucket with both hands interlocked and walked out of the kitchen.

Chapter 25

THE RAT PACK

GILBERT AND JOSE's caseworker, Sandra Maloney, made the following documentation about the two foster boys:

DESCRIPTION OF CHILDREN'S APPEARANCE: *Gilbert Curry and Jose Underwood are very attractive thirteen year old Negro boys. They are very friendly and introvert in nature. They are of average height and weight for their ages. They are always neat and take pride in doing this.*

PHYSICAL GROWTH AND HEALTH: *There have been no health problems reported on Gilbert and Jose during this dictation period. Mrs. Bessie Mae Willingham, the foster mother, is always good and conscientious about taking care of the children's medical and dental appointments.*

FEELINGS TOWARDS FOSTER PARENTS AND FOSTER SIBLINGS: *There seems to be a very good relationship between Gilbert, Jose, and the other siblings, and the other foster parents in this household. They seem to have a very harmonious home life, and Mrs. Willingham has never had any problems to report. There seems to be a very warm and affectionate relationship between Gilbert, Jose, and Mrs. Willingham, as there is between the other children in the household.*

CHILD'S RELATIONSHIP TO WORKER: *There has been no necessity to establish a close relationship with the foster children in this*

home, as Mrs. Willingham is an excellent foster mother and meets all of their emotional and physical needs without much help from the caseworker. Since there has been no agency contact with their natural mothers and fathers and no regular visit schedule made, there is little reason for the caseworker to play a role in the foster home setting.

CLOTHING BUDGET AS OF THIS DATE: At this time, there is nothing in Gilbert and Jose's clothing budget for the fiscal year. Mr. and Mrs. Willingham are very good about not over-spending the budget which is allowed.

CONCLUSION: Since Gilbert and Jose are doing quite well in this foster home, there are no immediate plans to move them. Mrs. Willingham is doing such a conscientious job of raising them.

Gilbert, Jose, and Vincent were never able to read over the documentation that their caseworkers or caseworker supervisors made. Things were mentioned in the documentation that weren't true. No, Bessie Mae wasn't a good and conscientious foster mother. She'd always put on a front whenever the caseworkers came to visit the Willingham residence. They were never told about all the abuse and neglect. As far as harmonious was concerned, that was the furthest from the truth.

*   *   *

Bessie Mae hadn't heard from Vernon in over two months. When he told her not to worry about his return, he meant what he said. Within those two months, he hadn't called or stopped by for a visit. Gilbert, Jose, and Vincent were in the front room watching television. They each fell back on the sofa, laughing hard and stomping their feet to an old episode of *"Sanford and Son"*. J.D. had walked into the front room

jingling his car keys. He blocked the entire screen of the television. He demanded that they go out on the porch. They quickly jumped up and stood out on the porch. From the bottom of the stairs leading to the second floor, J.D. called for Braun to come downstairs.

"Brawns!" J.D. called out loudly.

"Yeah, yeah, you wanna see me, J.D.?" Braun asked, rushing down the stairs beating the middle of his right hand with one of the thick wires, chewing a mouthful of gum that stuck to his rotten dental work.

"Put dat goddam wire up, Brawns!"

"Okay, okay, I'll put the wire up, J.D."

"Where ya git dat gum fum?"

"Yeah, yeah, Bessie Mae gave me this gum."

"Bessa Mae ain't gave ya no gum."

"Yeah, yeah, she sure did give me this gum."

"Why ya lying, Brawns!"

"No, no, I'm not lying, J.D."

"Take dat gum out yo mouth."

"Okay, okay, I'll take the gum out of my mouth."

"Lemme see dat gum, Brawns."

Braun kept trying to stall, sliding the wire down into his pocket.

"Alright, alright, I'll let you see the gum," Braun said, removing the large ball of black gum from his mouth and holding it right in J.D.'s face.

"Bessa Mae ain't gave ya dis gum."

"Yes, yes, she did give me that gum."

"Not lookin lack dat."

J.D. frowned as he closely observed the dark ball of gum in his right hand. He wanted wanted Bessie Mae to verify that she had given him the gum.

"Bessa Mae!" J.D. called from the front room.

"What is it, J.D.?" Bessie Mae answered from the steamy kitchen.

"Come in da funt woom."

"In the front room?"

"Yep."

Bessie Mae limped into the front room and stood right beside J.D. They both observed the nasty looking ball of gum.

"You gave Brawns dis ball of gum?"

"I never gave Braun any gum," Bessie Mae said, observing the gum that looked like a ball of charcoal.

"Less go up to his woom," J.D. suggested.

"I think we should."

Bessie Mae and J.D. traveled up to Braun and Junior's room. The bland smell of sour body odor and tobacco filled the entire room. Junior sat in his usual chair staring at the wall straight ahead.

"Open your drawers, Braun," Bessie Mae ordered.

"Okay, okay, I'll open my drawers," Braun replied, sliding open the top drawer.

"Look at this, J.D."

"Well, I say."

"This drawer is filled with a bunch of mess."

"Sho is."

"Black balls of old chewing gum."

"Dat's a shame."

"Gum that's months old."

"Dat's nasty, Bessa Mae."

"Trifling is more like it."

Bessie Mae and J.D. nodded their heads and gulped strongly as they scanned the top drawer with the months old balls of black chewing gum.

"Where did you get this gum, Braun?" Bessie Mae asked.

"Yeah, yeah, I get gum from other people."

"What people?"

"Yeah, yeah, I sure get it from other people."

"First, you told J.D. you got it from me."

"No, no, I never got no gum from you, Bessie Mae."

"Then, where did you get it?"

"Yeah, yeah, I can't remember."

Bessie Mae took a moment to do some brainstorming. She did chew gum, but would throw it in the trash, sometimes using the trashbarrel in the kitchen or the small wastebasket in the bathroom on the second floor.

"You got this gum out of the trash," Bessie Mae said. "Didn't you, Braun?"

"No, no, I didn't get no gum out of the trash."

"Yes, you did, Braun."

"No, no, I didn't go in the trash to get no gum."

"You pull gum out of the trash when you go looking for butts."

"No, no, I wasn't looking for no butts or no gum."

"Throw all of this gum away!" Bessie Mae shouted.

"Okay, okay, I'll throw all of this gum away, Bessie Mae."

"Don't you know that you can get sick?"

"Yeah, yeah, I can get sick from that."

"It's nasty putting that gum in your mouth," Bessie Mae retorted. "You don't know who's mouth that gum has been in."

Bessie Mae knew that she had to coach Braun and Junior on almost every move they made. That was one of the challenging parts of keeping men in their home who were mentally retarded. She now discovered that Braun wasn't only digging around in the trash for cigarette butts, but gum that she and others in the household had thrown away.

"Open that second drawer."

"Alright, alright, I'll open the second drawer."

"Isn't that what I said," Bessie Mae smarted off.

"Yeah, yeah, that's what you said, Bessie Mae."

"I'll be damned, J.D.!" Bessie Mae scowled. "This retarded fool done probably kept every hanger that I've ever thrown away. Get rid of every ball of gum and wires in both of these drawers."

"Okay, okay, I'll get rid of all the gum and wires, Bessie Mae."

Braun and J.D. went to the kitchen for trashbags. While he cleared out his drawers, J.D. took some of the trashbags out on the porch, giving Gilbert, Jose, and Vincent one a piece. He told them to wait in the backyard while he went into the toolshed. As they traveled towards the backyard, they laid their eyes on a horrible sight that almost reminded them of a horror movie. Gilbert frowned with every muscle in his face. Jose clutched the center of his stomach.

Vincent covered both eyes, then spread his fingers apart to watch the ghastly sight. The backyard was filled with dead rats. They were everywhere! Some were lying on their backs. Some were turned sideways. Some lied perfectly on their stomachs. A colony of hungry flies swarmed over the dead creatures. The problem with the rodents had gotten out of hand. Bessie Mae decided to call The City of Chicago's Rodent Control Division to bring bait out to the house.

The rats had been dead for about three days and the foul odor was evidence. Not only were the oversized rats trying to dig tunnels out by the dog pen and toolshed, but they tried digging holes that would lead inside the Willingham residence. J.D. unlocked the toolshed and brought out four rakes and four shovels.

"I want yall ta kean up every wat out here," J.D. instructed Gilbert, Jose, Vincent, and even Braun.

"Clean up all these rats, Mr. Willingham?" asked an astonished Gilbert, scanning the entire backyard and looking at every visible rat.

"Yep, all dese wats."

"But, we . . ."

"But nuttin, boy," J.D. said. "I don't wanna see one wat leff out here."

"Not one rat left out here?"

"Dat's wight."

Without further delay, everyone assumed their positions and started performing their grotesque duties. Gilbert and Vincent took their rakes, shovels, and trashbags over to the section that was separated from the next door neighbor's yard. When they arrived over there, they looked to the ground and saw six large rats that were lying on their stomachs and backs. One of the rat's feet were curled up, proving that the poison must've been potent.

Since they weren't far apart, Gilbert used his rake to move them close to one another. Vincent used his rake to move the others beside one another. Together, they joined the six rats into a pile and moved to another section of the yard. On the other side of the dogpen, facing a large green and white garage, there were more than a dozen other dead rats.

People walking up the street noticed the yard filled with dead rats. Instantly, embarrassment came upon the faces of Gilbert, Jose, and Vincent. Jose pinched his nose with one hand while trying to rake with his other hand. Over on the far right side of the dogpen, Braun was talking to himself, constantly mentioning his earlier life in St. Louis, Missouri, and how great Joe Louis was as a boxer, probably even searching for some cigarette butts.

Gilbert and Vincent continued raking the deceased rodents. They found it unbelievable that there were so many rats that bred in such large numbers. These were definitely Norway rats, having long bodies, short tails, teeth like beavers, and weighing up to thirteen ounces. The soil was moist around the backyard and inside the dogpen. There were small rat footprints and tail marks left behind.

One rat in particular was heavy. Vincent found it hard to rake it across the yard. Using the strong edges of the rake's teeth, he poked the side of the rat, rolling it around until it was joined with the others. Gilbert discovered something that was truly disgusting.

"Vincent!" Gilbert called from across the yard.

"What?" Vincent answered, stepping around the many different rodents.

"Come here."

"What?"

"I've got something to show you."

"I'm raking right now."

"Stop raking for a second."

"What is it, Gilbert?"

"Come over here."

Vincent traveled to the other side of the backyard to see what Gilbert so desperately had to show him.

"Yuck!" Vincent shook, taking a strong swallow and nodding his head in total disapproval.

"Looks nasty, don't it?"

"Nasty's not the word."

"It stinks, don't it?"

"Smells worse than a sewer."

Gilbert and Vincent stared down at a very large rat that was filled with thousands of hungry maggots. The maggots had eaten their way down to the rat's vertebrae, devouring all the internal organs that were nearby. Before the end of the day, the rat would be reduced to nothing but skin and bones.

"Hee! Hee!" Gilbert chuckled, poking the rat with his rake.

"How can you do it?"

"What?"

"Stand here and watch this junk."

"I've seen it before."

"Where?"

"At one of my other foster homes."

"Can't stop talking about your other foster homes?"

"Guess what, Vincent?"

"What?"

"This rat reminds me of a commercial on tv."

"What commercial?"

"The snicker bar commercial."

"What about it?"

"A snicker is chocolate covered outside."

"Right."

"It's also caramel and milk chocolate inside."

"True."

"Know what that means?"

"What?"

"This rat's dark covered outside and maggot-filled inside."

"Yuck!" Vincent moaned. "You're nasty, Gilbert."

"Remember that movie *'Ben'*?"

"About the rats?"

"Yeah."

"What about it?"

"This backyard looks like they made that movie here." It did appear as something right out of a movie, maybe a movie like *"Food Of The Gods"*.

Rats! They give most people the creeps.

Rats! They sneak in people's houses and eat up their food.

Rats! They eat holes through walls and floors.

Rats! They carry nasty diseases like rabies.

Rats! They cause millions of dollars in damage to property.

Rats! They tear open trash bags looking for food to eat.

Rats! They have been known to jump up in baby cribs and bite them.

Rats! They breed and breed and make millions of more rats.

Rats! They are nasty, sneaky, greedy, and evil creatures.

Rats! They remind Gilbert, Jose, and Vincent of Bessie Mae and J.D. Willingham.

Bessie Mae limped over to the kitchen window that gave her the perfect view of the backyard. She raised the window up to blow out a long drag of smoke.

"Didn't J.D. tell you all to clean up those rats?" Bessie Mae asked.

"Yes, mam," Vincent answered.

"Well, clean them up."

"There's a rat out here filled with maggots."

"So."

"It stinks real bad."

"The smell's not gonna kill you."

"These maggots are everywhere."

"I don't care if the rat's filled with bees."

"Yes, mam."

"Put it one of the trashbags."

Bessie Mae left the window to check on a large pot of spaghetti. Because there were so many other dead rats to worry about, Gilbert and Vincent left the rat filled with maggots lying there. Meanwhile, inside the smelly, fly swarming, flea infested, and dusty dogpen, Braun and Jose were raking soft and hard defecation waste left behind by the beagle hounds, even some of the tiny droppings were left behind by some of the rats.

Jose avoided further damage after accidentally smearing some of the soft defecation on the side of his sneakers. He also noticed that some had been smeared around the top portion. Some of it was wiped off when he ran his sneakers along the side of the links on the fence. He began raking in the corner that was opposite of Braun. Trying to rake all the junk into piles, he continuously stepped over and off to the side of the waste.

The large horseflies and small fleas became annoying. It was hard trying to rake and swat them away at the same time. The flies and fleas landed all over their bodies, buzzing around their faces and close to their ears. Braun and Jose

repeatedly slapped the back of their necks, the side of their faces, and around their ears.

The beagles jumped up on their legs. They wanted to play, but Braun and Jose knew that J.D. wanted that dog pen spotless. The beagles were sent back over to their dog house. Even after the swatting and slapping and jerking, the pesty insects wouldn't leave Braun and Jose alone. Jose began raking faster. Shedded hair from the hounds floated around the pen. Strands of the hair blew into Jose's mouth.

With no breeze coming through the air, Jose and Braun were forced to inhale the odor of the defecation. Mists of saliva spurted out of the mouth of Jose, eliminating him of the brown and white hairs that were on his tongue. Stepping back, he landed on a long piece of moist defecation. He stepped forward and landed on another piece. Both sneakers were smeared with defecation. Moving to the middle of the dog pen, Jose ran into a swarm of bloodsucking mosquitos, eagerly ready to put bites all over his body.

Right then and there, he wanted to stop and leave the dogpen, but knew that Bessie Mae kept her watchful eyes on everyone, making sure that they performed their bewildered tasks right down to the finish. Right outside the dogpen, Gilbert and Vincent had raked three piles of dead rats. They moved to the middle of the yard, where more dead rats had formed a circle, having eaten the poison around the same area and about the same time.

"God!" Gilbert inclined. "I can't believe these rats could get this big."

"Believe it," Vincent said. "Whatever food the dogs won't eat, the rats sneak out of those holes and finish."

"Wow!"

"They go over to their pans and eat the rest of the food."

"That's how they got that big?"

"Eating all that good food from the kitchen."

"You ever seen them eating the food?"

"All the time," Vincent said. "Right after I dump the food into their pans."

"Where do you be when they're eating the food?"

"Standing in the kitchen window."

"How many be eating at the pan?"

"I've seen about fifteen rats gathered around the pan."

"Really?"

"Yes."

"What's some of the food they eat?"

"Don't you feed the dogs, too?"

"Yes, I do."

"Then you should know."

"Come on, tell me, Vincent."

"All kinds of stuff," Vincent said. "Grits, sausages, eggs, pancakes, greens, cornbread, pork and beans, neckbones, spoiled milk, molded bread, rotten potatoes and tomatoes. You name it, those huge rats have probably eaten it."

"Where are the dogs?"

"Inside their dog house or on top of it."

"While the rats are eating up their food?"

"Yes."

"Why don't they gang up and kill them?"

"They're scared of them."

"Why?"

"Four beagle hounds are nothing compared to about thirty big rats."

"You're right," Gilbert agreed."But even when I was living at those other foster homes, I never saw this many rats."

"I'll bet you all didn't feed any dogs slop from a slopbucket."

"No, we didn't."

"That's why."

"We only had little mice running around the house."

If Gilbert only knew, the female rats around the Willingham residence were producing fourteen to sixty

young per year. The litters remained large because there was
ample food and shelter. The kitchen window facing the
backyard came up. The scratching of the old wood caused
Gilbert and Vincent to turn around and look up. Bessie Mae
had her eyes rotating from where they stood and out towards
the dogpen, where Braun was stooped down like he was
searching desperately for something.

"Quit talking and get back to work," Bessie Mae ordered
Gilbert and Vincent, blowing out a last drag of smoke from
her cigarette.

"We're working," Gilbert responded bravely.

"No, you're not!" Bessie Mae argued, poking her finger
onto the screen and down towards Gilbert.

"Yes, we are."

"I said, you're not."

"I said, we are."

"Don't argue with me, boy!"

"Then don't argue with me, Mrs. Willingham."

"Shut your goddam mouth, boy!"

"What have I said wrong?"

"Do you want me to send J.D. out there?"

"What?"

"You heard me."

"Send who?"

"J.D., boy!" Bessie Mae snarled. "I'll send J.D. out there
with his extension cord to beat the color off you, boy."

"Yes, mam."

"You're getting to big for your britches."

After straightening Gilbert out, Bessie Mae turned her
attention out to the dogpen, where Braun continued scanning the ground for something. She moved closer to the
screen and shouted, "Braun, what are you out there doing?"

"Yeah, yeah, I'm not out here doing nothing," Braun
replied quickly, grabbing the rake and pretending as though
he was trying to finish with the pen.

"You're lying."

"No, no, I'm not lying."

"You're looking for cigarette butts, aren't you?"

"No, no, I'm not looking for no cigarette butts."

"Yes, you are."

"No, no, I'm raking up this pen."

"Don't be sticking no butts in your pockets."

"No, no, I won't be sticking no butts in my pockets."

Bessie Mae limped away from the window to add some onions and peppers to her large pot of spaghetti. Gilbert and Vincent resumed their tasks. After Braun and Jose looked over at the stairs on the side of the house, they began working faster, raking up clouds of dust inside the pen. Someone on the side of the house caused them to become alarmed.

J.D. stepped from around the side of the house, holding tightly onto his long brown extension cord. His eyes were fire red. His chapped lips were puckered inwards. He was breathing heavier than ever before. This indicated that he was willing to inflict severe punishment on anyone who were disobedient.

Several people walking up the street were passing the Willingham residence and staring hard at the dead rats. They were astonished to see J.D. swinging his extension cord back and forth. J.D. gave Gilbert the look as though he was guilty of something. The only thought that crossed through the mind of Gilbert was receiving a severe beating. While he hung his head low, Vincent continued raking. They waited for a response from J.D.

"What's yo muttapucking problem, Gillbutt?" J.D. questioned Gilbert, gripping the extension cord tighter, kicking dirt from under his legs and into the face of Gilbert.

"I don't have a problem, Mr. Willingham," Gilbert answered modestly, fear filling his eyes.

"Bessa Mae say ya gittin smart wit'er."

"I wasn't getting smart with Mrs. Willingham."

"She say ya gittin too smart fo yo britches."

"I'm not too smart for my britches."

"Ya callin Bessa Mae a liar?"

"No, sir."

"Ya ain't had no old-fasson ass whippin yet."

"No, sir."

"Why ain't yall got dese wats keaned up yet?"

"Me and Vincent are raking them into piles."

"Yall should be finished."

"We're gonna put them in the trashbags later."

"When I come out here a'gin," J.D. said, pointing around the entire backyard. "Yall betta have all dese wats keaned up. I don't wanna see one leff out here."

"Yes, sir," Gilbert said. "We'll have them all cleaned up and there won't be any left out here."

"It betta not."

J.D. left the backyard and Gilbert and Vincent moved their rakes at a rapid pace. Gilbert didn't expect Bessie Mae to send J.D. out to the backyard to chastise him. They continued making more piles. Vincent rolled one of the rats over on their back and discovered that it had some of the poison left between it's teeth.

"This rat died eating some of the poison," Vincent told Gilbert, scraping the surface of it's sharp teeth with the rake.

"You better keep working," Gilbert whispered to Vincent, turning to look up at the kitchen window, hoping that Bessie Mae wasn't looking.

"Mr. Willingham's gone."

"You never know, he might come back."

"You're right."

To be on the safe side, Gilbert kept his lips sealed, dragging his rake back and forth across the grass. Another pile was completed, so they went to another section of the backyard. Vincent pointed out six more rats. Two were at the foot of the toolshed, three in the front of the dogpen, and one

lying curled up near the sidewalk. Gilbert and Vincent knew that teamwork would get the job done faster.

While they made piles over by the toolshed, Jose took a break to watch them perform their duties. For his sake, the break wouldn't last too long. Jose watched Gilbert and Vincent puncture the thick coats of the lifeless rodents with the teeth of the rakes.

"It looks like a *cemetery for rats*," Vincent said to Gilbert.

"A cemetery without tombstones," Gilbert said, taking a quick look up at the kitchen window and still moving his rake.

"May these big rats rest in peace."

"I hope I never have to see another rat."

"Never in our lives."

Inside the dog pen, Braun and Jose formed several small piles, which consisted of shedded dog hair, old bones from beef, pork, and chicken, loose dirt, and some smelly defeca-tion waste. Concurrently, everyone completed their duties. Braun and Jose stepped out of the dog pen to grab the shov-els and trashbags. Gilbert suggested that he and Vincent start dumping the rats in the trashbags. Vincent held the shovel in place while he raked the rats. Braun opened the sack while Jose dumped everything inside. The pesty fleas and flies followed the trash down into the bag.

The mosquitos flew out in the open, buzzing around their faces and ears. Gilbert and Vincent filled two and a half trashbags with rats. As much as they resented it, they moved over to the really large one that was filled with the devouring maggots. These same maggots had crawled off the rats and through surrounding grassy areas, searching for more dead rodents to devour.

"I hate flies," Gilbert commented sourly. "I hate them everytime I see them."

"Flies are nasty!" Vincent sneered. "They land on anything and start eating."

"They carry diseases."

"Diseases that make you sick."

"Make you have to go to the hospital."

"Somebody should kill these maggots."

"How?"

"Burn them up."

"Before they turn into flies?"

"Exactly."

"My foster mother at the other home used to burn them up with gasoline."

The maggot filled rat went inside the bag and they were almost finished. The trashbags had to be placed near the side of the house for trash day. Gilbert walked over to the window facing the backyard and looked up. "Mrs. Willingham!"

"What do you want?" Bessie Mae asked.

"Where do you want the sacks?"

"Somewhere near the street."

"Right here, Mrs. Willingham?"

"Anywhere's fine, boy."

Gilbert and Vincent grabbed opposite sides of the first sack that they had to haul. It was quite heavy. The dense weight of the rats made it difficult to lift, so they slid it through the grass. As they strained every muscle they had and planted the heels of their sneakers into the soil, they leaned and pulled until the sack was on the side of the house. Each trip took a lot of muscle work, but every sack made it to the side of the house.

Braun and Jose left the dog pen to bring their heavy sacks out. Gilbert and Vincent went inside the pen to help them bring out the rest of the sacks. Together, everyone took the sacks and placed them with the other ones. A line of green trashbags sat in the grassy strip near the street.

Jose went to lock the gate to the dog pen. In a flash, a large rat ran from behind the toolshed. The swift rat made

EYN

it's way past the pen and right down into a hole that was near
the large garage. Other holes were nearby, mainly
surrounding the shed and the pen.

"I just saw another rat!" Jose frightfully told Gilbert and
Vincent. "I thought all of them were dead."

"Where?" Gilbert asked.

"Over by the dogpen."

"Yeah, yeah, that was a great big ole rat!" Braun inter-
cepted, throwing his hands up to show them the size of the
rat.

"Where did he go?"

"Down one of those big holes."

"I bet there's some left," Gilbert said.

"That poison should've killed all of them."

"It should've, but it didn't."

"You know what that means?"

"What?"

"We might have to do this all over again."

"Oh no!" Vincent snarled. "Not this junk all over again. I
don't ever wanna see another rat, dead or alive, in my whole
life, again."

They were hoping that this mortifying nightmare was
over. Didn't they consider that rats bred in large numbers?
The slop fed to the beagle hounds was the rats only source of
food.

J.D. pulled out of the driveway. He cruised up the street
and stopped at the corner of Milwaukee. Since the backyard
had trash scattered everywhere, Bessie Mae told them to police the area. They picked up paper, soda cans, fruit juice
jars, and branches from the trees. Between an open space
behind the dog pen, Jose glanced into the window of a garage that no one ever went into. Inside, there were long
wooden benches, a short wooden podium, and torn dusty
pages from the Bible. Carved on the front of the podium was
a fancy cross. Around the benches, there were four small

white packages. A picture of camels was drawn on the front of these packages.

"I found something," Jose informed Gilbert and Vincent, bending over to look further into the garage.

"What did you find?" Gilbert asked.

"I don't know."

"You can't see?"

"It's got camels on the front."

"Camels?" Gilbert nodded. "It's probably what I think it is."

"What do you think it is?" Jose asked.

"It's probably some cigarettes."

"Let's go inside and see what it is."

"Make sure Mrs. Willingham isn't looking."

"Where?"

"Out that kitchen window."

Jose looked up at the window and no one was there. Gilbert and Vincent stood on opposite sides of the garage window. Curiosity hit them after they seen the white packages. Before climbing into the garage, Gilbert and Vincent took another glance up at the kitchen window. They climbed through the window and waited for Jose.

"Come on, Jose," Gilbert said, waving his hand repeatedly.

"I'm scared," said Jose, constantly looking back and forth.

"You better hurry up."

"You're right."

"Mr. Willingham might come back in his truck."

"I hope not."

"Mrs. Willingham might come back to the kitchen window."

"I better hurry up."

Jose quickly climbed through the window. He landed on the edge of one of the benches, gently hurting his elbow and kneecap. Gilbert went between the benches and picked up the dusty white packages. Since they hadn't been opened,

he rubbed the two packages together to smear off some of the dirt.

"I wonder who left these cigarettes in here?" Gilbert wondered, discovering those packs of Camel cigarettes.

"Probably somebody who went to church here," Vincent said.

"This was a church?"

"Yes."

"I can't tell."

"These are church benches."

"Nobody has church in a garage."

"Yes, they do."

"What's that wooden thing up there?" Gilbert asked.

"That's where the preacher stands when he's preaching."

"Do church people smoke?" Vincent asked.

"Yes."

"Like Mr. and Mrs. Willingham?"

"Yes, they do."

"God doesn't like church people to smoke."

"But they do it anyway."

"I thought it was wrong."

"As long as they don't smoke weed."

Vincent switched subjects quickly after glancing around the dusty garage. "Where did all these holes come from?"

"What holes?" Gilbert asked.

"The ones right there," Vincent pointed.

"Where?"

"Right there, and right there, and over there."

"They might be rat holes."

"Oh God!"

"They might come up out of those holes."

"And bite us!" Jose fretted.

"We'll just stomp them if they do."

"That's a lot of stomping."

"It might be a whole lot of them."

"Don't worry."

"Why not?"

"That poison took care of them."

Gilbert, Jose, and Vincent forgot about the holes and concentrated more on the packs of cigarettes they found. The packs of Camels were ripped open. They sniffed the top to check for freshness. Bessie Mae and J.D. always sniffed the top of their packs of cigarettes before smoking them, sometimes putting them in the freezer to insure complete freshness. Gilbert slid one out of his pack and wanted to fire it up. He needed matches and there were none around. Someone had to leave the garage to get some. Jose volunteered to go inside the house and search for Gilbert.

"Where can I find some matches?" Jose asked Gilbert.

"Inside the house," Gilbert said.

"Where inside the house?"

"Look wherever Mr. or Mrs. Willingham lay their cigarettes."

"Where do they lay their cigarettes?"

"Check in the front room."

"What if they're not in there?"

"Check in their bedroom."

"In their bedroom!" Jose quivered.

"Yes."

"Do you want me to get beat into a heart attack?"

"Quit being a scary cat."

"Alright, but if I get caught, I . . ."

"You won't get caught," Gilbert interrupted. "Mr. Willingham's bald-head self is gone."

"What about Mrs. Willingham?" Jose asked.

"Her crippled behind is in the kitchen with Granny Dear."

"Doing what?"

"Fixing dinner."

"Okay."

Jose kicked through the dirt and over the window. He cautiously looked down at the holes, making sure there were no rats coming out. A green Pontiac Bonneville came cruising down the street and parked in the driveway on the side of the house. Carmen stepped out of the car with a large sack from "Sears and Roebuck". She made her routine visits, still borrowing money and collecting old furniture from Bessie Mae.

"What are you waiting on?" Gilbert asked Jose.

"Carmen just drove up."

"Where?"

"In that big green car."

"Is she in the house yet?"

"Not yet."

"Where's she now?"

"Walking up the stairs."

When Carmen wasn't in sight, Jose jumped through the garage window and raced for the house. Gilbert was anxious to try and smoke one of the Camels. Vincent became questionably quiet, his face losing all expression. The mention of Carmen's name sent him into anger frenzies, bringing back haunting memories of the bathroom sexcapades.

*   *   *

Vincent had developed thoughts that traveled back to when he was six years old, the second floor of the Willingham residence. He couldn't forget the exact moment when Carmen had sexually molested him. His mind was stuck on the exact episode of when he and Carmen were in the middle of having unusual sexual intercourse.

"Does it feel good to you, Vincent?" Carmen asked Vincent.

"Yes, Vincent answered, not fully aware of what was going on.

"Do you like it, Vincent?"

"Yes."

"Do you love it, Vincent?"

"*Yes.*"

"*Say you like it, baby!*"

"*I like it.*"

"*Say you love it, baby!*"

"*I love it.*"

"*Say you want more, baby!*"

"*I want more.*"

*   *   *

Vincent had come back to the present day and glanced mysteriously around the gloomy garage. He suddenly exploded and shouted, "That bitch!"

"Who are you talking about?"

"Carmen."

"Why'd you call her that?"

"She's one."

"But, why?"

"She's what she is."

"You had to have a reason."

"You really wanna know?"

"Yes, I do."

"I hate her guts."

"Why, Vincent?"

"Don't think I'm lying."

"I won't."

"She made me do it to her."

"Have sex with her?"

"Sure did."

"When?" Gilbert asked, becoming more interested in details.

"I was a little kid."

"How old?"

"Six."

"Where did it happen?"

"In the bathroom."

"Which one?"

"On the second floor."

"Down the hall from Mr. and Mrs. Willingham's room?"

"Yes."

"She got away with it?"

"Of course she did."

"How would she do it?"

"Wait until everybody went to sleep."

"She'd make you do it to her?"

"Yes, she did."

"What happened when you all were doing it?"

"She'd pull me close to her."

"With all of your clothes off?"

"Yes."

"What happened next?"

"Then, she'd try and do it to me."

"Fuck?"

"Yes."

"Who else knows about this?"

"Nobody."

"I don't believe you."

"Nobody, but me and her."

"You never told Mr. or Mrs. Willingham?"

"No."

"Why?"

"Too scared."

"Scared of what?"

"Getting a beating."

"I see, now," Gilbert paused. "If you told Mr. and Mrs. Willingham, they wouldn't believe you, and they'd believe Carmen, and you would get a beating for lying."

"That's right."

"They show her favoritism?"

"Always have."

"They've always been nicer to her?"

"Yes."

"Carmen looks good."

"You think so?"

"Yeah!"

"She's ugly to me."

"I wish she would've took me in the bathroom."

"Very funny."

"I'm serious."

"I bet you are."

"We never had any cute girls at my other foster homes."

Jose jumped through the garage window, not even check-ing to make sure Bessie Mae wasn't looking. Gilbert and Vincent waited between the benches, waiting to fire up one of the cigarettes.

"Where're the matches?" Gilbert asked Jose.

"I couldn't find any," Jose explained, stepping over the holes.

"There's a bunch in the house."

"Where?"

"You didn't look in the right places."

"I looked in the front room."

"Where else?"

"I looked in the dining room, too."

"Mr. or Mrs. Willingham don't leave matches in there."

"Where do they leave them?"

"I'll go find some."

Gilbert stared out the garage window and up at the kitchen window. No one was standing up there. He jumped through the window, bending down by the dogpen, pretend-ing like he was picking up the remainder of the trash. To retrace Jose's tracks, Gilbert went into the front room and dining room to search for the matches. He didn't have any luck finding any. Going into the Willingham's room wasn't a bad idea, but he knew that it would be risky. Around the

coffee tables inside Bessie Mae and J.D.'s room, he searched
for the matches.

Bessie Mae or J.D. were subject to walk into the room at
any time. Under Bessie Mae's brown leather coin purse, there
was a book of matches that came from one of the famous
casinos out in Las Vegas. Gilbert took the matches and returned to the backyard. Stopping between the garage and
the dogpen, he turned to look up at the kitchen window.
Before attempting to jump through the garage window, he
made sure Bessie Mae was nowhere in sight. He quickly lifted
himself through the window.

Because Gilbert took the risk of getting the matches, he
had the pleasure of firing up the first cigarette. The matches
were passed to Jose, who passed them on to Vincent. He was
reluctant about pulling out one of the cigarettes.

"What're you scared of?" Gilbert asked Vincent.

"I've never smoked before," Vincent said.

"Never?"

"Not in my whole life."

"Don't be scared."

"Have you ever smoked before?"

"When I was at the last foster home."

"How did it feel?"

"Good."

"Even after you inhaled?"

"Yes."

Gilbert and Jose took their second puff and blew the
smoke straight into the air. Jose coughed in short spurts,
patting himself lightly across the chest. Before taking another puff, he waited a few minutes. The fire consumed most
of the cigarette. Vincent finally pulled one out of his pack.
An expression of uncertainty came upon his face. He jerked
one of the matches from the book. Nervousness made it difficult for him to apply enough pressure between the match
and the striker. His hands shook constantly.

"Can't light your cigarette?" Gilbert asked Vincent.

"I'm trying, but . . . ," Vincent stuttered.

"But what?"

"These matches, they . . ."

"They what?"

"They won't strike."

Gilbert was handed the book, lighting the match on the first try. Vincent leaned forward with a cigarette planted between his lips. He took a puff and didn't inhale. Gilbert and Jose were taking strong puffs, but were inhaling lightly. The dusty garage was filled with cigarette smoke.

"I hope the smoke don't go through the window," Gilbert fretted, blowing his smoke in the opposite direction of the window.

"Why not?" Jose asked.

"Mrs. Willingham will probably think this garage is on fire."

"The smoke will disappear."

"Hopefully, before it gets to the window."

"We better hope Mr. Willingham don't see no smoke coming out of this garage."

"What if he caught us smoking?"

"You already know the answer to that."

"What?"

"Beat us into next week."

"You're right."

They continued inhaling the smoke into their adolescent lungs. Vincent's mouth was filled with smoke. His jaws were poked out as far as they would go. The smoke was released like hot air coming out of a balloon. Gilbert and Jose wanted to see him inhale. Vincent had nothing to prove, but he was curious. He took a strong puff and slowly inhaled. Like having a bad cold, he coughed and pounded on his chest, trying hard to resume normal breathing. Spurts of saliva came rushing out of his mouth. His face was flushed. His

eyes turned bloody red. There was a slight case of dizziness that swayed him back and forth.

"Vincent!" Gilbert panicked, rushing to his assistance. "Are you alright, man?"

"I . . . uh . . . ," Vincent coughed, feeling the effects of Gilbert pounding on his back.

"Are you okay?"

"Yeah, I'm okay."

"You were right."

"About what?" Vincent asked.

"That you've never smoked before."

Vincent was still spitting and blowing thick mucous from his nose. When the effects wore off, Vincent smashed the cigarette into the dirt. It was no more cigarettes for him. Watching Gilbert and Jose blow the smoke in and out of their noses and mouths was enough to make him sick. Gilbert was far from being an amateur. He even knew how to french inhale. Everyone in the garage became silent.

"Aren't you all ready to get out of this foster home?" Gilbert asked, breaking the brief silence while taking hard puffs.

"I was ready to go the first day," Jose added.

"When Mrs. Maloney first brought us here?"

"Yes."

"Why were you ready to go, Gilbert?"

"When I saw those mattresses and boxsprings."

"Yuck!" Jose shrugged.

"Shit and piss stains."

"That's nasty."

"Knowing that we had to sleep on that stuff."

"Braun's black teeth scared me."

"Junior staring without blinking scared me."

"I knew that this was a weird foster home that we were coming to."

"I've never lived with retarded people before."

"What about Mr. Willingham?"

"Him too."

"I took one look at him and wanted to run."

"A big, black bear, huh?"

"No, a big black niggah who talked like he was dumb."

"Did he ever go to school?"

"Probably, to kindergarten."

"What about Mrs. Willingham?"

"Her being crippled sort of scared me."

"Limping up and down?"

"Hopping around like a bunny rabbit."

"Did Granny Dear scare you?"

"Not really."

"She didn't scare me, neither."

"An old woman in a wheelchair."

"How did she get in that wheelchair?"

"She's got arthritis real bad."

"For real?"

"That's why her legs are twisted like that."

"Why did Braun's black teeth scare you?"

"I've never seen teeth as black or as rotten as his."

"Beating his hand with that wire scared me."

"Me too."

"What did you think when you saw Junior?"

"A man who was off in a daze."

"Me too."

"I wanna call Mrs. Maloney."

"And tell her what?"

"I wanna leave this fucking foster home!"

"We should run away."

"And get chased down by Mr. Willingham's beagles hounds."

"You're right."

"Get beat like an animal in the jungle."

The sounds of a truck engine clattered off the pavement

on the side of the house. The noise ceased and Gilbert went
over to the window.

"Who's out there?" Jose asked, quickly mashing out his
cigarette.

"It's Mr. Willingham," Gilbert squealed, carefully keeping
his head ducked.

"Mr. Willingham?"

"Yes, it's him."

"What's he doing?"

"Getting something out of his truck."

J.D. walked around Carmen's car and went up the side
stairs. Moments after J.D. came up on the porch, Gilbert
crushed out his cigarette. Everyone was afraid to come out of
the garage. They had to worry about Bessie Mae or J.D. catching them in there. Gilbert quickly jumped through the garage window without J.D. seeing him. The timing couldnt've
been more perfect.

"Gillbutt!" J.D. called loudly from the middle of the
porch.

"Sir," Gilbert answered, standing before J.D. like a recruit
in bootcamp.

"I want ya ta find my mezzrin tape."

"What kind of tape?"

"My mezzrin tape, boy!"

"I don't know what kind of tape you're talking about, Mr.
Willingham."

"Mezzrin tape, dummy!"

"Did you say measuring tape?"

"Ain't dat what I said?"

"Yes, sir."

"You dumb bassard!"

"Where is it, Mr. Willingham?"

"Look in da funt woom."

"The front room?"

"Yep, dummy."

The longer anyone lived with J.D, they realized how illiterate he really was. His words were pronounced in the most wreckless manner. Sometimes, it was extremely difficult communicating with him. Gilbert rushed into the front room to begin his search. He opened the drawers to an antique cabinet behind the front door. He rambled around many objects, hoping he would find something that resembled a measuring tape. The search became frustrating, taking a quick break from the madness. Gilbert remembered that he had a blowpop in his back pocket. He reached back there and unwrapped it.

J.D. sat on the flatbed of his truck. He impatiently waited for Gilbert. Jose and Vincent were too afraid to come out of the garage. They peeked from opposite sides of the window, wanting J.D. to turn his back so they could come out. J.D. felt that Gilbert was taking too long. The screen door slammed and Gilbert quickly turned around. He was licking the top of his blowpop. Standing above him was an angry J.D., blowing hot air from his wide bull nostrils.

"What da fuck ya doing?" J.D. snapped at Gilbert, his eyes flaming red from lethal anger.

"Looking for the measuring tape," Gilbert said, ready to pass out from sudden fright.

"Where ya git dat sucker fum?"

"I bought it at the store."

"Who said ya could have a sucker in yo mouth?"

"Nobody."

"Den why ya got it in yo mouth?"

"I don't know."

"You dunno?"

"No, sir."

"What?"

"No, sir."

"Git yo ass in da utta woom!"

"What other room?" Gilbert asked, removing the blowpop from his mouth.

"Don't pay dumb, niggah!"

"The dining room, Mr. Willingham?"

"Yep."

J.D. stormed upstairs to get his extension cord. When he returned, he jetted into the dining room swinging the cord wildly through the air. He grabbed Gilbert by the arm and started swinging the extension cord across his chest and back. Gilbert jumped up and down, screaming as loudly as possible, as J.D. held the tightest grip around his arm and onto the extension cord. He could be heard from outside by people walking up the street. Jose and Vincent stood motionless inside the garage, knowing that their foster brother was receiving another severe punishment. Would they be next to get a beating? They jumped through the window and pretended as though they were picking up trash in the backyard.

*　　*　　*

J.D. had traveled back in time once more. Only this time, he recalled his father, Henry Willingham, beating him severely for not remembering to bring a set of molasses jars from the porch into the house. His mother, Callie Mae Willingham, was also furious at J.D., because she needed the molasses jars to pour some new molasses inside and stock on the shelves. Henry was thrashing J.D. with a thick strap that he used to sharpen his straight razors.

"Don't beat me, pappa!" J.D. screamed mercifully, running all through the old house that was like a shack built with thin plywood.

"Ya know daggone well Callie Mae needed dose lasses jars."

"I knows pappa, I know!"

"Den why ya didden git da lasses jars in da house?"

"I don't know, pappa!" J.D. replied, jumping up and down from the stinging effect of the powerful strap.

"Ya betta fess up, boy."

"I don't know why, pappa!"

"Me and Callie Mae sick'a yo mess, J.D," Henry said, stroking
the strap across the back and chest of J.D.
"I's sorry for what I do, pappa!"
"You done got too smart fo yo britches, niggah."

*   *   *

Merciful responses came from Gilbert. He tried jerking away
from the tight grip of J.D., but he wasn't about to let him go.
Bessie Mae and Granny Dear stood in the kitchen doorway.
They watched J.D. beat Gilbert senselessly. As spectators, they
watched in delight. Gilbert actually got a break, because J.D.
didn't make him take his clothes off.

"Why ya have dat sucker in yo mouth?" J.D. asked Gilbert,
taking long and hard strokes directly across his chest and
back.

"I don't know!" Gilbert screamed, using every muscle in
his vocal chords, rolls of tears and spurts of saliva dropping
onto the carpet.

"You ain't gone have no mo suckers in yo mouth?"

"No, sir!"

"Aint'cha?"

"No, sir!"

"What?"

"No, sir!"

"Can't hear ya."

"No, sir!"

"Ya know I don't like suckers in yo mouth?"

"Yes, sir!"

"Dont'cha?"

"Yes, sir!"

"Ya know what's gone happen next time?"

"Yes, sir!" Gilbert replied, the loudest scream of them
all.

"Dont'cha?"

"Yes, sir!"

"What?" J.D. asked, the muscles in his arm rippling, as he swung the extension cord up and down Gilbert's body.

Bessie Mae stood over Granny Dear's wheelchair smoking a Pall Mall Red. Jose and Vincent moved closer to the house. They listened as Gilbert was being severely punished. Everytime J.D. swung the extension cord at Gilbert, the painful memories kept coming back. His father, Henry Willingham, beating the young J.D. with the long strap.

Bessie Mae limped over to the kitchen window facing the side of the house. She looked out the window and shouted, "You all better get back to work!"

"We're working," Vincent said, holding trash items in both hands.

"Don't make me send J.D. out there."

"We're not doing nothing wrong."

"Don't look like you're working to me."

"We're trying to find somewhere to put this trash."

"You're going to be next."

"For what?"

"For a beating, boy!" Bessie Mae said.

Jose and Vincent traveled over to the toolshed and dogpen, picking up any object that was in sight. J.D. finally stopped beating Gilbert. He sent him back into the front room to search for the measuring tape. Inside one of the drawers, under a pile of papers, there was a square metal object. Gilbert took the object out to J.D. to make sure it was the measuring tape. J.D. was sitting at the edge of the flatbed. Gilbert stepped up to him and he snatched the object out of his hand.

"Is this what you were talking about, Mr. Willingham?" Gilbert asked, tears having dried all over his face.

"Yep, you dummy!"

"Okay."

"You about a dumb bassard."

J.D. sent Gilbert to the backyard to help Jose and Vincent finish cleaning up. Gilbert bent down rubbing his eyes and snorting thick mucous out of his nose.

"Why did Mr. Willingham beat you?" Vincent asked, whispering into the ear of Gilbert.

"For having a blowpop in my mouth," Gilbert whispered back, a serious look of rage on his face. He knew that their punishments were always unjustifiable.

"A blowpop?"

"Yes."

"Are you serious?"

"Yes."

"But, why would he beat you for something like that?"

"He's probably mad at something else."

"That's messed up."

"I'm calling my caseworker."

"Mrs. Maloney?" Vincent asked.

"Yes."

"When?"

"Whenever I get the chance."

"I don't blame you."

"He used the blowpop as an excuse."

"Just like when he beat Sean for breaking up that ink pen."

"And spilling the ink on his pants," Gilbert added.

"I wish somebody would shoot him."

"I'll do it if somebody gave me a gun."

"Anybody probably would."

Gilbert, Jose, and Vincent finished cleaning up around the backyard.

Chapter 26

THE STRANGEST STRANGER

VINCENT THREW A pigskin football autographed by Walter Payton to Gilbert. He threw the football over to Jose. They stood in the front yard enjoying the mild and breezy Fall weather. A 1977, Cadillac El Dorado convertible, slowed the traffic up on Milwaukee Parkway. The El Dorado flashed it's bright yellow signal and turned left on the side street.

Vincent embraced the football under his right armpit, taking a strong glance at the man parking the fancy red auto-mobile on the right side of the street. He stepped over to the sidewalk to get a better look. Gilbert and Jose were right behind him. Vincent stuck his neck forward to get a better picture of this strange man. Gilbert and Jose moved back slowly.

He moved further towards the street. The strange man smile graciously. Vincent suspiciously observed his body language. The well-dressed and well-groomed man, who wore a charcoal gray suit, which was double-breasted with thin white pinstripes, had his speckled gray hair slicked back, mustache trimmed neatly, and teeth were whiter than pure winter snow.

"Come closer, son," said the strange man, stretching his left arm out of the car. He signaled innocently with his hand.

"Who are you?" Vincent asked nervously, stepping closer to the car.

"I won't harm you."

"What do you want?"

"Do you know who I am?"

"No, I don't," Vincent said, checking out the expensive watch and diamonds he wore.

"I'm your father."

"You're who?"

"Your father."

"What's your name?"

"Vito."

"Vito who?"

"Carvelli."

"You're really my father?" Vincent asked, his heart pumping overtime and fingers quivering.

"Come over here."

"For what?"

"Give your old man a hug."

Vito leaned over the door to give Vincent a tight, warm hug. The son that he had abandoned nearly thirteen years ago stood before him.

"The family services people said that my father's name was Vito."

"They were right."

"They also said you were Italian."

"The wop everybody wants to drop," Vito casually joked, gleaming with pride.

"My mother's black?"

"Yeah, she's colored."

"Colored?"

"I meant, she's black."

"Where's she at now?"

"I'm glad you asked," Vito said. "She's been asking about you all."

"Why didn't she come with you?"

"Marion's been in the hospital."

"That's her name?"

"Yeah."

"What's she in the hospital for?"

"She's been having trouble with her emphysema."

"What's that?"

"Breathing problems."

"Is she gonna be alright?"

"She'll be okay."

"Do you and my mother live together?"

"We're married, son."

"Can I ask you a serious question?"

"Anything, son."

"Why didn't you all come by and see us?"

"We couldn't."

"Why not?"

"The family service people."

"What they do?"

"They wouldn't let us get you all back."

"Why not?"

"Our parental and visitation rights were terminated."

Neglect reflected all through Vincent's eyes, as he stared into the eyes of his flamboyant, criminally-inclined father.

"How did you know that I was still in this foster home?"

"I know people."

"Which people?"

"My buddy, Tony Castellano."

"How would he know?"

"He told me he saw a mulatto boy on Milwaukee Parkway."

"He knew that you were my father?"

"Said that you were like my twin."

After all these years of abandonment, Vincent had every right to ask all the questions that he wanted.

"Can I ask you another question, my father?" Vincent asked.

"You sure can, my son."

"Why did you all leave us in this foster home?"

"Where can I start?" Vito asserted. "Your mother and I were doing a lot of illegal things."

"What kind of things?"

"Things that were dangerous."

"Dangerous? How?"

"Something that children shouldn't be a part of."

"I see."

"That's why we had to leave you all here."

"I wanna know what you all were doing."

"Think you're old enough to hear this?"

"Sure I am."

"We had a house on Fitzgerald that we used to sell dope, liquor, and run whores in and out of."

"Are you still doing those things?"

"Well . . ."

"Are you?"

"Son, your old man's trying to get out of pimping women and pushing dope."

"I know what pimps and dope pushers are."

"How do you know about such people?"

"We see those kind of people on Rush."

"Rush Boulevard?" said a shocked Vito. "What in God's name are you doing up on Rush? It's a jungle all along that street."

"We sell The Baldwin Express up there," Vincent said. "We always see the men who are pimps and the women who are prostitutes. They hang out in front of Bennie's Hotel all the time."

"Well!" Vito grunted. "I see Bennie Caputo's still making big bucks off those hookers and junkies and queenies who hang inside his stinking hotel. Him and Fat Tony should've been in the can a long time ago."

"What's the can?"

"It's jail, son. It's somewhere that you never wanna go."

"Rush is the closest place to sell the papers."

"How are they treating you in this foster home?"

"Bad!" Vincent charged. "We're treated real bad."

"Whaddaya mean, bad?"

"Mr. Willingham beats on me and the others all the time."

"Is that right?"

"And usually for nothing."

"That non-talking moolie!" Vito growled. "I knew that watermelon and fried chicken eating, chitterling cleaning and cotton picking nigger, was nothing but trouble when I first set eyes on him."

"I'll be glad when I can leave this foster home."

"I understand that Vernon left here a while back."

"He did."

"Why?"

"Because of Mrs. Willingham."

"What'd she do?"

"Kept trying to take all of his money."

"Didn't she want him to keep a red cent in his pocket?"

"She wanted his whole paycheck."

"But, why?"

"I don't know."

"The state's already paying them for keeping you all."

"She's a mean lady."

"And a greedy bitch!" Vito added. "Your mother and I regret that we had to leave you all in this foster home."

"Do you, really?"

"Some of these foster homes don't care about the children."

"You're right, my father."

"It's a guaranteed check every month."

"Mrs. Willingham waits for the mailman to come with the checks."

"Vernon did the right thing leaving."

"I think he did."

"Have you heard from Valerie?"

"Not since they took her away."

"I heard what that Willingham guy did to her."

IN THE CARE OF EVIL

"When he raped Valerie?"

"Yeah."

"It's true."

"Lowlife cocksucker!"

"Who told you about it?"

"I know people, my son."

"That's good."

"Which foster home did they take her to?"

"Mr. and Mrs. Willingham wouldn't tell nobody."

"Your mother's sister might know."

"Aunt Caroline."

"Yeah."

"I'd like to see her."

"Sure hope Valerie's doing okay."

"I think she is."

"When we find out which home she's in, we need to go by and visit her."

"Sounds like a good idea."

"That Willingham guy," Vito recalled, a quick memory of their first meeting.

"What about him?"

"He's wicked."

"That's true."

"He's like a perverted demon, preying on young girls like Valerie."

"He always lied about raping Valerie."

"It's good he doesn't molest little boys."

"Why'd you say that?" Vincent asked.

"Had he molested you," Vito bragged. "I would've taken my magnum and blew his head clean off his shoulders. I probably would've pissed straight down his throat afterwards." The tough, Italian side of Vito had surfaced. During his years as a low-level mobster, he had witnessed more than his share of executions.

"Mr. Willingham's an evil man."

"He should be locked up in a cage like the animals at the zoo."

Suddenly, Vito locked his tongue and lips in place. All of his attention was directed up at the porch to the Willingham residence. J.D. had walked up the stairs and was headed for the front door. He stopped at the middle of the porch to stare over at Vito. To overpower J.D.'s ruthless, knaving attitude as a southerner, Vito conveyed a cocky, uncaring East coast attitude.

They stared at one another in the most sarcastic manner. Two men hating one another's guts! It became a battle of staring. J.D. placed his right hand on his waist, swinging his lunchbucket in short, horizontal strokes. He tried throwing Vito off by twisting his mouth sideways and gritting his teeth. He rotated his tongue around his back molars. The red and watery eyes, puckered lips, and heavy breathing, didn't intimidate Vito one bit.

"Look at that dumb nigger up on that porch," Vito thought to himself. "It's animals like him who screw it up for all men."

Meanwhile, Vito was across the street, all stretched back in his convertible, gripping the top of his steering wheel with his left hand. To magnify his low-level gangster image, he slid his hand under his suit jacket, pretending as though he was reaching for a gun. While they continued giving one another nasty stares, Vincent looked over at Gilbert and Jose. They were nodding their heads, watching J.D. and Vito stare furiously at one another. J.D. finally ended the senseless charade and started walking towards the front door. The patches of tar from his blue work uniform nearly matched his shiny

black skin. Vito nearly got physically sick from just laying eyes on J.D. There was officially bad blood between the two men.

"What does that moolie do for a living?" Vito asked Vincent, gradually sliding his hand from his expensive suit.

"He's a roofer," Vincent said.

"Oh yeah."

"That's his type of work."

"I recall him telling us that."

"When?"

"The first time we brought you all here."

"That was a long time ago."

"The dumb sonofabitch walks in hot tar all day?"

"Yes, he does."

"Putting roofs on houses and other buildings?"

"Yes, that's right."

"That's all that nigger will ever be good for."

"He didn't go past the first grade."

"Animal!" Vito whisked. "He needs to go back where he's from."

"Do you carry a gun, my father?"

"I have to, my son."

"What kind of gun do you have?"

"A .357."

"Magnum?" Vincent asked.

"Yeah."

Vito opened his suit jacket and slid the large gun from in between his waist. Vincent got a glimpse of the shiny handle.

"Are you going to shoot somebody?"

"If I have to."

"Have you ever killed somebody?"

"Came close."

Vito had been involved with a murder or two, but he would never tell his son the truth.

Jose threw the football on the side of the house and

Gilbert went to pick it up. Braun was biting on the remainder of some tobacco, which was left from one of Bessie Mae or J.D.'s cigarette butts. Both of his pockets were filled with butts. He would wait later to start eating them. Gilbert grabbed the football and went back to the front yard to watch Vincent and Vito have their *father-to-son talk*.

In front of the house, Carmen drove up behind Bessie Mae's Cadillac in her Bonneville and parked. Resentment immediately came upon the face of Vincent. Why couldn't he let go of the past? Everytime he saw Carmen, memories came crashing through like a wreckless driver. She got out of her car with a large sack from "J C Penney". Vito noticed that the expression on his son's face had become sullen.

"What's wrong, son?"

"Nothing, father."

"Come on, you can tell me."

"I hate her."

"Who?"

"Carmen."

"Who's that?"

"My used-to-be foster sister."

"What'd she do?"

"Oh, nothing."

"You don't go around hating people for nothing."

"It's nothing, father."

"She's a cute colored girl."

"I guess."

Carmen was always shopping. With the money that she made from her job, and the money that she borrowed from Bessie Mae, she was never broke. She strained her devious eyes to see what was going on across the street.

"Who's that well-dressed and handsome man driving that fancy car?" Carmen questioned herself silently. "He's probably one of those

older Italian men who's crazy about young black girls. His face sure looks real familiar."

Vito had business to take care of. Legally or otherwise, he knew how to make money. And a hefty sum of it, too!

"I've got to get going, son," Vito told Vincent.

"When are you coming back to see me?" Vincent asked, sadly watching Vito start up his fancy El Dorado.

"I don't know, son," Vito said. "Hopefully, it'll be soon."

"When do I get to see my mother?"

"When Marion gets out of the hospital, I promise you, I'll bring her by to see you. Okay?"

"Okay," Vincent smiled.

"Here's some money for you," Vito said, pulling out a fresh twenty dollar bill.

"Wow!" Vincent thumped. "Thank you! Thank you! Thank you!"

"You're welcome, my son."

"I can't believe it."

"Put the money up."

"I will."

"Don't want your greedy foster mother taking it from you."

"I'll hide it somewhere in my room."

"Good boy."

"Bye," Vincent said, bending forward to give Vito a tight, heartwarming hug.

"Love you, my son."

"Love you, too, my father."

"Be a good boy."

"I will."

Vincent waved goodbye to Vito as he drove down the street. As far as Vito telling him that he would come back to see him soon, Vincent knew that it was one big lie. His father

only gave him the twenty dollars to try and pacify him. In the end, Vito was nothing but a *sperm donor*.

He walked back to the front yard where Gilbert and Jose were tossing the football to one another.

"Now I see where you get that good hair from," Gilbert told Vincent, spinning the football around in his hands.

"Where?" Vincent asked.

"Your father."

"My father?"

"The white man who just left."

"He's not white," Vincent validated.

"What is he?"

"Italian."

"White and Italian are the same."

"No, they're not."

"Yes, they are."

"How would you know, Gilbert?"

"Check this out, Vinnie," Gilbert said. "Just like white people, your father's got the same type of hair, skin, nose, and lips."

"What type is that?"

"Straight hair, real bright skin, long and pointed noses, and the thin red lips." Gilbert couldn't have given a more accurate description.

"Guess what, Gilbert?" Vincent said. "And just like you, your daddy's got real nappy hair, real black skin, a big wide nose, and some thick liver lips."

Their discussion had become a heated racial issue. They outlandishly insulted one another's fathers.

"Are you dogging my father?" Gilbert accused Vincent.

"Yeah."

"Why?"

"You talked about my daddy first."

"So what, you've got good hair."

"Nobody said nothing about good hair."

"Who cares if you're half-Italian."

"You shouldn't care."

"You're still a niggah!"

"No, I'm not."

"You're a niggah with light skin and good hair."

"Who're you calling a niggah?"

"You, that's who."

"Your mamma's one!"

"Your daddy's one!"

"At least my daddy came by to see me," Vincent imposed, sticking his red tongue out at Gilbert.

"So what!" Gilbert shouted. "You're still living in this foster home, punk!"

"My daddy gave me some money."

"So."

"I'll bet your daddy never gave you any money."

"I should go and tell Mrs. Willingham."

"You snitch!"

"I will tell her."

"I don't care."

"She'll take the money that your daddy gave you."

"No, she won't."

"You'll never see it again."

"If you do, I'll . . ."

"You'll what?"

"Show her your secret hiding place."

"I don't care."

"She'll go behind that piece of tile and take all that money that you've been saving."

After listening to Vincent say that, Gilbert shut right up. The game of rude and obnoxious insults ended when Bessie Mae drove up in the front yard. In the backseat of her car, there were three tall stacks of The Baldwin Express. Gilbert, Jose, and Vincent went over to the car, as she wanted them to count the papers before taking off.

*   *   *

The sounds of B.B. King's song, "The Thrill Is Gone", rocked the entire front room. The only outlet for J.D. escaping the madness was blues music. He grew up listening to the blues, leaving Mississippi on the weekends to travel to Memphis to see the legendary B. B. King and Bobby "Blue" Bland perform in clubs on Beale Street. The most famous blues singer in the world could mesmerize the soul of an evil, nasty man like J.D. Willingham.

J.D. came into the front room dusting off one of his old B. B. King albums entitled, "Live In Cook County Jail". Being in Cook County Jail himself for the rape of Valerie would bring back memories. Whenever he felt that the mood was right, he'd put on some of Richard Pryor's, Redd Foxx's, or Moms Mable's comedy albums. A bit of humor did him some good from time to time. The use of strong language on the albums was definitely his forte. Carmen came into the front room. From the front door, she watched Vincent bring his stack of papers out of the backseat.

"What nationality is Vincent's father?" Carmen asked J.D.

"One of dem Italians," J.D. answered offensively.

"Isn't his father white?"

"Naw, he ain't."

"Yes, he is."

"Bleeves me, he one."

"I guess I believe you."

"I know I'm wight."

"Wasn't that him outside in that convertible?"

"Dat's him."

"Italians love black girls."

"Yep, dey lack colored gals."

Bessie Mae limped into the front room and dropped her purse to the ground.

"Vincent's daddy was outside?"

"We just saw him," Carmen said.

"What did that dago-pimp want?"

"Guess he came by to see Vincent."

"He knows the state don't allow him around his kids."

"Driving a nice car, too."

"He's probably still trying to push dope and pimp whores."

"Probably," J.D. agreed.

"Dope-dealing-dago!"

"He sho is."

A noticeable smirk came upon the mole covered face of Bessie Mae. "Guess who I saw today?"

"Who?" Carmen asked.

"Valerie."

"Where'd you see her?"

"On Rush Boulevard."

"Rush?"

"That's right," Bessie Mae grinned. "I saw that yellow tramp hanging around up there."

"What was she doing up there?" Carmen asked.

"What else?"

"Tell me."

"Whoring."

"Mrs. Willingham, that's not nice."

"Yes, I saw our used-to-be foster daughter whoring."

"She's prostituting?"

"Sure is."

"A whole lot of drugs are being dealt up there."

"She looked like she was strung out."

"Who knows?"

"She must've gotten kicked out of that other foster home."

"What other foster home?"

"I don't know."

"Hope she's okay."

"That yellow bitch is out on the streets!"

"You're mean, Mrs. Willingham."

"She got what she deserves."

"You didn't stop and talk to her?"

"Street trash?" Bessie Mae purred harshly. "No way!"

"Mrs. Willingham!" Carmen rejected. "How could you say something like that?"

"I don't care what happens to her."

"You're cruel."

"She's running wild with those other whores up on Rush."

"Can't believe you'd turn so cold."

"Well, believe it."

"You've become blackhearted."

"Some of them whores've been getting killed by Bennie Caputo's Hotel."

"The whore hotel?" Carmen asked.

"Exactly."

*   *   *

Bessie Mae had seen the movie "The Godfather" several times. She even read the novel by Mario Puzo. Her bitterness towards most of the Italians persisted. All through high school in Memphis, and after spending only one year at Memphis State University, she read much literature about organized crime and gangsters in America. She read about their infiltration into American life.

Some Italians may have felt that blacks were animals, worthless forms of beings, but Bessie Mae considered some of them to be the true animals. A lot of them didn't respect themselves or their wives and children, some who would sell their own mothers and fathers and brothers and sisters for control and power, and those who would steal money out of a dead man's pocket.

Bessie Mae once made the comment, "Bennie Caputo and those other dago-wop bastards brought that mafia junk over from Italy and Sicily and totally fucked up America. They probably got something to

*do with the whores who've gotten killed up on Rush, allowing the tricks
to mistreat the women right inside the very rooms that they rent inside
his hotel."* The names Charlie "Lucky" Luciano and Alphonse
"Scarface" Capone disgusted Bessie Mae everytime she heard them
mentioned.

*   *   *

As they counted through their papers, Gilbert, Jose, and
Vincent rested on the stairs. They listened to the harsh remarks that Bessie Mae made about Valerie and the Italian
people. Vincent wasn't too happy. Bessie Mae gave him every
reason to be upset, turning him red all over the face. She was
badmouthing his sister and there wasn't anything that he
could do or say about it.

After they counted through every single paper, they left
the house and walked down Milwaukee. When they came to
Rush, where things were busy as usual, Jose glanced over at
Vanzetti's. He couldn't resist going over there. Many
customers were trafficking in and out of the popular liquor
store. Quarters came from every direction the second he made
it over there. It was another Friday and payday for most
Chicagoans.

Business in front of the bank was very slow. Gilbert had a
business resourceful mind. He knew there were other places
that they could sell The Baldwin Express. Gilbert and Vincent
traveled one block east of Rush. The street was somewhat
noisy, with lots of traffic coming through. The houses were
run down badly, and it was evident that drugs and prostitution flourished rampantly. The impoverished conditions were
more evident than ever.

Chapter 27

VULTURES

NARCOTICS KINGPINS WERE making major bucks off the hookers, queenies, dopeheads, and even some upper-class people from the elite suburbs. Heroin, also known as "junk" among the older mobsters, came in by the pounds. It was sold to junkies everywhere.

Gilbert traveled south up the block. Vincent contemplated on going up to a house that was halfway up the block. A canary yellow Cadillac Fleetwood with donut whitewalls was parked out front. He walked towards the three-story house that was made of red brick. A car drove off Rush and sped up the street. The car was a rusty orange Malibu and it was in pursuit of Vincent. The horn was sounded to get his attention.

"Hey, can I get four of those papers?" the man asked, stopping the car and holding up four shiny quarters.

"You want four, sir?" Vincent happily asked, strolling quickly over to the car.

"Yeah, four of them."

"That'll be a dollar," Vincent said, pulling out four papers from the large stack, and then exchanging them for the money.

"Here you go, young brother."

"Thank you, sir."

"You're welcome."

From the same house that Vincent had intended to walk up to, there were women peeking from behind some curtains.

Because the curtains covered their bodies, only their heads were visible. Vincent sold four papers and had forty-six to go.

"Excuse me, little boy," said a dark complexioned woman, who happened to be wearing a long curly wig, a pair of tight blue hotpants, and a white halter top that drooped. Food stains covered most of the halter top.

"What?" Vincent said, carefully watching the suspicious looking woman.

"Are you selling The Baldwin Express?"

"Yes."

"How much are they?"

"A quarter."

"Do you have change?"

"Yes."

"How much change do you have?" the woman asked, staring down at Vincent's pocket.

"A dollar."

"I'd like to buy one of the papers."

"Okay."

"Would you like to come inside?" she asked, a mischevious smirk on her face.

"Come inside?"

"Yeah, I wanna buy one of the papers."

"Okay."

Vincent went inside the house. He was led into the front part of this smelly residence, where much trash was scattered all over the floor. Vincent found it extremely foul to see dog and cat waste, jugs half-filled with spoiled milk, shredded paper, empty beer cans and whiskey bottles, empty jelly jars full of cockroaches, and old musty and molded clothing, all lying around the nasty house. The odor from the filth annoyed him. The smell of the animal waste dominated the air. In a room that was right over from the front section, there was only one piece of furniture. A lime green sofa sat against the wall.

Vincent waited for the return of the woman who wanted to buy one of the papers. Three more women were coming downstairs. They wore the same type of *whorish* attire as the first woman. They slid their hands along the dark railing. They tapped their toes against the bars underneath. The woman in the very front tried enticing Vincent. Her black hotpants were shorter than normal. Strands of coarse pubic hairs and her flabby buttock cheeks were visible. The front part of her blue halter top showed a small set of breast prints, letting anyone know that she wasn't wearing a bra.

The other two women who were standing a few stairs behind her, were wearing similar attire. All three came to the bottom of the stairs. They surrounded Vincent, running their rough hands through his large curly locks. Their hands eased down to his mid-section and down by his legs and buttocks. They went under his shirt and started rubbing on his chest and stomach, trying to create some arousing foreplay.

"Stop!" Vincent shouted, scooting back towards the front door.

"What's wrong, sugah?" the woman wearing the black hotpants asked.

"Get your hands off my butt and my private!"

"What's wrong, baby?"

"Nothing's wrong."

"Ain't you never had none?"

"What?"

"Some coochie."

"I don't want no coochie!"

"Don't know what you're missing."

"Where's the lady who was supposed to buy the papers from me?"

The woman in the green hotpants went to the middle of the stairs. She stood at the edge of the bannisters and shouted, "Ramona!"

"What do you want?" Ramona answered from upstairs, sounding like she was rambling through some drawers.

"This light skinned boy is waiting for you."

"I'll be right down."

Ramona came downstairs with a dollar folded up in her hand. Vincent was escorted into the other half of the house. She wanted to negotiate the sale of the papers. They whispered in one another's ears. Were they plotting? There were more beer cans and whiskey bottles, soiled tampons, and empty packets that had drugs inside, all lying around on the floor. These people were living very foul! Most people who lived around Rush were simply bad news. Vincent began feeling unsafe. He tightly held on to his stack of papers. His paranoid eyes circled the room.

"Now, listen to this," said Ramona, a street-slick woman. "I'll give you this dollar when you give me four papers and those four quarters."

"You're trying to cheat me!" Vincent rebelled. "I'm not stupid, lady."

"I'm not trying to cheat you."

"Yes, you are."

"No, I'm not."

"I know how to count."

"You're supposed to give me the dollar and four papers, and I'm supposed to give you this dollar."

"Let me see the dollar," Vincent requested, staring into the dark, deceitful face of Ramona.

"Let me see the quarters."

"I need to see the dollar first."

"Not until you show me the quarters."

Vincent took a moment to think. He reached down into his pocket and pulled out all four quarters. His fist was balled up tightly. Ramona gripped the dollar in her left hand.

"Give me the dollar," Vincent said.

"Give me the papers and the quarters," Ramona said.

They tried to figure out one another's moves. When Vincent opened his fist to show her the quarters, Ramona

DEWEY REYNOLDS

snatched all four quarters from the palm of his right hand. With the other three women behind her, she sprinted out of the room. Vincent ran right behind them. He stopped at the bottom of the stairs that led to the upper part of the house and shouted, "Give me back my dollar!"

He walked halfway up the stairs and looked around the bannister. Where in the name of God did they run to? He wasn't familiar with the house. They couldn't hear him plead for the return of his money. The thought of J.D. beating him for letting someone steal his money crossed his mind. For those four impoverished women, a dollar had a lot of value. Vincent left the house and ran up the street. Tears trickled down his face. Gilbert happened to see him crying.

"What's wrong, Vinnie?" Gilbert asked, wanting to know why Vincent was acting hysterical.

"They took my . . . ," Vincent cried hesitantly, slinging tears off his face.

"They? Who's They?"

"Those women in that house."

"Which house?"

"The brick house over there."

"How did they take it?" Gilbert asked.

"I showed it to them."

"Remember what Mrs. Willingham told us?"

"What?"

"Don't ever pull your money out and show it to nobody."

"I forgot."

"We're going to get your money back," Gilbert bluffed, charging the house full speed.

They proceeded over to the house and Gilbert bammed on the door with a closed fist. No one answered after several hard knocks. He pounded and pounded on the door with greater impact.

"I'm coming! I'm coming!" replied the rough voice of

some woman. She opened the door and was surprised to see Gilbert and Vincent standing there.

"Where's my brother's money?" Gilbert barked, standing up on her like he would beat her into submission.

"What money?" asked the frivolous woman.

"The money you stole from my brother."

"Ain't nobody took your brother's money."

"You're lying!"

"Who's lying?"

"You're lying and you know it."

"Your brother never came to this house."

"Why's he crying like that?"

"I don't know and really don't care."

"We're not leaving until we get his money back."

"I'm not giving you nothing."

"I'll call my foster mother."

"Call 'er."

"She'll come over here with her gun."

"So."

"She'll blow your head off!"

"She's not the only one who's got a gun."

"Just give us the money back."

"Nobody's got his money, niggah."

"We need to finish selling our papers."

"Nobody has nothing of his."

She wasn't expecting a youngster like Gilbert to be so militant. Also, he had violent and irrational tendencies. While the arguing continued, neighbors along the block came out on their porches. They witnessed the altercation over a stolen dollar. Vincent never said a word to defend himself. Standing to the side, he watched Gilbert and the woman shout and curse at one another. They pointed and spit and growled in one another's face. To end this turbulent confrontation, a tall man, appearing to be in his late thirties, stepped onto the porch with a silverish .357 magnum clutched in his right

hand. The gun hung down by his side. Everyone became silent! Gilbert and Vincent saw the gun and moved towards the stairs.

"What the hell's going on?" the man asked, dressed sharply in a sharp blue suit, a Panama straw on top of his head and diamonds on every finger.

"My foster brother said somebody in this house took his money," Gilbert explained, keeping his eyes directed at the large gun.

"How much did they take?"

"He said they took a dollar."

Vincent stepped around Gilbert to gain the attention of the flamboyant man. He wanted to speak with Vincent.

"Would you recognize who took your money?" he asked Vincent.

"Yes, sir."

"Are you sure, young brother?"

"Yes, I'm sure."

Momentarily, he went inside the house and had the other three women come out. Of the three, Ramona stood in the very back. She tried hiding her black face, but she was told to come to the forefront.

"Which of these four women took your money?" the man wanted to know.

"It was her," Vincent pointed.

"Ramona?"

"Yes, sir," Vincent said. "It was her right there."

Rage boiled inside of Ramona. She gave Vincent an evil stare.

"You're lying!" Ramona yelled.

"No, I'm not."

"You little yellow pussy!"

"Hey, hey, watch your mouth, girl," he ordered. "Don't call this youngblood no names like that."

"I'm not lying," Vincent defended himself.

"I never took any of your money."

"Yes, you did."

"No, I didn't."

The man stepped in front of Ramona and dug into his pocket for a big roll of money. "Was it only a dollar?"

"Yes, sir."

"Here you go, young brother."

"Thank you, sir."

"You're welcome, youngblood," he recriprocated. "Now, go finish selling the rest of your papers."

"Okay."

The altercation was over. Gilbert and Vincent were glad that they didn't get hurt. It wouldn't have been a pretty sight if the man had come out of the house shooting. While he held the door open, the four women made their entrance. Before she went all the way inside, Gilbert and Ramona made twisted faces at one another. She threw the finger up and slammed the door. His once elevated temper had cooled off.

"Stay out of people's houses," Gilbert warned Vincent.

"You're right."

"Especially around Rush."

"That's it for me."

"Those ladies stand in front of Bennie's Hotel."

"That's right around the corner," Vincent recalled.

"I know."

"They're prostitutes?"

"All of them were prostitutes," Gilbert vindicated.

"Who was the man with the gun?"

"Probably their pimp."

"How could you tell?"

"They did everything he told them."

"Sure did."

"That's what pimps do."

"What?"

"Keep control over their whores."

"Remember the lady who tried to sell you some?"

"I remember."

"Bennie Caputo cursed her out real bad."

"Wanted to call the cops and have her taken to jail."

"I'm glad we didn't have to call Mrs. Willingham."

"I'm glad, too," Gilbert added. "She would've come up here with her gun."

"You know how crazy she gets when it comes to money."

"Let's try and finish selling our papers."

"I'm ready."

By now, Vincent had learned a good lesson. Don't ever go into a strange house anywhere near Rush Boulevard.

Chapter 28

STICKY FINGERS

During MONDAY AFTERNOONS, Bessie Mae spent a great deal of time in the basement doing many piles of laundry. She sorted through piles of badly soiled socks and underwear, not to mention the tarred-up blue shirts and pants that belonged to J.D. She also had to sort through the piles of sheets, pillowcases, and draperies. Pinching the waistband of a pair of underwear, which had dark yellow urine stains, quickly put a frown on her face.

Vincent was in the next room. He watched Bessie Mae sort through the piles of musty and dirt-embedded clothes. Paranoia made him observe her perform this nearly all day task. Because he had wet the bed the night before, then stuffed the sheets under a large pile of bed linen, he had reason to be afraid. Now what happened to throwing the sheets away or hiding them under his mattress? Eventually, the missing supply would become noticeable. His bed would become elevated to a height that would show the hidden linen underneath.

Bessie Mae had most of the socks, underwear, shirts, and pants in the washing machine. Afterwards, she sorted through the pile of bed linen. Vincent timidly stood at the edge of the dresser once occupied by Vernon. He wanted to see if Bessie Mae would detect any differences in any of the sheets. She separated the white sheets from the colored ones. The white sheets were folded over her left arm. Since there were several occupants in the home, she never payed much attention to the small saliva and urine stains on some of the sheets.

Two piles were placed at the front of the washing machine. The remainder had to be sorted through. Bessie Mae still never noticed any differences in any of the sheets. She unexpectedly came across a white sheet that had a very large yellow stain on it. It covered more than seventy percent of the sheet. Bessie Mae held it under the bright light in the middle of the laundry room. After taking a closer observation, she realized that only one person in the entire household could've left a stain that large. Vincent stood in the next room, watching Bessie Mae thoroughly overlooking the sheet. He rushed over to his bed to try and avoid any humiliation. Bessie Mae limped to the doorway with the sheet hanging over her left arm.

"Did you try and hide this pissy sheet?" Bessie Mae asked Vincent, stretching her left arm forward to confront him.

"No, mam," Vincent denied, rubbing his sweaty fingers inside his sweaty palms, eyes filled with resentment.

"Where did this sheet come from?"

"I don't know."

"How did it get in with the rest of the sheets?"

"I don't know, Mrs. Willingham."

"Why are you lying, boy?"

"I'm not lying, Mrs. Willingham."

"When are you going to stop pissing in the bed?"

"I don't know."

"You're pitiful, boy!"

"I use newspaper and plastic," Vincent said. "It usually stops the pee from getting on the sheets."

"Newspaper and plastic, huh?"

"Yes, mam."

"What good does that do?"

"It works, sometimes."

"Sometimes, huh?"

"Yes, mam."

"Don't you know that that crap isn't gonna stop the piss from getting on the sheets?"

"Yes, mam."

"Whaddaya doing using my newspapers, anyway?"

"I don't know."

"I use that paper to wrap my china and crystal in."

"I know."

"You're thirteen years old and still pissing in the bed."

"I can't help it, Mrs. Willingham."

"You can help it, alright."

"Really, I can't."

"Why can't you?"

"I don't know."

"What's so hard about getting up in the middle of the night?"

"Nothing's hard about it."

"Then, what's the problem?"

"Nobody will wake me up."

"You need to wake yourself up."

"I try, but . . ."

"But what?" Bessie Mae intruded. "You're the only foster child that I've ever kept who pisses in the bed."

"I'm sorry, Mrs. Willingham."

"I'm gonna stop you from drinking water."

"Water?"

"Yes."

"When?"

"After twelve o'clock."

Bessie Mae limped back into the laundry room to finish the rest of the laundry. Knowing that she wasn't going to take any disciplinary action, Vincent took a deep breath of relief. The washing machine stopped and she was ready for another load. Bessie Mae filled the washing machine with a load of sheets and pillowcases. She sprinkled a large cup of Cheer on top and started up the machine.

Since J.D.'s work clothing were done separately, she limped to the corner of the dryer to make other piles. The

toil and agony of the laundry ludicrousness had her sweating and bending sideways. She was definitely fatigued. She
tried scraping off some of the small patches of tar from J.D.'s
pants and shirts. Bessie Mae attended to the laundry while
Granny Dear was in the kitchen stirring up a large pot of
pinto beans. The beans became tender and she placed the
top back on the pot.

The fire was turned down low. She rolled over to the
refrigerator to search for some milk. Eggs, sugar, and butter
were already sitting on the table for a pan of fresh cornbread.
Her head was planted between the last two shelves. Bowls
and pans of her leftovers were moved aside, searching for a
gallon or a half-gallon of milk. No milk was found. Granny
Dear rolled to the top of the basement stairs. She opened
the door slightly and bent forward in her wheelchair.

"Bessa Mae!" Granny Dear called. "Hey dere, Bessa Mae!"

"What is it, Granny Dear?" Bessie Mae answered, her
voice ringing with tiresome.

"I'm gone need some milk ta make da conebread."

"There's none in the refrigerator?"

"I hunt fo some, but ain't none in dere."

"Are the beans almost ready?"

"Dey gittin tenda."

"Alright," Bessie Mae said. "I'll send somebody to go to
the store for some milk."

Bessie Mae limped into the next room. She reached
down into her bra for a ten dollar bill.

"Vincent," Bessie Mae said, unfolding the bill.

"Do you want me, Mrs. Willingham?" Vincent asked, hoping that she forgot about him trying to hide the sheet.

"Go to the store and get a gallon of milk."

"Yes, mam."

"And bring me all of my change back."

"Yes, mam."

Vincent went out on the porch. Gilbert and Jose were

sitting in the shade watching the cars travel up and down Milwaukee Parkway.

"Where are you going?" Gilbert asked.

"Mrs. Willingham wants me to go to the store."

"And get what?"

"Some milk."

"A gallon?" Gilbert guessed.

"Yes."

"You're gonna need some help carrying it?"

"I probably will."

"Let's go."

As Gilbert, Jose, and Vincent approached Rush, they saw much street-oriented activity going on. People were gambling on the street corners, tilting up beer cans and whiskey bottles, fighting over God knows what, and doing all types of drugs. Whether they were smoking marijuana, shooting heroin into their veins, snorting cocaine up their noses, or popping pills like barbituates, it was evident that drugs had been distributed heavily around Rush Boulevard. The plan that Bennie Caputo and the other mobsters had conspired worked out perfectly, simply because most of their loyal customers were blacks. The Summer and Fall months always attracted more addicts.

Gilbert, Jose, and Vincent crossed over Rush on their way to the grocery store. As soon as they came to the next corner, they heard the sounds of a basketball pounding on the pavement. They looked back and there were four teenage boys walking behind them. It appeared that they had just left Rush. Among the four, two of them had braided hair, shirts with the arms cut off, and scars all over their chest.

The other two had blasting afros, brand new jogging suits, and lots of jewelry around their necks and on their hands. All four appeared as though they were born and raised somewhere near Rush Boulevard. Their *thuggish* image showed across their faces and in their mannerisms. The expressions

on their faces were that of someone looking for trouble. Vincent walked several feet in front of Gilbert and Jose. There was a shiny looking object in the grassy strip to the right. Vincent approached the unknown object.

"I found a quarter!" Vincent shouted, throwing his arm to the sky to let the sun shine down on the quarter.

"You did find a quarter," Gilbert said, also looking up at the sky.

"I'm gonna buy me some candy when we get to the store."

"Won't you buy me some candy, too?"

"If I have enough left, I probably will."

Vincent tossed the quarter up in the air as they walked up the street. The intense sounds of the basketball pounding on the concrete indicated that the four *rogues* were getting closer.

"That's my quarter!" cried a voice from behind.

"Who said that?" Vincent asked, turning around to stare at the four street thugs.

"I said it, punk!" answered the same thug bouncing the basketball, wearing lines of braids all over his head.

"How could this be your quarter?"

"I dropped it when I came pass here earlier."

"You're lying!" Vincent charged.

"Are you gonna give me the quarter or what?" the ruthless thug asked.

"You're not gonna get this quarter," Vincent said.

"Are me and my boys gonna have to take it?"

"You're not taking anything."

From under his pants, the thug quickly pulled out a switchblade and rushed up to Vincent, holding it steadily under his throat. The basketball dropped to the ground. Gilbert and Jose jumped back, fearful that he might stab them or poke Vincent right through the throat. With no resistance, Vincent handed over the quarter. The thug slowly

pulled the switchblade away. Vincent took the deepest swallow of his life.

"You talk a lot of junk for a little punk," the thug said, boastfully tossing the quarter right in Vincent's face.

"I'm sorry, man," Vincent pleaded, shaking all over his body.

"I should slice your throat," he said. "I hate half-breed sissies like you."

"I don't want no trouble, man."

"I know you don't."

"Don't cut me, man."

"Start walking and don't look back."

Gilbert, Jose, and Vincent cautiously walked up the street. The four thugs kept their eyes on them until they were more than a block away.

"I'm glad that he didn't cut you, Vincent," Gilbert said, knowing that it was smart walking away from the confrontation.

"I should've picked up a brick," Vincent said.

"For what?"

"And busted him across his head."

"No, you shouldnt've."

"Why not?"

"He would've cut you up in a thousand pieces."

"I wasn't scared of that niggah."

"Plus, it was four of them and only three of us."

"Is that why you and Jose moved back?"

"At first, I thought he was going to cut all three of us."

Gilbert, Jose, and Vincent made it safely to one of the larger neighborhood grocery stores. After walking into the store, they began their search for the gallon of milk. Gilbert traveled down the aisle that had mostly canned goods. Jose and Vincent searched along the aisle that kept the produce and meats. At the end of the aisle, there was a special section which had cakes, cookies, pies, and an assortment of candy. They traveled to the end of the aisle and stood in front of the

candy. Candy bars, now and laters, lollipops, and ice cream gum, were a treat to their eyes.

The ice cream gum came in flavors like vanilla, chocolate, strawberry, raspberry, and cherry. Their savory eyes were glued to the packages of gum. They fantasized about their tastebuds getting a sample. It was too irresistable to keep a secret, so Jose and Vincent left that aisle to search for Gilbert.

Gilbert happened to be in the third aisle. He strolled along the shelves that kept the soaps, detergents, and cleaning products. Jose and Vincent walked into the third aisle. Gilbert was looking at a large box of Cheer washing detergent.

"You're not gonna find any milk in this aisle," Vincent told Gilbert.

"I know, I'm just hanging out over here."

"We've got something to show you."

"What is it?" Gilbert asked.

"Believe me, you'll like it."

"Tell me, what is it?"

"Come with me and Jose."

Jose and Vincent led Gilbert back over by the aisle where the candy was. They picked up packs of the ice cream gum. Gilbert had a pack of strawberry, Jose had a pack of chocolate, and Vincent reached for a pack of raspberry. They held the gum up to their noses and sniffed.

"Ummm!" Gilbert smiled, sliding his nose across the gum wrapper. "This gum smells just like strawberry ice cream."

"Mine's smell like real raspberry ice cream," Vincent incremented, taking repeated sniffs.

"It's not yours yet," Gilbert reminded Vincent.

"I know how we can buy some."

"How?" Gilbert questioned.

"With the money that Mrs. Willingham gave me."

"She gave you the money to buy the milk with."

"Yes, she did."

"No way!" Gilbert objected.

"Why not, Gilbert? She won't find out."

"Mrs. Willingham knows how to count money," Gilbert said. "When she looks at that receipt, she'll know how much change she should have coming back. She's not dumb like Mr. Willingham."

"She won't find out."

"Yes, she will."

"Does she really look at those receipts?"

"Hell yeah!"

"Let's do it anyway."

"And get a vicious beating from Mr. Willingham?"

"You're right."

They still wanted the ice cream gum. The desire to taste the gum that was relatively new on the market was overwhelming.

"I know what we could do," Jose suggested, staring right into Gilbert's face.

"What?" asked Gilbert.

"When nobody's looking, we can stick a pack in our pockets."

"You're saying that we should steal the gum?"

"Yes."

"What if we get caught?" Gilbert feared, nodding his head at Jose.

"We won't get caught," Jose assured Gilbert.

"What if we do?"

"If we hurry, we won't get caught."

"I don't know, Jose."

"What're you scared of?"

"Getting beat all across Chicago with Mr. Willingham's extension cord."

"Come on, quit being scared."

Gilbert and Vincent took a moment to think about the

sinnister plan of Jose. They glanced up at the ceiling. Cameras could have been everywhere. Gilbert and Vincent scanned every aisle. The grocery store was known to have had at least one security guard on duty. But there were no guards in sight. Jose and Vincent watched closely while Gilbert leaned against the shelves that had the gun. He swiftly grabbed a pack of strawberry gum and stuffed it down his pocket.

Customers pushed their carts pass the aisle they stood in. They didn't want to look suspicious, so they pretended to search for items to buy. When there wasn't any customers in sight, Jose grabbed a pack of chocolate gum and stuffed it down his tight pants pocket. Vincent was left to execute his plan. Coming from opposite ends, more customers walked past the aisle, pushing their carts, holding their babies, and searching for different items.

An elderly woman pushed her cart over to the candy section. Using her thick bi-focals, she strained her eyes to search for the items. She grabbed a handful of candy bars and went down the opposite aisle. In a matter of seconds, Vincent grabbed a pack of raspberry gum and quickly slid it down his pocket. They knew time had passed considerably and it was time to find the milk. In the last aisle at the opposite end of the store, there was the dairy section.

They came to the checkout counter and there were two customers standing in line. The line moved up and Vincent placed the milk on the counter. He bravely waited for the cashier to ring up his item. The milk moved up the conveyor belt. The cashier picked up the gallon and looked for a price. A security guard suddenly appeared and stopped on the other side of the checkout line. The juvenile hearts of Gilbert, Jose, and Vincent pumped with fear. The security guard took a quick glance at them and moved on. This was truly a sense of relief. The cashier picked up the gallon and looked for a price.

"Do you know the price of this milk?" the cashier asked Vincent.

"No, mam," Vincent replied, thinking that the price was stamped in an unsightly place.

"Did you see a price in the section where you got it?"

"No, I didn't."

The cashier decided to get on the intercom. She spoke into a microphone that was to the right of the register. "I need a price check on a gallon of homogonized milk."

Gilbert, Jose, and Vincent became paranoid. The square shape of the gum packages bulged from their pockets. Moments later, one of the store managers came up front. He stepped over by the register to give her the price of the milk. If only they could keep their composure, no one would notice anything unusual. Their hearts pounded hard. He walked away without noticing anything. Their hearts were beating normal again. The cashier tapped on the keys to her register and told Vincent, "That'll be one dollar and twenty cents."

Vincent dug into the pocket that was opposite of the one that had the ice cream gum inside. There was no money inside. Ironically, the money was under the pack of gum. To avoid pulling the gum out of his pocket, he twisted his fingers around the package until the ten dollar bill slid out. The cashier handed him his change and Gilbert quickly grabbed the sack off the counter.

They rushed out of the store with the noticeable gum package prints bulging from their pockets. Their plan worked out perfectly. Once they made it out in the parking lot, they started walking towards Rush. They were more frightened than ever, because this was their first shoplifting experience. It felt good not getting caught. Smiles were on all of their faces. Some of the tension from inside the store was gone. Gilbert reached into his pocket and pulled out the strawberry gum. Jose placed the sack down in the grass. Along

with Vincent, he was ready to open his pack of chocolate gum.

"This calls for a celebration," Gilbert said, shoving a piece of strawberry gum into his mouth.

"Gosh!" Vincent concurred. "It tastes like I'm eating raspberry ice cream. Boy, this gum is real good."

"I didn't know that there was such a thing as ice cream gum."

"Me neither."

"Now that we know, I'm coming here to get some more," Jose told Gilbert and Vincent. To them, the gum was truly delicious.

All three rotated their jaws, grinded their teeth, and rolled the gum around in their mouths. They made smacking noises, like they were malnourished youngsters. Their tastebuds were overly satisfied. One stick of the gum wasn't enough. They stuffed their mouths with three, four, and even five sticks. There were only a total of eight sticks in the packs. When Vincent opened his mouth, it looked like he was chewing a ball of red rubber.

"We better hurry up and get home," Vincent reminded Gilbert and Jose.

"Why're you in a hurry?" Gilbert asked.

"Granny Dear's waiting on the milk."

"Oh, that's right."

"We better hurry up before Mrs. Willingham finds an excuse to get Mr. Willingham to beat us."

"You're right, Vincent."

While crossing Rush, they noticed someone on the ground screaming. Several guys were beating up on one guy. He tried protecting himself, but a host of feet and fists pounded onto his entire body. A deep cut from behind his ear was visible. Blood gushed from the side of his head, forming a small puddle on the sidewalk.

"Where's my money, niggah!" said one of the men who pounded his foot on top of the helpless man's head.

"I'll get it, Tony! I'll get it, man!" the man yelled mercifully, nearly in the process of getting beat into a coma.

"Why don't you have my money, fool?"

"I'll get it to you, Tony!"

"I'll kill'ya, you know that?"

"Yeah, Tony, I know that!"

Gilbert, Jose, and Vincent watched in awe. They witnessed *black-on-black crime* first hand.

"What did he do?" Gilbert inquired, feeling great sympathy for the man who was being used as a punching bag.

"He must've done something bad," Vincent assumed, watching the spectators stand around with beer cans, wine and whiskey bottles, and marijuana joints in their hands.

"I think he owes somebody money," Jose said.

"You know black people'll kill over their money," Gilbert said.

"They're car, too."

They were absolutely right, because money was too hard to come by for most black people, and when somebody stole from them or didn't want to pay them, they nearly imposed a death sentence on that person.

"They're kicking his ass real bad."

"He's bleeding real bad, too," Jose said.

"I hope he don't die."

"He'll need to go to the hospital after that beating."

"They're stomping him into the concrete," Gilbert said, stepping a little closer to get a better view.

"Man, they're gonna kill him!"

"That's how we should do Mr. Willingham."

"Yes, we should."

"Stomp him for all those beatings that he's given us."

Gilbert, Jose, and Vincent actually pictured the man on the ground as being J.D. Willingham.

"Kick him and stomp him and punch him until he dies."

They witnessed enough of one man getting brutalized

by a group of hard street thugs. They walked across Rush and made it home. Granny Dear got the milk and Bessie Mae was given her change. Vincent joined Gilbert and Jose out on the porch. They chewed the flavor out of the rest of their ice cream gum.

Chapter 29

EASTER

LETTERS CONTINUED TO come to the Willingham residence, addressed directly to Bessie Mae. An inter-office communication letter from Annette Spizziri, of The Department of Children and Family Services, Cook County Division, read as follows:

Subject: Vincent Carvelli/ Load #754

From: Annette Spizziri

To: Bessie Mae Willingham

We removed Vincent from the County-State payroll for March. For the month of March, his room and board of $96.50 was paid from his accumulated Social Security funds. In April, we again paid his room and board partially from County-State funds and partially from Social Security funds. ($36. 29 Social Security—$72. 30 County-State.)

Bessie Mae often read the letter and filed them along with the others. She had yet to deal with the letters concerning her continued payments for the foster children that she presently kept. The Department of Children and Family Services weren't asking much when they sent the letters about the relicensing of her foster home.

Sincerely,

Annette Spizziri

Another year came around at the foster and handicapped
care home of Bessie Mae and J.D. Willingham. Not only was it
another year, but it was another Easter Sunday. It was one that
everyone would remember. Gilbert, Jose, and Vincent had
been ready for quite some time. They walked into the front
room, all dressed up in their leisure suits and patent leather
shoes. Bessie Mae was in the kitchen putting the finishing
touches on the Easter dinner. She was listening to the radio
ministry of Reverend Ike. His *"Blessing Plans"* and *"Secrets for
Health, Happiness, and Prosperity,"* always captivated Bessie Mae's
attention. All of her life, she had been looking for ways to get
rich quick. Whenever Reverend Ike sent her literature in
the mail, she'd mail him back money. The flamboyant minister had a church right there in Chicago.

J.D. walked into the kitchen and took a seat at the kitchen
table. He fired up a cigarette and tuned in closely to the
radio. Bessie Mae stood over the stove cutting off big chunks
of Kraft cheese to go into the pan of chicken casserole. Granny
Dear was over at the table preparing a pan of rice pudding.

"Who dat on da wadio, Bessa Mae?" J.D. asked Bessie
Mae, turning around to look at the portable radio on the
countertop.

"It's Reverend Ike, J.D.," Bessie Mae said, placing the
casserole in the oven.

"Revving who?"

"Reverend Ike."

"You still lissin to dat mane?" J.D. asked.

"Yes, I'm still listening to him," Bessie Mae reciprocated
sarcastically, wiping sweat from her face.

"Dat mane ain't nuttin but a crook."

"How's that?"

"Taking colored folks money."

J.D. reached over to turn up the volume on the radio. He
believed that Reverend Ike was in the wake of a ministry

scandal. But what would a man of his limited intelligence know about any scandal?

"He's a good man," Bessie Mae said.

"Good mane, huh?"

"Yes, that's right."

"Den why's he wich and colored folks po?"

"What colored folks?"

"Da ones sennin him da money."

"Everybody sending him money aren't poor."

"Ya sho, Bessa Mae?"

"Of course, I'm sure."

"White folks ain't sennin him no money."

"White people do send him money."

"Dey do?"

"Yes, they do."

"Dat niggah ain't doing nuttin but pimping folks."

"People are only supporting his ministry."

"Alwight, if ya say so."

J.D. wasn't optimistic when it came to Reverend Ike's ministry. After all, Reverend Ike had a fleet of Rolls Royces. Bessie Mae didn't have a fleet of Cadillacs. He dressed in expensive suits, wore expensive jewelry, and lived in a big fancy home. Bessie Mae didn't wear expensive dresses, wore fairly nice jewelry, but certainly didn't live in a very nice home. To J.D., he was nothing but a professional shyster.

Bessie Mae left the kitchen to come into the front room. She intended on inspecting her three foster sons before they took off to church. Gilbert stood over by the television. He wore a brown leisure suit, a white shirt, and a matching brown tie with white stripes. Jose stood in the doorway. His navy blue leisure suit fitted him perfectly. The light blue shirt and matching blue tie with white stripes complimented the suit. Vincent was proud to be wearing the black leisure suit that came with a pure white shirt and a solid black tie. Their black patent leather shoes matched their suits perfectly.

This was the first time that they had gotten any new clothes in a few years.

Bessie Mae sent them out the door. They stepped onto the porch, staring up and down Milwaukee Parkway, trying to see if the neighbors were leaving for church. Hoping that someone would notice them, they walked out to the sidewalk and stood around. Halfway up the street, four girls came out on their porch. They wore pretty pastel-designed dresses and matching bows on top of their heads. Gilbert, Jose, and Vincent became the center of their attention. Bessie Mae nor J.D. never let them travel up to that part of the block. They were total strangers to these girls. As they stepped off the porch, they pointed down at Gilbert, Jose, and Vincent. They made comments that couldn't be heard down the street.

"Who are they talking about?" Gilbert asked, pointing to himself.

"They're talking about me," Vincent replied, also pointing to himself.

"You know they want me."

"That's what you think."

"I know they think I'm cute."

"Whoever told you that?"

"Nobody."

"They lied."

"I already know it."

All four girls returned inside their home. Gilbert and Vincent felt like complete fools. While they made their journey to the church, Gilbert jumped in front of Jose and Vincent.

They interlocked arms and began shouting, "I am blind and I cannot see! If I knock you down, don't you blame it on me!"

They shut their eyes tightly and scuffed their brand new shoes across the hard concrete. Under their arms, they perspired heavily. When a person's underarms began having that musty odor, they were definitely approaching that age. After becoming exhausted, they decided to stop the horseplay. Several blocks past Rush, Saint Mark's Missionary Baptist Church sat on the corner. Rows of cars were lined up on both sides of the street. Several men, women, and children were going inside the church. They wore fancy suits and dresses. They were truly dressed for Easter Sunday.

Gilbert, Jose, and Vincent arrived inside the church. They went straight to the men's dressing room in the basement. Off the rack against the wall, they grabbed their blue and white robes and slipped them on. The vibrant sounds of an organ played. The crooning of gospel hymns followed. They knew that the junior choir would be marching soon. One of the organist, Mother Marcia Davenport, who was also an ordained minister, played a gospel tune for the junior choir to march to.

Gilbert, Jose, and Vincent, and the other young choir members, marched right behind the director of both choirs, Mother Lynette Carter. They sang, clapped, and slid their feet across the white carpet. She led them to their designated choir section. People in the congregation joined in as the organ echoed all through the church. Mother Davenport led the adult choir down the consecrated aisle and into their choir section. The church became silent. Easter Sunday at Saint Mark's brought members to church who hadn't been there in a long time. The sounds of the large motor fans cluttered near the ceiling. The babies and children were restless. Wax dripped down the iron cast holders. More cars pulled up on the side of the church.

The pastor of Saint Mark's, Bishop John Burgess, came from the back of the church. Bishop Burgess was a tall and very bright complexioned man, with a thick mustache and

wavy hair that rippled with a generous amount of hair grease. He wore a black and white minister's robe that had a large cross embroided near the chest. His heavy wingtip shoes sent echoes through the cracks of the wooden floor. Mostly everyone knew when Bishop Burgess was walking from the back.

Three altar boys carried crosses from the back altar and up to the altar in and around the pulpit. The altar boy carrying the tallest cross knelt at the altar before a large statue of Jesus. In a loud voice, he said, "We come now to carry the cross for all of Christianity."

Hitting the bottom of the cross on the pulpit floor three times, he said, "In the name of the father, the son, and the holy ghost."

The altar boys holding the shorter crosses on the outside of the pulpit, said, "He gave his life that we could have life everlasting."

The altar boy to his right, holding a cross of the same height, said, "That whosoever believeth in him shall not perish, but have everlasting life."

Two more elders of Saint Mark's, Mothers Earnestine Simpson and Carla Wagner, took their seats in the pulpit, along with Bishop Burgess. One of the church's popular deacons, Brother Zeno Bluett, brought the offering table and baskets to the front of the pulpit. A long line of church members and visitors came down the consecrated aisle. They dropped coins and bills into the basket. With the money that Bessie Mae gave them the day before, Gilbert, Jose, and Vincent gave their offering of one dollar a piece.

After the blessed offering, Mother Simpson came to the podium to announce that the junior choir was going to sing a selection. Mother Carter came around the pulpit and stood before the choir. Gilbert left the back row and stood at the edge of the pulpit. He was never shy, facing the people in the congregation with pride. Mother Carter gradually lifted

both arms. He was going to be the lead singer of the selection entitled, *"The Candy Man"*. The junior choir began singing. There was much participation from the adult choir and people out in the congregation. Mother Carter pointed over to Gilbert and he began singing:

The candy man makes
everything he bakes
satisfying and delicious
talk about your childhood wishes
you could even eat the dishes

Members of the congregation laughed and made comments about the lyrics from the song. Mother Carter pointed back over to the choir and they began singing:

The candy man can
cause he adds a lot of love
to make it all taste good

In harmonious voices, Gilbert and the choir ended the song. Gilbert took a seat back in the choir. People clapped loudly, then said "amen" several times. *"The Candy Man"* was truly one of Bishop Burgess' favorite tunes from the junior choir. After a couple of selections from the adult choir, Mother Simpson came back to the podium. She wanted all visitors to stand. It was Easter Sunday and members of Saint Mark's brought relatives and friends with them; several people stood up.

Mother Simpson welcomed them and expressed how they were free to come and worship at Saint Mark's anytime.

Vincent restlessly sat in the junior choir section. As much as he wanted to play a game called, "thump the knuckles", he behaved himself everytime he attended church. Those early days of having to sit out in front of the congregation were totally embarrassing. The time had come for testimonies. From the right side of the congregation, Sister Tamara Davidson stood up. On this bright and sunny Easter Sunday, she wore her long white church robe, along with a long white rosary around her neck. She began to speak before everyone.

"Giving an honor to God, to Bishop Burgess, Mothers Carter, Simpson, Wagner, and Davenport, the members of Saint Mark's, and all of my brothers and sisters in Christ. I truly thank the Lord for allowing me to see yet another Easter Sunday. The other day, I saw one of our former church members hanging around up on Rush Boulevard. She was running with a group of people who were considered bad influences. I'm really concerned about this young lady. I've always been concerned about her. I'm concerned about her safety and overall well-being. She's very special inside my heart and I'm sure she's probably very special to some of you all. My brothers and sisters in Christ, it might not happen today. It might not happen tomorrow. It might not happen next month. But I do believe that our Lord and Savior Jesus Christ is going to deliver this young lady from those dangerous streets of Chicago. I ask that you all pray with me, so that the Lord will bring her back into his house of worship. Amen."

Sister Tamara sat with tears coming from her eyes. Vincent thought momentarily about Sister Tamara's testimony. Could she have been speaking of his sister Valerie? Bessie Mae spoke of seeing Valerie hanging around up on Rush Boulevard. It was in the same vicinity where all the prostitutes solicited. Mother Simpson came back to the podium and told the church to receive the pastor.

"Let the church say amen."

"Amen," said most of the people inside Saint Mark's.

"Let the church say amen again," said Mother Simpson. "Amen."

Bishop Burgess stepped out of the pulpit and strutted his tall frame joyously with his index finger pressed to his lips. He had a beaming smile on his face.

"Let the church say amen."

"Amen."

"Didn't you all love that selection, 'The Candy Man', by the junior choir?" Bishop Burgess asked the entire church.

"Amen," responded some of the people.

"Let the church say amen again."

"Amen."

Vincent's eyes followed Bishop Burgess down the consecrated aisle. He always admired the bishop for being the master orator that he was. He eventually would spot his foster parents coming into the church. Bessie Mae and J.D. were strolling up into the church. They were dressed for the occasion. Bessie Mae wore a bright yellow dress, with a matching yellow hat and a set of white pearls.

J.D. walked behind her, sporting a two-piece, black and white checkered suit, with a matching white shirt and black tie, along with a pair of black polished wingtips. For some strange reason, J.D. always wore a pair of dark shades to church. Maybe he didn't want to be noticed. Him coming into a church was like Satan making a grand entrance, seeing what evil that he was going to do next. J.D. Willingham was an unbeliever and only came to church to satisfy Bessie Mae.

Bessie Mae went around the wooden railings so she could kneel and pray at the back altar. She had many sins to confess. J.D. found a seat in the middle row on the right side of the church. Up in the junior choir section, Gilbert turned around to give Jose and Vincent the signal that Bessie Mae and J.D. were present. Bishop Burgess began to get the church fired up. He paced up and down the consecrated

aisle, shouting and pointing at members of both choirs and the entire congregation.

A strong expression of resentment abruptly came upon the shiny black face of J.D. Something that Bishop Burgess had said or done caused his eyes to turn bloodshot red. He perspired heavily! This time, his chapped lips were really and truly puckered, and his breathing was heavier than ever. From under those dark shades, his eyes became as red as scarlet. Bishop Burgess had gotten well into his Easter Sermon.

"This is a day of celebration, all of my father's children," said Bishop Burgess, pointing all around the church with the index finger of his right hand. "This is a day that all of mankind should be thankful for."

"Amen!" shouted several people inside the church.

"Thankful because he saved us from destruction."

"Yes Lord!" shouted several others from all over the church.

"Thankful because he loved us so much, that he shed his own blood," Bishop Burgess crooned, working up a serious perspiration, pointing directly to the sky.

"Go on and preach, Bishop Burgess!"

"Not only your blood!"

"Yeah!"

"Not only my blood!"

"Yeah!"

"Not only your mamma's or daddy's blood!"

"Yeah!"

"Not only your brother's or sister's blood!"

"Yeah!"

"Not only your aunt's our uncle's blood!"

"Preach on, Bishop, preach on!"

"Not only your best friend's or worst enemie's blood!"

"Preach on, Bishop, preach on!"

"Do you love the Lord like I do?" Bishop Burgess shouted

very loudly, pointing over at the adult and junior choir sections, jumping up and down wildly with both legs clamped
together, slinging sweat off his vibrant face.

"Yeah!" the entire adult choir section responded.

"Do you love his son, Jesus Christ, like I do?" Bishop
Burgess asked, turning around to point at both sides of the
congregation.

"Yeah!" shouted both sides of the charged congregation,
people standing to confess their love for Jesus Christ.

"If you love him like I do, say, 'thank you Lord'."

"Thank you, Lord!" yelled everyone present in the
church.

"Say, 'thank you Jesus'!"

"Thank you, Jesus!"

"Say, 'thank you for saving me'!"

"Thank you for saving me!"

"Say, 'thank you for loving me'!"

"Thank you for loving me!"

In the first row on the right side of the congregation, a
rather obese and medium complexioned deacon named
Gerald McNally was always heavily involved with the sermons.
Gerald came behind Bishop Burgess and said, "You know
he's right, say amen!"

"Amen!" the church shouted accordingly.

"You know the man's right, say amen again."

"Amen!"

"Say it louder."

"Amen!"

Further back, on the right side, J.D. shook his head in a
dismal disapproval. Making it appear as though he didn't
want to be in attendance, he bit down on the edge of his
bottom lip. His heavy frame slid back and forth on the pews.
That would come as no surprise for an *atrocious aetheist* like
J.D. Willingham.

Bishop Burgess stomped his feet and clapped his hands

three times. He pointed around to every section of the church with a steady finger. Last, he pointed to the large statue of Our Lord and Savior Jesus Christ in the pulpit. "He arose on this day!"

"Yeah!" people shouted in joyful voices.

"He arose, children!"

"Yes, he did!"

"He arose for all of us!"

"Yes, he did!"

"Let the church say amen."

"Amen," the people said calmly.

"Let the church say amen one more time."

"Amen."

Bishop Burgess, a true man of God, was filled with the Holy Spirit.

His hair-raising, nail-biting, throat-clearing, facial-stretching, heart-pounding, eyes-rolling, and body-perspiring sermon, enlightened the entire church.

He thoroughly depicted the resurrection of Jesus Christ. Several women were jumping up and down. They ran into the pews in front and in back of them. Some ran out into the consecrated aisle, throwing both arms up to the sky, jerking their heads back and forth with both eyes shut tightly. Some were loudly shouting, "Yes, Lord! Yes, Lord!" Others were screaming, "Thank you, Jesus! Thank you, Jesus!"

Judging by the way J.D. had both fists balled up and moved forward in the pews, it appeared that he wanted to jump up and strike Bishop Burgess right in the face. It was the type of restlessness that any angry person like him possessed. The sermon was offically over.

Bishop Burgess walked up into the pulpit wiping sweat

off his face and neck. Mother Simpson came to the podium to announce that it was time for the blessed offering. Bessie Mae rambled inside her purse. J.D. dug down into his pocket for money. She limped to the back of the church with a five dollar bill in her left hand. She surprisingly met up with Sister Tamara Davidson. She requested to speak with Bessie Mae in privacy over by the stairs. They went over to the stairs for a private discussion.

"How've you been doing, Sister Bessie Mae?" Sister Tamara asked, a serious, buy yet cordial look on her face, her beautiful hazel eyes glistening like the sun shining down on sparkling Spring water.

"Doing just fine," Bessie Mae replied. "How about yourself?"

"I'm doing just fine. How are things over at your house?"

"They're okay."

"Are you still keeping the same foster children?"

"Some of them."

"Are you still keeping the same handicapped men?"

"Yes, I am."

"Oh, I see."

"There've been some changes in our home."

"What kind of changes?" Tamara asked.

"Let's see, now," Bessie Mae paused. "One of the handicapped men named Morris died of brain cancer. Another handicapped man named Sean was taken away and put in a home for handicapped people. Vernon left over a year ago. They took Valerie away a long time ago."

"I'm glad you mentioned Valerie."

"Are you?"

"I saw her hanging around up on Rush."

"That's funny, I saw her up on Rush, too."

"I'm really praying for Valerie, Sister Bessie Mae."

"Praying for what?"

"She's out there on those streets."

"Where she belongs?"

"That's a horrible thing to say."

"It's true, Tamara."

"She's out there being . . ."

"A whore, huh?"

"How could you say something like that?"

"All the praying in the world couldn't help that girl."

"How would you know?"

"She's helpless."

"You're not God."

"She didn't act right when she lived in my foster home."

"There's still hope for her."

"She's never gonna act right."

"Were you ever concerned about Valerie?"

"Not one least bit."

"You and your husband had her taken away from your foster home."

"And if we did?"

"I've got a serious question to ask you."

"And what might that be?"

"Did your husband rape Valerie?"

"J.D.?"

"Yes, J.D.?"

"That's none of your business!" Bessie Mae snapped.

"I'm making it my business."

"What goes on inside my home isn't none of your business."

"There's something you should know," Tamara mentioned. "The night that Carmen brought Valerie over to my house, I could tell that she'd been bothered."

"What night?" Bessie Mae asked.

"You were in Memphis, Tennessee."

"Get to the point, Tamara."

"I'm saying that your husband raped Valerie."

"That's a lie!"

"Your husband ruined her."

"Ruined her?"

"Yes."

"How?"

"Any teenage girl would be ruined after being raped by her foster father."

"I've got news for you, Tamara."

"What?"

"Stay the hell out of my business!" Bessie Mae growled.

"You need Jesus, Sister."

"I already have Jesus, *miss holier than thou.*"

"It hurts, don't it?"

"What hurts?"

"The truth."

"Get some business and stay out of mine's."

"I really feel sorry for you and your husband."

"Why?"

"You're headed for the eternal fires in hell."

"You'll be there before me."

"I'll be praying for you."

"What goes on inside my house will never be any of your business."

"It's a shame what those foster children and handicapped people have to go through at your home."

"You've got a whole lot of nerves."

"Sure do."

"I'm taking care of those people the best way that I know how."

"I don't believe you."

"I don't know where you get your information from."

"Reliable sources."

"You need to tell those people to get their lies straight."

"It's good that a lot of those foster children left your home."

"What are you talking about?"

"I know why Vernon left."

"Why?"

"You kept trying to take all of his money."

"That's a lie!"

"You wanted to clean him out."

"Now, you're lying, Tamara."

"I think it would be nice if someone had the nerves to tell The Department of Children and Family Services."

"What lies are they going to tell them?"

"About the unnecessary beatings that those kids get."

"That's crazy."

"Not to mention the unnecessary beatings the handicapped people got."

"Who's feeding you all those lies?"

"It's a small world, sister."

"You can tell those white folks at family services. You can tell the colored folks at family services. They're not going to come in our home and tell me and J.D. how to run things."

"I know a few people who work for Cook County family services."

"Hip hooray!"

"But, I'm really concerned about Valerie."

"Why're you concerned about her?"

"Don't you even care if she dies?"

"Look, Tamara!" Bessie Mae grunted, gritting her teeth and twisting up her nose. "I didn't choose being a whore for her. I didn't choose being a yellow bitch for her. She chose them dam streets for herself."

"Sister Bessie Mae, watch your mouth," Tamara reminded Bessie Mae. "You're still in a house worship."

"Why don't you take Valerie off the streets and bring her into your home?"

"Since nobody else wants to, I will."

"Good!" Bessie Mae grumbled."End of conversation."

"Have a blessed Easter, Sister Bessie Mae."

While Bessie Mae and Tamara continued exchanging mixed feelings about the way that she ran her foster home, and rescuing Valerie from the vicious streets of Chicago, J.D. lustfully observed the gorgeous young ladies who were dressed pretty in their Easter attire. Their tight dresses hugged their breasts, hips, and buttocks, just the way J.D. liked to see women in their clothing. Even for the ones who wore clothes loosely, he still imagined how their figures may have looked underneath. The manner in which he spoke to the young ladies was much too friendly. He was waving and winking at them. He was a devil who had no respect for God's house.

"How ya doing, t'day?" J.D. asked an attractive woman in front of him.

"I'm doing great," she replied cordially.

"Ya sho lookin good t'day."

"Thank you."

"Dat's a pretty dress ya got on."

"Thanks."

"I'd lack to get ta . . ."

"Alright, alright, I have to go," she said irritably, quickly walking away from J.D.

What did J.D. care? Flirting with another woman while his wife was in attendance meant nothing to him. He turned to look up in the pulpit at Bishop Burgess. Everytime he set eyes on someone bright complexioned, he slipped into another one of his resentful dazes about growing up in Clarksdale, Mississippi. Since the much brighter blacks were given preferential treatment, this deeply angered him everytime he saw someone like Bishop Burgess.

*   *   *

"We can't use ya round here, boy," a clerk in a store told J.D., an extreme racist white man who resented negroes for being as dark as they were.

"Why not, suh?" J.D. asked, standing on the other side of the store counter, looking sad and feeling sorry for himself.

"We can't use tarbaby niggers like ya round here."

"My pappy tells ma dat I needs ta find work."

"Why, boy?"

"He gone put ma outdoors."

"Let ma tell ya again, boy," the bigot white man told J.D. "We can't use no black spook like ya round here."

"Pease, hep ma, suh!" J.D. said, tears rolling down his greasy black face.

"Customers don't want no niggers round them."

"Pease, pease, I's do anythang ya say, suh!"

"Get out of here, you tarbaby-coon."

✳   ✳   ✳

Bessie Mae and Tamara eluded from the conversation to put money in the collection basket. Brother Bluett took the table to the back of the church. Church services at Saint Mark's ended.

At the same pews, or from different sides of the church, people fellowshipped with one another. People were still elated from Bishop Burgess', *good old raise the roof off the church* sermon. Since Bessie Mae and J.D. were the only ones who rode in her spacious Cadillac, Gilbert, Jose, and Vincent were able to catch a ride home.

Once everyone was inside, J.D. slammed the door harder than ever. He quickly twisted the ignition and jerked the gear down to drive. He pounded his feet down on the accelerator. Bessie Mae was barely given enough time to close her door. She was thrown backwards as a result of the sudden takeoff. Gilbert, Jose, and Vincent bumped one another, sliding around in the backseat.

"J.D.!" Bessie Mae said in a shocked voice. "What the hell's wrong with you?"

"I tell ya what's wrong wit ma," J.D. replied, the red watery eyes, chapped puckered lips, and strong breathing surfacing, meaning that he was filled with anger and wrath.

"Why did you rush up the street like that?"

"Dat Bissup Burguss is what's wong."

"What did Bishop Burgess do?"

"Pointing his goddam fanger!"

"What's wrong with him pointing his finger?"

"Somebody gone break dat muttapucker off!"

"Quit saying things like that about Bishop Burgess."

"I can say anythang I wanna say."

"Nobody's going to break his finger off."

"I am."

"And don't use the 'MF' word when you're talking about Bishop Burgess."

"Let'em point his fanger at ma again."

"He didn't mean no harm by pointing his finger."

"Yep, he did."

"Bishop Burgess gets happy when he starts preaching."

"I'm gone make'em mad next time he points his fanger."

"He has a habit of pointing around the church."

"Dat's one habit I'm gone break dat muttapucker fum!"

"J.D.!" Bessie Mae grumbled. "Quit calling Bishop Burgess a 'MF'."

"Don't tell ma what ta do."

"Listen to what you're saying."

"What?"

"You're a blasphemer."

"I ain't no bassfeemer," J.D. said, not even knowing the true meaning of the word.

"Yes, you are."

"Naw, I ain't."

"A lot of preachers point when they get happy."

"I don't give no dam."

"Hush up!"

"Naw, you huss up."

"Drive, niggah!"

"Shut up, woman!"

"No, you shut up, man!"

"Git out'a my face!"

"God's going to strike you down."

"Like hell he will!"

"You really are a blasphemer."

Gilbert, Jose, and Vincent sat perfectly still, watching in complete silence, as they watched their foster parents argue. The adrenalin was strong. It had the Willingham couple pointing and shouting in another's faces. They swapped spit from across their seats. Bessie Mae obviously was still upset after the confrontation with Tamara Davidson. J.D. was still upset from Bishop Burgess pointing his finger all around the church.

Near the corner of the backseat, Vincent had his body curled up. Gilbert and Jose's bodies were pressed together near the middle of the backseat. Bessie Mae slammed her fist onto the dashboard. She was angrier than ever at J.D.

"I don't understand it," said Bessie Mae, turning sideways to glance at the side of J.D.'s angry black face. "You're talking about how much you don't like Bishop Burgess pointing his finger. Why in the hell did you point your crusty finger in my face?"

"Cause I felt lack it," J.D. responded wittingly.

"You felt like it?"

"Dat's wight."

"Hypocrite."

"Go ta hell, woman!"

"You go to hell, man!"

"Ya git on ma nerves."

"You've been getting on my nerves."

Everyone instantly got quiet in the car. The evil in the red eyes of J.D. was strong enough to break the windshield in

front of him. Bessie Mae scooted closer to the passenger door. Gilbert, Jose, and Vincent never saw them disagree so strongly. J.D. drove up in the front yard and rushed into the house. To avoid any further annoyance from Bessie Mae, he ran upstairs and jumped in the bed. Bessie Mae limped into the kitchen to tell Granny Dear about church services.

Granny Dear was bending over in her wheelchair to dice up an onion. There was a pan of candy yams in the oven. They needed cinnamon sprinkled over them, so Bessie Mae limped over to the cabinets to find some cinnamon spice. She scrambled through the spices and couldn't find any of that type of spice. The oven was on a low temperature, giving the yams only a short time to finish cooking.

Gilbert, Jose, and Vincent were in the front yard, cutting through Bessie Mae's specially planted flowers. These beautiful flowers included poinsettias, lillies, roses, and daffodils. All three had Ball jars, the same jars that Bessie Mae had stored in the basement for future use. They waited for butterflies to land on one of the flowers so they could start a collection. They cautiously kept their distance, because large wasps, bumble bees, and hornets flew down on some of the flowers. Vincent crept over by one of the poinsettias. A large hornet was flying around the flower next to it.

"Vincent!" Gilbert hissed. "Stay away from that flower right there."

"Why?" Vincent asked.

"It's a hornet close by that flower."

"So."

"Have you ever been stung by a hornet?"

"Nope."

"Do you know what it feels like?"

"Nope."

"It feels like somebody sticking you with a hot pin."

"Are you for real?"

"Yes, I'm for real."

"How do you know?"

"When I was at the other foster home . . ."

"There you go talking about your other foster," Vincent charged.

"Shut up and listen, boy!"

"Alright, alright, I'll listen."

"My foster brother there got stung by a hornet."

"What happened?"

"It left a big red knot on his arm."

"I'll bet it hurt."

"All I'm saying is be careful."

A large swallowtail butterfly with an array of brilliant colors landed on one of the daffodils. Gilbert tiptoed past the other flowers. He tried keeping out of the butterfly's sight. A honeybee landed on one of the poinsettias to his left. A large bumble bee landed on another one of the daffodils. Gilbert stood between the two bees that had the potential of stinging him. A slight wave of the hand made both bees fly away.

With skilled eye and hand movement, Gilbert reached up and caught the swallowtail. The wings were clamped together by his tightly pinched fingers. Vincent took Gilbert's advice. The hornet wasn't about to fly away from the flowers. Several more butterflies hovered above. The screen door shot open. They quickly turned to stare up towards the porch.

"Leave them dam bugs alone!" Bessie Mae shouted from the front door.

"Yes, mam," Gilbert, Jose, and Vincent said, stepping away from the flowers.

"Where did you all get my canning jars?"

"From the basement," Gilbert answered hesitantly.

"Don't you know that I use those jars to can fruit?"

"No, mam."

"And you all are putting those nasty ass bugs in my jars!"

"I'm sorry, Mrs. Willingham," Gilbert apologized, Jose

and Vincent standing there in silence, looking as innocent as ever.

"You should be sorry," Bessie Mae said. "Now, put my jars back in the basement."

"Yes, mam."

Bessie Mae remembered that she needed someone to go to the store. She turned to Jose and gave him a five dollar bill. He was told to get the largest size of McCormick cinnamon spice. On the way to the grocery store, Jose took the same route. Upon arriving at the store, he noticed a security guard walking up and down the aisles. The store was crowded with last minute shoppers. Many of these shoppers were placing cartons of eggs in their carts.

Easter eggs were on display all over the city. Jose hadn't visited the store in several weeks. Along the aisles, items were arranged the same. He intentionally traveled down the aisle where the cakes and candies were. He stared at the ice cream gum so long, until it almost jumped off the shelf and into his hands. Short memories paid him a visit. He recalled the time when he, Gilbert, and Vincent stuffed some of the gum down their pants pockets. Though they made a clean getaway, Jose realized that if he tried stealing some more gum, the risk would be higher.

The security guard was towards the front of the store. Jose left the sweets section to search for the cinnamon spice. He went down the aisle that kept the canned goods and spices. The same security guard strolled up that aisle. Jose wondered if it was coincidental or was he being watched. He picked up a container of the McCormick cinnamon spice and opened the top. The tantalizing aroma rushed up his nose.

The temptation to steal some of the ice cream gum only intensified. Inside his young mind, there was some serious debating going on. Since the guard hadn't been seen for awhile, he went back to where the ice cream gum was. Right

next to the gum, a woman reached for some candy bars. Next to her, there was a woman reaching for some blowpops and Boston baked beans.

For Jose, they were a distraction. When they left the aisle, he stepped up to the shelf. To make sure everything was in the clear, he glanced down both ends of the aisle. He quickly grabbed a pack of chocolate ice cream gum, his favorite flavor, no doubt, and stuffed it down his left pants pocket. Right before he could get into any of the long lines, someone grabbed him from behind. They clutched the middle of his belt and jerked him softly by the pants.

The security guard escorted him to the back of the store. He was taken to a small office that had a desk and two chairs. Inner conversation had him asking himself, *"How did I get caught?"* Jose would soon find out. In the wall above, there were two, eight inch black and white monitors. These monitors covered every inch of the store. But where were they installed? Along with the security guard, the manager and assitant manager were in the office. Jose had to answer some vital questions.

"What's your name, son?" the security guard asked, sitting on top of the desk, as he stared seriously at Jose.

"Jose," Jose replied submissively, sitting in the chair shaking mildly.

"Jose who?"

"Underwood."

"How old are you?"

"Fourteen."

"Where do you live?"

"Thirty-eight, Thirty-eight, Milwaukee Parkway."

"Have you ever been to this store?"

"Yes, sir."

"When?"

"Some weeks ago."

"Have you ever been caught for shoplifting?"

"No, sir."

"Know what?"

"What?" Jose asked.

"We're going to have to call your parents."

"Are you?"

"Yes, we are."

Jose sat in the chair that was next to his desk. All he could envision was J.D. beating the living hell out of him with that painful extension cord. The manager picked up the phone and dialed the number that Jose gave him. The phone at the Willingham residence rung. Inside the kitchen, Granny Dear heard the rings. She rolled her wheelchair over to answer it. Since the personnel at the store requested to speak with the head of the house, Granny Dear called for Bessie Mae.

Bessie Mae was in the front room, relaxing on the sofa with a cigarette. Television station WGN was airing a special episode of *"The Jeffersons"*, and she was heavily involved in watching the popular sitcom. As much as she regretted leaving the front room, she limped into the kitchen to answer the phone.

"Hello," Bessie Mae said, her voice sounding frustrated.

"Are you Mrs. Underwood?" the manager asked.

"No, I'm not."

"With whom am I speaking?"

"This is Bessie Mae Willingham."

"My name's Stanley Caruthers."

"Yes?"

"I'm the manager of Food Kingdom."

"Do you need something?"

"Are you related to Jose Underwood?"

"I'm his foster mother."

"I see."

"Is Jose in some type of trouble?"

"Yes, he is."

"Well?"

"He's in the security office here at Food Kingdom."

"What'd he do?"

"He was caught shoplifting."

"Shoplifting!" Bessie Mae screeched. "What was he trying to steal?"

"Some chocolate ice cream gum."

"Say what!"

"That's right."

"I'll be up to the store shortly."

"Okay, Mrs. Willingham."

Bessie Mae jumped into her Cadillac and quickly drove out of the yard. She slammed down on the accelerator and sped down Milwaukee. She looked very upset from behind the wheel. People in other cars glanced over and saw the angry look on the face of Bessie Mae. Slowly, a group of teenage boys crossed the street. They watched Bessie Mae drive full speed from down the street. She sounded her horn repeatedly, but they continued walking slow.

"Get out of the street, niggahs!" she screamed, slowing her car up and sticking her head out of the window.

"Shut up old lady!" one of the teenagers said, pointing his finger at the windshield.

"Don't make me run your black ass over!"

"I dare you."

"You thug-bastards!"

Bessie Mae ignored their insulting responses. She continued her journey to the store. Finding a parking space in the lot at Food Kingdom wasn't easy. When someone pulled out of their space, Bessie Mae parked near the front of the store. She grabbed her purse and the long black strap that fitted around the massive waist of J.D. She stormed into the store in search of the security office. Customers standing in line noticed the black strap in her hand. One of the clerks

led her to the back of the store. The security guard stood
outside the office.

"Are you here for Jose Underwood?" the security guard
asked, watching Bessie Mae limp and down, holding the strap
with a demanding grip.

"Yes, I am," Bessie Mae replied ragefully.

"He's right here in the office."

Bessie Mae was taken into the office. Jose sat in the chair
palming both knees, gritting his teeth, and looking more
nervous than he'd ever been. The manager and assistant
manager came into the office.

"How are you doing, Mrs. Willingham?" the manager
asked Bessie Mae, standing to the left of the door.

"I was doing good until I heard that my foster son was up
here stealing."

"Whenever someone's caught shoplifting, they're subject
to prosecution."

"Yeah, I saw that sign out front," Bessie Mae said. "You
can prosecute him, but I'm going to persecute him on the
way home."

"I understand."

"Too bad he didn't take heed to the sign out front."

"Since Jose is a minor, there are certain guidelines that
our store follows."

"Does it make a difference if he's a foster child?"

"I don't think so."

"Well, let me tell you this," Bessie Mae told the manager.
"Since I'm his foster mother, I'm going to call his caseworker
and let her know what he did."

"Caseworker?"

"Yes."

"The Department of Children and Family Services?"

"Yes."

"We'll need you to contact us once you've contacted
them."

"I'll gladly do that."

"Thank you, Mrs. Willingham."

"You're welcome."

Once they were out of the office, Bessie Mae began swinging the strap wildly across the chest and back of Jose. For him, it was terribly embarrassing. After several strokes, he ran up and down the aisles crying, rubbing the spots where the strap made the strongest impacts. Bessie Mae and Jose got inside the car and she rushed out of the parking lot like a race car driver. She came down on him like an avalanche coming down a mountainside.

"Why did you come up here and steal that gum?" Bessie Mae asked Jose, barely watching the cars in front of her.

"I don't know!" Jose cried, wiping the salty tears from his eyes.

"Didn't I send you to the store to buy some cinnamon spice?"

"Yes, mam."

"Why didn't you buy what I told you and leave the store?"

"I don't know."

"Your caseworker is going to take you away."

"Take me where?" Jose asked.

"To a boys home."

"I don't wanna go to no boys home."

"You should've thought about that when you stole that gum."

"I'm sorry, Mrs. Willingham."

"Sorry didn't do it."

"I didn't mean to do it."

"Do you know what they do to you in a boys home?"

"No, mam."

"They never let you go outside."

"Why not?"

"You have to go to bed before six o'clock every night."

"Why?"

"They make you wear the same clothes everyday."

Bessie Mae had put a big scare on Jose. He sat next to her with his eyes bucked.

"I don't wanna go to no boys home."

"Well, you're going," Bessie Mae said. "Whether you want to or not."

Chapter 30

DEPARTURE FROM HELL

J.D. WAS in the toolshed looking for some fishing poles that he wanted to take to the lake. He reached for one of his reels and three others that were made of plain bamboo. The bamboo fishing poles were to be used by Gilbert and Vincent. J.D. picked up the tacklebox and made sure all the hooks, bobbles, and bait were inside.

Jose was in the basement preparing for his departure from the Willingham residence. His caseworker, Sandra Maloney, was on her way to pick him up. Gilbert and Vincent were helping their soon-to-be foster brother pack his belongings. With the same suitcase that he came to the home with, they folded shirts and pants and stuffed them inside. Bessie Mae was courteous enough to wash all of his clothes, sending him away with fresh laundry.

"I'm going to miss you," Gilbert expressed sadly to Jose, handing him three pairs of pants that were folded up.

"I'm going to miss you all, too," Jose said thoughtfully.

"Aren't you glad you're leaving?" Gilbert asked.

"I'm real glad."

"I'm glad you're leaving, too."

"Thanks a lot."

"Stealing that gum may have been good."

"You're right."

"You don't have to worry about no more beatings from Mr. Willingham."

"I know."

"Guess what, Jose?"

"What's that, Gilbert?"

"I've got a quizz for you."

"What's that?"

"Who's real black?" Gilbert asked.

"Real black?" Jose asked.

"Who's real ugly?"

"Real ugly?"

"Who's real fat?"

"Real fat?"

"Who's real dumb?"

"Real dumb?"

"Who's real stinky?"

"Real stinky?"

"Who's greasy and bald-headed?" Gilbert asked Jose, running out of harsh adjectives to describe someone very familiar.

"You're talking about Mr. Willingham."

"You've got it!" Gilbert cheered, smiling from ear to ear.

"Put all that together, you definitely get Mr. Willingham."

"You also don't have to worry about Mrs. Willingham."

"What about her?"

"Trying to take all of your money away."

"That's true."

"I wish I was leaving with you."

"You could leave, too."

"How?"

"Tell Mrs. Maloney when she comes here to get me."

"Mrs. Maloney?"

"Yes."

"Is she still my caseworker?"

"Of course she is."

"How do you know?"

"I heard Mrs. Willingham talking to her on the phone."

"When?"

"Yesterday."

"I don't know if I should tell her when she comes by."

"Then call her and tell her."

"You're right."

The suitcase was filled to capacity. Jose opened a small garbage bag and placed the rest of his belongings inside. Bessie Mae called from the top of the basement stairs. Sandra Maloney was in the front room to pick him up. Gilbert and Vincent followed him to the living room, carrying the suitcase and garbage bag. Sandra had a new look and it was very noticeable. She had cut her hair to shoulder length, got a gorgeous tan, and gained a few pounds after having a child. She wore a different style of clothes to keep up with the latest trends.

She was ready to take Jose to his next foster home. It was difficult finding a home for him, because most boys his age were considered too old to be placed. J.D. happened to walk into the house carrying his tacklebox. He held the door open so they could exit. He deceitfully smiled right into Jose's face. Jose frowned, because he knew that J.D. was putting on a front. It was the last time he would have to look at the evil J.D. Willingham.

Sandra stepped onto the porch with Bessie Mae. Gilbert, Jose, and Vincent walked out to her car. They placed his belongings in the back of her sky blue, 1979 Ford Mustang. Jose was getting a final look at the Willingham residence and Milwaukee Parkway. Leaving their home permanently felt good. He figured that there couldn't be a foster home worse than the one run by Bessie Mae and J.D. Some of the nosy neighbors came out on their porches to see who was departing from the Willingham residence. Having lived on Milwaukee Parkway for many years, most neighbors had seen many foster children come and go.

"Do you know what foster home Mrs. Maloney's taking you to?" Gilbert asked Jose.

"I asked Mrs. Willingham, but she told me that she didn't know."

"Do you think Mrs. Maloney told her?"

"Probably."

"Hope your new foster home's nothing like this one."

"No foster home could be worst than this one."

"I think you're right."

"I know I'm right."

Sandra stepped down from the porch. She said goodbye to Bessie Mae. Jose was ready to be taken to his next foster home. Gilbert gave his former foster brother a warm and tight hug. It was strong and emotional. He stepped aside and Vincent embraced him for a few seconds. Sandra was elated to see the three youngsters express so much gratitude amongst one another. Sadly enough, she was never notified of all the abuse that took place inside the Willingham's residence. Her attitude reflected that of one who would not hesitate to make some changes.

Bessie Mae and J.D. came out on the porch to wave goodbye to Jose. In a vengeful manner, he quickly turned towards the traffic out on Milwaukee Parkway, ignoring them in the most notorious fashion. Sandra got inside and started her car up. Jose slid in on the passenger's side. As she pulled out into traffic, Jose waved goodbye to Gilbert and Vincent. They walked up to the porch and J.D. asked if they wanted to go fishing. It sounded like a good idea, so they jumped into the back of the camper and the journey to Lake Michigan began.

The strong breezes of the windy city blew through the cracks of the camper. They traveled quietly out the busy highway. Gilbert and Vincent discreetly listened to a conversation that Bessie Mae and J.D. were having in the front of the truck. Gilbert leaned forward and pressed his right ear against the thin glass. To keep Bessie Mae from thinking that he was eavesdropping, he pretended to use the glass as something to lean against. The conversation came in much clearer.

"I sure hate Jose's gone," Bessie Mae asserted.

"We both gone miss'em," J.D. said, traveling about fifty miles an hour down the busy highway.

"That's going to be one less check."

"Ain't nuttin we could'a done ta keep him dere."

"You're right, J.D."

"Dey caught'em stealing, and he had ta go."

"Everytime we lose a foster child, we lose money."

"You wight, Bessa Mae."

"We can't afford to lose any money."

"We gone git mo falsta chilluns."

"I guess."

"Watch what I tell ya, now."

"Alright."

In the back of the camper, Gilbert signaled over to Vincent. His left hand hung low, throwing up his three middle fingers. Vincent responded by nodding his head, with an uncertain look already on his face.

"What're they talking about?" Vincent whispered over to Gilbert.

"Mrs. Willingham said something about losing money," Gilbert said.

"What about losing money?"

"Had something to do with foster children."

"What else're they talking about?"

"Mrs. Willingham said something about a check."

"A check?"

"Yes."

"What is Mr. Willingham talking about?"

"He said something about getting more foster children."

"Who can ever understand what he's talking about?"

"I tried to listen to all of it, but the wind kept blowing in my ear."

"I'll bet they were talking about Jose."

"You know they are."

"Greedy fuckers!"

Gilbert and Vincent had a relatively good idea of what the Willinghams were talking about. Losing money and a check were the two elements that had something to do with the crippling of their finances. About a half mile up the road, there was a large green sign that informed motorists that they were approaching Lake Michigan. J.D. hit his right signal and drove behind other motorists. They followed the road that led to the lake area. The reflection of the sunlight shimmered off the beautiful lake.

The lake was occupied with boats of all sizes. The roaring of the boat motors excited Gilbert and Vincent. J.D. parked his truck in an area that was a few yards from the lake. He came around to the camper to give Gilbert and Vincent the bamboo poles. They were told to meet him down by the lake.

J.D. brought his reel and tacklebox to the banks of the lake and began setting things up. With the door open, Bessie Mae sat at the edge of the camper. She wanted to see who would catch the most fish. J.D. pushed the metal stakes into the dirt and threw the attached rope into the water. It would serve as the line to hold the fish in the water. Out of the tacklebox, Gilbert brought out a rubber worm and attached it to the hook. His line was thrown out about ten feet. Vincent stood several feet away, throwing his line out closer to the banks.

J.D threw his line out very far, then reeled part of it back, and laid it on the ground. Other fishermen were gathered around with their lawn chairs, with cans of beer, peanuts, portable radios, and fishing gear. Everyone waited for that important bite. Gilbert and Vincent decided to put the orange and white bobbles on their lines. They wished for a nibble, a slight yank, or somewhat of a jerk on their line.

Unexpectedly, the bobble on Gilbert's line took a plunge. When he jerked his line out of the water, there was a large perch flipping up and down on the ground. Gilbert's prize

catch tried to work it's way off the hook, but it was too far away from the shore. He broadcasted his catch to everyone around. "I caught a fish! I caught a fish!" He jumped up and down, holding the fish high up in the air, wanting everyone to see him. Bessie Mae cheered and clapped from up in the parking area.

She stretched her arms to the sky. Other fishermen congratulated him. They made wise cracks, like he had some type of lucky charm. Seconds before Gilbert threw his line back in the water, Vincent's line got a strong jerk. Swinging the pole backwards, he jerked a large perch out of the water. They were two excited youngsters, beating their feet along the wet shores.

J.D. hadn't said a word. The red watery eyes, the chapped puckered lips, and heavy breathing, indicated that he had become angry. His line was submerged far out into the lake. Before another word was said, Gilbert's line took another plunge. The strong force of both of his arms pulled yet another perch to the shores. Like before, the fish flopped around on the ground. Gilbert unhooked the fish, placed it on the rope in the water, and went into the tacklebox for another worm.

Almost immediately, he threw his line back into the water. Minutes after Gilbert's second catch, Vincent's pole jerked to the extreme left. The struggle with this fish was hard, because he was being forced towards the water. He pulled himself further away from the water, exerting more force in his pull. The large perch came out of the water and pounded across the ground. It was the largest fish that they had caught. Vincent felt mighty proud. Compliments came from other fishermen who hadn't caught a single fish. Gilbert and Vincent wanted to break the tie, so they waited patiently to see who would catch the third fish.

J.D.'s pole rolled around on the ground a couple of times. He picked the pole up and reeled in part of the line. He

diligently reeled in the rest of the line and the hook was empty. This greatly angered him. The steadfast reeling was useless, making him look like an idiot standing at the shores of Lake Michigan. The fish took the bait and got off the hook. He slammed the pole on the ground and went into the tacklebox for another worm. The hooks, bobbles, extra line, and small lead weights, were thrown around inside the box like they were of no use.

Gilbert and Vincent stood perfectly still at the shores. All of their attention was directed at the lines in the water. J.D. threw his line back in the water. Everyone waited patiently for their next bite. Several boats sped past the area and made high waves. For the third time, Gilbert's pole moved forward. After several jerks, he pulled in another perch. The ferocious anger of J.D. was on the rise! He maliciously kicked dirt and grass that was in front of him into the water.

"Put dose goddam poles up!" J.D. snapped at Gilbert and Vincent, his barritone voice exploding like dynamite.

"What did we do?" Gibert asked, thrown completely off guard.

"I said, put dem muttapucking poles up!"

"We weren't doing nothing wrong, Mr. Willingham."

"If ya don't put dose poles up, I'a go all da way home and git ma stanching code!"

"Alright, alright, I'll put my pole up," Gilbert smarted off, bravely standing up to J.D. for the first and only time.

"Don't git smart wit ma no mo, boy!"

"You got smart with me first."

"I'm gone knock da shit out'a ya, boy!"

"Whatever."

"What'cha say?"

"Nothing."

"You didden say what I thought."

"Why do we have to put the poles up?"

"Cause I say so."

"Okay."

The other fishermen watched J.D. go beserk. These group of white people witnessed this angry black man saying harsh things to his foster sons. Gilbert and Vincent started walking towards the truck. Bessie Mae sat quietly in the doorway of the camper. She also watched J.D. get angry for no apparent reason, saying harsh words at their two foster sons. With their pride shattered, they stood at the front of the truck with sour expressions on their faces.

"Why did Mr. Willingham make us put our poles up?" Vincent asked Gilbert, glancing down at the lake to watch J.D. hope for a fish to bite.

"Because we were catching more fish than his black ass!" Gilbert answered with raging hostility, the glare of fury in his eyes.

"Why would he get mad over something like that?"

"The same reason he gets mad at anything else."

"He just got mad all of a sudden."

"Can't stand for nobody to be better than him."

"Oh, so that's it?"

"He's got a lot of nerves."

"For cursing at us like that?"

"Yes," Gilbert said. "And for embarrassing us in front of all those white people."

"Did you see the way they were looking at Mr. Willingham?".

"The white people?"

"Yes."

"They could tell that he was a dumb niggah."

"You're right."

"Using words like 'muttapucking' and 'stanching code'."

"I'm still wondering where he got those words from."

"From being a stupid ass dummy from Mississippi."

"I bet those white people think all black people are like that."

"Hope not."

"Me, too."

"I wish I could've left with Jose."

"Really?"

"I'm going to call Mrs. Maloney."

"For what?"

"Tell her that I want to leave this foster home."

"When?" Vincent asked.

"As soon as we get home."

"Are you gonna do it for real?"

"Hell yeah!" Gilbert said, not calling anybody's bluff this time.

"You're serious?"

"As a heart attack."

"Aren't you scared of Mr. Willingham beating you?"

"What's he going to do to me that hasn't already been done?"

"You're right."

"He'd better not try and beat me for calling my caseworker."

"You sure?"

"Vincent, let me tell you something," Gilbert validated, pointing down towards the lake at J.D. "If you don't want to be in any foster home, you can call your caseworker and tell her that you want to leave. That's why I left those other foster homes, because I didn't want to be there."

"Is this the worst foster home that you've been to so far?"

"Hell yeah!"

"Why's that?"

"At the other foster homes, we got whippings, not beatings."

"I don't even know who my caseworker is."

"Why not?"

"Mrs. Willingham's never told me."

"You should find out."

"How can I find out?"

"Make Mrs. Willingham tell you."

"What if she doesn't tell me?"

"Call down to the family services and ask them."

"How can I find the number?"

"Look in the phone book."

"Under what?"

"Under Cook County."

"I might be leaving right behind you, Gilbert."

"I'll bet you're scared to call your caseworker."

"No, I'm not."

"I'm getting out of this crazy foster home," Gilbert boasted. "I'm leaving just like Sean did, Vernon did, and Jose did."

Since Lake Michigan expanded to other areas, including places where more people fished, boated, and played sports, Vincent got permission from Bessie Mae to journey to other parts. Gilbert decided to hang around the truck. He needed time to think some things over. As far as calling his caseworker, he was definitely serious. While Vincent traveled further down the lake, the scenery became more alluring. He projected a deep blue spectrum of the water. The illustrious beauty of the water was too irresistible, so he moved closer to watch the waves splash on the banks. The swiftness of the large boats sped across the lake. The motors roared and treads of water caused even greater waves to form. For Vincent, it was exciting watching the boats race across the lake and spin around in circles. On the other side, J.D. continued standing at the shores. He felt disappointed, simply because after standing around for more than an hour, he only got one bite. He believed that the fish weren't biting in the place where he stood. J.D. felt that his luck wouldn't change. He reeled his line in and gathered everything to go inside the tacklebox. The fish caught by Gilbert and Vincent were thrown back into the lake. It was jealousy on the behalf

of J.D. He repulsively stormed towards the truck. Bessie Mae and Gilbert were ready to take off.

"Less go," J.D. said, pointing towards the front of the truck.

"Vincent hasn't come back," Bessie Mae informed J.D.

"Fuck Vinsun!"

"I told him he could walk around the lake."

"I ain't waitin on him."

"Let Gilbert go looking for him."

"Hell naw!"

"He's on the other side of the lake."

"Den let'em stay over yonder."

"We've got to find him, J.D."

"Fo'get dat yella fucker!"

"Why did you throw the fish back in the water?" Bessie Mae asked.

"Cause I wanted to."

"We could've eaten those fish for dinner."

"You want dose fish?"

"Of course."

"Den go out in da lake and git'em."

"You're about a lowdown sapsucker."

"Shut up, woman!" J.D. griped.

"You shut up, man!"

"Ain't nobody gone argue wit ya."

"What if something happens to Vincent?"

"I don't care."

"Who do you care about?"

"Myself."

"Nobody but yourself, huh?"

"You dam wight, Bessa Mae," J.D. proclaimed. "I ain't never cared bout nunna dese falsta chilluns dat ya brang to da house."

"Since you don't care about none of the foster children," Bessie Mae said. "I wonder if you care about me?"

"What chu thank?"

"I think you should stop acting stupid and help us find Vincent."

"Lack you care bout Vinsun?"

"Yes, I do."

"Naw, ya don't."

"Yes I do, J.D."

"Woman, you can't fool ma!"

"Man, I'm not trying to fool you!" Bessie Mae blasted back.

"Ya keepin dose chilluns fo da money."

"That's a lie."

"Ya know I'm tellin da truth."

"Money isn't everything."

"Den why ya wait outdoors fo dem checks?"

"Checks?"

"At da first of da month."

"To keep people from stealing them."

"Who gone steal dose checks?"

"Thugs will."

"What tugs?"

"Around the neighborhood."

"I don't bleeves dat."

"Believe what you want," Bessie Mae said. "We live around a lot of thieves who would steal the stink out of shit."

"Whateva."

"Yeah, J.D., whatever."

"Go ta hell, woman!"

"You go to hell, man!"

J.D. slammed the poles in the back of the camper. Once he got inside the truck, he jerked the gear down to drive, then sped away from the lake. Bessie Mae remained unhappy with J.D.'s decision to leave Vincent behind. J.D. wasn't even concerned about Vincent's safety. In the back of the camper, Gilbert sat impatiently. The argument between Bessie Mae

and J.D. revealed some things that he never thought existed. Whether it would be as soon as they got home, tomorrow, or the next week, he wanted to leave the Willingham's foster home.

*   *   *

Vincent wasn't aware, but they departed from the lake. After traveling back to the other side, he glanced at the parking area where J.D.'s truck used to be. Several cars were parked down there. Vincent realized that he had been left. There was nothing to do but start walking. If he had some money, he would make a phone call. As he walked around the lake near the boardwalk, there were people in cars, trucks, and vans looking back. They wondered if Vincent was lost. He ventured off into a residential area. A small white house, that was surrounded by a black iron gate, was less than a block away. A Corvette and a Camaro sports cars were parked in the long cemented driveway.

Vincent went inside the fence and knocked on the door. Seconds later, an attractive woman with strawberry blonde hair answered. The tight jeans that she wore hugged every curve of her figure. Her complexion was smooth and tanned, with a small black mole flanking her upper right cheek.

"What can I do for you, young man?" she asked courteously, speaking with a cocky, midwestern accent.

"I got left at the lake by my foster parents," Vincent explained, flabbergasted at her beauty, because he only saw beautiful white women on television.

"Oh, that's too bad."

"Can I use your telephone?"

"Wait right here," she told Vincent, closing the door slightly.

There was absolute silence inside the house. Vincent

listened closely to a conversation near the front part. The sounds of a large dog barking came from the back.

"There's some mixed-race boy at the front door," the woman told her husband.

"What does he want?" the man asked.

"He says his foster parents left him at the lake."

"I see."

"He asked to use the telephone."

The woman returned to the door with her husband. He stood around six feet five, had a thin build, a dark bushy beard, and thick black hair that was pushed back. He cordially opened the door for Vincent and allowed him to come inside. Vincent stepped to the middle of their front room and was surrounded by shelves of books. It reminded him of being in a miniature library. Pens, pencils, erasers, and lots of paper were lying on a desk in the far left corner. The man introduced himself and the woman who answered the door. "My name's Theodore Wallenstein IV, and this is my wife, Stacey Wallenstein."

"My name's Vincent Carvelli, and I'm pleased to meet you," Vincent said, reaching forward to shake both of their hands.

"Ha! Ha!" Theodore laughed, throwing his head back and patting his wife across the back. "How did you get an Italian name like Carvelli?"

"My father's Italian." Vincent replied seriously.

"What nationality is your mother?" Theodore boldly asked, noticing the negro features in Vincent's face and hair.

"She's black."

"Black?"

"Yes, sir."

"Don't call me sir," Theodore said. "I prefer you to call me Theodore, because it makes me feel much younger."

"Okay, Theodore."

"I only asked you that, Vincent, because I'm Jewish and I

grew up with a lot of Italians on the near north side of Chicago."

"Jewish, huh?"

"Yes."

"Wasn't Jesus Jewish?" Vincent asked, sort of moving more towards religion.

"Yes, he was," Theodore said. "My wife tells me that your foster parents left you at the lake."

"Yes, they did."

"How long have you been in this foster home?" Theodore asked, getting sort of personal with Vincent.

"Since I was a baby," Vincent answered unobjectively.

"A baby, huh?"

"Yes, that's right."

"Where are your real parents?"

"I don't know."

"You don't know?"

"No, I don't know."

"Would you like to know what I do for a living?"

"Yes, I'd like to know."

"I'm a microbiology professor at The University of Chicago."

"That's cool."

"Would you like to know what my wife does?"

"Yes."

"Stacey teaches fifth grade at an elementary school."

"You're both teachers?"

"You've got it."

"Do you teach people about animals and plants and bugs?"

"Exactly," Theodore said, honored to be a well-educated man.

"You've got a lot of books in here," Vincent mentioned, revolving his head around the room.

"I must say so."

"I like to read."

"Are you hungry, Vincent?"

"A little."

Theodore's wife, Stacey, went into the kitchen to prepare Vincent something to eat. Vincent wanted to contact his home; Theodore handed him the phone. When Bessie Mae answered the phone, he explained that he was in a house somewhere by the lake. Theodore was handed the phone, and he gave Bessie Mae the directions to their home. Vincent sat forward on the leather recliner. Stacey returned with a salami sandwich and a glass of fruit punch. When Vincent finished, Theodore wanted him to come to the basement. They walked down the basement stairs and the area down there was huge. Inside a set of cages, there was a sight that Vincent considered breathtaking. They were considered Theodore's prize possessions.

"Where did you get these funny looking rabbits?" Vincent asked Theodore, stepping closer to the wide cages.

"They're not funny looking rabbits," Theodore corrected Vincent, then opening a cage to bring out one of the bushy animals.

"What are they?"

"They're called chinchillas."

"Chin who?"

"Chinchillas," Theodore said. "They're small, fur bearing rodents from South America."

"They make fur coats out of them?" Vincent asked.

"They sure do."

"I've never seen animals like these before."

"Go to South America, you'll see lots of them."

"Why do you have so many of them?" Vincent wondered, his eyes traveling around to every cage.

"A friend of mine's manufactures fur coats out of them."

"Wow!"

"It's exciting."

"My foster mother has a lot of fur coats."

"Does she have a chinchilla fur?"

"I don't think so."

"Would you like to hold one of them?"

"They don't bite, do they?"

"No, not at all," Theodore said, handing the small chinchilla over to Vincent. He rubbed the chinchilla gently across the back. Theodore took him around to every cage, showing him the young and old, the large and small. He even had cages that were used specifically for breeding. On top of one of the cages, there were several fur pelts. They were kept as souvenirs from the fur manufacturers. As a token of his gratitude, Theodore gave Vincent one of the pelts. He ran his fingers along the smooth fur of the pelt.

A loud car horn sounded in the front yard of the Wallenstein residence. Stacey came to the top of the basement stairs to inform Vincent that the Willingham couple had arrived. Bessie Mae and J.D. were waiting at the front door. Before returning upstairs, Theodore made sure that all cages were secure. He came into the front room and Stacey had gotten acquainted with the Willingham couple. They were introduced to Theodore and everyone was seen out of the house. Bessie Mae expressed many thanks to the Wallenstein couple for allowing Vincent to stay at their home. J.D. sped away so they could start their journey back home.

Chapter 31

DISCLOSURE

THE BIG DAY for Gilbert had finally come. He was all packed and his belongings were sitting at the doorway near the laundry room. This time, he didn't bluff when he said he would call his caseworker, requesting to be removed from the Willingham's foster home. When he called Sandra Maloney, she had a long talk with Bessie Mae, who had a long and grueling talking with J.D. They both agreed that he should be removed from their home.

It was early Monday morning and Vincent was getting ready for school. While rambling through his drawers, he searched for clothes that he wished he had. The basement door opened slowly. Bessie Mae shouted down the stairs, wanting Gilbert to come to the front room.

It wasn't long ago that Jose had left. Sandra was in the front room, sitting on the sofa having a friendly conversation with Bessie Mae. The Department of Children and Family Services wanted Sandra to take a position in the offices that would be a promotion. She wasn't sure if she would take the position. Gilbert and Vincent came upstairs with his belongings. Sandra told Gilbert that they had to make his departure quickly, because she had other foster children to check on. While throwing the suitcase in the backseat, Gilbert called Vincent to the front of Sandra's car.

"Does your brother Vernon still live at the Willingham's foster home?" Sandra asked Vincent.

"No, he doesn't," Vincent answered truthfully.

"Where does he live?"

"I don't know. He left here a long time ago."

"Why?"

"Him and Mrs. Willingham got into an argument."

"Why did they get into an argument?"

"She tried to take his whole paycheck away," Vincent confessed, shedding light on a matter that had been left in the dark for too long.

"Did you know that Mrs. Willingham was still getting checks from the state for keeping your brother Vernon?"

"No, I didn't know that."

"Well, she is."

"How did you find that out?" Vincent asked.

"Gilbert informed me today."

"Isn't she supposed to stop getting checks for keeping my brother?"

"Absolutely," Sandra made clear, staring seriously into Vincent's eyes.

"Couldn't Mrs. Willingham get into trouble for that?"

"Possibly."

"Why?"

"That's considered stealing from the system."

"Can't people go to jail for that?"

"It all depends."

"Depends on what?"

"Whether or not we could prove that she knowingly and willingly received the checks for keeping Vernon after he left this home."

"How would you do that?"

"Start an ongoing investigation."

"How would you do that?"

"It would be a long process."

"It'll take a long time?"

"Lots and lots of paperwork."

"Why?"

"We don't know the exact date that your brother Vernon left the Willingham foster home."

"I don't know exactly when Vernon left, but I know that it was a long time ago."

"Where's your brother now?"

"He joined the Air Force."

"When did he go into the Air Force?" Sandra asked.

"When he got out of school."

"How long has he been out of school?"

"A long time ago, that's all I know."

"Mrs. Willingham's robbing the system," Sandra clarified, a veteran caseworker who knew a crook when she stumbled upon one.

"What do you mean when you say she's stealing?" Vincent asked.

"Her checks should've been stopped when your brother left this home. She's been getting free money and she knows very well that that's illegal." Sandra had a real good point, but there were so many people across America who were getting this free government money, some receiving extra welfare checks and food stamps, constantly being indicted for fraud.

"Is Mrs. Willingham in trouble now?" Vincent asked, hoping that she would be questioned about the ordeal.

"She could very well be."

"What does that mean?"

"We'll soon find out."

Gilbert and Vincent could go on forever telling Sandra about all the illegalities going on inside the Willingham's foster home. Sandra had deadlines to meet, and Vincent had to make it to school on time. There wasn't much left to talk about between Gilbert and Vincent, because they spent most of the night talking about all the hardships that they'd experienced at the Willingham home. Unfortunately, Vincent was still faced with some of those same hardships. They embraced one another tightly for several moments. As a part of the regular pattern, the nosy neighbors up and down Milwaukee Parkway came out on their porches, anxious

to see which foster child was leaving the Willingham residence.

"I'm going to miss you, Gilbert," Vincent said sadly, patting Gilbert across the back.

"Same here, man," Gilbert said, also patting Vincent across the back.

"Come by and see me sometimes."

"I will."

"Things're going to be different now that you and Jose are gone."

"You'll be leaving here one day."

"Yes, but when?"

"Soon."

"I hope it's real soon."

"See you later, Vincent."

"Later, Gilbert."

As he watched the Mustang travel down Milwaukee Parkway, Vincent waved goodbye to Gilbert.

* * *

The noise inside the fifth hour social studies class had gotten out of control. At the third desk, in the fourth row, Vincent sat quietly. Their instructor, Mildred Kercheval, a short and medium complexioned woman, who wore goggle style glasses and an assortment of wigs, was considered one of the strictest women at George Washington Junior High. The noise rose to a higher level.

"Quiet down!" Mildred told her disruptive students, patting her hand lightly down on her desk. "Quiet down or I'm gonna start writing conference cards."

"Shut up, you old bitch!" one of the disruptive students yelled from the back of the class.

"Who said that?" Mildred asked, coming around her desk to look between the rows of students. No one in the classroom

admitted to saying the outlandish statement. Mildred didn't like being called a bitch, but she knew that some of Chicago's worst kids were in her class.

"Shut up, you old cockeyed weasel!"

"Alright, who said that?" Mildred asked, her vision poor from just old age.

"Sit down, you old crusty dirtbag!" shouted yet another student from the back.

"That's it!" Mildred shrugged. "The next time somebody calls me a name, I'm going to send the whole class to the principal's office. Is that understood, class?"

"Yes, Mrs. Kercheval," the entire class responded, sitting at their desks looking innocent.

Tonya Raymore, a bronze complexioned girl with glistening brown eyes, sat behind Vincent with her feet rested on the back of his seat. Tonya was different from most girls at George Washington, merely because she had a fully developed body as a seventh grader. Most boys at the school admired her curvaceous figure. Her feet nearly pressed against Vincent's posterior. Vincent turned around and gave Tonya the stare that he was experiencing some discomfort from her feet resting against his seat.

"Did you lose something?" Tonya asked, jerking forward in her chair as though she was going to hit Vincent.

"I can feel your feet on the back of my desk."

"So!"

"So, won't you take them off."

"I'll put my feet anywhere I want to."

In order to turn in the absenteeism list to the office on time, Mildred had to leave the classroom. Since there wasn't any instructor present, the rowdy students stirred up much chaos. They threw textbooks at one another. They used foul language in the jokes they old and obscenities in describing certain people and objects. Some even went to the blackboard and wrote offensive words. To make matters worse,

three students ran out in the hallway and screamed down the hall.

Students like Vincent, who refused to be part of the pandemonium, had his head buried in his social studies textbook. Mildred wanted her class to read an upcoming chapter on the Native Americans. Tonya had her right leg drawn back. She powerfully kicked the back of Vincent's seat. The impact caused his seat to bump the girl in front of him, which was the second seat in the fourth row. She ignored what had happened and continued what she was doing.

The classroom instigators stopped what they were doing. They would do anything to cause a fight between Tonya and Vincent. She kicked his chair again and he turned around. She leaned forward with those brown eyes bucked wide.

"What are you gonna do, you half-white sissy?" Tonya challenged Vincent, leaning further over her seat, snarling her nose up.

"Why don't you stop kicking my desk?" Vincent pleaded, trying to review the chapter before Mildred returned.

"I'll kick it again, you half-breed punk."

"I'm not a half-breed."

"Yes, you are."

"Why are you trying to start a fight with me?" Vincent asked, his nervous heart beating fast.

"Because you're a pussy," Tonya said, trying to strike fear into Vincent.

"I can tell you where that's at."

"You can't tell me nothing, you half-breed faggot."

"The pussy is between your legs!" Vincent snarled ferociously, turning red all over his face.

"You punk!"

"You bitch!"

"You high yellow sissy!"

"You fat ugly pig!"

The classmates jumped around in their seats. They cheered Tonya on. Vincent never liked fighting. He actually couldn't fight. Trouble was on the rise! Tonya bent both legs backwards and kicked Vincent's seat again. It caused a greater impact than the first time, because the two seats in front of him were bumped. She had gone too far this time. Vincent stood up, pointed directly into Tonya's face, and in a hard voice, he told her, "You better stop kicking on my chair, you black ugly bitch!"

"What're you gonna do, you half-white pussy?" Tonya said, jumping out of her seat, bucking right up to Vincent. 'Pussy' seemed to be Tonya's favorite word. Where did she learn to say the word?

"I'm gonna kick your ass!"

"Here it is, kick it," Tonya dared, who was practically glued to Vincent's body.

"I really don't want to fight you, Tonya."

"But, I want to fight you."

"Why don't you sit down?"

"You're scared, punk!"

"Of what?"

"Getting your ass kicked."

Tonya and Vincent waited to see who would throw the first punch. Moving around in circles, they had both fists balled up. Their bodies were pressed together like glue and paper. Almost all the classmates were in Tonya's corner.

"Kick his ass, Tonya!" shouted one-half of the classroom, loud cheers and the pounding of desk tops sounding off.

"Kick his half-breed, white-honky ass!" instigated another half of the classroom.

From the doorway, one of the classmates informed everyone that Mildred Kercheval was coming. They ran to their seats and pretended as though nothing happened. The discrepancy between Tonya and Vincent ended. Mildred walked into the classroom and told everyone to turn to the chapter

on the Native Americans. They turned to the designated chapter and she read over the first four pages.

In a loud tone, the bell rang. Tonya and the other classmates rushed out of the classroom. They waited for Vincent to come out, but he stalled for time. Since everyone was on Tonya's side, Vincent felt that he was against incredible odds. As much as he dreaded, he walked out of the classroom and Tonya threw her books and pens to the ground.

"What're you gonna do now, you half-breed pussy?" Tonya brisked, pointing to the middle of Vincent's face, wishing he'd throw the first punch.

"What're you gone do, you ugly black bitch?" Vincent reciprocated, pointing right back in her face, waiting to see what she would do first.

"I'm going to kick your ass."

"You're going to get your ass kicked."

"Here I am."

"No, here I am."

Suddenly, Tonya rushed Vincent, swinging and kicking wildly. She hit him several times across the head and chest. After his books fell to the ground, he retaliated by landing a few blows right across Tonya's forehead and lower jaw. Like fans at a heavyweight championship fight, the exchange of blows had everyone around cheering. Vincent backed away and Tonya charged him like a raging bull. She rammed his head against the lockers behind him. He was able to grab her into a headlock and held a tight grip. She tried breaking loose by steadily ramming his head against the lockers. Vincent wouldn't let go. Using the hand that was free, Vincent sank his fingernails into Tonya's forehead.

"Kick his white ass, Tonya!" the spectators standing around harshly commented, jumping up and down like they were at a world series game.

It was evident that the students at George Washington Junior High weren't too fond of mixed-race people like

Vincent. There were others that they picked on who were bi-racial, but Vincent happened to be their main target. Was there racism that existed with the black race? Was it the black-on-black racism that black leaders spoke of over the years?

Rushing down the hall was a science instructor named Earl Butler. Earl forced himself between Tonya and Vincent and separated them. Tonya's forehead was bleeding from the deep clawing of Vincent's fingernails. Blood trickled down onto her face.

"Somebody take this girl to the nurse's office!" Earl ordered, holding Tonya around the waist, watching the bleeding on her forehead continue.

"Where's the nurse's office, Mr. Butler?" a group of students asked, those who were gathered around Tonya.

"It's on the first floor."

"Where on the first floor?"

"Down the hall from the main office."

"We don't know where that is."

"Look for the sign above the door," Earl instructed the students.

Tonya was taken down to the nurse's office. In the meantime, Earl had his hand clamped around Vincent's arm. He was highly upset, and it showed.

"What are you doing fighting girls?" Earl asked Vincent, pulling him by the arm while escorting him to the first floor.

"She started it, Mr. Butler," Vincent rejoined, his entire face as red as a ripe apple.

"You're not supposed to be fighting girls, young man."

"But she hit me first."

"I don't care," Earl said. "You're supposed to walk away from things like that."

"But she started swinging at me."

"It doesn't make no difference."

"My foster mother always told me to fight people back."

"I'm sure she didn't tell you to fight girls."

"Yes, she did."

"I don't believe that."

"Where are we going, Mr. Butler?"

"I'm taking you to the principal's office."

"We're going to Mr. Goldberg's office?" Vincent asked, who'd never had to go to the principal's office for anything.

"That's right, young man."

"But..."

"Sorry, but you have to go."

Earl walked into the school office with Vincent. One of the secretaries was informed that Vincent had been fighting. He was told to step into the principal's office. Minutes later, Tonya walked in with three bandages taped across her forehead. The school principal, Harold Goldberg, sat behind a large oak desk. As he stared at Tonya and Vincent, he scratched through his snow white hair, brushed his snow white mustache, and glided his hands across his wrinkled face. As the principal of George Washington for more than twenty years, he had dealt with many students who had gotten into fights. His office was gloomy. The moment was dead silent. Tonya and Vincent sat restlessly on the other side of his desk.

"Alright, Miss Raymore," Principal Goldberg paused. "I want you to explain to me what happened."

"Okay, it's like this, Mr. Goldberg," Tonya said. "When we were in Mrs. Kercheval's social studies class, I had my feet on the back of Vincent's chair and he got mad."

"What happened next?"

"Vincent jumped up and told me that I better take my feet off his chair."

"Did you give him any reason to jump up out of his seat?"

"No, I didn't."

"What happened after he jumped up?" Harold asked.

"He wanted to fight me."

"Who threw the first punch?"

"Vincent did."

"Did you rehearse this story before you came into my office?"

"No, no, I didn't."

"Are you sure?" Harold asked, his blue Jewish eyes burning right through the lying eyes of Tonya.

"Yes."

"What happened to your forehead?"

"Vincent scratched me with his fingernails."

"How bad was it?"

"The nurse had to put some alcohol on it."

Harold turned to Vincent. He wanted to hear another side of the story. Vincent moved forward in his chair and looked Harold directly in his face.

"She's lying, Mr. Goldberg!" Vincent charged, jerking his head sideways to glance furiously into the weary eyes of Tonya. "Tonya kept kicking the back of my chair and I told her to stop."

"What happened next, Vincent?"

"She wouldn't stop."

"And?"

"I jumped out of my seat and told her what I would have to do."

"What did you do after that?"

"Everybody sit down after Mrs. Kercheval came back into the class."

"When did the both of you start fighting?"

"When the bell rang and we got out into the hallway."

"Is that when Mr. Butler broke you two apart?"

"Yes, sir."

"What about this name calling?"

"Tonya was calling me names like *pussy* and *punk* and *sissy* and *faggot*."

"Hey, hey, watch your language young man."

"But, that's what she kept calling me."

"I know, but you didn't have to be so detailed."

Instantly, the office became quiet. It appeared that Harold was trying to make a decision. Tonya and Vincent ferociously stared into one another's eyes. Was this a love-hate discrepancy? Did they like one another? Tonya began breathing like she was about to explode.

"He's the liar!" Tonya shouted in the silent office, pointing right into Vincent's face. "He kept calling me names like *fat bitch* and *ugly bitch* and *slut.*"

"You're the one who's lying!" Vincent shouted back, then pointing his finger right back into Tonya's face.

"We can ask the people in Mrs. Kercheval's class."

"They're gonna lie for you, anyway."

"No, they're not."

"Yes, they are."

"Shut your mouth!"

"Why don't you shut your mouth!"

Harold Goldberg stood up, slammed his fist down on the desk, then pointed at Tonya and Vincent, and demandingly said, "Be quiet! The both of you!" There's two sides to every story. I'm going to call your parents and let them know what happened."

Harold pulled their student files and reviewed them briefly. On the other side of his desk, Tonya and Vincent sat calmly. Since Vincent's file was on top, Harold decided to call his home number first. He dialed the number and waited for an answer. After the first few rings, someone answered.

"Hello," Bessie Mae answered from inside the kitchen.

"Hello, Mrs. Carvelli," Harold said in a low voice, staring across the desk at Vincent. Vincent nodded his head, because he knew that Bessie Mae wasn't a Carvelli.

"I'm Bessie Mae Willingham," Bessie Mae rectified. "May I ask whom I'm speaking with?"

"My name's Harold Goldberg."

"Yes?"

"I'm the principal of George Washington Junior High."

"Is Vincent in some type of trouble?" Bessie Mae asked.

"Actually, he is," Harold told Bessie Mae. "He got into a fight with a young lady named Tonya Raymore."

"What is he doing fighting?"

"That's why I have them in my office."

"Why is he fighting girls?"

"Good question."

"What were they fighting about?"

"It had something to do with Tonya having her feet on the back of Vincent's seat."

"Every since Vincent was a little boy, he's had problems with fighting girls."

"That's what you get for having a handsome son," Harold joked.

"I guess."

"Are you Vincent's stepmother?" Harold asked.

"No, I'm his foster mother."

"Oh, you're his foster mother?" Harold repeated, glancing stronger than ever at Vincent. Vincent bowed his head in complete shame.

"I've been his foster mother since he was a baby."

"Since he was an infant?"

"Yes."

After Harold spoke with Tonya's mother, he sent she and Vincent back to class. It was the seventh and final hour of school. Vincent stopped at his locker on the third floor. Students walking past his locker made insulting remarks like, "Vincent got his ass kicked by a girl!" Some of the others were shouting, "Tonya kicked Vincent's white ass!"

At this point, there was that possibility that Vincent had gained a reputation for getting beat up by girls. School ended and Tonya was waiting at the front doors of the school. She was surrounded by nearly half of the students at George Washington. They waited for Vincent to make his presence.

At the opposite end of the school, Vincent happened to be walking out of the doors that led to the street.

Someone out of the crowd spotted him. They rushed down the hallway towards his direction. Like a contagious disease, Tonya had spread the news about Vincent living in a foster home. Living in a foster home and his classmates knowing about it was one of his worst nightmares. A small riot was formed by a group of junior high schoolers. They began releasing a titanic of insults.

"Roots! Roots! Roots!" the crowd of seventh and eighth graders began chanting, referring to the movie made famous by Alex Haley, which depicted the brutalities of slavery.

"Leave me alone!" Vincent cried, having immediate flashbacks of the humiliation that he suffered at Abraham Lincoln Elementary, especially when Jerry Grayson and Clinton Marks followed him home and discovered that he lived in a foster home with handicapped men.

"Don't beat me, master!" they joked unconsciously, mocking the slave owners portrayed in the movie. "Don't beat me, Master Carvelli!"

"Stop it!" Vincent rumbled, walking faster to try and get away.

"I'll be a good nigger, Master Carvelli!"

"Shut up!"

"Vincent is an orphan! Vincent is an orphan!" Tonya and her classmates chanted repeatedly, galloping closer to Vincent as he walked up the street.

"I'm not an orphan!"

"Vincent is an oprhaned, half-white punk!"

"Quit calling me an orphan!"

Vincent got closer to his home, and Braun was on the porch beating the middle of his hand with one of his wires. The slapping of the wire against his tough skin were enough to stop Tonya and the others. Braun smiled and showed all of his grimy black teeth.

"Yuck!" Tonya frowned, afraid to step any further. "What's all that black junk on that man's teeth?"

"Look like he's been chewing tobacco," someone from the back said.

"Why's he beating his hand with that wire?" Tonya asked, moving further back among the crowd.

"I know his hand probably hurts."

"All of his teeth are rotten."

"They're blacker than tar."

Like a freak in the Ringling Brothers and Barnum Bailey Circus, the crowd of youngsters stared exclusively at Braun. They weren't aware that he was just a harmless, mentally retarded man, someone who ate tobacco out of old cigarette butts and beat the middle of his right hand with a thick hanger wire. Vincent ran up the side stairs and right into the house.

*   *   *

Bessie Mae was waiting in the front room. She was obviously upset, because a distraught expression was on her face. Sitting at the edge of the sofa, she took a quick drag off her cigarette and said, "Who told those people down at the family services that I was still getting checks for keeping Vernon?"

"I don't know," Vincent answered uncertainly.

"Then, who was it?"

"It wasn't me."

"I'll bet'cha it was Gilbert," Bessie Mae said. "I'm glad they took that thuggish black bastard away from here."

Bessie Mae was highly upset, simply because Gilbert had blown her cover. Sandra Maloney moved faster than anyone would have thought. The check that Bessie Mae once got for keeping Vernon, would be no more, thanks to Gilbert speaking up. Sandra informed higher authorities down at the Cook County family services division.

Chapter 32

RUNAWAY

PROBLEMS FOR VINCENT at the Willingham residence increased. Vincent's caseworker, Jason Richburg, made several home visits and discovered that there was serious friction between Bessie Mae and Vincent. Bessie Mae tried convincing Jason that Vincent had gotten out of control. Jason drew up an agreement that read as follows:

AGREEMENT

In the interest of: Vincent Carvelli

I, Vincent Carvelli, agree to abide by the following conditions:

1. If I am allowed to leave the house evenings, I will let my foster mother know when I am leaving, where I will be going, and when I will return. I will never stay out past 8:45 p.m., unless I get special permission.

2. I will make my bed every day and keep my room clean.

3. I will help feed the dogs, pick up the trash, and work in the yard as part of my contribution to the household.

I, Bessie Mae Willingham, agree to abide by the following conditions:

1. *I will continue to provide for Vincent's needs, such as meals and shelter.*

2. *I will support and reward Vincent for performing chores and at other times when it is appropriate.*

3. *I will enforce Vincent's curfew hours of 8:45 p.m., unless I give special permission for late hours.*

I, Jason Richburg, agree to assist and support Vincent and Mrs. Willingham in following the conditions stated above.

Bessie Mae felt that Vincent wasn't adhering to this agreement. According to her, he started developing strange behavior. She took him to see a psychiatrist at The Cook County Children's Hospital. While inside the office, Bessie Mae told the psychiatrist the following things:

"Doctor, he puts hot food in his mouth. He still wets the bed and he just turned fourteen. When I call him, he acts as though he doesn't hear me."

The psychiatrist listened to Vincent's life history. Not once was Vincent asked any questions. The following information was recorded as a result of the evaluation:

THE COOK COUNTY
CHILDREN'S HOSPITAL

I consent for Vincent Carvelli to receive medical evaluation and treatment today for the condition that necessitated this visit or for any other condition that is discussed with me during this visit. I authorize the release of medical and social information to any appropriate health, welfare, or community agency and the taking of photographs for medical purposes.

MEDICAL CLINIC

CHIEF COMPLAINT: *Foster mother states social worker said Vincent needs to see a psychiatrist. The foster mother states that the child is hard to manage at home and that he has a defensive attitude. She said that he gets into fights regularly at school. Recently, he had a fight with a girl at school, and as a result, the social worker referred him to the psychiatric clinic. The foster mother also stated that he gets along okay at home, but doesn't do much around the house. As an eighth grader, Vincent does okay, but doesn't really like school, except for his friends and girlfriend, who are in the same classes. She states that he does nothing in his spare time, and after his homework is done, he just sits around the house and stares at the walls. The foster mother believes that Vincent might be using cigarettes, pot, or other heavy street drugs. Also, he may drink a beer, maybe two or three times a week.*

Throughout the entire evaluation, Vincent's confidence was never shattered. He had nothing to prove to the psychiatrist, Bessie Mae, or anyone else. He knew that he wasn't smoking drugs or drinking any type of alcohol. Who dreamed

up these lies? In the end, Bessie Mae was the liar. During the evaluation, Vincent wanted to tell the psychiatrist that part of his problems stemmed from being sexually molested by his foster sister. It seemed as though it was one secret that he would take to his grave. Vincent felt that Bessie Mae was the one who was emotionally disturbed.

Vincent's philosophy was: *"Anybody who stays in this foster home long enough, will end up going crazy anyway."*

*   *   *

Bessie Mae shouted for Vincent to come and feed the dogs. With an angry look on his face, he left the backyard and came into the kitchen. He pouted as he walked towards the slopbucket. Bessie Mae closely observed his facial expression and awkward body movement. Vincent walked out of the kitchen mumbling different words. He didn't mumble low enough. Bessie Mae thought she might've heard some things that he said. Surprisingly, she didn't respond, allowing him to go out to the dogpen. The slopbucket was filled close to the top. From the kitchen window facing the side of the house, Bessie Mae watched Vincent spill some of the food on the ground.

"Stop swinging that bucket like that!" Bessie Mae shouted out to Vincent, pressing her face close to the screen.

"This bucket's heavy, Mrs. Willingham," Vincent replied, turning to look up at the window, a strained look on his face.

"You're dropping food all over the ground, boy!"

"I can't help it. Can't you see that?"

"I can see J.D. beating the hell out of you with his extension cord."

"Whatever!" Vincent said disobediently, purposely swinging more food to the ground.

"Don't get smart, you yellow bastard!" Bessie Mae fired back, pointing her finger on the screen. "I wanna hear you get smart when J.D. comes home."

Vincent made it to the dogpen, leaving trails of food that started from the side stairs. Bessie Mae limped over to the window facing the backyard. Her view of Vincent was perfect. He bent down to pour out the mass of slop. The beagles rushed over to the pan, growling at one another as they made their choice of portions. They wasted no time sinking their teeth into the leftover table scraps. After every drop of food fell out of the bucket, Vincent locked the pen, wiped his feet off in the grass, and walked through the backyard dragging the bucket on the ground.

"Stop dragging that bucket on the ground!" Bessie Mae opposed, blowing a long drag of cigarette smoke through the screen, pointing her finger right down at Vincent.

"I'm not dragging the bucket!" Vincent abruptly responded, kicking his feet while traveling towards the side of the house.

"I'm sitting here watching you drag that bucket, boy!" Bessie Mae observed. "Are you trying to call me a liar?"

"No, but you're calling me a liar."

Vincent faded out of the backyard and came to the waterhose on the side of the house. Bits and pieces of food were stuck at the bottom and on the sides of the bucket. He took the jet gun and sprayed all around the bucket. Water splashed on the windows near the dining room and kitchen. The bricks were dripping with lots of water.

"Stop splashing that water on this house!" Bessie Mae shouted from the kitchen window facing the side of the house.

"I'm cleaning the bucket out, Mrs. Willingham!" Vincent shouted back, irritated from Bessie Mae's constant scolding.

"You clean that bucket out everyday, and you don't ever splash that much water on the house."

"The bucket's real dirty."

"It ain't that dam dirty."

"Yes, it is," Vincent argued, still splashing water every direction.

"No, it's not."

"How would you know?"

"Because I know, you yellow sonofabitch!"

Vincent was absolutely fed up with Bessie Mae's demands. She became extremely annoying. Stop this! Stop that! Don't do this! Don't do that! In her opinion, he may have been a *"yellow this"* or a *"yellow that"*, but in his personal opinion, she was still a greedy and arrogant woman, a crippled bitch who was selfish.

The slopbucket was spotless, and he carried it back into the kitchen. The second that he arrived in the kitchen, Bessie Mae was sitting at her favorite spot at the kitchen table. She looked like an atomic bomb ready to explode in his face.

"What's wrong with you, boy!" Bessie Mae snapped, blowing a thick drag of smoke right into Vincent's face.

"Nothing's wrong with me," Vincent answered belligerently, holding the bucket down by his right side.

"Why can't your yellow ass act right?"

"I am acting right."

"No, you're not."

"Why do you keep calling me those yellow names?"

"That's what you are, Vincent."

"No, I'm not."

"Do you want me to call Jason?"

"Jason Richburg?"

"Yes."

"My caseworker?"

"Yes, your goddam caseworker!"

"I don't know."

"Going to see that psychiatrist wasn't enough?"

"I don't know."

"Are you happy being here?"

"I don't know."

"What do you mean, you don't know?"

"I don't know if I'm happy or not."

"Don't you know that you can leave when you get ready?"

"No."

"Ain't nobody forcing you to stay here."

"I know."

"You can pack up all of your shit and get the hell out of here."

Vincent left the smoke filled kitchen. He stepped onto the porch and there was J.D., his shiny black face looking angry, swinging his lunchbucket and strutting in his tarred blue uniform. J.D. was the last person that Vincent wanted to see after dealing with Bessie Mae. It depressed him to see his foster father come home with the same red watery eyes, the chapped, puckered lips, and heavy breathing. They passed one another without saying a word. J.D. went into the kitchen and took a seat at the table. Bessie Mae and Granny Dear were overjoyed to see him. He fired up a Pall Mall Gold and leaned back in the chair. As always, he complained about the white people on his job, how they supposedly mistreated blacks when it came to the work and getting promotions.

"How did your day go, J.D.?" Bessie Mae asked.

"Same ole shit," J.D. complained, wiping the thicks oils and sweat off his face.

"What happened now?"

"Boss mane don't wanna give ma no waise."

"Boss man? No raise?"

"Yep."

"Have you talked to him about a raise?"

"All da time."

"Stay on him about your raises."

"Dey make us colored folks walk in da tar all da time."

"What do they make the white folks do?"

"Easy thangs."

"Like what?"

"Handin us da tar paper and working in da office."

"That's a bunch of crap."

Braun, Junior, and Vincent were called to dinner. After smoking his cigarette, J.D. went to lie down on a big cot that was right behind Junior's seat. In an evil manner, he rolled over and glanced up at Junior. He was eating at a moderate rate, so J.D. rolled the other direction and shut his eyes. J.D. rolled over again to take a second glance. This time, Junior wasn't eating at all. His fork sat in the plate of tuna casserole.

"Eat yo goddam food, Joanyer!" J.D. yelled, unbuckling his belt and sliding it off his massive waist, and then forming a loop in his hand.

"Eat your food. Eat your food," Junior repeated, picking the fork up and scooping it down into the casserole.

"Quit peating everythang I say."

"Quit repeating what you say. Quit repeating what you say."

"Put dat food in yo mouth."

"Put the food in the mouth. Put the food in the mouth."

Junior was still able to repeat some of J.D.'s badly mispronounced words. Quickly, Junior scooped a portion of the casserole on the fork and took a bite. J.D. sat aside to observe, trying to see if he would eat at a rate that was suitable for him. Looking from a side view to see if the fork was moving, he had the belt drawn back, ready to strike at any second. Junior had the spoon lodged halfway in his mouth. Because he had no teeth, he pressed down on the food with his gums, trying to break part of it off.

Junior was struck harshly across the middle of his back with a stroke from J.D.'s powerful arm. His already reddish complexion turned even redder. Every muscle in his face rippled. Both arms flew up into the air and his back twisted from side to side. The painful impact from the belt had him moaning. J.D. lied down and rolled over towards the wall.

Apparently, the stinging from the thrash dissipated. Junior tried finishing his meal. Vincent was on the other side of the table feeling great sympathy for him.

Vincent asked himself, "Why is Mr. Willingham always picking on Junior?"

J.D. rolled over facing the table to check on Junior again. He was eating slow. J.D. raised up and reached for the belt. Like before, the fork was lodged halfway in his mouth.

"Eat yo goddam food, Joanyer!" J.D. warned Junior, becoming extremely intolerable. He cocked his right arm back and waited a second.

"Eat the food, Junior. Eat the food, Junior," Junior said repetitiously, sliding the fork further into his mouth.

"What's yo muttapucking problem, Joanyer!" J.D. asked, drawing back further with the belt.

"What's the problem, Junior? What's the problem, Junior?"

"Put dat food on dat foke."

"Put the food on the fork. Put the food on the fork."

Again, J.D. thrashed Junior across the back. Junior dropped the fork down into the plate. Only this time, he jerked his head back, moved his shoulders in circular motions, greatly trying to ease the sting from the belt. He bit down on his lower lip. Tuna juices from the casserole and thick saliva ran down his chin and part of his neck. He made low moaning noises, almost resembling that of a crying baby whose mouth was covered.

J.D. gradually slid the belt across the cot. He was prepared to strike Junior again. He ate slow, so J.D. whacked him again. His body displayed that of sheer affliction. Vincent was across the table crying. The sensitive spirit came to pay

him another visit. The tears were so heavy until they fell into his plate of casserole. He couldn't help but sob for a help-less, retarded man like Junior. He tried minimizing the agony from the thick and wide belt of J.D.

Vincent started having homicidal fantasies. He pictured himself taking a large butcher knife and splitting J.D. from the top of his head and on down to his feet. It was exhilirating for Vincent to imagine J.D. lying in a pool of blood and no one there to help him. Since he was convinced that Junior would eat at a desirable rate, J.D. laid the belt under the cot and rolled over facing the wall. When he finished dinner, Vincent ragefully stormed out the front door. He ran wildly down the street. There were feelings about his foster home that he had been holding in for a long time. So many feel-ings he had bottled up as a result of abuse and neglect. Bessie and J.D. never cared one way or another. For Vincent, enough was enough.

He thought of many harsh statements like:

"I'm sick of this motherfucking foster home!"
"I'm sick of Mrs. Willingham's crippled ass!"
"I'm sick of Mr. Willingham's fat, black ass!"
"I'm sick of seeing mentally retarded people dogged out!"
"I wanna get the fuck out of this insane foster home!"
"I wanna shoot Mr. Willingham and watch him die!"
"I wanna slap Mrs. Willingham until she walks straight!"
"I wanna leave here, just like Valerie, Vernon, Sean, Gilbert, Jose, and anybody else who left this crazy foster home!"

*   *   *

Vincent had reached a conclusion. He had decided to run away from a home that he considered to have no feelings or affections for the foster children and handicapped men. Vincent was running away, but did not know where he was running to. Actually, there was no one he could run to. There weren't any dependable relatives, church members, friends, or associates.

As he walked down the street, he kicked soda cans and rocks along his path. His estranged eyes were buried into the pavement. A weary expression occupied his face. He came to an intersection and the lights turned red. Cars traveling along the intersection noticed the confused Vincent. They sadly saw the loathsomeness on his face and the fatigued contour of his posture. These motorists knew that he was wandering aimlessly.

The light turned green and he crossed the street dragging his feet. Both hands were stuffed in his pockets. His head swayed back and forth, as he turned to stare at the houses on opposite sides of the street. The journey continued until he came to several busy streets that stretched north and south. Vincent had the option of going either way.

To turn around and start the trip back towards Milwaukee would defeat his purpose, so he made a left turn and started walking towards one of the busy streets that led up to one of the congested highways. Nearly three blocks from where Vincent stood, there were several exits where the highway had split into different sections. Once he walked those three blocks, he began his journey down one of the noisy and polluted highways.

His head was hung low, kicking loose gravel in his path. He ignored the loud cars and trucks speeding down the road. Just like the world around him, Vincent didn't care. After covering more than three miles, his feet got tired. The

effects from the hard and rocky pavement had the soles of his feet aching. This definitely called for a rest. He leaned against one of the guard railings, watching the mass of cars and trucks jet down the highway.

There were those motorists who knew a runaway. There were those who could only speculate. Vincent didn't care. For once in his life, he felt free. He freely viewed the constant flow of traffic. The three miles of traveling down the highway caused him to stretch out on the rocks, glass, and sticks. Had Vincent lost his mind? Two highway patrolmen were driving on the same side of the highway where Vincent was laying. They turned on their flashers and began slowing down.

Vincent swiftly jumped up and continued walking up the road. After everything seemed okay, they sped up the highway. Further and further, Vincent traveled up the congested highway. He had no idea where he would end up. Less than two city blocks up the road, a group of men were working on a construction site. It wasn't unusual, because Chicago's highways were always in need of repair. Some operated heavy construction machinery, while others had tools to dig around the pavement.

Vincent came within a half-block radius and one of the construction workers stopped his machine. In a strange manner, he observed Vincent walking his direction. He climbed out of the machine and stepped closer to the road. Walking along Chicago's busy highways weren't the safest thing to do, and he knew it.

"Are you lost, son?" the man asked in a kind voice, walking closer to Vincent.

"I'm running away from home," Vincent answered honestly, a dull tone ringing in his voice.

"Running away?" he said. "What're you doing that for, son?"

"I don't wanna live where I'm at no more."

"Why come?"

"I'm tired of being in this foster home that I'm in," Vincent explained, frustration filling his speech.

"Where's this foster home at?"

"Milwaukee Parkway."

"What's the exact address?"

"Thirty-Eight, Thirty-Eight, Milwaukee Parkway."

"Tell me, truthfully, why are you running away?"

"My foster mother is real mean to me."

"Is she?"

"My foster father is real mean to me, too."

"Is he?"

"Yes."

"How're they mean to you?"

"They curse at me."

"Do they?"

"They beat me all the time."

"Why?"

"No reason."

"Why are they keeping you in their home?"

"They only keep me for the money."

"They do?"

"And they keep mentally retarded people for the money."

"What's your name, son?"

"Vincent Carvelli."

"My name's Reverend James Driscoll," the strange man said, dusting off his hand to make his acquaintance with Vincent.

"Are you a preacher?"

"I'm the pastor of Starlight Baptist Church."

"Where's that at?" Vincent asked.

"It's on the south side of Chicago."

"Are there a whole lot of people who go to your church?"

"We have quite a few members," James said. "Can you wait until I get off work?"

"I don't know."

"Don't be afraid of me," James told Vincent, an innocent look filling his eyes. "I wouldn't hurt you, son."

"Why do you want me to wait?"

"I wanna take you back home."

"I'm not going back there."

"Why, son?"

"I don't never wanna go back to that crazy home!"

"It can't be that bad."

"Yes, it is."

"I'm sure you can sit down and work things out with your foster parents."

"No, I couldn't."

"All you have to do is tell them about some of the things that you disagree with."

"They won't listen to me, Mr. Driscoll."

"Please, call me Reverend Driscoll."

"Alright, Reverend Driscoll," Vincent said. "I've been living in this foster home all of my life, and they haven't listened to me yet."

"I'll be getting off in a few minutes. Please, wait right here."

James Driscoll said lots of things to try and convince Vincent to return home, but he was thoroughly convinced that he didn't want to live with the Willinghams anymore. He went down to the machine and shut it off. In the kindest manner, he threw his arm around Vincent's neck and promised him that everything would be okay.

"Guess what I have for you?" James said gleefully to Vincent, reaching into his pocket for something.

"What's that?" Vincent asked.

"Here's a dollar for you."

"Thank you, Reverend Driscoll!"

"Now, will you let me take you back home?" James Driscoll asked, using the crisp dollar bill as a positive reinforcer.

"Yes, sir."

"Are you gonna talk to your foster parents when you get home?"

"Yes, sir."

Parked up the road was James Driscoll's money green Cadillac El Dorado. Vincent climbed in on the passenger's side and sank into the plush leather seats. The smell of strawberry air freshener filled the inside. Since James was a minister, he turned the radio on to a gospel station. The flow of traffic was heavy. Most people had just gotten off work and were in a rush to get home. When traffic slowed up, they made an exit to the left. Milwaukee Parkway wasn't far away. James sensed that something was wrong. Vincent sat quietly in the seat with the dollar bill pressed between his hands.

"What's wrong, son?" James asked, studying the nervous expression on the face of Vincent.

"Nothing," Vincent answered blatantly, his hands perspiring heavily.

"Everything's gonna be alright, son."

"I guess."

"You seem scared to death."

"I'm okay."

"Trust me, everything's gonna work out fine."

Vincent's mind was cluttered with frightful thoughts. At that moment, he wished that Milwaukee Parkway didn't even exist on the map. James Driscoll drove to the corner of Milwaukee and parked on the opposite side of the street. J.D. saw James and Vincent coming across the street. He pushed the screen door open with great force and threw both hands around his waist. Bessie Mae had already informed him that Vincent ran away when she couldn't find him nowhere around the house or along the block. Vincent came to the porch stairs and J.D. was looking like he wanted to strangle him with his extension cord. Bessie Mae came to the door

and stood right behind J.D. Vincent knew that he was in serious trouble.

"How do you do, sir?" James said to J.D., extending his arm to shake hands.

"I'm doing alwight," J.D. said. "How bout ya'self?"

"I'm fine, thank you," James smiled. "I saw your foster son walking along the highway, and I knew he was probably lost or running away."

"Thank ya very much," J.D. acknowledged. "He ain't gone be runnin way no mo."

"Take care of yourself, sir," James told J.D., waving goodbye to Vincent and taking off in his car.

"Ya do da same."

J.D. held the screen door open, then pointed right towards the dining room. Vincent wouldn't move a muscle.

"Git in dis house, Vinsun," J.D. demanded, swinging the screen door backwards.

"I'm not coming in there, Mr. Willingham!" Vincent screeched, standing there trembling, biting his nails, and moving further away from the porch.

"Git yo ass in dis house."

"No."

"Now!"

"I told you, I'm not coming in there."

"Don't make ma come down dere."

"I'm still not coming in there."

"Ya want ma ta go git ma stanching code?"

"You can go and get your extension cord."

"I'm goin ta get ma stanching code."

The only thing that crossed Vincent's mind was another vicious beating. Vincent was fourteen years old, and he was tired of getting beatings. There had to be other ways to be disciplined. J.D. stepped onto the porch, holding the screen door open with his left leg, pointing into the house. It wasn't

easy trying to persuade the stubbornly frightened Vincent. J.D. and Vincent closely watched one another's moves.

When J.D. moved forward, Vincent moved backwards. He eventually took off running down Milwaukee Parkway. Because of his evil ego, J.D. wasn't about to let his foster son run away twice. He dashed upstairs to grab his extension cord, which was lying on the side of their closet. Afterwards, he jumped into his truck and sped off down Milwaukee.

An instant, yet painful memory entered his mind as he was speeding up the street. Everytime he wanted to inflict punishment upon someone else, he remembered the punishment that his malicious father, Henry Willingham, would gladly inflict upon him. Having these excruciatingly painful memories became an endless pattern, like a generational curse that always came back to haunt him.

*   *   *

"What I do dis time, pappa?" J.D. asked Henry, afraid to come inside their shack, facing another one of Henry's vicious beatings.

"Git yo hiney in dis house, J.D.," Henry told J.D., holding his long black strap down by his side.

"But I didden do nuttin, pappa."

"Don't try and run from ma, boy!"

"Why ya gone beat ma dis time, pappa?"

"Git in dis house, niggah!"

"I ain't wantin ta come in da house, pappa."

"I'm gone beat da skin off yo hide."

"Pease, pease, don't beat ma dis this time, pappa."

"Me and yo mammy gone make ya mind us."

"I does mind ya, pappa."

"Naw ya don't, J.D."

"Yeah I does, pappa!"

*   *   *

Vincent was nowhere in sight. Near the corner of Rush Boulevard, he was trying to flag cars down. It was useless, because it was like he didn't even exist. The cars moved along the median. Vincent was definitely feeling the squeeze of a cold and cruel world. He desperately tried to find someone who would help, anyone who would rescue him from another vicious beating. J.D. was less than a block away. He sped near Rush, swurving around other cars like he had an emergency in the truck. Vincent ran further up Rush. An obese man with a long beard on a Harley Davidson motorcycle was caught at one of the lights. The opportunity couldn't have been better.

"Help me sir, please!" Vincent pleaded, pulling on the biker's faded blue jeans.

"What's wrong with you?" the biker asked, revving up his motorcycle's engine, ready to take off when the light turned green.

"My foster father's gonna beat me!"

"I can't help you, son," the rough-looking biker said, shunning Vincent like he was the plague.

"You've got to help me, sir!" Vincent begged, trying his best to climb up on the motorcycle.

"There's nothing I can do for you."

"My foster father's coming after me!"

"What the hell did you do?"

"I ran away from home."

"For what?"

"I don't like my foster home."

"Get back!" the biker told Vincent, pushing him away from the motorcycle.

"I need you to help me, sir!"

"Get away from me!"

The biker switched gears and Vincent tried jumping on

the back. While trying to hold on to the back of the moving motorcycle, he was pushed away. The biker built up enough speed to leave Vincent behind. He had to decide whether he would surrender to J.D. or continue running. Speeding from the north end of Rush Boulevard was J.D.'s truck. He rushed over to the curb, pulled the lock up on the passenger's side, and pushed the door open. The extension cord was clutched tightly in his hand. Vincent came within a foot from the door and stopped.

"Git in da twuck, Vinsun," J.D. said, keeping his evil red eyes on the heavy traffic while trying to watch Vincent at the same time.

"I'm not getting in that truck, Mr. Willingham," Vincent trembled, ready to start running down Rush.

"I ain't gone do nuttin to ya, boy."

"You promise?"

"Yep."

"Why do have the extension cord with you?"

"I ain't gone use dis stanching code."

"Okay."

"Bessa Mae gone call dose white folks."

"My caseworker?"

"Dey gone take ya away."

Vincent suspiciously walked over to the truck and stopped at the door. Other motorists were sounding their horns, wanting J.D. to move his truck. Vincent got inside, and he drove off. When they returned home, Bessie Mae let Vincent know that she was going to request that he be removed from the home.

Chapter 33

SNAKES DO BITE

J ASON RICHBURG WASN'T expecting to pay the Willingham residence another visit anytime soon. Bessie Mae notified him immediately following Vincent's runaway attempt. After Jason sat and talked with Bessie Mae and Vincent, he documented the following information:

Transfer: The situation with Vincent has not changed since the last time I visited. This case is being transferred to the same worker in the agency, because new caseloads are being created.

Description of Child's Appearance: Vincent is a nice looking, fourteen year old teenage boy. He is bi-racial and has curly brown hair.

Intellectual Growth and Schooling: Vincent is in the ninth grade at George Washington Senior High and his grades are good. He gets along well most of the time with other children at school.

Feelings Toward Siblings and Natural Parents: Vincent has no emotional ties to his natural parents. Parental rights were terminated between Vincent and his natural parents.

Child's Relationship To Worker: Vincent is friendly toward the worker and no problems have existed between us.

Finances of Child Care: *Vincent is supported by county and state funds, which is approximately $177.00 dollars per month.*

Feelings Toward Foster Parents and Foster Siblings: *I, Jason Richburg, went to the foster home of Bessie Mae and Jesse Dewayne Willingham to talk with Vincent Carvelli regarding the problems that he was having at the Willinghams. Vincent stated that he was unhappy and wanted to move, but he did not know where he wanted to live. Bessie Mae and Vincent got into an argument while I was there. Vincent stated that Bessie Mae was saying harsh things about his biological mother and father, as well as constantly picking at him for things that were considered petty.*

Bessie Mae called Vincent a liar and said that she wanted him to be moved the next day. I told her that this probably would be impossible, because it would be difficult to find a home that would take a teenager. Bessie Mae stated that she wanted Vincent moved as soon as a home was found. Several days later, Bessie Mae stated that she and Vincent had a long talk and they agreed that Vincent should not leave the Willinghams. Bessie Mae also stated that Vincent admitted that sometimes he can't control his temper, but would try and improve his behavior. She claims that his behavior has improved since my last visit.

*   *   *

The sun scorched into the faces of Vincent and five other boys, who jumped up to grab the basketball coming off the rim. One of the neighborhood boys named Kenneth Tatum looked at his watch, and it gave the time of 5:30 p.m. Since Vincent had to leave, he told someone else to take his place

in the basketball game. He ran across the empty lot and right up the street. The hot sun had him dehydrated. Sweat drenched his white shirt like he'd been sprayed with a hose.

On his way into the kitchen, Vincent cut through the dining room. Sitting in the chair that faced the kitchen door, with her legs crossed like a slut, was a very dark complexioned girl. She had an extremely thin build, short and nappy hair, a pugged nose with wide nostrils, clothes that were badly faded, which made her seem that she came from a disadvantaged background.

Bessie Mae sat in the chair facing the windows in the dining room. She appeared to be in a deep conversation with this strange girl. It seemed like they were communicating quite well with one another. Vincent came out of the kitchen with water dripping from his chin. Bessie Mae stopped him at the dining room table.

"This is my foster son, Vincent Carvelli," Bessie Mae said cordially, reaching into her bra for her pack of Pall Mall Reds. "I've been keeping him since he was six months old."

"How're you doing?" Vincent asked, reaching forward to shake her bony chapped hand.

"I'm fine," she answered monotonously, staring at Vincent like he was the filth of the Earth.

Vincent studied her closely, and right away, he didn't like what he saw. She reminded him a lot of J.D. The only difference between them is that she was *small, black, and ugly*.

She was probably the ugliest girl that Vincent had seen in quite some time. The old clothes that she wore had him wondering if she was some whore off the street, someone who had been taken in by the state of Illinois and taken to the home of some sympathetic foster parents.

"What's your name?"

"My name's Rhonda Davis."

"I'm pleased to meet you, Rhonda."

"Same here."

The attentive eyes of Vincent studied her body language. He paid close detail to her facial expression and overall appearance. Bad vibes wavered all through him. Rhonda gave him the impression that she was a bad omen. He didn't find her appealing at all. She was much too dark, hair was too kinky, and body didn't have any type of curves. The thoughts going through his mind were very much derogatory.

She looks like she could suck a mean dick.
She looks like the type that any dude could fuck.
She looks like somebody Mrs. Willingham drug off the streets of Chicago.
She looks like what the white man would consider a 'no good nigger'.
She looks like she's coming to this foster home to start trouble.
She looks like one of those drugged-up rundown whores from up on Rush Boulevard.
She looks like somebody that I could never get along with.

On the contrary, Rhonda found Vincent to be very attractive. From his curly hair, to his young and innocent face, and on down to his muscularly, maturing body, her eyes traveled lustfully. She would have never let him know that he was someone to be desired. Like Vincent, she had many thoughts swimming around inside her disillusioned mind.

I'll bet he think he's better than other black people.
I'll bet he thinks he's cute because he's light-skinned with good hair.
I'll bet he thinks all the girls want to talk to him.
I'll bet he tries to act white when he gets around white people.
I'll bet he tries to talk bad about black people with

nappy hair and black skin.
I'll bet he tries to fuck a lot of girls since he thinks he's a
pretty boy.
I'll bet he's somebody that I can never learn to like.

In a derogatory manner, Rhonda and Vincent stared at one another. Bessie Mae sat aside and stared at both of them. She sensed that they weren't getting off to a positive start. Vincent left the dining room and went to the top of the basement stairs. It was his favorite spot when he wanted to eavesdrop. He easily closed the basement door. Having his ear pressed against the thin wood, he allowed himself to listen to the conversation that Bessie Mae and Rhonda were having. Valerie's name was mentioned in a crunched voice. Vincent pressed his ear harder against the door.

"Me and Valerie Ramirez were in the same foster home," Rhonda told Bessie Mae.

"Which foster home was that?" Bessie Mae inquired, taking a hard drag off her cigarette. She was always willing to listen to any negativity on Valerie's behalf.

"It was over on the south side."

"Who ran this foster home?"

"A woman named Barbara Johnson."

"Was it a good home?" Bessie Mae asked.

"No, it wasn't," Rhonda answered negatively.

"What was wrong with it?"

"Girls fighting and getting high all the time."

"How many girls stayed there?"

"Including me, it was six."

"Including Valerie, too?"

"Yeah."

"How many bedrooms were in this house?"

"It was four."

"You all were cramped up like sardines."

"Or like packrats."

"Which room did Valerie stay in?"

"She stayed in the room next to our foster mother."

"Was she clean?"

"The most trifling girl in the house," Rhonda told Bessie Mae, fanning some of the thick smoke out of her face.

"What were some of the trifling things she was doing?"

"Leaving bloody tampons and shitty panties all over her room."

"You know she's a whore, don't you?"

"I heard."

"Right up there on Rush Boulevard."

"One of the other foster girls told me."

"That yellow tramp accused my husband of raping her."

"Valerie accused your husband of rape?" Rhonda asked.

"She sure did," said Bessie Mae. "That's why she's not in my foster home right now."

"Are you strict around here?"

"Why'd you ask?"

"My foster mother at the last home would let the girls do anything they wanted."

"Like what?"

"She used to let the other girls bring men over and they would have sex and smoke dope in ther rooms," Rhonda explained, making it seem that she was left out and some jealousy lingered on. Judging by her sinfully ugly appearance, she probably was left out.

"Well, we don't allow any of that here," Bessie Mae made clear.

Their conversation continued until Bessie Mae heard someone coming towards the dining room area. The unknown person made slapping noises. Bessie Mae threw her hand up in Rhonda's face, afraid that it might have been Vincent going back into the kitchen. She silently told Rhonda to discontinue their conversation. Vincent remained

at the top of the basement stairs, listening to every word, especially the negative things that were said about his sister.

Braun instantaneously turned the corner beating the middle of his hand with a silverish wire. Rhonda jumped to the side of the chair. She was alarmed at the sudden appearance of Braun.

"Put that dam wire up, Braun!" Bessie Mae ordered Braun, sliding her last Pall Mall Red out of the package.

"Okay, okay, I'll put the wire up," Braun replied, slipping the wire down into his left pocket.

"Rhonda, this is George Braun," Bessie Mae said."Everybody around here calls him Braun. He's a mentally retarded man that I've been keeping for a long time."

Rhonda took a moment to study Braun. She cut a slight frown when his mouth opened up. The black rotten teeth were unveiled.

"How are doing, Braun?" she asked, hesitantly reaching forward to shake his rough, wire-beaten right hand.

"Hey, hey, how'ya doing there?" Braun said, squeezing Rhonda's hand lightly, but still causing a somewhat painful effect. As he was talking, Braun had spit some of the dark saliva and moist bits of tobacco kernels on her arm.

"My name's Rhonda, and I'm glad to meet you," she said, wiping the disgusting saliva and kernels off her arm.

"Yeah, yeah, I'm glad to meet you, too."

Once he made his acquaintance with Rhonda, Bessie Mae sent Braun into the kitchen to take out the trash. Vincent heard the impact of footsteps coming towards the front room. He quietly ran to the other half of the basement stairs. Bessie Mae was at the bottom of the stairs with Rhonda. She summoned for Junior to come downstairs. Junior left his room and walked down the stairs with his head positioned straight ahead. Rhonda checked out his glossy eyes that never blinked. As always, his face displayed no expression at all.

"Junior," Bessie Mae smiled, placing her hand across his

back, blowing smoke the other direction. "This is a new foster girl who came to live with us today."

"New foster girl coming to live here. New foster girl coming to live here," Junior replied twice, nodding his head quickly and rotating his jaws in circular motions.

"Don't repeat what I said," Bessie Mae coached the retarded Junior. "Ask Rhonda how she's doing."

"Ask Rhonda how she's doing. Ask Rhonda how she's doing."

"No, no, Junior!" Bessie Mae said frustratingly. "Ask her how she's doing."

"Ask her how she's doing. Ask her how she's doing."

Bessie Mae was usually patient when it came to introducing Junior to someone new at the Willingham residence. She didn't want to become frustrated by trying to teach him to speak properly. His jaws moved rigorously, like he was trying to get rid of something in his mouth. Bessie Mae knew that he didn't have a single tooth in his mouth, so he couldn't have been biting on anything.

"Open your mouth, Junior," Bessie Mae said, bending forward to look into Junior's mouth.

"Open the mouth. Open the mouth," Junior repeated, as he spread his jaws.

"I'll be dam!" Bessie Mae relinquished, guiding her hand towards his mouth, raking along his gums to check for anything in there. "This fool's got chicken bones in his mouth from this morning. Go spit those dam bones out in the trash!"

"Spit bones in trash. Spit bones in trash," Junior said, as he walked towards the kitchen.

Granny Dear must've forgot to take the meat off the chicken bones. The big breakfast consisted of chicken, rice, and biscuits, all smothered in a thick gravy. On occasions, Junior would keep bones in his mouth. Bessie Mae feared one day that he would choke himself to death on those very bones.

Bessie Mae and Rhonda went back into the dining room to grab her two trashbags that she came with. They went upstairs and dumped all of her clothes across the bed, inside the same room that Valerie once slept in. They sorted through the clothes that appeared unsuitable to wear. The socks had holes at the toes. The panties were badly soiled with light blood and urine stains. The faded, tight-fitted jeans had rips up and down the legs. Bessie Mae had much sympathy for Rhonda.

"I'm gonna have to buy you some new clothes," Bessie Mae explained to Rhonda, a girl who seemed to be very underpriviledged.

"I really need some new ones," Rhonda expressed in a charitable voice, thumbing through the clothes that she'd had for many years.

"Did your foster mother at the other home ever buy you clothes?"

"No, she didn't"

"And why's that?"

"She didn't care."

"That's bad."

"Plus, there was a lot of other foster girls there."

"If I have to spend my own money, I'm gonna buy you some new clothes"

Vincent had traveled from the basement stairs to the stairs that led to where Bessie Mae and Rhonda were. He was outraged at this stage! He became extremely angry when he overheard Bessie Mae tell Rhonda that she would buy her new clothes with her own money. The only gut reaction that Vincent had was:

"I've been in this foster home all of my life, and Mrs. Willingham's never bought me any new clothes with her own money. As a matter of fact, she's hardly ever bought me any new clothes, period. Now, she's going to buy this ugly girl some new clothes with her own money."

Junior waited in the hallway after spitting the bones in the trash. Vincent came out of the basement and saw him standing there. "Go upstairs, Junior."

"Go upstairs. Go upstairs," Junior said, nodding his head.

*   *   *

The rattling noises of an automobile engine came from outside. J.D. was parking on the side of the house. His truck was badly in need of repair. Vincent knew that it was J.D. returning home from work, so he ran back to the basement stairs and sat quietly. J.D. strutted across the porch, swinging his lunchbucket, kicking the lawn chairs out of his way. He went into the kitchen and sat down to relax with one of his Pall Mall Golds.

Bessie Mae and Rhonda returned downstairs with some of her old clothes cuffed under their armpits. Bessie Mae insisted that some of her clothes had to be thrown away, or given to the Salvation Army or The Goodwill. They walked into the kitchen to dump the clothes into the large trash barrel. J.D. quickly crushed out his cigarette. Smoke rushed out of both nostrils and his mouth at the same time.

"J.D.," Bessie Mae smiled. "This is our new foster daughter, Rhonda Davis."

"Dis our new falsta dawda?" J.D. asked surprisingly, expelling the redness and water from his eyes, and then turning them into clear and lustful eyes.

"Yes."

"How long our new falsta dawda gone be here?" J.D. inquired strongly, studying Rhonda from head to toe, saturating his chapped lips with his moist tongue. For horny bastards like J.D. Willingham, Rhonda having short and nappy hair, a very dark and greasy complexion with pimples, and a thin and unshapely figure, none of these unattractive features seemed to matter to him.

YN

"Rhonda's going to be here until her caseworker decides if this'll be her permanent foster home," Bessie Mae explained, catching a glimpse of J.D.'s strong attraction to Rhonda. Rhonda stepped closer to the kitchen table. She stared straight into J.D.'s eyes.

"How're doing, sir?"

"Call ma J.D., pease," J.D. said, smiling charmingly up at Rhonda.

"Alright, how're you doing, J.D.?"

"Doing juss fine. How bout ya'self?"

"I'm doing fine, too."

"We gone be gad ta have ya here."

"Thank you, J.D. I'm gonna be glad to be staying here."

"I sho hope dis can be yo new falsta home fo good," J.D. plotted, undressing Rhonda's unattractive figure with his clear eyes.

"It'll be nice," Rhonda agreed, especially since her last foster home seemed like a tragedy.

"We gone git along juss fine."

"I'm sure we are."

J.D. just couldn't take his eyes off Rhonda. Be it ugly or attractive, a new face is what he longed for at the Willingham residence. *It became evident that J.D. would fuck anything that had a tail and wasn't nailed down.*

"What woom ya gone put our new falsta dawda in?" J.D. asked excitingly.

"Well, J.D.," Bessie Mae remitted, sensing that he was conspiring to do something immoral. "Our new foster daughter's going to be in Valerie's old room."

"Dat'll be good."

"Yes, I guess."

"We gone be close ta our new falsta dawda."

For a long time, J.D. and Rhonda stared seductively into one another's eyes. The attraction between them was

exceptionally strong. Bessie Mae left the kitchen to allow them to become better acquainted.

* * *

The clock that rested on the bedside table of Bessie Mae said 1:30 a.m. J.D. quietly got dressed and crept out of their room. Rhonda met him downstairs and they took off in his truck. She hadn't been living at the Willingham residence for a solid day, and she was already taking off with J.D., on a sinnister mission.

Rhonda and J.D. arrived at Lincoln Park and he parked in a dark area. They got out and locked their doors. J.D. unlocked the camper and they jumped inside, climbing onto a mattress that he had placed in there earlier that day. He knew the chances were good for him to take advantage of the new foster girl coming to their home, some fresh meat that he'd been craving for quite some time.

They began undressing and threw their clothes off to the side. Being that J.D. was a large man, he allowed Rhonda to get on top of him and insert his large black penis into her. He embraced her around her waist and began thrusting in and out of her. He gripped her breasts, which were no larger than radio knobs. Rhonda definitely wasn't a virgin. She was penetrated easily and the sex was totally enjoyable for her. The camper was filled with a musty genital odor. The windows steamed up, and with the rhythm created, the back of the truck began rocking. Rhonda slipped into a world of total ecstasy.

"Feels good to me, J.D.!" Rhonda squeaked erotically.

"Ya lack it, Wonda?" J.D. asked, nearly ready to have an explosive orgasm.

"Yes, yes, I like so much, J.D.!"

"Ya want mo of dis big black dick, Wonda?"

"Yes, yes, give me more of that big black thang, J.D.!"

Rhonda purred erotically, not even caring that J.D. was pronouncing her name all wrong.

"J.D. gone give it to ya, Wonda."

"Yes, yes, give it to me, J.D.!" Rhonda moaned intensely, leaning forward and palming the massive chest of J.D.

"Dis feelin so good."

"Feels good to me, too!"

"Ooooh!" J.D. wheezed exhiliratingly, feeling maximum sexual ecstasy, especially since it was an extreme rarity when he and Bessie Mae would have intercourse.

"Gonna cum, J.D.?"

"Yep, yep, gone comb."

"Go ahead, baby!"

They switched positions, allowing Rhonda to fall on her back and J.D. to climb on top, careful not to press too much of his weight on top of her. The intercourse continued until J.D. shot a big load up into Rhonda, sending tingling sensations throughout her entire body, a feeling that was greatly exhilirating. They got dressed and drove back home.

* * *

Before the sun could rise, they crept back into the house, with Rhonda going to her room first, and J.D. walking softly back into his room. The two lowlives didn't even have enough common courtesy to wash their nasty asses before entering the house. Quite typical for people of their calibre. The clock on the table said 2:45 a.m., which gave them more than an hour to slip away and have a rendezvous. Bessie Mae rolled over and looked up at the clock. She sniffed an odor that was very familiar. She watched J.D. get undressed and quickly became suspicious.

"Where you been?" Bessie Mae asked, trying to identify the odor that came from J.D.'s body.

"Been out checkin on da dogs."

"What's wrong with the beagles?"

"Dey was out dere bawking."

"I didn't hear no barking."

"Dey stopped bawking."

"What's that smell?"

"What smell?"

"Smells like . . ."

"Lack what?"

"Like musty underarms."

"I ain't smellin nuttin."

"Smells like somebody's ass, too."

"Don't smell lack nuttin ta me."

"Smells like somebody's been fucking."

"Yo mind's paying ticks on ya, Bessa Mae."

"My mind's not playing tricks on me, J.D."

"I thank it is."

"No it's not."

"Ya sho?"

"Sure I'm sure."

Bessie Mae was too tired to further inquire about the foul odor that surrounded their room. Once again, the evil, lowdown J.D. Willingham executed another masterplan and found a way to squeal out of it.

Chapter 34

THE LONGEST STROKE

NOT LONG AFTER Rhonda's arrival, she and Vincent were having problems getting along. Vincent was convinced that she was considered the *evil foster sister*. She came to the Willingham residence to be nothing but a serious troublemaker. He tried warning Bessie Mae that she was a no good bitch, who would eventually wreak pure havoc in the home.

Ironically, Jason Richburg was called back out to the Willingham residence to speak with Bessie Mae and Vincent. Of course, it was his duty as a caseworker to check on Vincent and make sure he was trying to improve his relationship with Bessie Mae. Over a week's period, Jason recorded the following documentation:

CHILD: Vincent is an attractive fourteen year old bi-racial boy who has curly brown hair.

HEALTH: Vincent has had no physical examinations during this dictation period, but he has been in good health. The foster mother, Bessie Mae Willingham, reported that Vincent had had no recent dental checkups, but the dentist's office always sent notifications when checkups were due. Bessie Mae reported that Vincent occasionally wets his bed at night. When further questioned about this, Bessie Mae stated that Vincent has done this since he was an infant and that physical examinations revealed no medical problems. Apparently, this does not represent a great problem for Vincent, as he changes his bed

whenever necessary, and this is known and accepted by other members of the household.

SCHOOLING: *Vincent is presently in the ninth grade at George Washington High School. He very much enjoys school and is a very conscientious student who makes above average grades. Vincent has expressed interest in attending college.*

ADJUSTMENT TO FOSTER CARE: *Periodically, Bessie Mae reported that Vincent was presenting behavior problems at home, such as using "dirty language", destroying other's property, refusing to cooperate, leaving the house without asking permission, staying out late, and calling his foster sister names. Several conferences were held with Bessie Mae and Vincent. Bessie Mae expressed the opinion that Vincent was jealous of his foster sister and that he was being influenced by older "street kids". Vincent expressed the opinion that he was being "dogged" and singled out for punishment. Because there are numerous adults in the household, I questioned Bessie Mae about how and by whom Vincent is disciplined.*

She stated that she is usually the one to discipline Vincent and it is usually by withdrawing his privileges. Conditions for the contract were discussed with and agreed upon by Bessie Mae and Vincent. The contract was signed by the both of them. She reported that he had not been following the contract. Vincent readily admitted this and stated that he forgot. Counseling was discussed with Vincent, but he would not participate in this as, "counseling is for kids who have problems in school and he has none". During the summer months, Vincent complained of being bored and stated that he would like to work.

However, he was not interested in the Summer Youth Employment Program, Job Opportunities for Youths, better known as "J.O.Y.". He was unsuccessful in obtaining a job on his own. Knowing that Vincent likes to read, I offered to assist him in obtaining a library card, but he was not interested in this, either. Recently, Vincent called me to request

that he be moved from the Willingham's foster home. Apparently, he and Bessie Mae had been fighting and he complained that the house was "evil", Bessie Mae "fusses" too much, and she does not appreciate what he does. I talked with Bessie Mae and we decided that once school resumed, Vincent's behavior would improve. My impression is that Vincent was at least partially right in his feeling that Bessie Mae is, at times, irritable and intolerable.

✳   ✳   ✳

Vincent was in the front room running the vacuum cleaner across the filthy floor. Braun was in the second floor bathroom giving Junior a bath, telling him more stories about St. Louis and the brown bomber himself, Joe Louis. Occasionally, Bessie Mae would give Braun instructions to bathe Junior and put fresh clothes on him, also giving Vincent instructions to shave them, which is something he learned over the years. Granny Dear sat up near the kitchen table. She chopped up a green bell pepper that she was going to put in a large pot of chili. Bessie Mae was leaning against the wall near the stove. As she talked on the phone, she displayed a sad and disappointed look on her face.

"It's like this, Bishop Burgess," Bessie Mae said, holding the phone halfway over her ear, talking in a very depressed tone. "J.D. has been having sex with our seventeen year old foster daughter and he's done got her pregnant."

"Dear Jesus!" Bishop Burgess yelled softly into Bessie Mae's ear. "How far along is your foster daughter?"

"She's almost due."

"How do you know Brother Willingham's the father?"

"He admitted to it."

"Did he?"

"It's almost like he's going around bragging about it."

"Say what!" Bishop Burgess exclaimed, assuming that

J.D. was the ideal family man. Not hardly! "What does your foster daughter have to say for herself?"

"She admitted to it, too."

"Can I get personal, Sister Bessie Mae?"

"Go ahead, Bishop Burgess," Bessie Mae replied painfully.

"Were they sneaking away from the house to have sex?"

"Sometimes."

"Is that right?"

"I believe that they were having sex right here in the house."

"That's statutory rape."

"You're right."

"They'd lock Brother Willingham up for having a girl that young."

"J.D. should've been locked up a long time ago."

"Where's he at now?"

"He's living somewhere around Chicago."

"What do you plan on doing now?"

"I'm filing for a divorce next week," Bessie Mae said courageously, finally seeing the light that she had been blinded from. She tried greatly holding back a rush of tears.

"Do you think Brother Willingham'll come back to church?"

"I don't know."

"Do you think you can get him to call me?"

"I don't care if he does or not."

"I'm so sorry, Sister Bessie Mae."

"Don't be, Bishop Burgess."

The discussion with Bishop Burgess ended. Bessie Mae slammed the phone down on the receiver. As a result, a loud ring echoed in the kitchen and into the dining room. She limped into the front room and stood at the bottom of the stairs. Carmen walked into the house with a large sack from Macy's. A newly acquired American Express credit card moved

her up into the ranks of big shoppers. Vincent was rolling the vacuum cleaner from one corner to the next. He was still upset with Bessie Mae after she used his money to finance a trip to Las Vegas, in which she took Rhonda with her.

Carmen had trouble trying to step around him. Looking at the crumbs on the carpet, he turned the machine off and went into the dining room. Carmen glanced across the room and noticed the distraught look on Bessie Mae's face. She knew that something was troubling her.

"What's wrong, Mrs. Willingham?" Carmen asked her former foster mother, staring at all the pain that was in Bessie Mae's eyes.

"That lowlife bastard, J.D.!" Bessie Mae screeched, fighting back the rush of tears coming down her face. "I was always good to that black sonofabitch! How could he end up doing me like this?"

"What did he do?"

"Haven't you heard, Carmen?"

"Heard what?"

"About Rhonda and J.D."

"Oh yeah," Carmen said. "The foster girl who's pregnant by Mr. Willingham."

"Goddam right!"

"Have you confronted him about it?"

"It's too late for that."

"Why?"

"I found out a month ago that J.D. was the father."

"Who told you the truth?" Carmen asked.

"Rhonda came to me and told me the truth."

"Who did she say the father was at first?"

"Some boy at her school."

"How do you know she's telling the truth?"

"She's telling the truth."

"Are you sure?"

"J.D. even admitted to it."

"Did he?"

"Look what thanks I get from her."

"What are you talking about?"

"I took that black heifer to Las Vegas with me."

"So, that's how she shows her appreciation?"

"I used Vincent's money that I promised that I would save for him."

"You did?"

"Sure did."

"Wow!"

Bessie Mae began thinking to herself. She now had nurtured a hatred for Rhonda, not knowing that she would end up betraying her trust. She dreamed up some fairly raw obscenities about Rhonda:

She's as black as coal.
She's got real nappy hair.
She's shaped like a toothpick.
She's as dumb as a betsy bug.
She flunks every class at school.
She sits around the house and does nothing.
She starts a lot of bullshit between other people.
She seduced my husband and he ends up getting her pregnant.

"You know something, Carmen?" Bessie Mae said. "Who, besides a sex hound like J.D. wants to screw around with somebody as ugly as Rhonda?"

Bessie Mae's anger had kicked into full gear. She wasn't talking that way about Rhonda when she first came to their home. Carmen didn't believe that she had the capacity to say such harsh things. But Rhonda and J.D. had gone too far.

DEWEY REYNOLDS

Her becoming pregnant was the ultimate sin. In the end, who was to take the blame?

"You're right," Carmen thought. "She's not attractive at all. As a matter of fact, I've heard other people in the neighborhood call her all kinds of 'black ugly this' and 'black ugly that'."

"I didn't believe it at first."

"What?"

"But now I really believe it."

"Believe what?" Carmen asked.

"It's all coming to the light."

"What're you talking about?"

"J.D. really did rape Valerie."

"You believe it after all these years?"

"I'll die believing it," Bessie Mae confessed, conjuring up more painful tears, making herself sick from holding in all the hurt.

"Why've you changed your mind after all these years?" Carmen questioned.

"Love blinded me into believing that J.D. didn't rape Valerie.

"How's that?"

"Black Mississippi niggahs like him love those yellow women."

"Light skinned girls with the long pretty hair?"

"Yes."

"Why's that, Mrs. Willingham?"

"It's the closest they can get to a white woman."

"I've heard that before."

"It's true, Valerie."

"I know."

"Where J.D.'s from, they weren't even allowed to look at white women."

"Clarksdale, Mississippi?"

"They used to lynch colored boys for batting their eyes at white women in Mississippi."

"I've heard that, too."

"J.D.'s a lowdown black bastard!" Bessie Mae grouched. "First, he rapes one of our foster daughters. Second, he gets another one of our foster daughters pregnant. "

"Know what?"

"What is it?"

"Rhonda's probably used to being molested by other foster fathers in those other foster homes."

"Probably."

"What's gonna happen now?" Carmen asked.

"I'm divorcing the lowlife, black sonofabitch!"

"When?"

"Next week."

"You've got a lawyer?"

"I'm going to his office to start filing."

While moving the chairs away from the dining room table, Vincent was listening to the entire conversation. All the sinnister tactics that J.D. had executed over the years were brought to the forefront. Vincent plugged in the vacuum cleaner. He began cleaning under the dining room table.

The squeaking sounds of the screen door opening indicated that someone was coming through the front entrance. After moving over to the end of the table where Braun ate, Vincent discovered that J.D. and Rhonda were walking into the house. Once inside, J.D. traveled up to the second floor. Rhonda had a mighty large stomach. Her one-time thin, unshapely body had picked up a few pounds. The shedding of hair strands made her scalp visible. She was much uglier than before, because her bull nose had spread across most of her face. Vincent ran the vacuum cleaner all over the dining room carpet.

The sounds of someone arguing came from the second floor. There was the pounding of objects against the floor and walls. Vincent turned the vacuum cleaner off. He moved

closer to the front room. There was extreme vulgarity in the heated argument.

"Shut up, motherfucker!" Bessie Mae screamed, pressing the hard barrel of her .38 calibre handgun into the left temple of J.D.'s head.

"Don't shoot ma, Bessa Mae!" J.D. pleaded, cautiously standing firm in the middle of the floor.

"Shut the fuck up, goddammit!" Bessie Mae responded defiantly, moving her index finger further back on the trigger. J.D. was possibly seconds away from his death. "You had to fuck her, didn't you?"

"Pease, pease, don't shoot ma, Bessa Mae!" J.D. compromised strongly, praying that Bessie Mae wouldn't blow his brains clean out of his skull and across the room. His entire body shivered like a prisoner being led to his execution. Sweat rolled off the top of his shiny bald head. For once in his life, J.D. now had the chance to see what it was like to be intimidated by a woman.

"Why did you have to fuck her?"

"I ain't did no such thang."

"Quit lying, niggah!"

"I didden mean ta git'er pegnant, Bessa Mae."

"Yes, you did!"

"Naw, I didden."

"Why did you have to rape Valerie?"

"Ain't nobody waped dat gal, Bessa Mae."

"Shut the fuck up, you lying sonofabitch!"

"Pease, pease, put da gun down, Bessa Mae."

"I should blow your goddam head off with this motherfucking thirty-eight!" Bessie Mae viciously erupted, gradually moving the trigger back further. A loaded pistol would make any abusive man become the most humble man before any woman. Even a ruthless, blackhearted man like J.D. stood submissively at the middle of the floor.

"Pease, pease, don't shoot ma, Bessa Mae!" J.D. said. "I'm sawry fo all da wong I did to ya."

"You're not sorry!"

"Yes, I am."

"You're lying, niggah!"

"I loves ya, Bessa Mae."

"You don't know what love is, niggah!"

"I cares a lot bout cha, Bessa Mae."

"You don't care about nobody but your goddam self!"

Bessie Mae continued holding J.D. at gunpoint. Any suddenly wrong movement of her finger would discharge a bullet from the gun. Carmen had analyzed some of this drama from the bottom of the stairs, and she quickly ran into the kitchen to tell Granny Dear.

"Oh my God!" Carmen said to Granny Dear. "Mrs. Willingham's got a gun on Mr. Willingham."

"Where bouts dey at?" Granny Dear asked.

"Up in their room."

"Less go over yonder to see what's happening."

"Alright."

Carmen pushed the back of her wheelchair and they stopped at the bottom of the stairs.

"Bessa Mae!" Granny Dear called from the bottom of the stairs.

"What is it, Granny Dear?" Bessie Mae answered loudly from inside her room.

"What cha up dere doing?"

"I'm about to blow this black niggah's brains out!"

"Put dat gun away."

"No, I'm going to kill him, Granny Dear."

"He ain't worth it, Bessa Mae."

"I'm going to put him out of his misery."

"Don't do no such thang."

Slowly, Bessie Mae lowered her arm and moved towards the side of the bed. She opened the top drawer to her bedside table and placed the gun inside. J.D. released a long wind of relief, wiping sweat off his bald head and face. At the

bottom of the stairs, Carmen, Vincent, and Granny Dear had waited to see what would happen. Vincent was hoping that Bessie Mae would have shot J.D, ending a streak of evil in the home. J.D. rushed down the stairs. He perspired heavily all over his body. Minutes after things cooled off, he left the house with Rhonda. Instead of going downstairs to tell Carmen and Granny Dear what had happened, Bessie Mae locked her door, got undressed, and lied across the bed in a horizontal position.

*   *   *

At exactly 4:00 a.m., everyone at the Willingham residence was resting comfortably. Since Bessie Mae and J.D. were officially separated, she slept alone, moving around in the bed in only her underwear. While snoring loudly, she rolled her head back and forth. Two doors over, Braun and Junior snored even louder. Beyond the kitchen, Granny Dear embraced her pillow tightly. She made groaning noises as she grinded her false teeth together. Crackling noises traveled from the kitchen and into Granny Dear's room. She wanted to know who was creeping that direction. She raised her head and reached for her cane, slowly moving the curtain back.

"Who dere?" Granny Dear asked, her voice drowsy.

No one answered. The crackling proceeded towards the refrigerator. The long cane hit against the wall that separated the kitchen and Granny Dear's room. Vincent was trying to sneak into the refrigerator. His stomach growled from hunger, because the dinner that consisted of vegetable stew without any beef, wasn't too tasteful.

Vincent crept to the right side of the refrigerator. He waited to see if Granny Dear would pull the curtain back. Granny Dear didn't want to slide into her wheelchair. Scooting to the foot of the bed, she was far enough to push the curtain back with the cane. Before the curtain was drawn

back fully, Vincent dashed over to the counter where Bessie Mae kept the sugar and flour containers.

A large rat was at the opposite end of the counter, sniffing around for food. Vincent was stuck in a tight spot. Since the sugar and flour delighted its senses, the rat was coming in the direction of Vincent. Granny Dear was at the foot of her bed rubbing both eyes for better vision. She took a short yawn. The curtain was drawn back all the way. Her head moved all directions to see if someone was prowling around the kitchen. Vincent stood perfectly still. Both arms rested on the sides of his body. He drastically tried controlling the volume in his breathing. Efforts to scare off the large rat were useless. It moved closer to the flour and sugar containers.

"Shewww! Shewww!" Vincent whispered in the lowest voice, fanning his hand wildly, praying that the rat wouldn't jump over and bite him.

After taking a final glance around the kitchen, Granny Dear gradually allowed the curtain to drop. She laid the cane against her wheelchair and climbed back up to the head of her bed. Despite the void of hunger, the slight turbulence of gas was also rumbling around inside Vincent's stomach. The rat had gotten even closer. Vincent became exceptionally nervous. Very quietly, he said:

"Where did that big ass rat come from? I thought they were only supposed to be out by the dog pen and toolshed."

Brmmmmp! Brmmmmp! With no intention whatsoever, Vincent farted real loud. The rat rapidly ran towards the

594   DEWEY REYNOLDS

opposite end of the counter. Thanks to the turbulent noise of gas, probably even the foul smell, he effectively ran the rodent off.

"Who in dere?" Granny Dear asked, raising her head and reaching for her cane again. Afterwards, she lied down and threw the covers over her body. Vincent came from around the counter and opened the right side of the refrigerator. It was the perfect opportunity to search for something to eat. The bright light from the refrigerator shone under the curtain and right into the dark room of Granny Dear. She moaned in a cluttered voice. The cane thumped onto the floor to scare off the intruder.

Vincent snatched two jelly glazed donuts off the top shelf and rushed out of the kitchen. After returning to the basement, he sat in the middle of his bed, sinking his teeth into the delicious donuts. A loud chime came from the front room. The small grandfather clock that sat on the antique desk, gave the exact time of 5:45 a.m. Except for Bessie Mae, everyone in the house slept peacefully.

Inside her dark quiet room, she was stretched across the bed, kicking every direction. At the foot of the bed, she held a tight grip on the top sheet. The top sheet grazed against the bottom sheet. Her head jerked back and forth. She was breathing heavily, almost like she was having a cardiac arrest.

All types of memories came crashing through. Bessie Mae was recalling all the bittersweet memories between she and J.D. The troubled past wouldn't leave her alone. Significant memories of she and J.D.'s first meeting, their wedding day, the establishment of their foster and handicapped care home, the coming and going of many foster children over the years, the brutal abuse of these same foster children and handicapped men, the rape of Valerie, and maybe worst of all, seventeen year old Rhonda becoming pregnant by J.D.

*   *   *

The middle nineteen fifties couldn't have been a better time for two people to fall in love. For Bessie Mae Pierson and Jesse Dewayne Willingham, love seemed to have filled the air. As the two waited in a line to get their tags renewed on their cars, they couldn't take their eyes off one another. There stood this young woman wearing a blue scarf wrapped around her neatly permed hair. In the line opposite of her, there stood this extremely dark complexioned man with a serious receding hairline and a bulky physique. The attraction was like electricity, ready to send strong charges into the air.

"How ya doing, t'day?" J.D. asked the young and innocent Bessie Mae.

"I'm a blessed woman," Bessie Mae replied invitationally. "How about yourself?"

"Doing juss fine."

"You have a strong accent."

"Yep, I do."

"You can't be from Chicago."

"I'm fum Mississippa."

"What part?" Bessie Mae asked.

"Clarksdale."

"That's funny."

"What's dat?"

"I'm from Memphis, Tennessee."

"Is dat wight?"

"I sure am."

"What's yo name?" J.D. asked attentively.

"I'm Bessie Mae Pierson," she said with a smile. "What's yours?"

"I'm Jesse Dewayne Willingham," he said with little pride. "Most folks call ma J.D."

"Pleased to make your acquaintance."

"Ya fum down south, too."

"How long have you been living in Chicago?"

"Bout, couple'a years."

"What part do you live in?"

"I'm on da wess side."

"The west side, huh?"

"Yep."

"I'm living on the south side with my mother."

"Yo mammy, huh?"

"Yes, my dear old mother."

"Where bouts ya work?"

"Right now, I'm taking care of some white kids out in Cicero."

"Tendin ta white folks chilluns, huh?"

"Yes."

"Ain't dat where da wich white folks stay?"

"The big moneymakers," Bessie Mae said. "Where do you work?"

"I put woofs on places fo da white folks."

"You're a roofer?"

"Yep."

"Where's your wife at?"

"I ain't got one of dose."

"You've never been married?"

"Once befoe."

"Any children?"

"I got thwee chilluns."

"Three children?"

"Yep."

"Where do they live?"

"Wit dey mammy down in Mississippa."

"What do you have, all boys, all girls, or some of both?"

"Two boys and one gal."

"That's nice."

"Ya got any chilluns?"

"None."

"Why's dat?"

"Can't have any."

"And why's dat?"

"Problems that we women have."

"Dat's da way life goes."

"Know what I'd really like to do?"

"What's dat?"

"Start a home for foster children and the mentally disabled."

"Is dat wight?" J.D. asked, thinking Bessie Mae might be running head on into a tragedy.

"I've always wanted to take care of disadvantaged people."

"It's plenty of dem folks out dere."

"So many children are given away."

"All da time."

"I'm good with children and I think I can start a home like that."

"I thank so."

* * *

Bessie Mae began trembling from head to toe. Foams of thick saliva gushed from the sides of her mouth. Her eyes rolled around inside her head and her tongue stretched out of her mouth.

"Why me, J.D.? Why me, J.D.?" Bessie Mae repeated in her deep, turbulent sleep. "Why did you hurt me so bad? Why did you hurt me so bad?"

No one in the house was aware that Bessie Mae was suffering a stroke. Her upper body trembled even moreso. Large rings of saliva were on the sheets. Technically speaking, J.D. was killing her softly. The present stroke that she was suffering, was a result of years of deception. A loud cry made by Bessie Mae carried into the room of Braun and Junior. Braun jumped out of bed and rushed into her room. He stood in the doorway.

"Hey, hey, Bessie Mae, are you alright in there?" Braun asked, observing all the foamy saliva around her head.

"What did I do to you, J.D.? Why did you have to treat me

so bad?" Bessie Mae cried out, her head jerking profusely, her eyes rolling around like pinballs.

"Yeah, yeah, something wrong in there, Bessie Mae?"

Bessie Mae didn't respond. Even a mentally retarded man like Braun knew that something was wrong. He went down to Granny Dear's room and pulled the curtain back. Granny Dear raised up and grabbed her cane.

"What's wong wit ya, Brawns?" Granny Dear asked Braun, pulling her wheelchair closer to the bed.

"Something's wrong with Bessie Mae," Braun informed Granny Dear, showing every front black tooth in his mouth.

"Sumthang wong wit Bessa Mae?"

"Yeah, yeah, something's wrong with Bessie Mae."

"What is it, Brawns?"

"I think she's sick."

Granny Dear threw on her nightgown, jumped into her wheelchair, and rolled to the bottom of the stairs going to the second floor. She leaned forward to try and look over the bannisters.

"Bessa Mae, you alwight up dere?" Granny Dear asked, sliding forward in her wheelchair. There was no answer. Granny Dear became extremely worried. In order to get Vincent's attention, she bammed on the basement door. The vibrations traveled down into the basement. After tossing and turning a few times, he took heed to the signal. He awkwardly struggled to walk up the basement stairs. When he stepped past the basement door, Granny Dear snatched his arm and pointed up to the second floor.

"What's wrong, Granny Dear?" Vincent asked, shaking his head to wear off the hard sleeping.

"Bessa Mae's up dere sick!" Granny Dear explained, looking worried as ever.

"What's wrong with her?"

"I dunno," Granny Dear nodded. "Gone upstairs and find out."

"Okay."

Vincent sprinted up to the second floor. Braun followed him into Bessie Mae's semi-lit room. Since her bed faced the bright street lights outside, Vincent could clearly look upon the nearly lifeless body of his foster mother. Braun hit the light switch. They ran over to the bed and noticed the thick saliva rings around the head and neck of Bessie Mae. Vincent rushed down to the first floor to give Granny Dear the tragic news.

"I think Mrs. Willingham's dying!" Vincent said hysterically, clutching the armrest on Granny Dear's wheelchair.

"What's wong wit'er?" Granny Dear inquired strongly.

"Her eyes are wide open."

"My goodness!"

"There's a whole lot of spit and foam around her head."

"Oh my Lawd!" Granny Dear exhalted, raising out of her wheelchair, like she was ready to walk on her arthritis-stricken legs.

"It looks pretty bad, Granny Dear."

"Call da ambalance folks!"

"Yes, mam."

Vincent raced into the kitchen and scanned the list of emergency numbers that were on the wall near the phone. A number that read, *Emergency Medical Services,* was at the bottom of the list. It had the logo of a small, red and white ambulance next to it. With the swift movement of his fingers, he dialed the 911 digits.

"911, operator thirty-seven," the operator answered professionally.

"We need an ambulance at Thirty-Eight, Thirty-Eight, Milwaukee Parkway," Vincent said hurriedly.

"What's the problem?"

"My foster mother's dying!"

"We'll send an ambulance with paramedic units out there as soon as possible."

"Thank you."

Vincent hung up and returned to the front room. He informed Granny Dear that an ambulance was on its way. Granny Dear impatiently moved around in her wheelchair. She silently prayed that Bessie Mae wouldn't die. Meanwhile, Vincent went upstairs to check on Bessie Mae. By every fading second, she was breathing slower. Vincent wished he could do something to rehabilitate his foster mother. He was never taught any life-saving techniques. Still, Bessie Mae trembled and gushed out spurts of saliva. Vincent stepped over to the bed and placed his hand across her forehead.

"Don't die, Mrs. Willingham!" Vincent crooned.

The roaring sounds of sirens came from the south end of Milwaukee Parkway. The flashing of red and yellow lights shone up and down the block. Along with a long yellow fire truck, the ambulance had arrived. Vincent looked out the front door to make sure they were coming to the right house. Three paramedics and five firemen came up on the porch with a long stretcher and their medical supply kits. Granny Dear was at the bottom of the stairs to greet them.

"How yall doing?" Granny Dear said, reaching for the paramedic's hand.

"We're doing fine, mam," the tall and stocky paramedic responded. "What's wrong?"

"My dawda's upstairs sick."

"Do you know what happened to her?"

"I reckon she had a stroke."

"We're gonna go up and find out."

"Thank ya."

The paramedics and firemen followed one another up to Bessie Mae's room. Immediately upon entering the room, they began their life-saving techniques. Her vital signs were taken with the blood pressure cup, stethescope, and thermometer. They could tell that a considerable amount of oxygen had been lost to her brain. Time was extremely crucial!

Once she was placed on the stretcher, the paramedics and firemen rushed her downstairs.

Granny Dear waited restlessly at the bottom of the stairs. Bessie Mae was being carried out in nothing but her underwear. Her large breasts hung over to the side of the stretcher. Granny Dear made the ones carrying the stretcher come to a complete stop.

"What's wong wit ma dawda?" Granny Dear questioned the paramedics, tears forming at the corner of her eyes.

"She suffered a severe stroke," one of the paramedics explained.

"She gone be alwight?"

"We must rush her to the hospital, mam."

"Will ya call when ya git'er to da hospital?"

"We sure will, mam."

"Thank ya very much."

"You're welcome."

Vincent held the door open while they carried Bessie Mae out on the stretcher. When they got her inside the ambulance, tubes were stuck down her nose and into her arms. The ambulance sped north down Milwaukee Parkway. Several neighbors up and down the block stood on their porches. Some of them were still in their nightwear, watching the noisy ambulance rush towards Cook County Hospital.

Granny Dear wanted Vincent to contact Carmen. She knew that Carmen could reach several other important people. Since Vernon was away in the Air Force out in California, he had to be notified through the Red Cross. They hoped Valerie would find out through a reliable source like Tamara Davidson. As far as other foster children were concerned, it remained to be seen if they would show up at the hospital. Important church members, such as Bishop John Burgess, would learn about Bessie Mae's crisis through other church members. Since J.D. and Rhonda were of no account, they wouldn't bother trying to notify them.

*   *   *

Vincent stood at bedside where Bessie Mae was hooked up to total life support. His emotions got the best of him, because he shed light tears and glanced around at the ventilator in her throat and the feeding tubes in her arms. The room was silent and the only sounds made were that of the total life support system. Vincent reached forward and rubbed the ashy forehead of Bessie Mae. During this heartfelt moment, Vincent wanted to tell her about all the things that he was sorry about:

> *I'm sorry if I wasn't a good foster son, Mrs. Willingham.*
> *I'm sorry if I pissed in the bed too much, Mrs. Willingham.*
> *I'm sorry if I didn't make the grades in school that I should've, Mrs. Willingham.*
> *I'm sorry if I didn't clean my room when I should've, Mrs. Willingham.*
> *I'm sorry if I stayed out too late when I wasn't supposed to, Mrs. Willingham.*
> *I'm sorry if I used bad language around you, Mrs. Willingham.*
> *I'm sorry if I got mad when you told me to do something, Mrs. Willingham.*
> *I'm sorry if I didn't feed the dogs when I was supposed to, Mrs. Willingham.*
> *I'm sorry if I ever did anything to make you mad, Mrs. Willingham.*

*   *   *

A charge nurse entered the room of Bessie Mae to check her chart. Vincent continued to stand over her bed with the saddest expression on his face. He found it terrible to see her in that condition. The nurse checked the ventilator and feeding tubes, and then marked some items on her chart.

"How are you doing today?" the nurse asked Vincent.

"I'm okay," Vincent said.

"Is this your grandmother?"

Bessie Mae must've appeared to be older than she was, especially while laying up in the hospital.

"No, she's my foster mother."

"I see."

"Can I ask you a question?"

"Sure, anything."

"Is she gonna live?"

"It's hard to say right now," the nurse explained. "We're doing everything to keep her alive. You can rest assure of that."

"What causes people to end up like this?"

"It's different things that can cause people to have a stroke."

"Like what?"

"Smoking, drinking, not eating right, and maybe things related to stress."

"Thank you."

"You're welcome."

The nurse left the room and Vincent stepped closer to the bed to plant a kiss on the right cheek of Bessie Mae. He embraced her hand as a well of tears trickled down his face.

Chapter 35

REST IN PEACE

IT WAS A SUNNY Saturday morning and Vincent was preparing for Bessie Mae's funeral. After being in a coma for three and a half months, she was finally being laid to rest. Along with Carmen and Vernon, Vincent made several trips back and forth to the hospital. It wasn't easy watching Bessie Mae being hooked up to a total life support system. She couldn't eat or breathe on her own. It was absolutely terrible. As he was slipping on his pants, he pictured Bessie Mae lying down in a casket. He envisioned countless flowers surrounding her casket. The very woman who kept him from the time he was six months old, had his mind occupied with lot of memories. Many were bad, and very few were good.

Vincent opened his top drawer and brought out a letter that Vernon had written to him about seven months prior to Bessie Mae's death. The one page letter, which came from Edwards Air Force Base in California, read as follows:

Dear Vinnie:

What's been going on in Chi-town? I've been having a really wonderful time out here in California. The weather's much nicer out here, little brother. I'm only a hundred miles away from Los Angeles. My service buddies and I go down there to party at some of the disco clubs or just check out some of the beauties in their bikinis on the beach. The girls in California are really beautiful. I'll send you some pictures so you can see

what I'm talking about. Have you heard from Valerie? Is she living with Sister Tamara Davidson from St. Mark's? I sure hope she's okay wherever she's at. I truly do love our sister, Vinnie. I know you feel the same way.

What have Mr. and Mrs. Willingham been doing? I suspect that Mrs. Willingham's still trying to take people's money away from them. Listen to me, little brother, and I want you to listen good. Don't let her crippled ass take a penny of your money away from you. Do you hear me? Not a single penny! When you work hard for your money, you should be able to keep it and spend it on whatever you want. Because if you don't, she'll gladly spend it for you. What has Mr. Willingham been doing? Is he still going around beating on people for no reason? Sometimes, I wish I could come home and straighten him out. I hate that black sonofabitch for what he did to Valerie. I hate him with all of my heart! I mean that, Vinnie. I'll have my day to confront him for raping Valerie. How has Carmen been doing? She was supposed to be writing me, but I never heard from her. Maybe I will see her when I come back to Chicago and visit. The next time you go through Roselli's Market, tell Mr. Roselli and Martha, and all the other people there that I said hello. Well, I have to end this letter, but make sure you write me back and let me know how Valerie's doing. Tell everybody back in Chicago that I said hello, and will see them soon. Take care of yourself, little brother, and I'll see you soon.

Love you dearly,
Vernon Ramirez

*   *   *

A host of Bessie Mae's relatives from Memphis, Tennessee, Kansas City, Missouri, Buffalo, New York, Jackson, Mississippi, Tulsa, Oklahoma, and Springfield, Illinois, all came to pay their respects. In the front room and dining room, they waited to see Vincent. Since he was wearing blue slacks, Vincent opened the top drawer, searching for a white dress shirt. The bottom drawer had a blue tie that could easily clip on. Gilbert accidentally left that tie behind.

Vincent was a sharp dressed young man who was ready to pay his final respects to his longtime foster mother. The basement door opened and the light inside the laundry room came on. The audible voices from upstairs motioned down into the basement. It was clear that there were lots of people up there.

"Vincent!" Carmen summoned loudly from the top of the stairs.

"Yes," Vincent answered, running a comb through his curly hair.

"Everybody's up here to see you."

"I'll be up there."

"What's taking you so long?"

"I need to finish getting dressed."

Vincent finally made his presence upstairs. There were many people standing around and sitting on the sofa in the front room. They hadn't seen Vincent since he was a little boy. Bessie Mae's closest cousin from Memphis, Bruce Bennett, and his wife Opal, along with their three daughters and one son, Gail, Nicole, Stephanie, and Carlton, came to attend the funeral. They raised up off the sofa to give Vincent a big hug, smiling graciously into his face.

"My goodness!" Bruce said to Vincent, embracing him under his six foot four inch frame. "Boy, we haven't seen you

since you was a little kid. Why'd you stop coming down to Memphis with Bessie Mae?"

"I had a lot of things to do," Vincent smiled, staring up at the smooth, cleancut face of Bruce.

"We sure missed you coming down to see us."

"I missed coming down, too, cousin Bruce."

"You should get out of Chicago sometimes."

"I will."

"Come down to Memphis and see your folks."

"How would I get down there?" Vincent thought, especially since Bessie Mae was dead.

"Get on a Greyhound bus and come on down."

"The bus?"

"We'll send you a ticket if you don't have no money."

"Okay, that sounds real good."

Vernon walked through the front door wearing his neatly pressed Air Force uniform. His jacket proudly displayed the first stripes that he had earned since enlisting. Vernon had returned from the home of his wife's parents. He decided to marry Daphne Sinclair, his longtime, high school sweetheart, especially since she was the only prize catch. He knew that she would eventually steal his heart.

Like Vincent, the Bennett family gave him a tight, warm hug. It had been even longer since Vernon saw them last. The front room was filled with hugging, kissing, and handshaking. There was the sudden outburst of laughter in the room. Starting time for the funeral was drawing near. Vincent was ready to walk out of the house.

"We can give you a ride to the church," Bruce told Vincent.

"I can walk," said Vincent.

"Are you sure?"

"Yes, I'm sure."

"Okay, we'll see you there."

Granny Dear rolled into the front room to greet some of

her relatives. While standing over her wheelchair, they bent down to hug her. There were too many good old days in Memphis to reminisce about. Booker T. was always the focal point of attention.

Vincent left the crowded, noisy front room and started his trip to St. Mark's church. When he came to a busy corner of Rush Boulevard, he quickly fell into a daydreaming state. Startling questions traveled through his mind:

"Could Mrs. Willingham have been a better foster mother if she wasn't married to Mr. Willingham?"

"Did Mr. Willingham make her the evil woman that she was, or was she like that before she met him?"

"Why did she let Mr. Willingham get away with so much wrong-doing crap?"

Vincent snapped out of the daydreaming. Many anxious motorists traveled up and down Rush, trying to make it to the nightclubs, gambling parlors, and drug and prostitution houses. The traffic was clear, so Vincent crossed the street. From a short distance, he could tell that St. Mark's was lit up brightly. The bright lights, which came through the large windows, on the opposite sides of the front entrance, also beamed down onto the sidewalk.

Vincent was very reluctant to go inside the church. He stood around on the sidewalk tapping his heels on the rough concrete. He spun his hands around in his pants pockets. Though he didn't have a watch, he realized that precious minutes had ticked away. There was a reason for him to go inside and view the body of Bessie Mae. He gently turned the knob to the front door and closed it with much ease. Once inside, he glanced up at the tall ceiling, over all the walls, down the dim and narrow hallway, which led to the lower

IN THE CARE OF EVIL

section across the green carpeted floor, and up the stairs that led to where the service was to be held.

There was absolute silence in the church. The smell of incense burned from upstairs. Even the heating and cooling vents weren't making their usual revving sounds. Vincent went towards the first stair and grabbed the railing on the left side. Throughout his entire life, he couldn't have been more nervous than at that very moment. Not even the vicious beatings from J.D. were more scarier. As he took a quick glance up at the ceiling, he traveled halfway up the stairs and stopped.

At the top of the stairs, there was a short wooden podium that had the obituaries for Bessie Mae on top. Vincent went all the way to the top and stopped in front of the podium. A small black and white photo of Bessie Mae was on the front of the obituary. The photo showed her wearing a designer hat with a set of pearls and matching earrings. Below the picture, there was information that gave her date of birth and date of death.

Vincent picked up one of the obituaries and held it in front of his face. His heart pumped at a steadfast rate, and stomach churned out low growling sounds. Not a soul was in the pulpit or out in the congregation. But to the right of Vincent, there rested a soul in a beautiful, black lacquered casket that was trimmed in gold. The long casket sat in front of the wooden railings that separated the back altar from the consecrated aisle. The bright sun beamed down onto the white carpet of the consecrated aisle. The candles glowed brightly and incense burned lightly on both altars.

The silence inside St. Mark's was intense. Vincent could hear his own heart pumping. Regurgitating sounds rumbled inside his stomach. He apprehensively strolled across the carpet, afraid to view the body. Upon arriving in front of the casket, a gloomy expression showed on his face. He leaned forward to view the body of Bessie Mae. His sixty-one year old

foster mother was wearing a pure white robe that had a matching white veil that fitted perfectly on her head. Between the
middle of her hands, she held a pearly white rosary. Vincent
froze this moment in time.

He found it hard to believe that Bessie Mae Willingham
was a deceased woman. It was reality to the highest degree.
Tears flowed from his eyes after he placed his hand across
her shoulder. The tears began flowing at a rapid pace, coming all the way down his face and onto his collar. Vincent was
truly sad, because he would now miss his foster mother. He
came to terms that she could've been a better foster mother,
still considering the man that she was married to, and the
other circumstances that surrounded her.

From her shoulder and up to her face, Vincent's hand
moved vigorously. Bessie Mae's face was as hard as concrete.
It was the embalming process that changed her body
completely. She still looked like herself, but there were
defections that showed around the facial area. Mother
Davenport came up from behind and placed her arm around
the waist of Vincent. She handed him some tissue so he could
wipe away the constant flow of tears. Someone like Vincent
needed words of consoling during this time of grief. Mother
Davenport was always there to cheer someone up.

"Sister Bessie Mae's at peace now," said Mother Davenport, drawing Vincent closer to her body, while smiling down
into his face.

"At peace?" Vincent couldn't understand, looking down
into the casket.

"Yes."

"What do you mean when you say peace?"

"It means she's leaving this world for a better one."

Vincent smashed his tears back into his eyes before they
would come out.

"Better?"

"She's going to a place without any problems or worries."

Mother Davenport reached into the casket to straighten the top of Bessie Mae's robe.

"Why did Mrs. Willingham have to die?"

"It was her time."

"She had to die to have peace?"

"You can have peace on Earth."

"Can you?"

"But when you die, you go to have eternal peace with God."

"Is Mrs. Willingham going to heaven to have eternal peace?" Vincent asked, staring sadly over at the casket.

"Yes."

"I'm glad."

"She lived according to God's will."

"I don't never wanna die, Mother Davenport," Vincent said, reaching into the casket to hold Bessie Mae's hand.

"Everyone has to die, Vincent."

"Do they?"

"If you wanna see God, you're gonna have to die."

The sounds of someone gliding their feet across the stairs caused Vincent and Mother Davenport to turn around. Bishop Burgess was making his way towards the casket. A big smile was on his face to greet the sad Vincent. He reached into the casket to straighten the rest of the wrinkles in Bessie Mae's robe. He wasn't too happy with the overall job that the funeral home did.

"Jackson and his people know better than this," Bishop Burgess complained, moving the veil on her head to the right side of the casket. "They should've had Sister Bessie Mae's robe pressed better than this."

Frederick T. Jackson and Sons Funeral Home was responsible for Bessie Mae's body.

"Don't it seem like they rushed through to dress her?" Mother Davenport asked Bishop Burgess, moving the rosary closer to Bessie Mae's hand.

"I wasn't expecting to see nothing like this."

"Neither was I."

"Somebody needs to get on them about this."

Vincent watched Bishop Burgess pinch different areas of Bessie Mae's robe. There were too many wrinkles to try and pull out. When he left the casket, one of the representatives from the funeral home came upstairs in his neatly pressed, black and white suit. Deep voices of men came from the bottom of the stairs. With Bruce and Vernon lifting the wheelchair from the front and back, they carried Granny Dear up the stairs. Vernon rolled Granny Dear over to the casket. On her badly, arthritis-stricken legs, she lifted herself up to view the body. She moved closer so she could touch Bessie Mae.

"Dey sho got Bessa Mae fixed up pretty," Granny Dear commented, viewing the body closely. She reached into the casket to hold Bessie Mae's hands.

"I think so, too," Vernon agreed.

"I really lack dis white robe dey got'er in."

"The rosary fits the robe and veil real good."

"Dey sho do."

Granny Dear sat down in her wheelchair and Vernon rolled her over to the first bench on the right side. Vincent continued standing in front of the casket, sadly observing the foster mother who left him behind. This was the day that he would put all irreconcilable differences aside. A spark came to the eyes of Vincent when he saw Valerie coming upstairs with Sister Tamara Davidson. Tamara wanted to rescue her from the cruel streets of Chicago. She wanted to help her clean her life up, and made sure she moved in the right direction. Several years had passed since Valerie and Vincent had seen one another. To make up for lost years, they embraced each other tightly. It lasted a long time. Afterwards, she planted a big kiss right on his lips.

"How've you been, Vincent?" Valerie asked her little brother, holding him tightly by her side.

"I'm doing okay. How've you been?"

"Thanks to Sister Tamara, I'm doing better."

"I haven't seen you since you left the Willingham's home."

"And how long ago was that?" Valerie wondered.

"A long time ago," Vincent remembered, elated about seeing his sister.

"I'm really, really glad to see you."

"I'm glad to see you, too."

Valerie stepped over to the casket. She stared hard into the ashen face of Bessie Mae. It appeared that she had fallen into a trance. The rape dilemma didn't matter anymore. Bessie Mae was deceased and it was her duty to pay her final respects. Carmen and her husband and children came over to the casket and stood beside Valerie. Together, they took a few minutes to view the body.

"Go over and talk to Granny Dear," Carmen told Valerie.

"Where's she at?"

"She's up front."

"Wouldn't you say that Mrs. Willingham looks nice?" Valerie asked.

"Very nice," Carmen nodded, brushing the top of Bessie Mae's shoulder.

"I'm really going to miss her," Valerie said compassionately, shedding a light tear under her right eye.

"We're all going to miss her."

Valerie left the casket to go up front and speak with Granny Dear. Opal and Bruce and their children walked up to the casket. They took a good glance at Bessie Mae and then left to find a seat. More of Bessie Mae's relatives from Kansas City, Buffalo, Tulsa, and Springfield came upstairs. Following behind them were many more men, women, and children. Some of them were former foster children, those who came to pay their respects after going years without seeing Bessie Mae. Everyone took turns in viewing the body. They had obituaries curled inside their hands.

Both sides of the church began filling up. Bishop Burgess went over to the casket with the funeral home staff. They closed the casket and rolled it down the consecrated aisle. The casket was placed directly in front of the pulpit. Everyone in the church remained silent.

J.D. walked upstairs with Rhonda and their baby that she had given birth to. Judging by the matching physical attributes of the baby boy, which were the large forehead, the wide bull nose, and very dark complexion, it was like J.D. had spit him out. That was definitely J.D.'s son. J.D. often bragged to people that he had fathered the child, still able to produce potent sperm to impregnate any woman.

Nearly everyone in the church turned around to watch them. J.D. was wearing a two-piece brown suit and a pair of dark shades. Rhonda was wearing a lavender dress that was clinging to her body. Their son was dressed in a blue and white sailor's outfit. They found a seat in the fifth row on the right side.

Vernon and Vincent had rage in their eyes. If they could, they would jump up and rip J.D.'s heart out, and then politely hand it to him. J.D. stared straight ahead, hiding those evil red eyes behind the shades. After the choir gave a selection, Mother Davenport came up to the podium to say some words of comfort. As a faithful member of St. Mark's, she knew Bessie Mae very well.

"First of all," Mother Davenport said, taking a strong breath inward, then grasping the podium firmly. "Giving an honor to God, to Bishop Burgess, and to all of my brothers and sisters in Christ. I come to you today to let you know that when God sees that you're tired, he'll come and give you rest. I want you to know that he came to give Sister Bessie Mae rest. She was tired and I know that her burdens were many. I want you to know that Sister Bessie Mae has gone on to a much better place."

Bishop Burgess went up to the altar in the pulpit and grabbed a set of brass bells. In a clustered formation, these bells had a short handle at the top. After stepping out of the pulpit, he stood at the foot of the casket. With a swift flick of his wrist, he rang the bells three times.

"Hallelujah! Hallelujah! Hallelujah!" Bishop Burgess shouted, circling the casket while ringing the bells over the top. "Bessie Mae used to respond to these bells, but she don't respond anymore!"

He was filled with the Holy Spirit. A chosen man of God like him always paced the consecrated aisle. His index finger was pressed to his set of sealed lips. Before officially giving anyone's eulogy who belonged to St. Mark's, Bishop Burgess would always stand at the middle of someone's casket, point to both sides of the congregation, clap both hands up to the sky, and then shout in a very loud voice, "I've said it many times before, and I'll say it many more times! If you die wrong, you're gonna wake up wrong!" It was his way of warning those who were living in sin.

Bishop Burgess placed the bells back on the altar in the pulpit and returned to the consecrated aisle. He was ready to give the eulogy. The pacing up and down the aisle and swaying side to side, indicated that he was ready to fire away.

"Bessie Mae! Bessie Mae! Bessie Mae!" the bishop yelled three times, hitting part of his body against some of the pews. Sweat dripped from his handsome face. "You left this old Earthly temple, and now, God has allowed you to put a down payment on another one!"

People in the choir section and out in the congregation watched Bishop Burgess falter up and down the aisle. He constantly moved to the back and in the front of the casket. The man was charged with pure spiritual energy. He continued with the eulogy.

"God has given you a holier temple!" the bishop hummed exhiliratingly.

"Yeah!" most of the church responded.

"A much higher temple!"

"Yeah!"

"An everlasting temple!"

"Say it, Bishop Burgess, say it!"

"She came to me and told me all about it!" the bishop yelled once more, the electricity of God charging him up.

"Yeah she did, Bishop Burgess!" the church cheered, some standing up and waving their hands through the air.

"She told me all about her sorrows, and I understood!"

"Yeah!"

"She told me all about her headaches and heartaches, and I understood!"

"Yeah!"

"She told me all about her misfortunes and mishaps, and I understood!"

"Yeah Lord, she did!"

"She told me all about her faults, her failures, and her fears, and I understood."

"Go on preacher, and preach it!" the congregation yelled, creating steam about the entire church.

"But now, Sister Bessie Mae, I say to you, that God has taken you away from all of that!"

"Yeah, he has!"

"You now have everlasting rest!"

"Say it, Bishop Burgess!"

"The rest that riches can't buy!"

"Preach the truth, Bishop Burgess!"

"The rest that man can't give you!"

"Keep on, Bishop!"

"The rest that only the Almighty can give you!"

"Yeah!"

The powerful and moving words of Bishop Burgess had the entire church saying *"yeah this!"* and *"yeah that!"*, and *"amen this!"* and *"amen that!"*.

Carmen jumped up and started shouting. She fell between Vernon and Vincent. The Holy Spirit filled her body
with power. Bishop Burgess strolled up and down the consecrated aisle. From the back of the church, he raced to the
middle of the aisle and stopped. The sudden stop surprised
everyone in the church. With the exact same finger that J.D.
had often vulgarly criticized him for pointing too much,
Bishop Burgess stood at the fifth pew, clapped his strong
hands three times, stomped his feet twice, pointed his finger right in J.D.'s shiny black face, and shouted in an explosive voice, *"Brother Willingham, you need to straighten up and fly
right! You need to fly right, you hear me!"*

J.D. instantly became the center of unwelcome attention. The entire church looked his direction. From the way
that he moved his head, and balled up his fist, it was evident
that he was angry and terribly embarrassed. But who cared?
Many of the same foster children who Bessie Mae kept over
the years, turned around in the pews and gave him the look
of the greatest satisfaction.

Vernon and Vincent turned around, happy that J.D. had
been put on the spot. From under those dark shades, J.D.'s
red eyes were burning with fury. Everyone knew that Bishop
Burgess was dead serious. More tears fell from Vincent's eyes.
Opal moved forward to hand him more tissue. It would only
take a few seconds for the tissue to become soaked. The
eulogy ended and everyone stood. Forming a single file line
on both sides of the church, everyone walked down the
consecrated aisle for a final viewing of the body.

Vernon pushed Granny Dear up to the casket. She raised
up from the wheelchair to take one last good look at Bessie
Mae. It would be the last time that she ever saw her daughter.
Crying at Bessie Mae's funeral seemed contagious. Granny
Dear dropped tears into the casket.

"Oh Lawd!" Granny Dear cried, climbing further into

the casket to give her daughter one last hug. "I'm gone be wit'er one day real soon!"

She sat down in the wheelchair and Vernon leaned forward to give Bessie Mae a farewell kiss. Individually, Valerie, Vincent, Carmen, Bruce, Opal, and other relatives and friends came to the casket to give her a kiss.

J.D. and Rhonda were the last ones to come to the casket. The two lowlifes couldn't stare down at Bessie Mae's face. They had to turn their heads to the side while standing at the middle of the casket. They knew that they had done her wrong. After everyone viewed the body, Bishop Burgess instructed the funeral home staff to come up front. They closed the front of the casket, and it was rolled to the back of the church. Bruce and Vernon picked Granny Dear up and brought her out to one of the limousines. Many rows of cars surrounded the church.

Inside the two limousines, which were parked directly in front of the church, family members waited for others to get inside their cars. The journey from the church to the cemetery was going to be long. Vincent sat quietly in the second limousine. The curly locks in his head pressed against the window. His fingers thumped on the armrest. One certain memory jetted through his mind. He slipped into a trance that took him back a few years at the Willingham residence.

Twelve year old Vincent rushed upstairs to tell Bessie Mae about some of the horrible things going on in the basement.

"I don't want to sleep down there, Mrs. Willingham," Vincent told Bessie Mae.

"Why, Vincent?" Bessie Mae asked.

"I saw a bunch of mice running across the floor."

"Those mice aren't going to bother you."

"They try and jump up in the bed with me."

"If they do, just throw them off your bed," Bessie Mae said, making it seem easy sleeping in a basement that was mice infested.

"There's a bunch of roaches crawling on the wall by my bed."

"Take a shoe or some paper and brush them off the wall."

"They're going to crawl right back on the wall."

"There's nothing I can do."

"Can Mr. Willingham do something about it?"

"Maybe."

Vincent left the kitchen sad, knowing that he would have to continue to sleep in the basement with all of that filth.

*   *   *

The officers on the motorcycles were ready to lead the motorcade out to the cemetery. The limousines and multitude of cars were practically bumper-to-bumper. Measuring almost a mile, the long line followed the officers up the street with their lights on. At the end of the ride, which consisted of many twists and turns through Chicago's streets and highways, Chapel Memorial Cemetery was slightly off the road.

The officers directed everyone to find a parking space. The long funeral car drove into the cemetery, parking close to the plot where Bessie Mae was to be buried. Bishop Burgess and the funeral home staff brought the casket out of the car. Vernon pushed Granny Dear through the grass. Under the large tent, Valerie, Vincent, and Carmen sat in one of the padded seats. The casket was placed on top of the opening where Bessie Mae was to be buried, surrounded by an assortment of flowers.

Once everyone was gathered under the tent, Bishop Burgess opened his large black Bible. He turned to the twenty-first chapter of Revelation, beginning with the fourth verse. The bishop read: *"And God shall wipe all tears from their eyes; and*

there shall be no more death, neither sorrow, nor crying, neither shall there be any more pain: for former things are passed. "

Though the scripture said that God shall wipe all tears from their eyes, more tears swelled in Vincent's eyes. Starting from his red cheeks, tears flowed under his chin and on down to his collar. Vernon left his seat to go over and console Granny Dear. It was hard containing herself, especially after she lost her only daughter.

All the grief that Vincent had locked inside, came out through the tears that he cried. Carmen reached over to hand him more tissue. From a small cardboard box, Bishop Burgess scooped up a handful of dirt, sprinkled it lightly over the casket, and then he said, "From ashes to ashes, and from dust to dust." When he stepped aside, the multitude of people came forward to take one of the flowers. It was the last memory they would have of Bessie Mae. The woman who spent most of her life operating a home for foster children and handicapped men, was about to be lowered into the ground. Bessie Mae's reign as "foster mother" had ended. Vincent stood at her casket crying. The sorrow was deep. There was a love for Bessie Mae that had finally prevailed. Braun and Junior couldn't attend the funeral because they didn't have the proper dress attire. Of course, they only had three pairs of pants and two shirts to their name.

With his eyes shut and hands interlocked in prayer, Vincent leaned over the casket. Cemetery workers who were dressed in gray uniforms were ready to lower the casket into the ground. They wondered what he could possibly be praying about. He turned around and Mother Davenport was standing right in front of him.

"Everything alright, Vincent?" Mother Davenport asked, sliding her arm around Vincent's waist for consoling purposes.

"I'm going to miss her, Mother Davenport," Vincent confessed, taking a final look at the casket.

"If you be a good boy, you'll see her again," Mother Davenport said affectionately, moving closer to the casket with Vincent.

"Where?"

"In Heaven."

"Mrs. Willingham's in Heaven right now?"

"She's resting right now."

"I loved her, Mother Davenport."

"I know you did."

"I really, really did."

"And she loved you, too."

"You think she really did?"

"Sure."

"I believe you."

"She loved you as though you were her own son."

Vincent took one of the flowers and walked from under the tent with Mother Davenport. It would've been too painful to watch the cemetery workers lower Bessie Mae into the ground, so he kept his back turned until he got inside one of the limousines.

Chapter 36

A FALLEN DYNASTY

JASON RICHBURG MADE documentation that was recorded before and after the death of Bessie Mae. The Department of Children and Family Services sent him to the Willingham's foster home several times during Bessie Mae's illness. He recorded the following information and eventually sent a letter to the Willingham home afterwards:

> *I, Jason Richburg, was informed that Mrs. Bessie Mae Willingham had suffered a severe stroke and had been hospitalized. A conference was held with supervisors and it was decided that Vincent would remain in this foster home under the supervision of Bessie Mae's mother, Ida Lou Pierson, until further planning could be done. Frequent contacts were made with Vincent; he continued to attend school regularly and presented no problems for Ms. Pierson. Vincent did have some anxiety regarding his future if Bessie Mae died and support was given to aid him in this. When Bessie Mae died in mid September, several alternative placements for Vincent were explored. A foster home request had been submitted, but a home had not been found. I had some difficulty getting Vincent to cooperate in making plans; he was having trouble accepting Bessie Mae's death and the necessity of moving elsewhere. Possible placements which were explored included:*

(1) Vito and Marion Carvelli (natural parents, parental rights terminated)

(2) Vernon Ramirez (half-brother), in Air Force at Andrews Air Force Base in California.

(3) Zeno Bluett (church deacon and youth counselor)

Sincerely,

Jason Richburg (Caseworker For Vincent Carvelli)

*   *   *

Those who remained at the Willingham residence included Vincent, Granny Dear, Braun, and Junior. Technically, J.D. and Rhonda were still residents, coming back and forth to the house. Whether it was a foster home, or an institution for the handicapped, everyone had to vacate the premises by the end of the week. Rhonda was supposed to be a temporary foster girl, but stayed longer than anticipated. Bessie Mae was to never know, but J.D. arranged for her to stay longer.

As darkness filled the house, Vincent was on the second floor laying clean clothes across the bed. Inside the room that Rhonda used to sleep in, he was preparing himself for school. Fifteen years of that mice and roach infested basement was enough. Vernon came into the room to give Vincent some important news.

"Your caseworker found you a new foster home," Vernon informed Vincent.

"Jason Richburg?" Vincent asked in a low tone, throwing his old clothes back on the bed.

"Yeah."

"When did you talk to him?"

"Today."

"Which new foster home am I going to?"

"It's over on the west side of Chicago."

"I hope it's better than this one," Vincent wished, something that he had prayed about for a long time. He survived the abuse and neglect at the Willingham residence and that was all that counted.

"I'm hoping, too," Vernon said.

"Why can't I go with you out to California?"

"I talked with your caseworker about that, too."

"What did he say?" Vincent anxiously asked, though he really knew the answer.

"Since I'm in the Air Force and travel a lot, it would be impossible for you to travel with me."

"Why's that?"

"You couldn't stay in one school and one home all year long."

"Oh, I see," Vincent pictured, knowing that Vernon was looking out for his best interest.

"Look at it this way, baby brother," Vernon said. "You've only got two more years of school left and then you can get out of this foster home crap. You'll be free to do whatever you want to do."

Vernon sure had a way of explaining things to Vincent. He always cared about his younger brother in ways unseen.

"That's a good way of looking at it," Vincent smiled.

"You'll be alright."

Vernon realized that it was getting late. He knew that Vincent had to get some sleep for the upcoming school day.

After Vernon left the room, Vincent slipped into his pajamas, cut the light out, and pressed his eyelids together tightly. A quick clinch of the pillow and turn over onto his back, caused him to fall into a deep sleep. During the night hours, the hands of the clock made their revolutions. Vincent moved around in the bed, sucking the sticky residue from inside his mouth. A strong urge to get up and go use the bathroom came to him.

It was unfortunate that that same urge never came during his early childhood and adolescent years. Vincent threw the bed covers back and sat on the edge of the bed. When he walked into the pitch dark hallway, he discovered a light that probably only lit up half the bathroom. That same light wasn't on when he was preparing for bed. Since the body weight of Vincent was light, no squeaking noises were made through the cracks underneath. He strolled towards the bathroom rubbing his eyes and yawning lightly.

The dim light was useful in helping him find his way down the hall. The surprise of a lifetime hit Vincent right smack in the face. While trying to shove his long black penis into her dark and bushy vagina, J.D. had Rhonda leaned over the edge of the bathtub. Since she had recently given birth, stretch marks and stitches were showing across her stomach. Her pink nightgown was held up past her waist. J.D.'s pants and underwear were dropped to the floor.

Little did they know that Vincent stood right in the doorway watching them. His mouth opened wide with astonishment. He was bewildered to witness J.D. trying to fuck Rhonda on the edge of the bathtub. Rhonda held the edges of the tub, then wrapped her legs around his waist for better leverage. Vincent maintained his position at the edge of the bathroom door. Consciously, he asked himself several logical questions:

"How could these two black monkeys do this to Mrs. Willingham?"

"Don't they have any morals left in their evil bodies?"

"I wonder if Mrs. Willingham'll come back and haunt them?"

"Does Mr. Willingham feel bad about doing this?"

"Does Rhonda feel bad about doing this?"

"Why did they both have to fuck in a dark bathroom in this house?"

"Why couldn't they just go to a hotel or over someone's house?"

"Will God punish them both for doing this to Mrs. Willingham?"

"Is Mrs. Willingham's spirit looking at them?"

J.D. thrusted his big black penis in and out of Rhonda. He held firmly to the sides of her waist. Her head was tilted back far. They continued to engage in some raw sex, heating up the bathroom with their hot breath and unhibited intercourse.

"Give it to me, J.D.!" Rhonda requested erotically, her needle shaped nipples turning hard.

"Yep, I'm gone give it to ya, gal," J.D. said, pounding his heavy frame up against her much smaller frame.

"Don't stop, J.D.!"

"I ain't gone stop, gal."

"Please don't!"

"I'm gone keep it comin, gal!"

"Keep that big black dick coming, J.D.!"

"I'm bout ta . . ."

"Getting ready to cum, J.D.?"

"Yep, dat's what I'm gone do. I'm bout ta comb in ya, woman."

"Go ahead and shoot that hot cum up in me, baby!"

"Aw shit, here it comes!"

J.D. released a load of semen up in Rhonda and wouldn't stop stroking her contracting vagina until he felt that every

drop was in her. Their breathing was heavier than ever, perspiration saturating every inch of their upper bodies.

Vincent couldn't stand to watch or hear another second of what he considered to be *two black barbarians*. Unannounced, he stepped into the bathroom, pretending as though he didn't know that someone was in there. J.D. expeditiously jerked his hard penis out of Rhonda's smelly and wet vagina. The foul odor of raw sex had traveled into the air. He quickly pulled his underwear and pants up to his waist, and then ran over to the sink, pretending as though he was searching for something in the medicine chest.

As for Rhonda, she jumped off the edge of the tub, slid her white panties up around her waist, dropped her nightgown down to her knees, and ran over to the stool. She tore off a piece of toilet paper, threw it inside the stool, and flushed it several times. What great pretenders those two lowlives were. Vincent had rained in on their *fucking parade*. He knew that his eyes hadn't deceived him. They knew it also.

J.D. turned around and smiled at Vincent. "What ya say dere?"

"I don't have nothing to say," Vincent said insubordinately.

"How ya doing in school?"

"Why'd you ask?"

"Juss askin."

"It's strange of you to ask."

"Ya gittin yo lesson alwight?"

"You've never asked me those things before."

"Juss checkin ta see if ya learnin anythang in school."

"What's that smell in here?" Vincent asked pretentiously, knowing good and well that that type of odor was too familiar.

"I ain't smellin nuttin."

"You don't smell nothing?"

"Naw."

"Are you sure?"

"Yep."

"Smells like somebody just got through fucking."

"Brawns or Joanyer probably came in here and used da bathwoom."

"Braun and Junior are sleep."

"Yep, dey are."

"Do you mind?"

"What's wong?"

"I just have to use the bathroom."

"Alwight."

Rhonda and J.D. rushed out of the bathroom. They knew that they had been busted. Vincent used the restroom and returned to bed.

*   *   *

Friday evening arrived and J.D. was selling every piece of furniture and expensive item that Bessie Mae had ever accrued. Most of the customers were wealthy white people from the elite suburbs of Cicero and Chicago Heights. Some came as far away as Joliet, Elgin, and Springfield, Illinois. J.D. had already started auctioning off the furniture to interested parties.

"How much are you asking for this sofa, and the matching loveseat and chair?" a very wealthy man from Cicero asked, holding a blank check in his hand.

"Give ma bout five-hunted dollars," J.D. said, nodding his head at the very people he hated so much. But now that it came down to business, J.D. didn't have an ounce of hatred for whites. Money was neither black nor white, even to a man as illiterate as J.D.

"How much are you asking?"

"Five-hunted dollars."

"Five what?"

"Five-hunted," J.D. tried explaining somewhat clearer. "Dat's what I's asking."

"Oh, you're asking five-hundred for it?"

"Yep."

"You've got yourself a deal."

"It's some nice stuff."

"Do you take personal checks?"

"Sho do."

"That's great."

"Long as I can cass it."

"You'll be able to cash it."

"Alwight."

"Who do I make the check out to?"

"Make it out ta Jesse Willingham."

After dealing with that customer, J.D. traveled up to the second floor bedroom with a wealthy couple from Joliet. They were interested in purchasing the furs and jewelry once owned by Bessie Mae. Carmen and Vernon wanted to get their hands on everything in the house before J.D. was able to, but since he and Bessie Mae were still legally married at the time of her death, he was allowed to come in and clean the house out. This caused Vernon a lot of anguish. The couple viewed some of the furs lying across the bed.

"How much do you want for this fox fur?"

"I'a take a hunted fo it," J.D. told the prospective buyer.

"How much?" the man asked, not understanding J.D.'s illiterate dialect.

"A hunted."

"I'm sorry, sir, but I still can't understand you."

"One-hunted dollars," J.D. explained a little clearer.

"Okay, a hundred-dollars," he said. "That's a deal."

"Alwight."

"How much do you want for that rabbit fur?"

"Give ma a hunted fo dat one, too."

"Sounds great."

The wealthy customer wrote J.D. a check for five-hundred dollars after several of the furs were auctioned off. The

customer was actually getting off dirt cheap. Someone as illiterate as J.D. didn't know smart business anyway. Before the end of the day, he would have auctioned off more than five thousand dollars worth of merchandise, including Bessie Mae's Cadillac Sedan de Ville.

While J.D. sat at the dining room table counting large sums of money, Vernon and Vincent waited in the front room for his caseworker. Braun and Junior waited in their room for a representative from The Illinois Division for the Handicapped. Granny Dear was in her room with the television turned up loud. She rolled out of her room and went to use the bathroom.

J.D. snuck into her room and unplugged her television. Most of Granny Dear's belongings had been gathered by Vernon and Carmen earlier during the day. They were preparing for her to return to her native Memphis, Tennessee. Her brother, Booker T., and some other relatives arranged to have her moved down there. J.D. opened the curtain to her room and Carmen and Vernon were right there to rudely greet him.

"You're not going to take Granny Dear's television," Carmen told J.D., bucking up to him very bravely.

"Who gone stop ma?" J.D. asked, holding the small television down by his side.

"You don't wanna find out."

"Yep, I do."

"It's bad enough that you've sold everything that Mrs. Willingham owned."

"Some of dose thangs was mine's."

"No, they weren't."

"Yep, dey were."

"Put her television back in her room."

"You betta git out'a my way, gal."

"I'm not going nowhere."

"You betta move or . . ."

Vernon jumped in front of Carmen and said, "Or what, motherfucker!"

"What cha say ta ma, boy?" J.D. asked, lifting the television like he was going to hit Vernon with it.

"I don't stutter."

"Ya betta gone somewhere."

"You are a lowdown sonofabitch!"

"Ya talkin to ma, boy?"

"Who else am I talking to?"

"Not me."

"You're trying to steal an old woman's television."

"I ain't doing no such thang."

"You're a thieving bastard!"

"Gone now, boy."

"You've never cared how lowdown you are."

"I ain't lowdown."

"You're trying to sell the television, too?"

"Dat's my bizzness."

"Me and Carmen are making it our business."

"If ya don't git out'a my face, I'm gone . . . ," J.D. said, drawing the television back as though he was going to strike Vernon with it."

Vernon lifted his shirt and snatched out a .38 service revolver. He stared deeply into J.D.'s red eyes and said, "Or what? What're you gonna do?"

J.D. stood there speechless and his body was absolutely motionless. Vernon held the pistol down by his side, with his finger planted firmly on the trigger. "I've always wanted to confront you about raping my sister."

"Ain't nobody waped yo sista," J.D. said, his body shivering all over.

"Now, I dare you to hit me."

"Put dat gun way, Vernun."

"When you put Granny Dear's television back in her room."

"Yall acking lack yall own thangs in dis house."

"We just made ourselves owners," Vernon said authoritatively, raising the gun closer to the greasy black face of J.D. "Now, put the television back before you be feeling a hot slug in your ass!"

Surprisingly, J.D. threw the curtains back and placed the television on a nightstand in Granny Dear's room. The altercation ended and everyone went their separate directions. This was yet another humbling experience for J.D. He had enough .38 handguns up in his face.

Around the nearly empty home, everyone had their belongings packed and ready to leave. Someone knocked at the front door. Vincent went to the door and it was his caseworker. Jason Richburg arrived to take him to his next foster home. He went back into the kitchen to say farewell to Granny Dear.

"I'm leaving, Granny Dear," Vincent announced, standing in her doorway.

"Make sho ya lemme know how ya doing," Granny Dear said, raising forward in her wheelchair to give Vincent one last hug.

"I will," Vincent assured Granny Dear, giving her a kiss on the cheek.

Vincent left Granny Dear's room and passed J.D. for a last time. He stared at his evil former foster father as though he never wanted to see him again in his lifetime. Rhonda stood behind J.D. holding their baby, while he counted large sums of money. He looked at Vincent and asked, "What's wong wit ya, boy?"

"Do you really want to know?" Vincent said, not worrying about anymore vicious beatings.

"I ask, didden I?"

"I should've done what Mrs. Willingham started to do."

"What's dat?"

"Took that same thirty-eight and blew your brains out."

"Don't talk ta ma lack dat, boy."

"You know what you are?"

"Tell ma."

"An illiterate motherfucker from Mississippi."

"Don't make ma . . ."

"You're fat and black."

"I'm gone go and git ma . . ."

"You're nasty and greasy."

"I should git up and . . ."

"You're ugly and dumb."

"Ya say one mo thang bout . . ."

"You're going to burn in hell forever," Vincent said, effectively cutting J.D. off everytime he tried to say something.

"Dat's it, boy!"

"The next time you raise that extension cord to beat someone with, you're going to be hung with it."

Vincent walked out of the dining room with his head up to the ceiling. J.D. badly wanted to run and get his extension cord. He knew that those days were over, and that Vernon and Vincent would take the same extension cord that he lifted to strike someone with, and use it to choke him around his thick black neck.

Vincent went upstairs to say farewell to Braun and Junior. Finally, he came downstairs to say goodbye to Vernon. They gave one another a heartwarming hug.

"You have my number," Vernon told Vincent, patting him across the back. "Give me a call when you've settled into this new foster home."

"I'll call to let you know how I like it."

"If you have to, call collect."

"Are you sure?" Vincent asked.

"I'm sure your new foster parents won't accept any long distance calls."

"You're right."

Vincent turned to look at his caseworker. Jason stood by the front door with a notepad in his hand.

"All ready to go?" Jason asked Vincent, fidgeting with the handle of the door.

"I was ready to go almost fifteen years ago," Vincent joked, reaching down to grab his suitcase and trashbag.

"Well, it's off to your next foster home."

"Let's go, Jason."

"Alright, Vincent."

Vernon came out on the porch with Vincent and Jason, wanting to wave goodbye before Vincent departed. They went out to Jason's Datsun B-210 and placed his belongings in the back of the car. Vincent took a final look at the big brick house on the corner of Milwaukee Parkway.

He glanced up and down the block. The nosy neighbors came out on their porches to watch another foster child leave. Vincent looked up to the sunny blue sky and thought to himself:

> *I no longer have to worry about getting beatings from Mr. Willingham.*
>
> *I no longer have to sleep in a basement with mice and cockroaches.*
>
> *I no longer have to sleep on a bed with piss and shit stains on them.*
>
> *I no longer have to worry about getting cursed out by Mrs. Willingham.*
>
> *I no longer have to worry about being snuck into a bathroom to have sex.*
>
> *I no longer have to worry about sneaking around at night to change pissy sheets.*
>
> *I no longer have to live in a home with mentally retarded men like Braun and Junior.*
>
> *I no longer have to live in the care of Bessie Mae and J.D. Willingham.*

For Vincent, it felt good knowing that he didn't have to live in care of foster parents who mistreated him and others so badly. Finally, Vincent felt exceptionally good about not having to live *IN THE CARE OF EVIL.*

Dewey Reynolds

DEWEY REYNOLDS WAS born and raised in Kansas City, Missouri. At six months old, he was abandoned by both parents who were involved with crime on a large scale. After his abandonment, he was left in foster care and became a permanent ward of the state. Years following his release from foster care, Mr. Reynolds attended a community college and decided to research the history of foster care in America, and found some startling statistics. The extremities of abuse that he read about in foster care were very similar to the same abuse that he suffered at the hands of his brutal foster parents. With careful preparation and endless research, Mr. Reynolds has written a disturbing and provocative story about the misuse of sex and power within the foster care system. In The Care Of Evil offers insight into the brutal and complex world of one foster child. Dewey Reynolds currently resides in Kansas City, Missouri.

Printed in the United States
4602